Stars In The Deep
~Destiny~

Book 1

Destiny's Children

By

David F. Snider

Stars in the Deep
Volume 1: Books 1-3

ISBN: 978-0-9890703-0-0

DEDICATION

To Laura, my best friend of 35 years. Her love, loyalty and encouragement has been valuable.
And, to DJ, Lisa, and Emily, three of our five grown children, whose conversations and brainstorming sessions helped to spark and develop this tale.

ACKNOWLEDGMENTS

I'd like to thank all those who test read all or portions of this work. Your comments and ideas were most helpful.

Also, in the area of language, I wish to thank, in advance, the rich culture of the people of India for the language of Sanskrit, from which I borrowed heavily in creating the language of the Aambüka. My heavy use of several online Sanskrit and Tamil dictionaries was instructive.

I do tender my apology, in advance, to all those who are familiar with Sanskrit and hold this rich and ancient language dear to their hearts. I fear I have bent spellings and grammar past their breaking point in the adoption process. My purpose was to create a language that would be vaguely familiar, yet believably alien. I assure you there was NO INTENTION of causing angst over the use and, probable abuse of Sanskrit. I have the deepest respect for the language and cultures of the peoples of the Indus region.

Stars in the Deep
Volume 1: Book 1

Table of Contents

Chapter Sections	Starting Page
A Change of Plans 1 - 5	1
Major Complications 1 - 4	27
Discovery 1 - 6	43
Committed 1 - 8	64
Fallout 1 - 6	87
Cleaning House 1 - 7	118

A CHANGE OF PLANS — 1

THU 01.21.2094
Deep Space; location unknown
ECS Destiny, 0545 Hrs

Daryl McIntyre started from sleep to the persistent sound of the COMM signal. Tapping the patch that clung to the back of his left hand, he dragged himself irritably from the bunk and the warm body next to him.

"Daryl here!" The screen lit up to present Franklin Drake, Navigations and Computer Tech Officer. He looked worried.

Daryl, the Chief Engineer, glanced at the ships clock. Third shift was coming to a tired end. *Why was Frank up there?* Then he noticed the flash of the NAVCOM alarm on his display.

"Daryl, we're in deep sheep! NAVCOM blew us way off course. You gotta get up here quick!"

Daryl blanched. Going off course was bad enough. Going off course in Multi-Space Level 2 was deadly serious. He ran a hand through his short stubborn hair. "Crap! Ok, nobody's going to like it, but you better yank us out of MS."

Frank grimaced. "Ouch!"

Daryl shrugged, stifling a yawn. "Yeah, I know, but we can't afford to let things get any worse."

"Good point..." Frank shook his head, "...one rude awakening coming up."

"All right, I'll roust the captain. We'll be right up." Daryl closed the link and ducked into the sanitary cubicle to douse his face. He stepped back into the bedroom and looked longingly at the bed. His young bride, Naomi, rolled over, mumbling about lights.

He shrugged into a uniform, explaining why he was up. He needn't have bothered, she'd gone back to sleep. Brushing the interface patch on the back of his hand, he darted out the door, the lights already dark.

He stopped at the captain's door and tapped the announcer tab...and waited. It took three tries to get an answer. The door snapped open for an athletic looking, bleary-eyed man who stood unhappily in the opening. "I hope you're aware of the God forsaken hour. This had better be good." The captain motioned Daryl to enter.

Daryl explained as he crossed the threshold. "Captain, we're in trouble. NAVCOM fouled up and we're way off course."

"When?" The captain was suddenly wide awake.

Daryl shrugged. "I don't know. It looked like Frank had been working on the problem for a while. I didn't get much detail, but I'd say at least a couple of hours. I told him to get us out of MS and we'd be right up."

The captain grimaced. "Well, I said, 'it had better be good...' All right. Go on ahead. I'll splash my face and be right there."

"Got it." Daryl headed back out the door.

Captain Anatoli Chernov stepped into his own sanitary cubicle. He stopped before the small mirror, glancing at the grumpy image. A kindly face with a faint overnight shadow peered back. The deep brown eyes looked like they'd seen too much for their age. After a quick rinse he directed a tiny hot air hurricane over hands and face.

Suddenly, he felt like he'd been shoved blindfolded off the edge of a three hundred foot cliff, followed instantly by the gut-wrenching lurch of a premature landing. He reflexively grabbed the chicken bar next to the mirror. Even with the fledgling tech of grav-plates and inertial dampers, 'chicken bars' came in handy from time to time.

A damn fast fall, he thought. They'd safely, if abruptly, returned to normal space. As he strode across the small grassy park toward the forward lift well, Vincent Leoni, his first officer, darted from his cabin like a startled rabbit.

"What the...Captain, what's going on?" The captain motioned him to follow. Vince, madly tucking his shirttails, hurried after. They stepped off the lift, crossed the corridor and bustled onto the command bridge of the colony ship *Destiny*. The tension could be cut with a knife.

Daryl noticed their presence, "Captain on the Bridge!"

Instant silence, or nearly so, ruled the moment. "As you were." Captain Chernov scanned the room as he rounded the cluster, approaching his command chair. "So, what's going on up here?"

The captain passed the patch on the back of his hand near a sensor, activating his command codes as Franklin Drake extracted himself from NAVCOM and approached the CONN. "Sir, according to the log, at about 0200 hours NAVCOM decided to make a random course change. What's worse, since the computer initiated the course change, the alarm didn't sound and no one noticed the problem till about 0420 hours.

"I was called to the bridge, confirmed the assessment and notified the Chief. On his authority, I performed an emergency dive from Multi-Space. Now we're in normal space, trying to figure out what happened and where we are."

"Thank you, Mr. Drake." The captain thought for a moment. "What happened and why is clearly important, but I need to know where we are and where we're headed."

Daryl stepped close and murmured. "Captain. If we can't trust the computer, we'll not be able to trust the information. I recommend a thorough system check and calibration. We need to know this problem isn't coming back at any moment."

Captain Chernov nodded. "Yes, of course, quite right."

He spoke up for the benefit of everyone else. "All right. The Chief says we do a complete system check and calibration. I agree. Helm, slow us to 'point two five-c' and hold our current heading until we can sort out this mess."

"Sir."

He glanced towards the COMM station where a young ensign was on duty. "Yes, Finny."

"Sir, I've been flooded with anxious calls about the sudden bucking of the ship."

Chernov forced a grim smile. "What are you telling them?"

Finny hesitated. "Well, sir, I set up a message, saying we're experiencing minor difficulties, so people should remain calm and wait for a general announcement."

"Very good, Finny; I commend your ingenuity. Please open a ship wide channel. They'll get their announcement."

Finny nodded and turned to his console. He murmured to the computer and tapped a couple of prompts. He pointed a finger, "You're on, sir."

The Captain paused for a moment. "Attention, all personnel. Due to computer trouble, we've made a quick exit from Multi-Space. Don't worry, the ship is in good physical shape. Necessary repairs to the computer are being made as I speak.

"We hope to be under way soon, so in the mean time, please remain calm and go about your usual business. Please try to refrain from unnecessary calls to the command center. We'll keep you informed as needed. Chernov out."

Captain Chernov made a chopping motion. "Finny, why don't you cut a new message that covers the salient points? Then we can ignore distracting chatter."

Finny nodded, "Certainly, sir."

Captain Chernov tapped a 'change' command and stood. "Vince, you have the CONN. I'll be next door." He strode to the port side door to his standby cabin.

* * * *

Vincent Leoni left the cluster of techs at NAVCOM and stepped up to the command chair. After registering the official change of command he sat, quietly pondering the implications of their situation. Two hours off course while in Multi-Space 2 could mean the difference between minimal fuel surpluses to reach their goal and barely making it at all.

It could have been worse. He thought. If they hadn't caught on when they did they wouldn't have been able to finish the trip. Then, there was the limited service-life built into the MS drive itself. After all, *Destiny* was a colony ship. It had made a sort of economic sense to use a low cost, one way Multi-Space drive. The ship wouldn't be returning. It's role was to deliver the colonists to the target planet and then be disassembled to provide ready materials for building the first settlement.

* * * *

About an hour later, Frank got up from his seat at NAVCOM. He scrubbed his face tiredly with one of his big hands as he approached Vince's station.

Meanwhile, the tech team began cleaning up the tangle of light-wire and component cards in the back of the station.

Vince put on his hopeful face. "What's up Frank?"

"Well, Vince, I think we can put NAVCOM back on line." He was clearly worried. "As you can imagine, our situation's not good; not good at all."

"Yeah? Go on..."

"Well, as it turns out, a sub-processing unit turned glitchy. It chose a crucial moment in the auto course confirmation phase to signal a recalc. So far as I can tell, the recalc wasn't needed. We pulled the faulty unit and installed the back up. The tests are all good, so I think the problem in the computer is gone."

Vince nodded. "Well, that's something anyway."

Frank countered, "You'd think, but there's more news."

Vince raised an inquisitive eyebrow.

Frank looked frustrated. "I went through the auto-log history. That glitchy chip has been sending course correction commands since shortly after we transitioned to Multi-Space this last time. I counted three previous course change commands. That's about one per week plus this one we caught in progress."

Vince gave a sharp intake of breath, eyes wide.

Frank continued, "To make matters worse, I don't have the slightest idea where in the universe we are right now. I've got the scopes running and the computer crunching away, but it'll take a couple of hours, maybe more, to figure it out."

Vince considered for a moment. "Look Frank...You can't do any more till the computer gets done, right?" Frank shook his head. "So, go get some rest. I'll tell the captain the glorious news."

Frank smiled. "OK. Thanks, Vince." He turned to go.

Vince turned his attention to the techs around NAVCOM. "All right, guys. Go ahead and finish buttoning up. Then grab a bite to eat and get some rest.

"Oh! What's happened here stays here till we can fill everyone in officially. We don't need a panic on top of everything else." He looked serious. "Got it?"

The techs nodded silently.

"Very good. Carry on."

Vince caught Daryl's attention. "Daryl, would you take charge here while I fill the captain in?"

Daryl shrugged, "Sure. Have fun with your report."

Vince relinquished his command status and made his way to join the captain.

* * * *

Though inspired by old wet navy tradition, the standby cabin bore only a vague likeness to the historical captain's sea cabin. For one thing, it was bigger. There was a small conference table in the middle of the room. On the outside port bulkhead were the coffee and snack dispensers conveniently stationed a couple steps from the captain's desk. At the forward end of the room was a broad curtain, much like the kind found in vintage movie theaters back home. It curved invitingly along the bulkhead, looking mysterious.

Vince went straight to the coffee dispenser where he drew two cups. He stepped over to where Captain Chernov was working on reports at his desk.

Anatoli turned in his chair and accepted the proffered cup gratefully. "Well, what do we know for sure?"

Vince snorted before taking a sip of his coffee. "They found and corrected the problem. We should see no more NAVCOM errors from that station..."

Anatoli started to relax when Vince continued, "...but, Frank tells me this screw up was the fourth since we entered MS about three weeks ago. He has the computer busily crunching away, trying to figure out where we are. It could be several hours before we get any definitive answers."

"Oh...Delightful." Anatoli mumbled his heartfelt sarcasm. He stood and took the few steps to the curtained wall. With a small waving gesture, the curtain slowly parted and the lights dimmed to reveal a panoramic window on the universe.

After a long moment of silence, "This..." he nodded at the star studded view, "...has got to be the loneliest place to be lost in."

Vincent joined him, captivated by the expansive view.

Anatoli continued. "Let's hope and pray we find our way...there are so many lives at stake."

Vince glanced at the captain. The man stood staring fixedly into the blazing glory, lost in thought. The moments stretched and the captain's stare never wavered. Vince was starting to worry. Psychologists didn't recommend long stints of immersion in this type of stargazing.

"Tolya?" He prompted quietly.

Anatoli visibly shook himself from the hypnotic depths. "I'm fine...Once we have the information, I want a staff meeting. We need a new plan."

Vince nodded. "I'll tell you when we have an answer."

The captain nodded and settled himself on a small couch facing the window. He composed himself with his coffee as Vince returned to the bridge.

A CHANGE OF PLANS — 2
ECS Destiny, Quarterdeck, MedCentral, 0755 Hrs

Dr. Daniela Jacobs peeled off the gloves and tossed them unceremoniously into the recycle bin. "Well, Jeanette, your arm should be good as new in about two weeks. Till then, I want you to keep it in the sling. The bone should set nicely thanks to the nano-bond and I don't think there'll be any visible scars." She offered an encouraging smile.

Jeanette smiled wanly as she stepped gingerly down from the edge of the bed. "I was so scared. Suddenly I was falling...I thought I was gonna die."

Daniela patted her good shoulder. "You'll be OK. You heard the captain's announcement. Right?"

Jeanette nodded her head uncertainly.

"Everything will be fine. You'll see." Daniela watched the worry working across the woman's face. "How about this? Try encouraging your coworkers. I bet they're pretty upset."

Jeanette flexed her fingers and shrugged her shoulder, checking for pain. Finding none she smiled hopefully. "Thank you, doctor. I'll do that."

Daniela smiled back and Jeanette left MedCentral. She picked up the small BGS unit and followed her recent patient through the curtain and down to the end of the row of cubicles that passed for exam rooms. She placed the unit carefully in its recessed home in the equipment rack. The device helped to stimulate accelerated bone regrowth by activating the nano-bots injected at the site.

Brianna, Daniela's personal assistant looked up from her station. "That was the last one, Dannie."

Daniela sighed. "Thanks, Bri. Are Freddy and Janice done?"

"Yeah, they left about twenty minutes ago."

Daniela grunted in acknowledgment as she slipped out of her lab coat. "How many were there anyway, ten? I was too busy cutting and pasting to count."

Brianna got up and came around the desk. "Surprisingly, there were only six."

"Just six from this deck?"

Brianna nodded, "Yup. There were the two working out in the gym, that guy who was in the showers, and the two, including Jeanette, setting up for breakfast in the diner."

Daniela shook her head, "I wonder what it was like on the residential decks? Six wasn't too bad really, after that rude roller coaster ride."

Brianna rolled her eyes. "That was fun, wasn't it?"

Daniela gave her a sidelong look and shook her head. "Oh, loads of fun..." she said with a chuckle. "You know, it could have been a lot worse if it had happened during the 'day'."

Daniela could never get over the arbitrary terms 'day' and 'night' on shipboard. There were no natural references for the mind to grab hold of, ships programmed lighting not withstanding. It'd be so good to breath fresh air, alien or not.

She smiled tiredly at Brianna and stepped into her office cubicle. "Now, I'm going to get my inside source to cough up some answers. They're supposed to announce when we're dropping out of MS."

Tossing her lab coat over a hook, she made a rag doll flop into her chair, reached over and tapped the COMM icon on her terminal. This opened a window awaiting her pleasure.

"Routing?" The cheery voice of the AI prompted.

"Bridge," she muttered.

The window flashed, revealing a pleasantly familiar face. Vincent Leoni, the first officer, blinked in surprise. "Ah! My favorite doctor. How can I help, my dear?"

Daniela grinned wickedly. "Right now, Vince darling, you could start by telling me what's really going on up there. That little roller coaster ride we had kept me busy the last couple of hours patching up after your driving."

Vince feigned mock innocence. "My driving? That wasn't me this time." He grinned weakly. "I was just about to call you."

Daniela nodded, "Yeah, but I got there first, so cough it up."

He turned serious. "Sorry, Dannie. Things could be a whole lot better up here. Captain asked me to pass on a call for a general staff meeting at 0830 hours in the staff conference room. You'll be completely filled in then."

Daniela blinked. A general staff conference this sudden meant serious issues. She looked him in the eyes, as much as that was possible on a vid-link.

Vince looked around uncomfortably. "Let's just say things have taken an unhappy turn, but I CAN tell you that the ship is just fine. It's the mission that's a mess."

He paused. Leaning closer, he spoke quietly. "We'll be reviewing our itinerary."

Daniela sat forward, eyebrows reaching for her hairline. "Itinerary? Vince. We only have ONE destination! This is not a pleasure cruise, you know!"

Vince winced. "Yeah, well, like I said, we'll be reviewing that issue. Look. NAVCOM screwed up big time and Captain doesn't want a panic, so...well, you know the drill. He wants hard facts before word gets passed around."

Daniela frowned. "OK. I'll be there, of course."

Vince smiled tiredly, "Thanks, Dannie. I'll see you then."

Daniela returned the smile and his face was replaced with the ship's logo. She sat back, lost in thought.

Brianna brought coffee which she gladly accepted. "That didn't sound so good." She commented.

Daniela look up at her. "The truth is, I think things are about to get more exciting. I'm going to a full general staff meeting in about half an hour. We'll know more then. Oh, and Bri, we probably shouldn't discuss this with anyone till we have a better idea just what's happening."

Brianna looked a little worried. "Of course, Dannie. You go ahead and I'll watch the shop. At least all the injuries from that horrid bump have been dealt with."

She gave a little conspiratorial grin. "Now I'm going to switch roles for a minute. I'm prescribing a stop at the diner for a quick bite on your way to that meeting. You've been running half awake on empty for a couple of hours."

Daniela got up. She grabbed her power-tab from her desk and squeezed Brianna's arm in a friendly gesture. "Thanks, Doctor Bri. I'll get right to it." She grinned and as she started for the door, "I'll let you know what I can when I get back."

A Change of Plans — 3
Quarterdeck, Staff Conference Room, 0825 Hrs

Tanya Nydel, Chief of Security, arrived at the conference room a few minutes early. She was of medium height, in excellent physical shape and reasonably attractive. She'd been a last minute addition to the command staff, presenting herself at the entry ramp twelve hours before departure.

Being a woman of action, the last twenty-five months had been almost boring. There'd been few incidents to truly test her mettle; an occasional petty theft report, one case of public drunkenness. Apparently there was a private still somewhere on board. Her team had yet to find the thrice-damned thing. This emergency would be her first time seeing the staff under truly stressful conditions.

The first to arrive was Dr. Emily Strauss, Chief Science Officer and the colony's Director of Education. She was intelligent, inquisitive and a good communicator. She was attractive, at least by the scale most men kept to measure such things.

Emily smiled at Tanya as she took her place at the table. Tanya considered some small talk when the next staff member entered.

Dr. Daniela Jacobs was probably the friendliest woman Tanya had ever met. The Chief Medical Officer was tall and slender, almost willowy. She seemed to lend strength to everyone she met. Tanya couldn't think of anyone else she'd rather have as her personal doctor. Everyone knew there was a special chemistry developing between Daniela and the First Officer, Vincent Leoni.

Daniela murmured a quiet greeting to Tanya and sat next to Emily. The two began talking in soft, concerned voices.

Predictably, the next two staff members arrived together. Daryl and Naomi McIntyre were one of two married couples on the command staff. Daryl was the ship's Chief Engineer, while Naomi was their Chief Mechanical and Design Engineer.

They were quietly talking shop as they entered. "Hey Tanya; good to see you." Naomi offered. Tanya brightened and smiled. Daryl nodded absently, ushering Naomi to a set of seats near the head of the table. In spite of his brusque veneer Daryl could be warm and friendly. Right now his ship was having trouble, and that brought out the grumpy old bear. In contrast, Naomi always seemed warm and friendly. She was an artist in her craft and passionate about designing and building things.

Tanya left her place and went to the counter and coffee dispenser unit. Though it was clearly not part of her job description, Tanya had taken on the role of coffee lady. As she began her rounds, Franklin Drake, the Navigation and Computer Tech officer, came in looking worried. He made his way to his seat opposite Emily.

Emily gave Frank a little smile that seemed to work wonders on his nerves. *Interesting. More chemistry?* Tanya gave a cup to Naomi, who murmured a quiet 'thanks.' *I wonder whether anyone will ever have any chemistry for me?* She shook her head. *Stop it.* She focused on more important matters.

Frank was an artist in his own right. His navigation skills were amazing, and he seemed to have a second sense for all things computer. He doubled as the colony's historian.

The staff's second married couple entered, engaged in quiet conversation. Ichirou Akari was of medium height; slender, almost wiry. His tiny wife, Midori was only tiny in stature. She was quite the fiery one, once excited. This couple was responsible for the successful management of Ag-Deck. He managed the program, but Midori was the unchallenged expert on hydroponics.

They glanced about the room and spotted Tanya. Ichirou smiled, dipping his head in her direction. Tanya returned the gesture with a grin. This couple had kept her busy in the quiet times. They were great neighbors. Midori offered friendly chatter to the others as the two made their way around the table to sit next to Tanya's place.

Vincent Leoni and Captain Anatoli Chernov entered, engaged in an earnest discussion, which ended as they approached the last available seats.

Vince sat, winking conspiratorially at Daniela, as he got comfortable. He was a tall, muscular man who seemed to exude charm. A very capable first officer, his command style was somewhat laid back compared to the captain.

The captain was of medium height, slender in a solid, muscular way. He stood for a moment at the head of the table looking around at his senior staff. His eyes lingered momentarily on Tanya as she was making her rounds with the coffee. She didn't notice him tearing his gaze away with a determined look as he took his seat.

Tanya finished the circle, bringing the last cup to the captain. She harbored a soft spot for him, but tried valiantly to suppress such inappropriate notions. She assumed she wasn't his type anyway.

She handed him the cup. "Here ya go, sir."

He glanced up, took the cup, offering a gracious "Thanks." Their eyes locked momentarily. Tanya flushed, feeling foolish, and with a little self-conscious grin, hurried back to her seat.

Nine speculative sets of eyes followed her progress. She buried her burning face in a sip of coffee, not noticing Daryl nudging Naomi's arm with a grin. Again, Captain Chernov tore his eyes away. He stood, clearing his throat. All eyes snapped back to him.

"OK folks. Let's get this meeting going." He tapped a spot on the corner of his power tab, bringing the recorders to life. "I'm sure everyone's dying to know what happened this morning. The nasty ride we experienced, putting the good doctor to work in earnest," he glanced with a grin at Daniela, "was the result of an emergency dive from Multi-Space 2." He placed the power-tab on the table in front of him. "NAVCOM developed a faulty sub-processor which threw us way off course."

Tolya sipped his coffee and continued. "As bad as that sounds, the problem was compounded further. During the scramble to find and correct the problem, Frank discovered this was the last of four similar events in the last three weeks. Because NAVCOM ordered the course changes, the navigation fault alarms did not go off. We knew nothing until early this morning when Frank checked the auto-log history against the real-time data."

Much muttering and a general stir ran like electricity around the room. Anatoli shook his head. "I would remind everyone that during MS flight we maintain skeleton crews on the bridge, essentially to baby-sit the computer. The computer generates an interpretation of the view of space around us because our brains are unable to interpret the physical reality. Simply put, we became too dependent on the computer."

Anatoli folded his arms over his chest, looking around the room. "Obviously, three weeks on the wrong course in MS yields horrific problems. The good news is, we've solved the NAVCOM mess and have a fix on our current position. So, technically we're not lost."

He paused to take another sip and Dr. Jacobs piped up. "Technically? Technically, we're not lost? That sounds mighty ominous. So, what's the bad news?" All eyes swiveled towards the doctor. Tanya tensed at the challenge in her voice. Like a tennis match, the eyes swiveled expectantly from the doctor back to the captain for his answer.

He stood and began to pace behind his seat like a caged tiger. "We know *Destiny* was equipped with a one-way MS drive and a matching supply of fuel. Normally, we'd have a small surplus of fuel once we reached our goal. However, after very careful calculations, painstakingly checked and verified, we find we've gone so far along this new course, we can no longer reach *Terra Nova* on our remaining fuel."

He stopped, grabbing the back of his chair. "If we tried, we'd wind up dropping painfully out of MS generations from our target, unable to complete the journey." He shook his head in frustration. "Even if we could find more fuel, the drive system wasn't meant to work indefinitely."

There was an ominous silence as everyone digested this information. Daniela voiced the unasked questions. "So, what are we to do? Are there alternatives? Could we go back to Earth; maybe try again?"

She stopped her noise with a nervous hand. She truly wanted to take that last question back. It was impossible. Even if they made it back, there'd be little they could expect from that source. By now, all those they'd known would be old enough to be long retired, if not actually dead.

By the time they got back, if they could get back, who knew what condition Earth would be in? Multi-Space significantly minimized the time dilation effects of near light-speed travel, but it didn't eliminate it. It only made longer voyages, like theirs, a little more practical.

"Sorry. That was stupid!"

There were a few nervous chuckles as Captain Chernov moved around his seat and leaned on the table with his knuckles, smiling, "I understand, Dannie. Thank you for the comic relief."

More chuckles… Daniela blushed slightly.

Anatoli continued. "The answer is, 'yes.' There's room for cautious optimism." He straightened up. "Once we found ourselves and confirmed our situation, we began considering our options, which were hovering close to zero.

"In the middle of the star mapping survey we found something very interesting in our current neighborhood. It seems we're in easy range, a short MS-1 hop, of a very favorable star. Emily pointed it out in our survey, so I asked her to give us some details. Emily?"

He nodded in Emily's direction and sat down. Tanya noticed a curious spark in the back of his eyes. She wondered if there was something between them. *No, it looks like Emily has eyes for Frank.* She mentally kicked herself. *Get your brain in gear, girl!*

Emily stood. "Before I start, I thought it might help to see a visual of our situation."

She tapped the surface of the table where she'd been sitting. Nearly the entire table lit up and the room lights dimmed. There, under several elbows, was a realistic star field. Everyone sat back from the table and watched closely.

"This is a…well, a bird's eye view, of the area of space we're in." She reached towards the middle of the table and tapped a star. It brightened and the label, *18 Scorpii* appeared. "This is the star we were headed for." She touched the edge of the table near her and drew a quick arc towards the star, leaving a green line that ended at a point a little over half way to the labeled star. "This line is the path we followed until this last MS transition about three weeks ago"

Emily tapped the end of the green line and a blue line meandered oddly off to the right and further across the table to stop facing the end opposite the captain. "And this is where we've gone since." She tapped the end of the blue line and a little blue triangle lit up. "We're about here right now."

She glanced around the table. "Calculating the remaining distance from where we first went off course…" she ran a finger from the end of the green line to the labeled star, leaving a red line, "…and point that line from our current position back towards our target …" she pinched the red line, dragged a copy over to the blue triangle and spun it around to point as she described, "…you can see it doesn't come close."

Emily paused to let the visual speak for itself. "While surveying the local neighborhood, looking for navigational cues and potential candidate stars, we noticed this one." She reached out and gently tapped a star near Daryl's elbow. He grinned and politely removed the offending space monster. The star brightened and another label lit: *20 Leonis Minoris*. The two selected stars were over half way across the table from each another.

Placing her fingers like a giant spider on the screen, she dragged it towards the captain. The star field scrolled as if painted on the inside of an immense sphere. As the selected star reached the center of the table she removed her hand. The star field expanded in every direction, stars vanishing off the edge of the table. The outward expansion slowed as a single star became prominent.

"Being much closer than we would be on Earth, we quickly found several planets orbiting this star. Our catalogues of candidate stars don't include this one, but one of the planets shows potential signs of earth type attributes."

She clustered her fingers over the star and splayed them outward as if opening a small bag. The computer quickly zoomed the star in question and put a faint globe of light around it. Data points appeared and resolved into planet icons with faint traces showing projected orbital paths.

She tapped one of the icons and the computer highlighted it. Compact lines of data scrolled beneath it. "This planet is within the desired, habitable zone for this star; what we call the Goldilocks Zone. Spectrographic analysis proves this star is a bit richer in heavy elements. It's a little brighter and slightly larger, but otherwise, very similar to Sol. Because of the higher degree of heavy elements, the tentative target planet is most likely richer in usable metals than Earth."

After a few moments to allow everyone to absorb the implications, Emily swept a hand across the table, banishing the scene from the room as the lights slowly brightened.

She resumed her seat and the captain waited, watching his team's reaction. Curiosity seemed to be the predominant expression. He stood up and took the floor.

"Thank you, Emily. OK folks, I think maybe we can turn disaster into opportunity. Frank, Daniela, I'd like you to assist Emily any way you can. We need to get all the information we can from this distance. If the results are positive, I think we should make the short hop into the system and study it in detail. We've got to get this right because we've run out of options. Vince, I want you to help coordinate this project.

"Daryl, Naomi, if we're fortunate, we could find a new place to colonize. If so, it'll be a totally new world. We'll have to survey it ourselves and, probably, we'll need some changes in our settlement plans. I want you to double-check our readiness for a landing."

His attention switched to Ichirou. "Ichi, Midori. There's not a lot you two can do until we get closer. If we make the hop we'll be needing all of your expertise."

Ichirou gave a small respectful nod and the captain returned it before looking Tanya's way.

After a short, hesitant pause, he continued. "Tanya, I need you to stay for a few moments after the meeting. We have to tell everyone what's going on, but I'm concerned about panic. It's going to get rough when everyone discovers things are not going as advertised."

Tanya looked apprehensive. Whenever she wound up close to the captain she turned into a tongue-tied idiot, *but a private meeting?* She quietly bit her lip and nodded.

Anatoli smiled and looked around the room. "Questions?" No one spoke. "OK. Lets get to it; any problems or questions, talk to me. In a few days we'll meet again to discuss results and solidify plans. We're gonna get through this. We have to!"

He stepped away from the table and the thoughtful postures of the staff officers melted into action as they stood, clustering together to discuss assignments.

* * * *

The room was empty except for Tanya, who stood nervously by the door, and the Captain, who was busily going through his notes. Tanya took a deep breath and approached. "Could I get you another coffee, sir?"

Captain Chernov looked up from his power tab. "Oh, no. Thanks anyway. I've probably had more than enough." He sat and motioned for her to join him. She sat nervously on the edge of the seat, the corner of the table between them.

He looked at her earnestly. "Tanya, I need your thoughts on how we're going to explain all this to the colonists. Your profile says you've a knack for dealing with large groups of people. Our people sacrificed everything for this venture. When they learn we're not going where promised, there's going to be a great deal of unhappiness." He placed his power-tab on the table between them. "So, how can we turn dreadful news into a positive outcome?"

Being this close to Anatoli Chernov distracted Tanya. She firmly pushed her jumbled thoughts into 'Ms. Efficient' mode and considered the situation.

She brought her hands from her lap and rested them on the table as if setting herself for some physical activity. "Well, sir, it's never easy working people through a major disappointment, but a few ideas come to mind."

She turned one hand over and tapped a finger into the exposed palm. "Sir, first..." Anatoli stirred restlessly but held his peace. "First. Whatever we do, we must be honest and stay that way. If the people ever think we're trying to pull the wool over their eyes, they'll explode. Their lives are now in limbo. They don't know it yet, but they're truly in God's hands now."

Anatoli nodded and Tanya rushed on, tapping two fingers into her palm. "Second, after the shock they'll want to find a way to fix it. Never forget; you have a vast resource in the people on board. There are bright minds here that need to be plumbed for the knowledge, experience and wisdom we're going to need to get through this. As governor, according the colony charter, they're YOUR people, but you have to make them WANT to be your people. Make them feel needed."

Sometime or other, Anatoli had reached for his power-tab and started taking notes.

Tanya tapped three fingers. "Third." She was in her element now. "You must show them you have a firm grasp of where we're going, what the goals are and that you have the determination to see them through to the bitter end."

Anatoli looked up at her. "Let's pray the end is not so bitter." He said quietly.

Tanya found her eyes diving into his. She mentally jerked herself back, "Agreed," she replied nervously.

Tanya cleared her throat and tapped four fingers into her palm. "Finally. No matter what you do, we're going to run into a handful of troublemakers. Believe me, there's always someone with an axe to grind who'll seek personal advantage in the face of any crisis."

She sat back and looked at the captain. Dropping her hands back to the comfort of her lap, she concluded. "I suggest you hold a ship wide meeting. You could give a general explanation of the nature of our situation. Then, present the solution we've come to recommend. Then solicit questions, comments and suggestions."

Tanya noticed him gazing at her and stopped, feeling a slight flush color her face.

He smiled, "Go on..."

"Well, ah...once the meeting is over there should be a time for communication. People would have the harder questions answered and their suggestions and comments considered." She shifted nervously in her seat. "After a time, you could announce the decision and give a date of execution."

Anatoli sat back and stared thoughtfully at his notes. Tanya fidgeted a little as the silence grew.

"You know something?" He looked up and considered her, as if seeing her for the first time. "In all this time I've never stopped to appreciate how bright and articulate you are. There's a lot more to you than meets the eye."

His face flushed slightly as he replayed that last statement. *Oh man! That sounded like the winner of the 'cheesiest pickup line of the year' award. What the heck am I doing?*

Tanya looked uncomfortable. She'd never been good at accepting people's praise. Her problem was compounded with the captain. "Aw, sir...it's nothing really..."

He interrupted. "Tanya, please. Unofficially, my friends call me Tolya. I'd like to think of you as a friend."

Tanya looked at him as if he'd grown a third eye. "Is that really...you know, appropriate...sir?"

Tolya chuckled. "Probably not, to someone somewhere, but think of it this way. We're no longer active officers of the ESN or any other Earth agency. Once we get our feet on firm ground we're going to be just regular folks trying to survive in a new world. Whatever happens, we'll be working closely together for the rest of our lives. It's time to drop formalities."

Tanya thought for a moment. "I guess it can't hurt."

"Good," He said happily.

Tanya took a deep breath. *Good grief. Where was I? First names? Nicknames? This is embarrassing. Oh, yeah, the problem. Focus! Focus!* "Well, sir..."

He looked at her, one eyebrow raised mischievously.

She flushed. Her mind was muddled with impossible possibilities. She tried again. "OK, um...Tolya..." He grinned. She wrung her hands nervously in her lap under the table. "Anyway, to the problem..." She brought her hands up to count off points.

Tolya reached out and gently stopped them. He gave her a searching look. "Tanya? We just discussed it."

Tanya's furious blush went from her scalp to under her collar.

Anatoli continued. "I've got the notes right here. I'll study them and tell you in the next few days what we're going to do. OK?"

Tanya nodded wordlessly. She realized he still held her hands. She snatched them back as if they burned. They probably did.

A CHANGE OF PLANS — 4

SAT 01.23, 2094
Quarterdeck, Open Gym, 1357 Hrs

Tolya tightened the three-striped, black belt of his *gi* and headed out to the gym floor. He stopped in the doorway. As expected, Tanya was already working out.

He stood, watching in appreciation of her graceful motions. Though he'd noted her history in martial arts from her profile, he'd never seen her work through the katas. Being somewhat private about his own workouts, he chose late hours when few people were about. He was taking steps to correct this oversight.

He remembered how, about six months out from Sol system, Tanya had requested permission to begin a program to train her security team in Karate. He'd been quite willing to grant her permission; not that he expected a serious need.

Tanya was unaware of her singular audience. She flowed in constant motion. Her hands flashing in precise arcs, stopping abruptly as if hitting solid objects. Blocks, kicks, punches, spin kicks; she covered the floor in dominant strides, ending with her back to him.

Once he was certain she'd completed her katas, he clapped slowly, but firmly. Tanya spun, the ends of her two striped black belt whipping about, to stare in surprise. Tolya gave her the ritual bow, cupped hand over fist extended forward in her direction. She blushed and returned the gesture.

"Excellent. I'm sorry I never watched you before." Tolya said.

Tanya grinned. "I see."

She looked him up and down, appraising his *gi,* a traditional fighting uniform. "Your outfit looks nice. Does it mean anything?" The challenge in her voice was welcome.

Tolya grinned back. "Well, now, we could find out." He walked out onto the gym floor, stopping a few paces from her. "Tell you what. If you don't mind helping me warm up, we could spar a couple rounds afterwards."

Tanya nodded, a mischievous twinkle in her eyes. "Now, this could be fun."

Tolya smiled and they moved to the center of the gym floor. They faced each other and knelt on the mat. After the breathing and stretching, they rose smoothly, assuming ready stances. They worked through the forms; low, mid, high blocks, strikes. Turning, they went through the kicks, side by side and finally came smoothly to the end.

Tanya's face was flushed from the exercise. Tolya felt great. They turned and faced each other.

Tolya raised an eyebrow. "Two rounds?"

She shrugged. "Sure,"

He grinned. "Just to see how things go..."

"Watch yourself," Tanya grinned back.

They stepped back a few paces from each other, bowed in precise formal fashion and then snapped into fight ready postures, hands loosely bladed. Things started slowly, but soon escalated as they found the rhythm of their styles. The strikes and blocks met in the air with precision.

Neither was aware of the watchers gathering in the doorways. Daryl nudged Naomi and they leaned together in whispered comment. Daniela stood in the opposite entry and watched with great fascination.

The sparring went on for a while as both fighters sought to find an opening. They were more evenly matched than expected.

Finally, in a sudden flurry of blows, blocks and a surprise sweep, Tolya wound up on his back. Tanya's hand flashed like a knife blade to stop millimeters from his throat. They froze momentarily, and then Tanya backed off, offering her hand to help Tolya up. Motion caught Tolya's eye as he bounced to his feet. He glanced in the doorways. They'd acquired an audience. He grinned at Tanya, who returned the favor.

They bowed, and then the second round began. Now, they were hot and sweaty. Now, they were serious in their concentration. The give and take of blows, kicks and blocks were more calculated, more precise. Some of the moves were so blurred that the watchers barely saw them. The exchange went on even longer than the first. Finally, it was Tanya's turn to land flat and hard on her back, with Tolya coming down hard in a powerful lunge that left his pointed elbow resting rock steady just above her sternum.

They froze for a moment. Then, Tolya stepped back, put out a hand and pulled her up. They bowed, grinning from ear to ear like

Cheshire Cats as their impromptu audience clapped enthusiastically. Tolya, his breathing returning to its normal pace, looked over at Tanya and asked, "Call it a draw, or go around again?"

She shook her head. "That's...OK. I'll...let you slide...for now. We'll have to do that again sometime."

Tolya grinned. "Definitely!" They turned towards the locker rooms and he asked, "How about dessert and coffee in the lounge?"

Tanya glanced at him. She shrugged, "OK. Sure."

"Great! I'll meet you out front in a few minutes." Tanya grinned as they parted.

* * * *

The myriad colors of the endless star field made a magnificent backdrop to the low lighting in the lounge. They sat at a table near the transparent armoplast expanse. Tanya wore a casual outfit that complimented her form nicely. Tolya was in casual slacks and a short-sleeved shirt.

They flipped through the dessert section of the table top menu, finally settling on a single, large, decadent, Chocolate Mousse. Soon, the sinful confection arrived along with their coffees.

After a couple of bites, Tolya sat back and looked appreciatively at Tanya. "So, I've read the basics in your profile, but I'd like to hear it from you. Exactly how did you pick up your fighting skills?"

Tanya tilted her head slightly, carefully stirring her coffee to hide her nerves. "It started in high school. I was fascinated with the martial arts and my parents encouraged me to go for it. I got pretty good over the course of two years and was accepted on the school team as a junior.

"After high school I joined my college team. Between my personal training and my college days, I made a lot of progress." She grinned and looked impishly at him. "So, now it's your turn. How'd you get to *Sandan* black?"

Tolya leaned forward and snagged another bite of the mousse. "Well, my story is similar in some ways, except I started earlier than you. I was in the sixth grade when my folks thought it would be good for my self-discipline. I found I loved it and excelled. My high school didn't have a karate club so I continued with private instruction.

"I got my second and first *kyu* brown belt by the time I went off to college. Since my schooling was in the Earth Space Navy, my interest and skills in martial arts earned appreciation from some of my superiors.

"I got my Black when I was about to graduate from the Naval Academy and then, over the course of four years of service out on the rim, I earned *Shodan* and *Nidan*. My last one, the *Sandan* came a couple of months before I took this final command."

They sat in companionable silence, trading swipes at the chocolate mousse. Finally, Tolya spoke up. "Tanya. Do you remember Thursday, when I said I'd go over the notes from our discussion?"

Tanya was thankful for the subdued lighting. She could feel the blush and wondered if her face glowed of its own volition. She remembered quite vividly that private moment with him. She'd felt like an idiot at the time, but since, on reflection, she had no regrets. It was quite pleasant treating Tolya like a friend, rather than just a superior officer.

"I remember."

Tolya smiled. "I've gone over those notes so often I have them memorized. I told you I'd let you know my decision."

He leaned forward again and placed his elbows squarely on the table. "I'm going to have that meeting. We're going do it just like you said."

A surprised look crossed her face. "You took me serious?"

Tolya stopped. "You were serious, weren't you?"

"Well, yes." She looked down, somehow embarrassed. "I just, well… most people in authority don't take me very seriously."

Tolya winced. "Their loss."

She glanced up, one delicate eyebrow raised.

"I mean it. Anyone who doesn't take you seriously is missing out, big time." He thought for a moment. "Tanya, I told you before, but it came across sounding lame, maybe even stupid. The way I see it, some people's talents are obvious. They seem to wear them on their sleeves like badges of rank."

He shrugged. "Then there are others, like you, whose talents seem held in reserve, waiting for the right moment to surface."

Tanya looked puzzled. "What, so I'm hiding my talents now?"

Tolya shook his head. "No, not at all. It's just…well…you're just not flashy; you don't show off when it comes to your various skills.

"Take Karate. I've known since I first read your profile that you practiced the art, but it wasn't until I challenged you today that I got to see just how skilled you really are.

"More to the point, when I asked for your advice on this communications issue, I didn't know what to expect. When you got past the nerves and started talking, I discovered you had a natural wisdom and knack for addressing this kind of problem. Your profile says you're knowledgeable in that area, but I needed to see for myself."

Tanya looked searchingly at him, unconsciously nibbling the corner of her lip.

"Look. Forget all that. The simple answer is, 'YES.' I do take your advice seriously, and I intend to follow it."

Tanya glanced down with a shy smile. "Thank you."

Tolya gazed at her for a moment and then reached for his cup. "I wanted to tell you before the next staff meeting. You've probably noticed, most of the staff members are slowly starting to pair off. Since the vast majority of our people are in families of various sizes we need to be sensitive to that perspective."

He got that lopsided half grin she secretly found so cute. "Daryl and Naomi are an established couple and represent the people well. The same goes for Ichirou and Midori. Vince and Daniela are developing as a couple. They need to be seen as part of the future of the colony." Tolya let out a chuckle. "One of these days, poor Frank's going to figure out what to do about Emily."

"We'll be using three venues; this one, in theater mode, and the two Ed-center lecture halls to ether side of us. I want the various pairs taking leadership roles in the other two venues.

"Daryl and Naomi will take the Port side Ed facility and Ichi and Midori Akari will take the Starboard side. We'll have Vince and Daniela sit in with the McIntyre's and Frank and Emily with the Akari's. That leaves one venue. I want you here with me." He pointed to the floor next to his chair. "Right here."

Tanya looked up at him, eyes round. "Me? Why me? I'd think Vince, being your first officer, would support you in a public setting. I'm no public figure. Nobody really knows who I am."

Tolya shook his head. "No. You're no 'public figure.' You're a no nonsense person who doesn't give a rip what people think, so long as the right thing gets done."

Tanya gave him a sidelong glance. "And you want me here with you. So, what are you saying? You seem to have a number of little messages for the colonists."

Tolya was nonplussed. "I ah, well...I think we work well together...and I think couples working together lend a sense of comfort in an otherwise tense situation."

He paused, wondering what he was really saying. "I mean...if you'd rather not. I didn't mean...I know..."

Tanya placed a tentative hand on his arm, silencing him. "No. I don't object...I'm just trying to figure things out."

She released his arm. She couldn't explain the topsy-turvy emotions she felt. There was a sense of expectation. Somehow she was missing something important.

A CHANGE OF PLANS — 5

TUE 02.28.2094
Quarterdeck, Event Center, Theater Mode, 1800 Hrs

Even on a massive colony starship, space is at a premium. It took the three largest venues to accommodate the crowd. Tolya felt nervous. Tanya smiled at him. "You'll do fine."

He smiled gratefully and stood to start the meeting.

Before signaling the digicams, he began with a greeting to those in the crowded dining hall. "Folks, I want to thank you for squeezing in here. Sardines never looked so good!"

A few polite chuckles quickly trickled to nothing. "OK, well...The purpose of this meeting is to explain what's going on. We're broadcasting this meeting throughout the ship, so I'd appreciate if you'd hold all comments and questions for the Q&A time afterward."

Murmurs rustled through the room.

"With that said," he continued, "Let's begin the broadcast portion of the meeting." He signaled the tech and the digicams lit.

"Friends, colleagues and fellow adventurers, thank you for taking time out of your schedules to attend this meeting.

"Our three largest venues are crowded with people who are concerned about our future. To those of you watching from essential station assignments, thank you for your dedication. A recording of this meeting will be posted on ship's-net."

He scanned the hall. "Everyone knows we recently made an emergency dive from Multi-Space. Some of you had the misfortune of being in the wrong place at the wrong time, with no warning.

"I speak for the entire staff when I say, we regret your pain and inconvenience. Sadly, the action was unavoidable."

The crowed murmured to itself.

"The truth of the matter is, due to a simple manufacturing defect we have a major challenge to surmount... On Thursday, January 21, 2094 at 0547 hours, during a routine computer managed course adjustment, the navigation computer's sub-processor malfunctioned. As a result, we were thrown badly off course while in Multi-Space.

"We did an emergency dive from Multi-Space to minimize the drastic deviation. The computer problem was fixed, thanks to our capable tech crew. That's the good news."

He paused for a sip of water. Anticipation and apprehension were tangible presences in the room.

"There is some bad news, however. It would be dishonest and unfair not to tell you, so here it is. We are now so far off course, that even knowing exactly were we are, our limited fuel supply and the one-way nature of the ship's design prevents us from safely reaching *Nova Terra*."

The room erupted with exclamations ranging from dismay to anger. Tanya watched and her team members shifted nervously, anticipating trouble. As the tension mounted Tanya rose and tapped the pin-mic on her collar. "WAIT! Please, listen!"

The cameras panned to include her in the view as she raised her hands towards the crowd. The rumblings in the room, echoed by similar reactions in the other venues, continued unabated. Tanya put her fingers to her lips and blew a shrill, piercing whistle that left closer ears ringing.

The angry noise slowly subsided. She glanced at a bracelet with a small galaxy of red, amber and green lights. The lights, representing the signals from a team member in the other two venues, slowly shifted from red to green.

Tanya placed hands on hips, "That's better!" She looked around the room, daring anyone to interrupt. "We're all in this for the long haul. So, we've got to pull together to deal with the problem." She stood trembling, arms folded across her chest.

A voice shouted out above the quieting crowd. "Yeah, sure! We're depending on YOU to get us there safely. So, what happens? YOU go and SCREW it up!"

The crowd grumbled. The voice grew bolder as its owner sensed the mood. "What are we going to do now? Where are we going to go? Are we just gonna die out here?"

Tanya's hand flashed forward and pointed in the direction of the angry voice. "YOU must TRUST those you CLAIM to depend on!"

Her hand swept up toward the ceiling, pointing in the general direction of the ship's command bridge. "The problem was caused by equipment failure. So, if you want to whine and complain, if you just have to lay blame on someone, give Earth a call!"

She saw her team approach a tall, red-faced man near an entrance. She flashed a 'watch and wait' signal and then crossed her arms again. "I'm sure we'd all love to hear how they'd explain this."

She waited for the trickle of nervous chuckles and affirming expletives to subside. "Unfortunately, as you're fully aware, that option is truly out of reach!"

Her eyes swept the room. "All of us, from the youngest mother to the captain himself, were selected for the qualities necessary to found an independent Earth Colony, so I think some responsible, adult attitudes are exactly what we need right now."

Tanya dropped her arms and waved in Tolya's direction. "Tol... ah, Captain Chernov has more to say. There is a silver lining! So, I'd really appreciate if you'd reserve your CONSTRUCTIVE questions and comments for AFTER the captain finishes his piece!"

She abruptly sat down and snatched up her water glass. The silence that ensued slowly turned to polite applause, which escalated quickly. A number of catcalls and a few yelled exclamations of 'You tell em!' were added to the mix.

Tolya stepped forward and the cameras panned back to center on him. The room grew quiet as he looked at his security chief. "Wow! Thank you, Tanya!"

There was a pregnant pause.

"What I was about to say is...there's some cautiously optimistic news." All eyes were now riveted on him.

"While surveying local space, we discovered a nearby star that has a complete system of planets. This star is similar to our sun. One of the planets, located in the 'habitable zone' seems enticingly earth-like. After our teams studied everything they could from this distance we agreed that it's worth the short hop for a closer look. We think we've found a new, unexplored, earth type world."

Positive excitement worked through the crowd. Tolya sensed hope in the room. He held up his hands for quiet and finished his spiel. "Before we take this important step, we feel you deserve to know the facts and have some input. So, we'll field and record questions and comments. Every effort will be made to find answers before we come to a consensus. I appreciate your spirit of cooperation and seek your prayers and encouragement as we tackle this new challenge. Thank you!"

Tolya sat and the digicams went dark. The hall erupted in tumultuous applause as people, except for a cynical few, grasped the spirit of purpose their captain had invested in them.

The room quieted down as Tanya stood. "OK. We're going to start the Q&A time. Any questions we cannot readily answer will be researched with answers posted on Ships-Net.

Into the expectant pause that followed, she asked, "Questions?"

MAJOR COMPLICATIONS — 1

MON 02.8.2094
Quarterdeck, Command Staff Conference Room, 1210 Hrs

The conference room emptied quickly. A majority of the colonists were enthusiastic about the coming survey mission. Tolya scrolled through his notes and Tanya saved a few comments on her own tablet.

"So. It looks like we're good to go," she commented.

He looked up from his tablet. "Yeah. It went better than I thought it would."

Tanya smiled. "Well, we do have a good group..." Her smile faded. "Mostly."

Tolya cocked his head in silent query.

Her thoughtful look faded as she focused on the captain. "Do you remember that guy who yelled out last week?"

Tolya grinned. "How could I forget? Let's see, Jackson, right?"

Tanya nodded. "Yeah. I've an odd feeling about him. I'm told he's been trying to agitate folk. He says the leadership, translated YOU, should have been more on the ball. He thinks there's some kind of conspiracy."

Tolya frowned. "How'd a crazy like that wind up on board a colony ship?" He shut off his power-tab. "Let's just throw him in the brig and be done with him."

Tanya grimaced. "How he got through screening, I can't imagine, but Tolya, you know we can't just throw him in the brig. We don't have anything on him. He hasn't done anything against the charter...yet." Frustration washed across her face. "If we nab him now we'll make things worse. People will wonder if we're trying to cover something up."

Tolya grunted at the point. "Yeah. I guess you're right. I just can't stand the thought of a crazy man brewing trouble on my ship; especially in the middle of a crisis."

Tanya patted his forearm. "I know. You're under enough pressure. The last thing you need is some rebellious fool stirring up a bunch of trouble."

She leaned back and picked up her power-tab. "I wouldn't have brought it up except it's something you have to know about. Don't worry. I'm keeping a close eye on this guy."

"Thanks, Tanya." He smiled. "I know I'm in capable hands; keep me informed." His face brightened, "Let's hit the dinning room. I know I could use lunch."

Tanya arched an eyebrow and teased, "So...what? Was that a lame attempt at asking me out?"

Caught off guard, Tolya blushed, speechless.

Tanya hopped up, grinning. "OK! It's a date then!"

With a wink she headed for the door. Recovering quickly, he levered himself up and hurried after her.

* * * *

TUE 02.09.2094
Deck 3, Starboard Community Center, Forward,1245 Hrs

Ted Jackson sat at the table, drumming his fingers impatiently, glancing at the clock and mumbling profanities. Finally, the door opened and Jake Townsend slouched in and took a seat.

"Your late." Ted complained.

"Relax, Ted. We got lotsa' time." Pulling a flask from a pocket, Jake took a swig before offering it to Ted. "Sample?"

Ted tossed back a slug. With a slight splutter he handed the flask back.

The door opened again admitting Felix Hernandez. "Hey! Startin' without me?" He crossed to the table putting out his hand for the flask. Jake looked distastefully at Felix, shrugged his shoulders and surrendered it.

Felix snatched it and belted down a generous helping.

"Hey! Don't kill it. It's mine after all!"

Ted sat up and slapped his palm on the table. "OK boys! We gotta do somethin' about our problem. Sit down, Felix."

Felix' cool gaze regarded Ted before sitting. He was still leery of Ted. He looked over at Jake, holding up the flask. "This stuff would be very useful on the job. I wouldn't have to work so hard unclogging drains."

He scooted the flask across the table and Jake intercepted it, tightened the cap and stashed it in one of his plentiful pockets.

Ted plowed into his agenda. "Both of you heard the line of bull the captain fed everyone at that meeting. Does anyone really believe his story?" Two sets of bored eyes looked lazily back at him.

"Well, I don't. I think he's covering his hide. 'The ship went off course!' How lame is that, huh? The foundation couldn't even get us competent leaders!"

Ted's questionable companions looked pained.

"Come on, Ted. Are you still goin' on about that?" Jake asked. "What if the Cap'n's tellin' the truth?"

"Fat chance!" Felix commented, injecting a bravado he didn't really feel.

Jake shrugged. "Even still, what can we do about it?"

Ted sat back and considered his would be team. Felix was a thin, wiry young man of Hispanic background; medium in stature. He was a wily character with a dubious talent for acquiring other people's stuff without their immediate knowledge. Nobody paid him much notice. Being on the janitorial and maintenance staff, he could turn up anywhere on the ship.

Jake was of medium build. He spent his on duty time in the food services section. Off duty, his favorite pastimes were working his still, pedaling the products of the same (such as the industrial cleanser they'd just sampled), selling unorthodox medications and running personally profitable card games. His skills with knives didn't stop at carving meat in the kitchen.

Ted had been big in real estate before he'd signed up for this one-way trip to *Nova Terra*. He had managed to get himself into big legal trouble. The very real potential of doing prison time had reduced his options to one.

He hadn't been on the list of favorable types for the colony recruiters and his chances of getting off planet had been slim to none. So, he'd called in every favor he'd ever finagled over the years. The result had been a place on *Destiny* and a small piece of property on the new world. He was getting away clean and moderately wealthy. Correction! He would have been wealthy had they actually gone where advertised.

Ted answered Jake's question. "I think somebody wasn't paying attention. I don't think the problem's as bad as he says. Further, I think this whole thing about findin' a 'new world' is just a way of gettin' us to forget that they screwed up big time, and to make himself look like some kinda hero.

"So, I think we gotta get us back on plan before Chernov gets us all killed!"

Felix began cleaning his fingernails with a small knife. "Suppose you're right. They say we can't make it to *Nova Terra*. We're too far from Earth to make it back and…"

"Back to Earth?" Ted interrupted. "That's the last thing I want! I ain't got nothin' there but a prison term! Besides, we've been out here for about twenty-six months. If there's one thing I know about space, it's that it's friggin' huge. In just over two years, we can't really have gone too far. I refuse to believe we've gone too far to find our way back on course and home free! This guy's lookin' for personal glory and power!"

Felix switched hands and shrugged. "Believe what you want. I'm still not sure what we can do 'bout it. Can you pilot this tub? Can you figure out where we are and if we're goin' the right way? Do you even know where the 'gas tank' is?"

Ted drummed his fingers irritably on the table; his ruddy face getting redder. "Of course not, you idiot! Look. We gotta stop this side trip to this new star and get 'em to focus on gettin' on with the plan. We all have a lot vested in gettin' to *Nova Terra*. All this adventurin' crap's gonna do is waste more of our fuel. You know, that fuel the good captain's so worried about?"

He paused and sat staring at nothing for a moment. He took a calming breath. "Felix, do you have any connections in the drive section; somebody who's unhappy with this nonsense? Maybe we could, you know, delay the trip 'till we can bring the captain around to the right way of thinkin'."

Felix flipped the knife in the air, caught it deftly, folded it and made it vanish in one of his pockets. "Well, yeah... I know one or two down there. One's kinda worried about this whole deal. So, what's up?"

Ted leaned forward and dropped his voice. "What if a harmless little glitch made the main drive, the ah, yeah, that MS drive, fail to start up? They'd have to stop, figure out the problem and fix it before we could go anywhere."

Felix looked speculative. "Well, I think one of 'em could pull it off…" A calculating look crossed his face. "What's in it for me?"

Ted shifted uncomfortably. "Look, I got a chunk of prime real estate comin' to me on *Nova Terra*. According to the charter, that gives me a little clout over what happens when we get there. So...I can make it worth your while."

Felix calculated for a moment. He had a gut feeling something was going to go wrong. He shrugged it off. "Ok. I'll see if one of 'em's interested."

Ted grinned happily. "Great! Tell 'em to come talk to me."

"Well, I gotta get to work. I'll refer him to you." Felix reached out and the two slapped fingers. Felix stood..

"All right," Ted grinned, "but hurry it up. I think they're ready to make a move."

Felix waved a negligent hand. "Hey, I'm just the messenger boy." Then he headed out the door.

Jake scratched his nose. "So, wadda I gotta do?"

Ted thought for a moment. "Well, Jake. We need a way to persuade the good captain to our way of thinkin'."

Jake slouched even lower in his seat. "Ya know? I never liked that cocky SOB. Maybe we need a change of command."

He pulled on his ear as he considered. "Everybody's gotta eat and drink. Right?" Ted nodded. "Plus, we all know how big coffee is up there in elite country."

Ted nodded again, waiting for Jake to commit himself. "So, we could put a little somethin' in his coffee soz' he stops being a problem, ya know?"

Ted raised an eyebrow. "My, my. I see you're bein' creative here. I like creative, but we don't want the situation to be permanent; just bad enough to scare the crap out of people. How can we convince the man if he's out permanent like?"

Jake nodded wisely and grinned. "Well...at least he could get really, really sick. Then he'd know he's not so high and mighty in control of everythin'."

Ted smiled delightedly. "I like it. It needs some work, but it's very promising."

Jake grinned. "Course, like my boy, Felix, nobody plays for free. I mean, I'm stickin' my neck out farther than he is coz I'm the one's gotta deliver the message."

Ted grimaced. "So, why am I not surprised? Tell you what. What I told Felix goes the same for you. You could be a small landowner instead of just a laborer.

Jake considered. "Yeah, Ok. It'll take a little while to come up with the stuff; maybe a couple of days."

Ted nodded. "That's fine. It gives Felix time to find somebody. We need to coordinate with Felix' guy in drive and see if we can get our message off clear, like."

Jake rose fluidly from his chair and slapped fingers with Ted. "I'll be in touch," he said, leaving Ted to ponder his progress.

Ted left much happier than when he'd arrived. He was so self-satisfied he didn't notice Lieutenant Robert Franc from ship's security ducking down the cross corridor. Ted hurried off to his stateroom and Robert went to the security office.

MAJOR COMPLICATIONS — 2
THU 02.11.2094
Command Deck, Command Bridge, 0745 Hrs

Destiny completed the course change at three quarters-c. All stations reported green and Anatoli nodded, giving the signal to initiate MS-1 transition. Tremendous energies had been winding up for the shove and the moment of release was upon them.

The count down reached zero and Anatoli absently grabbed the arms of his chair in anticipation of the surge. Instead, as the surge began there was a lurch and a sagging sensation as the transition failed. Both the MS drive and the conventional space drives went into emergency stop. Alarms on the Engineering console began to flash and beep.

Franklin at NAVCOM looked up in surprise. Daryl threw up his hands in disgust, supplying heart felt, and descriptive expletives. These earned him the captain's stony stare.

"Sorry! What else can go wrong? First it's NAVCOM, now it's the drives. He stood up from his station. "Captain, I'm headed below to check it out."

Anatoli nodded, released command status and rose from his command chair. The star field slowly drifted in a diagonal arc across the screen. He made his way to the engineering console and watched the displays tell a story of destruction below. "Frank. Get this tub pointing in just one direction. I hate a tumbling ship."

He shook his head in disgust and headed for his standby cabin. "Vince. Take the CONN, please. I'll be at my desk."

Just as the door snapped open, he turned and said, "Oh. When Daryl gets back let me know."

Vince took the command station and the captain disappeared into his sanctum.

As Vince sat, Tanya dashed onto the bridge. "What's going on?" She demanded.

Vince shrugged his shoulders. "The MS drive failed as we were about to transition. Everything shut down and Frank is pulling us out of a slow tumble. Once more, everything has gone crazy."

Tanya shook her head. "Where is he?"

"He's at his desk next door."

She started for the door. "Careful. He's reached a new level of total disgust."

Her smile was grim. "I'll see about cheering him up."

She stepped through the door as Vince logged on.

Tanya found Tolya staring at the coffee dispenser as if confronting a friend who'd betrayed him.

"Hey. One of those days?" She offered softly.

He sighed and turned to greet her. "Yeah, you could say that. First the MS drive fails in the middle of executing transition, and now I can't even get a coffee."

Tanya squeezed the little tab in her collar.

"Routing?" The AI asked.

"Main kitchen."

"One moment."

A rather unhappy voice responded. "Yeah, what's up?"

"Chief Nydel here. We need a coffee service here in the captain's standby cabin. This coffee dispenser's not working. We'll need that serviced too."

There was an exaggerated sigh. "Yeah well...we're having all kinds of 'stuff' like that today. I'll be right up."

Tanya frowned. "Thanks, Nydel out."

She pinched again and the connection closed. Her brows furrowed as she replayed the short exchange in her mind. 'We've had all kinds of stuff...today?' Why today? Something stinks.

She turned to face the captain, who'd settled at his desk during her chat. "I think there are just a few too many problems cropping up all at once. Why today? You know, call me paranoid, but I don't like the trend."

Tolya glanced up. "Well, the coffee I can live with, I guess. This screw up in drive's another story."

Tanya gave a grimace of a smile. "I know. I need to check out a couple of things. I'll be back in a little bit."

She turned to go and he smiled fondly. "Hurry back."

* * * *

Tanya stepped off the lift on her way to her office. Jake Townsend came out of the kitchen, heading for the lift with a tray of fresh coffee and some pastries. Tanya nodded absently and continued on her way.

She stalked into her office and, flinging herself down at the computer, began browsing through the various reports that had been catalogued for the past week.

She glanced up and leaned towards her door. "Sherry, would you please snag a cup of coffee for me?"

Sherry was her personal assistant and one of her few close friends. "Sure, Tahnie. Just a moment."

Tanya went over the reports quickly. Something nagged at the back of her mind. She found the report she was looking for. It was from the second shift lead officer, Lieutenant Robert Franc.

Mr. Irate, better known as Ted Jackson, had been seen, wandering Deck 3 alone around 2300 hours. He'd let himself into one of the starboard community centers, unoccupied so late, and stayed for about forty minutes. During that time, two of the more unsavory types on board were seen entering the room, staying for a while and then leaving.

They'd arrived separately and left separately. After this apparent meeting, Ted Jackson had left the room and gone, almost blissfully, back to his quarters.

Tanya knew Ted was trying to stir up trouble. He'd been chatting up a number of people, but for the most part, his efforts seemed unsuccessful. There didn't seem to be a clear indication of a specific cause for alarm.

She reached over and touched an icon of a video screen, dragging it to the center of her desk screen.

The icon blossomed into a window that accessed the security vid files. She looked for various approaches to the center during the time indicated.

The file she wanted finally showed up in the long list. Tanya pinched the file name with a thumb and finger and placed it into the playback window. The player obediently lit up and she swirled a finger clockwise.

After a moment, Ted Jackson emerged from the starboard side lift well. He strolled by the security station and the education suites, past the mezzanine and along the balcony corridor overlooking the Promenade before turning to starboard.

The view changed to a new camera. Ted was walking along the wide cross-corridor divided by a long planter with dwarf trees. After looking around hesitantly, he approached the community center and the camera that supplied Tanya's perspective. He reached the door, glanced around again and then ducked inside.

A long, agonizing time later, a slouchy looking fellow of mid height ambled into view and entered the center without hesitation. Tanya thought he looked familiar.

After a few more moments, a young, slender Hispanic fellow strolled casually down the same corridor and entered the room.

Tanya racked her brain. Where've I seen him before?

She switched the view to a camera that looked towards the community center door. She dragged a finger to the right, speeding up the playback significantly, and then tapped 'stop' as movement in the doorway resumed.

She back-stepped several frames and swirled the scene to motion. The second guy came out and hurried away. A few minutes later the face that had tickled her brain reemerged from the room and the 'slouch' ambled back the way he'd come.

Finally, Ted Jackson emerged with a Cheshire cat's grin on his face. He strode purposefully away and Tanya tapped stop.

She backed the recording and froze the image where the Hispanic guy came out of the room. Placing a cropping frame around the man's head and shoulders, she pinched the cropped image and dragged a copy to a small box with a question mark in it, sending the computer on a quick personnel search.

Soon, a small window opened displaying a replica of the face on the video. Information filed down the page.

The man's name was Felix Hernandez. He was on the ship maintenance and janitorial crew. She made a note to check him out before running the video forward to freeze on the 'slouch' making his exit.

The same procedure rendered the name, Jake Townsend, listed as a lead in food services. Suddenly, the missing piece clicked sickeningly into place.

This was the guy with the coffee service she'd passed near the lift well. He'd been headed for command deck.

She remembered her request for coffee service and in a momentary flash of panic, *Tolya!* She leaped up and, knocking the chair into the wall, dashed for the exit.

Sherry was on her way to Tanya's office with a hot cup of coffee when her boss came flying out of the room as if shot from a cannon. She barely avoided Tanya's charge and cried out in dismay as coffee sloshed everywhere. When she looked up, Tanya was gone.

* * * *

Jake set the coffee service on the conference table near the captains work desk. Captain Chernov turned his chair to watch the man at work.

Jake poured the coffee and offered it and a plate of pastries to the captain. Anatoli took the cup and after a moment's hesitation, selected a pastry. "Thank you," he said simply.

Jake responded. "My pleasure, captain. I apologize for the coffee machine. I've arranged for servicing."

The captain shook his head, "Well, don't worry about it. It seems today's the day for screw-ups all over the ship."

Jake laughed and replied. "You should see the insanity in food services. Sometimes I think there's a plot to ruin everybody's day. Anyway, I should get back before something else goes south."

The captain nodded and took a sip. He frowned. "What type of coffee is this? It has an unusual bite."

Jake replied, "Oh. It's not an Arabica. It's a Liberica, which is a rare type of bean. It comes from the Philippines, back on Earth. They call this one 'Baraco.' It means 'wild boar.' I guess I make it kind of strong."

Jake grinned. "Some say it's an acquired taste. You might try a little more sugar. I brought some just in case." He slid the dispenser towards the captain. "It's my favorite. It's kind of a gift because of the coffee service problem."

Anatoli nodded and smiled politely. "That's all right. Nothing else is going well. Why should this?"

Jake grinned.

The captain added a little sugar and took another sip. "Hmmm. Well, that's not so bad. I hope the rest of the day goes better for you," he said by way of dismissal.

Jake left the room. *What a fool. He was totally clueless.* He strode quickly from the lift back to the event center kitchen.

MAJOR COMPLICATIONS — 3
Lower MS-Drive Interface, Control Room, 0755 Hrs

Daryl McIntyre stormed the drive control room like a schooner before a typhoon. "Report!" he snapped.

A young, smooth faced technician approached. "Sir! We have a fault in the cascade initiation control node. Robin is scoping it out right now."

Daryl growled a silent epithet and brushed past the tech to peer angrily at the displays for the cascade controller. *Yes, there's the fault alarm. These numbers are WAY off the scale!* He nodded to the tech and hurried over to a closeted area. He slipped in next to another tech crouched over an open panel, studying readings on a scope.

Grey-white smoke slowly wafted up from the opening. The acrid stench made his own eyes water. He could only imagine how the tech could possibly put up with it.

The tech looked up as Daryl approached. Daryl prompted, "What do we have?"

Robin, brushed a stray lock of hair from her face, wiped her watery eyes and jerked her face-mask down. "Sir! I think there's been some damage in the cascade control sequencer. One of the boards blew. See the readings here?" Daryl looked and invented a whole new inventory of curses.

After a moment of thought, he said. "Ok. Sorry kid. You've done well. Let's isolate this unit and pull the board. I want to have a good look."

Robin was becoming accustomed to her chief's mercurial moods. She smiled shyly and got to work. She rerouted the power coupling, effectively isolating the controller. Daryl snapped the latches to slide the reluctant rack out of the chassis. He tugged sharply to get it moving as clouds of smoke billowed out.

Robin waved irritably at the offending smoke and then traced her fingers along the ID codes at the base of the rack of cards.

The metal frame of the rack was hot and slightly warped. Some of the fine light-wire bundles were melted. She found the slot she wanted and tried to pull the card. The slot tried to come up with the board and Daryl tapped the edge carefully as she tugged and the board broke free. After one quick look, her face suddenly took on a look of horror. She offered the board for inspection.

Daryl's face was a study in anger management. He pressed his lips together to stop the flood of angry verbiage that came to mind. The young tech didn't need to hear that right now. ·

Robin tendered a comment. "It almost looks deliberate, sir."

Daryl nodded grimly, finding useful communication to offer. "Yes, lass, someone did a first class job of frying a crucial board."

He looked more carefully and then raised an eyebrow. "We're very fortunate, don't ya know."

She looked questioningly at him. He pointed out a particular undamaged spot on the board. "See here?" Robin nodded seriously. "Well, if this component to the left of the burn had been damaged... well, let's just say we would have cascaded into a mini nova. Earth might have seen a new, very temporary star in a few years!"

Robin looked more horrified, if that were possible. Her face turned so pale, her red hair positively glowed.

Daryl patted her shoulder. "Let's just be thankful that whoever did this was either very lucky or very skilled. We survive to sort it out and deal with the son of a..." He glanced at Robin. "Well, you get my meaning!"

Robin smiled tentatively as Daryl peered along the rack at the card directly behind the one they'd pulled. It too was damaged, and would need to be replaced.

"OK kid. Go get me a storage bag. I want to show this to the captain. Meanwhile, I'll check inventory and pray we have a back up board. I don't want to have to rebuild this one. It doesn't look terribly hopeful."

Robin dashed off as Daryl headed for a nearby terminal.

MAJOR COMPLICATIONS — 4
Command Deck, Captain's Standby Cabin, 0845 Hrs

Tolya was fighting sleep. *I slept well last night.* He thought. *Why am I so tired?* He nodded off, then jerked awake again. This was the third cup of coffee. He reached over and took another long sip. The coffee was assuming room temperature. *How long have I been here?*

He glanced at the upper left corner of his display. *How odd, I've been here for forty minutes, but I just sat down.* He couldn't put his finger on the source, but he didn't feel well at all. It was getting cold. He considered checking the thermostat settings when Tanya burst through the door.

Tolya turned around slowly at the sudden entrance and grinned in surprise at a very agitated Tanya. *She really did hurry back.*

He got up to greet her, but felt dizzy. There was a rushing sound in his head and the floor suddenly seemed to be calling for him.

* * * *

Tanya found Tolya sitting at his desk. There was a partial cup of coffee on the desk next to a napkin with a bit of pastry on it. She started to relax when he got up from his seat, only to tense in horror as his face turned a pasty white. He reached for one of the chairs at the conference table, missed and started to collapse.

Tanya dashed impossibly across the room and caught him before he hit the floor. She almost fell with him, but managed to lay him out and loosen his collar. She dropped to her knees and put her face down close to his. He was breathing very quickly, but she could barley feel his breath on her face. His pulse was thin, slow and difficult to find, the skin, cold and clammy.

She leaped up and smashed the emergency alarm on the wall by the door. Then she dashed through the door to the bridge and in a hoarse stage whisper called, "Vince!"

He glanced up, startled. She frantically motioned him over. He hesitated for just a moment when he saw her look of panic and horror. Then he realized the alarms for the captain's standby cabin were going off.

All eyes on deck had swiveled in unison to take in the developing drama. He jumped up and grabbed Frank by the shoulder. "Quick!" he said, "Take the CONN! Something's wrong with the captain!"

Frank gaped at Vince for a second before nodding and moving silently to the captain's chair. Vince hurried over as Tanya disappeared back through the doors.

She was on the COMM as he ran over to see the captain stretched out on the floor.

"Brianna! It's Tanya. I need Daniela, now!"

"But Tanya, she's taking a br…"

"Brianna! The captain's unconscious on the floor! I think he might have been poisoned."

There was an audible gasp. "I…I'll get her right now."

"Thanks, Bri'! Be quick! Please!"

Tanya broke the connection and shakily turned as several security officers dashed into the room looking for trouble. Somebody killed the raucous alarm.

"I don't want anyone leaving the quarterdeck. I think the captain's been poisoned. Cordon off all lifts. I'll follow up with instructions when I can!"

The ranking officer nodded, "Yes ma'am!" He instructed two to guard the door. The rest filed out to carry out orders.

Vince approached where the captain lay. "What happened?"

Tanya raced through the story and hurried to the captain's side to check his pulse. Nothing had changed. *Don't you die on us now you big turkey! We need you…Damn! I need you!*

Vince, feeling useless, wandered over to the desk to see what the captain might have been working on.

Tanya snapped. "Don't! Don't touch anything!"

Vince stopped; startled. "Easy, Tanya. Are you OK?"

She rose from her knees, pain lancing through her back and shoulder, and stumbled over to the desk where she caught herself. "Sorry, Vince. I guess I'm a little shook up. That's all."

Slowly she straightened and indicated the desk area. "This is a crime scene. I think there's a plot to get the captain. I'm pretty sure I know who it was!"

Vince shrugged. "Sure. I understand. Who was it?"

Tanya wanted to blurt out her accusation, but she hesitated. "I have to be certain before naming names."

Vince nodded. "OK. Are you sure you're all right?"

She nodded and cast another fearful look at the captain. Vince looked speculatively around the room. "You know, this is an awfully inconvenient time for this kind of thing to happen."

Tanya cast a sidelong glance at him. "Understatement seems to be a common talent lately." She quipped tartly. "I can't think of any time this would be convenient."

The door snapped open. Daniela and the par-med team dashed in and hurried to the captain. She physically checked his vitals as the techs pulled out equipment. She moved smoothly aside as a tech attached various monitoring devices and began running the scans.

The door snapped open again and another team nudged an emergency lifter into the room. An ELU interacted with the grav-plates in the decking. It literally floated at about waist height waiting for its newest burden.

Tanya heard numbers and medical terms flying about the room like ghosts at a dance party. She stood staring at the scene, looking lost and tired.

Daniela approached and laid a hand on her arm. "Tahnie... Tahnie! You OK?"

Tanya blinked from her momentary fugue and looked at the ship's doctor. "Yeah," she replied shakily. "I...I tried to get here faster...but I was too late!"

She forced back an unwelcome sob. "God! Don't let him die! I tried! I did!"

Daniela pulled Tanya to her in a sisterly hug. "Come on Tahnie. Tolya needs you more than ever."

Tanya pulled back, brushing her face. She took a deep breath. "I'm fine. Really."

"Good. You said you thought he'd been poisoned." Daniela waited patiently.

"Oh, yeah!" Tanya was all business now. "We should check his coffee cup and the pastry on his desk. There's also the coffee service there on the table. We should get the necessary proof there."

Daniela smiled. "Great. We'll get him stabilized and move him to MedCentral. You get the samples over to my lab and we'll figure this out."

"OK! Thanks, Dannie. Sorry. I guess I kinda got a little worked up there. I'll take care of the samples."

"Good!" Daniela gently squeezed Tanya's arm before moving to confer with her team.

Tanya took a deep, cleansing breath and leaned out the door, grabbing a guard. "Tom! Go back to the office and get the field forensics kit from the lockers and bring it back... No...wait! I'll call Sherry. We must secure the evidence. Run down to MedCentral and take up station there. Someone made a try on the captain. We don't want them to get another chance. We'll get a team to relieve you. When they do, report to Sherry for instructions."

Tom murmured a quick "Ma'm" and loped off.

Tanya cleared the door and pinched her COMM tab. "Routing?"

"SecCentral... Hey Sherry, I need a forensics team in the captains lounge right away. Thanks..."

* * * *

ECS Destiny, Command Deck, Command Bridge, 0855 Hrs

Daryl marched purposefully onto the bridge, an avenging angel looking for a victim. "Cap..."

He looked around. "Frank. Where's the captain?"

He was faced with anxious looks. "All right, what else is wrong?" He looked around suspiciously.

Frank pointed soundlessly towards the captain's standby cabin. At Daryl's blank look, he replied. "He went that way. Then the alarms went off and Tanya came out lookin' like she'd seen a ghost. Vince put me on CONN and raced in there with her." He shook his head. "So, I get stuck here and nobody tells me nothin'!"

Daryl grimaced and marched through the doors where controlled pandemonium reigned supreme. The center of focus was the captain lying on an ELU with medical equipment attached all over. The doors to the corridor snapped open and they made a surprisingly orderly exit.

Daryl hurried over to Vince, who was talking quietly with Daniela and Tanya. They paused as he approached. "What the heck's going on here?" He hissed.

A forensics team scurried through the door and quickly began going through the area around the Captain's desk as Vince responded. "The captain collapsed; we think he was poisoned."

"Poisoned!" Daryl spluttered his disbelief before remembering the vandalized board he carried. "So! Sabotaging the drive system wasn't good enough?"

Vince blanched. "What? Sabotage?"

Daryl unwrapped his package, handing it to Vince.

Vince looked it over carefully. "God save us!" he murmured. "This looks deliberate. It's too precise!"

Daryl nodded. "Yep. If the cretin had burned just a little to the left…" he indicated the spot on the board, "Well…let's just say the moment we went into transition, the board would have caused a cascade of failures. We'd have become a big flash in the night!"

Vince examined the indicated component. It looked as if he was about to be sick. Finally, he looked over at Daniela, who, along with Tanya, was looking in horrified fascination at the offending power board. "Dannie… Dannie?" She jerked her gaze up to his.

"I assume you two have this situation," he waved a hand about the room, "fully under control?"

She nodded and gave him one of her special little smiles before glancing at Tanya. "Don't worry, we'll have our captain right as rain in no time."

Vince smiled his thanks. "Good. He's in the best two sets of hands a man could ever want."

He handed the useless board back to Daryl. "Well, Daryl and I need to get down to business with THIS problem. Tanya, drive section has to be another crime scene. We'll be careful not to compromise anything."

Tanya nodded. "Thanks, Vince. Would you call Sherry, in my office, and have her send another team down there?"

He nodded.

"And Daryl, if you could fill them in on everything you can recall, I'd really appreciate it."

Daryl growled his assent. The ladies headed for MedCentral and the guys turned towards the bridge. As they reached the door the forensics specs finished securing the evidence. One of the three took the sample case and followed the ladies, while the other two purposefully approached the bridge officers. "Mister Leoni."

Vince turned. "Yes, Veronica, isn't it?"

"Yes, sir. Sir, we're finished here. We could accompany you to drive section and get started there. The sooner that scene is secured, the better."

Vince nodded. "Sure. Thanks. Daryl, if you would escort them down, I'll fill Frank in on what's going on and then catch up."

Daryl headed for the corridor access. "Come on, you two. Let's catch us a first class piece of…!" The door snapped shut.

DISCOVERY — 1

THU 02.11.2094
Quarterdeck, MedCentral, 0900 Hrs

Tanya watched as the par-meds transferred Tolya to the bed. They quickly and expertly switched over the monitors to the more powerful shipboard instruments. One of the forensics team members entered and headed for the lab.

Tanya turned to Daniela. "Dannie, I'll be in the lab to see about typing the poison. Let me know the moment he regains consciousness, please?"

"Sure, Tahnie. Once you get the data, you should get some rest. There's a small bunk in the back of my office you can use."

Dannie waved Tanya out and turned back to the captain. *OK fella; let's not get too comfortable here.* She watched the monitors and fretted for a while.

The lab work was pretty straightforward. The lab tech, a young man named Jeffrey, deftly took the sample and slid it carefully into the reader. He tapped in the data for the known substance, waved a hand across the tiny screen and stood back to watch.

Several spectrograms flashed up on the screen. The black bands with rainbow bars made odd patterns as they rapidly lined up in columns down the screen. Numbers and other data spun to the right of each spectrogram as the computer sorted out the chemical compounds found in the sample. Jeffrey kept up a running description of what was going on.

Tanya figured he was just trying to be helpful. "...So the computer analyzes the chemical components of the sample. I have just entered the description for this one. The computer has a database of the chemical compounds of a whole raft of common substances; in this case, coffee, with cream and sugar."

After a few seconds, several of the bars blanked out to leave gaps in the display. "Now the computer is comparing the actual signature of the compounds in the sample to the expected signature stored in the database. Any moment now it'll list the expected substances from the display and, hopefully, identify any foreign compounds. Any out of place substance will be highlighted in blue."

Soon, only four bars remained. The computer rearranged the remaining bars into a column with descriptive text and data listed to the side of each one. One of them was backlighted in pale blue so it stood out from the others.

Tanya stepped forward to get a better look. The young tech moved politely to one side, but continued to monitor the run. There, for the discerning to read, was the computers' description of the contents from Tolya's coffee cup.

Jeffrey stepped forward and entered a few commands. The run results and process was saved for review and a printout of the information emerged from a slot below the screen.

"Here you go ma'am. I hope this helps. Would you give this printout to Dr. Jacobs?"

Tanya smiled and took the slightly curled strip of paper. "Sure, Jeffrey. Thanks for your help."

He shook his head. "I can't believe someone would want to hurt the captain. I really like him."

Tanya checked her move for the door and turned back to face the young man. "So do I, Jeffrey."

He could feel the intensity of that statement from across the room. "There are a lot of us who can't believe it. I promise you this, though. The person who did this will dearly wish he hadn't done it on my watch. I'll do whatever I have to, to get him!"

Jeffrey looked mildly surprised. "You said, 'He,' Do you have someone in mind?"

Tanya grimaced. "Yeah. You'll learn soon enough!"

Jeffrey looked her in the eye, seeing something alive and angry lurking there. "Ma'm, I could almost feel sorry for the man...not sorry enough, though." He smiled. "Good luck!" He began resetting the scanner as Tanya turned and walked briskly out of the lab.

The rustle of cloth as Tanya entered stirred Daniela from her moody stare. Tanya offered up the printout and waited for Daniela to read it.

Daniela studied it, her lips moving slightly as she followed the formulas. She pursed her lips in a low whistle. "Damn!" she breathed fervently.

She turned to Tanya. "Chloral Hydrate. Where the heck did they find that here in the middle of nowhere?"

Tanya opened her mouth to express her opinion when an alarm went off on the monitors above Tolya's head.

Daniela reached up and tapped a call tab. Immediately they heard running feet. She pulled up one of Tolya's eyelids for a quick look. The assistant quickly entered the cubicle and placed himself opposite Daniela. "Jorge, his heart rate and blood pressure are falling. Let's give him something to counter it.

She reached up and slapped a tab on the monitor. The extremely irritating alarm fell silent.

Jorge grabbed a vial from a small cupboard. He scanned the label, nodded and snapped off the seal. Expertly, he pressed the vial into one of the waiting sockets in the IV line. After a few tense moments the numbers slowed their steady decent and then, finally stopped. Sluggishly, the numbers crept back to desired levels.

Daniela glanced at the look of relief on Tanya's face. "OK hon, we've got this under control."

Tanya commented, "Chloral Hydrate. That's a sedative isn't it? It couldn't do all this, could it?"

Daniela shook her head. "No, Tahnie. Normally you'd be right." She picked up the print out from the counter where she'd dropped it. "but, well…look at the concentration." She indicated a number next to the chemical name. Tanya looked blank and Daniela went on to explain.

"First, CH is a very old sedative, discovered way back in the mid 1800's. It's still around, but it's seldom used in modern medicine. Normally, if I were to use it, say for someone who had trouble sleeping, the dose I'd prescribe would be much lower than this. CH can be beneficial in small doses, but it's an addictive substance that functions like some barbiturates you'd find back home.

"Taken at these levels," she slapped the print out angrily, "it can make a person very sick. God forbid, they can be fatal."

Tanya blanched. "No!" she whispered. She turned to move closer to the bed and stumbled, grunting in pain.

Daniela stepped forward and gently, but firmly grabbed Tanya's arm. "You're hurt!" she accused. "Where?"

Tanya looked a way. "Just about everything hurts."

Daniela shook her head and released her arm. "Why didn't you say something? What did you do?"

Tanya seemed almost shy. "When I saw Tolya falling I went into automatic. Somehow, I caught his fall. He's a solidly built guy! Did you know that?"

Daniela shook her head slowly and started prodding Tanya's neck muscles. "You must take care when catching heavy loads!"

Tanya winced at Daniela's probing. "You don't say…"

Daniela grinned. "I know, another one of those understatements you're always going on about. Anyway, you pulled some muscles. You should rest before I have to put you in the next cubicle."

Tanya started to protest, but Daniela raised a warning hand. "Look, Tahnie. You won't be any good to anybody; let alone Tolya, if you're laid up with a strained back. Give it some rest before I sick Jorge on you with a sedative; Doctor's orders."

Tanya sent a pleading look. Daniela smiled sadly. She pulled out a spray injector and loaded a vial of something. "He's going to be OK. We know what the problem is and we'll get him stabilized and conscious, probably by the time you wake up."

She pressed the injector against Tanya's back and tapped the stud. Then, reaching into a cabinet she pulled out a foil with a couple of pills in it. "Here's something to ease the pain. Now go to my office and get a little rest. I'll try to look in on you."

Tanya seemed to deflate. "OK."

Brianna looked up as Tanya entered. "Hey. There's a bunk in the back of her office. I'll let you know if something happens."

She got up and gently took Tanya's arm. Tanya was too tired to care. She hated being babied.

Brianna helped her onto the bunk, draped a light blanket over her and turned to go. She stopped and crossed the room, pulled a small, foil-sealed pill from the cupboard and poured a cup of water. Putting them on the shelf next to the bunk she said. "If you have trouble sleeping I've left a mild sedative for you." She turned, waved her hand just so, dimming the lights, and left the room.

Tanya rejected the sedative idea. It would be a cold day in hell before she messed with sedatives. She tore open the pain medication, tossed it down with the small cup of water and rolled over to face the wall.

Brianna returned to her station to find Daniela hunched wearily over the desk. She was paging through a long list, searching for something. "You OK, Dannie?"

The doctor looked up from her search. "Yeah. Thanks, Bri. How's Tanya?"

"She'll be fine after some sleep. I could say the same for you."

Daniela shrugged eloquently. "The good doctor must first save the patient. I'll take a break later."

Brianna radiated concern. "Look, Dannie. Why not just stabilize him and take a break? You can cure him later if he's out of danger."

Daniela shook her head. "I won't take that chance. We need him too much. I refuse to loose him. Besides, we know what the poison was. It's just a matter of finding the right way to counteract it without putting him in more danger."

Brianna looked just a little stubborn. "Ok, Dannie, but if you don't take a break soon, I'm going to sick Vince on you." She grinned impishly.

Daniela stopped and took on a dreamy look. "Ah, If only there was time…"

Brianna wagged a finger, "I didn't mean that, silly. You know how unhappy he'd be if something happened to you. I mean it, Dannie. Take care of yourself. You're the best we got." She gave her a tight little smile and headed back to her station.

Daniela bent over the monitor, mumbling to herself.

DISCOVERY — 2

ECS Destiny, Lower MS-Drive Interface, Control Room, 0915 Hrs

Daryl left the forensics crew to their work, heading for his office. He snagged the printout from his inventory search that he'd left on the desk. A non sequitur flashed through his brain. It was close to a hundred and fifty years since the invention of the personal computer and people still had to use these ubiquitous printouts.

He scooted his chair to the door and looked out over the work area. "Hey Jeryk. Come here a sec."

Jeryk looked up from his station. "Sure boss." He climbed out of his chair; his nearly seven lanky feet towering over everyone on the floor. "What's up?"

Daryl scooted back to his desk. Taking a pen, he signed the printout. "Here. Take this over to stores and collect these boards for me. Be extremely careful. If those babies get damaged, there aren't any others within' forty light-years. Then we're in worse trouble."

"Sure boss. I'll treat 'em like eggs; nice and gentle like."

Daryl grinned. "Thanks, Jeryk."

Jeryk left to carry out his solemn duty.

As Daryl turned back to his desk to catch up on reports, the forensics team appeared at his door. He sighed and waved them to sit. "What's the good news?"

Veronica looked frustrated. "Well, sir, we've done the standard work up on the crime scene. I've never seen one so clean. There's not a single fingerprint. That board is clean too; except, of course, for the prints from you and Mr. Leone. If not for the obvious damage, you'd think it had come fresh off the shelf."

Daryl frowned. "How? It's way too precise to just be random."

Veronica shrugged. "That's true, sir. There's no doubt it was sabotage. We think this person was wearing gloves and possibly a face-mask. There was absolutely no usable genetic material either."

Daryl sat back, absently drumming his fingers on the arms of his chair. "OK, no sense beating a dead horse. I'll talk with Tanya."

He stood, as did his guests. He shook Veronica's hand. "Thanks for your trouble."

She smiled, "No problem. If you need anything further, just let us know."

He shook her partner's hand and they turned to go.

That's when Jeryk came dashing in with a look of irritation painting his face. The two from forensics backed quickly out of his way as he barreled into the office. "It's not there, sir! We looked everywhere!"

Daryl held up a hand. "Slow down. What's not where?"

He froze... "You mean our boards?"

Jeryk nodded vigorously. "One of 'em anyways."

Daryl thumped the arm of his chair. "But, the computer says they're there. Who else could possibly need them? They only serve one purpose!"

Veronica raised a delicate eyebrow and looked speculatively towards her partner.

"Lord, please no!" Daryl breathed fervently.

He looked at his guests. "Come on, let's check it out."

Everyone filed out and Daryl closed and locked the door; something he'd never done the whole trip. Jeryk looked at him.

"Apparently you can't be too careful," Daryl mumbled.

* * * *

Victor Romero was seated behind the counter, scrolling through the inventory list when the agitated parade filed into the room. He recognized the chief and leaped to his feet. "Can I help, Chief?"

Daryl slapped the printout he'd retrieved from Jeryk, down on the counter. "I believe my man here," he nodded towards Jeryk, "came just a few minutes ago, to requisition this board." His finger jabbed meaningfully at the inventory number listed on the paper. "I understand you're unable to find it."

Victor looked nervous. It was never terribly pleasant to get the chief's blood pressure up. "No, sir... I mean, Yes, sir. I searched everywhere, but I got the other." He pointed to a small box with another board in it.

"I even let Mr. String Bean here, look for himself." He shrugged eloquently. "What else can I do?"

Daryl snatched the print out and made his way to the end of the counter where the lift top door controlled admittance. "Open up. I want to take a look."

Victor hurried over and raised the counter top and the four filed into the main stores vault.

This was one of the larger rooms on board except for the landing docks for the shuttles and the manufactory spaces. For its size the ceiling was very low. Poor Jeryk had to stoop as he entered.

Row upon row of storage shelves stretched back into the room. Victor led the way to the place where the board was supposed to be stored. Daryl checked the printout with the shelf labels to confirm their location. There was nothing in the place indicated.

Veronica gently snagged his arm before he reached into the shelf. "Sir. If you touch things, we can't do an accurate investigation."

Daryl looked irritable, but he stopped. Instead he turned to Victor. "Any other requisitions or pickups?"

Victor looked nervous. "I'm not sure."

Daryl physically turned Victor towards the front counter and said pointedly. "Let's check the records, shall we?"

He and Jeryk followed Victor, as Daryl spoke back over his shoulder. "Veronica, you two do your magic. We'll be up front."

"Yes, sir," came her reply.

They rounded the end of the row and disappeared.

The computer was clueless regarding any requisitions other then the one Daryl sent earlier. Victor was worried. "Sir, I never release anything without a printout verifying an original computer requisition. I have no idea what happened."

Daryl looked into Victor's eyes and sensed nothing more than the fear of someone falsely accused. "I haven't accused any one of anything. Yet!" Victor swallowed.

Veronica and her shadow turned up and she shook her head. "I can see something was removed, from the faint pattern of dust, it was dragged from the shelf fairly recently.

Daryl nodded. "Apparently someone doesn't want us replacing the board."

Victor seemed confused. "Sir, what's this thing anyway? I mean. Why's it such a big deal? I'm sure it'll turn up, whatever it is. Where can it go?"

Daryl loomed over Victor and put a thick finger against his chest. "Whatever it is, is the only way we're going anywhere significant, anytime in our lifetimes! It's the only replacement for the board that failed, preventing our transition into Multi-Space. No board, no go!"

Victor paled and sat heavily on the stool behind the counter. "Believe me," he breathed. "The last thing I want is to be stranded forever in the middle of nowhere."

Daryl nodded. "Fine." He pointed towards the entrance. "Nobody comes in here and gets anything from stores until we get this sorted out. Got it?"

Victor nodded, "Yes, sir."

Daryl motioned his little procession towards the door.

Veronica's partner, Wayne, spoke up. "Sir, how about I stay here until we can get an officer down here?"

"Good idea, Wayne. We'll try to get someone right away."

Wayne nodded, "Very good, sir." He picked a seat near the door and parked.

DISCOVERY — 3

ECS Destiny, Quarterdeck, SecCentral, 1130 Hrs

The COMM chimed and Sherry swished the pickup. "Security." She said sweetly.

"Hey Sherry. It's Daryl. Can I speak with Tanya?"

Sherry frowned. "I'm sorry, sir. Tanya hasn't come back to the office since the captain went to MedCentral."

"Really! OK, then I'll check there. Oh, by the way, do you have anyone you could send down to keep an eye on stores? We have another problem down there."

Sherry tapped a fingernail against her teeth. "Yeah, I think we can pull a couple and send them there."

"Great. I'd appreciate it. No one but security personnel and myself are permitted entrance to stores until further notice. Tanya or I will lift the order when appropriate. I'm on my way to MedCentral. Later!"

The connection went dead and Sherry turned to relay the orders. She sure wished she knew what was going on. This whole mess had started with Tanya tearing out of here like the devil was after her.

* * * *

Who's shaking me? Don't bug me! Stop it! Tanya woke to the gentle shaking of her arm and struggled to recall where she was. She rolled over and squinted in the light coming from the doorway. She finally focused on her tormentor, locking eyes with Brianna.

"Hey, Tahnie. Sorry to wake you. Daryl's out in the office. I guess we can't quite live without you."

Tanya struggled to sit up, finally connecting the dots and realizing where she was. "How long have I slept?"

"Almost three hours."

Tanya winced. "Three hours!"

"It's OK." Brianna said reassuringly.

Tanya looked up at Brianna. "Tolya?"

"The captain's asleep. They finally got him stabilized. Daniela thinks the worst is over, but he'll be pretty sick for a few days." She saw Tanya's relief and smiled. "Come on, Tahnie. Daryl doesn't seem terribly happy."

Tanya got up from the bunk. "Ok. Give me a couple of minutes to freshen up. I'll be right out."

A few minutes later, Daryl hopped from his seat as Tanya came striding out of Daniela's office. She looked a lot better for the rest. "Hey Daryl, what's up?"

"Hey, yourself." Daryl replied. "You look better."

"Thanks. Brianna says your unhappy. I'd say she's right."

Daryl sighed. "Yeah, well, our saboteur seems to have been more thorough than we thought."

"Really! Tell you what; let's head back to my offices and you can fill me in."

Daryl bowed and waved a flourish towards the door. "After you, my lady." They chuckled as they disappeared down the corridor.

DISCOVERY — 4

ECS Destiny, Quarterdeck, SecCentral, 1155 Hrs

Sherry looked up when the door snapped open. Tanya and Chief Daryl were still chatting as they stopped at the desk.

"Hey Sherry." Tanya offered.

"Hey yourself! You had me worried!" Sherry sniffed. "You took off like a shot, knocked the coffee you wanted so badly all over me and then disappeared leaving me for hours wondering what was wrong. Meanwhile, things have been hopping around here like some precinct police station during a gang war. All I know is that something bad happened to the captain, and that somebody broke something that makes it so the ship can't go!"

Tanya grinned sheepishly. "Yeah, I guess I kinda blew by awfully quick." She sobered quickly. "I'm sorry, Sherry. Captain Chernov was poisoned. I caught on almost too late and tried to get back there before it happened." Sherry's look of horror was priceless.

"It's OK. We got him to MedCentral in time and he's going to be fine. By the way, thank you very much for handling all the excitement around here. From what I've heard, you handled things quickly and professionally." Sherry blushed at the praise.

Tanya continued, "I'm sorry I didn't get back to you sooner to let you know what was going on. I managed to hurt myself while stopping the captain's fall. Doctor Jacobs insisted I lie down and you never want to buck the good doctor.

Sherry nodded. "Sure. I was just worried. Anyway, let me fill you in." She picked up a sheet she'd filled out and handed it to Tanya. "We have a team cordoning off Command deck and Quarterdeck per your orders. We have people on guard at MedCentral, also per your orders.

"The forensics crew finished in the captain's lounge and accompanied the chief and Mr. Leoni down to drive section. They've conducted a preliminary investigation at the crime scene down there; something about a damaged power board. And, as of the last report, the same team has been chasing after the chief here because of a problem in stores. Which reminds me; I sent a couple of our guys down to stores per the chief's request to secure things down there."

Tanya suppressed a chuckle and beamed a big smile instead. Turning to Daryl she said, "See what I mean, Chief? Where would we be without her at the wheel?"

Sherry blushed prettily, looking self conscious.

"OK Sherry. Why don't you get something to eat? Then I want you to take the rest of the day off."

Sherry gave her a grateful look. "Thank you."

"You deserve it. Tomorrow, I'll probably have something new for you to do. Now," she winked. "Get outa here while you still can."

Sherry grinned as Tanya turned for her office, Daryl at her heels.

He mused, "How'd you manage to get such devoted people? Coming on at the last minute must've been something of a handicap after everyone was already used to the other guy."

Tanya gave the extra chair a shove in his direction with a short grunt of pain. She shrugged before sitting at her desk. "I don't know, really. I don't like talking crap about the deceased, but...well, that guy was a real piece of work. If what I hear is true, nobody liked him. Supposedly, he was arrogant, a know it all, and treated everyone else as if they were totally incompetent."

She offered a lopsided grin. "As sad as it is, I found it remotely amusing that the man was the only casualty in that botched emergency airlock drill."

Daryl chuckled. "You've pegged him well, Tahnie..." He considered his words. He was aware of her lengthy struggle to fit in socially with the staff.

"You know, to be honest, I had some doubts about you when you showed up twelve hours before departure, but I'm very glad to have you aboard. You've proven your mettle in my book."

Tanya flushed down to the collar. "Ok... Thanks."

She moved on, trying to change the subject. "So, let's get on with the fun part."

She turned to her computer and started rearranging things on the screen. "Come on. Hitch up a chair and look at what I found. It's what sent me running for the captain when I did."

* * * *

The video clip ended and Daryl looked thoughtful. "Ok. I'm no expert on criminal investigations, but how did you come up with, 'the captain's in danger?' I recognize the second and third guys. One works in the event center diner just down the hall. The other seems to be all over the place. He does maintenance and janitorial work. I don't know either of their names but everybody recognizes them at a glance; especially the younger guy."

Daryl scratched his head. "But the first guy? I don't recognize him at all."

Tanya considered the information. "Well, you're right about the other two. Now, the first guy..." She swiped her finger over an icon and a window came up with a file photo of the man.

"Do you remember that ship-wide meeting? There was this disturbance in the crowd where Tolya and I were presiding?"

Daryl nodded.

"Well," she tapped a finger gently on the screen. "That's him."

Daryl looked thoughtful. "You've been watchin' him ever since then, haven't you?"

Tanya nodded. "Yep. We have no way of knowing what those guys talked about, but you can bet it wasn't about the prospects of fishing next month."

She turned to face the chief. "This guy has been agitating amongst the colonists. He's been trying to put together some type of organized thing to get this voyage 'back on track.' Apparently he refuses to believe the circumstances that prevent it."

She smacked her palm on the desk. "My problem is, he's done nothing strictly illegal; not yet, anyway."

Daryl scratched his chin and thought about it. "So what about the other two guys? They all got together, as proven by your surveillance video. What about them?"

Tanya grinned evilly and turned back to the display. She waved her hands, swept her fingers and tapped a couple of times. The faces of two men flashed up in a separate window with personnel info listed below.

Daryl sat forward as Tanya pointed to one of the men. "This guy, the one you said was in maintenance and janitorial, is Felix Hernandez. Because of his occupation, he has much greater access to sensitive areas of the ship than most others of the civilian crew."

She pointed to the second face. "This guy...is mine!"

Daryl saw an eager, predatory look on her face and made a mental note not to cross this lady.

"His name is Jake Townsend. As you pointed out, he works in food services."

Tanya hesitated, looked at Daryl and then away. She looked unhappy. "It was me," she mumbled. "I...I was the one who ordered the coffee for the captain. He was frustrated with the transition failure and then he found his coffee service out of order."

She pulled absently on a strand of hair. "So, I called down to the diner and requested coffee and someone to come service the machine. I didn't know exactly who I was talking to until later."

She took a deep breath. "I LEFT the captain to come back here and go over reports because something about this chain of screw-ups was happening all in one day.

Daryl sensed something was about to break.

Tanya was struggling for control. "I ah...I got off the lift on my way here and guess who I saw with a coffee service, headed for command deck?"

She tapped the face on the screen. "Him. I thought nothing of it at first. I got here and began going through reports, looking for something to connect the dots on the 'day of screw-ups' problem. That's when I found the footage I showed you just now." Daryl raised his eyebrows in expectation.

"I saw that face," she tapped the display, "and I just knew Tolya was in danger."

"Daryl, I broke all the rules getting back to his standby cabin...to find I was right."

She looked at Daryl, working to hold back tears that tried to spill from dark pools. "I'm the one who put him in danger, and if I hadn't figured it out when I did…"

Her voice broke and she stopped for a second, struggling to finish the thought, "He…He'd be dead right now."

She looked away. "Do you still think I've proved my mettle? I nearly failed my captain…my…my friend." She tried to ignore the tears sliding down her face.

After an awkward silence, Daryl reached out and tugged her chin, gently turning her head around to look at him. "Don't you ever think that again, Lass. Nobody around here is Superman or Wonder-Woman. You're not all knowing and almighty. There's only ONE in the universe who has that advantage and you should be thanking HIM for helping you save your…friend."

Tanya nodded, sniffling and feeling foolish. "You're right. I'm just feeling sorry for myself, I guess."

Daryl patted her hand. "Forget it."

Tanya pulled a box of tissues from a desk drawer as Daryl continued. "Look, this is way off topic and probably none of my business, but…well…it's obvious to everybody except you and our captain that you two have become more than just…friends. I think things would run a lot more smoothly around here if you two got on the same page and quit pretending it's nothing."

Tanya snagged another tissue from the box in front of her, dabbed her eyes and threw it in the recycle basket. She sat back and considered Daryl's statement.

The silence grew and then Daryl continued. "Frankly, I think the two of you deserve each other." He grinned, "As a matter of fact, since I'm giving unsolicited advice, I might as well go give the captain a little as soon as he wakes up."

Tanya tried to offer an objection, but Daryl held up a hand. "Come on Tanya, don't deny it. The people of this colony, wherever it winds up, need strong, kindly leadership. You two, when you're working together, just…I don't know, it's like…it's perfect. I've watched you in your sparring sessions; you're a team. I think you need to acknowledge what's obvious to everybody else so you can get on with the business of rescuing this voyage and running this colony."

Tanya sat quietly, looking off in the distance.

Daryl got a sudden inspiration and spoke again. "Just look at me and my Naomi. It's the same with us. We figured it out a couple of years before *Destiny* left orbit. We work together like a hand in a surgical glove. Everyone sees that in you... in spades."

Tanya nodded slowly, as if waking from a dream. "Yeah, I suppose you're right. I think Tolya's been trying to get us there, but I've been trying to ignore the signs."

She dabbed at her eyes. "I haven't had an interest in anyone. I don't deny I'm taken with him. I guess my goofy behavior of late shouts the fact. It's just...it seems now's not the right time. Just look at the mess we're in!"

Daryl shrugged, "all the more reason to get past the goofy stage and get on with the mess, stronger and more resolute than before."

Tanya nodded, *why is it the important things in life that make us act so stupid?*

Daryl saw something shift behind her eyes and smiled. "So, that's enough of Uncle Daryl's lectures. Let's see if we can fix some of this mess."

Tanya nodded. "Thanks, Daryl."

She stopped, took a breath and looked thoughtfully at the faces on the screen.

"You know." She said, dabbing away at her face, "I think there's some connection between Mr. Felix here and your mess in drive section. We know that Mr. Jake is connected with the poison thing. He had the means and the opportunity. He was seen going to and emerging from a meeting with our principle ringleader, Mr. Ted."

"OK..." Daryl prompted.

"Well," Tanya turned back to look at him. "I don't think Mr. Felix is equipped to do the damage himself. I think he's more a messenger boy. What if he has an acquaintance with someone in your section that would have been sympathetic to their cause and able to accomplish the task?"

Daryl looked thoughtful. "Maybe. Your friend Felix has nearly unlimited access to most areas of the ship; he and others in his department. He knows lots of people. After all, he and the rest of the custodial staff are seen regularly by most everybody on board."

Tanya grinned, "My thinking exactly!" She sat back in her chair and considered the situation. "Now we need to figure out who in drive section was unhappy enough to be tempted to act? This person would then need to have a connection with Mr. Felix."

Daryl added, "And, this person would have to have the expertise to do the damage without causing his or her own death along with everybody else's."

Tanya was becoming enthusiastic. "OK. I think a good way to figure out who we're looking for, is by figuring out where your missing board is."

Daryl grinned. "I like it."

"I thought you might."

Tanya stood up and Daryl followed her lead. "Daryl, I'm going to organize an official search for your board. I need an accurate photo and a description. Then we're going to turn this ship inside out till we find it. While you're getting me that information, I'm going to go throw our good friend, Mr. Jake, into the deepest corner of the brig on charges of attempted murder and anything else I can dig up. I owe him that much!" Her evil little grin didn't bode well for the good Mr. Jake.

Daryl laughed, patted Tanya gently on the back and headed for the door. "I'll get that info back to your office today. Oh, and Tanya, please think on what we discussed."

DISCOVERY — 5
ECS Destiny, Deck 2, Starboard Community Center, Forward, 1200 Hrs

"Do you have it?" Ted looked eager, like a child at the morning's Christmas tree.

Felix nodded and pulled out an object wrapped diligently in anti-static plastic. Ted took it eagerly and looked it over, as if he'd know what he was looking at.

Ted was ecstatic. "This, my boy, is the insurance policy I was talking about. This board is a major bargaining chip. You watch. They'll do anything to get this thing back."

Felix was a lot brighter than he acted. While his education had been limited, he was quite capable of figuring out the tremendous amount of trouble Ted was creating for the rest of the population.

"Ted, you didn't say anything about poisoning people, like the captain. You didn't say anything about causing damage that could have killed us all. I never wanted to do so much as what you've made us do. I'm tired of this insanity and I don't want any more to do with it."

Ted gave him a withering look. "Listen boy. You should know about taking risks…"

"Yeah, but I never take deadly risks."

Ted shrugged. "Just consider it upping the stakes. You know, bigger risks for higher stakes equals better rewards. Now I don't want to hear any more whining."

He handed the board back. "Go put this somewhere safe. I don't want them to find it near me. When I'm ready for it you just bring it back."

He gave Felix a contemptuous sneer. "Stop your sniveling boy. We'll make a man of you yet. Now, git!"

DISCOVERY — 6
ECS Destiny, Quarterdeck, SecCentral, 1630 Hrs

A little over four hours after Daryl left the office, the COMM chimed. Tanya swished the pick up icon "Security."

"Hey Tahnie, it's Brianna."

Tanya's attention perked up. "Hi, Bri, what's up?"

"Someone here's demanding your presence. I think you better get over here. They seem very insistent."

Tanya frowned. "I'm kinda busy, can't they come over here?"

Brianna replied, "I don't think so. They're giving Daniela fits. I think she'd appreciate your intervention."

Tanya sighed, looked over at the time display and raised a surprised eyebrow. *Has it really been four hours? I guess I could use a break.* "Oh, all right. I'll be right over."

Tanya secured her terminal and grumbled her way out the door. *What the heck's going on? Don't we have enough trouble without crazy people makin' more?*

She walked the few short steps and turned to enter MedCentral. Brianna met her at the door. "Hey, Tahnie. Come on, this way."

Tanya's curiosity was in high gear. She couldn't hear any raised voices or other signs of tension. They went past the various examination cubicles and Brianna stopped at the last one. She looked questioningly at Brianna who just smiled and motioned her to enter.

Tanya turned to enter the cubicle and almost collided with Daniela, who was backing out. "Oh, sorry, I didn't see you."

Tanya nodded. "That's OK. So, What's up?"

Daniela's grin was infectious. In fact, it was starting to look suspicious. "Somebody's been asking for you; very insistent!"

She pulled the curtain back and Tanya saw Tolya propped up on several pillows, watching her enter the cubicle.

"Hey Tanya. Miss me?"

Tanya grinned till she thought her face was going to split. "Tolya! They didn't tell me you were awake!"

"They weren't supposed to yet." His mischievous smile looked a little tired.

Tolya was still a bit pale and not quite his energetic self, but he looked much better than when she'd left him almost seven hours ago. Behind her, Daniela and Brianna exchanged conspiratorial smiles and withdrew from the cubicle to find things to keep themselves…elsewhere.

Tanya suddenly felt shy. "So…you look a little better than the last time I saw you."

He smiled wanly. "I hear I wasn't much to look at."

"Yeah. I… I'm sorry I didn't get back sooner. I shouldn't have even left."

Tolya waved a hand negligently. "It seems you got back soon enough… Thanks."

"No charge." She grinned. "You're a pretty solid catch. Did you know that?"

He raised an eloquent eyebrow that Tanya failed to translate. "Dannie got mad at me 'cause I wasn't careful when I tried to catch you when you fell."

"Oh." He said noncommittally. "Maybe you should start from the beginning. I don't remember much. I remember you barging into the room and I remember getting up from the desk. That's it. The next thing, I'm waking up to find Dannie and Bri looking down at me."

Tanya looked grimly at the wall above his head for a moment. Just remembering the incident stirred strong emotions she thought she should hide. "Well, let's just say it was the worst moment of my life. You see, after I ordered the coffee…"

* * * *

It was Tolya's turn to look grim. "We've really got a serious problem here."

Tanya arched an eyebrow and he grinned mischievously. "Yeah, I know; all those horrible understatements." They laughed quietly.

"Tahnie… can I call you that?" She nodded her head, not trusting her voice. "Tahnie, I've been doing some thinking. A mutual friend came by a couple of hours ago and gave me a gentle, but very sensible chewing."

Tanya's face flushed as she remembered her own awkward talk with Daryl.

Tolya continued. "I was led to believe you got a similar lecture."

Tanya nodded, a smile peeking through her nerves.

"Well, I've been thinking." He reached over and took the hand she'd placed on the lowered railing of his bed. "Haven't we avoided the obvious long enough?"

She nodded, butterflies madly cavorting about inside.

"I...I'm not really very good at this. I've never met a lady like you before."

Tanya's face went crimson. *Stop blushing! Stop Blushing.* The blush just got worse. *Nobody's ever called you a LADY that way.*

Tolya continued, looking inward, trying to explain himself. "I've never been the kind to give chase. My career always came first and...by the time I accepted this mission, the thought of lifetime bachelorhood didn't bother me so much."

He looked up into her face. "But, when you showed up at the boarding ramp twelve hours before departure with orders to replace the dearly departed Chief Steinberg...I found myself...distracted. Ever since, I've found myself distracted ...pleasantly so, I might add... whenever you're near."

He released her hand to scoot up on his pillows. "Tahnie. Have you...ah...are you seeing someone?"

Tanya reached behind her with a foot and hooked a chair up so she could sit.

"Well, not really." She mentally kicked herself. *'Not really?' You don't really know anybody well enough.*

She rushed into the tense pause before she could insert the other foot. "No! I've been too busy trying to prove myself to everyone and, well, you're pretty distracting yourself."

She looked down. "I have always assumed you had more qualified choices."

Tolya laughed, a rich, comforting laugh that rumbled pleasantly in his chest. "Tahnie, I don't know where you got that notion. Like I said, I've never had an active interest in pursuing lasting relationships. No-one's ever caught my eye this way. So, no I don't have a line of applicants." He gave her a solemn look and reclaimed her hand. "Just you."

A look of surprise flitted across Tanya's face. She'd spent so long believing there was nothing in common between them; that he'd never find her that appealing.

"You know? We have more in common than I ever imagined. I've always been...Miss Efficient, you know, Miss All About Business. I've ignored the occasional attempt to get my attention.

I've never been interested. I've always been too busy proving myself to someone."

She shrugged, "I signed up for this assignment so I could be a part of something new and challenging; no attachments, no family, no real friends, I could just disappear.

"Since I came aboard, I've been yearning for a lasting relationship. I suppose the growing realization this was a 'rest of my life' arrangement shifted my thinking.

Tanya looked into his eyes. "Meeting you was a jolt of lightning in that direction." She looked down at their clasped hands. "It's not until the last couple of months that I felt I had a hope of fitting in with the rest of the command staff."

Looking thoughtful, Tolya gave her hand a squeeze. "Do you remember when we were figuring out how to approach communicating with the colonists, we agreed to drop the formalities and just be friends and partners?"

Tanya remembered back to their first truly private conversation and grinned at the memory, "I remember."

"Since then, we've truly become friends. We work well together, we fight well together, we seem to complement each other at every turn." He looked at her quietly for a few moments. He seemed to be gathering strength of will.

"I think I finally know what I'm feeling. I don't have flowery words so I'm going to be horridly blunt."

Tanya felt a rush of expectation.

"Tahnie, I've done something a captain's forbidden to do. I've become attached to one of my officers."

He took a long breath. "I've fallen in love with you...I just wish it had been under better circumstances."

Tears welled up in her eyes unbidden. "I've been trying to resist my feelings for a long time. I thought they were somehow misguided and stupid; that you could never return them." She hugged his hand close, "...but I think I finally admitted to them when I saw you lying there on the floor."

She searched his face, "I suddenly realized I could never bear to lose you." She reached over and gently stroked the hair over his ear. "I love you too."

There was no avoiding the subject; no hiding behind obscure notions of propriety. Their feelings were mutual. They'd been expressed aloud.

Out here among the stars, isolated from all civilization but the other two thousand some odd souls on board, there was a sense of the need to seize the moment. The time for lengthy courtships was simply impractical. The future seemed even more tenuous given the circumstances.

"I ah...this seems...well, it's way too fast, but well..."

Tanya stood and leaned over him, silencing him with a gentle kiss on the lips. Tolya's eyes widened at the sweet surprise and she pulled away. "Yes."

Tolya's surprise was complete. "Yes? You don't think it's too fast; too soon?"

Tanya grinned through her tears. "Someone, somewhere will think so, but not me. We've been acting like confused teenagers for months now. That should count for something, shouldn't it?"

Tolya gazed into her eyes, coming to grips with what she was saying. "You mean it? You'll be my wife, my first lady?"

Tanya nodded her head. "Absolutely. I don't want to loose you. So, you're stuck with me for good."

She bent over the rail for a repeat performance of that first kiss. Tolya's eyes lit up and he reached up, took the back of her neck and pulled her into a passionate response that got her heart pumping.

"When?" He half whispered.

Tanya clung to his hand. "Well, if I had my way, I'd say right now...but I seldom get my way."

She sighed. "We have this horrid mess to deal with and I think it's going to get worse before it gets better."

He was clearly disappointed. "Yeah, I know." Then he perked up. "I want to make this a public event. I want everyone to know...but you're right. With everything that's going on right now, it's a bad time. Besides, I don't want a wedding in a hospital bed."

They both laughed at the absurd picture.

Tanya brightened with an idea. "How about when we get to this new system? We could celebrate that success along with ours. It would give the whole colony a joyous break from the stresses of our current troubles. And...it would send a positive message about our expectations for the future."

Tolya smiled. "I love it."

Tanya grew serious. "We need to get down to business. I've a lot of work to do."

Tolya gave a mock pout. "That means you're going away?"

Tanya grinned. "Yes, I'm afraid so, but the sooner I go away, the sooner I can come back!"

She leaned over and gave him a final, parting kiss before leaving the cubicle.

Daniela and Brianna took one look at Tanya's face and quietly slapped high fives. Tanya never noticed as she floated out the door.

COMMITTED — 1

FRI 02.12.2094
ECS Destiny, Quarterdeck, Tanya's Cabin, 0745 Hrs

Tanya finished her light breakfast and straightened up her cabin. After her stunning conversation with Tolya the evening before she'd wandered back to her office. Unable to concentrate and, having no appetite, she'd returned to her cabin and gone to bed early.

Now she was fresh, energized and full of purpose. She entered her offices before Sherry, an unusual event. A note from the forensics lab flashed on her display. It was about the findings from Tolya's work lounge.

On the coffee cup, they could only find the captains smudgy fingerprints. However, the coffee service tray had yielded a solid set. The computer had matched them to those of Jake Townsend with a probable accuracy of ninety-seven point eight two seven percent.

"Gotcha, you s.o.b!" She sat back considering her next step. She checked the time. It was 0840.

The AI responded to the pinch of her COMM tab. "Routing?"

"Deck 1 Security."

"One moment."

A short pause… "Franc here."

Tanya smiled. "Hey Robert. I'd like you to take a couple of your boys up to the main kitchen on Quarterdeck and bring Mr. Jake Townsend to me for questioning. He's my prime suspect in my investigation on the attempted murder of the captain."

She heard the grin in his voice. "Yes ma'am."

"Oh, Robert; when Mr. Townsend has been secured, report to MedCentral. I'll have Dr. Jacobs accompany you to his work area, lockers and personal quarters. Find and bring anything that contains, or might have contained the substance, Chloral Hydrate. Dr. Jacobs is along as expert advice. She'll be able to confirm if you've found it."

"Yes, ma'm," came the enthusiastic reply.

* * * *

Brianna swiped the COMM icon. The display window popped open and a very self-satisfied Tanya smiled back.

"Hey there, Tahnie. What's up?"

"Hiya, Bri. I need a quick chat with Dannie."

"Sure thing. Hey, you gonna fill us in…you know?"

Tanya flushed and grinned. "All in good time, Bri. By the way, even if that tricky little charade played out wonderfully, it was a very cruel trick to play…Thanks!"

Bri chuckled in delight. "Hang on. I'll get her."

The window blanked for a couple seconds. Dannie's face flashed up. "Hey there! Have you landed yet?"

Tanya looked puzzled for an instant.

Dannie laughed. "Sorry kiddo, but you came out of Tolya's cubicle at least three feet off the deck."

"Ha! Like I told Bri. That was a nasty trick to play…Thanks!"

Daniela offered a warm smile. "No charge. It was Tolya's idea, really. So, what can I do for you?"

Tanya got down to business. "Dannie. In about a half hour, I'll have my chief suspect in custody. I'd appreciate if you would accompany my man, Robert Franc, on a tour of this guy's work area, lockers and personal quarters. He's looking for any trace of Chloral Hydrate. He'll need your expertise identifying it."

Dannie glanced at the time display on her screen. It was 0900. "Well, Tahnie, you picked a really good day. I have nothing pressing on my schedule except for a dinner with Vince early this evening. That's nonnegotiable, you know."

Tanya smiled. "Sure! How about in a half hour?"

Dannie nodded. "Sure; anything for you and Tolya."

"OK, enough of that." Tanya winked. "Thanks."

She closed the link and then pulled up the image of the missing board that Daryl had sent her along with a concise description. She copied and pasted it into a new file and added a public notice to the digital bulletin windows about the ship. She provided the COMM code, and on the reward line, a short poignant phrase: WITHOUT THIS BOARD, WE'RE ON AN ETERNAL RIDE TO NOWHERE.

COMMITTED — 2

ECS Destiny, Quarterdeck, SecCentral, 0925 Hrs

The door snapped open and Robert Franc ushered Jake Townsend into the room, flanked by two burly security officers. Tanya went to the door of her office and looked out into the reception area at the object of her most intense displeasure. Sherry, who'd just settled in for her shift, took in the growing drama with wide eyed concern.

Jake Townsend smirked at Tanya, but his cockiness faded as he sensed the barely controlled urges percolating behind her eyes.

She slowly approached, staring intently into his eyes. Her urge to spit in his face died, whimpering. That was hardly lady like, let alone professional.

"Mr. Jake Townsend. I am placing you under arrest on charges of attempted murder of the ship's captain, Anatoli Chernov. I am also charging you with conspiracy and possession of a controlled substance for sale or illicit use."

She turned to Franc. "Log him into maximum security. Make sure everything is properly done. I'll question him later."

Robert Franc smiled grimly and said, "Ma'am."

Then Jake spoke for the first time. "You know, where I come from, a man's supposed to be read his rights and allowed at least two calls."

Tanya stuck her nose nearly in his face. "Rights, Mr. Townsend? Have you forgotten where you are? We're not on Earth anymore. We make our own laws. While the charter contains some cautionary restrictions, we're free to design our own system of justice.

"Right now, you have the right to shut up. We'll talk later."

Tanya turned back to Franc. "Thanks, Robert. When you get done, head to MedCentral. Dr. Jacobs will be waiting for you."

Robert snapped off a sharp salute, uttered 'Ma'am,' and marched Jake off to maximum security.

Tanya turned to find Sherry watching. "Mornin' Sherry."

Sherry smiled back. "Morning, Tanya." She gave a quick nod in the direction of the detention center. "That was exciting. How are you doing this morning?"

Tanya grinned broadly. "Sherry, I've never felt better in my life! Besides my obvious pleasure in having that man," she waved in Jakes general direction, "behind bars, I have some news for you."

Sherry turned to face her boss squarely. "News? The way you look, it must be awesome. Tell me!"

Tanya sat on the edge of Sherry's desk. "Well, it comes in two parts. First, Captain Chernov woke up last night and he's totally out of danger."

Sherry grinned broadly. "Great!"

Tanya held up two fingers. "Second, if number one wasn't great enough, this will blow your socks off."

She leaned closer, lowering her voice conspiratorially. "He proposed last night!"

Sherry's jaw dropped and her eyes got hugely round.

"No way!" She exclaimed.

Tanya stood up and laughed. "It's true!"

Sherry jumped up from her seat and threw her arms around Tanya's neck. "Oh, Tahnie, that's so wonderful. Everybody's been wondering when…"

She stepped back. "Tell me you said, 'yes.'"

Tanya grinned. "Of course. How could I refuse?" She looked at Sherry. "We were that obvious?"

Sherry beamed and nodded her head. "Yep. Every time you two got close enough, people could feel the electricity, like you were fighting an irresistible force."

Tanya nodded thoughtfully. "Yeah, I guess we were."

Sherry resumed her seat. "So, when's the big day?"

Tanya smiled. "Well, with all that's going on, we're going to have to wait till we've reached Emily's new system. We'll have a big celebration over our successful arrival, topped with a wedding."

Sherry grinned. "Awesome! Hey, if you need any help, you know, getting ready, let me know."

"Absolutely! We'll talk more, later. Right now, I need you to do me a more mundane favor."

Sherry nodded, "Of course."

Tanya went on with her instructions. "I need you to mind the shop for a little while."

Sherry grinned, "Sure, what's up?"

"Nothing big, I'm off to MedCentral…"

"Of course. I've got this covered."

"Thanks, Sherry."

* * * *

Brianna looked up from her station, grinning from ear to ear. "Hey, Tahnie. You look chipper this morning!"

"Why thank you, Bri. Is Tolya awake?"

Brianna nodded. "Oh, yes! He's getting very restless. Daniela said if he didn't settle down she was going to have to chase him out of here."

Tanya grinned. "Yeah, he can be pretty determined."

"So, what happened last night? You've gotta tell me."

Tanya blushed a little. She seemed to be doing a lot of grinning lately. "Well, we had a heart to heart talk and decided everyone else knew something we didn't."

Brianna raised an impatient eyebrow.

"Anyway, after that...he proposed and I accepted."

Brianna laughed and clapped her hands together. "I knew it! You were in another galaxy when you left last night. I called a bet with Dannie that he'd propose. She turned me down because she'd thought the same thing."

Tanya came around the counter and Brianna got up to give her a hug. "Please, don't tell Dannie. I want to tell her."

Brianna winked and crossed her heart. "Mum's the word. Dannie tried to get Tolya to spill the beans but he said we'd have to ask you."

Tanya chuckled. "That's Tolya, all right."

"Hey, my ears are itching; you talking about me?"

They both whirled around to see the captain standing in the entryway of the lobby in hospital style PJs.

Brianna feigned outrage. "Captain! You're supposed to be quietly convalescing in your cubicle!"

He grinned unrepentantly. "I keep telling you two, I feel fine. In fact, I'm so itchy to get moving I'm going to have a break down from sheer boredom."

Brianna put hands on hips and started to protest some more.

Tolya waved his hand in dismissal. "Besides, how am I supposed to stay patiently in my cubicle when you're selfishly hoarding the one person who holds my greatest source of joy?"

He entered the room and Tanya hurried forward.

She stopped him in a warm embrace. She stepped back, looking him up and down. "Are you sure you're ok? Dannie keeps saying you need more time."

Tolya grinned. "I kind of get a kick out of bugging her, but really, I feel great."

He looked thoughtful. "I think it's your fault."

He gave her a quick kiss before she could object to the barb.

Brianna shrugged in mock resignation. "You haven't heard the last of this, sir. Just you wait till the doctor gets back."

She couldn't suppress the grin that invaded her face. She looked across the lobby. "The waiting room's empty. If you two need to... talk, you could go in there. I'll let you know if someone's coming." Tanya smiled gratefully. "Thanks Bri."

* * * *

ECS Destiny, Quarterdeck, MedCentral, 1010 Hrs

The two sat, cuddled together on a couch in an obscure corner, out of direct view of the office. Tanya sighed as she leaned on Tolya's chest. "Tolya, I came to see you for a couple of reasons; first, just because I couldn't stay away another minute; but second, because I did something today that's going to start a lot of mess."

Tolya looked down at her and grunted inquisitively.

Tanya continued. "Last night I didn't get to tell you everything I knew about the attempt on your life. We kinda took a left turn there...not that I minded."

Tolya chuckled.

"Anyway, I figured out it was the guy who brought your coffee. He was seen recently going to a secret meeting with Ted Jackson. When I saw that guy on the surveillance vid coming out of the conference room, I realized who the guy was who had taken you the coffee. So, I raced back to catch you...thankfully, in time."

Tolya replied. "Yeah, that's what I've been thinking. Do we have enough proof?"

Tanya sat up and pushed her hair out of her face. "I almost have enough; enough that I had the man arrested this morning and sent my guys and Dannie to search for the final piece of evidence. If they can find even traces of Chloral Hydrate in his possessions I am confident it'll be sufficient."

"I'd love to get something settled and behind us." Tolya said. "The missing board; how's that coming along?"

Tanya grimaced. "Well, I put a notice on the public bulletin displays. It says we're headed nowhere if it isn't found."

Tolya looked worried. "How do you think the people are going to react to that? We mustn't start a panic."

Tanya shrugged. "I don't think so. Remember when I told you people would need to feel they're a part of the solution?"

Tolya nodded.

"I think most of them know we have their best interest at heart. When they find out someone's trying to ruin their chances, they're going to be furious with him. They'll go out of their way to help."

Tolya pulled her back down to cuddle in the crook of his arm. "Well, it looks like you've made mighty good progress for a distracted security chief."

Tanya grinned and gave him a playful punch in the ribs. She mimicked claws and grabbed his arm. "I don't know...having your prey firmly in your grip can really focus your mind."

Their laughter faded after a few moments and they sat in silence for a while. Finally, Tanya brought up another subject that had been troubling her.

"Tolya, when I confronted Jake this morning and charged him, he had the temerity to criticize my methods, citing the old Miranda laws. I told him we're no longer bound to Earth laws."

She swiveled around so she could look into his eyes. "Before we get much further, I want us to sit down and hash out what the charter says about our governing forms. I want to do this right so things don't come back to haunt us later."

Tolya sat up. "You're right. When I pry myself out of here, I have a whole library dedicated to government. We can sit and talk to our hearts content!" He grinned as Tanya pummeled him playfully on the chest and then they kissed before getting up to rejoin the community at large.

Before they returned to the lobby, Tolya peeled the interface patch off the back of his hand. "Let me see you're pocket-tab."

Tanya unclipped the small, but powerful computer node from her belt and handed it over. Tolya placed the patch on the small screen and tapped in some instructions on the pad.

The pocket-tab chirped and Tolya retrieved his patch, reaffixing it to his hand.

"If you don't mind?" He held out his hand. Curious, Tanya peeled off her own patch and handed it over.

Tolya placed it on the little screen and tapped in some more instructions. Another chirp signaled the end of whatever process he'd just completed.

Tolya carefully peeled the patch off the screen and handed it back. "You now have all my recognition codes. You may enter my cabin and you may access my personal files."

He gazed at her. "You're the only person I've ever entrusted with so much...Would you please get a few things from my room?"

She smiled. The notion that he'd just included her in the heart of his most personal information was numbing.

"Certainly." She thumbed her pad. "What do you need?"

"Well, let's see..."

COMMITTED — 3

ECS Destiny, Deck 3, Starboard Community Center Forward, 1040 Hrs

"Damn, Ted! Are you out of your stinkin' mind?"

Ted gave Felix a blood-chilling stare. "You better watch your attitude 'messenger boy!' If that vile woman gets Jake to spill, he'll implicate both of us."

Felix licked his lips and wished again that he'd never met this crazy s.o.b. "Listen Ted. I ain't no action hero, see? If I get caught, you still get fingered. Security will really want answers if I get caught, and I don't know if I can hold out."

Ted was losing his patience, not a difficult task for him. "You get your skinny little ass up there and get Jake out of this mess! The fool got himself caught, but we cant' let him stay there."

He stared at Felix, thinking hard. "Look, you're a lot sneakier than you give your self credit for. Not getting caught's all the motivation you need. Now, git! Go on!" He gave Felix a shove.

Felix had grown to fear Ted. He didn't know just why, but he swallowed a nasty answer and left the room.

COMMITTED — 4

ECS Destiny, Quarterdeck, MedCentral, 1105 Hrs

Brianna looked up from her work as the captain and his bride-to-be came out of the waiting room chuckling happily together. They approached the counter and Tanya looked at her.

Brianna smiled. "So, all caught up?"

Tanya grinned. "No, but it'll have to do for now. I'm going to get some things for Tolya and be right back."

"Oh," Tolya reached for Tanya's pocket-tab. "You'll need filenames. I want to catch up on some reports." He jotted down the filenames he needed and relinquished her unit.

"My power-tab is in the top left drawer of my desk."

Tanya started to go then turned to Brianna. "Bri. If Dannie gets back sooner, would you ask her to wait?"

"Sure, no problem."

"Thanks Bri."

Tanya turned back to Tolya and gave him a petite little wave. "I'll be right back. You'd better behave."

Tolya grinned innocently as she walked out.

* * * *

71

Tolya's door recognized her patch and opened happily. She went inside and looked around for the items he requested. She smiled at the room's appearance, very neat and orderly.

Everything was exactly where he'd said it would be. She found a small suitcase in the bottom of his closet. After laying it out on his bunk she started filling it. There was a complete working uniform set: a shirt, a pair of pants and socks. His shoes, shiny enough to see your own reflection, were in a little cubby in MedCentral. The uniform he'd worn the horrible day before was at the laundry.

It felt awkward fishing about his small dresser, but everyone needs underwear. She flushed a little as she tucked them into the suitcase. She found his shaving kit on the shelf above his sink. In the cabinet behind the little mirror, she found toothbrush, toothpaste and cologne. Tolya would be happy to get those. He was using a generic hospital toothbrush, but he wasn't happy with it. *Picky, Picky,* she thought. She tucked them into an outer pocket. She closed the suitcase and set it down by the door.

Next, she went to his desk and pulled his power-tab. She sat down in his chair and started up his computer, which accepted her patch and opened up for business. She placed the power-tab next to the desk computer, turned it on and waited the couple of seconds it took for it to start up. She set up a file transfer routine and keyed in the file names.

The clock-calendar said it was 1150. She stood, peering about the room as the computers chuckled happily together. Tanya's eyes were drawn to an old-fashioned digital photo frame set back near the corner of his desk. The picture being displayed showed a middle-aged couple standing in front of a beautiful little cottage. Two boys stood between them. One looked to be about ten or twelve. The other was older, probably around sixteen or eighteen. Apparently, Tolya had a younger brother. Tolya looked sharp at sixteen. The boys stood together, the younger one trying to look distinguished and grown up.

She smiled at the family photo. *I wonder why his brother didn't come?* The parents seemed a little older than she'd have expected. *They must have started late,* she thought.

She paged forward. The next photo was of Tolya, probably eighteen or nineteen years old. He stood next to his mother, who looked much older. Tanya wondered where his dad and younger brother were. She paged forward again.

Here was Tolya in a Fighter Squadron dress uniform. The picture was superimposed over a slightly blurry image of a triangle folded

United States flag. Being unfamiliar with military flag protocols, she wondered at its significance.

Her breath caught in her throat when the next picture came up. This was a photo of Tolya standing next to a very attractive young woman. He was holding a baby girl in his arms with the proudest look on his face.

Tanya stood trembling, absorbing what the photo depicted. *What's this?* She sat heavily in his chair, staring at the photo, confused. *He said he'd NEVER had any relationships before. This looks like a pretty solid relationship to me.*

She didn't hear the job complete chime sound right away. She just sat staring, teetering between dismay and despair. Some time passed before she surfaced enough to notice that the computers were done working.

She set the photo frame back where she'd found it. Her world was crashing in around her. *Did he lie to me? Why? What happened to them? Why didn't they come?*

She worked on automatic; shutting down the power-tab and his computer, putting the carrying strap over her shoulder and picking up his small suitcase.

It was 1210 when Tanya numbly secured the door behind her and, hefting Tolya's things, trudged the long two-minute hike back to MedCentral.

Daniela wasn't back yet and Brianna was out for lunch. Tolya must have gone back to his cubicle. She peered in. He was sound asleep. Relieved, she placed his things by his bed and slipped out without a sound.

She couldn't face anyone just then, so she went to her cabin and sat numbly staring at the computer. She stumbled through a simple message to Sherry, the characters on the screen swimming before her watery eyes. She forced her way through the message, and then collapsed onto her bunk. *Did I misplace my trust yet again? Am I just cursed?* In her devastation she cried herself to sleep.

COMMITTED — 5

ECS Destiny, Crew Country, MedCentral, 1245 Hrs

Daniela returned late from the search of Jake Townsend's haunts. Brianna looked up with a worried frown. "Dannie, did you see Tanya on your way back?"

Daniela shook her head. "No, and I need to talk to her about her suspect. We found her evidence, and more."

Brianna's frown deepened. "That's weird. Tanya went off to Tolya's cabin to collect some things for him. That was about 1110. She was only going to be gone maybe a half hour and then come right back."

Daniela turned and glanced out into the corridor.

Brianna continued. "She didn't come back when expected and Tolya got tired. He took a nap and I slipped out for a quick lunch. As far as I know, she hasn't come back."

Daniela glanced at the time display. It was 1255. Lunch was half way through. This wasn't Tanya's normal pattern. She looked in on Tolya to find him propped up, reading from his power-tab.

He looked up with a quizzical expression. "Hi. Where's Tahnie? I think she brought my stuff in while I was asleep."

After some quick discussion, they decided it was most unlike Tanya to just disappear like this.

Tolya prevailed on Daniela to release him. He was apparently well on his way to recovery and there seemed little point in keeping him. He gathered his things while Daniela called Sherry in Security.

He approached the reception desk and Daniela looking puzzled. "What's up?"

She shook her head. "Tahnie's been in the clouds all day, but Sherry just said she wasn't feeling well. She's in her quarters."

Tolya looked askance. "I just saw her this morning. I don't think she could've felt better if she'd wanted to."

"That's right," Brianna opined. "She was practically walking on air. I've never seen her so alive and happy."

Tolya hefted his gear. "Well, I'll get this stuff back to my cabin and then go find out what's wrong. I'll let you know." With that, he headed briskly down the corridor.

He let himself into his room and as the door closed behind him, stood, breathing in the familiar scents of 'his space.' He sensed Tanya's delicate fragrance as he dropped his suitcase on the bunk and sat at his desk.

Something seemed out of place. He started up his computer and put his power-tab in its drawer before his eyes locked onto the minor the discrepancy.

The photo frame on the back corner of his desk wasn't displaying the same picture he'd selected. Instead, it was showing the picture of his late brother with his wife and their little baby. He picked it up and wondered how the pictures had been switched.

It dawned on him, if Tanya had sat in this chair to transfer his files, she'd have seen the photo frame and been curious.

But, why did she leave that picture up? He sat staring, remembering the day he'd taken it. He still missed his brother. Yasha had been so full of life. His wife, Tamara, quietly went mad after his death. Her passing had been God's act of mercy for her. *I'm glad I could bring little Lyubova along.*

Tolya roused himself from his melancholy reminiscing and got to his feet. *This isn't going to help figure out what's bothering Tahnie.*

It was 1330 hours. He left the room and walked the short distance to Tanya's door and tapped the call tab. All was quiet and no one was out and about. He tried two or three times before becoming concerned. He tried calling. "Tahnie?" Nothing. "Tahnie, it's me, Tolya." Still nothing. Now he was worried.

He tried the call tab again before deciding to take extreme measures. He swiped the back of his hand over the security pad. The door snapped open and he leaned into a darkened room. In the light coming from the computer screen saver he could see Tanya lying on her bunk with her back to the door.

Tolya quietly stepped into the room and as the door snapped shut, flicked his hand as if striking a match. He held his hand in a palm down position to complete the move. The room lights came up to about half-light.

He saw she wasn't really asleep. "Hey, you OK? What's wrong?"

COMMITTED — 6

ECS Destiny, Quarterdeck, SecCentral, 1335 Hrs

Felix stopped on the forward bridge that accessed the lift bank across from the Mezzanine on Deck 3. He left his equipment cart against the rail overlooking the Promenade below. It wouldn't do to have it found near the security office.

He stepped around the parked tramcar and called the lift. The lift took him up to Quarterdeck where he cautiously stepped off. As he walked aft, towards SecCentral, he noticed there was very little activity at the moment.

Pausing near the sky view structure, he glanced down on the vast expanse of the central core of the ship. The Mezzanine was directly below. Farther below was the Promenade with its massive park and water fountains.

He finally set his nerve and turned towards SecCentral. He elected the bold approach and strode confidently into the lobby. He spotted an attractive young lady working industriously at her computer station.

Felix cleared his throat and she looked up startled. "Yes? Can I help you?"

"Yeah, well... I was told to come and take care of a mess in the detention block."

She looked puzzled and then frowned. "I don't think my boss wants anyone back there right now. Besides, if there was a mess to clean up, I'd know about it."

Felix shrugged, "Yea, well... I got my orders, same as you. Just toss me the key card and I'll take care of it."

She half turned and cast a nervous glance at the small cabinet behind her station. She turned back to her workstation. "I'll tell you what." She tapped the COMM tab. "Let me get that cleared with my boss first, OK?"

As the connection was going through, Felix darted behind her chair and fumbled for the latch to the key cabinet. "Hey Tahnie, it's Sherry..." She turned as Felix went for the cabinet, lunging to stop him. "Hey! What're you doing? Where do you...?"

Felix jerked the door open and scooped up the cards hung by lanyards inside. The cabinet door swung hard and Felix tried to push the fiery young lady out of the way. The door hit her in the forehead. "Ow! Stop it!"

She lost her balance and fell. Felix, in an awkward position and his hands full of lanyards, tried uselessly to stop her fall. She hit the floor as her head struck the side of the counter. He heard bone snap as her arm bent under her in an odd direction.

Felix froze, staring in horrified fascination at the young woman with a bloody face, lying broken like a rag doll.

The COMM came to life. "Sherry? What's going on? Sherry?"

Felix raced for the detention area yelling, "Jake!"

Jake responded. "In here!"

Felix passed each of the three cards over the lock in quick succession till one of them worked. He tossed the card on the floor. "Move it! Someone's comin'!"

He pulled Jakes arm and headed back to the front. The sound of running feet increased their desperation. There was the armory. He found the right card and ducked inside, pulling Jake after. The door snapped shut and the waiting game began.

* * * *

Tanya kept her back turned to him. "I don't feel like talking right now." He could hear tears in her voice. It felt like someone had slammed a door in his face.

"Tahnie?" He felt an urgency he'd never felt before, but he struggled to keep his voice gentle. "I don't understand. You...you were the light in the room this morning. Now it's gone and you're pushing me away."

She rolled over, looking at him like he was a stranger. Her eyes were puffy and his heart fell into his shoes.

Just then the COMM chimed. She surged up from her bed, eager to escape the conversation. She tapped the tab on her screen and snapped at the air. "Nydel here."

"Hey Tahnie, it's Sherry. I..."

Something or someone interrupted her train of thought. "...Hey, what are you doing? Where do you think you're...Ow... Stop it..."

Tumultuous sounds ensued before all went quiet.

"Sherry? What's going on? Sherry?"

Tanya looked over at Tolya and then reached up to grab her utility belt. She'd never felt the need for a weapon on board before. She reached into a small closet and brought out a long, hard nightstick. She tossed it to Tolya who caught it expertly. Wordlessly, they headed out the door and down the corridor.

Tanya had a look on her face that would've given a Roman gladiator pause. They rushed into the security office lobby and stopped in exasperation.

Sherry's station was a littered mess. She lay crumpled on the floor by her overturned chair, one arm twisted in an unnatural way with a bruised, bloody gash across her forehead. Tolya knelt down to check her pulse while Tanya dashed back to the detention area.

Tolya determined Sherry was unconscious but not in danger. It was 1340 hours. He squeezed his COMM tab.

"Routing?" The ship AI responded.

"MedCentral."

A voice responded. 'MedCentral, Connie speaking." Apparently the second shift had already started.

"This is the captain. I need emergency response in SecCentral, now. We have one unconscious with a probable broken arm."

"Right away sir!" Came the response.

Tanya returned to the room. She looked ready to chew steel spikes and spit poisoned bullets. "He's gone." She hissed, holding up a keycard dangling from a lanyard. "Somebody busted their way in here and sprang the filthy cur!"

She looked down at Sherry and her face softened immediately. "How is she?"

Tolya replied. "She's unconscious, but her breathing and heart rate seem fine. I think that arm's broken."

Tanya nodded. "I thought I heard you on the COMM; you called MedCentral?"

"Yes, they're on the way."

She put a call through.

"Deck 3 Security."

"Nydel here, I need forensics up here in SecCentral; yesterday!"

"Yes, ma'am!"

Tanya turned to look at Tolya. "He's gone. They came and broke him out."

She checked the P-MS pistol on her belt. "You better start carrying one of these for a while."

She went to a locker and swiped her patch. She pulled out another belt with a P-MS pistol and spare power pack. After a quick, expert check out of the equipment she handed it to Tolya.

"We can't use fire arms...I guess you knew that already. Sorry." It was common knowledge among space going professionals. With firearms, if you shoot the wrong direction you could get a hull breach, the private nightmare of all space travelers. Besides, it was thought that firearms tended to be the last resort of the desperate. They were less common at the end of the twenty-first century.

The par-med team showed up just then. They got to work immediately. Tanya absently pocketed the detention passkey she'd found on the floor by Jake's cell. They got Sherry's arm set and immobilized, placed her on an ELU, and hurried back to MedCentral. Tolya stepped out and Tanya followed.

After a few minutes the door to the armory opened manually and Felix stuck his head out and looked around. All was clear. He made his way quickly to the exit, Jake right behind him.

Felix tossed the armory keycard on the floor near the front desk. There was still blood on the floor. The sight sent a chill up his spine.

The halls were clear, so they sprinted aft down the starboard corridor, called one of the lifts and dove inside. Just as they started down, the forward lift disgorged the three officers sent to secure the crime scene.

* * * *

Daniela came bustling in, dressed in civvies and looking mildly annoyed. Vince followed in her wake. She checked Sherry's vitals and looked sternly at Tanya. "I'd chew YOU out, but she comes first. What happened here?"

Tanya looked properly chastened. "Someone barged into my offices and broke Jake Townsend out of maximum. In the process they injured Sherry."

Daniela shook her head. "Why am I not surprised?" She checked Sherry's eyes. "She may have a mild concussion, but it could have been worse"

She took a careful look, gently probing the arm. "Yeah, I think it's a simple break. We'll scan it to be sure, but with the nano-bond procedure she'll be out and about by tomorrow evening." Tanya visibly calmed.

Daniela consulted briefly with the second shift intern before turning to leave.

"I'm sorry they disturbed you, Dannie. I'm sure they could have handled things."

Daniela smiled. "It's OK. I've a couple of hours before our dinner. As they say, the night is young, yet."

She gave Tanya a stern look. "Still, I do have a bone to pick with you. The next time you take it in your head to vanish into thin air, I expect a warning. You had absolutely everyone worried about you.

"By the way." She pointed to a cabinet behind the desk. "You have all the evidence you need in there. We'll talk later."

Daniela left and Vince hurried after with a roll of the eyes and a quick shrug. This brought a chuckle to the captains' lips.

COMMITTED — 7

ECS Destiny, Quarterdeck, MedCentral, 1406 Hrs

Tolya checked the waiting room. It was empty. He turned to Tanya. "Tahnie, I think we have something to talk about." He stepped inside and turned to watch her.

Tanya hesitated. It still hurt, but with the recent insanity, the raw gash of betrayal had faded to a throb. *Now, I'll get some answers!*

She followed him into the room. Tolya sat in an armchair. She sat opposite him trying not to fidget. She launched her attack without warning. "So, what happened to them?"

Tolya blinked in confusion. "Them?"

Tanya continued. "Why didn't you bring them? That must have been like twisting the knife in their back." Her voice was cool.

Tolya was totally lost. "Wait, Wait! Them? Who are you talking about? You're making no sense!"

Tanya sat forward in her chair. "Did you think I wouldn't see the photos? I saw them…You…You had a family before you took this assignment. You told me there had NEVER been anyone in your life before who…what was the phrase, '…caught your eye like this?' What was that if it wasn't someone who'd caught your eye?"

Tolya put his face in his hands and sat, quietly shaking his head. Then he looked up at her with a strange expression on his face. *This is what happens when people make commitments before they get to know each other more thoroughly.* He thought. "Oh, Tahnie, that picture you left up on my desk? That was a picture I took of my older brother and his wife and child."

Tanya was startled. "You never said anything about a brother."

He smiled sadly, "That's because we've not had time to explore each other's lives."

She wilted. Anger vanished leaving confusion in the vacuum.

"I promise you on all that's holy, I've NEVER touched another woman romantically."

Tanya was confused and embarrassed. "I feel so stupid."

Tolya thought, desperately trying to salvage things. Then he smiled. "All right. Come with me to my cabin. I'll show you my albums. See everything for yourself."

Tanya hesitated. "What about the escape?"

Tolya waved a dismissive hand. "You're stuck till you can question Sherry and hear back from forensics." He looked her in the eyes. "So, you have some time to kill. Better time than me!"

Tanya winced at the play on words. "All right."

Tolya got up and, breathing a sigh, ushered Tanya out of the waiting room.

She stopped to talk with the intern. "Say, I need to talk with Sherry. Would you page me when she's conscious?"

"Sure, Chief."

"Great. If it's urgent, call the captain's quarters."

He quirked an eyebrow. "No problem, Ma'am."

* * * *

ECS Destiny, Quarterdeck, Tolya's Cabin, 1420 Hrs

The quick walk to Tolya's cabin was in thoughtful silence. He offered his office chair and then pulled out an old, well worn, wooden dining room chair. He turned it and sat astride it, leaning over the back. "Go ahead."

Tanya looked over to see a gentle smile on his face. She started up the computer. Tolya made a complex gesture. The screen rearranged itself and new icons appeared.

"See the archives folder?" Tanya nodded. "Put the file 'Family Album' into the display window."

She complied and a slideshow utility started up.

"Tap voice control, please?"

Tanya complied.

Tolya scooted forward in his chair, his head just above her shoulder. "How about we start at the beginning. Ask any questions you like."

* * * *

Two hours later they ran out of pictures and stories. Tanya felt like a total idiot. She'd made stupid assumptions. Then she'd acted childishly, without asking questions.

She turned to face him. "I'm so sorry. I should have asked you instead blowing my cork...I...I almost threw everything away."

Tolya leaned over and kissed her gently. She responded in kind. Finally they separated, just looking at each other.

Tolya gently brushed a tear from her cheek. "Please Tahnie. I'd cut out my tongue before I'd ever try to hurt you or lie to you. Confront me. Ask the hard questions, but don't ever think that I'd willingly hurt you."

Tanya looked down for a moment. "I'm learning to trust, Tolya. My childhood taught me trust is expensive. I doubt easily. Maybe that helps me do my job well, but...well, that's probably why I've taken so long to fit in with everyone around here. I choose to trust you because I really want to. I hope I can be worthy of your trust."

Tolya leaned forward and kissed her forehead. "I do trust you. How can you love someone you can't trust?"

They embraced again and the COMM sounded. Tolya waved a hand and called out to the room at large. "Yes!" There was just a hint of impatience there.

"Sir, this is Connie in MedCentral. I was instructed to contact Chief Nydel when her assistant was conscious."

Tolya nodded to Tanya who responded. "Go ahead Connie, This is Chief Nydel."

"Yes, ma'am. Sherry regained consciousness shortly after you left, but after we finished treating her, she went back to sleep. I'm happy to report that she just woke up a few minutes ago and is asking for you. She's very insistent."

Tanya grinned. "Thanks Connie, we'll be right there."

Tolya had a crooked grin on his face as he stood up. "Do you realize? This is an example of some of what we can look forward to for the rest of our lives."

Standing, Tanya gave a throaty little chuckle and pulled him in for a long kiss. When they came up for air she said, "I think you're worth it."

COMMITTED — 8

ECS Destiny, Quarterdeck, MedCentral, 1630 Hrs

Sherry was sitting up in her bed when they entered her cubicle. She looked up and gave a smile of greeting.

"Hey, Sherry. I'm glad to see you awake. How are you feeling?" Tanya gently gave her a hug.

"I'll be OK." Her faced screwed up in an angry frown. "I'm sorry, Tanya. I guess he got away. This guy came in and demanded the passkey...something about a mess in the detention block. I told him no and he tried to get it from the cabinet. I tried to stop him but..." She bit her lip in frustration. "I'm really sorry. I know how much you wanted that ass in the cell."

Tanya looked grim. "It's OK Sherry. I never expected you to have to risk your life in there. You're a great help to me, and a good friend. We'll get him back."

Sherry looked hopeful. "You think so?"

Tanya gave feral grin. "You can count on it."

Tolya moved into the sphere of conversation. "That's right. These guys don't know who they're messing with. Anybody hurts our friends; they get two to deal with."

Tanya looked Sherry in the eye. "Sherry, I know you've had a rough day, but could you look at some pictures and see if you can point out who did this?"

Sherry nodded. "Sure. That's why I was asking for you. I know who it was. It was that young guy who's always going around cleaning the offices."

Tanya glanced at Tolya who nodded his recognition. Tanya looked back at Sherry. "I think I know exactly who you mean. I'm going to get my pocket-tab. When I get back I'll show you a photo. I want you to tell me whether the man in the photo is the same man who hurt you today. OK?"

Sherry nodded. "Sure."

"Great. I'll be right back."

Tolya touched her arm. "I'll keep her company."

Tanya smiled. "Thanks."

She left the cubicle and Tolya pulled up a chair. "So, how'd you wind up working for Tanya?"

Sherry looked at him. "Well, sir, I applied for a job working for security before she came on board, but the other chief, you know the one that died?"

Tolya nodded.

"Well, he wasn't interested. So, I gave up. Then, when Tanya showed up I tried again."

Sherry smiled, remembering. "She posted a job opportunity after we left Earth and I resubmitted my application. At the interview, we hit it off really well. I was so impressed with her attitude I wanted the job more than ever. Tanya gave me a shot and I've enjoyed working with her ever since."

Tolya nodded. "She's fun to work with."

"Captain?"

Tolya nodded, "Yes?"

"Well, I've never seen Tanya this happy since I first met her. I'm so happy for her. Congratulations on your engagement. I think you're really good for her."

Tolya blushed. He wasn't used to getting personal praise from the office staff. "Thank you Sherry. Believe me, I plan to keep her."

Sherry grinned and Tanya breezed back in the room, "I heard that!"

Tolya glanced up, a twinkle in his eye. "Good!" He offered her the chair.

She graciously accepted. "Ready, Sherry?"

Sherry nodded.

"OK," Tanya touched the screen of her power-tab. She touched an icon on the screen and a window opened with a digital high-res photo. She held up the picture for Sherry.

Sherry's face blanched and an angry look possessed her features. "That's him! How'd you know?"

Tanya lowered the power-tab to her lap. "I've been waiting for him to do something I could arrest him for. You see, he's the other guy's partner."

Sherry's jaw dropped. "There are two of those guys? Isn't one murderer on board, one too many?"

Tanya smiled. "I agree, but until now he hasn't done anything obvious I could get him for. Now…"

Sherry grinned. "Now you can get him!"

"Absolutely! I'm just sorry you had to get hurt because I waited. I didn't expect him to do this."

Sherry waved her good hand as if shaking off some water. "It's no big deal. It hurts a little, but the doctor says I'll be fine."

Tanya smiled back at her. "Ok, but trust me! We'll get this guy; both of them!"

"I'd like to see that!"

"Oh, you will! I guarantee it!"

Tolya spoke up. "I hate to break this up, but it's getting late and I think Sherry could use some food."

He turned to Sherry. "I'll get the staff to scare up something to eat. We'll be back tomorrow to see you to your quarters when you're released."

"Thanks Captain."

He smiled at her.

Tanya got up and he escorted her out of the cubicle.

He approached Connie at the reception counter. She looked up. "Can I help you, Captain?"

"Yes, I think Sherry's feeling a bit hungry. She missed lunch and it's coming up on dinner time."

"Of course, Captain, I'm on it."

Tolya gave her his most charming smile. "Thanks."

Out in the corridor, "In case you forgot, you still have an invasion to investigate."

Tanya looked startled. "I've been so distracted. I was in there to get this photo and I totally forgot about the forensics report." They hurried to the security office.

* * * *

ECS Destiny, Quarterdeck, SecCentral, 1645 Hrs

The door to her office recognized her patch and snapped open. Sure enough, there was a message from the forensics team. It was concise. They'd found no prints. The only genetic material was of Sherry, where she'd fallen, and of Jake, in his cell.

Tanya sighed. "Well, I guess it's a good thing we have a positive ID from Sherry. The guy was somewhat more careful than his partner."

Tanya reviewed the message. "It says everything's been tagged and catalogued. We may tidy up. There's a note saying the detention pass key's missing."

Tolya laughed. "That's because it's in your pocket."

Tanya's mouth dropped and her face turned red. "Oh! I forgot." She broke out laughing and pulled it out of her pocket.

Tanya opened the cabinet to hang the card and lanyard on its peg, but stopped. Here was the detention pass. There was the vault pass, but where was the armory passkey?

They found it under the edge of Sherry's station where it probably fell in the tussle. She hung it up, but a strange feeling of dread hit her. "Tolya...call me crazy, but I've got a bad feeling."

Tolya frowned and followed her back up the aisle and around to the armory. The armory door snapped open and lights came on as they moved down the narrow room with neatly racked weapons. Tanya's face went white. One of the pistol drawers was just barely open. When she pulled it the rest of the way she saw the piece was missing. The tag read ' .357 Magnum.'

Frantically, she whirled, pulling out the corresponding ammo drawer. Two boxes were missing. "God help us! Tolya! The little fool lifted a gun and ammo!"

She slammed the drawer closed and turned back to the gun drawer. Taking the tag, she turned to exit as Tolya backed quickly into the aisle. It seemed a very good idea to get out of her way.

Tanya hurried back to her office unconsciously breathing a prayer, "Oh God, we don't need this!" She seldom prayed, but right now it sure seemed like a really good idea.

Tolya was inclined to agree. Firearms loose on board a spacecraft were a major nightmare, but now they were talking about a .357, a magnum no less. A lot of people could die a horrible death if an outer bulkhead was punctured.

Tanya pulled up the armory inventory list on her computer and traced down the drawer tag number. A photo of the weapon appeared and information filed down. Noting the serial number, she copied it and the photo into a new file and created a security alert message, which she forwarded to all the security substations on board.

Tanya stood. "We've gotta handle this very carefully. If it gets around that someone has a weapon on board, there could be a minor riot."

"So, what do you propose?"

"I just sent a security alert to the substations so my people know what to look for. We've got to find that thing fast."

Tolya nodded. "OK. Tell ya what. Let's go personally to these stations. You can explain things quietly and make sure no one overhears. Afterward, I'm going to take you somewhere for a little treat. You need to calm down and I have just the ticket."

She tried to object but he wouldn't have it. "Tahnie. You have a solid team of professionals working for you. Their job is to make yours doable. Let 'em work. You'll have your chance to wade in with both feet. And when you do, I'll be right there with you."

Tanya shook her head, "Oh, no! The last person we need facing a .357 magnum is the captain and governor of this colony."

Tolya was looking very stubborn. "Look...OK, technically you're right, but I won't let you face that alone. We're in this together, so we fix it together."

Tanya saw she'd lost this argument on two levels.
As her captain and as her husband-to-be, he was taking command. She'd learned to choose her battles. This was lost before it began.

She shrugged in resignation. "Fine, but I don't like it. I nearly lost you once, I can't chance loosing you again."

"Yes, but now I can see it coming. I'm prepared, and when I'm prepared, you know I'm no push over."

She expelled her breath in frustration and said, "Yes, dear," in her sauciest voice.

He had the temerity to grin.

Tolya placed a hand on the side of her face, gently caressing her cheek. "So, why don't you go freshen up? I'll go make a call before we go." He pulled her to him. She leaned into his chest and finally began to calm down.

"I'll meet you at the port side lift well in..." he glanced at the ship's clock. "Let's say twenty minutes. That'll be about 1750."
She nodded. "OK."

FALLOUT — 1

FRI 02.12.2094
ECS Destiny, Deck 3, Starboard Community Center, Forward, 1750 Hrs

Felix brought Jake to the lounge Ted had assigned. The ships clock read, '1750.' They selected chairs and sat nervously for several minutes. The tension was mounting to unbearable levels when the door snapped open and Ted entered the room.

He wore a casual suit that made him look like a wealthy businessman. There was a sense of self-importance that was grating on Jake's nerves. Felix wasn't much impressed either.

Ted sat down in a comfortable recliner and presided over the room. "Felix. Did anyone see you, or recognize you?"

Felix fidgeted a bit and answered. "Nobody was there except the office lady. She tried to stop me, but I...I shut her up."

"So she saw your face." It was a statement, not a question.

Felix' nerves were starting to jump. "Come on man; the idiot got her head bashed. She...she's dead and can't say nothin'. Nobody else was there."

Ted nodded. "Fine. That's very reassuring." He turned to Jake, who obviously wasn't happy with the tone of the conversation.

Who made this guy the high and mighty one? He thought.

"So, how much did you tell 'em, Jake?"

Jake was getting mad. "You really think I'm that stupid, Ted? I didn't say nothin'! The filthy witch never got to question me."

"Ah, so you didn't get the opportunity to babble."

Jake sat forward as if to get up, but stopped.

Ted continued, "Do I think you're stupid? Consider who it was got caught. You're one arrogant SOB." Ted seemed to enjoy pissing Jake off.

"She wasn't supposed to connect me with anything. There was no reason I can think of to suspect me!"

Ted shook his head sadly. "They found your prints all over the coffee service. You just had to go and handle it yourself. You could've put the stuff in the coffee and sent some flunky to deliver it. Your not only arrogant, you're stone stupid!"

Jake jumped up and bunched his fists as if he planned to pound his tormentor. "I think I did a fine job of whacking the captain. It just pisses me off he didn't stay down. What I put in there would've finished most people. I don't even know how he managed to live."

Ted leaned forward menacingly. "But I told you specifically I wanted him alive; sick, but alive. It's a very good thing that he's still alive."

Jake's face started turning red. "You have no idea what trouble I went through to get that stuff into him. You're just a petty dick head with delusions of grandeur who thinks he's God or something."

He turned for the door. "Screw you…"

"PHAP! PHAP, PHAP!" The odd sound barely registered in the brain. Jake stumbled and dropped to his knees, his hands flung out to either side as if trying to reach for his back.

Felix sat numbly, staring fixedly at the tiny black pistol barely visible in Ted's hand.

Like a severed tree limb, Jake flopped forward, hitting solidly on the carpet. His body spasmed once and went still.

Felix stared at Ted as if he were seeing a demon from the bowels of Hell.

Ted stood up and turned to face Felix, The gun arcing lazily in his general direction. Faint wisps of smoke curled from the beady eye of the muzzle as it stopped, not quite pointing directly at him. "I think we're about to have a new understanding, Felix.

"Poor Jake here; he forgot who he was working for. You, on the other hand seem to have a firm fix on facts. You're mine and you know it, so I'm giving you a choice. You say one word and you join Jake, here. See, if I go down, you go along for the ride."

Felix was frozen. He felt like peeing his pants. He was seated with no way to run. By the time he got up he'd be dead. He was trapped as effectively as a fly on flypaper.

The insane man continued, "I can still use you. You did a first class job arranging that transition failure, and you did fine acquiring that remaining board, which you've put in safekeeping. Right?"

Felix nodded numbly.

"See? Then you successfully got Jake out of that woman's jail. I like talent, so don't screw up and not only will you survive this little adventure, you'll profit even more without Jake, here."

"Come on, Ted! Be cool! I know whose team I'm on. I haven't failed you, just like you said!" He hated himself in that moment. He waved a trembling hand at the cooling body he tried not to look at. "I don't have any idea what happened to this guy here."

Ted smiled. "I think we understand each other just fine." He set the safety and stuck the deceptively tiny gun in a small holster inside his jacket.

Quiet, just as advertised, Ted thought. "Drag this fool over behind the couch over there and then get outa' here. Not a peep!" Felix jumped to comply. "Sure thing, Ted. Sure thing."

Felix was used to cleaning up messes. That had been part of his job for years, but this was different.

Blood had gushed from Jake's nose and mouth, slowly soaking the carpet. The body had relaxed...everything. The stench of excrement was horrid. Felix tried not to retch as he dragged the inert form behind the couch.

It was 1802 when Ted followed Felix out of the room. He looked back, gauging the condition of the room. The bloodstain on the carpet was unfortunate, but it would probably be dry when discovered. That might not be for a little while.

He chuckled at the thought of the smell someone was going to experience when the door opened next, and Felix scurried away, trembling from head to toe, Ted's demented chuckle driving him to greater speed.

FALLOUT — 2

ECS Destiny, Quarterdeck, Captain's Cabin, 1730 Hrs

Tanya went off to her cabin to freshen up. Tolya, back at his cabin, selected the COMM channel and put through the call. Shane O'Connor's face brightened in pleased surprise. "Tolya, you old buzzard. Did you just remember we're down here?"

Tolya gave one of his lopsided grins. "Well, Shane, I'm sorry to say, things have gotten so exciting up here I've not given you much thought, but I'd like to make up for that tonight if you don't mind."

Shane grinned back. "Tonight? Wow, that's sudden."

"Yeah, well, there's business to attend to down there tonight. I thought it a perfect excuse to drop by."

"Oh, you know you don't need an excuse!" Shane's voice took a serious tone. "Tolya, some ugly rumors are percolating down here. Some even said you'd been killed."

"I was afraid of that." Tolya grimaced. "As you can see, the rumors of my death were slightly in error. When we get there, I'll tell you all about it."

Shane nodded, "Wait! We? I thought you said, 'we.'"

"Oh, sorry. I forgot to mention, my security chief will be with me. You don't mind another plate, do you?"

"Security chief. Interesting."

"Shane, you have no idea." Tolya grinned.

"Well, there's no reason why you can't bring a colleague with you." Shane raised an eyebrow. "This should provide great dinner conversation."

"Thanks Shane. You'll love this. Oh, we probably can't get there before 1900. I hope that's not too late."

"Ah, no problem. That'll just give Kaitlyn a little more time to expand her plans."

He looked off screen and back again. "Oh, someone's practically yanking my leg off to get in the pickups."

Tolya chuckled. "Sure, put her on."

There was a flurry of motion as Shane backed away and a pretty, young face sprang into his place. "Uncle Toly! You didn't come see me last week!"

"I know princess! Things haven't been going well up here and I couldn't get away. Can you forgive me?"

Lyuba looked stern. "Well, I guess, but you have to promise you'll visit more often."

"Da! I'll do the best I can. I promise, cross my heart!" Tolya grinned. "Besides, I can make it up."

"Yeah? How?"

"How about I come see you tonight?"

"Tonight?"

"Yes, tonight. Plus, I'm bringing a nice lady friend with me for you to meet!"

Lyuba's eyes glowed before getting that look, "Hmph! What's her name?"

"Well...I'll tell you if you promise not to tell Uncle Shane or Aunt Kaitlyn."

"Ok, fine. It'll be our secret. Cross my heart."

"Ah, well then, her name is Tanya."

"Tanya? That's a pretty name."

"Yes, well, for now that should be Ms. Tanya to you."

"Yeah, OK. Uncle Toly, is she pretty?"

Tolya grinned from ear to ear. "Yes, I think you could say she's the prettiest lady I ever met!"

Lyuba sniffed, "Oh? Prettier than me?"

"No! Never! Well...she's almost as pretty as you."

"Oh! I guess that's OK."

"OK, sweetheart. If I don't get off the COMM, I'll never get there. Can I talk to Uncle Shane again?"

"Sure. I'll see you tonight, right?"

"That's right, my Lyuba."

"OK. Bye!"

Another flurry of motion brought Shane back.

"All right, you old fox. What's this about a pretty lady?"

Tolya grinned. "You'll know soon. We'll try to get there no later than 1900 hours."

"Sure. You know you've made her night, don't you?"

"Da! I thought I might. See ya soon. Bye."

* * * *

Tanya stood in a fresh uniform, tapping her toes, arms folded...waiting. When he saw her look he put on his penitent face. "Sorry, I didn't think it'd take so long."

Tanya sniffed. "So, what was this mysterious call?"

"Ah, it's part of the special treat I promised you. If I told you...then...I'd be telling, wouldn't I?"

She gave him a sidelong glance and motioned to the open lift door. She noticed that Tolya was holding a small, flat, rectangular package wrapped in ornate gift-wrap. She gave him one of her eloquent eyebrow lifts as they stepped inside. He glanced at the package and winked. "I can't say just now."

She shrugged and leaned back against the wall of the lift as the doors slid shut.

FALLOUT — 3

ECS Destiny, Promenade Deck, O'Connor Residence, 1855 Hrs

Tanya was growing more curious by the moment. They'd finished the last briefing, ending up on the Promenade. Tolya strolled happily out onto the edge of the grand park area, periodically greeting someone. Many, he called by name.

It was the dinner hour and most people were headed home for the evening. The lighting had dimmed to the ship's notion of nighttime levels. Here on the Promenade it was beautiful. The trees and plants added a wonderfully fresh feel to the air.

They watched the beautifully lighted cylindrical rain curtain that showered into the long pool. The water streamed like natural rain down from its starting point up underneath the Mezzanine three decks above.

Finally they moved on across the park. Tanya was about to prod him for an explanation when they stopped at a door that faced onto the park on the starboard side. He smiled nervously and pressed the announcer tab.

The door slid open to reveal a beautiful young lady of about thirteen years old. Tolya stepped into a major hug. "Uncle Toly!"

Tanya suppressed a grin as she made the connection. This was the infant in the photo she'd so egregiously misinterpreted. She'd seen pictures of her in Tolya's albums, but she was so much the sweeter in real life.

She extracted herself from the hug and turned to face Tanya. Tolya made introductions, "Tanya, this is my niece, Lyuba. Lyuba, this is Ms. Tanya, my security chief."

Lyuba made a picture perfect curtsy and said, "Welcome, Ms. Tanya. Won't you please come in?"

Tanya didn't even try for a curtsy. *I've never been good at those darn things!* Suppressing a grin, she inclined her head, "I'd love to. Thank you, Lyuba."

The girl stepped aside and waved them grandly into their home away from home. Tolya handed the package to Lyuba and whispered, "Not till after dinner." Her eyes got big.

Tanya whispered in his ear, "Sweet!"

Shane and Kaitlyn stepped in from a room adjoining the entryway and took turns hugging Tolya. He introduced Tanya. "This is my Chief of Security, Ms. Tanya Nydel."

They shook hands all around and Shane ushered them toward the dinning room. "Hey, what's with the hardware?" He nodded down at Tolya's hip.

Tolya glanced down involuntarily and then looked sheepishly at Shane. "Uh, Sorry. I forgot I was packin'. Would you mind putting them up for us?"

Shane looked quizzically at him.

"I'll explain later." Tolya removed his utility belt and handed it over. Tapping Tanya on the shoulder, he motioned for her weapon.

Realization dawned and she followed suit. "Sorry."

Shane smiled and headed for the hall closet.

He quickly returned, "You're just in time for dinner."

Tolya grinned, "Why, what a coincidence."

His eyes twinkled as he helped Tanya to her seat. Kaitlyn came bustling in with the last steaming dish, wiped her hands on her apron and assumed her seat at one end of the table.

"Hey, Princess," Tolya said, "why don't you go call Owen and Aileen for dinner."

Her eyes gleamed. "OK."

She hurried off to collect her 'cousins'.

"Hey! Uncle Toly's here! And it's dinner time!"

A pretty, dark haired girl of thirteen hurried after Lyuba. A tall young man of fifteen made his entrance.

Shane introduced them. "Tanya, this is my daughter Aileen..." she curtsied and took her place.

"...and this is my son, Owen." Owen made a barely noticeable bow, eyes locked on Tanya. He realized he was being watched and blushed furiously, murmuring a greeting.

Shane stood opposite Kaitlyn at the other end of the table. Aileen and Owen sat along one side to Shane's right. Lyuba was seated across from Aileen with Tolya in the middle and Tanya to the left near Kaitlyn.

When all were settled, heads bowed and Shane said Grace: "Bless us, Oh Lord, and these your gifts which we are about to receive, from your bounty through Christ our Lord. Amen."

All repeated, "Amen," and Shane took his seat.

Kaitlyn spoke up. "Since we have guests, I thought it'd be fun to try some traditional, down home dishes. So, tonight we're having Coddle and Champ with Soda Bread Cakes." She winked at Tanya. "I threw in steamed carrots, too."

Tanya basked in the warm, friendly atmosphere. It was home cooking like she'd only had a few times in her life.

Coddle was new and very interesting. It was a layered conglomeration of sausage, bacon, sliced potatoes and onions that warmed the heart as well as the belly. Champ was creamy mashed potatoes liberally sprinkled with small cut scallions.

Tanya was delighted with the steamed carrots. They were nice and crunchy with a simple butter sauce. The soda bread cakes were surprisingly good. Just add a little butter or use it to sop up the juices from the meal; it complimented the comfortable experience.

This was probably one of the most evil meals her waistline would ever experience, but her taste buds were thanking her.

The conversation was restricted to small talk and reminiscences on the past. Tanya heard more battle stories from Shane and Tolya than she thought possible.

Apparently, Tolya's time as a fighter pilot for the Earth-Space Navy had been more eventful than he'd let on in their tour of his photo albums. They recounted thrilling fights with the asteroid pirates in a war of rebellion that had raged for four years. Shane had been Tolya's wing-man through that campaign.

Tanya watched the youths. Lyuba sat in worshipful bliss listening to the stories her favorite men were telling. Aileen occasionally rolled her eyes at some of the obviously exaggerated parts. Owen seemed to drink in every word; asking questions and exclaiming at the amazing scenes the two men painted. Tanya could tell the guys were enjoying the attention.

Kaitlyn kept Tanya company with questions and stories of her own. Tanya could tell that she was fishing for information. Apparently Kaitlyn had her suspicions.

Finally, the main part of the meal was done and Kaitlyn rose to clear the dishes. Tanya joined her, making companionable comments and keeping the woman company. She really liked this couple. They'd been good to Tolya and his niece through the years.

Eyes glowed and happy laughter rebounded as the ladies doled out dessert. It was a decadent Chocolate Mousse Pie. At this point Tanya gave up ever repairing the damage this was going to do to her waistline.

Shane quipped, "Well, it may not be Bailey's, but my Kaitlyn makes the best Chocolate Mousse Pie this side of the Milky Way!"

Kaitlyn gave Shane a sidelong look and then said, "Aye, my man's fishing for brownie points tonight!"

The men laughed heartily.

Tolya sat back in his chair and gazed at Tanya till she turned and noticed. He held her gaze and she gave him a quizzical quirk of eyebrow. He seemed to come to a decision and turned back to the table. He asked for everyone's attention. All eyes focused on him as the table became quiet.

"You may or may not know that Tanya here, has been instrumental in helping us through the difficulties we've recently experienced on this voyage. What most people don't know is, she's become much more than a key player on my team."

Sudden expectation hung in the room. Tanya caught his glance. He quirked an eyebrow as if to say, *Well?*

She smiled self-consciously and nodded.

Tolya continued. "Well, Shane, you know I've been a stubborn non-participant in the great chase. Right?"

Shane's eyes twinkled and he nodded with a grin.

Tolya went on. "Well, I guess I've been avoiding the chase for so long I got careless and got myself caught."

Kaitlyn raised her eyebrows and looked at Tanya, a smile slowly creeping across her face. Tanya could almost see the words *Yep, I was right*, scrolling brightly across her forehead.

Tolya continued, "I want to correct the introduction I made earlier this evening." He stood and took Tanya's hand coaxing her from her seat. She stood, knowing what was coming and looked nervously around the table.

"Shane, Kaitlyn, kids, this is Tanya Nydel, my Chief of Security. She's also the one who managed to really set the hook." He pulled her close. "Please welcome the soon to be Mrs. Tanya Chernov."

There was polite applause around the table and Shane let out a long whistle. "Man! When you fall, you fall hard!"

Kaitlyn got up, came around the table and gave Tanya a sisterly hug. "Welcome. I gotta give you credit. You've got good taste."

She grinned and Tanya chuckled. "I don't know, it took a collective slap in the face to get our attention and make us realize what the rest of the staff had already figured out."

Kaitlyn nodded. "Sometimes we have the toughest time accepting the good things that come our way."

Tanya glanced over at Lyuba, who sat, staring at her, a confused look on her face. Tanya looked at Kaitlyn and nodded towards Tolya's niece.

Kaitlyn bit her lip and whispered. "You might have a tough sale there. Go, talk to her. It couldn't hurt." She squeezed Tanya's arm and turned to say something to Tolya.

Tanya stepped behind Tolya and approached Lyuba. She smiled warmly. "Hey there. Can we go talk somewhere?"

Lyuba hesitated and looked towards Tolya who, while chatting with the rest of the family, had been watching. He gave his niece a wink and a grin. That seemed to help some.

Lyuba turned her gaze to Tanya. "Um, OK... I guess we can use the front room."

She got up from her chair and led the way. Tanya followed, wondering what she should say.

She remembered the many times she'd thought she was going to have a wonderful family, only to be taken away to another center. It had only been in her last two years of high school that someone had determined to honestly love her. She thought she might just understand the fears of a girl who'd lost her real family as an infant; who had an uncle who loved her, but because the weight of his responsibilities, didn't have the time to pay the attention he wanted to give.

Tanya sat on the edge of a couch and patted the seat next to her. Lyuba slowly approached and sat, nervously perched on the edge of the seat.

Tanya smiled. "So, I guess you might be feeling a little blown away; maybe even a bit confused. Right?"

Lyuba nodded. "Uncle Toly called you the future Mrs. Chernov. Are you really getting married?"

"Yes, Lyuba. We just decided...yesterday." *Was it only yesterday?* "We decided we really loved each other and wanted to marry. We have a lot of plans to make."

Lyuba nodded. She looked at nothing for a minute. "I only see Uncle Toly once a week, but he's always busy...and lots of times he can't come. Now he's going to be busier."

Tanya understood more than this young lady could imagine. "Oh, Lyuba. I don't want to take your uncle away from you. I just want to share him. You're his most favorite person in the universe. You know that don't you?"

Lyuba nodded her head slowly.

Tanya continued. "I don't think I could change that if I wanted to, and I don't." Lyuba looked doubtful.

"I think you have the greatest uncle ever. I bet you're really proud of him."

Lyuba smiled slowly. "I am proud of him. I brag about him a lot, but...he doesn't have much time for me." Her smile was starting to drown in the tears that were welling up in her eyes.

"But he wants to so much, Lyuba."

Tanya's heart almost broke for this girl. "Lyuba honey, I'm gonna tell you a secret. Your uncle doesn't even know it yet. You get to know about it first."

"Yeah?" She wiped her eyes vigorously.

"Yeah. See, when I was eight years old I lost both of my parents. I didn't have an uncle to comfort me and make sure I was taken care of by somebody who loved me. I lived in an orphanage for a while. Then I was bounced from one foster family to another.

"I was in high school when I finally found a family that truly loved me and wanted to keep me. They adopted me, but I only got to live with them for three years, because when I was in my first year of college they died in a tragic accident. Nobody I loved saw me graduate."

That seemed to strike some chord with Lyuba.

Tanya put a hand on Lyuba's shoulder and gently pulled her into a light hug. Lyuba hesitated for a moment before returning the hug.

"What I'm trying to say is, I know how you feel about your uncle and I'd never do anything to stand between you."

She gently pushed Lyuba back enough to look into her face. "In fact, I'll do everything I can to make sure you get to spend even more time with him."

Lyuba eyes snapped up to meet Tanya's. "Promise? I can see him every day if I want to?"

Tanya smiled. "Please, try to understand that sometimes things don't always happen as fast as we want them to. I promise that I will do everything I can to make sure you can be with your uncle as often as you like, but it might take some time before you really see it happen. I don't make empty promises. I take them very seriously."

Lyuba wavered for a moment and then came to a decision. "If Uncle Toly loves you like he loves me, I guess it's OK."

Tanya chuckled. "Yeah, I guess you could say that. One day you'll figure out there ARE a few minor differences, but that's OK."

Tanya gave Lyuba a big grin. "I'm going to need a friend; someone to help me figure out how to take care of Tolya.

"And...I'm going to need help planning a wedding."

Lyuba's eyes lit up. "I always wanted to go to a wedding."

Tanya grinned. "How would you like to be IN one?"

The girl's eyes glowed like live coals. "That would be so awesome!" She breathed.

"So, can we be friends? I'm gonna need your help."

Lyuba looked tempted. "You really meant that stuff you said?"

Tanya drew a cross over her chest. "Cross my heart."

Lyuba grinned. "I'd like having you as a friend."

Lyuba got up and turned to go back to the dinning area. Tanya got up to follow when Lyuba stopped dead in her tracks and turned around. Her mouth hung open a moment and then she said. "That mean's you're gonna be my aunt. I never had a real aunt before."

Tanya chuckled and reached out a hand. Lyuba took it and Tanya said, "You know? I think you're right. I didn't even think of that. So, is that a good thing?"

Lyuba grinned, "Sure! This is really cool!" They walked together, hand in hand, back to the dining room.

* * * *

The kids hurried to the back rooms to resume playing on the game consoles while the adults quickly cleared the table and cleaned up the kitchen. They adjourned to the living room where coffee made its rounds and the serious discussion began.

Shane started things off. "OK, Tolya. We're so excited for you I can't adequately express it, but there are less pleasant things going on that we have to talk about, I'm sorry to say."

Tolya nodded sadly. "Yes, you're right. I don't know how much you know, so I want to hear from you before I fill you in."

Shane nodded. "Well, I don't know where to start. Rumors are running thick and fast down here since that meeting you and Tanya presided over. The initial jolt of fear turned into hope as everybody got on board with the new plan. Then the entry into Multi-Space failed and we started hearing rumors of criminal activity up-top. With so many conflicting stories no one knows what to believe."

He shrugged. "Like I told you when you called, we're even hearing stories that somebody killed you. We worked hard to prevent that one from reaching Lyuba. That would have been a disaster. Now we have an official posting asking for help finding some missing power board."

Tolya looked grim. "I'm truly sorry the communication has been so poor."

He sat back next to Tanya who scooted closer. "OK. If there's anybody I can trust besides my full time security chief here," he put an arm around her shoulders, "it has to be you two. I'm going to tell you a story that'll probably sound like some crazy novel. Unfortunately, it's all true."

Kaitlyn looked nervously over at Shane.

"First, because you weren't able to be in the venue Tanya and I oversaw, you only had a vague idea of what was happening there. There was this guy who went ballistic when we made our initial announcement. You might have heard part of that exchange; but, believe me, it was a very nasty few moments. Tanya put him in his place and got the crowd under control so I could finish the presentation; but wait! The story gets better.

"See, this guy, apparently put together a couple of scum-bag types and they decided to take things into their own hands. One of those guys managed to recruit someone to damage the drive control systems that govern the MS drive. That failure was the result of a deliberate sabotage.

"While he was working, the other accomplice successfully managed to spike my coffee with something and I wound up in MedCentral for a couple of days."

Shane's eyebrows reached vainly for his receding hairline. Kaitlyn took a sharp breath and put a hand to her mouth.

Tolya looked over at Tanya and said, "Take over for a while will you? That's where I was out of commission."

Tanya collected her thoughts and began. "Understand...all this happened so close together it seemed like one huge incident.

"I caught on to the plot against Tolya just in time. When I got to his work lounge, next to the bridge, he was just succumbing to the poison. I was able to get help for him immediately and the doctor was able to reverse the damage."

She shuddered visibly. "Believe me. That was one of the worst day of my life. Anyway, we found out about the sabotage to the MS drive during Tolya's emergency.

"After I got him settled, I found out the replacement board for the damaged one had been stolen. I was able to figure out who the would be assassin was and I had him arrested."

A smile crept onto her face. "When Tolya was recovering, I went to see him. We finally acknowledged what we'd been avoiding and worked out our relationship."

"After that, the other guy, the one who recruited the saboteur, broke into the security office while I was away and broke the first guy out. On the way out, he helped himself to a .357 magnum from the armory."

Kaitlyn murmured, "Oh no!"

Tolya looked at Shane. "You know what a nightmare having that cannon loose on the ship could be."

"The crazy bastard!" Shane said fervently.

Tanya spoke up. "My thought exactly."

Tolya took up the narrative. "Anyway, that was the business we were about that brought us down here and gave us the perfect excuse to come see you."

Shane thought for a moment. "So, we have two fugitives at large; one carrying a hand cannon. We're also looking for a missing power board that's the only hope of us getting anywhere, and in all that mess, you managed to go from confirmed bachelor to an engaged governor of a troubled colony. Did I miss anything?"

Tolya shook his head. "I'm afraid you have the gist of it."

Tanya spoke up. "Actually, there's one point missing. There are really four fugitives. We're pretty certain the heckler from that meeting is the ringleader. I've just been waiting for something definitive to pin on him. Then there's the person who did the physical damage in drive section. We still don't know who that is."

Kaitlyn said simply, "Wow! You're right. It sounds like some cheap drama, but I fear it's anything but entertaining."

Shane leaned forward. "Well, I can see why you two are carrying. I wouldn't want to go up against a .357 with those little pop guns, though."

Tanya grimaced. "Believe me, I'd be much happier with the magnum, but you know our hands are tied."

"Damn straight." Shane replied. "So, how can we help?"

The last thing Tolya wanted was to have civilians taking on gun toting crazies, but he knew they were at a point where every eye and mind was going to have to be brought to bear on the problem.

"Well, I need eyes and ears. I don't want anyone up against firearms. If I could use your COMM, I'll download some photos. You can float them around; see about drawing in the net."

Shane nodded and indicated the household unit. "Be my guest."

Tolya continued. "Also, I'd like it made known that I'm very much alive and well. Maybe even let it slip that we know for sure who sprung the would-be-assassin. Let's let them squirm."

He got up and crossed to the COMM station and navigated his way to Tanya's office computer. He looked up at her. "You want to do the honors?"

She got up and smiled evilly. "I'd be delighted. We really need to get you my codes."

She swiped her patch and ordered a transfer of the pertinent photos to the O'Connor's COMM station.

She put the three photos up for review. "Here are the three guys we know about. This one," she indicated the photo of Jake. "This one is the would be assassin. This guy," she tapped the photo of Felix. "...is the guy who recruited the saboteur and sprang Jake from my jail. This one here..." she indicated Ted, "...is the ringleader. I think he may be more dangerous than we know, but I don't have anything solid on him yet."

Shane and Kaitlyn gathered around the view screen and examined the photos.

Shane tapped Felix' picture. "I've seen this guy. Doesn't he work for janitorial and maintenance?"

Tanya nodded. "That's right. It would be nice to find him fast. He's the one who snatched the hand cannon."

Shane grunted. "OK. I'll get some of the guys to start keeping their eyes open."

"Great!" Tolya responded.

* * * *

There were hugs all around. Tanya even got one from Lyuba.

As they started across the Promenade hand in hand Tolya made an observation. "Well, that went nicely. I noticed you and Lyuba worked things out. What was that all about, anyway?"

They stopped on the path that traveled nearly the length of the park and turned to watch the beautiful rain curtain going through its color cycle.

"Oh, she was feeling like she was about to lose you. I had the job of convincing her otherwise."

He raised an eyebrow. "Where'd she get that idea?"

Tanya laughed out loud. "Well, let's see. You've been the darling of your uncle's eye since you can remember. Suddenly, someone comes along and starts looking very much like they have become more interesting than you. Not only that, you're told this is going to be rather permanent and that your uncle, and everybody else, is happy with it.

"Now. Top that off with the feeling that in spite of having been your uncles' favorite, you've had a constant sense of competition for just a chance to see him. Wouldn't you feel just a bit threatened?"

Tolya pondered this as they headed for the forward lift well. "Yeah, I guess I might. I never thought of it like that."

"No, I don't suppose you have. Most men have a little trouble with the whole sensitive female thing. Although," she gave his hand a big squeeze. "You don't do so badly."

They reached the lift well as Tolya asked. "So, how did you go from impending disaster to glorious victory?"

Tanya sighed. "Actually, I made some promises that we're going to have to work on keeping. First I told her I'd never, ever take you away from her. Then, I told her about my childhood and how, because of it, I could really understand how she felt."

Tolya looked quizzically at her. "I haven't even heard all that yet," he complained.

Tanya called for the lift. "Well, when have we had the time? Basically, I lost my real parents when I was eight years old. It was some kind of building collapse that killed a lot of people. I was visiting my grandma that summer and didn't find out about it till they failed to show up to get me."

The lift arrived and the doors snapped open. "Anyway, like I told Lyuba, I lived in an orphanage for a while."

They entered the lift and Tolya sent them to Quarterdeck. "My grandma was too old to take care of me permanently and then she got really sick. I bounced from one foster family to another until half way through high school. Then a family took me in and we all fell in love. I was so happy..."

The doors snapped shut and the familiar surge of motion signaled the beginning of their four-deck ride.

"But, three years later, while I was away at my first year of college, they were killed in a terrorist attack on the hotel where they were staying." She shrugged. "I had no one to celebrate my graduation with."

They stepped out in front of the Event Center. Tolya stopped and gently hugged her close. "I'm sorry to hear that. You should've had the joys of loving parents."

Tanya hugged back and then pulled his arm to lead the way towards her cabin. "Yeah, well anyways, I told Lyuba I truly understood how she would feel losing you. I said I wasn't going to ever let that happen. I promised her she'd get to help me plan the wedding and that she'd be in it."

She stopped him in front of her cabin and turned him to look at her. "I told her I'd do everything in my power to help her to see you any time she wanted."

Tolya smiled. "That's a tall order."

It was 2200 hours and few people were out and about. Tanya stood looking into his eyes, searching for something. "Tolya, in all these years, why haven't you adopted Lyuba?"

Tolya looked like he'd been slugged in the gut. "Tahnie, I've wanted to for years. I was always away on short haul voyages to Ganymede, Io and the like. I didn't want to drag her all over the solar system without a home or friends or a solid family life. I had hoped when I became a regular run captain things would be better than when I had been in the Navy. It didn't work out that way.

"When I decided to take the plunge and accept this final mission, I'd hoped, with her on board, I'd be able to spend more time with her. You can see how that's worked out.

"Once a week worked OK until a couple weeks ago." He stared into the distance. "Shane and Kaitlyn have put a lot of love and effort into caring for Lyuba, but I'd really like to take her on and be the father my brother never got to be."

Tanya squeezed his arm and he looked back at her. She looked into his eyes. "Why don't we?"

Tolya was shocked.

"I mean it. Lyuba's the sweetest young lady I've ever met. She reminds me a little of me when I was her age."

Tolya saw the shimmer of water in her eyes and realized she truly meant it. "Tahnie, that's a lot to expect of you so soon."

She shook her head. "She's become a part of you over the years. I'm signing on for the whole package."

He pulled her head to his chest and hugged her close. "Do you really want this?"

She looked up. "Don't you?"

"Yes, love. Yes, I do"

After a few moments Tanya chuckled and pulled away, wiping her eyes. "You know you're the one who's going to have to sell this one. Don't you?"

Tolya grinned. "Yeah. I guess you're right."

"So, sometime soon, you need to sit down with her and discuss it. If she's OK with the idea, I'll have a chat with her too. If all goes well with that, I'd like to make it public as part of the conclusion to our wedding."

Tolya raised his eyebrows. "You've given this some real thought haven't you?"

Tanya grinned. "Well, yeah, I guess. Sometimes, a lot of thought happens pretty fast. It wasn't until I saw her at the door tonight. After you spilled the beans, I just couldn't get it out of my head."

"OK, Tahnie. I'll talk to her before the week is over. I think your idea of including her at the wedding is wonderful. She's going to be like a real princess!"

They got close enough to her cabin for the door to recognize her patch and open.

She gave him another lingering hug. "It's getting late and tomorrow's a busy day. So, as much as I hate to say it, 'Good night.' I'll see you in the morning."

Tolya hesitated. "I guess you're right...This is taking forever."

Tanya arched her eyebrows. "Eager are we?"

Tolya actually blushed. "You could say that."

She offered up a long kiss. "It won't be so long."

"I know. Well...I love you...Good night."

FALLOUT — 4

SAT 02.13.2094
ECS Destiny, Deck 3, Starboard Community Center, Forward, 0800 Hrs

Francine went to the community center early to set up for Dennis' birthday party. She was grateful she'd been able to reserve it. This was a special day. Dennis was turning eight and was looking forward to seeing all his friends. Susan, her neighbor from starboard-forward, said she'd be there in a few minutes with the refreshments; cake, ice cream and punch.

She approached the door and it snapped open. The horrid smell that coursed around her nearly made her gag as she reflexively stepped around a dark red-brown stain in the carpet. She deposited her bundle of decorations and party favors on the table and turned to examine the stain. It was right in front of the door. Something about it sent a shiver up her spine.

She might have decided to ignore the stain, but the odor in the room had to go. The smell was worse than the worst fouled diaper she'd ever changed. It was a thick cloying smell; not at all the sort of smell you'd want to have at a birthday party. She hurried to the wall next to the door and tapped the small COMM screen.

The AI voice sounded in the room. "Routing?"

Francine always felt awkward talking to these machines. "Ah...yeah. I need Maintenance. Deck 3 Maintenance."

"One moment."

"Maintenance."

"Yeah, this is Francine Douglas. I'm in Community Center FS-333. I reserved this place for a birthday party at noon, but somebody spilled something nasty on the carpet in front of the door. Worse than that, there's a gagging smell in here that's starting to make me sick. I want somebody over here right now. There's no way I'm havin' a bunch of kids in here like this."

The voice on the other end sounded bored. "Yeah, yeah. Someone'll be there in about fifteen minutes."

"Oh no! You get someone over here right now! We need to set up and we can't till you guys get done. All the other centers are taken today."

"OK, OK! I'll be right there. Can you lock that door open? That might help air things out."

Francine replied. "Fine. I'll lock it open, but you better get right over here."

She closed the connection and turned to the door.

Under the actuation touch tab were two smaller ones, one red, one green. The green one was currently lit. She tapped the actuation tab and the door snapped open. Then she pressed the red tab. The green one went dark and the red one glowed brightly. Now the door would stay open till someone pressed the green tab again.

About then, Sue breezed into the room with a sheet cake and a bag of goodies. "Phew! Ohhh...Gaaach!" Sue felt like hurling and turned away to avoid a disaster.

The sheet cake hit the wall in the entryway as she turned and tumbled messily to the floor. She ran out of the room and took several deep breaths.

Francine stepped over the mess and hurried to her friend. "Are you all right?"

Sue slowly straightened up from her bent posture, the barf reflex averted. "Yeah, I'm OK. What's that horrid smell?" She looked back at the open door. "How can you stand to be in there?"

Francine patted her shoulder. "I know! I just got done calling the maintenance guy. He should be here already!" She looked around irritably.

Sue pointed into the room. "Look at that vile stain on the floor! No, I don't mean the cake; that dark nasty looking stain right in front of the entryway."

Francine glanced at the nasty spot. "I don't know. It looks pretty gross though. Do you think it's makin' the smell?"

Sue grimaced. "That's my bet. Some people are just pigs!" She said officiously.

"Where is that guy? We can't have a party like this!"

Then she remembered the cake and moaned. "Now I have to get another cake! You can bet the committee's gonna hear about this."

Sue had cake on her sweater and her hands. She braved the smell, which seemed a little less, to go to the small sink. She washed off her hands, rinsed the cake out of her sweater and wrung it out. She turned to shake it out and noticed something that stopped her in mid motion. Poking out from behind the sofa was what looked like someone's fingers. Curious, she walked over to take a look.

Just as Bob, the maintenance guy came through the door; Sue let out a startled scream and jumped back from behind the sofa.

Her hands went to clasp over her mouth. It seemed all the blood had drained from her face. The maintenance guy froze, startled. Francine darted in and looked at Sue in surprise.

Sue's mouth was working like she was trying to say something as she pointed a trembling finger at something behind the couch.

"Well, what is it?" Francine snapped. She hurried around the end of the sofa to see what is was and stopped dead in her tracks. Her face turned a pasty white. She backed away at some horror and waved at the maintenance guy to come see.

He looked warily at her before approaching to see exactly what horror they might have found. Only one word escaped his lips as he looked behind the couch. "Daaaamn!" He said it in a fervent, almost reverent tone of voice.

On the floor was a dead man with another stain spread out around his body.

Bob headed for the door. Sue spun around and hurled all over the floor up against the back wall. The horrid smell that had filled the room finally had a source.

"Come on, ladies! I'm calling security!" He turned words into action and hit the emergency tab on the COMM screen.

"Security."

"Yeah. This is Bob Jones from Deck 3 Maintenance. We need you guys in FS-333 right away. We've got a dead body in here. It looks like someone got shot."

"Shot! Wadda ya mean, shot? There ain't...Oh...uh...We'll be right there."

Francine helped Sue clean up and then they moved out into the corridor to rest against the opposite wall.

The three stood, fidgeting on pins and needles. Security was surprisingly fast. Three officers came trotting down the corridor, past the miniature trees, looking grim. Bob led them into the room and pointed out the obvious as the ladies hovered nervously near the door.

The lead officer turned to them. "Who found this?"

Sue shuffled forward. "I saw it first. Then I pointed it out to Francine, here. Bob called you guys after that."

The officer pulled out a pocket-tab and took notes as he asked his questions. Finally, he reached up and squeezed a little tab on his collar. "Yeah, we need the forensics team to handle a crime scene in FS-333. It's definitely a homicide."

He listened to someone through a tiny bud in his ear. "That's right. Oh, and call SecCentral. Tell her, it wasn't the missing one she warned about."

"No! It doesn't look right." "Yeah, OK. We'll secure the scene."

He turned to the three shaken colonists. "Sorry folks. I'd appreciate if you could join us at the security office. Once we get your statements, you'll be free to go."

Two officers stayed behind and the lieutenant escorted them to the deck security station. Francine absently wondered what was to become of Dennis' birthday party.

FALLOUT — 5

ECS Destiny, Quarterdeck SecCentral, 0850 Hrs

Tanya reached over and swished the COMM icon. A window popped open and one of her officers peered out. "Ma'am. I'm sorry, but we have a homicide on Deck 3."

Tanya paled. *Already?* "Homicide? Are you sure?"

The lieutenant shrugged. "I'd think three shots badly spaced through the back would qualify, Ma'm"

"Damn! Sorry lieutenant. You're right. Was it...?"

"No ma'am. I'm afraid not. We found the bullets. the lab guys extracted one and checked it out. They say it was a 7.62 millimeter; probably silenced."

7.62 mil? What the heck kind of weapon is that? "When?"

"They say it was probably around 1800 last night."

I was on Promenade with Tolya last night. She put the thought aside. They'd had no way of knowing.

"All right lieutenant, I'll be down in a few minutes. Are the folks who found the body still there?"

The lieutenant grimaced. "Yes, ma'am. I'd say they're pretty shook up."

"I can imagine. I'll be right down."

She swished away the COMM window and got up from her chair, squeezing a tab on her collar.

The computer voice asked for her party. "Captain Chernov."

There was a faint click and Tolya's voice blossomed in her ear. "Chernov, here."

"Tolya, it's Tanya. I'm going down to Deck 3. There was a homicide just before we got to Shane's place last night."

"Homicide? Tahnie, I'll meet you at the lift."

"No, honey. There's no need. My people have everything under control and there's no clue yet about who did what. I'll fill you in once I know something. Oh, don't forget. You promised we'd walk Sherry back to her quarters when she gets out. Daniela said she was going to release her about 1400."

"Ok. Take care of yourself."

Tanya purred, "Oh, believe me, Captain, sir. I have every intention of meeting you at lunch.

"Very good, Chief." She heard the grin in his voice.

* * * *

Francine and Sue looked up when the door to the waiting area snapped open. The lieutenant escorted a young, athletic looking woman of about medium height. She had a pleasant face and a kindly bearing. Despite her pleasant features, a sense of command and calm radiated from her. "Francine? Susan?"

They stood as Tanya approached and took both their hands. "I'm Tanya Nydel, Chief of Security. I'm told you have a story to tell."

Francine nodded. Her adrenaline high was gone and now she was just tired.

"Please. Sit." The chief hooked a chair with her foot and dragged it forward to sit down before them. They resumed their seats feeling comforted by her demeanor. "So, please. Tell me everything you can."

Tanya listened patiently. When the story was complete she knew little more than she'd gotten from her team. That was to be expected, but they needed to feel she cared about their experience. That she really did care was a bonus for them in her line of work.

She stood and asked, "Have you had opportunity to consider what to do about your ruined birthday party?"

They looked at each other blankly and then Francine started to tear up. She was trying hard not to make a scene, but today had just been too much.

Tanya's heart went out to them and then she had an idea. "If you'll wait just a couple more minutes, I want to check on something. Then we'll let you go."

She went into the station office and squeezed the COMM tab on her collar.

"Captain Chernov," she instructed.

"Chernov here."

"Hey you big captain, you. I have a favor to ask."

"Ah, anything for my favorite Chief of Security."

"Look honey, these gals who found the body have had a serious disaster made of their kid's birthday party. I'd like to give them the use of the Officer's Lounge in the Event Center. We can handle the load and it'll be great PR."

There was a light chuckle. "Tahnie, you don't always have to ask me. With the occasional exception, I'll honor just about any decision you make."

"Wow, that's almost like a blank credit voucher!"

She heard his grin. "Yeah. I guess I'm a big push over, especially with you. Well, I gotta get back to work. See you at lunch."

"You got it." She squeezed the tab again to release the connection before going to the station computer and checking the calendar. Today was clear.

She checked the ship's clock, '0930,' and punched the code for the main kitchen.

"Sarah here." Her eyes widened when she saw who was calling. Tanya smiled. "Sarah, I need a really big favor."

"Yeah?"

"I know its really short notice, but there was a horrid mess made of one of the meeting halls down on Deck 3. A party was reserved down there and now they're totally at a loss. Would you please set up the Officer's Lounge for a big birthday party? It's for an eight-year-old boy. His name is Dennis."

Sarah looked pained for just a moment and then shrugged. "Sure, why not? My staff's a little short since that idiot, Jake left, but I think it would be kinda fun to break the routine."

Tanya beamed. "Thanks Sarah. I owe you one. They expected to have their party at 1200. Is that doable?"

Sarah glanced at the clock in the kitchen. "Oh, sure; plenty of time. We'll partition off the lounge from the main dining area so the regular diners won't distract the group. Don't worry, we'll make it a screamer!" She said with a grin.

"Great!" Tanya said, "I'll send the mom up to confer with you in a little while. Do what you can, but don't let her get too demanding. You're the boss."

Sarah smiled. "Thanks, Tanya."

Tanya grinned. "No, Sarah. Thank you!"

She cut the connection and returned to the waiting room. "OK. It's a shame about your plans. The cake's ruined, the ice cream's melted. And honestly, with the investigation, it'll be a while before we can reopen that room."

She watched the depressed looks on their faces. "Besides, who'd want a party there after what happened?"

They nodded in glum agreement.

"So, I've been given permission by the captain to give you access to the Officer's Lounge in the Event Center."

Francine looked incredulous. "The big one?"

Tanya grinned. "Yes! I've already arranged for the kitchen to put together cake, ice cream and punch. They have decorations, and they're great at parties."

Francine looked at Sue, who just gaped in surprise.

"Francine, I told Sarah; she runs the kitchen up there. I told her you'd be up to give her all the information about Dennis and what you'd like for the party. I can't guarantee everything you want, but Sarah will do what she can. It is short notice for her, after all."

Francine stood and shook Tanya's hand. "Thank you so much. How did you work it out?"

"Well," Tanya grinned. "I have my sources."

She looked at Sue. "How are you doing?"

Sue smiled tentatively. "I'm fine, really. It was just too much all at once."

"I understand. Tell you what. While Francine chats with Sarah, why don't you go through your guest list and tell them about the change. Just tell 'em you got a lucky break and leave it at that. OK?"

Sue nodded. "Sure. That's fine. Thank you."

Tanya turned back to Francine. "You have a couple of hours up there. Have fun."

She turned to go and then stopped. "Oh, no promises, but I might just get the captain to come by and say hi! He'll be off for lunch right about then."

The two moms looked dazed and then put their heads together as she turned for the door. *Now I've got a bigger mess to clean up.*

* * * *

Tanya got even less useful information from Bob, the maintenance guy. He'd just seen the body the ladies found and had the presence of mind to call security.

She made her way to the crime scene and chatted with the officers at the door, blocked with the ever-essential red tape.

She ducked under the tape and surveyed the room. The odor still lingered, but it was barely tolerable now.

There was the stain in front of the door. There was a chalk outline of the body behind the couch; a big stain there also. "Kelly. Where's the body now?"

The officer who'd accompanied her replied, "In the morgue ma'am. We had to start the freezer to going for the first time."

She shook her head. "Well, I guess it was useless to hope it'd never be needed."

She turned to face him. "Was the body I.D.'d?"

"Yes, Ma'am. The guy matches one of the photos you circulated recently. Jake Townsend, I think."

Tanya's eyebrows vaulted up her forehead. "Really!" *So, Jake; you pissed somebody off. I wonder who that might have been?* "Thanks Kelly. I'm off to the deck station."

"Yes, Ma'am."

Tanya strode quickly back to the station and borrowed the office computer. She navigated her way to the surveillance video archives. Indexing through the locations she found the cam near the meeting hall. Working her way through the time index, she selected 1700. An hour before time of death seemed sufficient.

The video file loaded and she started the playback. She set it for 2X speed and watched people scurry by like cartoon characters. She stopped play and zoomed in on two men approaching the Community Center. *Would you look at that; two birds with one stone.*

She watched Felix and Jake enter. She noted the time, jotting it down, '1750.'

It took almost ten minutes for Ted to show up. He was dressed in a casual business suit, looking cocky. 1758, she wrote. He entered the lounge and Tanya sped up the play.

The time index read 1817 when the door snapped open. Tanya backed the scene a little and hit normal play at 1815.

Felix was a changed man. She wasn't sure for better or for worse, but he was definitely changed. He was ghost white. He looked like he'd seen the devil himself, and barely lived to tell it.

Ted came right behind him. He looked like he was on top of the world; like a man who held all the cards. He stopped, patted his jacket and chuckled to himself. She could see Felix almost running down the hall, deathly afraid.

Tanya pulled the photos of Felix and Ted. She created a bulletin showing both men and sent them to all deck-security stations. Then she called for officer of the watch. She showed him the photos on the screen and informed him that they were to be apprehended immediately. "Consider them armed and dangerous. You can expect to run into at least two handguns. All officers must carry P-MS's till further notice."

"Yes, Ma'am."

Tanya left the station office and headed for the lift well. It was 1032. She went directly to the morgue, a small space situated between MedCentral forward and SecCentral aft. It was accessible from either office, a convenience for both the medical and security staffs.

She waved her hand and the heavily insulated door slid open slowly. Only one drawer had data showing on the tiny display. She touched the open tab and stood aside as the drawer slid smoothly open. Jake Townsend lay like a statue carved in ice. There were three ghastly bruises, two on his chest and one over his abdomen.

The rounds were obviously slow and heavy. What ever this weapon was it was not something she needed loose on her ship. Death had been quick. *Mores' the pity*, she thought.

Tanya touched the tab and Jake Townsend resumed his solitary confinement. She let herself out, securing the room.

She entered her office where she sat gathering her thoughts. She knew she had to work fast. There were two desperate men, both with deadly weapons that could not only kill people but also endanger many more. One was scared to death and liable to do something stupid in an attempt to save himself. The other had become a mad man seeking his own way no matter the cost.

She had something to pin on Ted Jackson now. She came to a decision and got up to head for MedCentral.

Brianna greeted her cheerily. "She's in her office."

"Thanks Bri." She breezed past and stopped to tap at Daniela's open door.

Daniela looked up and smiled. "Hey, Tahnie. You're a little early aren't you?"

Tanya entered the room, hooked up a chair and plopped. "Dannie, we're about to have a full scale manhunt."

Daniela blanched.

"Did you hear about the killing?" Tanya asked.

Daniela replied, "I saw when they brought the body. They didn't need any help so I left them to it. I've enough to do."

Tanya looked toward the door and thought about nearby ears. "Dannie, come with me, please?"

Daniela frowned, but nodded and rose. Tanya led her to the back of MedCentral to the morgue entrance.

"I'm not trying to be melodramatic or morbid, honestly. I want you to learn something where other ears can't hear." She spoke softly. Daniela was intrigued.

Tanya waved the door open and they entered the frozen world of the dead. She tapped the open tab on the single occupied drawer and Jake slid obediently from his hiding place. Daniela took one look and paled. "Firearms loose on board a space vessel?"

"I'm afraid so." Tanya confirmed as she returned Jake to his rest. "Let's go to my shop. Nobody's there right now."

They passed through the morgue and out into Tanya's office. She turned to Daniela. "Look. That was the result of a crazy man on Deck 3 running around loose with a gun."

Daniela grimaced.

Tanya continued. "The shooter was the ringleader. I'm sure of it, though we won't be able to verify it until we can catch him and question him,"

She leaned against the counter, "but the problem gets worse."

Daniela folded her arms firmly across her chest and asked. "Can it get any worse?"

"Sadly, yes. Things have been happening so thick and fast we haven't been able to keep everyone on staff up to speed. You know they broke Jake out of here."

Daniela nodded.

"Well, that body in there was Jake."

Daniela's eyes widened. "He got off easy."

Tanya smiled grimly. "I couldn't agree more."

Tanya continued. "The guy who broke him out was Felix. We know this because Sherry made a positive ID. What you don't know is, Felix used the armory passkey to get in there and help himself to a .357 and two boxes of ammo."

Daniela spluttered. She pointed back towards the morgue and stated. "That was no .357 that took Jake out! Are you trying to tell me there are two guns rattling around?"

Tanya's shoulders slumped in frustration. "That's exactly what I'm telling you. We have to end this. We'll take care of Sherry this afternoon like we promised. Then I'm taking every spare officer I can get and we're going to sweep the whole ship if necessary to get these two."

Daniela muttered something wicked under her breath. Tanya straightened up. "I'd probably agree with you if I'd heard that."

Daniela flushed. "It's OK. It shouldn't be repeated."

Tanya laid her hand gently on Daniela's shoulder. "Dannie. I need you to gear up for traumatic injuries. God forbid anyone gets in the line of fire, but we must be ready. Surviving a direct hit from that hand cannon is…well, it would be a miracle."

Daniela reached up and squeezed the hand that held her shoulder. "Thanks for the warning Tahnie. I'll be ready. You can count on it."

Tanya gave a grateful smile and dropped her hand. "Thanks. That's all I can ask."

She glanced at the ship's clock, '1112.' "I'd better go." She headed for the office exit. Daniela looked at the morgue door as if tempted to walk through to her office. She shuddered and followed Tanya out into the corridor.

FALLOUT — 6
ECS Destiny, Command Deck, Command Bridge, 1215 Hrs

Tolya turned as the doors snapped open. Tanya strode possessively onto the bridge to stand quietly behind him at the command station. Frank glanced over and grinned before going back to his calibrations. Vince was nowhere to be seen.

She leaned over and said quietly. "You ready for lunch?"

Tolya grinned. "Yep. We're just waiting for Vince."

"Good, I have another favor to ask."

"Yeah?"

"You know that birthday party from Deck 3 I rescued?"

"Yeah."

"Well, I sorta suggested you might happen by during lunch. I thought the birthday boy would be pretty jazzed about it."

Tolya looked askance at her. "If you want, why?"

Tanya put on her wise councilor look. "With all that's going wrong right now, people seeing you about, in control of things, helps calm frazzled nerves. These two have had their nerves frazzled to the breaking point. All of their friends will think you're the greatest."

He looked at her again.

"Hey." She said. "What could it hurt?"

"I guess your right. It couldn't hurt." He pretended to think it over. "OK. We'll go."

He pulled her closer for a quick peck on the cheek. "Besides, I can parade my favorite lady about on my arm and start all sorts of delightful rumors."

She punched his arm playfully. "You devil, you."

He chuckled as Vince strode onto the bridge. "Stop that!" he said in mock sternness. "You have reputations to preserve."

Tolya punched the change command and stood up from the chair. "So, how about you take the CONN and we can blow some more of that reputation over lunch?"

Vince made a terribly sloppy salute, "That would be more acceptable, sir!"

"Then I leave our limping guppy in your capable hands. Drift boldly where no man has drifted before."

Vince couldn't help it. He fell in the chair laughing. "You're impossible, sir."

Tolya patted him firmly on the shoulder. "Yes, My Security Chief perpetually reminds me of that. Carry on."

They left the bridge laughing quietly. Once the doors closed, Tanya's laughter died and she slowed their pace. "Tolya, things are going to get very stormy this afternoon. I have two fugitives, both with firearms rattling around on one of the residential decks. After we take care of Sherry, I'm conducting a manhunt."

Tolya frowned. "Maybe we should postpone lunch and get it over with."

Tanya shook her head. "No; for three reasons. One, we need to show people that things are under control. Two, we need to keep our promises no matter what, and three," she hugged his arm. "We need to take quality time to communicate. That way, when we need to be focused on the problems we avoid distractions."

"You're probably right."

"Of course I am," she teased.

They were on and off the lift in a matter of moments. It was 1220. The lunch crowd was filtering in and out. They could hear fun going strong behind the partitions.

Tanya stopped him just before they came in range of the door sensors. "Remember. We're doing fine. Progress is being made and you are on top of things. Therefore, you can smile confidently and carry on casual conversation."

He smiled at her seriousness. "Yes, dear..."

* * * *

The lounge doors snapped open and Francine saw the captain enter the room. To her surprise, the young security chief who'd been so sweet was on his arm in formal style, looking very regal for someone in uniform.

The noise level dipped noticeably as everybody took in who had entered the room. Francine hurried over to greet the captain and gave Tanya a raised eyebrow look. "Thank you so much, Captain, for allowing us to use the lounge, and thank you for taking the time to visit."

Tolya smiled graciously and took her hand. "You're quite welcome. I'm just sorry the day started so badly for you. I hope this helps."

Francine smiled her gratitude and turned. "Dennis. Hey Dennis! Someone's come to see you."

The birthday boy looked up from his ice cream, he gaped in delighted surprise. Then he jumped up and ran to present himself to the captain.

Tolya bent and offered his hand to shake. The boy shyly took it and shook it. "Well, Dennis. I just came to wish you a happy birthday. I hope you're having a wonderful time."

Dennis beamed. "Oh yes, sir. It's awesome!"

Tolya grinned. "You know, I didn't get an invitation until the last minute. So, I didn't get a chance to get you a present. I have an idea though."

The boy looked more eager, if that were possible.

Tolya escorted the small group that had gathered over to the great curtains against the long wall. He waved his patch-equipped hand and they parted.

The grand panorama of stars flooded the room as the lights automatically dimmed. All the kids in the room crowded to the line and 'Oohed' and 'Ah'd'. Tolya watched the glow of excitement in young eyes. Then he turned to Dennis. "How would you like to come watch how things work on the bridge sometime?"

Dennis' mouth dropped into a large round "O" and nodded his head vigorously. "That would be cool."

The captain laughed. "Well, we're having a few problems right now, so it would be terribly confusing, but when everything is all fixed, I'll send someone to come get you and you can come watch us fly the ship."

Tanya couldn't help grinning from ear to ear.

Francine leaned over and commented in her ear. "You've got quite a catch there."

Tanya touched her on the arm. "Oh, believe me. Not a moment goes by that I don't remember that."

Francine smiled. She gestured, pointing back and forth between them. "How long have you…"

"We started seeing each other in the last month or so."

Francine's eyes widened. "You look so right together. I'd have thought you were married if I didn't know better."

Tanya grinned. "Well, that little problem is going to be solved at the earliest opportunity." She leaned over and stage whispered in Francine's ear. "He proposed just a couple days ago."

"No!"

"Yes! And that's what I said. 'Yes!'

Francine grinned. "You said you had your sources. I guess you can't get better than the captain and governor. Congratulations."

Tanya looked over in time to see Tolya pat the birthday boy on the back and send him scurrying back to his friends.

Tolya turned and approached them. He made a slight, bow to Francine who flushed self-consciously. "Francine, is it?"

"Yes, sir."

"Well, Francine, you have a fine and bright lad there."

"Thank you, captain."

He nodded. "Not at all. I hope you don't mind. I promised Dennis that when we get under way again, he will be allowed to watch operations on the bridge."

Francine fairly glowed. "Captain, you don't know how much that boy dreams of seeing the bridge. He plays at being star ship captain with his friends. Sometimes I wonder if he might try to be one someday."

Tolya grinned. "Yes, he's very enthusiastic. Anyway, when the time comes I'll ask my very capable Chief here, to come get Dennis for his one shift tour of duty."

"Captain, you're too kind."

"Don't mention it. We'll be sure to give you a heads up before the event. All right?"

"That would be fine. Thank you."

Tolya reached for Tanya's arm. "Till then."

She gave a little wave and, feeling foolish, turned to manage a room full of enthusiastic children.

Tolya whispered to Tanya. "Why don't you introduce her to Emily. I think she'll need all the help she can get once we get settled. Francine seems to have the right temperament."

"You got it."

They made their way around the room, chatting with several parents, sampling the ice cream and cake, and cheering on several games in progress. Finally they bade a polite good-bye and slipped out of the party.

They strode in casual fashion across the dining area. Tanya laughed. "You are quite the charmer, sir."

He grinned. "Just practicing, just practicing."

He led her towards an empty table. "Why don't you fill me in over lunch?"

"OK, but I warn you, some of it's not very palatable."

Tolya chuckled. "Not palatable? Well, I guess it wouldn't be the first time."

CLEANING HOUSE — 1
SAT 02.13.2094
ECS Destiny, Command Deck, Command Bridge, 1315 Hrs

Earlier in the day, Felix had come out to discover that his name and likeness was on the bulletin display screens throughout the ship. Ted was displayed right along side.

He immediately went into hiding, choosing an empty classroom in the port side education wing. He sat on the sofa, trying to figure out how he'd gotten into this whole stinking mess. All he'd wanted was to pick up a few credits; just the usual deal.

Back on Earth...he almost wished he were back there now... emergencies, and the stupid antics people performed because of them, served as quick opportunities to make a little cash or earn a quick favor. He'd always been the quick, in and out kind of guy. Messing with a long-term project was far more risky. The results might be smaller his way, but they were more survivable.

He remembered when he'd decided it was time to reform. The recruiting drive for the *Nova Terra* colony project was going strong then. On a dare, he'd signed up and was surprised to be accepted.

It seemed like opportunity knocking. Everything would be brand new. Besides, if his attempts to reform met with the usual disaster, he'd have unrestricted access to a private goody land; things ripe for the pickin' and there was nobody to pay off or watch out for.

His experience through the first year had been surprisingly pleasant. He'd done well at his job on board *Destiny*. Occasionally, there'd be that, 'just for old times sake' opportunity he just couldn't pass up. He'd collected a few trinkets that way.

Then, he'd bumped into Ted Jackson. Ted seemed like a great guy, a man's kind of man. He had that worldly-wise look that suggested he was a good man to keep on his side. When the navigation screw up had nearly dashed his hopes, he'd decided there'd be something for him to do wherever they wound up. It was like a warning to stay on the straight and narrow.

Ted had gotten all bent out of shape with the navigation disaster and had even made a total fool out of himself in front of the captain. *Why'd I ever listen to that idiot?*

Felix had never wanted to make trouble. Yeah, he'd 'requisitioned' a few personal items, but he'd mostly tried to keep his nose clean. Something about Ted had started to bother him, but he'd fallen for the man's emotionally charged appeals. To his shame, Felix had managed to get himself into something truly evil. He'd even been forced, thanks to Ted, to kill that cute young lady so he could 'rescue' Jake Townsend.

He'd never killed someone before. She'd seemed like such a nice girl, but Ted had made it clear. If Jake squealed, the heat would be on everyone including himself. *I just didn't have a choice. I really didn't mean to kill her.*

No one would believe him, but the girl's death had really been a freak accident when he'd accidentally slammed the cabinet door in her face... He was a murderer. It ate at him like a cancer. His despair was nearly complete, but the capper on everything was watching the crazy bastard kill Jake in cold blood. There was no warning; just 'wham!' that's it. He realized rescuing Jake had really been a death sentence. *Some rescue!* He thought bitterly.

Felix just knew something was going straight to hell. That's why he'd snatched that beautiful gun he'd found in the armory. Now he knew he had to stop Ted.

Ted was one cold bastard, and if he could just off somebody like Jake, no one was safe, especially Felix. So, as crazy scared as he was, he knew he had to go out there and stop him. No one else deserved to get hurt because Ted was unhappy. He could see that now.

Felix had never kept a gun; never even fired one. Usually guns just meant trouble. He'd stayed out of trouble by avoiding them, but now he was up against a big fish and needed the advantage.

It was 1340. Felix pulled the gun from a small box he'd salvaged. It was a remake of the old Smith & Wesson Model 327 .357 Magnum Revolver. It was no six-shooter. This one was an eight shot cannon.

He didn't want to die, but he couldn't let Ted go on messing up everybody's lives. If this wasn't settled soon, he knew he'd be dead before they ever got to wherever they were going.

Felix filled the clip and slid it into the revolver, flipping the spinner up and snapping it into place. He made sure the safety was on and put the gun in his waistband. He dropped the extra clip in his pocket and crossed the room to the door.

Having made up his mind, he peeked out the door he'd set on manual. Nobody was nearby, so he stepped out and started walking. He knew Ted lived somewhere here on Deck 3. It was just a matter of time till he found the jerk.

* * * *

ECS Destiny, Deck 3, 1355 Hrs

Felix's eyes darted furtively, expecting trouble at any turn. He remembered the notices with pictures of him and Ted on display. Felix crossed the corridor outside the classroom and stepped out onto the mezzanine. He assumed a nonchalant air and forced himself to casually wander about.

He passed various merchant kiosks, looking at the various items available. The overhead tram quietly glided across his path, stopping momentarily to drop people off. It continued forward and he resumed his stroll to starboard.

When Felix got to the starboard dining patio, he turned and headed forward and in towards the center of the massive platform that bridged the open space above the Promenade. As he reached the backside of another cluster of kiosks, he spotted Ted, sitting at a table in the port side patio. Ted hadn't noticed, and Felix took opportunity. He pressed in close to the back of a kiosk and pulled his gun. He slipped the safety off and took careful aim.

Ted turned at some sixth sense and locked eyes with Felix. His eyes got so wide they seemed as if they'd pop right out. Felix was tightening his finger when a voice cried out. Ted leaped to his feet.

Startled, Felix quickly lowered the gun. He saw that a ship's security officer, at the walk where he'd first entered, was working his way through the crowd towards him. Felix turned and scooted behind the kiosks, hurrying to the forward railing, looking for Ted.

Ted was running along the balcony corridor of the forward, port side neighborhood. A second officer was trying to get through the crowd to take up chase. Felix considered making another try, but the first officer came around the corner at that moment. Felix whirled and desperately lunged toward the officer, surprising him and causing him to stumble back out of the way. Felix ran like the devil was after him.

He reached the aft starboard mezzanine exit and madly pounded along the balcony corridor. His ears tingled and a loud slapping sound came from the wall of the corridor just behind him. At the aft bridge he realized he was near a lift well.

Felix ducked down next to the bridge railing and looked back the way he'd come. The officer who'd been chasing him had apparently lost sight of him. The man reached the place where his shot had hit the corridor wall and stopped. He stood puffing for breath, looking around frantically.

Boy, it's a good thing I'm not shooting security. He'd be dead where he stands, Felix thought.

The officer spoke into his COMM device and then trotted back across the mezzanine to port. Felix duck-walked across to the lift well and called a lift. Ted had lost his pursuer and raced from the starboard side entrance, across the mezzanine and took Felix' rout to the aft lift well. Felix was not in sight, but Ted noted the destination on display and called the neighboring car to follow.

* * * *

The lift doors snapped open and Felix ran out onto the lift access bridge. In a panic he realized he'd hit Deck 1 instead of Promenade. The lift doors had already closed and a light indicated the next car was on its way down.

Felix ran to port and fairly flew around the Deck 1 balcony corridor. Deck 1 was sparsely populated at this hour. Most people were down on the Promenade or elsewhere, enjoying a peaceful Saturday. No one was about near the port side security and med stations, but he didn't want a chance meeting with security while waiting there for the lift. He dashed across and onto the forward balcony corridor heading for the forward lift access bridge.

Ted ran out of the lift and saw Felix crossing in front of the med and security station. He ran along the balcony and stopped. Taking aim he fired across the gap as Felix started around the far balcony. His shot missed and smacked the wall just behind Felix. Ted resumed the chase.

* * * *

Felix got the right tab this time. The lift doors snapped open and Felix dashed out onto the grass. The expanse of green stretched the length of the huge park, which comprised the Promenade. A few yards ahead, a giant planter box nurtured several small trees. Felix dashed for the spot, seeing an excellent place to hide.

A couple of minutes later, Ted emerged from the lift and moved out onto the grass. He stopped and stood, looking into the crowd, trying to figure out where Felix had gone. Seeing the opportunity, Felix took careful aim and squeezed the trigger.

To fire a pistol for the first time is, for most, a startling experience. To fire a .357 magnum, as the very first pistol, was almost enough to soil Felix' pants. The kick back nearly put the weapon into his teeth. The sound of the report left his ears ringing and his eyes tearing. He knew he'd missed, but he had to get out of there. He heard the smack of a bullet hitting the planter box under him. Ted had fired back.

Felix leaped from his hiding place and fled wildly down the stone path, dodging left and then right as frightened people scattered everywhere. *Oh God, a shoot out on a space ship in the middle of nowhere.* His world had just turned up-side down.

Ted picked himself up from the grass where he'd thrown himself. He'd make that little punk pay. He ran after Felix. The park was full of people, but their peaceful Saturday was being rudely disrupted. Ted nearly collided with a teenaged girl. He brandished his pistol and growled nastily. The girl shrieked and fled. Soon, yelling and screaming could be heard up and down the length of the park.

Felix almost tripped over a young boy running across the stone path. He yelled, "Sorry!" as he kept on running. Felix looked back and saw Ted duck. A flash splashed the low wall of the central fountain just behind Ted. Ted turned and fired at a security officer who'd just missed him. The officer spun and hit the grass, writhing in agony from a bullet wound in the leg.

Felix took another shot at Ted since he was distracted. Ted jerked and grabbed his side as Felix resumed his mad dash, heading for the aft lift well. Ted knelt down at the end of the pool and fired. The clacking sound of the action still surprised him. A gun should speak with authority, not make little noises like a child's popgun.

This time his shot was almost true. Felix spun halfway around as the round gauged the flesh of his shoulder. His weapon flew uselessly from his numbed hand. In desperation, Felix picked himself up and pounded the last few steps to the lift. He called the lift and then banged frantically on the lift doors. Just as he thought he'd be killed where he stood, the doors snapped open and he dove, slapping the close tab on his way in.

Oh, God, Oh, God! I didn't mean for all this to happen. Ah!! It hurts. He slapped the tab for Industrial Deck; a place for research and development and small to medium sized manufacturing projects.

Ted swore fervently as the doors closed behind his prey. He slapped the tab for the next lift and stood waiting.

* * * *

ECS Destiny, Quarterdeck, Event Center Diner & Lounge, 1355 Hrs

"So, now we are going to have to scoop these guys up before we have some sort of 'O.K. Corral' scenario in the middle of a residential area." Tanya stopped and took a sip of her iced tea.

Tolya shook his head, returned his glass to the table and leaned back in his chair. "You know, whatever happens, we have to figure out who did that damage to the drive system and recover that board. Otherwise, this situation, as bad as it is, will be just a circus side show on the road to nowhere."

"Yeah, I know. I've got to make sure that one of them survives this experience." She absently swirled her drink.

"The more I think about it, the more I think Ted instigates the actions of others. He doesn't have the guts to do anything he's ordered done; except the murder of Jake, of course."

She finished the tea and thumped the glass on the table for emphasis. "That didn't take guts, shooting a man in the back."

Tanya's COMM bud chimed in her ear, startling her. She held up a finger warning Tolya to wait and answered. "Nydel here." She listened and her face paled. "You're kidding, I hope!"

Her eyes locked on Tolya's for a moment as color returned rapidly and then deepened as anger took over.

"OK, take everyone you have and get down there after them...Oh! Leave enough to cover the lifts. Then if they double back, you have them."

She shook her head. "No, I'll meet you on Deck 1, the forward lift well. You're certain? Aft?"

She nodded. "OK. I'm on the way!" She squeezed the collar tab and stood determinedly. It was 1358.

Tolya rose to match her as she pulled her gun to check the charges and the spare power pack. "I misjudged the timing. 'O.K. Corral' just started."

"They're shooting it out?" Tolya couldn't believe it.

They strode rapidly out of the diner as Tolya quickly checked his weapon. Several diners stopped in mid bite, startled at the sight.

Tanya grimaced, "Yep! Apparently, Felix decided he'd had enough and tried to put Ted out of his own misery. The tables have turned and Ted's chasing him."

They crossed the corridor and faced the forward lift well. Tanya swiped her patch hand rather than hitting the tab. All lift calls in memory were shuffled down the queue and her call went to the top.

They stepped out on Deck 1 and two officers trotted over to meet them. "Ma'am, they took the lift down to Promenade Deck just a couple of minutes ago."

Tanya rolled her eyes. They'd almost stepped into the path of two gun-toting idiots. "Very good, Sergeant. Let's get down there." They turned and re-boarded the open lift.

They ran out onto the grass and Tanya addressed an officer who stood waiting. "Do we know where they are right now?"

About then, the unmistakable report of a .357 magnum made the question academic. "Come on, Sergeant. Let's get a little closer."

They trotted aft towards the stone path and the planter of trees. Tanya's COMM bud chimed. "Nydel."

She started running and everyone followed. "OK, keep him stable and get him up to MedCentral. They're ready for casualties. We're approaching from the forward port side. Nydel out." They sprinted past the pool and fountain as people scattered once again.

Off to the right, to port, a par-med team was raising an ELU and moving into one of the two lift cars facing them. Tanya veered that way and an officer trotted up and saluted.

Tanya returned his salute and asked. "What happened?"

"We came out when we heard chatter about the shoot out up on the mezzanine. We saw this guy running towards the aft lift well. Terry took off after him. We never heard the shot, but a bullet took Terry in the leg.

"While we were seeing to him another guy jumped up from the fountain and ran. I think he was chasin' the first guy. He had the weirdest little gun I ever saw. He shot at the first guy over by the lift well. I think he got him because the first guy spun and dropped his weapon. Then he vanished into the lift."

Tanya looked at Tolya. "That's the gun he used on Jake. It's one of the quietest handguns I've ever heard of. He must have some kind of silencer"

She thought for a moment. "Let me get this straight. The first guy, the one with the Magnum, never fired at you?"

Sanchez shook his head. "No. His shot was before, over by those trees forward of the pool." He pointed forward.

Tanya asked another question. "Did it look like the guy with the 'weird little gun' had been hit?"

"Yeah. He was holding his hip like it hurt. There wasn't much blood, though."

* * * *

On board Destiny, Promenade Deck, Aft Lift Well, 1438 Hrs

"OK. Take your people to Ag-Deck and wait there. I'll take Harrison, Sanchez and the captain down to Industrial Deck and see if we can't end this."

Tanya scanned the group. "Once we get down there, hit the emergency stop and keep all four cars stalled until I or the captain give the word." They saluted Tanya as the lift doors snapped open. There was a little blood pooled on the floor of the lift. Someone, probably Felix, had been wounded. Sanchez said Ted wasn't bleeding that much.

They stopped at Ag-Deck and most got off to assume their positions. Two of the four aft lifts ended on Ag-Deck; the same with the forward lifts. They entered one of the two that went on to the Industrial-Deck.

The doors snapped open and they filed out onto the top level of the industrial deck, Naomi McIntyre's domain. This deck was on minimal lighting. Its capacity of use was barely scratched at this stage of the voyage. Here were the machines and systems to produce a wide variety of necessary equipment and materials for colony construction. There were also the systems that ran the ship's critical life support functions.

They were on the gallery level that surrounded the main deck. There were two sets of stairs running from the gallery level down to the main floor for quick access, One in front of each the lift wells.

Tanya looked carefully around for a minute or two. She found no drops of blood on the floor. It seemed their fugitives had gone straight down to the main deck. She pointed down the stairs and signaled for silence. Quietly they made their way down to the main deck and spread out around the base of the stairs.

They went around to the back of the stairway and confronted the lift well. Again, Tanya carefully looked about and pointed to a widely spaced trail of blood. Tanya looked through the window and saw no one in the next room. She grunted in satisfaction. Their pray had gone all the way into the shuttle bay. She triggered the pressure doors and they quietly trooped inside.

They were in the port side wing of the anteroom. Here were storage racks with pressure suites used for working in the hanger while it was open to space. There was another wing to starboard.

They headed to the left and into the main room. The far wall was occupied with a long counter area where a control console complete with computer monitors was located. A huge, high-impact, high-pressure viewing window covered the upper third of the wall over and between four large airlocks opening onto the flight deck.

* * * *

Felix crouched shakily up in the nose-gear well of one of the huge shuttles, the pain so great he wanted to cry out. Tears flowed freely and blood from his shoulder dripped slowly, but steadily onto the deck below.

The airlock cycled and Ted spoke. "So, you decided to switch teams, eh Felix? Thought you could take me out and save yourself, did ya?"

He chuckled. Felix found nothing humorous in the situation. "You know I can't let you get away with that don't ya?"

Felix bit his lip. He could hear Ted's steps.

Ted passed the little service scooters squatting like odd little motorcycles at the top of the short ramp. "You got good taste in weapons. If you're going to make a statement, nothing does better than a .357; excellent choice. Just to salute your excellent taste in weapons, and as a thank you for the gift, I'm gonna use it to put you out of my misery!"

He laughed long and hard, delighted with his own wit.

* * * *

"Cocky bastard." Tolya murmured.

Lieutenant Harrison nodded "You got that right."

Tanya was peering through the observation window. She nudged Tolya and pointed to a control pad near an air lock.

He nodded and reached over, waving a hand over the pad.

She pointed down the row of locks.

Again Tolya nodded and repeated the procedure. None of the air locks could be opened from the hanger side until the lockouts were released.

She moved to the main hanger pressurization and door actuation station. "Lieutenant. We're going to finish this. You and Sanchez go suit up for EVA. I'm going to depressurize the hanger. This will cause them to pass out. When they do, you two cycle through and drag them in here. I'll have par-meds on the way. Got it?"

The two men nodded and went over to the lockers and began suiting up. Tanya squeezed the tab on her collar. "MedCentral."

A couple of clicks later, "Bri! It's Tanya. I need Daniela, now."

"Right away, Tahnie!"

There was a short pause. "Tanya, what's up?"

"Dannie, I am going to need a full team down in the hanger bay. They should be ready for gunshot wounds and sudden depressurization trauma. There'll be two patients."

"That doesn't sound too good, Tahnie."

"You're right, but it's that or one of them will be killed in cold blood and the other will be flushed into space naked."

"I see. Well, I guess you have a point. A team's on the way."

"Thanks Dannie, it's almost over."

"That's good. Oh! Your guy wasn't hurt too badly. It was a deep flesh wound, no bone damage; he should mend well."

"Thanks Dannie. Tanya out." She squeezed the collar tab twice and rerouted a call to the team on Ag-Deck. "OK. Release the lift. I'm expecting a par-med team down here and I'll need them fast. Nydel out."

She turned to look Tolya in the eye. "I have to get this right. Too long in near vacuum and these guys are gone."

"Do what you can, Tahnie. I know you'll do your best." He reached over and squeezed her shoulder.

Tanya took a deep breath and turned back to the hanger deck console. She swiped her patch hand over the ID reader. The console obediently lit up.

Harrison and Sanchez approached, suited for a space walk. They stood, waiting at the airlocks. Tolya did a quick, but thorough check of their suits and gave them a thumbs-up. Then he stood at the ready.

The entry doors snapped open and the par-med team filed into the room, bringing along two ELU's. It was getting just a little crowded, but such was life in space.

Tanya saw that all was in readiness. She waved a hand over the display, swiping a flashing warning light.

The AI politely protested. "Chief Nydel, there are two unsuited individuals in the hanger bay at this time."

Tanya rolled her eyes and forced herself to keep her composure. "I'm aware. This is an emergency. You will comply on my authorization code."

The AI was maddeningly persistent. "Regulations state you must have higher clearance to perform this operation. I am sorry, Chief Nydel."

Tolya suppressed the urge to yell at the damn computer and stepped up to the console to swipe his hand over the ID reader. "This is Captain Anatoli Chernov. I trust this authorization code is sufficient for you to comply with ALL of Chief Nydel's commands from here out."

"Thank you, Captain Chernov. This code is satisfactory. Complying with the chief's command."

* * * *

Ted reached the end of the hanger nearest the great clam shell doors; no Felix. He began the return trip. He'd checked around the massive shuttle on the starboard side. He began checking the three smaller shuttles in the middle. He was almost in the center of the flight deck when he noticed the small pool of blood near the front gear well of the shuttle on the port side.

Just then the lights changed from their glaring, but poor imitation of sunlight, to bright amber. Red lights flashed all about the perimeter of the room and a loud, but pedantically polite voice began chanting a warning.

"Warning, Depressurization will commence in ten-seconds. All personnel. Seal your helmets or enter the airlocks."

A siren began to wail. "Depressurization in Five-seconds."

Ted flew to the airlock to the right. He slapped the cycle button; nothing happened. He stuffed the .357 into his belt and pounded on the door. Then he hurried over to the next airlock. After trying the other two locks, he began feeling panicky. There was an incredible sound like the mother of all hurricanes.

He dashed to the observation window and stared into the other room right into the eyes of that evil security witch who'd humiliated him back at that stupid meeting.

The sound was fading and his ears popped. He was starting to see spots before his eyes.

A soft 'plop' sound, barely audible above the thinning rush of air, drew his attention. Felix had fallen from the gear well and was crawling towards the airlocks, oblivious to Ted's presence.

Ted pulled the .357 and grinned wickedly as he tried to line it up on the pathetic little punk, but he couldn't hold the thing up. The gun kept sinking out of alignment and he was feeling weak.

As if in willful rebellion, the gun fell from Ted's suddenly flaccid fingers. Ted went to his knees sucking frantically at the rapidly thinning air. No good. Everything went dark.

Felix fell just short of the airlock. *It's over,* was the last coherent thought he had.

CLEANING HOUSE — 2

ECS Destiny, Quarterdeck, MedCentral, 1532, Hrs

Filmy, watery, light swam in his vision as Felix discovered it wasn't over after all.

He had a splitting headache. His shoulder throbbed fiercely, and his chest and back felt like he'd been run over by a freight train. His tongue felt five times normal size and his throat and sinuses hurt like crazy.

The next thing he discovered was that his hands were securely bound together, as were his feet. The light hurt and he turned his head to get it out of his eyes. As his vision slowly cleared, he found himself surrounded by medical equipment and people. Dr. Jacobs was reading the monitors above his head and a nurse checked his pulse.

Across the aisle in the recovery area he could see Ted similarly ensconced and looking around angrily. Their eyes locked and Felix was grateful the angry looks of an enemy weren't actually lethal.

* * * *

ECS Destiny, Quarterdeck, Tanya's Cabin then Tolya's, 1532 Hrs

Tanya stood in front of her sink. After washing her face and hands, she shook out her hair, the tension slowly fading from her muscles. Slowly, methodically, she redid her hair and stared at herself in the mirror.

Can you really execute a man that way? She asked her reflection. *Never mind how despicable he was, did they have the right to do something so horrendous?*

She shook her head. It wasn't her decision in the end. It would fall to Tolya to make the final determination, but she knew she had to make the recommendation. They needed to discuss this.

Tanya dried her hands and arms and left the tiny restroom in her cabin. She stepped out into the corridor and made her way to Tolya's cabin. She hesitated a moment and then decided.

She went to tap the announcer, but the door opened in response to her patch. She'd forgotten about her new access.

Tolya got up from his office chair, startled. He relaxed when he saw Tanya and invited her to take a seat at his small table.

She sat, looking tired and haggard. Tolya sat and reached across the tiny table. He took her hands, eyes searching her face. "What's bothering you, sweet?"

Tanya gripped his hands hard. "Tolya, I wish we could talk about anything else, but we need to work out our strategy. How should we proceed? We're going to have to have a public trial for those two."

He reclaimed one of his hands and brushed the hair from the side of her face. "So, what about this is bothering you? The procedures are clear."

"Yeah, well, I've never had to prosecute before. I never thought I'd have to actually play the part of D.A.; not out here in space."

"Tahnie, you've a tender heart under that competent, assertive, official presence. That's one of the thousand things I love about you. All I can say is, you have to divorce yourself from the emotion of the thing. Your emotions are fighting the toughness you project.

"Despite what you feel, you must maintain an objective distance. Simply state the facts. Make your lawful recommendations and let me make the decision."

Tanya smiled feebly. "Yeah, but I think I know what recommendations I'll have to make. I'll question them carefully and we'll examine all the facts, but I know enough about this thing to know someone is going to pay the ultimate price. That's a horrible decision to have to make."

Tolya sat back and thought for a minute. "Tahnie, as a fighter pilot out on the rim, I was constantly in situations where it was me or the other guy. I had that fraction of a moment to think, 'he's dead.'

"This afternoon when you pulled that little stunt down there, you made a decision. In spite of the risk of death for the two people out there on the flight deck, you decided the risk was an acceptable price for a peaceful resolution.

"If they'd continued to run about the ship taking pot shots at one another, others, perhaps many others, would've been hurt or killed. I'm still amazed that no-one besides your officer was hurt."

He leaned forward and reclaimed her hands. "What I'm trying to say is, like those situations, there are times when we're called upon to make tough decisions. This is similar. Once you determine the facts, you must decide between the lives of these two and the safety of everyone else on board.

"Once you make that determination we'll discuss it and make a decision. We'll present the case before the people and let them help determine justice. If they vote guilty, you will make the recommendation we've agreed upon and I will announce the judgment. It's one of the evils of governing."

He gave one of those half grins of his when he was thinking of something obscure or ironic. "At least it's an evil if you wish to govern justly. I do, and I think you do too."

Tanya nodded. "Absolutely."

Her eyes narrowed slightly as a thought hit her firmly for the first time. "You know, I never gave a thought to the whole governing part of our relationship."

Tolya grinned broadly. "I know. I found someone who loves me for me; not my status."

He looked at the time display. It was 1550. A sudden realization hit him. "Sherry! We forgot her!"

Tanya looked horrified. "Oh no."

Tolya went over to his desk, waving a hand at the COMM icon. His desk screen lit up with Daniela's face almost immediately.

She looked slightly startled and laughed out loud. "I was just reaching to call you. I see Tahnie's there too." Her eyebrows twitched a little to accompany the little grin that played briefly about her lips. "Anyway, Tahnie, your visitors are awake. You can come chat with them whenever you like."

Tolya's eyes gleamed mischievously. "We were just ending our conference. We just realized we managed to miss Sherry's release."

Daniela grimaced. "Oh, dear. I've been so busy playing patch-em up, I forgot to sign the release and send her off. If you're coming to see your charming guests, you could meet her as promised. No harm, no foul."

Tanya stepped closer to the pickups. "We'll be right there."

Tolya waved and closed the connection. "Let's go. We can take Sherry out and grab a quick bite with her before taking her to her quarters. Why not let our friends cool their heels just a bit longer?"

Tanya grinned and headed for the door. "You're just looking for another excuse to take me out."

They entered MedCentral, offering a quick hello to Brianna. On their way to Sherry's cubicle Tanya spied Felix in his.

She hesitated and then went up to his bed. He was watching them, a despairing look in his eyes. He'd clearly been crying.

She looked him over. "Felix, Felix. Look what a hell of a mess you've gotten yourself into."

He tried to swallow, his throat hoarse. "I know I screwed up. It was never supposed to go like this."

A painful cough forced a pause. "I never wanted to hurt anybody. Then Ted made me get Jake out of your jail...I was scared and I did what he said."

A look of sadness and self-loathing settled on his face. "I didn't mean to kill that girl. It...it wasn't supposed to happen that way...it was an accident."

Tanya looked up at Tolya's face. He nodded and she looked back at Felix. "You and I have a lot to talk about, Felix. I'm going to go get someone. Then we'll have a little talk. You'd best think about just how sorry you are for everything, because the better you cooperate, the better things might be for you."

She couldn't help it, "Don't go anywhere."

She led the way to Sherry's cubicle. It was 1600 hours.

Sherry was sitting up in her bed, looking very impatient. Her things were on a chair next to the bed and the eagerness to be off was clear in her eyes. She sat up straighter and Tanya leaned over for a hug. "Sorry we took so long. I see you're all better."

Sherry looked down at the cast on her arm. "Well, almost. I heard things went crazy while I was here."

She got a serious look on her face. "Is that the guy that knocked me down?" She pointed towards Felix' cubicle.

Tanya hesitated before nodding. "Yes, it is."

Sherry looked troubled. Then she leaned forward and whispered. "I've been listening to him sobbing; quietly, but I could tell. He must be a mess."

Tanya looked over at Tolya who was gathering Sherry's things. She firmed up an idea that had been percolating in the back of her brain. "Sherry, would you be willing to meet him, if I were with you? I need a positive ID for the record. He thinks you're dead... He thinks he killed you."

Sherry's eyes got big. "You're kidding. He just smacked me good with the key cabinet door so he could get at the card keys.

Tanya nodded. "Yeah, I think he's been a small time pickpocket. He's probably never hit someone in anger before in his life. When he saw you unconscious on the floor he thought he'd killed you. Part of him didn't want it to be true, but another part of him needed it to be true."

Sherry thought for a moment. "You know, he shouldn't go on torturing himself for something that's not really true," she whispered. "I mean, yeah, he hurt me, but I'm hardly dead."

She grinned. "Besides, it'll be fun to see the shock on his face when I show up."

Tanya returned the grin and whispered back. "Great. This just might seal a deal I hope to make with him. If I can get his cooperation, I can sink that Ted guy for good and we can find the person who sabotaged the drive system and get our board back."

Sherry slid off her bed and Tolya hefted her things. Tanya took her good arm and they headed for Felix' cubicle.

Felix heard the Chief's party coming down the aisle and turned to watch her return. She approached his bed and looked at him as if calculating the angle of a difficult shot. "Felix. I told you I had something to show you. I hope that by showing you this, you'll be willing to cooperate. Are you ready?"

Felix nodded. *What could be so amazing that it would affect me like she thinks?*

The curtain rustled and a young woman with a cast on one arm entered the room. There was a fine line on her forehead where she'd received a nasty gash. Recognition dawned and Felix lost any semblance of composure. This was the girl he'd knocked so brutally to the floor.

Not dead! The thought chased itself around his brain before the significance of this vision registered. *I'm not a murderer.*

Sherry approached his bed and looked him over. His face was one big bruise. His nostrils were still slightly bloody. One shoulder was wrapped and looked awkward. Apparently, he'd gotten his own drubbing. "Hello Felix."

Felix started. Wondering how she knew his name.

"Chief Nydel told me. I wanted to know who hurt me."

Tears welled up in his eyes and he turned to hide his shame.

Sherry waited a few moments. Felix mumbled something hoarsely. It was unintelligible. She didn't respond, waiting for him to turn and try again. Finally he turned to look at her again. "I...I'm so sorry," he rasped. "I'm sorry I hurt you. I'm sorry I ever went there at all. I never wanted to hurt anybody." He took a deep, painful breath. "I thought you were dead and it was because of me. I thought I'd killed you and...I didn't even know who you were." He turned away to hide his emotions.

Of all the expressions Tanya might have expected, Sherry's look of concern was not even on the list.

"Felix. Look at me."

He hesitated and then turned to look at her. "As you can see, I'm not all that dead. You just knocked me out. Chief Nydel explained what happened...I know you weren't really trying to kill me."

She paused as if trying to figure something out. "What you did was very wrong, and you know it, but I can see you're truly sorry for it."

She paused again, an awkward silence hung there. "I forgive you, Felix. I refuse to stay angry with you. I just have one thing to ask." She hesitated, "No, no. I'm begging you. Please, please tell the chief everything she needs to know. Maybe you can make up for some of what you did."

Tanya and Tolya stared at Sherry and then looked at each other as if to say, 'where'd that come from?'"

Felix nodded, tears running forgotten down the side of his face. "I don't know how you can say that. I know I don't deserve it, but I promise. I...I'll cooperate any way I can."

He shifted his gaze to Tanya. "I promise."

Tanya nodded. "We'll talk in a couple of hours." Felix nodded and turned his face toward the curtains. They turned to go and then Sherry turned back. "Felix?"

He turned back to face her.

"You said you didn't know who I was. My name is Sherry."

He tried to smile. "Thank you..." he whispered as she turned to go. "Sherry..."

Ted growled from across the aisle. "You little bastard...You wimpy baby-assed punk. You're done... I'll see to it you..."

Tanya suddenly loomed over him. "Shut your ugly pie hole, Ted. You've damaged enough lives for one voyage." She whirled and left the room, resisting the urge to knock him clean out of his bed.

On the way out, she stopped at Daniela's office entry. "Hey, Dannie. I'd appreciate if we could get some quality separation between our guests. Bring Felix out to one of the closer cubicles if you can. He doesn't need more from Ted."

"Sure, Tahnie. We'll get to it right now." She looked at Sherry and smiled. "You take care of yourself. The next time I see you, I want you well, happy and unhurt. Got it?"

Sherry replied seriously, "Yes ma'am." It was 1618.

CLEANING HOUSE — 3
ECS Destiny, Deck-3, Sherry's Quarters, 1730 Hrs

After a quick, early dinner, they saw Sherry to her quarters. Tolya excused himself. He had neglected responsibilities that needed attention. He looked at Tanya expecting her to follow, but she shook her head.

"I'll call you later." He nodded and left.

Tanya turned to look at her friend. She was a little worried about the way this Felix thing was turning out.

Sherry looked at her, puzzled at the scrutiny.

Tanya sat on a chair facing Sherry, who was in an armchair. "Sherry, I'm just a little bit...confused about your reaction to Felix this afternoon."

Sherry frowned. "I don't see the problem."

Tanya took the plunge. "Well, see, I...you...I've never seen you treat a guy so sweetly before."

Sherry blushed. "Say what?"

"Well, the way you treated this guy, Felix, is very unusual for someone confronting a recent assailant. He's not only committed a crime against the ship and colony, he's committed a personal crime against you. It's very dangerous to get emotionally attached to someone like that."

Tanya came up for air and Sherry jumped in. "Look Tanya. I don't know exactly how I feel about anything right now. I thought I could hate him for what he did to me and all, but...I can't. There's something about him that yearns to be free. There's a better person in there looking for a way to break out."

Tanya shook her head slowly. "That sounds like fairy tale material to me. You know you're going to have to press charges before I can prosecute him on the assault. Right?"

Sherry sat forward in her chair, "NO! I can't! I won't!" She paused, startled at her own vehemence.

Tanya backed off fast. "Whoa! Sherry, it's me here!"

Sherry continued, a little more calmly, "You have plenty to hang on him already. If I can forgive his actions, then I think you need to respect that!"

Tanya shrugged. "Look. I'm sorry if I hit a nerve here. I'll respect your decision on the assault charge." She looked long at her friend. "I'm your friend, even if I am your boss. I just hope you walk carefully here..."

She couldn't help the trace of a grin at the irony. "This guy, Felix...he doesn't know it yet, but he's just found himself a great big good luck charm."

Sherry looked away. "I...I didn't mean to yell at you...I don't understand what I'm feeling here. Just...I guess I need to work my way through this."

Tanya stood. "I can't say I fully understand. I've never seen this happen in my short career, but never forget, I'm here for you. So, if you need me, holler."

Tanya placed firm hands on her hips. "I'm going to make damn sure he treats you respectfully or all bets are off."

Sherry got up from her seat and gave Tanya an awkward hug. "Thanks, Tahnie...No assault charges?"

Tanya let out an explosive sigh. "No assault charges."

Tanya made her way to the door. Before taking her leave, she turned to Sherry. "Let's get this over with so we can get this ship moving again. We've a wedding to plan and everything keeps getting in the way."

Sherry brightened. "You're right!"

Tanya grinned. "And, no more wild adventures. I can't loose my maid of honor."

Sherry grinned, "I'm more than happy to avoid any more adventures. I..."

Her eyes lit up in total surprise and excitement. "Tanya! You mean it? I mean, 'Maid of honor?'"

Tanya went over and hugged her friend again. "Absolutely, if you're willing."

"I...I...Tahnie, I'm honored. Of course I'm willing!"

Tanya returned to the door. As it snapped open she replied, "Good. Something good happened today."

Sherry grinned. "I'll see you tomorrow in the office." Tanya waved and headed back to Med-Central.

* * * *

ECS Destiny, Command Deck, MedCentral, 1820 Hrs

Tanya signed Felix out of MedCentral. He was still a bit shaky. His voice was hoarse and he would be very sore for quite some time. She escorted him through the morgue and into her offices. He moved stiffly but managed on his own.

Felix very carefully avoided looking at the single lit drawer as they passed Jake's place. *That one really bothers him.* She thought.

She got him settled in a chair and then moved to her desk. "OK, Felix. Let me start with what I think are going to be the charges against you." She picked up a pad of paper and consulted a hand written list. "We have one count assault, one count robbery, one count aiding a prison break, one count illegal possession of a firearm on board a space vessel, two counts illegal discharge of a firearm on board a space vessel, one count collusion with a seditious person, and one count aiding and abetting in an act of sabotage."

She looked at him. "I was pleased to remove murder from the list. I decided not to add attempted murder to the list after that little rampage through my ship."

Felix was doing a fascinating study of the grain patterns in his shoes. Despondence lurked on his face.

Tanya continued. "I'm going to consider extenuating circumstances on that last one and work from there."

She sat forward and concluded. "Finally, your luck has raised another notch. There's a young woman who insistently refuses to press charges on the assault."

She flipped the pad with the list of charges onto her desk and looked squarely at Felix. "Felix. Look at me and listen closely."

Felix' eyes snapped up to lock on her face.

"I'm not sure what's going on in that girls head right now, but you had better think long and hard before you ever do anything to hurt her again. She's not just my assistant, she's my friend and you should know right now, I take good care of my friends."

Felix looked both relieved and troubled.

Tanya continued. "Now! I'll consider reducing some of these charges in return for honest answers and your willingness to testify against Ted Jackson." Felix blanched and looked nervous. "You'll be protected from anything Ted might do. Frankly, his days are numbered by the digits of my hands and feet.

Felix swallowed and nodded his head. "So, what do I gotta do?" He was just slightly less raspy. Tanya got up and drew a glass of water from the small dispenser in the corner of her office. She gave this to Felix before retrieving her notepad.

She tore off the list, sliding it into a drawer for later. Then she grabbed an old fashioned pen from the same drawer and sat ready to take notes. "I want you to tell me everything that happened from the day you first met with Ted and Jake till the day you decided to chase each other through this ship.

"Most important, I need the name of the person you recruited for Ted. He or she sabotaged the drive system and could have killed us all in a flash had there been the least bit of carelessness. Finally, I need to know where the replacement board went. All consideration hinges on how you answer these questions."

* * * *

ECS Destiny, Command Deck, SecCentral, Detention Area, 1900 Hrs

Tanya showed Felix to his new cell. It was a low security cell designed to accommodate as many as six people. Felix was considered a cooperating prisoner.

Felix sat on the bunk and stared morosely at his shoes as she closed the door. "You'll be safe here. Ted's not going anywhere. I guarantee it."

She went to a storage closet and pulled out a couple blankets. She passed them through the flat horizontal composite slats and tossed them on the bunk next to him. Those slats could, if necessary, shutter flat into a surprisingly strong wall.

"Have you had anything to eat? Do you want something?"

Felix shook his head. "They gave me some hot soup while I was waiting for you to come back." He was depressed. "I'm not very hungry right now."

"OK." Tanya replied. She went back to her office, took her note pad and pen and walked through to MedCentral.

* * * *

The interview with Ted was a bust. The man was impossible and refused to say anything that wasn't vile and unrepeatable. She threw up her hands and left.

Ted was securely manacled to his recovery bed and there was a twenty-four hour guard outside his cubical. She returned to her office and went over her notes again before paging Tolya.

It was 1950 when he called her back. "Hey there. It's been a while, how's everything going?"

"Well, I have news, but I think I need to include Daryl." She smiled, "I was thinking we could get together with Daryl and Naomi and have a double date in the officer's lounge. We can have our dinner and I can fill everybody in. Sound good?"

Tolya nodded. "That sounds great. I'll pass the word to Daryl and Naomi."

He glanced at the time. "Go ahead and get ready. I'll come in about twenty minutes and we'll go together."

She agreed and closed the connection.

Tanya hurried to her quarters. She freshened up, applied a sparing and judicious amount of makeup and got into one of her nicer casual dresses. It felt great wearing something besides a ship's uniform.

At 2010, Tolya tapped the announcer. Tanya opened the door and watched his reaction.

Tolya let out a low appreciative whistle. "Nice!"

She stepped into the corridor and Tolya looked at her. "Turn around. Let me see you." Tanya grinned and did a slow turn.

"Tahnie, you look delicious." He held out his arm and she took it. Together, they walked to the officer's lounge at the Event Center. Daryl and Naomi had arrived before them. They grinned and waved the new couple over to their table.

* * * *

Dinner was pleasant. Daryl and Naomi were very encouraging, offering great advice on relationships and ideas about wedding plans and such.

When the dessert dishes were cleared away and the coffee was replenished, Tanya reached down and pulled a slim folder from under her chair.

"I'm really sorry to have to turn this into business guys, but I need to catch you up. Since the final phase of this investigation is about to be completed, and since it involves your department Daryl, I thought it important I discuss it with you."

"My department? How's that?"

Tanya placed the folder down at her place and picked up her coffee. "I imagine you both have heard all kinds of scuttlebutt about the goings on in the last few days."

Naomi nodded. "Yes, stories are flowing thick and fast. There's been more excitement around here than the whole rest of the trip put together."

Tanya smiled at Naomi's comment. "Before I discuss what's going on, let me fill you in on the last few days."

The story unfolded with pertinent additions by Tolya. The looks of consternation on their friends' faces were manifold.

"So," Tanya concluded. "I just completed the interviews with Felix and Ted."

Tanya took another sip and put her cup down. She opened her folder and pulled out her hand written notes from her interview with Felix. She really didn't need them all that much. The contents were mostly things she'd already surmised or experienced, but she had them ready.

"Our friend, Felix has been a petty low grade thief for most of his life; at least since his early teens. His parole officer apparently dared him to take the opportunity of this colony trip to start anew. I suspect the parole officer was eager to get Felix out of his hair; permanently, but legally."

"Very professional!" Daryl quipped.

Naomi gave him a nudge. "Not now," she whispered.

Tanya suppressed a grin. "As I thought, Felix has been little more than the messenger boy in this mess. He barely knows which end of a gun to point at someone.

It appears that when he witnessed Ted murder Jake Townsend, Felix had already realized he'd gotten in way over his head. He claims he tried to back out before his messy jailbreak, but Ted threatened him if he didn't go 'rescue' Jake."

"Felix was worried about his own survival when he found out just what his recruited acquaintance had done to the ship and he was horrified about the attempt on Tolya. None of those things had been things he had anticipated being involved in."

She looked at her captive audience and then continued. "When he released Jake, Felix ran out of time as Tolya and I were approaching SecCentral. He used the passkey to get into the armory to hide. It was then that he discovered exactly what was in there and an idea formed. He had taken the .357 for personal insurance. Besides, Ted was going to get everyone killed if the whole operation didn't stop."

"Felix felt personal responsibility to make sure the operation did stop. Remember, he already thought he'd killed Sherry. That notion weighed heavily on him."

Naomi offered comment. "It seems to me Felix has been on a collision course with himself for a long time. "I wonder; even though Sherry knows nothing personal about Felix, do you think she somehow sensed this about him? Frankly, I think her response is nothing short of amazing."

Tanya shrugged. "I'm somewhat at a loss trying to understand what's going on with her. She has a kind heart. I just hope she doesn't get hurt in some other way, later down the road."

She returned to her notes and continued what amounted to a briefing. "The final phase of this business is to find the saboteur and get that board back."

"Amen to that." Daryl raised his coffee and mimicked a toast.

Tanya turned to address him. "Daryl. I need to know a little about someone in your drive section crew. Particularly, I need to know about someone named Enrique Ortega."

Daryl blinked a moment like he'd been taken off guard. "Enrique? Well, let's see. Besides the fact nobody's very fond of him, he's the best tech I have down there. He has an amazing skill with electronics and optronics. A circuit board is a puzzle that he delights in mastering. If it could be done at all, he'd probably be the only one I'd give a prayer of successfully repairing the sabotaged boar…"

A look of disgust mixed with dread came across his face. "No… you…no, he's a first class jerk but…"

He looked in her face and knew. "You think its him?"

Tanya shook her head. "I don't think it's him. I know it's him. Felix recruited him and passed the arrangement information on to Ted. Ted coordinated Enrique with Jake's attempt on Tolya."

Daryl sat back, stunned. "But why? He's a real complainer, but sabotage? Really?"

Tanya shook her head and put down a sheet of her notes. "Evidently Ted made some vague promises of land. I did some research. Ted somehow secured unusual amounts of land on *Nova Terra*. He was promising a small share of land, which would equate to a say in council politics. In his estimation, it was going to be a great source of personal wealth. He evidently told Felix to extend a promise to Enrique for services rendered."

Naomi shook her head. "So, let me guess. When we lost any hope of getting to *Nova Terra*, Ted panicked, thinking his hope of wealth and power was being snatched away from him, right?"

Tanya nodded. "He refused to believe what was only too obvious and instead, decided to fight what he thought was a personal attack."

Naomi quipped, "Obviously his lift doesn't reach the top deck."

Daryl nodded. "So, I guess Enrique bought the lie and agreed to help stop the hijacking of their good fortune. I remember him going on about how stupid it was; how we were 'just giving up before we even tried.'"

Tolya looked grim. "I say we pick him up tonight."

Tanya hesitated. "I thought to wait till his shift. I could take a couple of officers to your office, Daryl. Then you could call Enrique in for something innocuous. That would make less of a scene than marching down to the residential decks and banging on his door at bed time."

She glanced at Tolya and winced. "Sorry, honey. If you really want, I'll do it now."

Tolya shook his head. "No, I'm just tired of this mess. We have more important things to worry about." He shrugged and looked around the table. "Maybe Tahnie's right."

Tanya patted his hand. "Thanks, honey."

141

She turned to face Daryl. "Daryl, I'll bring a couple of guys and wait in your office just before the shift begins; say 0545. You can call Enrique in for something or other and then we'll take it from there."

Daryl nodded. "No problem."

CLEANING HOUSE — 4

MON 02.15.2094
ECS Destiny, Drive Section Interface, Control Center, 0607 Hrs

Enrique Ortega walked imperiously into the drive section control center, the usual disdain for his coworkers etched on his almost too perfect features. He didn't care much what anybody thought of him. He was the best and he knew it. It never occurred to him that his habit of claiming other's solutions and ideas as his own should garner any resentment. People acknowledged his presence grudgingly.

Today was no different. Since his little trick with the cascade power controller, the slowdown in the workload made the days drag by. People had become lax about arriving on time. He arrived about seven minutes late, no later than some, a bit later than others. He busied himself going over the third shift logs, checking readings, watching the others drift into their routines.

The PA pinged and Chief McIntyre's cocky voice called out. "Enrique. Come on over to the office, will you? I've a little something for ya."

Enrique strutted his important self to the Chief's office. The door snapped open and he stepped in. "Yeah, Chief?"

The door snapped at his heels and the features of the room came into sharp focus. Chief McIntyre was standing next to his desk with his perpetual cup of coffee. There were several new faces in the room. That awesome security babe was sitting in McIntyre's chair looking him up and down.

Whoa! I hope she likes what she sees. His speculative lear faltered as the rest of the scene unfolded. He noticed two armed security officers flanking the door. They seemed far too fascinated with his arrival.

Daryl pushed himself off the wall where he'd been leaning. Setting his coffee on the desk next to the security babe, he looked at Enrique in open contempt. "Enrique. I'm delighted to introduce to you our very capable Chief of Security, Tanya Nydel. She came all the way down here just to see you."

Enrique was getting a serious case of nerves. It was awfully stuffy in the room. He backed up to activate the door, but bumped into it instead.

Daryl continued. "Did you really think no one would discover who the genius was who doctored the cascade controller?" Daryl folded his arms over his chest and looked Enrique in the face. "I have to hand it to you. You pulled it off very efficiently."

He picked up the coffee again and perched comfortably on the corner of his desk. "I suppose I should thank you for being precise. Otherwise we'd all be so much stardust."

Enrique assumed the look of a trapped animal. He licked his lips and started to protest his innocence. The woman in the chief's seat stood in one graceful motion. It was more like the motion of a lioness, swift, with deadly precision.

"So, Enrique, let's get the formalities over with, shall we?" She pulled a pocket-tab from her utility belt and thumbed an icon. She glanced at the display and then looked at him. "Enrique Martinez Ortega. I am placing you under arrest, pursuant to the provisions of the colony charter. The charges are, willful destruction of colony property, willful disabling of a commissioned starship, willful endangerment of the entire population of this ship, and the cooperative participation in a plot to stop this mission. You will be taken into custody and remanded to a trial by jury as provided by the colony charter."

The officers to either side firmly took his arms and stepped him forward to stand before her. She pulled a set of cuffs from her belt, circled behind him and fit them snugly to his wrists.

It was some kind of bad dream. *How could this happen?* He'd been so careful covering his tracks. He'd left no clues. He thought with all the crazy crap going on elsewhere on the ship, they'd never figure out he was involved. *It's not fair!*

The trip across the control center, under the curious eyes of his peers, and up into the main ship was a demoralizing experience. The security chief walked briskly in front and the officers propelled him politely but firmly after. He was, for the first time, not interested in the view of the woman ahead of him.

* * * *

TUE 02.16.2094
ECS Destiny, Command Deck, Captain's Standby Cabin, 1900 Hrs

Tolya and Tanya sat in his standby cabin next to the bridge. They frequented it often to retreat from the craziness and just get to know each other. The place where she'd nearly lost him had become their private sanctuary.

Tonight, they sat at his desk poring over the files that made up the colony charter, studying the intricacies of criminal law.

The charter had been designed to cover all the necessary points of law, yet leave room for innovation. Given the people's predilection for a democratic society, it was modeled loosely after the constitution of the United States of America along with documents covering alternate methods of democratic governance as found in Great Britain, Canada and Australia. The first generation of colonists was supposed to hammer out the basics of their governmental forms as a unique people.

They poured through the sections covering various types of criminal law in the four great democratic societies of Earth. They decided great care would be given to finding all the facts and providing clear proof of guilt before any sentence was carried out.

The colonists generally agreed that the idea of 'innocent until proven guilty' should prevail. It was also a consensus that once guilt was established beyond any doubt, the sentence should be surely and swiftly carried out. Delay was seen as a weakening of the resolve of the people. Once sentence was passed, a short process of appeal was allowed. Then sentence was to be carried out swiftly.

They discussed capitol punishment in some detail. There were few options available to a people confined to the insides of a starship. The hope had been that there wouldn't be a need to deal with something so severe while plying the stars. Unfortunately the vagaries of human nature made such altruistic hopes futile.

Finally, in the wee hours of the morning, they fell asleep sitting on the couch facing the sea of stars. They'd covered much ground and had decided they were as ready as anyone could hope to be under the circumstances.

CLEANING HOUSE — 5

FRI 2.19.2094
ECS Destiny, Quarterdeck, Event Center, 0900 Hrs

Preparations for the trials went quickly. Like the emergency meeting that had started the whole cycle of events, the three main venues were full to overflowing. Digicams recorded. The mood of the ship was an odd mix of apprehension, anger, and anticipation.

Everyone had heard about the multi-deck shoot out and the murder. There was no secret about what had happened to the ship's drive; that power board was still missing.

Shane, Kaitlyn and the kids sat in the main venue. Lyuba nudged a friend next to her and pointed as the officers of the court entered for the opening of proceedings. "See? That's my Uncle Toly!"

"Wow! Cool!"

Captain and Governor Anatoli G. Chernov sat in the center with the Chief of Security to his right. All were resplendent in dress uniform. In spite of the formal dress, there was no sense of pompousness. Rather there was a sense of solemnity bordering on sorrow. The accused trio were escorted in and seated separately from the crowd, facing down the length of the table. There they endured much murmuring and finger pointing from the crowd.

The ships' clock read 0900. It was time to begin. Anatoli stood. "Attention, please."

The room quieted quickly. Silence was the chief sound as the vid-relays played out the events. "It is with a profound sense of sadness that I call this trial to order. It had been my fondest hope that we would not have to contend with the evils we left behind...before we ever got to our destination.

"This is a sad episode in the history of our colony that we will reflect on often in the years to come. My wish is that, in spite of the seriousness of this moment, we will find in it a new sense of unity and purpose when all is completed."

He picked up a wooden mallet and rapped firmly on a wooden block set on the table in front of him. "I call this trial to order and call on the citizens of this colony to witness the exercise of justice on their behalf."

He scanned the room and then continued. "I would first like to acknowledge the jury of peers that sits in attendance in the row in front of me."

The digicams switched focus to show a row of colonists in their Sunday best, gold pins affixed to their lapels. Six men and six women sat under the cameras.

"It seemed appropriate..." the cameras panned back to Anatoli. "...to appeal to the God of justice and mercy to guide in these proceedings. So, I have asked the Reverend Brad Hill to open with a word of prayer. All rise, please."

All over the ship, people stood; many in respect, some in nervous, polite deference to a practice they weren't so used to. The minister, a tall, young man, with a dazzling smile and a purposeful stride, stepped up from the front row next to the jury box and approached the microphone placed before the podium. In a strong Australian accent, "Let's bow in prayer...Heavenly Father..."

* * * *

After the invocation, all resumed their seats.

Anatoli stepped forward. "Thank you Reverend. Would you remain and swear in the jury, please?"

"Surely, sir."

The man turned and faced the jury. They stood and, as instructed, raised their right hands and swore to listen unbiased to the testimony and render a just and honest verdict. All returned to their seats.

Anatoli addressed the jury. "The three to be tried before you," he waved a hand in the direction of the three to his right, "face serious and damning charges if found guilty. Weigh carefully the facts and judge fairly. You are to determine guilt only. Any sentences will be the responsibility of this office."

He turned to the young woman to his right. "Will the prosecution please call the first defendant."

She stood, and in a clear, rich, low soprano, "The Prosecution for the Colony aboard the ship, *Destiny* calls Felix Xavier Hernandez before the court."

* * * *

Finally, the arguments were all presented, the evidence laid out. The time of decision was at hand. The mood in the room had long since moved closer to the angry side of the emotional spectrum. The reality of the evils and dangers they'd all been subjected to had been revealed and the outrage was nearly unanimous.

The jury had been ushered to the staff conference room to deliberate while the court was in recess.

The proceedings had been anything but boring. When Ted Jackson's turn before the court had come, he'd made a spectacular scene, hurling insults and wild accusations in the faces of the officers of the court. The interruption was not tolerated long. Governor Chernov ordered him gagged if he didn't shut-up.

Finally, the jury returned to their seats and court resumed.

Anatoli stood and tapped firmly with the gavel. "Court is back in session." He looked around and confirmed that all was in order.

Then he looked down at the jury. "You, the jury, have been instructed to deliberate and determine verdicts for each of the three accused. You have been charged with rendering a guilty or not guilty verdict. Do you have a representative?"

A nervous young woman approached the microphone. "We have, your honor."

Anatoli smiled his reassurance. "Please, proceed with the jury's decisions. Let's keep the order of verdicts consistent with the order of appearance of the accused."

The woman nodded respectfully and held up the three cards she carried. "Your honor, this jury finds the accused, Felix Xavier Hernandez, guilty on all charges."

There were a few mumbles from the crowd and Felix slouched down in his seat, head down in abject defeat.

The young lady shuffled to the second card. "The jury finds the defendant, Enrique Martinez Ortega, guilty on all charges."

The crowd was more animated now. Their approval was clear. Enrique jerked his head up and stared with impotent rage at the poor woman.

The jury representative looked around the room nervously and Anatoli held up a hand for quiet.

She concluded her task. "The jury finds the defendant, Theodore Daniel Jackson, guilty on all charges."

Pandemonium erupted as the crowd roared its approval. Ted jumped up and screamed his rage. "You filthy little ..."

Two officers gripped him firmly from behind and forced him back down in his seat. He opened his mouth to resume his tirade and officer stuffed a gag in his mouth, muffling the obscenities.

Anatoli rapped loudly and repeatedly for order. It took a little longer, but the room finally quieted.

Anatoli scanned the room sternly and then addressed the jury representative. "The court thanks the jury for its hard work in rendering these verdicts."

She nodded graciously and returned quietly to her seat.

"Now, the court will consider recommendations of sentence from the prosecution."

Anatoli sat and Tanya rose. "Your Honor, the prosecution makes the following recommendations regarding sentencing."

Anatoli nodded and said, "Proceed."

"In the case of the Colony on board *Destiny*, against the convicted, Felix Xavier Hernandez, the recommendations of the prosecution are as follows:

"In consideration of both extenuating circumstances and voluntary cooperation with the court, a course of mercy seems appropriate. This would consist of time in incarceration deemed appropriate by the court followed by time, deemed appropriate by the court, in community service under proper supervision."

The crowd seemed restless but there was little reaction. Many people tended to like Felix because he'd been kindly while serving in the maintenance department. Felix' head came up and the shock on his face was priceless. Tanya barely managed to suppress the humor from her voice.

"In the case of the Colony on board *Destiny*, against the convicted, Enrique Martinez Ortega, the prosecution recommends the following:

"Given the extreme and deadly nature of his crimes and the willingness to imperil this entire community with the very real possibility of instant annihilation, the prosecution reluctantly recommends the sentence of death by spacing."

The murmurs began. "A person willing to gamble the lives of over two thousand people for perceived personal gain can never be trusted to value the good of those he or she has betrayed."

The crowd rumbled with mixed horror and approval. Enrique's face turned death white and he leaned forward as if to bury his head between his knees.

"In the case of the Colony on board *Destiny*, against the convicted, Theodore Daniel Jackson, the prosecution recommends the following:

"Since time immemorial, the murder of another human being has cried for the blood of the murderer." Ted's face was already turning red. "The convicted has shown the ultimate disdain for the dignity of human life. Coupled with willfully risking the entire colony in a vain attempt to derail it's single chance for survival, the prosecution is compelled to recommend a sentence of death by spacing."

Ted tried to lunge up again but was anticipated by the guards who forced him back on his butt. "This man forfeited his own life the day he chose to take the life of another."

The crowd was on its feet, roaring and Ted was struggling to get out of the grip of the guards. The consensus was absolutely clear on this last recommendation.

Anatoli stood and pounded for order.

The room finally quieted and Tanya finished her say. "With these recommendations, the prosecution rests. Thank you."

Anatoli nodded solemnly as Tanya sat, keeping an iron grip on her emotions.

"In conclusion, the court agrees with the recommendations of the prosecution. Execution of sentences will commence no more than five days from announcement, as prescribed by the charter.

Executions will be digitally witnessed for the record, but will not be released for public viewing."

Anatoli paused for a few seconds as he looked in Felix' direction. "Felix Hernandez is hereby remanded to the custody of SecCentral." He picked up the gavel. "Court is adjourned."

The ship's clock flipped to 1640 as the gavel pounded three times on the block.

* * * *

ECS Destiny, Drive Section Interface, Stores, 1810 Hrs

Felix led the small procession from SecCentral down to stores in drive section.

Daryl was bemused. *Stores? I checked here myself! This guy better not be yanking my chain.*

Daryl released the lock down on the door and they filed into the waiting area. Naomi moved to the end of the counter and raised the folding part up to allow admittance. It was 1810.

Felix began explaining. "I ah...I had access because of my job, so I came after hours and let myself in. Then, I hopped the counter.

"Enrique gave me a piece of paper with the number on it and told me to find the one that matched. Ted wanted to use it to bargain with."

Daryl interrupted. "Look kid, I came in here myself, cross referenced the part and went straight to the spot. The board wasn't there. Then we searched all the shelves around to see if it had been misplaced. It was nowhere to be found."

Felix looked amused. "That's because it's not on the shelves."

He started down the rows and his audience followed. He passed the spot where the board was supposed to have been without so much as a glance.

At the back of the room was a long, low table where items were identified, sorted and temporarily stored until they could be properly placed on the appropriate shelves. He went to one end of the table where a number of plastic bags were stacked, awaiting sorting and placement. He pawed through the small pile and selected one of the larger ones. Gently, he picked it up and turned, handing it to Daryl.

Daryl stared at the bag for a moment before taking it and moving to the table. He gently laid it down and opened it. Everyone gathered around. Daryl pulled out a brand new power board; labels yet to be removed. He gently placed the board back in the bag and sealed it. Then he reached up and grabbed an appropriate box from a shelf above the table.

The box with the precious board went under one arm and he turned to give Felix the strangest look. Daryl was speechless. Tanya couldn't help it. She started laughing. The absurdity of the situation was more than she could stand and she laughed till her side hurt. Daryl gave her an injured look that disintegrated in an explosion of laughter of his own. It didn't take long for Naomi to join in. Felix stood grinning foolishly, feeling embarrassed.

The release of tension was cathartic. Daryl clapped Felix on the shoulder and looked at him with new eyes. "Amazing! What possessed you to put it in plain sight?"

Felix shrugged. "One time, I heard somebody say that the best place to hide something was right in plain sight. After Ted saw it, he told me to hide it till he was ready for it. He didn't want to get caught with it.

"I left it there and none of you ever thought to look anywhere but around where it was supposed to be." He shrugged, grinning. "People do it all the time."

Daryl looked Felix straight in the eye. "You know, kid?" He tapped Felix on the forehead. "You have plenty of smarts up there. I bet if you filled it with useful knowledge, you could go far in life."

Daryl looked over at Naomi. "I'll tell you what. If you're willing; once you dig yourself out of the present hole you're in, I think that between me and Naomi, and our friend Emily, we might make something of you."

Felix flushed self-consciously. "Thanks Mr. McIntyre. I think I'd like that."

Tanya beckoned them back out of stores and started the procession back to where they'd started. Daryl and Naomi left the party at the entrance to drive section control center. Tanya, Felix and a security officer made their way back up to SecCentral.

CLEANING HOUSE — 6

ECS Destiny, Command Deck, Captain's Standby Cabin, 1920 Hrs

The door to the standby cabin snapped open on a darkened room. Tanya saw the curtain open, revealing jewel strewn velvet.

"Tolya? Are you in here?" She called softly.

"Yeah. Please...come join me."

She saw motion near the window and realized he was on the small couch he used when he wanted to sit and think. She entered and let the door close behind her. She crossed the room in the vague wash of light from the vast star field.

"Are you OK?"

"Yeah. I'll be fine... just... thinking."

She stepped up behind the little couch. Reaching over the back, she began methodically messaging his shoulders and neck. It was like squeezing rock. "You're really tense, honey."

Tolya leaned forward and grunted appreciatively. "Yeah well, it's been a very tense week."

Tanya worked for a few more moments till she could feel his muscles slowly relax. "I was looking for you. I wanted to be first to give you good news for a change.

Tolya turned and looked up at her face, softly lit in the starlight. "Good news? You mean besides having you in here all to myself?"

She chuckled quietly. "Well, yes actually."

He patted the seat and scooted over to make room.

Tanya stepped around and slid contentedly next to him. "I just wanted to tell you Daryl has his missing board back."

Tolya smiled. "That is good news. After today I need all the good news I can get." He put his arm around her and she slid into the hollow of his side. They sat quietly staring out into the depths that insistently drew the eye.

Tanya remembered visiting a spaceport orbiting Mars that had an observation lounge. It was one of the grand tourist attractions of the solar system. The lounge was domed over with an incredibly strong, transparent polymer.

If you sat in the middle of the room with the lights off, you could get the growing sensation of floating; falling really, into the depths of the universe. A couple of people had been found catatonic.

Tanya always considered the view stark and cold. Now, it occurred to her that viewing it in the company of a loved one, it became a warm, calming experience.

Tolya murmured something quietly to himself.

"Did you say something, sweet?"

He leaned his head on hers. "I was just thinking. How can anybody imagine that all this," he waved his free hand across the star field, "could have just happened by random chance? The design is so beautiful."

"Yeah," she breathed.

They sat for a long time, just basking in the rare moment of peace and privacy.

"Um...Tolya?"

"Yes?"

"Have you ever seen an official spacing execution?"

Tolya's head came up and he looked at her.

"Being in the wars and all, I thought, you know..."

His eyes searched her face. "Spacing? It troubles you a lot doesn't it?"

She nodded.

"Well, it should." He said. There was a long pause. "I've never seen an official spacing. They're blessedly rare in the Navy."

He looked out at the lonely view, lost in thought. "I saw the results several times during my rim tour. It seemed to be the pirates' favorite occupation. It's not pretty, I assure you."

Her fingers absently traced random arcs over his knee. "I've never seen it done; never wanted to."

She looked up at him. "I've never seen the results either; Thank God." She saw a haunted look in his eyes.

He shuddered. "God knows I wish you didn't have to. It looks like...well, it must be one of the worst ways to go...I don't know."

He drew a long breath and expelled it in a deep sigh. "Words are inadequate. The people...the bodies...they were hideous. The horror on those faces defied description. They never had a trial; had never done anything to deserve such a brutal fate."

Tanya sat up and took his hand in both of hers. He could see the glimmer of tears in the starlight. "Are we doing any better? We're going to do that to...to two human beings in a few days."

Tolya pulled her to him, pressing her head to his chest in a gentle caress. "I know...Believe me, I know. It's nothing to take lightly."

There was a long pause. "I suppose we could keep them confined indefinitely, but...well, we're like fish in a bowl. If one of the fish gets sick, the water quickly becomes poisoned. If it's not removed and the water freshened, the rest of the fish will soon die."

Tanya sat back and looked at him. "It's an imperfect analogy, I know, but there's a parallel.

"These two are a poison to the community. You know that. You said as much today in your sentencing recommendations."

Tanya looked away, troubled.

Tolya sighed, "The problem is, knowing the facts and realizing the unhappy need for action, the soul of a good man or woman still shies away from carrying it through. No moral person wants to do such a detestable deed to another, no matter the reason or provocation. That doesn't change the painful truth that it has to be done."

Tolya stood and crossed to his desk, pulling a handful of tissues from a dispenser. He returned and offered them to her. Tanya took them gratefully and began patting her face down, trying to eliminate the evidence of her distress.

* * * *

TUE 2.23,.2094
ECS Destiny, Command Deck, Command Bridge, 1000 Hrs

Daryl strode onto the bridge looking very self satisfied. Tolya turned in his chair to watch his chief engineer approach. "Chief. Please tell me you bring good news."

Daryl grinned. "Aye! That I do, Keptin."

Tolya leaned over in his chair and spoke sotto voce. "That's enough, you jokester."

Daryl chuckled. "Seriously sir, I came to report all systems are green. All the damage has been repaired, the systems have passed their tests and we're ready to go on your word."

Tolya leaned back and breathed a contented sigh. "It has been a very long time since I had such good news."

He looked at the clock and his smile faded. "Daryl, in about two hours we'll have the executions and put paid to this little horror story we've been through. For the sake of propriety and for the record, I need two witnesses. I'd appreciate if you'd be one. I've asked Daniela to offer pain blocker."

He shrugged eloquently. "I wish to God it hadn't come to this. Tanya and I will perform the deed and it will be digitally stored for the record."

Daryl's face was grim. "I can't say I'd be glad to, but count on me to be there."

"Thanks Daryl. I'll be asking Vince as well." Daryl nodded and turned to go.

"Frank?" The captain stood and stepped away from his chair. "You have the CONN. I'll be back at 1300. Be prepared to get under way by 1330."

Frank grinned. "My pleasure, Captain." He stood, crossed to the command chair and Tolya followed Daryl out the door.

* * * *

Captain Chernov and Chief Tanya Nydel, Mr. Vincent Leoni and Dr. Daniela Jacobs, along with Chief Daryl McIntyre and his wife, Naomi stood at attention in dress uniform in the main airlock anteroom on the aft end of Quarterdeck. A security officer stood at parade rest, awaiting orders. At last the clock flipped to 1200.

Anatoli stepped forward. "Bring the condemned."

The officer came to attention, performed a crisp salute and stepped out into the central Assembly Area. He signaled the waiting officers to bring the two men.

Two digicams had been stationed to record the event for posterity. They stared in silent witness. Soon the officers brought the prisoners in and stopped before the captain.

Tanya stepped forward crisply to join him. The two men wore simple disposable hospital gowns and a pair of hospital slippers. Their hands were bound behind their backs. There was hate and anger boiling in Ted Jackson's eyes. He had not the slightest remorse. Enrique's eyes held sheer terror mixed with anger. He was convinced he was being wronged.

Captain Chernov signaled Enrique forward. "I truly regret this moment. Your crimes have bound you to your fate. What is done here is to satisfy justice and for the good of the colony. Do you have any final words?"

Enrique trembled where he stood. He shook his head, no.

Dr. Jacobs stepped forward with a hypo-aerosol in her hand. Tolya continued. "The ships doctor has provided a strong pain blocker. It's the only token of mercy we can offer. Do you wish to receive the injection?"

Enrique's eyes were watery. Finally he nodded his head. Dr. Jacobs placed the hypo-aerosol against his arm and pressed the stud. After a moment the medicine began to take effect.

Tanya, her mouth set in a rigid attempt to keep her emotions in check, stepped to the airlock controls and activated the inner door. It slid heavily to one side and the small room, looking a lot like a slightly over sized lift car, waited.

Enrique was escorted into the chamber and turned about to face them. The guards stepped back and the captain finished the formula. "May God have mercy on your soul."

The inner lock slid shut with a final click. Captain Chernov stepped forward and placed his hand over Tanya's on the outer door control. They looked at each other and then through the glass into the eyes of the condemned.

Together they pressed the emergency override and the outer door slid open quickly. The sudden evacuation of the air swept Enrique out over the massive drive jets, currently powered down. Terror filled eyes went wide and his mouth formed a silent scream. The glass iced over almost instantly, blessedly hiding the grim process of explosive decompression.

Captain Chernov and Chief Nydel turned and stepped smartly away from the frosted glass while a security officer got the outer door closed and reset the system. Tanya was struggling but stayed with the plan.

The operation moved over to the next airlock. The procedure began again with Ted Jackson, who was defiance personified. The captain asked for last words and the room was filled with vile invective. At a nod from the captain, a gag was stuffed into the his flapping mouth. "Do you wish the pain injection? Answer 'yes' with a nod, 'no' with a shake of your head."

Ted screamed through the gag, shaking his head in anger.

Tanya cycled the inner door open and the security officers struggled to get Ted into the airlock. They jumped back and Tanya hit the close tab. Ted threw himself against the glass, eyes wide, face red. Captain Chernov stepped up next to Tanya and again placed his hand over hers on the controls. "May God have mercy on his soul." He intoned. They looked the man in the eye through the glass and together, pressed the emergency override.

* * * *

As everyone began moving from the camera view, Tanya let out a sob and slumped, hands over her face. Tolya took her and held her to his chest, turning to shield her from the digicams. The techs stopped the recording and the ordeal was over.

Everyone gathered around the captain and Tanya. Daniela gently rubbed Tanya behind the neck while Naomi rested a hand on her shoulder.

Tanya finally regained her composure and pulled away from Tolya. She smiled her gratitude at him and then reached over and squeezed Daniela's hand. "Thanks. I'm sorry, I guess I'm being a big cry baby."

Daniela gently scolded her. "No, Tahnie. I'd be awfully worried about you if you'd come away from this unscathed."

She squeezed back. "It's the mark of a good person to abhor the taking of a life."

Tolya turned, looking around at his staff…his friends. "Thanks; all of you."

He exhaled as if to get rid of a bad smell. "Now, let's get things buttoned up for a long overdue transition." There was general agreement and the group quietly dispersed.

Tolya escorted Tanya to his own cabin and had her sit on the couch. He sat on the edge of the cushion next to her and brushed her cheek with the back of his hand.

He said, apologetically, "I have a lot to do to get this boat moving. I want you to just relax for a while. It's a lot quieter in here than down the hall. I'm going to make a ship wide announcement and then I'll be on the bridge. When you're feeling better, I'd love to have you come and keep me company when we make transition."

Tanya nodded, emotionally exhausted. She knew she was too keyed up to sleep, but she could at least stay and relax for a while. "I'm turning out to be a big cry baby."

Tolya brushed a lock of hair from her face. "No sweet. You have moments where emotion battles your will, but I think ninety-eight percent of the time you're one of the strongest women I've met.

He kissed her on the forehead, "I wouldn't be terribly excited about a woman who had a cold heart of iron. You have a warm beating heart with a steel core; strong on the inside, but tender on the outside." Tanya gave a little smile and nodded. She lay back on the couch. Tolya stood and lifted her legs, putting her feet where he'd been sitting. She gave him a smile and rolled over. Tolya watched her for a moment and then tearing his gaze away, crossed the room to his desk.

He sat down and contacted the bridge. "Hey Frank. I need to make an announcement. Give me COMM, please."

"Sure thing."

The face of a junior tech came up on screen. "Yes, sir."

"I need to make a general announcement. Can you patch me through from here?"

"No problem sir. Give me just a second."

Tolya watched the young man working precisely on the controls. It reminded Tolya of a concert pianist.

The tech looked back up at him. "You're on sir."

Tolya sat forward and assumed his 'official' voice. "May I have your attention? This is Captain Chernov speaking. Attention please."

He waited a count of five. "I reluctantly announce that the execution of the two convicted prisoners has taken place. I am asking for a minute of silence. I want everyone not manning essential stations to stand, face aft and take a minute of silence... We will begin...now!"

Tolya sat watching the clock. He waited till 1258, just to be sure. Then he sat forward and spoke again. "Attention please. Thank you for your participation. Now, I want everyone to get to his or her appropriate place for a transition that will commence at 1330 hours. I repeat. We will enter transition at 1330 hours." He looked at the ship's clock. It was 1300. "Captain out."

When he turned in his chair he found Tanya watching him. She smiled at him and sat up, pointing to the clock. "No time. Besides, I just had a thought that's cheered me up so much I'm ready to go right now."

Tolya arched an eyebrow and waited.

"This whole mess is over. So, once we transition to MS, I can start making plans for a wedding; our wedding!" Her smile was like a spring morning sunrise.

They both stood. "We're almost there," she said and gave him a quick hug. "Let's get going!"

CLEANING HOUSE — 7

TUE 02.23.2094
36.56 ly, line of sight from Sol
Between '6 Comae Berenices' in Coma Berenices and 'Denebola' in Leo
ECS Destiny, Command Deck, Command Bridge, 1315 Hrs

Tanya stood next to Tolya's command chair watching orderly preparations percolate about the room. She whispered in his ear.

His eyes widened and he slapped a palm to his forehead. "I totally forgot!" He looked at the clock. Fifteen minutes.

Apology was written all over his face. "I'm so sorry. Would you please fetch our young guest?"

Tanya grinned and made a very sorry salute. "Yes, sir, captain, sir; I'll be back before you miss me."

Tolya stage whispered, "I miss you already," as she glided off the bridge and out the door.

Tolya got back to work. So far, everything was going well. The power up cycle was progressing; the helm reported a clear board. He waved his hand over the control screen pad.

Daryl's face lit up on his screen. "Hello, Captain."

"Hello yourself, Chief. The power buildup looks good from here. How's everything down there?"

Daryl grinned, "Well, and good. The excitement is very infectious down here."

"I'm not surprised, Chief."

"Well, they've been doing make-work for nearly a week. It's good to be going somewhere again."

Daryl looked to one side, nodded and pointed before turning back. "I'd better get going...never a dull moment."

"Very good, Chief. I'll see you in Multi-Space." He flicked a dismissive finger, closing connection.

The bridge doors snapped open to admit Tanya and a young and very excited Dennis Douglas. The count down clock read six minutes, thirty-two seconds.

Tolya waved the boy closer. Dennis followed Tanya around the command cluster, eyes wide in wonder.

"Hello, Dennis. So, what do you think?"

Tanya winked at Tolya as Dennis replied. It was a one-syllable word, a long one, but just one. "Wowwwwww!"

Tolya stood up with a grin. "Yeah, I guess that sums it up. I have an idea."

He turned and raised his voice. "Attention everyone."

Most eyes looked up.

"I want to introduce our honorary captain of the hour. Please welcome Honorary Captain Dennis."

Welcoming grins swept the room.

He waved a hand towards his chair. "Have a seat, Dennis, but don't touch anything just yet."

Dennis scrambled up on the chair and sat, feet hanging nearly a foot off the floor.

Tolya looked at the count down clock, five minutes.

He moved next to the chair, putting a hand on Dennis' shoulder. "In a few minutes, we're going to count down from five to one."

Tolya pointed at the icon for the drive section. "When we get to 'one,' I want you to touch that little picture."

Dennis looked carefully at the display and nodded.

"Touch it and say, 'Go' as loud as you can. Got it?"

Dennis nodded enthusiastically. "Got it!" His shrill voice carried quite well.

"OK" Tolya said. He glanced at Tanya. She'd stationed herself to the right of the chair next to the Ship Systems monitor station. She grinned at his conspiratorial wink.

Tolya signaled the COMM station for ship-wide. "Attention Please. This is the Captain. We will commence transition in two minutes. If you haven't done so, secure yourselves for transition. This is the last announcement. Captain out." He glanced at the count down clock.

One minute. "Ready Dennis?"

"Yup! Ready."

"What are you supposed to do?"

"Count down from five. Then touch this picture and say, 'Go.'"

"Very good, Dennis. You'll make a great captain."

Thirty-seconds.

"OK people, get ready. Report, please." Rapidly the reports flowed. All was green; all was go.

"Thank you. OK, Dennis here we go."

He spoke so all could hear. "We have transition in…" He gently squeezed Dennis' shoulder. "…Five…four…" Two voices rang across the bridge. "…Three…two…one…"

Dennis carefully tapped the icon. It was the p.a. connection to drive section, but he didn't know that. He tapped the icon and yelled at the top of his voice, "Goooooooo!"

A raw surge of power welled up. Dennis, mouth agape in awe and just a little fear, grabbed hold of the arms of the chair, as did Tolya on one side, and Tanya on the other.

There was a stomach-lifting surge like the beginning of a roller-coaster ride at the top of its climb. The scene of stars on the main display screen washed to a ghosted grey before the computer compensated for the new rules of Multi-Space. The surging sensation faded to nothing and it was over.

Tolya roughed Dennis' hair and patted him on the back. "Good job!" He turned to address everyone. "Well done, people."

He signaled COMM for ship-wide. "Attention please. This is Captain Chernov. You may stand down from transition stations. Transition was successful."

Turning to Tanya, he grasped her hand and continued. "For better or for worse, we're on the way."

Stars In The Deep
~Destiny~

Book 2

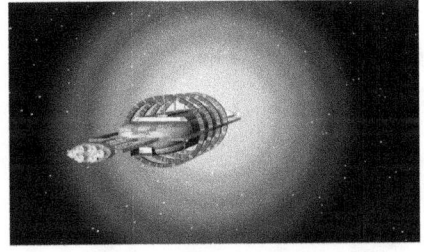

New Road to *Destiny*

By

David F. Snider

Stars in the Deep
Volume 1: Book 2

Table of Contents

Chapter Sections	Starting Page
On the Way 1 - 6	165
Preparation 1 - 9	220
Celebration 1 - 9	275
Wet Reception 1 - 5	331
Fundamental Changes 1 - 5	365
Healer by Default 1 - 6	394
Rite of Passage 1 - 11	413

ON THE WAY — 1

Tolya sat at his desk. He touched an icon and opened the COMM feature. Looking vacantly at a spot on the bulkhead, he reviewed what he'd say. Finally, he waved a hand and the screen displayed the ready window.

"Routing?" The AI asked.

"O'Connor residence; Promenade Deck..."

Kaitlyn's cheery face lit up the screen and she smiled her recognition. "Well, if it isn't our favorite Romeo! How ya doin'?"

Tolya grinned, "I'm doing great, Katie! Things are almost back to normal."

Kaitlyn nodded, "It's almost boring after all the excitement of the last few weeks."

Tolya's smile was just slightly strained. "Yeah, I hope one day, I can leave that chapter behind. Listen, is Shane home?"

"Oh, no. He's up on the Mezzanine. Today's artisan's market day. He said something about some special shopping.

Tolya looked thoughtful, "Artisan's market day? Hmm. So, when do you expect him home?"

Kaitlyn glanced at the time display. She thought for a moment. "I'd say in about a half hour or so."

Tolya shrugged. "Ok. I think I'll wander on down there and see if I can catch him in the act. When he gets back, would you tell him, I need to discuss something with him?

Kaitlyn smiled again. "Of course. Will you be dropping by the place, then?"

Tolya grinned. "Would I hear the end if I didn't?"

"Probably not!" She grinned back, "See ya soon."

"Sure. Bye now." He broke the connection and ran a comb through his hair before heading for the door. The door snapped open as he squeezed the tab on his collar. "Tanya," he intoned.

"Chief Nydel here."

He smiled fondly as he crossed for the lift well. "Hey sweet! How's it going?"

He heard her grin. "Things are cooking along fine. What's up?"

"Well, I wanted to let you know I'm off to have a chat with Shane. I'll be wandering around the Mezzanine. It's artisan's market day." At the lift well he waved for a car.

"Is it now?" she asked. The lift doors snapped open and he stepped inside. He tapped Deck 3 and the doors snapped shut. "Yes, indeed. After that, I'll probably be at Shane's place for a while. If you can get away, I could meet you there."

The lift stopped and the doors snapped open. Tanya replied. "Well, we'll see what happens. I'm going over plans with Emily on what we can do to...um, I mean, for our friend, Felix."

Tolya grinned as the lift doors snapped shut behind him. "Well, it looks like you have your hands full then. Tell you what; if you can't make it, I'll drop by after I'm done here."

Tanya replied, "OK. If I can get away, I'll call."

"OK, love you."

"Back at ya!" The connection closed as Tolya strolled onto the mezzanine on artisan's market day.

* * * *

Emily Strauss watched Tanya's conversation with Tolya. She suppressed a grin and glanced back at the list of activities the two conspirators were working up for the young man in the cell a few steps away. Tanya's 'Back at ya,' caused Emily to look up.

Their eyes met and both broke out with quiet laughter. "Tanya, you practically glow whenever he calls you."

Tanya grinned and shrugged her shoulders. She finally found the nerve to ask her question. "So, how are things going with you and Frank?"

It was Emily's turn to flush and gaze off into space. "I think we're doing well. He's kinda shy about the subject, but we've got plenty of time."

Tanya sat back and placed a boot on her desk. "You know, I remember watching everyone coming in for that first staff meeting after the NAV screw-up; you know, when everything went crazy?"

Emily nodded.

"Well, I remember watching everyone, trying to figure out who was with who. I remember Frank came in looking so worried, and when he sat down, you gave him a little smile. He seemed to gather strength and confidence from just that little smile. That was my first clue there was something there."

Emily grinned, remembering the meeting. "Yeah, that was the day Tolya decided I should make his presentation."

Tanya grinned and Emily continued. "I knew I was interested in Frank about three months ago. That was just after we started the transition that ended up off course. You know, he's been watching me for almost a year now. For a while, I just tried to ignore him.

"See..." she hesitated a moment and then made up her mind. "When I signed onto *Destiny* I was leaving behind a messy break up. I was engaged to this guy when I discovered he'd been screwing around behind my back."

Tanya frowned. "I've never had that happen." She realized how silly that sounded. "Tolya's my first relationship. I guess I was a social dud."

Emily smiled. "You got lucky, you know; the right one, the first try? Unheard of, at least in my world."

Tanya shrugged. "I guess you're right. So, what happened with the player?"

Emily seemed to look back in time. "Well, as you can imagine, I was devastated. I'd been warned he was going to hurt me, but I was so head over heals I wouldn't listen. When I learned the truth, I wanted to dig a hole, crawl into it and die."

Tanya shook her head. "I'm so sorry."

Emily put her list back on Tanya's desk. "Don't be. It all worked out for the better. Lacking the guts to go off and die, I decided to leave the jerk and everybody else behind and start my life over. Hence, my presence on *Destiny*."

She got back to the purpose of the history lesson. "Anyway, I started noticing Frank, who isn't hard to notice, mind you. He was always watching me, but if he caught my eyes, he'd turn away as if he'd been looking elsewhere."

She shook her head. "For months I tried to ignore him, but one day, I was sitting in the diner and it was really busy. Frank came up with his lunch and looked around. He actually worked up the nerve to speak to me."

Tanya was all ears. This was the first time she'd ever had an intimate conversation with Emily. It felt good to be accepted enough to share such a private moment.

Emily continued. "He was very polite and asked if I minded him sitting at my table. What was I going to say? Go away?"

Tanya grinned and Emily continued. "We had a very pleasant conversation. He went his way and I went mine, but from then on, he'd seek out my table and it slowly became a routine. We've had a long history of great conversations."

Tanya put her feet down and sat up. "So, when will the great conversations become something more?"

Emily grinned. "Well, a few weeks before that staff meeting you mentioned, he asked me if we could start seeing each other. I'm afraid I cracked up. We'd been unofficially seeing each other for weeks. I could see my mirth hurt him. I felt bad, so I reached out and took his hand. I explained I'd been taking it for granted for a while and he blushed."

Tanya laughed. "So, what's next?"

Emily shrugged. "I know he wants to move to the next level. He's the quintessential gentleman. I think you and Tolya have prompted him that way. He'll get there...and I'll be ready."

"You will, will you?" Emily grinned.

"Yeah, I don't know what's come over me in the last few months. I really think I'm ready to try again." She winked, "He's a keeper. I know it."

They laughed and then bent over the waiting list.

* * * *

Tolya wandered the mezzanine. Apparently, on artisan's market day, the open area was festooned with ribbon, posters, and colored paper. Small carnival booth tents were erected and strewn in a haphazard sort of organization. The whole affair lent itself a delightfully festive atmosphere.

He strolled about, watching the people interact. Gleeful, noisy children ran helter-skelter between the legs of haggling venders and their customers. Couples walked along or sat on benches or in one of the two dinning patios on either side.

Tolya went from booth to booth, inspecting the amazing array of wares. He found Shane checking out a small flower shop. His inquiry resulted in a boisterous reminder of Kaitlyn's birthday coming up the next day.

Tolya, feeling about three inches tall, started going over the flowers too.

A rudimentary barter system had asserted itself and worked reasonably well. Tolya and the shopkeeper haggled in good humor and agreed on a price. Tolya waved his patch at the reader, punched in the agreed upon credits and took his selection. He thanked the shopkeeper and followed Shane across the mezzanine.

"I can't believe I forgot Kaitlyn's birthday. After all these years, I feel so stupid."

Shane laughed. "Just wait, my friend. You've signed up for a great responsibility with that delightful security chief of yours. Just imagine all the dates you'll have to remember, like birthdays, anniversaries, Valentine's Day…the list goes on!"

Tolya laughed and shook his head. "You have a point, but I think the burden's worth bearing."

Shane glanced at him. "You've got it bad, brother."

They returned to Shane's residence. Kaitlyn came bustling from the back and exclaimed with delight at Shane's offering of a beautiful bouquet.

"Happy Birthday, my dear. I know it's a day early, but I could never hide anything from you and tomorrow would've been a bit too late."

She tipped up on her toes and delivered a very delighted kiss. "They're beautiful!"

She turned to greet Tolya. He bowed formally and pulled a single rose from behind his back. "Happy Birthday, Kaitlyn. You look younger than ever. What's your secret?"

She chuckled, deftly plucking the rose and gave him a quick peck on the cheek. "You'd better keep that silver tongue polished, mister. You've someone who'll be wanting your charming comments to herself."

Tolya grinned, "I expect you're right."

"I know I am."

Shane and Tolya exchanged commiserating looks and they all laughed heartily.

They sat down in the front room and chatted. Tolya had thought to discuss his concerns with Shane first, but now he decided to make it a joint discussion.

"Shane, Kaitlyn. I confess I didn't come just to visit. Tanya and I discussed something recently and I wanted to talk it over with you." His closest friends glanced at one another as if they'd been expecting this.

"First, before I go there, I want to ask you, Shane, if you'd be my best man at the wedding?"

Shane raised his eyebrows and then smiled broadly. "Absolutely, I'd be honored."

"Good. I could use some advice on weddings."

He turned to Kaitlyn. "My dear, I have a very strong feeling Tanya will ask her assistant, Sherry, to be her maid of honor. I hope you'll understand."

Kaitlyn chuckled. "Of course. I'd hardly expect her to ask me. We've just met. I do hope she'll let me be of some kind of help."

Tolya smiled. "Oh, I'm certain she'll be begging for help. We only have a month before we get to this new system. That's when we want the ceremony."

Kaitlyn smiled and glanced at her husband. "Just so long as Mr. O'Connor here doesn't forget 'who the fairest of them all' truly is, I foresee no difficulties."

Shane looked mortally wounded and they all laughed again.

Shane sobered first, "It's about Lyuba isn't it?"

Tolya winced. This had been a difficult topic over the years. The O'Connors' had been faithful and loving in their sacrifice, caring for his niece; but it was really unfair to them and their own children to expect it to go on forever.

They denied being put out by his perpetual failures, but he sensed deep down, they were just waiting for him to take hold of the situation.

Tolya looked down considering his words carefully. "Yes, it's about Lyuba. Tanya and I had a heart to heart talk about her. Actually, Tahnie brought the subject up. I was afraid to mention it, because I thought it would be too much, too soon. I guess I still have a lot to learn about her."

Kaitlyn smiled. "Yes, you've a very generous and considerate lady on your hook."

Tolya flushed and hurried on. "I know you've given of yourselves, above and beyond the call of duty, to help with Lyuba. I can't begin to express how grateful I am."

He cleared his throat. "We've decided we want to formally adopt Lyuba. It's something I've considered for a long time, but never discussed. Tanya left me speechless when she declared her wishes on this."

Kaitlyn grabbed her husband's hand and leaned in close to him. Hints of tears glistened in her eyes. "I thought that's where she was headed. I don't know her story, but Tanya connected with Lyuba in a way I'd never have expected."

She looked at Shane, and then turned back to Tolya. "You know we love Lyuba an awful lot, but I think Shane would agree, this is the best thing that could happen to her." She dabbed her eyes and continued. "I hope you know she practically worships the ground you walk on." Shane nodded, silent, letting Kaitlyn carry the ball.

Tolya felt awkward. "I know. I don't know what kind of dad I'd make, but I've always wanted to take on the roll. For Tanya to step right in, eyes wide open, with full support, it's something I never dreamed of."

Shane spoke up. "Tolya, I think, between the two of you, Lyuba couldn't possibly do better." He leaned forward. "Besides, it's not like she's going very far. I think both of us would be devastated if we never saw her again."

Kaitlyn smiled through her tears. "Of course. She'll just be up a few decks."

Tolya looked up from the floor where he'd been staring. "Certainly. She'd be free to come and go between decks. Besides, you've always been free to come up and see me. It's just nicer to come here."

He combed a hand through his hair. "I've got to talk with her. How do you think she'll react? Do you think she'd even want to be adopted...by me?"

He was suddenly full of doubt. Was he going to be adequate to the task? Could his little Lyuba really want to call him father? What about Tanya? Would Lyuba love her the same?

Kaitlyn leaned forward and gripped Tolya's arm. "Yes, Tolya. You must talk to her. Just tell her your feelings. Let her know you love her and wish to be there for her."

Tolya looked up and she smiled. "I know she loves you. She's never talked about it, but I think secretly she fancies you could be her dad." She sat back in her seat.

Shane gripped Tolya by the shoulder. "No matter what, we're here to help. I think this story has a happy ending for both of you; heck all three of you." He gave a brotherly pat.

Kaitlyn added, "Tanya will need to talk with her too. Once you settle things with Lyuba, you and Tanya should get together and talk it over. Frankly, I don't see much of a problem. Tanya's already managed to find a little corner of Lyuba's heart."

Kaitlyn glanced at the clock and got up quickly. She snagged a tissue from a dispenser by the couch and dabbed her eyes quickly. "Lyuba will be home...uh...here...any minute. Her classes ended about five minutes ago. Come on, let's have some coffee and cheer up. We're not talking about a funeral, after all."

She hurried to the kitchenette and started the coffee as the men followed. Shane pulled three cups from a cupboard and set them out at the table.

They'd just started in on their coffee when the front door snapped open and a whirlwind sailed in. Lyuba stopped in her tracks when she spied Tolya.

"Uncle Toly!" She tossed her things on the couch and hurried into the dining room and straight into Tolya's arms. Tolya grinned and buried his face in her hair and gave her a great big bear hug.

Lyuba pulled back and looked up earnestly. "You never come after school. Aren't you busy today?

Tolya grinned. "No Princess, it's less busy in MS."

He brushed hair out of her eyes and looked at her. "I thought it might be fun to come down here and surprise you. I got your aunt Kaitlyn a flower for her birthday and then waited around for you to get here."

Shane got up and subtly motioned for Kaitlyn to follow. "Hey Lyuba, we're going to go check out the market before it gets too late. You can visit with your uncle for a while till we get back."

Lyuba looked at Shane and Kaitlyn, her expression suggested she sensed a shift in the winds. "Um...ok. See you later."

"Sure thing." Shane said. Kaitlyn gave her a kiss on the cheek before taking her husbands arm.

Lyuba looked thoughtfully at the door and then faced Tolya. "What's up with them? They look sad."

Tolya smiled. "Oh, they'll be OK..." He struggled a moment, trying to get the topic going. "Lyuba, honey?"

She looked at him like she'd looked after the O'Connors. "Are you OK, Uncle Toly?

Tolya smiled. "Yes, dear heart. I'm fine."

He decided to just dive in. "I came to talk to you about something very important."

He reached over and pulled out a chair for her. "It's something I wanted to talk to you about a long time ago, but, well, I just didn't know how."

Lyuba sat on the edge of the chair and looked serious. "What's wrong Uncle Toly?"

Tolya kissed her forehead. She was so serious and concerned. "Nothing's wrong dear one."

He thought for a moment and then asked. "Lyuba, do you remember your dad and mom at all?"

Lyuba got a curious look on her face and shook her head. "Not really. All I know about them are the few things you've told me."

Tolya nodded his head. "Yeah, you were just a baby when we lost them."

He asked another question. "So, does it ever bother you that you don't have your own dad and mom?"

Lyuba got very quiet. Tolya feared he'd upset her when she finally answered him. "I think about that a lot. All of my friends have dads and moms and they're really happy; well, most of the time, anyways."

She tried to hide the tears welling up in her eyes. "A while ago, some of the kids at school said I was weird because I didn't have parents and they did." Her voice trembled as she said, "All I have is Uncle Shane, Aunt Kaitlyn and you...but that's not the same." The tears came hot and fast.

Tolya held out his arms and she hurried to them for another hug. "I'm so sorry. You're not weird at all. You're a wonderful, pretty young lady."

Lyuba sobbed into his chest for a few moments and he just sat there patting her back gently and stroking her hair. Suddenly she pushed back and looked into his eyes. "I wish you could be my dad...but you're too busy!"

Tolya felt as if he'd been slapped. Then he realized he had the perfect opportunity. "Dear one, that's what I came to talk about."

She wiped her tears. "What do you mean?"

Tolya would have picked her up and put her on his knee just a year or two before. He realized she was getting kind of big for that. He took the unused napkin from his place and handed it to her. "Princess, I've been trying to figure this out for a long time, but I didn't know if you'd be interested. See...I want to be your dad. I want you to be my daughter."

Lyuba's eyes got big as silver dollars. "Really?"

"Absolutely! There's a ceremony that people do sometimes. It's called adoption. Sometimes it's a really big thing like a wedding and sometimes it's just a quiet little meeting, but the result is that everyone knows the person in the ceremony just got a new dad and mom. It's what happened to Tanya when she was in high school."

Lyuba thought for a moment. "Ms. Tanya told me somebody adopted her, but I didn't really know what she was talking about. It sounded nice though."

Tolya smiled. "Yeah, it must be pretty nice."

He gently pulled on her chin, turning her to face him. "Lyuba, would you like to have a ceremony like that so I could be your dad and you could be my daughter?"

Lyuba threw herself into a fierce hug. "Oh, Yes, yes! I wished you were my dad for a long time!"

She stepped back and looked troubled. "...but what about you and Ms. Tanya? You guys are getting married. What's gonna happen then?"

Tolya smiled and, taking another napkin from the table, gently brushed a tear she'd missed from her cheek. "Do you remember the night Tanya came and I told everyone we were getting married?" Lyuba nodded.

"Do you remember the promises she gave you?" Lyuba nodded again.

"Well, she told me all about it. One of those promises was that she was going to do everything she could so you could be with me any time you wanted. Remember?"

Light dawned in her eyes. "She said she was going to fix it so I could see you any time, but she said she wouldn't make empty promises and it might take a long time."

Tolya smiled at her and took her by the shoulders. "Tanya talked to me that night when I walked her back to her quarters. You know what she asked me?"

Lyuba shook her head.

"She asked me why I hadn't adopted you before. I tried to tell her about how busy I was and how unfair it would be to keep you from your friends when I wasn't even going to be there all the time.

"Then she wanted to know why we couldn't adopt you together since we were getting married. Don't you see? She wants to adopt you too."

Lyuba stood there, a stunned expression on her face. The dawn became dazzling sunrise. "I'd get a dad AND a mom!" She seemed to lose focus as she considered the possibilities. "I like Tanya. She was very nice to me and she acted like she really understood me."

Tolya grinned. "She understands you more than you can guess, Princess. I love you just like you were my daughter. I think Tanya has grown to love you the same way. I don't understand it. She's only met you once, but when Tanya decides to love somebody, she puts her whole heart in it."

Tolya stood and took Lyuba's hand. "So, would you like to have your own dad and mom?"

Lyuba grinned. "I'd love it!"

"Well, then...how about coming up to my place, so we can talk about it?"

"Sweet!"

"OK, why don't you go freshen up? When you're ready, we'll go see Tanya."

Lyuba started for the back. "Ok, I'll be right back!"

His coffee was cold, so he poured more to heat it up. After a while the front door snapped open and Shane and Kaitlyn stepped in, question marks on their faces.

He gave a thumbs-up sign. "I hope you don't mind. I'm stealing her for a few hours. We're going to have a little chat with Tanya."

"Oh, Tolya. That's wonderful!" Kaitlyn hurried over and gave him a hug.

Shane shook his hand. "I'm happy for you, old man."

Tolya grinned. "Hey, watch that 'old' stuff."

Lyuba came bustling back into the room dressed informally in a basic pants and shirt outfit. It vaguely resembled the women's uniforms in cut if not in color. She looked grown up somehow.

"I'm ready! Hey, Aunt Kaitlyn, Uncle Shane, Uncle Toly and Ms. Tanya want to adopt me! Isn't that great?"

Kaitlyn gathered her in a hug. "Awesome honey." She blinked back the tears. "Truly awesome!"

ON THE WAY — 2

ECS Destiny, Quarterdeck, SecCentral, 1610 Hrs

They strolled into the lobby of SecCentral hand in hand. Sherry looked up from her desk and gave them a cheery greeting. "Hi Tolya, who do we have here?" She got up and came around the counter to greet Lyuba.

Tolya grinned, "This is my niece, Lyuba. Lyuba, this is Sherry, Tanya's assistant."

Sherry took Lyuba's hand and shook it gently. "So this is Lyuba. She looks just like you, Tolya."

Tolya laughed. "Is Tanya still in?"

Sherry waved her good hand towards the office. "Sure. I think she's finishing up with Emily."

Tolya thanked her and urged Lyuba on.

Tanya looked up as they entered. She took one look at Lyuba and switched her gaze to Tolya, an eyebrow arcing.

Emily shut down her power-tab. "Hey, Tolya. So, who do we have here?"

Tolya placed one hand on Lyuba's back. "This is my niece, Lyuba. She came up to see Tanya."

Emily grinned. "Everyone wants to see Tanya these days." She got up and approached Lyuba. "Hello, Lyuba. My name's Emily. I'm pleased to meet you."

Lyuba smiled and nodded politely. "Hello, Ms. Emily. You're the Science Officer?"

Emily grinned up at Tolya. "Oh, she's a bright one. Yes, I am. I'm also a teacher and a friend of Tanya and your uncle."

Lyuba smiled and Tolya asked. "So, how are things going with our young friend?" He pointed in the general direction of the security cells.

Tanya laughed. "Emily gave him a battery of tests. She's going to go over them to figure out just where he is in his schooling. He's very sharp, to hear Emily's comments."

Emily grinned. "Yeah, he shows some real promise. He just needed the right people around him to get motivated, and I think his recent brush with mortality got his attention."

Tolya smiled. "I'm glad. I hoped something good would come out of all that grief."

Emily picked up her power-tab and moved towards the door. "Well, I have to go over all this stuff now and figure out what we're going to do with him. So, I'll leave you three to chat. See you later."

Lyuba moved up close to Tanya, looking around.
"So, this is where you work?" She asked.

Tanya nodded. "Yep. This is it. If it gets too interesting, like the last couple of weeks, I work all over the ship, but this is it when things are normal."

Lyuba nodded and continued looking around the room. Tanya shot a questioning look at Tolya. "I have an idea," he announced. "Why don't we go up to my standby cabin? We can eat up there."

Tanya raised an eyebrow and then smiled. "Sure, how about it Lyuba, hungry?"

Lyuba smiled. "Yeah. We could eat and talk."

Tanya chuckled and got up from her chair. "Let's go then." She gently squeezed Lyuba's shoulder and they left the office.

Sherry winked at Lyuba. "Bye, everybody."

Tanya nodded and grinned. "Sherry, don't bore Felix to death in there. OK?"

Sherry's face turned pink. "Bore him? Never."

Their laughter drifted down the corridor.

* * * *

They stepped out of the lift on Command Deck and Lyuba drank in the view. It was the first time she'd been up here. Tolya wondered why he'd never thought to have her up before. He decided to include a side trip through the bridge.

The doors snapped open. Vince glanced up and called out, "Captain on the Bridge." Everyone snapped to working attention.

Tolya grinned. "As you were."

Lyuba stood rooted to the floor staring at everything at once. "This is it? This is the Bridge?"

Tolya stepped up and hugged her next to him. "Yes, Princess," he said quietly. "This is the command bridge; the heart and brains of the ship."

She began to wander from station to station. Touching the edge of the nearest console she uttered, "COMM."

Slowly she walked the stations clockwise around the room. At the next one she recited, "Graviton Pulse Deflector Control." Front center, "NavCom and Helm, where you steer the ship." On the right she touched another panel. "Engineering."

Tanya looked at Tolya and raised an eloquent eyebrow. Lyuba kept moving, reciting the station names and basic functions.

Tolya could no longer resist. "Honey, where'd you learn that?"

Lyuba grinned. "I always wanted to know what you did in here. So, I looked it up on ShipNet."

She finished her circuit, facing Vince in the command chair. "Hi. I'm Lyuba."

Vince grinned, offering his hand. "Hello, Lyuba. I'm Vince. I'm your uncle's first officer."

She shook his hand gravely. "So, you're kinda like the assistant captain, right?"

Vince grinned. He looked up at Tolya. "Well, kinda. Yeah."

Tolya came to his rescue. "Yes, Vince is the number two guy around here. I'd be in all kinds of trouble if he didn't come and help me out from time to time."

He chuckled and then turned to Vince. "We're going to have a mini-dinner conference next door. If I'm needed, I'll be in there. If possible, I'd rather not be disturbed."

Vince nodded. "You got it, sir."

Tolya started for the port side doors. "Oh, keep up the good work, everyone."

* * * *

They gathered around Tolya's desk, making selections from the menu. After Tolya sent the order, he motioned to the table. "Well, ladies? Let's sit and talk for a while. When the meals come we can take a break for dinner. OK?"

Lyuba grinned. "OK."

Tolya sat at the head of the table and glanced at Tanya on his right. "Tanya, Lyuba and I had a very interesting discussion and we thought it would be a good idea to discuss it with you."

Tanya's pulse quickened as she realized what he was saying. She looked across the table at the young lady. "So, what did you two talk about?" She wanted Lyuba to speak her own mind.

Tolya seemed to be reading her mind. "Why don't YOU tell her, Lyuba?"

Lyuba nodded her head, watching Tanya intently. "Uncle Toly asked me if it was OK to adopt me."

She was trying to be very serious about it, but Tanya could sense an underlying excitement that wanted to bubble out. "I kinda thought that might be it. Did he tell you we talked about it?"

Lyuba nodded, a smile winning its way onto her face. "Did you really say you wanted to adopt me too?"

Tanya blinked. *Why do these things always get me all teary eyed?* She smiled, "Yes, honey. I did."

Lyuba considered this. "Why? I mean, Uncle Toly said you only met me once."

Tanya chuckled through the tears and Tolya handed over the tissue box.

She squeezed his hand before snatching a tissue. "Why? That is a very wise question, one I wish I'd asked all those people who promised to love me and take care of me and then sent me back to the shelter."

She dabbed her eyes, trying to get control of herself. "The quick answer is, you remind me a whole lot of me when I was your age. I want your life to be happier...but there's more to it than that."

She considered her words. "Just because you've only met someone once doesn't mean you can't love them. I believe love is more than just feelings. It's something you choose to do, to give to someone else. I didn't know it when I first met your uncle, but I had already decided somewhere in the back of my heart that I wanted to love him. I was just too scared to admit it.

"When your uncle told me about you, and showed me the pictures in his album, I liked you already. When I met you the night we came over, I decided I could love you too. I just didn't know how much yet."

Lyuba thought it over. "I told Uncle Toly I'd always wanted him for my dad. I never thought I'd get a mom too."

Lyuba got up and came around the table. She put a hand on Tanya's arm. "I'd love to have you as my mom."

Tanya chuckled through her tears and grabbed another tissue. "You would?"

Lyuba smiled. "Cross my heart."

Tanya pulled Lyuba into a warm embrace. Just then the door announcer chimed. Tolya got up. "That's probably dinner."

He signaled the door open and a kitchen helper wheeled a cart in. He expertly set everything out formally on the table before turning to leave.

"Thank you Ruben." Tolya clapped the older man on the shoulders. "I appreciate the trouble."

"Not at all Captain, not at all." He grinned back at Tolya and trundled his cart back out into the hall.

They kept the conversation light over dinner. Tanya talked about the Felix project she was helping Emily with.

Lyuba talked about school and friends. She told them all about her study of the systems on the bridge; how it made her feel closer to Tolya by understanding what went on there. Finally, they stacked their empty plates and set them on the end of the table. Tolya got up and invited the women over to the couch in front of the huge window. Tolya sat with his favorite ladies on either side. "I'd open the curtain, but there's nothing to see when we're in Multi-Space."

He thought for a moment. "I think we all agree we want to adopt Lyuba and Lyuba wants to be adopted. Right?"

There was a pleasant duet of approval. "Ok, before we discuss how we want to do this, I think we should make sure we know what we're getting into."

Lyuba snuggled against him. "What do you mean?"

Tanya snuggled on the other side.

A man could get used to this! He decided. "Well, here's what I think adoption's about..."

They discussed at great length what it meant to adopt and be adopted. Near the end Lyuba asked. "So you mean, when we have this ceremony, it'll be just like I was your real daughter...like I was born that way?"

Tolya grinned and Tanya squeezed. "That's right. This isn't make-believe here. This is for real. Just like a marriage is supposed to be. In a way, I think marriage and adoption are very similar."

They sat cuddled together for a long while.

* * * *

ECS Destiny, Quarterdeck, SecCentral, 1700 Hrs

Sherry put her computer to sleep for the evening before walking across the aisle to the first detention block. Felix looked up from the book he was reading.

"Hey. Are you hungry? I'm done for the night and I was going to go for a bite at the diner. I um..I could get you something...if you'd like."

Felix put the book reader down on his bunk and came to the door. "I guess I could use a bite. I forget the time in here...Is it really closing time?"

"Yeah. Everybody's gone. So, what do you want?"

Felix regarded her frankly, still wondering how she could be so kind to him. "I don't know...you could surprise me."

Sherry grinned. "OK. I'll go get a couple of dinners and come right back."

"Thanks," he said simply.

Felix watched her walk away and wondered how he could have ever hurt her. He turned and went back to his bunk and resumed his reading.

He was startled when, twenty minutes later, he heard some clattering around in the front of the offices. He got up and looked out to see what was going on.

He was in time to see Sherry dragging a small card table out of the storage closet. She came up to the door and put the table in front of it. She glanced up at him, grinned and retreated to collect more things.

She did most of this one handed; her cast made things awkward for her. This only served to make Felix even more regretful of his treatment of her. Soon she placed a tray with two BLT sandwiches and a couple of salads on the table, arranging it so she could sit next to the door where he could reach items off the table. "So, pull up your chair."

Felix shrugged and dragged up the chair parked next to a tiny desk. He sat and watched her organize things.

"I couldn't decide what you'd like, so I just guessed. I hope you like BLT's." She grabbed a napkin, expertly wrapped the sandwich, placed it on a plate and carefully slid it through the horizontal slats. He took the plate and looked around. Reaching over with one hand, he nabbed the tiny desk and dragged it over.

They both laughed when it came to trying to get the salad through. Sherry didn't have leave to use the detention keys to open his cell, so she couldn't open up and hand him stuff.

Finally, she had an idea. She shook her head and said, "I'm sorry, but this salad's not going to look very pretty after I get done here."

She carefully shook the plate so the salad and dressing settled flatter on the plate. She was right. It didn't look like much. She set the plate on one of the slats and slowly slid it inch by inch under the one above.

The shaking had been just enough. Felix took it and finished pulling it through, placing it next to his sandwich.

"That's OK," he said. "It's gonna look a lot worse when I'm done with it."

Sherry got comfortable in her chair. "So, I don't know about you, but food tastes better if you eat with someone."

Felix was confused. Sherry had been pleasant with him ever since the trial. She hadn't said more than simple greetings, but she never seemed to miss an opportunity. Those greetings were always sweetly offered and he thought he might go crazy trying to understand her.

Finally, he could no longer stand it. "Um...Sherry?"

She looked up, happily chewing a bit of her sandwich.

"Why are you doing this? I mean, after what I did to you, you should be avoiding me; I don't know, giving me dirty looks or something like that."

Sherry shrugged and swallowed. "I don't know. Tanya asked me the same thing. In fact, she was mad at me because I wouldn't press charges."

She put her sandwich down and turned to look at him directly. "Honestly, I really wanted to be nasty to you when I first woke up. Then, when we were in MedCentral, I...I don't know. Something just changed. Like I told Tanya. I like you." She pointed at him. "I still think there's someone better hiding in there." She took another healthy bite of her sandwich.

Felix felt more perplexed. "Well, I appreciate your kindness. I just don't think I deserve it."

Sherry looked quizzically at him. "Does anyone 'deserve' to be liked, or loved by anyone? I'm not the brightest light on the light pole, but I do know that some things just are. It doesn't matter if you deserve friendship, but it does matter that it's offered."

Felix just sat and looked at her for a few moments. He grabbed his sandwich and took his first bite.

Suddenly, Sherry jumped up and dashed to the storage closet that still stood open. She took longer coming back, balancing a couple of covered coffees.

"I forgot them when I got the table."

She managed to safely deposit them on the table and then, since they were well sealed, tipped one on its side and handed it to him before resuming her seat.

"So, how about telling me a little about yourself?"

Felix shrugged. "There's not much to tell, I guess. When I was about ten years old, my old man ran out on my mom. She'd always hoped he'd come back, but a few years later, he got himself killed in a fight with some guy. She couldn't handle his death and started into using hard drugs. I grew up watching her slowly turn into a crazed animal. Only the drugs could keep her happy...but that was really a lie.

"I was doin' OK in school till she started fallin' apart. I got in with a small gang and discovered I had some very interesting talents. I could snatch things right off of people and they never knew about it till I was long gone.

"My 'friends' were amazed and thought I was cool. I kept a little food on the table that way. I had to help my mom keep her supply going. I thought she'd die without it. By then I was doin' terrible in school. I was always absent and never paid attention when I was there. When I stopped going to school, my mom yelled at me a lot, but I had to take care of her and us, so I got good at doin' my thing."

Sherry's eyes were wide. She forgot to eat.

"One day, I came home with a little food. She was really sick and I was worried. She'd been usin' that garbage even more than usual. I went to tell her we had something to eat and I found her on the floor by her bed. The empty syringe was there next to her hand..."

He looked up at her, a hint of moisture in his eyes. He shook his head trying not to get emotional. After a moment he continued. "I collected all her stash, took it out in the back alley and burned it. It made the brightest bonfire."

He stared off into a distance only he could see. "I never learned what happened to her body. The police and the par-meds came when I called, but I was under age and had no say about anything.

"They tried to put me in foster care because I had no other family. I was fifteen by then and I thought I could take care of myself, so I ran away and tried to set up business in another neighborhood."

He took a sip of his coffee and Sherry speared a tomato from her salad. "OK, so what happened when you moved to the new neighborhood?" Sherry prompted as she sipped her coffee.

"Well, it took me a while to establish my territory. I had some competition. I should have known I was headed for trouble, but I was determined to prove something; what, I don't even know.

"I wound up in jail three times in two years." He took another sip and a big bite of his sandwich.

Sherry remembered her salad and took another bite. She grabbed another napkin and then thought of another question. "So, how'd you wind up on *Destiny*?"

Felix shrugged. "After I got out of jail the last time, I knew I had to get away from everything and start a new life. My parole officer recommended me to the foundation. I didn't think they'd accept me, but they did. So, here I am.

"Unfortunately, my intentions at reform got side tracked by my old habits of snatching things. Then I met Ted Jackson and you know the rest of the story."

They ate in companionable silence. Felix finally got up the nerve to ask, "So, do I get to hear your story? I'd like to know how such an attractive girl wound up by herself, taking a one way trip to the other side of the universe."

Sherry turned a pleasant shade of red. She sat back and took a sip of her coffee before starting. "I was born in Greece. We lived there for about eight years. When I was nine, my dad's business changed somehow and we wound up moving back to the States. We lived in Monterey, California. You ever been there?"

Felix shook his head. "I never left Chicago."

Sherry smiled. "You'd have loved it in Monterey. It's on the South end of a deep bay on the coast of California. The wind off the bay keeps the air fresh and clean. Monterey was my favorite place in the world."

He looked up. "Didn't somethin' bad happen there?"

Sherry nodded and her face turned sad. "Yeah, you could say that. It was in 2082. My family went back to Greece for a vacation to see old friends. That's why I'm still in the land of the living. The terrorists targeted the Army base in town. They said it was a suitcase bomb.

"Anyway, somehow the police found out about what was happening and wound up chasing the terrorists all over the city. When the terrorists figured they wouldn't reach their target, they picked a spot and triggered the bomb as they drove through.

"For a nuke it was kinda small, I guess, but most of the town was devastated. My parents shortened their vacation and we flew back to the states. Of course we weren't allowed back into the city, so I never saw what was left of our home. All I know is thousands of people died."

She sat staring at her hands for a few moments. Finally she worked up a brave smile. "Anyways, that was a sad chapter, but we moved on. My parents moved to San Jose. It's a large city just north and east of Monterey. My dad was ready to retire by then and I went off to San Jose State University. I'd developed an interest in criminal justice. So, I entered the program there.

"When I graduated, I started looking around for a position locally. There were no jobs available and I was thinking about moving east when the foundation put out its add for volunteers. I was fascinated."

Sherry smiled fondly and stared at nothing for a moment. "My parents went crazy when I told them my plans. 'We'll never see you again.' They said. I just wanted to do something brave and new. I told them I had to do this. I love my folks, but they didn't want to come; 'too old,' they said."

She put her coffee cup down and organized the dirty tableware. Felix handed his plate and bowl through the bars and watched her stack them.

She looked at him. "I'll always miss them, but I'm glad I chose to come. I've found purpose, adventure and friends. I have people who treat me like family and trust me and take care of me. What more can anyone want?"

Felix thought for a moment. "I guess you're right. I've managed to alienate almost everyone in my life so far. I guess I could use friends like that."

Sherry stood and moved up to the door. She looked him in the eyes. "I'd like to be one of those friends if you want. I think you'll find Tanya and the McIntyre's are on your side, and if you have Tanya, you'll probably win the captain."

Felix looked doubtful. "You want to be my friend? Do you really think your friends will too?"

Sherry put her hand over the one he had gripping the bar. "Of course I want to be your friend. Why else am I here instead of off doing something else?

"As to Tanya and the Captain, Tanya wants to believe in you and she has a lot, I mean, a lot of influence with the captain, in case you haven't figured that out."

Felix looked puzzled.

"Man!" Sherry was amazed. "For such a bright guy, you don't pay much attention to people around you. Tanya and the Captain are engaged to marry. Once we finish this leg of the voyage, there'll be a wedding. You didn't know that?"

Felix shook his head, his surprise complete. "I never guessed. I've been sitting around in here, moping, so I guess I've not been very observant."

Then a light came on and his eyes widened. "She went to bat for me with the captain even before the trial, didn't she?"

Sherry nodded. "Part of that's my fault. I had a little argument with Tanya about pressing charges. I persuaded her not to, and then she had a talk with the Captain. Because you cooperated, they could justify lightening your sentence."

Felix sat staring at his shoes. "She's been working with Emily Strauss, planning all kinds of academic tests and stuff. They want to get me caught up on my education." He looked at her. "I didn't think Tanya was honestly that interested. I thought she was just, you know, doing her duty...just like everyone else did."

Sherry took his empty coffee cup and set it next to hers on the table. "Felix, I want you to try hard. I think you can do a lot when you put your mind to it. I think if you make every effort not to screw this up, you can even win the captain's respect and trust. Don't forget, he's the governor too. You could really use him on your side."

Felix looked up at her. "Thank you, Sherry. Thank you for being so kind to me. I was horrible to you, and yet you've been nicer to me than anyone else."

He paused, considering his words. "I want to do better. I'm tired of the stupid mess I've made of my life. You and your friends have given me hope."

Sherry grinned. "You're more than welcome...I better get going. I'll see you tomorrow." She turned to go and then looked back over her shoulder. "I'm betting on you, Felix."

ON THE WAY — 3

THU 02.25.2094
ECS Destiny, Quarterdeck, McIntyre's Residence, 1110 Hrs

Frank stepped from the lift and headed for his cabin.

Daryl left Tolya's cabin and gave a nod. "How's it goin' Frank?"

Frank shrugged. "OK. What're you two up to?"

Daryl grinned, "We were discussing the wedding. Tolya wanted some advice. Somehow, I've become the expert."

They stood near the micro-park situated between Tolya's cabin and the Conference Room.

"Well, Daryl. You're the senior married guy up here. I guess that makes you expert by default."

They chuckled together. Then Frank took on a more serious tone. "You know, speaking of advice, if you have a minute, I could use a little myself."

Daryl raised an eyebrow, motioned for Frank to follow, and headed back towards his stateroom. "Come on in. Naomi's off with Midori. They're trying to decide on a location for the wedding."

Frank shrugged. "That's nice."

Daryl grinned, "So, you can have my ear for a little while." Daryl scooted a chair from the dinette over and Frank snagged it. He grabbed the second one and sat down. "So, what's up?"

Frank shrugged. "Well, I...I guess you've figured out I've been seeing Emily."

Daryl chuckled. "Yeah, these things don't stay secret in such a small community."

Frank looked uncomfortable. "Why's this so hard? If I was trying to work out a difficult navigation problem or unraveling a software mess, I'd know just what to do and make it work."

Daryl was truly puzzled. "Wait, what's so difficult? You've got a thing for Emily and its clearly mutual."

Frank shrugged and looked more uncomfortable. "That's the thing. We get along just great. We have fantastic conversations, but it never goes anywhere."

Daryl raised an eyebrow as he started to see the difficulty. "Look Frank. I know you're familiar with the term, 'operator error'."

Frank looked at Daryl, puzzled. "Operator error? Yeah, but what's that got to do with..."

Daryl laughed. "Frank. One of the advantages of being married is that you get to hear things your woman hears from her friends. It's not always an advantage, mind you, but sometimes the volumes of data yield fantastic insights."

Daryl leaned forward and put on a conspiratorial tone. "Women tell each other things we men are seldom privy to. For instance, Naomi often chats with Tanya and Emily. They know things about Emily I bet you don't even know."

Frank looked dubious. "What's that got to do with it?"

Daryl grinned. "Everything Frank, because I'm about to let you in on a little secret. I listen to my wife's babble about conversations with her friends. Most of it I forget right away, but every once in a while, something sticks."

He raised an oratory finger in the air. "For instance, Emily told Naomi and Tanya recently that she's just waiting for you to make the next move. They're all wondering when you're going to get around to it."

Frank's face flushed. "I asked her a while ago if we could officially start seeing each other and she laughed at me."

"Yes," Daryl grinned, "but you were so busy feeling frustrated you didn't listen to her explanation. I know, because the ladies think the whole thing is very entertaining.

"See, Emily wasn't interested in a relationship, but the enormous amount of time you two have spent just being conversational friends has worked its magic better than any artful courting schemes. Somewhere along the way, Emily took it for granted the two of you were 'seeing each other' because of your routine lunch time sessions."

Frank scrubbed his face with a big hand. "She assumes we're already 'seeing' each other?"

Daryl laughed. "Frank, Frank. Have you ever dated before?"

"Well, not really. I mean...I had plenty of bright young ladies to talk to and work with on my projects in school, but nothing ever came of it."

Daryl shook his head. "I don't get you kids! Frank. Sometimes a woman reaches a point where she decides the guy she's landed as a friend would make a great mate, but for some reason, she waits for the man to point out the fact."

He got up and drew a couple cups of coffee from the dispenser in the mini-kitchenette. He handed one to Frank and sat down. "Frank. Do you love her?"

Frank stopped mid-sip and stared. "Well, yes, of course I do."

Daryl nodded. "Well, from what I hear, she's waiting patiently for you to say so."

"But...I've never said that to anyone but family. It's not that easy to say to...its...I don't know..."

Daryl shrugged. "You've got to tell her sometime. If you wait too long, she'll think she was mistaken about you and give up."

"How am I supposed to do that? I'm no hot blooded Romeo with slick gushy lines."

Daryl stood, reached over and clapped Frank on the shoulder. "Change the routine. Ask her to go with you someplace special, maybe the garden and fountains on Promenade Deck or something. Sometimes, changing things up signals an important moment...Then, you just have to tell her. If you really want to, you'll find the words."

He turned to refill his coffee and looked over his shoulder at Frank. "Oh. There are no magic words. There's no secret formula." He brought his cup back and stood next to his chair. "A woman wants to know that the affection she's found is not misplaced. She wants to hear the 'I love you' words from you.

Frank looked thoughtful. Then he stood up. "You're right, Daryl. Thanks. I'll let you know what happens." He tossed down the last of his coffee and put the cup on the counter before heading for the door. "Thanks for the 'Joe' too."

"No problem Frank. That's what friends are for." He grinned and waved as Frank headed down the row of cabins.

* * * *

ECS Destiny, Quarterdeck, Event Center, Diner and Lounge, 1230 Hrs

Frank came up to Emily's table just like all the other times. "Is this seat taken?" He asked politely.

Emily smiled, "I've been saving it for you." He grinned and took his seat. His lunch was a light sandwich and an apple juice, tiny when compared to his usual fare.

Emily was finishing her salad. She'd been taking her time, waiting for Frank to show up. "So, how's everything up on the bridge?" She asked, breaking the ice.

Frank shrugged. "It's kinda boring right now. As long as the computers are behaving, there's little to do in MS." He took another bite of his sandwich and watched her take her last bite of salad.

Emily excused herself and tossed her tableware in the recycle bin. Frank took a bigger bite and swallowed it down with a chug from his apple juice.

When Emily returned, Frank grinned and said, "You know? I have the rest of the day off. If you're not busy, let's go for a walk in the park and watch the dancing waters."

Emily arched an eyebrow. *That's weird. What's up?* She decided it might be fun to see what he was up to. Besides, she loved the water shows and the park. "Sure. Why not? I'm free today."

Frank smiled, but there was tenseness in his posture.
"Great." He popped the last of his sandwich in his mouth and washed it down with the last of his juice.

Emily found his behavior mildly mysterious and amusing at the same time. He scooped up the last of the items on the table and strode over to the recycle bin. A quick dump and his long strides brought him back to the table. "Come on. Let's go."

They got to the lift and Frank tapped Promenade. Emily stood to his left and slightly behind. She watched him as the lift began its plunge. She could see he was incredibly tense. They stepped out into a shipboard wonderland.

Over half the length of the ship's interior was one incredible park. There was a system of stone paths that stretched much of the distance. A combination of rock and plants went into a delightful series of gardens. Trees of various kinds were planted strategically in artfully made planter boxes.

In the center was a long rectangular pool. A beautiful circular rain curtain ran from the underside of the mezzanine high above, down into the center of the pool. At certain times of day and night, a system of fountains in the pool came into play to create beautiful dancing water shows with lights and music.

Two smaller play fountain pools were situated close to a couple of playground areas for the children. They were a favorite attraction for the little ones.

They walked for a while, admiring the view, reading the tags that described the plants and where on Earth they'd come from. Emily naturally took the role of tour guide and started talking about the various plants. Frank seemed to relax as she spoke and they continued that way for a while.

They finally reached the grand pool in the center of the vast indoor garden and stopped near a park bench; one of many strewn about the Promenade.

Frank took up the conversation for the first time since she'd begun her impromptu garden tour. "Let's sit for a while?"

Emily wondered where he was headed with this odd little side trip. The talk had been somewhat stilted, lacking its natural and comfortable flow. She nodded. "Sure."

They sat. He seemed to be gathering his thoughts.

Finally, he looked at her. Emily watched his face. *Is he trying to be romantic or something?* She had mixed feelings about that prospect. She wanted him to make some kind of move, but she wasn't quite sure what that should be.

"Emily? I uh…well…" *Say it, damn it. You're going to freak her out.* "You know, we've been friends for a little while now, and…well, it seemed to me that…Damn! I'm sorry, I'm so nervous…"

Emily felt a little heat on her cheeks. It had been a long time since someone made her feel this way. She turned to face him more directly, willing him to find his tongue.

Frank took a deep breath and moved closer to her. "Emily…I can't help myself. I've fallen in love with my chatting partner."

She sat, stunned. She'd figured something like this was coming, but the reality still hit her like a ton of bricks.

He reached out and touched her hands. She let him take them in his. "It's way too sudden, but if…if you care for me the same way, would you marry me?"

Emily stared at him. Her heart hammered in her chest and she couldn't decide whether to shout for joy or run gibbering in terror. She couldn't speak.

After a minute or so, Frank released her hand and watched her, his face taking on a look of dread bordering on despair.

Slowly, he stood and looked at her sadly. "I'm sorry. I…shouldn't have…" He turned and slowly headed for the path.

Something inside snapped and Emily realized she was going to blow the chance she'd been dreaming of for weeks. She jumped up, "Frank? Frank, wait!"

He stopped and turned, a question on his face.

Emily ran to him and stood, looking into his face, eyes misting. "Oh, Frank. I am so sorry. You caught me so totally by surprise. I…I wasn't expecting the whole deal all at once…"

She laughed at her foolishness while wiping the moisture from her eyes. "Oh, Frank, Yes! I do care about you the same way. I've been in love with you for a long time, now. I just wasn't sure how you felt."

She reached out and took his arm, looking into his eyes. "If you still want me…then yes, I'll marry you; gladly."

She pulled on his arm and they returned to the bench. He turned her to face him. "May I?"

She laughed nodding her head. They met in a long passionate kiss neither had expected was coming...They sat, hand in hand, watching plants grow. After a little while, "Frank? I really need you to understand what happened when I didn't answer you."

She gazed at the rain, ceaselessly falling into the pool. "It wasn't you. It was me. See...a year before *Destiny* pulled out of orbit, another man, one who was a fool and a jerk, proposed to me. He was all polish and debonair. I'd fallen for him in spite of my friend's warnings. I accepted and made all kinds of wonderful plans for our wedding and our lives together..."

She paused and gathered her thoughts. "Four days before the wedding, I caught him taking someone else into a hotel. I couldn't believe it, so I followed. They headed up the stairs. She was all over him like butter on bread."

Frank put his arm around her and listened as she relived her torture and shame.

"I lost it! I ran up the stairs after them and shoved her away from him. I yelled at him and demanded an explanation. He was drunk and laughed at me like it was all some big joke. The little witch on the floor was swearing and yelling at us. I turned and kicked her really hard and ran...I just wanted to die."

She paused, getting a grip on her emotions. Frank waited patiently, gently stroking her hair. "Some of my friends found me in a park and drove me home. I broke the engagement, canceled the wedding and headed straight for the foundation recruiting office."

She looked up at him, a sad smile on her face. "Frank. I didn't want to get involved with anybody ever again. When you started watching me, way back when we'd finished our first MS transition, I tried hard to ignore you.

"But you've been a friend to me; something that ass never dreamed of doing. You've respected me. I wasn't some personal prize. You gave me something I'll always cherish: uncompromising, genuine friendship.

Frank kissed her hair and whispered. "It's OK."

She turned and looked at him. "When you told me you'd fallen in love with me and then proposed marriage...it scared the hell out of me. I'm sorry I put you through that."

Frank kissed her on the forehead and then they dove for another breath taker.

* * * *

ECS Destiny, Quarterdeck, SecCentral, 1400 Hrs

Tanya looked up from her reports as Emily came in, power-tab under one arm. Something was different about her, but she couldn't quite place it.

"Hey Tanya, how's it going?"

Tanya smiled broadly. "Things are great. Remember when Tolya brought his niece to visit?

Emily nodded. "Sure. She's such a sweet girl."

Tanya continued. "The reason for the get together was to discuss her adoption. We've all agreed and we'll be formally adopting her at our wedding."

Emily glowed. "That's awesome. I didn't realize that she was without family."

Tanya put her reports aside. "Lyuba lost her parents when she was still an infant. Tolya was awarded custody in the courts and she became his ward, but because of his outrageous schedule, he was never able to be there long enough to really care for her. He has these very close friends; they're like family. They elected to come along on this venture. Anyway, they've been caring for her for probably seven or eight of her thirteen years."

Emily sighed. "That's beautiful; you two adopting her and all at your wedding. She's a lucky little lady."

Tanya smiled. "Emily? Are you going to tell me why you're so dreamy today? You're barely here."

"Hnh? Oh! He did it!" Emily was ebullient.

Tanya looked puzzled for a moment and then the light dawned. "Frank? Did he…"

"Yes, I told you I'd be ready...but I was wrong. After lunch, Frank invited me down to Promenade Deck for a walk in the garden. I thought that was kinda weird, but I like it down there so I agreed. While we were there he proposed! I was so shocked I couldn't say anything for a few minutes. When I didn't answer, the look on his face said his whole world had just crumbled."

Tanya looked horrified. "Em! What happened?"

"He turned to walk away and I realized I was about to loose him and I cried out. I ran after him and stopped him."

She smiled dreamily. "He was willing enough to stop, so I apologized...and then I said yes! The rest was just...wonderful!"

ON THE WAY — 4

FRI 02.26.2094
ECS Destiny, Quarterdeck, Command Staff Conference Room, 0900 Hrs

Tanya placed cups around the table as the staff slowly began filtering in for the first of several meetings scheduled for the duration of MS flight. She drew coffee from the dispenser and began the rounds. Someone had rearranged the seating order. She found her place moved from the end of the table to the head, just to Tolya's right. Tanya shook her head with a ghost of a smile. Someone was getting cute.

Tolya came in and took his place. She finished her circuit, pouring Tolya's cup and then hers last. As she sat at her place it occurred to her the places had been rearranged to reflect the many confirmations of pairings that had taken place recently.

She and Tolya were at the head of the table, Daryl and Naomi sat along the side to her right and Ichirou and Midori sat next to them. Vincent and Daniela and Frank and Emily sat on Tolya's left. The opposite end was unoccupied. Somehow she found the arrangement amusing.

Tolya gave her arm a squeeze and sat down. "Good morning everyone. As I mentioned in those net-mail messages, this is going to be a regular occurrence, at least for this leg of the journey. I want us to stay on top of preparations to take this new system."

He glanced around the table with a ghost of a smile. "I had the seating arrangements adjusted slightly. We need to stop thinking of ourselves as just a command staff aboard a starship. We should begin thinking of ourselves as the first leaders of a successful colony.

"Our colony is made up mostly of families. Since we're all busily pairing off and preparing to found new families of our own, I thought our seating should reflect the fact."

Daniela looked around the table and then at Vince. He shrugged as she spoke up. "OK, I can see you two, and obviously, we have the McIntyre's and the Akari's, but...I haven't heard any other special announcements."

Tolya looked at her, feigning shock. "Why Dannie! I believe you're falling down on the job. You mean you don't know?"

Daniela looked around, noting again the seating arrangements. Then it hit her. Frank usually sat across from Emily, but they were sitting rather comfortably together.

"I guess not. Emily? Am I missing something?"

Emily grinned and Frank fidgeted. "Sorry Dannie, but it just happened yesterday."

Daniela looked startled. "You're kidding. Right?"

"Nope, dead serious. Frank proposed and I accepted."

Daniela's mouth hung open in surprise and Vince reached over to gently close it, grinning at her.

Daniela swatted playfully at his hand before continuing. "Wow! I'm sorry Emily. You just surprised the heck out of me. Last I heard, it was going to be a waiting game."

Emily grinned. "You're surprised. I nearly blew everything, I was so surprised!"

Frank looked embarrassed. "It was either get it out there or I was going to mess it up myself."

Vince reached over and shook Franks hand. "Well, it's about time. Congratulations, man."

Daryl and Naomi expressed pleasure at the announcement. Naomi looked pointedly at Daniela. "So, it looks like you're the ones dragging their feet!" She grinned mischievously. Everyone looked their way and Vince and Daniela both started laughing.

Vince started. "Well, we've been bugging each other for almost the entire voyage. Somehow we've never gotten around to some romantic breakthrough."

Daniela stepped in. "No, we just started talking about the future one day and somehow in the conversation, we started assuming we'd both be in each others hair the rest of our lives. Vince has never proposed and I've never tried to get one out of him. We just sort of decided together that, once we get there, we'd get married."

Tanya chuckled. "You've been trailing us along waiting for the other shoe to drop. Well, I'm happy for you guys too. I guess everyone figures it out in different ways."

Tolya tapped his spoon on his coffee cup. "OK, gang. I didn't mean for this to turn into a grand soap opera. My point is, as a group, we're slowly becoming more of a microcosm of the colony. I think we need to remain aware of that fact."

He smiled to take any sting out and continued. "Now, let's move on to more pressing matters."

He swiped his power-tab to the next page. "First, a couple of days ago, I experienced something that really brought home just how separated we are starting to become from the rest of the community. "Some of you know I have close family friends down on Promenade Deck. I broke from my normal routine and went to visit with them during daylight hours. We spent some time up on the Mezzanine and then at their place."

He looked around the table. "How many of you have participated in Artisan's Market day?" Nobody volunteered.

"Just as I thought. We've developed our own social group and they, theirs. That day, I walked through the Mezzanine on what they call Artisan's Market Day. I didn't even know they had formal markets, let alone market days.

"The point is, we need to close this growing gap before it becomes a problem. We need to be part of the colony, not some appendage that must be put up with to function."

Naomi commented. "I agree. I haven't given it much thought, but it's very important we don't let a gap develop between the leadership and the rest of the colony. We've had our share of out of control people endangering the rest of us. We can't afford to give marginal folk an excuse."

Tanya nodded. "Yeah, when I talked with the ladies who found the murder victim, they were so surprised I was kind to them. It's like they weren't sure we cared. Tolya gave me leave to give them use of the Officer's Lounge for their birthday party. They fell all over themselves in profound gratitude over a gesture of kindness."

Before anyone spoke, she remembered something. "Oh. Emily, I totally forgot. I think it would be a great idea if you would have a chat with one of those ladies. Her name's Francine Douglas. She has a knack for working with school age children. I know you could use help. I'll connect you if you like."

Emily smiled. "I'd be delighted to meet her."

Tanya smiled at Tolya, half whispering, "Sorry, I forgot."

He smiled graciously and moved on. "We should participate with the activities of the colonists. We're one people. Let's not allow this people to fracture into factions. The idea is to mingle, make friends; essentially, become involved."

Vince piped up, "I have to agree. I have a couple of good acquaintances. By talking with them I've been learning a lot about stuff on the residential decks."

Daryl nodded. "I'm glad you mentioned it. I have a number of friends who live on various decks. Unfortunately, I keep myself so busy, I seldom get down to see them."

Tanya piped up, "I think we should get Tolya's friend, Kaitlyn O'Connor to show us girls around these markets. I can think of all kinds of shopping that needs to happen."

Dannie, Emily and Naomi agreed with enthusiasm.

Tolya reluctantly nudged the meeting along, "OK. I think we're on the right track on that topic. I have something else that needs to be dealt with."

All eyes were aimed his way now. "According to Emily and her teams' research, the system we're about to enter is richer in usable metals than Sol system. I believe," he turned to Emily, "and correct me if I'm wrong...when we enter this system, we're going to find the equivalent to Sol's Oort cloud, a rich bonanza to harvest and supplement our supply."

Emily nodded. "The supposition is sound enough. What do you have in mind?"

Tolya smiled. "Once we enter this system and figure out what's available, we need to be prepared to harvest whatever raw materials are needed."

He looked at Naomi. "That's where you're going to get busy. I'd like you and your folks to start working out practical methods of mining comets, asteroids and the like."

* * * *

Everyone crowded around Frank and Emily to offer congratulations. Tolya and Tanya slipped off for a workout. It had been a while since the last go round.

Daryl noted their departure. "Hey, hey, listen up."

They all quieted.

"Since the 'royal' couple went for their exercise, I think we should get down to some planning of our own. Naomi and I have been talking.

He looked around. "Ladies, I think Naomi wants to get together and discuss a few matters regarding a certain wedding. Guys, we've similar work to do."

He put an arm over Naomi's shoulder, pulling her close and she spoke up. "Daryl and I want to make this the most awesome wedding possible. It'll be one of our more notable historical events. Let's make it a great one.

She glanced at Midori. "I just had a wonderful session with Midori yesterday." Midori gave a smile.

"She's agreed to coordinate the conversion of Promenade Deck to a garden wedding fit for royalty."

Ichirou grinned. "Yes, she gets to coordinate and I get to move things around; so very exciting!"

Everyone laughed. They quickly organized where to meet and when. Naomi reminded Daryl to call Shane O'Connor and make sure he and the captain's niece were in attendance.

Daryl gave Naomi another squeeze. "How about this?" He glanced at the ships clock. "We'll meet at the agreed upon places in an hour. That'll give us time to collect the missing. Naomi and I will round up the O'Connors and Lyuba. Dannie can collect Sherry. Sound good?"

Everyone agreed and set off with a will.

* * * *

Shane considered the vaguely familiar face on the screen.

"Shane O'Connor?"

"Aye that'd be me."

"Hi, Shane. I'm Daryl McIntyre, Tolya's chief engineer?"

Shane brightened with sudden recognition. "Oh yes. We met at Tolya's Christmas bash last year."

Daryl grinned, "Exactly. Shane, I know it's been a while, but I was wondering. All of us on the command staff are trying to get organized and get Tolya and Tanya started in a big way. I know it's kind of sudden but could I impose on you and your wife to come up and meet with us?"

Shane grinned. "That'd be fun, I think. Let me check with the boss." He winked and turned from the pick up.

A moment later, the pick up pulled back to include both Shane and his wife, Kaitlyn. "Hello, Daryl. It's been much too long. How's your wife, Naomi?"

Daryl grinned. "She's great. Good to see you."

Kaitlyn smiled. "Shane told me of your plans. I'd like to change them just a wee bit if you don't mind."

Daryl raised an eyebrow. "Would you? How?"

She glanced at Shane and back. "Why don't you all come here? We've plenty of coffee and I think I could scare up a dessert or two."

Daryl grinned broadly. "That sounds mighty tempting. We want to split the guys and gals for specific planning."

Shane sat forward, "That's no problem. I've my own study and the ladies can have the front room or even the dining room."

Daryl considered. "How many folks can you handle? There's, let's see…nine of us if you include Tanya's maid of honor, Sherry; plus, you and your wife, and don't forget Lyuba. She figures into this more than I thought."

Kaitlyn's eyes twinkled. "Och, that's a mere twelve. Why, it'll be great fun!"

Daryl surrendered, "If you're comfortable with an invasion of this magnitude, who am I to say nay?"

Kaitlyn grinned, "Why, nobody of course...Let me see...Lyuba's due home from school any time now. When should we meet?"

Daryl glanced at the time display. "Well, we'd originally planned to meet in about an hour, but if you need more time, we could move it back."

Shane looked at Kaitlyn. "What about Aileen and Owen?"

Kaitlyn shook her head. "Aileen's visiting with her friend Ana, and Owen's at James' place."

She looked back at the screen. "An hour from now will be just fine, Daryl. I look forward to meeting your whole group. My, my; all of Tolya's friends at once!" She hurried for the kitchen.

Shane shrugged, moving closer to the pickups. "Well, this ought to be interesting. I better get to helping."

Daryl grinned. "Oh, where are you located?"

Shane smiled, "We're down on Promenade Deck. AP-P05. You can't miss it. We're in the Aft, Port Side arc facing out on the fountains and pool."

"That's easy enough. I'll see you in about an hour. Thanks for the hospitality."

"No problem."

Daryl closed the connection and headed for the door. He stopped at Frank's and told him about the change of plans.

Frank stepped out into the corridor and Vince looked out from next door. "Hey guys, what's up?"

"There's been a change of plans." Daryl grinned. "We're all going to the O'Connor's place. They have the room and his wife, Kaitlyn, mentioned something about coffee and dessert."

Vince brightened. "Ooh! Better and better."

* * * *

ECS Destiny, Promenade Deck, O'Connor Residence, 1130 Hrs

Lyuba answered the door page to confront nine adults dressed in ship's uniform. She recognized Emily, Sherry and Vince. The rest were total strangers.

Emily stepped forward. "Hey, remember me?"

"Oh, you were in Ms. Tanya's office the other day."

"That's right. These are all my friends."

From the back of the unit came a woman's voice. "Well, let them in, princess."

Lyuba's eyes widened as she realized her error. "Oh, I'm sorry. Please, come in." She stepped to one side as they filed in. Sherry winked at her with a grin.

Kaitlyn bustled from the back to greet everyone. "Come on in, have a seat." She waved towards the family room with a wealth of chairs and a sizable couch.

Everyone crowded in as Shane stepped out from his study. "Hello everyone."

Daryl crossed the room and they shook hands. "Shane. Good to see you again. It's been too long."

Shane indicated a seat and smiled. "All too true."

Lyuba came in behind everyone, eyes bright with curiosity. Sherry scooted over and motioned Lyuba to join her.

Lyuba squeezed in. "Where's your cast?" She whispered.

"Oh, Dr. Jacobs," she indicated Daniela, "removed it yesterday. I'm all better."

Lyuba whispered. "I'm glad."

Sherry smiled and patted her on the back.

Lyuba asked. "Hey! Where's my uncle and Ms. Tanya?"

Emily replied. "This meeting's a secret. We're making plans to help them get ready for their wedding. Are you gonna help us?"

Lyuba grinned, "Sure."

Daryl spoke up. "OK. There's much to think about, and not much time."

He looked at Sherry. "Sherry, do you have any idea what Tanya's been thinking for her wedding?"

"Sure. We've talked a lot in the last couple of days. I think she's written out several pages for the ceremony itself. I've never planned a wedding before, so any suggestions would be fabulous."

Daryl looked at Shane, who sat on the arm of Kaitlyn's chair. "How about you? Anything from Romeo yet?"

Shane grinned. "Yes, and no. Tolya's often quiet about what he wants. I know he's concerned about finding a ring."

Sherry piped up. "Yeah, that's something Tanya mentioned too. She wants a compete set."

Vince spoke up. "I may have the means to solve that little problem. I know a guy up on Deck 2. He was a first class jeweler back on Earth. They brought all his tools and equipment along. I believe we have enough raw materials in stores, so if my man could get his hands on the stuff, he could custom make something great."

Shane nodded. "Outstanding. How about introducing me in the next few days? We should get started right away."

"Sure. We have a chess match this evening. Come with me. I could use the moral support after the drubbing I'm liable to get."

Shane chuckled. "Why not? We'll find out what he's willing to do. Then I'll get the lovebirds together with him so they can hash out details."

A chime in the kitchen sent Kaitlyn hurrying off. Shortly thereafter, scents of tasty delights wafted into the room.

Shane stood. "I believe we're expected in the dinning room."

ON THE WAY — 5

THU 03.11.2094
ECS Destiny, Quarterdeck, SecCentral, Tanya's Office, 1000 Hrs

Tanya handed the test results across the desk and sat back in her chair. "So, we have a guy with a stellar IQ, who's managed to waste most of his youth on the streets as a petty criminal. He's bright enough to work his way to the equivalent of a PhD. in several fields, but he needs to catch up in his pre-college level work to get him prepped. Does that cover it?"

Emily grinned and put the power-tab in front of her. "Yeah, that fairly covers it."

Tanya nodded. "So, what can I do to help?"

Emily sat back and considered the question. "Well, if he's willing to work hard, he needs to get through the high school courses he missed. I don't mean the useless fluff they coddled us with. I mean the important stuff that'll help him to excel."

Tanya nodded, prompting her to continue, "OK..."

"Well, you've been there for many of our interviews. Surely you can see how much he wants to make something of himself. I think time and resources are wasted while he twiddles his thumbs back there." She pointed in the general direction of Felix' cell.

Tanya leaned her chair back, tapping a pencil against the wall above her head. She sat forward and dropped the pencil on the desk. "If we can square it with the charter, I'm thinking of some kind of house arrest arrangement. He'd have some freedom to get about giving you easier access. I'll talk to Tolya"

She looked up at Emily. "One problem I have is his living arrangements. I don't think his old haunts down on Deck 2 are conducive to a new lifestyle."

Emily thought for a moment. "Wait! I know this sounds crazy, but think about it. There are a few vacant staff cabins right here next to us. They've never been used. We could put him in one of those and get him going on an accelerated program to complete his pre-college subjects. He'd be right there under everyone's scrutiny."

"Hmm. I'm not sure." Tanya pondered the suggestion. She turned to her computer and pulled up a few files, cross-referencing to a couple of texts. Then she grabbed the pencil and tapped the eraser end on the desk, lost in thought.

She looked at Emily. "OK. I think we might get away with this little shenanigan with a little piece of insurance thrown in. It's possible to put a tracer bracelet on him."

Emily raised an eyebrow, "Tracer bracelet?"

Tanya grinned. "Yeah. It's linked to the ship computer. It would allow us to always know where he is. There's a little vibrator built in that warns the wearer if they're about to leave the restricted area and I can set those restrictions any way I like."

She leaned back. "For instance; I could make it so he has to stay on this deck. Everything he'd need would be here, so there'd be no need for him to go anywhere else."

Emily blew out a breath of amazement, "Whoooh! That'd probably do the trick. Felix gets a certain limited freedom, and we can help him realize his potential. Would you really do all that just for him?"

Tanya sat forward, dropping her pencil back on the desk. "Yeah, I guess so. I'm too big a softy." She grinned, "But I still have to square it with Tolya. If he approves the plan, we can put it into effect next week. That's...four days. Is it really Thursday, already?"

Emily grinned. "Thanks Tanya. I just know we can make something of this kid."

"No charge, Emily. I want him to succeed as much as you, but I do need a favor from you."

"Name it!"

Tanya stood and cleared her screen. "Remember our Monday meeting when I mentioned Francine?"

Emily stood and stretched. "Sure. You thought she'd be useful in my program."

"Yeah, well, I'm inviting her up here for lunch. I'd like you to come meet her. I really think you'll like her."

Tanya wagged an admonishing finger at Emily. "We need to get our younger kid's programs on course. You've mumbled about that on a number of occasions."

Emily nodded. "You're right, Tahnie. I've been a little distracted lately. I guess I kinda' forgot."

"I know. I've been sweetly distracted myself."

"I guess you have, haven't you?" She picked up her power-tab. "I'd be happy to meet Francine. Tomorrow? What time?"

"How about lunch hour tomorrow. Her son, Dennis will be in class so she should be free."

Tanya saw Emily hesitate and remembered her lunch included Frank. "Don't worry, you can bring him too."

Emily grinned. "You caught that did you?"

Tanya laughed, "Remember, I'm on the same roller coaster ride as you."

"I guess so... Oh! By the way, we were wondering if you could join us Saturday. We're all eager to talk wedding and we never seem to get together."

"Saturday? I don't see why not. OK. I'll bring my notes and we can talk for a while. When? Where?"

Emily grinned. "Oh, how about the Staff ready room next to the bridge, say 1300?"

"Sure, OK." Tanya grinned and glanced at the time. "It's about noon and I know at least one of us has a lunch date."

Emily glanced at the clock. "Wow. I'd better get going."

Tanya laughed. "Don't worry; I have one too. We'd both better get going."

Emily ducked out of the office. "OK, we'll meet you tomorrow, at noon. Bye!"

Tanya returned to her desk and tapped the COMM icon.

The AI responded, "Routing?"

"Francine Douglas, Deck 3."

After a moment Francine's face flashed on the screen. She smiled when she recognized Tanya.

"Hello. What a pleasant surprise. What's going on with you?"

Tanya smiled. "I'd like to invite you to have lunch with me and Emily Strauss."

"Me? Wow. What's the occasion?"

"Oh, nothing special. I just thought you might be interested in helping out in the colony's education department. We need good people and you seem quite talented in that department."

"I'd love to, but I don't have the appropriate accreditations."

"I know, but this isn't Earth. I think Dr. Strauss would be interested in you, and I sensed you love working with kids."

Francine was bursting with suppressed excitement. "Yes, I do. I used to be a teachers aid in the elementary schools back home."

Tanya smiled again. "That's what I thought. Why don't you come tomorrow to the main diner? We'll have lunch and Dr. Strauss can discuss it with you. She won't bite, you know."

Francine laughed, "Of course not. I'd love to come. It's at a good time too. Dennis doesn't get out of school till 1500."

"OK then," Tanya glanced at the ship's clock. "I have a lunch date with my captain. So, I need to hurry off. Can I count on you tomorrow at lunch?"

"I'll be there with bells on!" Francine exclaimed.

"Thanks Francine. Bye."

Tanya broke the connection and hurried to the lounge. There was Tolya, looking slightly lost. His face brightened when he saw her. "I thought you forgot me," he admonished.

"Me? Forget you? That'd be the day. No, I had a last minute chat with Francine Douglas. I'll be introducing her to Emily over lunch tomorrow."

"So, does that mean no lunch date?"

Tanya dug him in the ribs. "Of course not. Frank's gonna be there. I didn't think I'd get Emily to agree to miss her lunch date so I invited him."

They found a table and sat down. After ordering, they sat back, watching folk come and go. Tolya asked, "So, how did things go this morning?"

Tanya replied. "Today's been productive, so far. I spent the time with Emily."

She sat forward, elbows on the table, chin resting on her hands, looked him in the eye and said, "...which reminds me; I've an important request I need you to consider."

Tolya grinned. "Anything for you sweetheart."

Tanya made a little kissing motion, "I think it'll be the right thing to do."

Tolya raised an eyebrow. "My, it must be something pretty serious then."

Tanya sat back and gave him an approximation of his own famous lopsided grin. "Emily has been studying Felix' test scores. She showed them to me this morning."

Her face turned serious. "Tolya, his scores are nearly off the chart. He's bright. Emily wants to start a crash course to catch him up on his pre-college education. She said he's being wasted, sitting there in a cell."

Tolya looked grim. "I'm sure she's right, but we can't just let him off. That would make the whole sentence a joke."

Tanya looked down. "Yeah, I know..." She looked up, "...but we talked about that and we thought about putting him on some kind of house arrest status. Look, as far as his part in that whole mess, I think he's learned some powerful lessons. You know he was very repentant, and his behavior's been exemplary. I think we could make a house arrest work out."

Tolya used his table knife to draw imaginary lines on the table top, lost in thought. "It's risky. How would you go about it?"

Tanya reached across and took his hand. "I think I've worked it out. First, I don't want him back in his old haunts on Deck 2. He needs new friends."

She gave his captured hand a squeeze. "Emily pointed out that we have open cabins right here on Quarterdeck. They've never been used and it would put Felix under the eyes of every one of us."

She released his hand. "Second, I need to restrict his movements...for a couple of reasons. One, he has to remember he's still doing time, and Two, he needs to avoid contact with the bulk of the population till we can establish that he's paid his dues."

Tolya nodded. "So how about that little problem?"

Tanya grinned. "That's easy. I have access to all kinds of toys in my line of work. One toy is a bracelet that can only be removed by the owner of the equipment. The ship's computer would keep track of his location. I can assign set restrictions the computer can monitor. If he crosses a line, his bracelet will vibrate a warning, and the computer will notify us."

Tolya resumed his imaginary doodling for a few more moments. Their orders arrived and they set to eating. In mid bite, he stopped and looked at her. "OK. I'd really like to see Felix shape up and become something better. I'm a little uncomfortable with this plan, but I trust your judgment."

He looked her in the eyes. "So I'll go with it, but if he pulls anything stupid, he's back in his cell."

Tanya smiled. "Thanks, honey. I know it'll work."

Tolya smiled at her and took his aborted bite.

* * * *

ECS Destiny, Quarterdeck, McIntyre Residence, 1800 Hrs

Naomi sat at her desk in the cabin she shared with her husband. She poured over volumes of information, periodically jotting notes on her power-tab. Mining for raw materials on a chunk of rock and ice was a reasonably straightforward proposition. The captain had stipulated the word practical. She liked that. One needed the best results for the lowest expenditure of energy and fuel.

Fuel was likely to be very low on the list of problems. Raw materials for the fuel would be readily available, partially as a byproduct of the mining process. With the five shuttles and the six work bees, there were enough craft for a simple operation. She decided on a strip mining approach.

First they'd assess the stability of the target and take core samples to determine its make up. Simple robotic machines could be devised to scrape away the material in ever-deeper swaths. The material would be brought to a central location and run through a set of separators and the waste materials ejected.

A large percentage of the base material would most likely have sufficient amounts of hydrogen to process for fuel. They would hardly dent their supply for the shuttles and work bees.

She accessed her CADD station down on Industrial deck and ran various combinations of components through virtual tests. An idea was incubating.

About thirty minutes later, there was a three dimensional representation of a low mass ore collector. It had two powerful mining lasers mounted on articulated arms. A longer set of arms situated lower, were equipped with gripping claws. As the lasers cut away material, the grippers would grab the pieces and stuff them into a hopper built into the front between both sets of arms. The materials would be packed into the carapace.

This device looked vaguely like some kind of deformed insect. Instead of legs, wide treads were mounted, two in front, two in back. They were curiously articulated trucks that could flex over very rough terrain. A set of grav-plates was mounted under the chassis. Their function was to provide a pull on the surface of the body to aid in traction and to prevent flyaway due to the extremely low gravity.

Naomi sat back and considered her creation. All seemed right except for one minor detail. She started moving things around, adding here, adjusting there.

Little changed visibly, but the carapace section became detachable. Towing hard points were added and now it was possible for two work bees to attach to the carapace, pull it away and tow it back to the ship. Another set of work bees could bring an empty to replace it.

Daryl arrived and stood watching as she finished the last steps and saved her work. He leaned over, kissing her hair. "Looks great; what is it?"

Naomi looked up and grinned. "It's a new design for a robotic ore collector."

She turned around in her seat and stood. Daryl gave her a big hug and then she stretched getting the kinks out from sitting for so long. Daryl stood back, appreciating the stretch almost as much as she did. "I move we get dinner and then take a walk."

Naomi brightened. "I like it. I second the motion."

She stood on tiptoes and planted a kiss. Daryl grinned, ushering her out the door.

ON THE WAY — 6
FRI 03.12.2094
ECS Destiny, Quarterdeck, SecCentral, 0655 Hr

Tanya got to the office at about 0655; a little early. She went to the storage room, rummaging through the shelves till she found what she was looking for. She took the small box to her office. At her desk, she set the box down and woke her computer, opening a peripherals folder and selecting the utility she needed.

The box contained a functional looking bracelet. A slender boxy segment housed the circuitry and the rest was a heavy linked chain. She pulled a small device out of the box and tested it. The bracelet clicked open. Nodding, she snapped it shut and pulled. She smiled when it wouldn't open. She couldn't even see a seam.

Turning to the computer, she started up the utility, set up a profile and entered the limitations for the unit. The computer beeped happily, accepting the 'apply' command.

Sherry came in and set up her station for the day.

"Sherry, I could use your help." Tanya called.

Sherry swept into the office. "Good morning, and what can I do for you?"

Tanya grinned and tossed Sherry the detention pass card. "Would you open up and bring Felix? I have a little project for him."

Sherry stared at Tanya as if she had announced she could fly. Tanya chuckled. "Just get him. You'll understand soon."

Sherry shrugged and left the room.

Felix sat up on his bunk as Sherry approached. "Hi, Sherry."

Sherry smiled. "Hey. How are you this morning?"

She passed the card key and the lock snapped open.

Felix looked surprised. "Um...Sherry. What are you doing?"

"Tanya asked me to bring you to her office. She said something about 'a little project for you.'"

Felix got up from his bunk and approached the door. Sherry swung it open and he stepped out, looking confused.

Sherry tugged his arm. "Come on, she's waiting."

Tanya was indeed waiting. Felix came hesitantly into the office with Sherry following on his heels. Tanya indicated a chair near her.

Felix sat.

Sherry hovered in the entrance, unsure what to do. "Oh, sit down, Sherry. You'll make him nervous." Sherry blushed and sat in the remaining seat.

Tanya focused on Felix. "I've been busy the last couple of days. Dr. Strauss has persuaded me to give you a longer leash. In turn, I've managed to persuade my captain to permit it. Dr. Strauss has plans for you. These require that you have more flexibility, so I'm placing you on something like house arrest."

Tanya turned and picked up the bracelet and held it out for Felix to take. Felix looked curious as he took what looked like a man's medical bracelet.

"I'm taking a chance on you, Felix. Captain Chernov was a bit skeptical about this idea, and I am sticking my neck out, betting you'll be honorable.

She pointed at the bracelet. "The device you're holding is a monitoring bracelet. It's linked to the ship's computer. Your leash is getting longer." She sat back and glanced at Sherry who was trying furiously not to show too much excitement.

Tanya stopped a grin and resumed her lecture. "As it happens, we have a spare staff cabin available up here. Because our staff consists of two married couples, arrangements were made to accommodate them. This left a couple of spare units. You should feel privileged staying there. For a single person, it's surprisingly roomy as starship cabins go."

Felix was nearly speechless. Only one question really seemed appropriate, "Why?"

Tanya raised an eyebrow. "I see you appreciate your position." She sat back with a sigh. "The answer is probably very complex, but to put it simply, we believe you can be better than the sum of your deeds. When I say we, I'm talking about Me, Dr. Strauss, my captain, Sherry here, and of course, the McIntyres'. That's not a few well placed people putting faith in someone who, up until now, has given no good reason to deserve it."

Felix squirmed and glanced over at Sherry. Sherry gave him a happy grin. He wondered exactly what she was grinning about.

Tanya continued. "There are several restrictions. We can't have you running about all over the ship. First, people would be offended, at best, to learn that one of those who caused so much grief recently should appear to be getting off too easily. Second, frankly, I think you need a more wholesome environment than you are accustomed to.

"So, here's the deal. You're free to come and go on this deck so long as you follow polite behavior. Peoples' cabins are off limits unless they invite you in. You're free to use the Event Center diner and lounge. I strongly recommend you take advantage of the gym." She paused as an intriguing idea was born. "I think I'll come back to that one later."

She picked up her original train of thought. "If you attempt to leave this deck, your bracelet will vibrate a warning. If you do not reverse course immediately upon feeling the vibration, our security teams will be instantly alerted and you WILL be caught and returned to the cell you just left. Captain has made it clear that it will only take one deliberate screw up to land you back in the can."

Felix couldn't have looked more serious.

Tanya held her hand out for the bracelet. "Felix, do you understand and accept the conditions?"

Felix nodded.

Tanya raised an eyebrow. "I can't hear you."

Felix' face flushed. "Yes, ma'am. I understand and agree to keep the conditions."

Tanya smiled. "There, that wasn't so hard, was it?" She tapped a code on the computer and the cache on the bracelet clicked open.

She held it out to Felix. "If you agree to the conditions, and if you intend to honorably abide by them, I want you to put this on your right arm and clasp it shut."

Felix took the bracelet and looked into Tanya's eyes. Then he looked at Sherry who was quietly willing him to put it on. "I really do want to do better." He flipped the bracelet around his wrist and snapped the clasp shut.

Tanya nodded her approval. "Sherry. Take Felix out to your station and get his new profile written up. Then set him up with an active neuro-patch. You can key it to his new cabin. Let's put him in FP-Q024."

She turned to Felix. "Go with Sherry and she'll get you set up. When you're finished come back here."

She glanced at Sherry who was standing before her desk. Her stern look remained. "You too. I have something else to talk about when you get back."

Sherry nodded. Looking a strange combination of troubled and happy, she turned for the doorway.

Felix stood and offered his hand. Tanya raised an eyebrow and took it. Felix shook her hand, "Thank you. I won't let you down."

Tanya returned his grip with equal effort. "I certainly hope not. I'd like to see you succeed. Now, get set up and come right back."

Felix followed Sherry to her station. It was 0740.

Sherry slid into her seat and keyed up the neuro-patch assignment page. Reaching into a drawer, she pulled out a thin plastic case from a stack. "OK, Felix, come on. I'll have to ask some questions for the survey before we activate the patch."

Felix came up next to her and stood, a hand on the chair back, watching her handle her station. Her hands seemed to fly over the screen. She pulled his ID number from the colony roster and asked a few more questions like age and occupation. She put down 'student' for the occupation. She hesitated over the status question. Then she entered, 'House Arrest' in the blank. She looked up and grinned. "We'll have to change that someday."

Sherry popped open the case. The patch was a thin rubbery rounded rectangle. It was nearly crystal clear unless you held it up to a light for a good look. Then you'd see a barely discernible grid work of traces and odd shapes.

She pulled it out carefully, placing it on a small tray. The tray with the patch adhered, settled into a small depression in the desk next to the screen. The computer chuckled to itself for a couple of seconds. The tray rose from its receptacle waiting patiently for the patch to be removed. Sherry gently peeled it off and turned to Felix.

"OK, give me your right hand."

Felix held out his right hand and she carefully centered the patch, which had undergone a transformation. It was no longer clear. Rather, it was now a pale, translucent yellow color with a white slash through a tiny image of a house.

As he examined it, it seemed to conform itself to every fold and curve on the back of his hand. It would eventually look like it had been tattooed there.

"There you go. By the time you need to use it, this little guy will have gotten acquainted with your nervous system and will be able to open the door to your cabin."

Sherry gave him a curious look. "Maybe someday, we'll be able to add features. When that happens, it'll change appearance to reflect your new status." Sherry held up her hand. "See mine?"

It was a translucent blue with a darker blue shield in the center.

Sherry gave Felix a sweet smile and got up. "Come on, Tanya doesn't like to be kept waiting."

Tanya looked up from her computer. "Sit down; both of you. I'll be right with you." The two young people sat and waited. Tanya quickly finished her report, flicking it into the 'completed' icon.

"OK. Sorry. I forget how efficient Sherry can be."

She looked at them. "I've decided both of you could use the gym more often. If Dr. Strauss is to be your academic coach, then I'll be your athletics coach."

She glanced at Sherry. "The captain and I have specialized in Karate for a long time. You will be our first students."

A puzzled look crossed Sherry's face. She started to make a comment, but Tanya held up a hand and shook her head. "After your recent brush with violent behavior, I don't want to hear 'you don't need to learn to defend yourself.'"

Felix looked at Sherry and then ducked his head, feeling about two feet tall.

Tanya turned to Felix. "And you. I've determined that, for all your bravado and street smarts, you've never truly hit and hurt anyone before; present company excepted.

"While most of our people in this colony are decent sorts, there are those who would find you a convenient target for their displeasure. If you CAN defend yourself effectively, you're less likely to NEED to. Besides, the martial arts are an excellent way to develop self-discipline and if there's anyone who needs self-discipline it's you. Finally, there are the obvious health advantages."

Felix spoke up. "I've always wanted to learn martial arts."
Tanya smiled. "Well, now's your chance. Both of you, be at the gym this afternoon, say 1630 hours. Get into some sweats and prepare to...sweat."

Tanya grinned and looked over at Sherry. "Sherry. Felix' personal items were moved from his former residence. They're currently in the Vault. Why don't you help him get his things?"

Sherry, who was looking slightly overwhelmed, nodded and stood up. "Sure."

She turned and waited for Felix before heading across to the vault. She waved her hand near the lock and the door snapped open. They stepped into a fairly narrow room stacked on either side with deep shelves. Sherry made her way along one side and found the cubby with Felix' things. "Here you go...want some help?"

Felix stepped forward and began examining his things. It didn't take long to see the little he had was all there. "Maybe a little help would be nice. There's not much here, but it would speed things up a little."

Sherry shrugged. "Great. So, what should I take?"

Felix considered. "How about taking the folded clothes here. I'll grab the bags."

Sherry grinned. "What about that box?"

Felix hesitated. 'That box' contained things he shouldn't have had at all; things that he'd liberated from their original owners. He shrugged realizing it was a bit too late to worry about what she thought of him.

"It's a little on the heavy side. Can you handle it?"

Sherry raised an eyebrow with a look that suggested he could have worded that one better. "Of course I can, Felix!"

She piled his clothing on top of the box and was out of the room before he could collect the bags.

Felix followed her down the corridor. They passed the grand sky-view. It was a large rectangular area in the very middle of the deck. Thin, transparent armoplast wrapped up and over a framework that made it look like a huge see through half cylinder. There were park benches stationed along its length for people to sit and chat. One could look down on the Mezzanine and the Promenade, far below.

She stopped at Felix' new cabin and put her load down, waiting for him to catch up. He juggled the bags and freed his hand, passing it over the door lock. The door snapped open and the room lit up for the first time in almost twenty-eight months.

* * * *

It was 0840. Tanya looked up to find a troubled Sherry standing in the doorway. Tanya motioned to a seat. "What's up?"

She entered the room and slid into the seat. "Tahnie, are you mad at me?"

Tanya was genuinely surprised. "Mad? Of course not! Where'd you get that?"

"Well, I don't think you've ever talked to me like you did this morning; not even when I first started working for you."

Tanya thought back on the morning activity. "Sherry, if I was rude or abrupt with you, I'm sorry. I focused on making sure Felix understood he's still under my authority. I was a bit severe with him. I don't know why you thought I meant it for you."

Sherry considered this. "It's just that you treated me like I was one of two wayward students who needed to be reprimanded...and, I don't know anything about fighting and stuff like that. I've never been interested in that."

Tanya shook her head. "Sherry, I'm sorry. You're not a wayward student who needs to be reprimanded. You're my friend, but you're also my assistant. Its hard to split how you treat someone who's under your authority AND a friend."

Sherry nodded, "I guess I can understand that."

Tanya smiled. "About the fighting thing, the Karate... I'm serious. I want you to be able to defend yourself from people who'd hurt you like Felix did a few weeks ago."

"But, Felix isn't like that anymore."

Tanya stood and came around the desk. She put her hand on Sherry's shoulder and looked fondly down at her. "It's not about Felix, honey. You'll benefit from what Tolya and I can teach you.

She gave Sherry's shoulder a gentle squeeze. "It'd also give us something in common that we could enjoy doing together. At least try it."

Sherry nodded doubtfully. "I guess I could try."

Tanya smiled, crossing her arms. "Just think. You'll be doing something active and healthy and you'll have an excuse to hang out with Felix. I cant' imagine that would bother you so much."

Sherry blushed and Tanya followed the tangent. "I don't know what made you connect with Felix the way you did, but for what it's worth, I think you're right about him. There's a lot more to the guy than he lets on."

"...However..." Tanya perched on the edge of her desk. "Do yourself a favor. Take this slow. There's no big hurry. Let him prove himself beyond a doubt. Let him show a little initiative. Don't always be the one to start things."

Sherry seemed to relax. "Felix is still amazed that we...that I...could be so kind to him after what he did. I just knew a really a wonderful person was hiding in there somewhere."

Tanya shrugged, "I'm still amazed at how you made that leap. I think he can do better, but for you it's like nothing happened. Not many people can forgive that thoroughly."

She stood and Sherry joined her. "So, will I see you this evening? I'd love to work with you."

Sherry smiled. "OK...Oh! Are you coming Saturday to the meeting with the ladies?" There was a hint of amusement hiding in her eyes that eluded Tanya's curiosity. "Sure. It should be fun."

Sherry grinned. "No doubt. I'd better get to work." She turned and went to her station.

* * * *

ECS Destiny, Quarterdeck, Event Center Entry, 1220 Hrs

Francine Douglas stepped out in the entryway of the Event Center, looking around. She was ten minutes early and couldn't decide whether to wait in the lounge or go to the security office.

She wandered around the lift well and stood, looking down the main corridor of Quarterdeck. She'd only been up here once, twice if you counted the initial boarding experience. She heard the lift hum to life and turned to see who it was.

Frank and Emily stepped out and headed deeper into the dining area. They smiled and murmured polite greetings to the pleasant woman waiting at the entrance as they passed.

Francine didn't know who they were. They seemed a very nice couple. She considered following them when a voice called from the corridor behind her.

Tanya was striding toward her. "Francine?"

"Yeah, it's me."

Tanya put her hand on Francine's shoulder. "Good to see you. How's Dennis?"

Francine smiled. "Oh, he's just fine. He did a report the other day about what happened with his visit on the bridge." She chuckled. "He's still jazzed about that."

Tanya laughed, remembering the scene. "Yeah. It was hard not to laugh. He was so serious."

They started into the dining area when the lift hummed and the doors snapped open to disgorge the captain, himself. He saw them and hurried over.

They exchanged a short little kiss and Tanya turned to Francine. "Tolya, you remember Francine?"

Tolya grinned, "But of course." He shook her hand. "So, how's Dennis?"

Francine beamed. "He's doing great."

Tanya gently pulled Tolya's hand leading him into the dining area, "I think Frank and Emily are there."

Tolya smiled. "Then, let's not keep them waiting."

Frank saw them as they entered and waved them over to a large table they'd commandeered.

Tanya steered Francine next to Emily and made introductions. It turned out Emily was the young lady she'd seen moments before.

"Francine, I'd like you to meet Dr. Emily Strauss. She's the ship's Science Officer and Director of the education department."

Emily stood and shook Francine's hand formally. "I'm happy to meet you. Tanya says wonderful things about you."

She indicated Frank next to her. "This is my fiancée, Franklin Drake. He's the ship's Navigation and Computer specialist, and our Colony Historian."

Frank stood and shook her hand.

With formal introductions dispensed with, Tolya assisted Francine to a seat next to Emily and then did the same for Tanya before taking his place. As the lunch hour drew to an end, Tolya begged leave and, with a gentle kiss for Tanya, headed back to the bridge.

Tanya made her own apologies. "Francine, I have some preparation to make, so I'll leave you in Emily's capable hands. I hope you two work something out. I look forward to maybe working with you in the future." She smiled and gripped Francine's shoulder in a friendly gesture.

"Bye, guys." She offered to Frank and Emily.

After Tanya left, Frank realized it was his turn. He leaned over and gave Emily a peck and stood. "I'll leave you to it. Francine, it was nice meeting you."

He looked over at Emily. "Dinner?"

Emily gave him a big grin. "Absolutely."

With a wave, he left them to work out the future.

* * * *

ECS Destiny, Command Deck, at entrance to Bridge, 1340 Hrs

Tanya caught up with Tolya just outside the bridge. "Hey there! Not so fast, Mister."

Tolya turned at her approach and grinned, pulling her to him for a quick hug. "What can I do for you?"

"Well, how would you like at least a couple of people to start calling you *Sensei*?"

Tolya was caught off guard. "Huh? Sensei?"

Tanya chuckled. "I've decided to start instructing Felix and Sherry in Karate. I told them to come to the gym this evening."

Tolya raised an eyebrow and looked thoughtful. "Wow! You're just full of surprises today. Why?"

Tanya shrugged. "I think it'll do a world of good for both of them. Sherry needs to learn to defend herself if the need comes. She's already had a need she wasn't ready for."

Tolya nodded. "That makes sense. I'm sure you'll do a great job. So, what do you need me for?"

Tanya grinned. "That's a silly question, Mister. You know what I need you for, but back to Karate; I could use your help and support. I don't think either one of them realize you're skilled in this area."

Tolya asked, "What's your plan?"

Tanya held up a finger. "First, I'd like us to give them a demonstration, a taste of what's possible. Second," she held up two fingers, "I'd appreciate your help."

Tolya thought about it for a moment and a smile crept onto his face. "I think it could be loads of fun. Then, when they start fighting later on, they could do a really good job of it."

Tanya rolled her eyes and poked him playfully in the ribs. "OK you, enough of that. Are you going to help me or not?"

"Sure, why not? What time?"

"I told them to show up at 1630. Will that work for you?" He pondered the doors to the bridge. "Yeah, that works."

Tanya grinned triumphantly. "Great! It would be good to get there a little early."

Tolya nodded. "I'll try to get there about 1615 then. Ok?" Tanya moved in for a promising kiss. "Great."

She turned and headed for the lift, leaving him in a warm glow.

* * * *

ECS Destiny, Crew Country, Exercise Gym, 1625 Hrs

Sherry wandered out of the women's locker room in her workout clothes. The gym was surprisingly spacious. Even with a ceiling lower than a proper gym, it felt comfortable for exercise purposes. Felix came out in sweats. He spotted her and approached.

Sherry smiled, "Hey there. Are you all settled in?"

Felix grinned. "Yeah, that's a great cabin."

"I'm glad its working out for you."

The starboard entry snapped open and Tanya strode in carrying a small gym bag over one shoulder. She was dressed in a formal karate *Gi*. There were black, loose fitting pants and a top tied shut with a black, tie on belt. The loose ends of the belt were decorated with two small, red dragons.

She wore very lightweight black shoes, almost like dancing slippers. As she approached, Sherry could see that the cloth of the outfit was almost a silky material with a pattern of dragons embroidered in darker black.

"Hello Felix, Sherry. Are you ready?"

Felix nodded and smiled. "Sure."

Sherry still felt unsure, but she went along. "Yeah, I guess so."

The port side entry snapped open and Felix saw the captain enter the room. He was surprised to see he too was wearing a formal karate *Gi*. His was very much like Tanya's except for a few details.

The black cloth was similar, but it had no embroidered dragons. Instead, there was a small red dragon over his chest about where a shirt pocket might be. A larger version was done on the back. His belt, also black, had three darker black bands near the loose ends.

Tolya approached, gave Tanya a quick kiss and turned to the would-be students. He looked at Felix. "Well, we meet again." He held out his hand and Felix tentatively shook it. He still wasn't sure how the captain felt about him.

They released hands and Tolya said. "I'm glad we can meet on better terms."

He turned to Sherry and gave her a light brotherly hug. "Good to see you, Sherry. I believe you'll find this to be more pleasant than you suspect."

He stepped away and looked to Tanya. "Tahnie?"

Tanya nodded with a grin. "OK. I thought we might begin with the stretches. Then we can introduce the basic punches and blocks. After that," she turned to Tolya, "we can give them a little demonstration."

Tanya smiled, indicating the center of the room. "Lets form up. Stand side by side and leave plenty of room so we don't kick each other accidentally."

The younger two moved to the spot indicated and stood facing Tanya. She stepped back a ways and stood facing Sherry. Tolya moved up next to her and moved away to give her room. He stood facing Felix.

"Now." Tanya's tone took on a ring of authority. "Whenever we're working out like this, Tolya and I are your instructors. In the tradition of martial arts, and in particular, Karate, the instructor is addressed as *sensei*. When approaching the instructor at the beginning of a session, it is customary to bow slightly like this."

She put her right hand, closed into a fist across in front of her sternum and placed the other hand over it, cupped so it looked like a tent over the fist. She touched them together and then bowed slightly, keeping her gaze on Sherry. She resumed her normal stance and then had them practice.

"This is a sign of respect given to the *sensei* at any practice or tournament event. In practice sessions, we do it at the beginning and at the end." She looked at her charges. "Any questions?"

Sherry spoke up. "Why all the formal stuff. Isn't this about exercise and fighting?"

Tanya grinned. "First, this is about personal discipline. By observing certain forms, we train ourselves to express respect to others. There's a saying. 'When the fist goes forward, leave anger behind. When anger goes forward, leave fists behind.' Fighting is not the end in itself. It's only a necessary step to maintain life, peace and honor. To live this way, we learn to discipline ourselves."

Sherry looked thoughtful. Felix raised an eyebrow as he absorbed the information. They went through a series of stretches and bends, hands, feet, neck, back. Then Tanya began to show them various punches, blocks and kicks. By the time they were done they were both sore and sweaty. Tolya and Tanya performed all the moves along with them, but didn't seem to be the slightest bit breathless.

"*Yame!*" Tanya called. They ended the routines and assumed a relaxed stance.

Tanya turned to Tolya. "Would you mind demonstrating some of the katas?"

Tolya grinned. "No problem."

They bowed to one another and he turned to them.

"OK. Why don't you two move to the out of bounds line there and have a seat?"

Felix and Sherry looked back, found the bold line around the playing area, and sat on the floor.

"What I am about to do is called a *kata*. It's a series of moves that are combined to re-enforce the learning process. You could call it stylized fighting.

"I'll do a couple of simple ones, and then something a little more complicated." He moved to the middle of the room. Tanya glided over to stand next to Sherry.

Tolya assumed a ready stance and began a simple *kata*. It consisted of a series of blocks, punches and kicks that carried him a sizable distance across the floor. His movements were precise, flowing, and almost dance like. Yet, there was a sense of energy you could feel. Felix cringed at how horribly clumsy he must have looked by comparison.

Tolya turned and bowed to his audience. He performed another more complex version of the moves they'd practiced. Then he turned and motioned Tanya to his side. They spoke quietly for a moment and she nodded. She assumed a ready stance, as did he. Together they did a longer routine that amazed the two watchers.

The moves were carefully coordinated. It seemed like they should have hurt each other by accident any number of times. Yet not once did they cause injury.

When it was over, Felix and Sherry clapped politely. It was an amazing display. Tolya looked over at Tanya and raised an eyebrow. She grinned, facing their audience. "Now we're going to demonstrate a mock battle. In tournament mode, the objective is to perform the moves of a fight without seriously harming your opponent. It's all about control and discipline."

She turned to Tolya and they bowed formally to one another before assuming ready stances. After a moment a sudden blur of motion started the sparring session; strike, block, counter strike. Kick, block, punch, block, jump and kick, block. They were all over the floor. Finally, Tolya stumbled and wound up flat on his back. Tanya's rigid hand pointed, like the tip of a spear, inches from his exposed throat.

She stepped back, holding out a hand. Tolya took it and rose smoothly from the floor to stand before her. They bowed formally, grinning Cheshire cat grins, and turned back to face the two amazed watchers. Finally they showed signs of exertion.

Tanya took a deep breath, letting it out slowly. "That was a short sample of a tournament fight. If it had been a real fight, my opponent would have wound up either badly injured, or perhaps, dead. It's simply the discipline and the level of focus and skill that separates a tournament fight from a real one."

Tolya motioned Felix and Sherry forward. They approached. "Now we're going to show you some defense moves that could come in handy in real life."

* * * *

Sherry, face flushed from exertion, was grinning as they headed to the women's locker room. "I never thought this could be so much fun. You didn't say anything about fun."

Tanya grinned back. "The fun's the icing on the cake. The results are important, but if you enjoy it, you'll do even better. By the way, I thought both of you did very well for your first session. You both show much promise."

Felix and Tolya headed for the men's locker room. "Felix. You did well out there. I saw you looking discouraged after our demonstration. Don't worry. You'll get there if you apply yourself. I was the ugly duckling when I first started."

Felix felt awkward. He finally got up the nerve to speak. "Captain. I just want to say thanks. You and your friends have treated me way better than I would have ever expected. I...I won't disappoint you."

Tolya stopped at his locker and turned to face Felix. "You know, Felix, in spite of myself, I can't help but like you. I truly hope it's the real reform we're working on here. You apply yourself in your studies and in your training and you'll shape up to surprise all of us. You've probably already figured this out, but there are a number good people betting on you right now. Make us proud."

PREPARATION — 1

FRI 0.12.2094
ECS Destiny, Deck 2, Aft Lift Well, 1630 Hrs

"So," Shane asked. "Where'd you meet this guy?"

"Samuel? I met him in the training sims during the six months before we left orbit. We wound up in line for...Huh. You know? I don't even remember."

He grinned. "You remember that last crazy six months...Anyway, we got to talking and struck up a friendship. I've been down here for chess at least once a week. His son, Saul works for Naomi McIntyre in the Nano-Tech department."

Vince tapped the announcer. A young man greeted them. "Vince, how ya doin'?"

"Hey Saul. Doin' great, thanks."

Saul glanced at Shane. "Who's your friend?"

"Ah! This is Shane O'Connor. He lives on Promenade Deck. I brought him along as sort of moral support. Your dad always trounces me so badly on these games. If I didn't like him so much I'd probably give up."

Saul grinned. "Dad sure likes his chess. Come on in." He stepped aside.

Samuel came from the back. "Vincent, you sly devil. What have you been up to these days?"

Vince grinned, giving the older man a friendly grapple. "Just the usual; staying out of trouble."

Chuckling merrily, Samuel shook his head as if that were a preposterous idea. "You? Out of trouble?" He ushered them into the front room. It was homey, with warm colors. There was a corner group consisting of a long couch and a recliner. Two chairs had been set at one end of the room bracketing a small game table. A beautiful chess set of marble inlaid with fine gold threads outlining each of the squares sat ready for use.

"How's that lovely doctor of yours?"

Vince grinned. "Oh, she's as beautiful as ever."

Samuel nodded sagely. "So when will you complete the catch?"

Vince shrugged. "All in good time, my friend."

They sat, except for Saul, who went for some coffee.

"Samuel, let me introduce you. This is my friend, Shane O'Connor. He's a close friend of Captain Chernov. I brought him along for two reasons. One is to help me not feel so bad when you roast me over that board of yours."

Samuel laughed. "I'm pleased to meet you." He looked to Vince. "...but you mentioned two reasons.

Saul returned with coffee to go around.

They sat, sipping and Vince answered. "Samuel. You get to be one of the first to learn this officially. Captain Chernov has found himself a woman to share his life with. Her name's Tanya. She's the ship's Chief of Security."

Samuel's eyes gleamed. "Was she the one who told that fool off; the one who heckled the captain during that ship-wide meeting?"

"Yes, exactly."

Samuel chuckled. "I thought there might be something there. She came to his defense like a lioness for her cubs."

He turned to look at Vince, mischief in his eyes. "I hate to tell you this Vince, but rumors of this are floating around. I've heard this Tanya has become very popular around here."

He sipped his coffee then asked, "So, what has that to do with your second reason?"

Vince grinned. "I was coming to that. They decided to have their wedding right after we drop into this new system we're headed for. That leaves us about a month and a half to get everything ready."

Samuel nodded and Vince hurried on. "We, on the staff, got together and began working on plans. I mentioned you to them while we were talking."

He took another sip. "Samuel, I think it would be a great honor to take the commission of making the wedding set for the colony's first governor, and his first lady.

The gleam in Samuel's eyes brightened. "Truly, that would be an honor. I have my equipment set up, but what about the materials?"

Vince held up a rhetorical finger. "I did my homework. We have a reasonable supply of gold and silver in stores. I'm not sure what the foundation was thinking, but it's there.

"Shane here is the captain's best man. I'll leave it to him to work things out."

Samuel sat forward placing his cup on the table. "Let me show you something."

A look of pride crossed his face as he got up and moved to the small corner table between the couch and the recliner.

He picked up a folder and handed it to Shane. "These are samples of some of my best designs. Some are original drawings and some are photos of finished pieces."

Shane began pouring through the contents of the folder. He did plenty of wide-eyed staring. He looked up at Samuel. "These are fantastic. They're worthy of royalty."

Samuel bowed his head in humble acceptance. Then he got up and moved towards the corner table again. "I have never told anyone, but…"

He squatted down and touched a spot on the front of the table. With a soft click, a small door swung open. He tapped a code on the revealed panel and pulled a couple of small velvet bags from the small cavity.

Returning to his seat, he undid the string on one of the bags and carefully spilled an impressive quantity of gems on the coffee table. "I brought my collection with me, hoping that some of these darlings would come to good use."

His fingers deftly sifted through the little pile, separating out a number of beautiful diamonds. His visitors admired the small fortune lying there.

Vince spoke quietly. "I can see why you might not have mentioned it."

Samuel looked up with a smile. "Yes, it could be just a little too tempting for some. So, what do you think they have in mind?"

Shane shook his head as if to clear a hangover. "I don't know particulars just yet. I can say they want a three-piece set; two rings, one for him and one for her, and he's been fretting about not having a proper engagement ring."

Samuel thought for a minute. "Why don't you bring them tomorrow afternoon, say around 1600. I'll get sizes and show them some of my work."

Vince grinned. "How much of what metals do you need?"

Samuel looked into the distance, pursed his lips in thought and then said, "I'm not certain just yet. I'll know more once I have a chat with your captain."

Vince nodded. "We have some variety in gold. If you go on ShipNet to the Stores site, you can see what's available."

Vince grabbed his pocket-tab and wrote down a code. "Is your computer active?"

Saul nodded. "Yes, Dad doesn't care for it much, but I use it all the time."

"Great." Vince tapped send. "There. The code I sent you will give you access to the protected materials section. What you're looking for is in the first category, which you now have access to. The other categories will remain unavailable.

"Once you get things settled with the captain, you can get him to authorize an order from Stores."

Samuel grinned and looked over at his son. "My son thinks I'm an old savage. Actually, I'm quite conversant with the computer.

He looked at Vince, "Thank you Vince, for the access. It makes things easier."

He turned to Shane. "So, Shane. If you'd bring the happy couple here tomorrow at around 1600, I'd be delighted to work out something wonderful."

Shane smiled, "Thank you, Samuel."

Samuel stood and started for the game table. "Come on Vince. It's time for your weekly beating."

Vince rolled his eyes. "We'll see about that, old man."

Saul nodded at Shane. "You want a short tour of our workshops? It might be instructive"

Shane grinned, "Sure. Why not?"

Saul led him back to one of the bedrooms. The first had been handily converted to a fine jewelers' workshop. Saul walked him through, showing the steps in the process for making a ring. Then they moved to the second room.

Here, the room had been turned into a pristine laboratory, complete with computer, some complicated looking instruments, a couple of solution tanks, a faraday cage, and a small glassed-in cube mounted on a pole.

Shane whistled. "This is quite the setup. What's it for?"

Saul smiled broadly. "This is my private research lab. I work for Naomi McIntyre on her Nano-Tech research team."

He led the way to his computer station. "In my free time, I like to hang out in here and work on projects I've been working on down below. I thought of an interesting application for the little critters that compliments Dad's art."

Saul woke the computer and got his lab online. Like a little boy about to show off his favorite rock collection, he took a small case out of a locker and moved to the table in the center of the room. "Look at this."

He waved Shane over to peer into the box. Inside was a tiny mound of what looked like metal flakes.

Using a fine pair of tweezers, he gently snagged some flakes. He put them into a micro-viewer and twiddled the controls. Soon the screen displayed a few blocky shapes with six tiny legs. They looked like microscopic toys waiting for a child to pick them up.

Saul looked proud. "These are my big boys."

He pulled the viewing tray, placing it in the glass cube. Tiny camera's mounted around the cube were aimed at the center of the platform. A screen above the cage showed a magnified view of the little bugs.

Saul picked up a pocket-tab and started inputting commands. Motion caught Shane's eye and he focused on the screen. The nannites began moving around, marching in a little circle as they sorted themselves out.

Saul put the pocket-tab down and watched the action. The movement stopped and they were lined up in a perfect row. The unit on the left rotated ninety degrees right and marched across the backs of the others. Upon reaching the end of the row, it turned left and stopped at the head of the line. When the next unit in line was cleared, it performed the same maneuver. The process sequentially repeated with each unit in the lineup.

The result was a line of tiny machines creeping to the right as one unit. As they neared the edge of the screen the process reversed and the line crept back to its starting point.

Saul grinned and, reaching down, tapped his pocket-tab. All movement stopped.

Shane grinned. "That's cool, but what can they do on a more practical level?"

Saul reached in and retrieved the viewing stage. "There are a wide variety of these little guys. One type is in common use in the medical field. Dr. Jacobs probably uses them for any number of broken bones. Those little guys assist in the building process. Someone found a way to get them to stimulate bone growth."

He set the viewing stage next to the tin where the nannites were stored. "We have nannites that have made old-fashioned welding nearly obsolete. They're suspended in a gelled solution. When you paint the gel on a steel surface and place another steel surface against it, the nannites in the gel manipulate the molecules of the two pieces and cause the metal to bond into one solid piece. You can't find a seam once the process is complete.

Saul looked up at Shane and grinned. "The only problem is, you'd better be damn sure the two pieces are exactly where you want them, because you'll have to cut them apart if they're not. It only takes a few seconds for the process in most cases."

Shane raised an eyebrow. "You said you had something that complimented your dad's art," he prompted.

Saul grinned. "Right! I'm sorry. I get so engrossed with these guys I forget where I'm headed from time to time. Come. Have a look at this."

He put his 'big boys' away before pulling out another tin, which he placed reverently on the desk. There didn't appear to be anything in the tin at first. Then, Shane noticed an unusual smear, a rainbow sheen in the bottom.

Saul took out a glass probe and a velvet bag like the one his dad had emptied on the coffee table earlier. He fished with a pair of tweezers, producing a small diamond. "I don't mess with Dad's good stones unless it's for one of his projects. This is an inferior stone, but it'll suffice for a demonstration."

He put the diamond on a special glass stand and placed it in the viewer. After some adjustments Shane had a marvelous view of the facets of a diamond, close up.

Saul took the glass probe and tapped the rainbow smear at the bottom of the tin. Shane took a close look and saw that the tip of the probe had a rainbow film on it.

Saul pulled out the viewing tray and touched the probe to the glass stage. He pushed it back into the viewer and quickly located the smear.

What showed up on the screen was fascinating. There were extremely tiny boxy shaped objects. Each had four legs. Each randomly flashed through the colors of the rainbow, changing from one brilliant color to another.

Saul touched the probe to the bottom of the tin and approached the viewer. He pulled a monocle from a small pouch at his belt and put it up to his eye. Then, using the tweezers, he picked up the diamond. Gently, he painted the bottom side of the diamond, covering the whole thing with a rainbow film. The almost wet look faded and the base of the diamond took on a dull pearlescent sheen.

After placing the diamond back on the glass stand, Saul carefully slid it back under the viewer. Once in focus, the screen showed a radically changed diamond. It had a luster and flash that would have been hard for a prime stone to duplicate.

Shane wondered what the same application would do to a priceless gem. As he watched, the color flash seemed to meld and merge in random order.

Saul pulled the diamond out of the viewer and set it in its stand on the floor of the glass cage. Even at its normal size, the diamond had more life than it had before. "Watch!" Saul said with a grin.

He reached into the air and starting with his fingers far apart, slowly brought them closer together, like he was pinching something. The room lights faded to black. There, in the glass box, the diamond glowed and glittered in rainbow colors as if it were generating its own light.

Shane was amazed. "How?"

In the dark, Saul explained. "The nannites in the mix gather power whenever light strikes the surface of the diamond. Then, when the light is off, they shed the energy in whichever frequency they're set to at a given moment. There's a random generator that determines what color to emit. They'll function for hours on the energy stored up while exposed to light."

Shane considered what that might do to a quality stone."

Saul opened the door and headed out onto the lighted hallway. Shane followed. "It's absolutely amazing. If I was back on Earth I could have made a fortune with it. If your captain friend is interested, I'd do it just for fun."

* * * *

SAT 03.13.2094
ECS Destiny, Command Deck, Command Bridge, 0650 Hrs

Tolya strode onto the bridge and assumed his station. All was in order. The two or three people that comprised the MS third shift nodded pleasantly, greeting the captain as they continued to scan their instruments.

"Report!" he called. The officer on watch approached. "Sir, all is in order. All systems are functioning nominally. There were no significant events to report."

"Thank you Mr. McKinley. You stand relieved."

McKinley nodded. "Thank you, sir." He turned and left the bridge. Before the doors could close, Vince stepped onto the bridge. He approached the command chair and leaned over to address the captain. "I'm here, sir."

Tolya looked up and grinned. "That was probably the most informal report to duty I've ever heard."

"Yes, sir. I'm inclined to agree." The men laughed quietly and Vince leaned over, speaking quietly.

"I have something for you and Tahnie to check out. You need to meet with Shane. I introduced him to a guy who can make very fine jewelry from scratch. The man has the tools and the stones. All he needs is the metal, which, by the way, we have in decent supply."

Slowly the other first shift crew-members filtered in. Tolya looked up, a gleam in his eye. "When?"

"He asked to see both of you at 1600 on Deck 2."

"Great! I'll have Shane join us for lunch."

Vince grinned. "I tell you, this guy's a wizard. You gotta see his stuff, and his son works for Naomi. He's quite the expert on Nano-Tech. While you're there, be sure to ask about his application of Nano-Tech to jewelry."

Tolya raised an eyebrow. "Wow, such high acclaim! I can't wait to meet them."

* * * *

ECS Destiny, Quarterdeck, Event Center Diner, 1200 Hrs

Tolya and Tanya were seated at their favorite spot. "...So you think Pastor Hill should do the wedding?"

Tanya nodded. "I thought he was both professional and personal. He just seems a very sincere person."

Tolya squeezed her hand. "I agree. Don't forget, he was the staff choice for the minister at The Trial."

Tanya stirred her lemonade for the hundredth time. "This guy's been Lyuba's pastor for over two years. Who better to do her adoption ceremony?"

Tolya chuckled. "Love, you don't have to sell me on this. I just said I agree."

He grew thoughtful. "Why don't we go to this little church they have on Deck 3 next weekend? Shane and Kaitlyn have been pestering me to come to church for nearly the whole voyage. We can put that little pest to rest and have a talk with this Pastor Hill."

Tanya grinned. "OK...I haven't been to church in probably six or seven years."

Tolya shrugged. "I've been away from church since my teens. I hope the shock won't be too great."

About then Shane showed up. Tolya got up and they shook hands. Shane came around and gave Tanya a gentle hug before sitting down.

"So," Tolya said, "I hear you found a master jewelry wizard."

Shane grinned. "Yeah, I guess you could say that. I've seen awesome samples of his work. Kings would vie for his services, and get this. His son has a trick using nannites."

They gave their orders to the server and Shane continued. "You should see the life nannites can bring to a diamond!"

Tanya perked up at that. "What do you mean?"

"Well, it's hard to describe. He found a way to bond nannites to the underside of a diamond; you know the rough side that's hidden by the mount?"

She nodded.

"Well, once the process is completed they get their energy from light that shines into the diamond. They're programmed to change colors in every hue of the rainbow in random order. The result is more fire in the light that flashes off the diamond."

Tanya's eyes lit up.

"Now, if you think that's good, when the lights go off, the pent up energy stored from the light they've received all day is slowly released. The result is, a slightly subdued flash and fire from the diamond even in total darkness. It's beautiful. You'll have to see it to believe it."

Tolya shook his head. "It sounds like they really are wizards."

PREPARATION — 2
ECS Destiny, Deck 2, Perlman Residence, 1600 Hrs

Samuel Perlman answered the door chime. Shane and his two friends stood smiling at the door. "Hello Shane, Captain, Ms. Nydel. Welcome. Please. Come in and make yourselves at home." He ushered them into the living room. "Sit, sit."

They settled on the large sofa and Samuel sat on the front edge of the recliner. "I take it coffee's fine?"

He got smiles and reached for the decanter in the middle of the coffee table. He poured into beautiful cups; porcelain with fine vines with leaves of gold. The coffee was very good.

"So, Captain. I've heard it from official sources that you two are to marry. Congratulations." He shook Tolya's hand.

Turning to Tanya, he took her hand, examining her fingers, turning the hand over to see the palm side. "Exquisite."

Tanya blushed.

"Don't be embarrassed, my dear. It's quite all right to have beautiful hands...Captain, you have a precious catch here."

Tolya grinned. "Yes, I'm very lucky. Oh, and please, call me Tolya. This is Tanya."

Samuel smiled. "All right, Tolya. Just call me Samuel."

He grinned and reached over to pick up a folder from the coffee table. "Before we discuss what ideas you have in mind, I thought it might be helpful for you to take a look at some of my past work."

He handed the folder to Tanya and sat back in his chair to sip his coffee and wait. He glanced at Shane with a smile.

Tanya was quickly absorbed in the amazing craftsmanship found cover-to-cover. Tolya was equally amazed. Nothing they'd ever seen compared to the artistic care represented in these pictures.

They got to the end of the collection and Tanya gently put the folder on the table. "Samuel. If your finished work is as beautiful as these I couldn't be more fortunate."

She sat back on the couch and took Tolya's arm. He offered, "Truly amazing work. I'm excited."

Samuel nodded his thanks and pulled out a pocket-tab. "Now, let's talk about you. What exactly are you looking for?"

Tolya went first. "Well, I think both of us want to wear a wedding band. I'm particularly fond of a combination of Yellow and White. I don't want a huge stone in mine; maybe some small ones would be good." He squeezed Tanya's hand, "Tahnie?"

She sat forward and considered. "I agree. We both want bands, and I'm more than happy with a two-tone look, as long as it's not too overdone. A light dusting of diamond chips on the band would be beautiful."

Samuel jotted down notes on his pocket-tab. Tanya remembered something. "I'd like to see him with two or three small stones."

Samuel smiled and sat forward in his chair. "Ok. Tolya, what about the engagement ring? Do you want it to fit in with the band as if it were part of a set, or do you want it to be a separate design?"

Tolya considered for a moment. "I've always liked the look of the engagement ring and the wedding band somehow worked together. They compliment each other."

Samuel nodded and selected a photo from the pile. "You mean something like this?"

Tolya took the photo and considered it. "Yeah, something like that." He handed the photo to Tanya who looked for a few moments and then smiled. "This is getting pretty close." Samuel placed the photo back in the folder.

The discussion went back and forth for a little while and Shane began feeling like a second left foot.

The entry door snapped open and Saul strode in. He took a package to the kitchen before returning to see the guests.

Samuel introduced the couple to Saul. "This is my son, Saul. He has a particularly intriguing talent for very tiny things."

Saul smiled and mumbled welcomes. "If someone will hand me the decanter, I'll get another round of coffee going."

Tolya, being closest, snagged the decanter, handing it over. Seizing the opportunity, Shane excused himself and went off to chat with Saul in the kitchen.

The coffee soon arrived and the talk got back to rings and things. Samuel pulled out his velvet bags and poured his amazing collection on the coffee table.

He deftly sorted, making his selections. "Here are four diamonds that I think are just right. The larger one..." He slid one aside, "...would be for Tanya's engagement ring."

"The smaller ones..." He scooted the smaller three together to the other side. "...would be for Tolya's band."

He looked up at them. "For Tanya's, I have another bag with some very fine diamonds and diamond chips."

He sat back and thought for a moment. "Well, I think we've made some progress."

A thought struck him and he looked at Tanya. "I see your ears aren't pierced. Have you considered piercing so you can wear a set with your gown?"

Tanya grinned. "No, you're right. I never had my ears pierced. In my line of work, it's not wise to have things dangling in your opponent's reach."

She smiled to take away any sting in her answer. "Besides, I've never been a big jewelry buff. I have a couple of basic necklaces but not much else."

Samuel nodded. "Very well. Is there anything else you'd like to have done?"

Tolya pondered the question for a moment and was about to shake his head no.

"We mustn't forget Lyuba." Tanya supplied

Samuel looked alert, "Lyuba? Who's Lyuba?"

Tolya grinned. "Lyuba's my niece. She lost her parents when she was an infant and has been my ward ever since. Shane and his wife have cared for her for a number of years."

Samuel sat forward. "So, where does she fit into your plans?"

Tanya answered. "Tolya and I have decided to formally adopt her. We'll be having the ceremony of adoption at the conclusion of ours. We thought it might be nice to design a pendant as a reminder of the vows we'll make together as a new family."

Samuel smiled. "How beautiful. This'll be a momentous occasion indeed." He began scooping the remaining gems back into their bag. "So, what of this pendant?"

Tolya pulled out his pocket-tab and keyed up an image he and Tanya had been working on. He handed it to Samuel for inspection. "We thought by adding a third ring to the traditional twined ring symbol we would have a wonderful representation of the bonding of our new family. The colored stones are birthstones representing each of us as individuals. The diamond in the middle represents the one family."

Samuel examined the drawing. "Indeed. You have an excellent concept here."

He looked into nowhere for a couple of moments. "So, tell me what you think of this; an oval medallion of white gold; say an inch and a half wide by an inch and a quarter. The three twined rings would be of highly polished yellow gold. I could place the four settings pretty much as you've drawn them here."

He looked up with a grin. "After all, I have an awful lot of birthstones right here." He patted the second bag that had remained closed.

Samuel picked up his pocket-tab and had Tolya transfer his drawing. "How will this be hung; from a chain? I'm afraid I don't have chain."

Tanya leaned forward. "No, I'm thinking of either hooking it on a velvet choker, or using it as a clasp for a small cape that'll go over her dress."

Samuel nodded, "Well, I'll put a couple of loops at the top and one on either side. They'll be hidden behind the medallion. If you like, I can devise hooks to sew into the cloth to fasten to."

Tanya responded. "Wonderful. You're so kind."

Samuel nodded his acceptance and then had another idea. He turned to Saul, who had seated himself at one of the chairs bracketing the chess table. "Saul, why don't you take them to see the workshop and lab?"

Saul hopped up with a broad grin. "I'd be delighted to. Please, come with me." He headed for the back and his guests followed.

The workshop was small, but well outfitted. It was amazing the array of tools a master jeweler had. Saul explained the casting process involved in making their items and then led them back out into the hall.

"Now this," he indicated the next-door down, "is my lab. I found a unique application of Nano-Tech to the making of jewelry."

The door snapped open and the lights came up. Here was the laboratory that Shane had seen the day before. Saul showed them his collection of tiny, colorful creations. Then he performed the same demonstration he'd given Shane with the diamond.

Tanya's eyes glowed with avarice at the thought of such enhanced diamonds. "I love that. It's beautiful. What about the tiny diamonds and diamond chips?"

Saul grinned. "I've wondered about that. I'm fairly certain if you got enough of the chips painted with my little guys, and sprinkled together on a surface, you'd have a subtle rippling color display. It wouldn't be really bright like the bigger diamonds, but it might make an awesome accent."

Tanya was excited. "Give it a test and let me know. I think it would set off my wedding band nicely."

Saul beamed. "Cool. I'll work on it tonight." He had another thought. "Oh, that pendant for…Lyuba, was it?" Tanya nodded.

"I could put a fine groove around the circumference of the circles. Then, if the treated diamond chips idea works out, I could fill the grooves with the treated chips."

Tolya chimed in. "Delightful! Let us know what happens with your tests."

They returned to the front room, topped off their coffee and Samuel addressed the last bit of discussion. "So, Tolya. I'll need at least two…let's say three to be safe; three, twelve inch long lengths of large gold wire. One of them should be white gold.

"Also I'll need a two inch, square sheet of yellow gold, and a two inch, square sheet of white.

"We want at least 14 karats; better yet, 18 karats for a really quality set."

He looked up from the pocket-tab that displayed his notes. "Vince tells me there's a reasonable supply of the stuff. He gave me net access to the area where the gold is kept, but he said you'd have to authorize the actual requisition."

Tolya nodded. "I can do that for you right now. Then one of you could pick it up right away."

Samuel smiled. "Excellent. Let's go to the computer and handle the red tape."

The two laughed and, coffee in hand, headed for Samuel's study.

* * * *

Felix walked back to SecCentral. It was 1320 and the lunch crowd was thinning. He entered the lobby and saw Sherry working.

She was focused on her screen and didn't see him, so he slipped quietly up next to the entrance to her station. He leaned against the wall behind her, watching her talk with someone on the COMM.

"Kaitlyn, it's Sherry."

"Hello, Sherry. Good to see ya."

"I was just reminding you about tomorrow."

Kaitlyn frowned. "Tomorrow? Oh! I can't believe it's Friday already. You're talking about the party?"

Sherry grinned. "Exactly! So far Tanya's clueless. She thinks its just going to be a planning meeting."

Kaitlyn chuckled. "Wonderful! What time again?"

"It's 1300 hours in the Staff Ready Lounge on Command Deck. Don't forget to bring Lyuba."

Kaitlyn glanced slightly off to one side as she spotted Felix in the pickup. Sherry wondered what was distracting her. Kaitlyn's eyes went a bit wide as if something had startled her.

A sudden sixth sense caused Sherry to quickly look to her right. There was Felix, leaning against the corner of the entrance to her station, grinning like a fool.

Sherry put a hand to her chest and blushed furiously. "OH! You scared the heck out of me!"

Felix straightened up and stepped closer. "I'm sorry, I didn't want to interrupt. You better tell your friend all's well before she has a fit."

Sherry turned back to the COMM. Kaitlyn had sensed her alarm was premature. "Sorry. It's OK. Its just Felix."

"So I see!" Kaitlyn didn't look her happiest. "Why's he running around loose?"

Sherry glanced at Felix nervously. He smiled and nodded. "Tell her. It's going to get around soon enough. Better to have the truth rather than speculation."

She turned back to the COMM. "Tanya and Tolya have decided he's behaving well enough to be shifted to house arrest. He lives here under the watchful eye of the staff. That way, Emily Strauss can torture him with all kinds of class work."

Kaitlyn looked askance. "I wouldn't let that get around too quickly. Folks might be a wee put out."

Sherry was a bit defensive. "Oh believe me, he's restricted to the Quarterdeck and it's not widely advertised."

"Well, OK...I guess they know what they're doing."

She shrugged. "Anyway, Lyuba and I'll be there tomorrow at 1300. See you then"

"OK. Thanks, Kaitlyn. Don't worry, Tanya's on top of things."

She cut the connection and turned to look at Felix. She seemed a little vexed. "Felix...It's a good thing that was a good friend of Tanya and Tolya. Kaitlyn's right. If it got around to the wrong people that you're running around, they'd be very unhappy.

"You're the last person left who was involved in that whole mess. So even if you didn't do the worst of it, some folks will probably attach it all to you."

Felix looked thoughtful. "I'm sorry. I should have stayed out of the pick up." He hesitated. "I just dropped by to see if you'd like to go to lunch. It's late. Most of the lunch crowd is heading back to their assignments."

Sherry brightened. "Lunch?" She glanced at the time. "I didn't realize the time."

She looked up at him. "I'd love to." She hopped up from her seat and stopped to log off. "OK, let's go!"

PREPARATION — 3

ECS Destiny, Industrial Deck, Naomi McIntyre's Office, 1330 Hrs

Daryl made his way into the warren housing Naomi's offices. He found her at her computer, pouring over yet more data on her mining project. He put the two sub-style sandwiches on the desk along with her cup of coffee.

She looked up and offered a grateful smile. "Thanks honey. How's everything in drive section?"

Daryl wagged his eyebrows. "Boring. Everything' running perfectly and I'm almost caught up on my reports. I thought of you, slaving away and decided to bring lunch."

He reached into the bag and pulled out one of the sandwiches. "Chicken, avocado with the works."

Naomi's eyes glowed. "You sweetheart!"

Daryl grinned and handed it over. Then he dug for his roast beef monstrosity. "So, why don't you take a break, turn your back on your work and have lunch with your husband?"

Naomi chuckled and obediently turned to face him.

"So," Daryl began, "have you heard what's going on with our young friend?"

Naomi nodded. "I just chatted with Tanya last night. What have you heard?"

Daryl shrugged. "Not much. Tolya told me he was upgraded to house arrest. I'm not sure what that means, but he said he was leaving it up to Tanya. He did say he had high hopes Felix would benefit from the arrangement."

Naomi nodded. "Well, the way Tanya told it, Emily prevailed on her to find a way of letting him out of his cell. She says he's passed all the tests Emily's given him. His scores are almost off the charts."

Daryl whistled. "Off the charts?"

Naomi grinned. "Almost. He shows great aptitude for the sciences. Anyway, he moved in next to Vince yesterday afternoon, and on Monday, he'll be starting on a program Emily is designing to get him through his pre-college work."

Daryl grinned, "So how long before we can put him to work?"

"We?" Naomi teased. "Emily said he has a head for mechanical things; making things work."

Daryl winced, "Nice for you!"

Naomi grinned. "Gotcha! I think we still have a while to wait. Tanya wants to take her time. It wouldn't be good to cause trouble with the colony because our guy looks like he's getting off early. I'd guess, we'll be safely in orbit before he ever gets free enough to leave the upper decks."

* * * *

SAT 03.20.2094
ECS Destiny, Command Deck, Staff Ready Room, 1304 Hrs

Tanya hurried to the Staff ready room. She'd promised to meet the girls there and was running a couple of minutes late. No one seemed to be about on Command Deck. The door snapped open on a darkened room.

Curious, she stepped in and raised a hand to turn on the lights. The instant the lights came on there was a hearty feminine yell.

The lights revealed a room full of friends and colleagues. It was decorated in the shades of green she'd selected for her wedding and there was a wonderful cake prominently arrayed on a table in the middle of the room.

Sherry gave her a hug. "Congratulations, Tahnie."

The room erupted with laughter and everyone took turns giving hugs and kisses.

Tanya was thoroughly surprised and deeply touched. The last people in line for a hug were Kaitlyn and Lyuba. Kaitlyn gave a hug and a wink.

Lyuba took her place and hugged for all her might. "I love you," she whispered.

Tanya hugged back fiercely and laughed through tears of happiness. "I love you too, princess."

Tanya took Lyuba's hand and they walked to the table. Everyone was getting seated and Tanya found herself at the head of the table.

Sherry stood and spoke. "Tanya, we didn't have time or resources to do a more traditional shower, but we just wanted to give you a little party to let you know we love you and are excited for you. Our gifts are small, but from the heart."

Tanya grabbed a napkin from the small stack next to the cake plates. She dabbed at her treasonous eyes and grinned. "Well! One thing I can say, you know how to keep a secret."

That earned her a few laughs. "That's tough to do in a tiny community like this."

She looked around the room. "Thank you. You can't begin to know how much this means to me. Thank you, Thank you."

She dabbed her eyes again. "I don't care how big or fancy the gifts are. You could've dispensed with them all together. Your love and support are enough."

She took a closer look at the decorations. "Oh, my! You got the colors just right. If we can find materials for the dresses that are close, it'll be fantastic."

She sat and Lyuba parked in the chair to her right.

Before sitting down, Sherry concluded. "I figured we could be crazy for a while and then sit down and start doing some planning. I vote we start with the cake and ice cream."

There were hearty sounds of approval all around and everyone got up to form a line around the table.

PREPARATION — 4

SUN 03.21.2094
ECS Destiny, Promenade Deck, then Deck 3, 0952 Hrs

The door snapped open and Shane smiled out at them. "Come on in. The ladies are almost ready."

They entered, gravitating to the front room to wait. Lot's of rustling about and urgent murmuring indicated a household scurrying to meet a deadline.

"Well, Owen, if you'd put things away, you wouldn't have so much trouble!" Kaitlyn's frustrated voice drifted from the back.

In another few moments, Aileen entered the family room, followed by Kaitlyn. "Oh! Good morning. I didn't expect you."

Tolya put up his hands in surrender. "Sorry, I didn't want to just barge in there. I thought we could all go together."

"Come, come, Tolya, the room won't collapse in shock at your sudden appearin'." She chuckled before calling to the back of the house. "Owen! We're waiting!"

Lyuba came into the room dressed in her finest. "Uncle Toly." She hurried over for her hug. Then turned for another from Tanya. Meanwhile, Shane went to the back of the house to get Owen motivated. Finally, everyone was ready and they all started off.

Happily, Kaitlyn had spoken the truth. The meeting hall did not collapse when Tolya stepped through the door into the pre-service activities of a lively church congregation.

A small band was set up in the front of the room, playing some inspiring, upbeat music that was surprisingly well done. People were friendly. It took a while before they realized the new visitors were the governor and his new lady. The greetings had been sincere, not feigned or self-serving.

They sat with the O'Connor's during the service. Tolya wasn't used to the contemporary church, but the style was pleasant and the joy in the music contagious. Tanya seemed familiar with the flow of the service, but remained somewhat distant. Shadows of the past distracted her.

Finally the pastor, Brad Hill, got up from the front row and mounted the low platform. He'd been very professional at THE TRIAL when he'd opened with prayer and sworn in the jury. Now, he seemed just another member of the group. There was an air of authority, but no sense he exulted in it.

"Good morning everyone. It's great to see you." His gaze swept the room and lingered momentarily on Tolya. A brief glimmer of surprise registered. "I see we have a number of new visitors this morning. I hope we've made you comfortable here. We like to make our visitors welcome. We're so glad you all chose to get up a little earlier and visit in the house of the Lord.

"On the back of the seat in front of you, you'll find a card. Please put your name and ShipNet address on it and leave it on your seat when you leave. Our ushers will pick them up after the service. I'd like to send you a message of appreciation for your visit and a short word explaining what *New Destiny* is all about. Now, let's give our visitors a warm, friendly *New Destiny* welcome."

The room erupted with hearty applause. Brad continued with announcements. They sang a couple more songs and then he opened his Bible and began his message.

One thing was certain; the man could preach. He brought a sense of authority to the passages he read and his points really made a person think.

* * * *

The music ended and people began visiting, shaking hands and slowly filtering out of the room.

Brad approached. "Captain, Governor." He took Tolya's hand and they shook firmly. He gave Tanya a brotherly hug. Then, after a quick hug for Lyuba he turned back to Tolya. "Well, I'm pleasantly surprised to see you here. I didn't know you had any interest in church things."

Tolya shrugged. "I confess it's been far too many years since I've darkened the doors of a church. I teased Kaitlyn O'Connor with the notion the church walls would collapse in shock if I came. I'm happy that she was right in denying it."

Brad grinned. "Yes, many folk have that feeling. I'm glad to see you this morning."

He turned back to Tanya. "G'day, my dear. I'm so happy to see you too. I'm starting to wonder about certain rumors about you and this fine gentleman here." His eyes twinkled as he took them both into his gaze. "Is there any truth to them?"

Tanya grinned and nodded. "Absolutely. In fact, we were hoping you might have time to chat."

"Oh?"

Tolya stepped in. "Yes, we've been working on wedding plans, and we had hoped you would do us the honor of marrying us."

Brad raised an eyebrow. "Wow! The last time I spoke with you, Ms. Nydel here, was your Security Chief, Chief Prosecutor and Counsel. Now she's to be your bride. I'm excited for you."

The last few people passed by, making polite compliments as they left. Brad shook a few hands and a young lad of about three ran up to hug his leg. He looked down and grinned, "Evan, I'm not a tree. You can't climb me."

Brad's wife came, trying to rescue Brad. She smiled. "Hello. I'm glad you could come."

Brad grinned. "Jodi. This is Captain Chernov and his new fiancé, Tanya. She's the ship's security chief."

"Oh! I thought I recognized you. You're Lyuba's Uncle right?"

Tolya grinned. "That's right."

Brad stepped in again. "This is my beautiful bride, Jodi, and this..." He lifted the young lad from the floor and held him close. "...is our son, Evan."

Tanya gave the boy a quick smile and a wink. He seemed charmed. "Hi, Evan." Evan turned suddenly and buried his face in his father's shoulder. They all chuckled.

"So captain, when would you like to meet? We have much to talk about before I make promises."

Tolya smiled. "I thought, if you weren't terribly busy today, we could have lunch and talk privately."

Brad glanced over at Jodi. She smiled and nodded, a resigned look on her face.

"I can't think of anything that could prevent me from enjoying a lunch with you."

The band had finished boxing up their equipment. The little bit of specialized furniture and the chairs were put away, leaving the place cold and empty.

Brad turned to the break down crew. "Thanks guys; see you all Wednesday?"

They chorused affirmatively.

"Great!"

He gave his wife a gentle hug and whispered something in her ear. She grinned and nodded. Handing over his energetic package, he turned for the door. "OK. Let's go."

* * * *

They finished ordering lunch and sat around the conference table. Lyuba was acting the hostess, putting out cups and pouring coffee. She finished pouring and sat next to Tanya.

Tanya gave her shoulders a squeeze. "Thanks, honey."

Lyuba grinned. She was curious about the purpose of the meeting, but kept silent and just listened.

"So, Captain..."

Tolya interrupted. "Pardon me. My friends call me Tolya. I'd be happy if you did the same."

Brad smiled. "Thank you…Tolya. I was about to ask, why me? There are at least two other ministers on board. Mind you, I truly appreciate the honor, but I'm curious."

Tolya pondered the question and Tanya watched, mildly amused. Finally he spoke. "Well, Brad, I've heard good things about you, and, frankly, I know absolutely nothing about the others you mentioned. My good friends, Shane and Kaitlyn O'Connor have sung your praises for most of the trip. You seem to be a no nonsense man with a sincere faith. Now I know you preach a great sermon."

He shifted in his seat, mildly uncomfortable. "The few times I've ever been in church since my teens, I've never met a pastor who was so matter of fact about faith; someone who could make it seem real.

"Officially, you served well at the unfortunate trials we just endured and I felt you'd do very nicely as the man to marry us."

Tanya spoke up. "After that trial, I had to agree with Tolya's appraisal. I liked the way you handled your role."

Brad nodded, sitting back, fingertips together, hands steepled in thought. He sat up and snagged his coffee. "I thank you for the compliments. I don't really work at making impressions. As you suggested, I'm quite satisfied with just being myself as I try to follow the Lord. So…"

The door chimed and a kitchen staffer rolled their lunches in. Tolya helped the young man distribute the food. "Thanks Jack."

"No problem, captain. Have yourself a great day." Tolya followed him to the door and saw him off down the corridor.

He returned and sat. "Pastor, would you please?"

"Certainly."

They all assumed prayerful postures and Brad said grace.

As the lunch progressed Brad looked up and asked. "Tolya… Would you mind sharing your faith background? What was your upbringing? How did you come to where you are now?"

Tolya sat back with his coffee and considered the question. "I haven't given it much thought for a long time. My parents were of Russian Orthodox tradition. My earliest memories were of this big, beautiful place with grand, stately music.

"They were quite faithful in the early years, but by the time I was about eight they'd become less attached somehow. When my father died my mother grieved for several years, and, for a while, we went to church more often.

"Then my big brother was killed in action during the first rim rebellion. It's like my mother lost her will to live. Church disappeared completely.

"While I served in the second rim rebellion I sent everything I could to keep her going financially, but I had become somewhat jaded to the idea of religion. I've always thought there has to be a God, but wherever He is, He doesn't seem interested in my problems. I still look out that window..." He waved at the closed curtain at the end of the room, "...and I wonder how people think it all happened by accident."

Brad finished off his sandwich and sat back with his coffee. "Thank you, Tolya. People sometimes find it hard to talk about things like this. I appreciate your candor."

He turned to Tanya. "May I call you Tanya?"

She nodded; somewhat sobered by the story Tolya had just finished. "Sure."

"Tanya. Would you mind telling your story?"

Tanya was clearly uncomfortable, but she dove in gamely. "Well, I don't remember much about my early years. My parents died when I was eight years old. They were never much for going to church. So, I didn't think much about it. I grew up bouncing between orphanages and foster homes. There were some Catholics who came on Sundays to one of the institutions I lived in. I liked them, but never really got involved.

"It was the last family that fostered me. They went to a church. Yours really reminds me of that one. The people were friendly, open and sincere. I even considered joining at one time. My foster parents were active there and they moved to adopt me. Those were the happiest years of my childhood."

Tanya paused to gather her composure. "Anyway, I went off to college, excited about a normal life with loving parents. I was seriously thinking about trusting in God when my world fell apart.

"My adoptive parents went on a short missionary venture to the Philippines while I was off to college. They were in their hotel when terrorists blew it up...

"I ah...I never saw them again." She looked up at the ceiling, blinking back the beginnings of tears. Then she looked back at Brad and continued. "The funeral was closed casket because there was little left to identify."

She was struggling to keep her voice steady. "My interest in church evaporated after that. I finished college and went on with my career. I could never come to grips with how the only people who ever truly loved me since childhood, who served God so faithfully, with such joy..." She snagged a napkin and dabbed her eyes. "I could never understand why God let that happen."

She struggled to put a smile on her face. "I'm sorry. I try not to think too much about it...because..." She waved the napkin at her face, "...this always happens."

She wiped her eyes and tossed the napkin onto her plate. "Someday, I'd like to understand."

Lyuba reached over and patted her on the back, looking concerned. Tanya attempted another smile and pulled her into a generous hug.

Brad watched the interplay with interest. "I'm sorry the story is such a sad one."

He considered. "Tolya, what about Lyuba? How does she figure in all of this?"

Tolya smiled. "Well, you know the O'Connor's have been caring for her?"

Brad nodded. "They've told me a little. She's actually your niece, right?"

"That's right. She's my older brother's daughter. He died while she was an infant and her mom wasted away. She died about a year later. Lyuba's more than just my niece, she's also my ward."

Brad's eyebrows rose. "That I didn't know. What happens to her in your plans?"

Tolya smiled and pointed to where Tanya and Lyuba were sitting together, Lyuba comforting her. "We're adopting Lyuba as our daughter. That's another reason why we wanted you. She knows you and trusts you as her pastor because she's spent nearly two years under your care. We thought, who better to perform her adoption ceremony?"

Brad sat back and stared, as if seeing Tanya for the first time. "How long has Tanya known you two?"

Tolya shrugged. "Tanya came on board as our security chief twelve hours before we shipped out of the system. I've been aware of her since then. We finally admitted an interest in each other about a month ago. She met Lyuba shortly after that."

Brad pondered the information. "I hope you know, Tolya, God's blessed you above and beyond normal expectations. I pray you never forget that."

He was silent for a moment. "Tanya?"

Tanya straightened up and put on a brave face. "Tanya, I can't give you a perfect answer to your question, partially because you have yet to understand the nature of the relationship God has with those who've given themselves fully to Him.

"All I can say, at this point, is that your adoptive parents loved you very much; that they loved God very much to give themselves to the effort of missionary work. It's a lot harder than most people will ever imagine. They served their purpose in your life, and in their mission, so God chose to bring them home."

He leaned forward. "I grieve your loss, but you need to understand that for them, it was like a promotion. That's the best I can tell you right now. Someday, soon I pray, you'll come to understand this on a personal level. I know God can and will heal your heart if you truly ask Him."

Tanya smiled again and sat up straighter. "Thank you, Brad. You're very kind."

"Not at all," he countered. "I care for people because the Lord cares for me and has called me to do the same." Brad sat back and surveyed the little family that was forming before his eyes. "I'd love to do the ceremonies."

He focused on Tanya. "I think Lyuba is most fortunate to find such total acceptance from you."

Then he turned to Lyuba. "Sweetheart, do you realize how much God has smiled on you, with a new mom?"

Lyuba nodded. "Yes, sir. I love her very much."

Brad smiled, "Well. I'm very happy for you."

He turned to Tolya. "I reserve the right to insist on doing some counseling. Some will be with just the two of you, and some will include Lyuba.

"I want you to fully understand just what you're getting yourselves into. You seem to have a reasonably good idea, but, before God, you need to understand His expectations."

Tolya looked over at Tanya. She nodded quietly and Tolya turned back to Brad. "Thank you. We're committed to this, and we accept your counseling."

Brad smiled. Then he stood and asked them to join him. He took Lyuba's hand and she grabbed Tanya's. Tolya caught on and gripped hands to complete the circle.

"Thank you Tolya, for a fine lunch. I should get going, but I'd like to pray with you before I go. Then we can meet…Oh, let's make it three meetings in the next three weeks. Call me tomorrow for times."

He smiled around the circle. "Let's pray…Father…"

PREPARATION — 5

MON 03.22.2094
ECS Destiny, Quarterdeck, Staff Conference Room, 0930 Hrs

Tanya finished pouring the coffee and sat. Tolya finished his notes and looked up. Everyone was present. "Good morning everyone. We've a lot to cover today, so I'm going to get right down to it. We'll start on my left with Frank, and go around the table."

The usual morning chatter was somewhat subdued. Apparently the Monday morning coffee had yet to take effect. "OK. Frank, you're on."

Frank sat forward. "Well, I don't have much to report, really. Everything is going just fine. If we weren't going in a totally new direction, one would think nothing had ever gone wrong.

"I have good news. My calculations say we should be dropping from MS by some time Sunday evening or Monday morning, early."

Daniela perked up. "Sunday or Monday? That's almost a week early, isn't it?"

Frank grinned. "Yes, it is. Our initial estimation had to take in a number of uncertainties, but our numbers firmed up significantly and progress has been excellent. That's all I got, so if there are no more questions, I'll hand it off to Emily."

Emily smiled. "Where to start..."

She sat back and considered. "I guess I'll take up where Frank left off. Like he said, we're going to come out of MS almost a week early. From what we've been able to calculate, we'll be dropping out at a sharp angle to the local plane of the ecliptic.

"That means we'll have about two weeks of reasonably free cruising before we have to consider possible debris. The local Oort cloud will be our first goal, so that means a bit of maneuvering to enter the cloud at the right angle."

She sat forward and set her empty cup on the table. "Next, I guess we could talk about Felix. I'll let Tanya give the details, but I'm starting a crash program to get his education on track. He shows great promise, particularly in the sciences. I think Naomi will be seeing more of him in a few months. He's very determined."

Frank grabbed the decanter and poured her another cup as she continued. "In other areas of education, I am very excited to announce, I brought on a new associate. Her name is Francine Douglas. It was her little boy, Dennis, who got to participate in our insertion into MS."

There were several heartfelt chuckles. That event had become a fond memory; the little guy seriously counting down and shouting 'Go!' during transition.

Daryl grinned. "I still can't get over that sudden cry on the intercom. I didn't expect the sound of a little boy, gleefully howling 'Go!' as the cascade started."

Emily continued. "Francine has a wonderful way with children, and she has plenty of experience working in the school systems back on Earth. I'll be putting her directly in charge of the early childhood and elementary programs. We'll probably see more of her at the occasional staff meeting, giving reports."

Tanya smiled. "I told you she was a great choice."

She glanced at Tolya. "It was Tolya who first noticed she had a talent with kids. I think you're all going to like her."

She sipped her coffee and then continued. "I know I'm out of turn, but since I'm involved in the Felix story, I'd like to put my two cents in while the subject is fresh."

Nobody objected so she continued. "Well, Emily prevailed on me to find a way to lengthen Felix' leash, so to speak. So, I did a little research and came up with a plan. I have Tolya's approval." She looked over at him with a little grin. "It was a little reluctant, but I got it." A couple of surreptitious chuckles circled the table.

She grinned self-consciously and continued. "Long story short; just in case nobody's noticed, we have a new neighbor in FP-24. Felix has been upgraded to house arrest."

She looked around the table. "I'm counting on you to help keep an eye on him. He wears a security bracelet, so the ship's computer knows where he is all the time. Without a special pass, he can't go anywhere but Quarterdeck."

Daniela started to say something and Vince gave her a gentle nudge. "Sorry. Tanya, don't you think we're going a little too fast?"

Daniela looked at Vince and nodded. Tanya understood. "Yeah, I thought about that myself, but as Emily pointed out, he's wasting his time staring at four walls. Trust me, he's serving his time. He's forbidden from the rest of the ship."

Tolya stepped into the gap. "Vince, Dannie, believe me, I had strong reservations when Tanya first brought up the subject, but I figure with all of us interacting with him, and keeping him honest, he stands a good chance of staying on this 'new leaf' he claims to have turned.

"Frankly, I'm impressed with his handling of the situation so far. He's gone out of his way to be respectful and helpful. Tanya hasn't mentioned this, but I might as well since I've started gabbing. We've taken Felix and Sherry on as students in Karate. I know most of you have peeked in to watch us work out from time to time."

He looked around with a grin. "So, while Emily is going to be his academic coach. Tanya and I have taken on his athletic coaching. Believe me..." He looked at Daniela. "Felix will get stretched in every way possible. Don't think he's getting off easy. Besides, he knows the instant he violates his restrictions, he's back in that cell."

Daniela nodded. "It's not that I don't want to see him rehabilitated. It's just, if people get the impression he's getting preferential treatment, some of them at least, will certainly be very put out."

Tolya nodded. "I understand that. That's one reason why we won't let him down on the residential decks. I've also noticed that Felix is very sensitive to what people might be feeling. He makes a point of staying out of the public areas like the Diner until most of the folk from the residential decks have left.

Daniela relaxed. "Well, I truly wish him well. Something good has to come from all that grief."

Like sentiment circled the room and Tolya looked about. "I guess it's Daryl's turn."

Daryl poured himself another coffee. "Well, like Frank, there's very little to report. Everything is running as advertised. The MS and the NS drives are happy. We've done a complete test of the shuttles and the work bees. All are ready for use when we get in system." He looked to his left.

Naomi patted his hand and then pushed her coffee cup back. "I've been busy. We've been looking at ways to extract raw materials from the various bodies in this system's Oort cloud. Since we had no actual micro-g mining equipment on board, I sat down and drew up plans for making our own equipment.

"I designed a specialized robotic ore extractor. It's programmable to cut and ingest the raw materials on a given body. Its container is removable, and I've made it compatible with the work bees for towing purposes.

"I also designed a self-contained processing rig. It's designed to be stationed in a clear area between targeted bodies. The bees can tow this thing as well, all to minimize the number of people who must be exposed to the extremely hazardous environment."

Naomi sat back. "Your turn, Dannie."

Daniela grinned. "You've been very busy." She looked around the table. "Well, I've been working on basic medical supply issues;

making sure we have no serious shortages. I'm happy to say we're doing well. There are no shortages, yet."

She smiled and continued. "We've been surprisingly fortunate over all in the basic health of the population. There have been no major outbreaks of the usual nasties, like influenza. The few individual cases have been quickly treated and the afflicted person effectively isolated from the general population. Let's just hope things continue that way."

Daniela looked at Vince. "Your turn."

Vince grinned. "I've been busy 'coordinating.' I've been the troubleshooter, and I'm pleased to report that nobody has had any trouble worth shooting."

That brought a few chuckles and a groan or two. "All seriousness aside, I'm looking forward to seeing this new system. By the way, has anyone given thought to a name?"

Blank looks abounded. "Well, I think it might be fun to come up with a name for it. People identify more readily with things they can name."

Tolya took the floor. "Thanks Vince. I think you have a good point. I'm not sure anyone has given much thought to a name."

Emily grinned. "Well, the images I had to study gave me a couple of ideas. The grouping of the visible stars in the vicinity of our target made me think of a circlet of jewels. I thought of a princess' tiara…"

She looked around self-consciously, "I know, silly, but that's what came to mind. The star we're headed for is at the closed end of a partial circlet of stars. It is brighter than the rest, which made me think of a gem covered tiara."

Tolya smiled. "Well, it has a nice ring to it. Let's give it some thought." He turned to the last members of the staff, "Ichirou, Midori, anything?"

Ichirou smiled. "Everything is growing well…"

A couple of groans rewarded his effort. "And, I have no problems to report."

He turned to Midori, "Mi'chan?"

Midori gave Ichirou a generous smile and nodded respectfully towards Tolya. "I am happy to say that hydroponics is rich and fertile. I've managed to improve the yields on my crops. So, I foresee no shortages. I have started my husband and his crew to working on Promenade Deck for a certain wedding. That's about all for now."

Tolya inclined his head. "Thank you both."

He looked around. "Well, if there are no questions, I'll let you all dig in."

He stood, stowing his pocket-tab on his belt. "Since we're dropping out of MS near our meeting time next week, we'll switch it to the Friday before. Let's get to it!" He grinned and all got up to go about their day.

As everyone was moving for the exit, Ichirou approached Tolya. "Tolya, about your teaching Karate to the two young people, I was not aware you practiced the art. I would like to come and observe one of your sessions. I regret not working out since leaving Earth."

Tolya was surprised. "Ichirou. I'm delighted to hear that you also practice the art. I'd be honored to have you come visit. You're welcome to work out with us if you wish."

Ichirou seemed relieved somehow. "Thank you, Tolya. I didn't know that Tanya also practiced."

Tolya grinned. "I knew from her files, but I'd never seen her in motion. I walked in on one of her practice sessions one day. She's good! If you don't mind my asking, what's your current rank?"

Ichirou grinned. "I am Nidan black, but it has been a long time since I worked out."

Tolya gave a slight bow. "Second degree black. That's great. Tanya is also Nidan black. I earned Sandan black a few years ago."

It was Ichirou's turn to offer a slight bow. "Third degree, Congratulations. I look forward to working out with you."

His glance darted quickly to find Midori finishing her chat with Tanya. "I regret we must leave for now. Please leave me a note with times so I can come. Thanks, Tolya."

They bowed in the fashion of the martial artist, with one difference. Rather than with covered fists, the left hand remained open, resting against the flat of the right fist. It was a simple gesture of peace and friendship.

"I'll get that note to you today." Tolya smiled and turned to join Tanya as Midori took Ichirou's arm and they made their exit.

* * * *

ECS Destiny, Quarterdeck, Event Center Lobby, 1030 Hrs

Felix and Sherry left the Diner. "Well. I gotta get to work."

"Yeah, me too. Dr. Strauss said after breakfast she wanted me in her office."

Sherry gave a look of mock horror. "Ooh! You're in for it now. Your nose will be on that grinding stone for sure."

Felix laughed. "I expect you're right. So, how about lunch?"

"Lunch would be great. What time?"

Felix pondered. "Most folk are gone by around 1330. Can you wait that long?"

Sherry considered. "You're trying to stay away from everyone, aren't you?"

Felix looked down. "Yeah. I don't like the looks I get from those few who really recognize me. I don't want to make any more trouble for everyone."

Sherry reached out and touched his arm. "I'm sorry, Felix. Someday they'll see the guy I see."

Felix looked puzzled, trying to parse the spectrum of meanings in her comment.

"It's OK Felix, 1330 will be just fine."

He smiled. "OK, I'll come by the office then."

Sherry smiled and headed down the corridor for SecCentral. He watched her go for a few moments and then turned and headed for the Port Side Education Wing. He had a date with Dr. Strauss.

As he stood at the entrance, he heard a voice call to him. Dr. Strauss approached from the Command Staff Conference room. "Good morning, Felix."

"Good morning. How was your meeting?"

"Very good. Things are progressing nicely."

She led the way through the lobby to her offices. The door recognized her patch and snapped open on a reasonably comfortable room. In one corner was a desk and chair facing into the room. Four chairs stood in an arc facing the desk. Various cabinets were ranged about the edges of the room.

She indicated a chair facing the desk, and as Felix got settled she moved around the desk and sat down. "Felix. You've probably heard this till you're tired of it, but many of us think you show great promise. I don't know what happened in your past to maroon you in this mess, but now you have the chance to turn adversity into opportunity. All that's needed is hard work."

She stopped, giving Felix a chance to comment. "You're right. I've heard this a lot in the last couple of weeks. I've never had so many people tell me I'm worth something, but I don't resent it. I know I'm not stuck in a rut in the streets of Chicago or some other hellhole anymore."

He sat looking at nothing, thinking. "I have new friends; even some enthusiastic friends I am perpetually aware I don't deserve." He looked directly at her. "Believe me. I know I have everything to gain and nothing to lose from busting my butt, and that's exactly what I plan to do."

Emily smiled as she woke her computer. "You're very articulate for someone in your situation. I've worked up a program for you. You'll be happy to hear I'm skipping most of the 'fluff' the public schools thought so necessary. I'm aiming for the basics. If you can sprint through your English, History, Math, and Sciences, I think we can cover the ground in about six months. Then we'll test to see where you are best suited to concentrate your efforts."

Emily opened a drawer on one side of her desk. "I have a fair idea where that might be, but I want you to discover it and own it for yourself."

She pulled out a power-tab. "This is for you to use indefinitely. I've stuffed it with a number of texts. All of your subjects are here. There's an interactive menu that'll guide you to what assignments you must complete.

"Start with the reading. You'll have a fairly flexible schedule. If you're diligent, I'll not hold you to a fixed daily routine, but start slacking off and you'll be glued to these rooms."

She handed the device across the desk. "You can send your assignments on ShipNet. I set up a special account. You'll find instructions for activating it when you power up."

Felix took the device and Emily stood. "Come. Let's meet Gregory in the lobby. He knows everything about this facility. Later, I'll have him give you a quick tour."

* * * *

ECS Destiny, Deck 1, 1045 Hrs

Kaitlyn checked off another item on her list. The gowns were in progress and the cake was ordered. Lyuba grinned as they left the seamstress' residence. "It's gonna be a beautiful wedding."

Kaitlyn smiled. "I agree. Tanya has good taste in decorating."

Lyuba grinned. "I love my dress. It's kinda like Ms. Tanya's, except it's ivory with green trim."

Kaitlyn grinned. "It's a lovely touch. The other dresses have green with ivory trim. They're opposite"

Lyuba puzzled for a moment. "Oh, yeah. I never thought about it."

* * * *

ECS Destiny, Quarterdeck, Captain's Cabin, 1320 Hrs

Tolya answered the COMM. It was 1320 and he was headed for lunch with Tanya. His impatience was replaced with expectation when he recognized Saul Perlman on the screen. "Saul! What's up?"

"Tolya, I have good news for you. Remember that process with the diamond chips we discussed?"

Tolya nodded. "Yeah."

"Well, I ran the tests and I'm delighted to say the results exceeded all expectation."

Tolya grinned. "Great. So what's the plan?"

"Tanya said she wanted a fine spray of diamond dust on her band. She was also interested in the idea of outlining the circlets on Lyuba's pendant with the same thing."

Tolya considered. He remembered Tanya saying if the tests came back positive, she'd like Saul to do what he had described.

"Yeah, well, Tanya hasn't said anything to the contrary. So, since she was very excited about the prospect, I'll stick my neck out and say, 'go for it.'"

Saul grinned like a child let loose in a candy store. "Great. You guys are gonna love it. By the way, Dad says the engagement ring should be ready by Wednesday, noon."

Tolya whistled. "Wow. That was fast."

Saul shrugged. "Yeah, he got on it the night you guys came over. I haven't seen him so focused on a project in a long time."

Tolya glanced at the time display. "Listen, Saul. I don't mean to run on you, but I've a lunch date with my bride and I'm running to get there on time."

Saul laughed. "Well, I won't keep you. Why don't you come Wednesday for lunch? You can pick up the ring then."

Tolya grinned. "Excellent idea. Thank you." He glanced at the time display. "I better go now; see you Wednesday."

"Ok! Later." Tolya ran for the dining hall.

Felix stepped out of the port side education center as Tolya approached. "Felix. What's up?"

"I promised to get Sherry for lunch."

Tolya chuckled. "Well, I'm headed for lunch with Tanya right now. We'll save you a couple seats."

Felix replied, "OK. Thanks. We'll see you in a few minutes." Both men trotted in opposite directions.

* * * *

Sherry wrapped up her morning work and put the computer to sleep. It was 1335. She puttered around her station organizing and reorganizing things, keeping an eagle eye on the lobby entrance.

She was finally rewarded to see Felix hurrying in. She bent to her desk, fidgeting and reorganizing things until he presented himself.

"Hey! Sorry I'm late. I got caught up on an assignment and forgot the time."

Sherry looked up with a smile. "That's OK. I was just closing up for lunch."

Felix grinned, "I bumped into the captain and stopped to chat. He said he was going to save us a place in the lounge. You still want to come, right?"

Sherry, smiled and grabbed her bag. "Of course."

"Come on. You said Tanya doesn't like to be kept waiting." They walked briskly down the corridor to the diner.

* * * *

TUE 03.23.2094
ECS Destiny, Industrial Deck, Main Shuttle Bay, 1320 Hrs

Tuesday proved to be just as busy as Monday. Naomi finished examining the tow linkages on one of the work bees in the hanger bay. She'd decided to add some reinforcement to account for the stresses of all the heavy towing they were about to do.

Her ore extractors were going to be somewhat massive. The processing barge she'd just finished the last computer simulation on would be even worse. It would take at least four of the six work bees to lift and tote the thing out to its assigned station.

A flash of inspiration hit; if the four work bees were fastened to the tow points and then slaved together to a synchronized control module, the process of maneuvering the ungainly contraption would be much more efficient.

After jotting down this thought, Naomi left the hanger bay and headed back to her offices. *Yet another session of brain wracking creativity*, she thought. This brought a grin. She was having fun!

* * * *

ECS Destiny, Quarterdeck, Emily's Office, 0930 Hrs

Emily looked up from a report when Felix entered. "Good morning. I went over your English assignment a while ago. Your writing is surprisingly good."

Felix smiled. "Thank you."

Emily grinned, pointing him to a chair. "Oh, don't thank me quite yet. You've a long way to go, but I was happy to see you show some promise. I want you to read the next assignment and then write a well thought out report.

She sat back, watching Felix take lightning quick notes. "What I'm looking for here is comprehension. Different people show different rates of comprehension from the same body of reading. I want to see what you truly understand from a couple of readings."

She leaned forward at her desk. "So, tell me in your own words the basic idea of what the author's trying to say. Did the author present the information in a way that helped you understand, or did he or she muddy the waters so you had to dig to understand it?" She smiled. "That's it."

Felix finished his notes. "Got it. When do you want it?"

Emily grinned. "How about tomorrow evening. Just send it on ShipNet to my mail. I'll read it over and we'll talk Thursday."

Her eyebrows furrowed till the elusive thought yielded to her probe. "Hmm, I almost forgot. For math, just skim the first three chapters. Do the practice exercises at the end of each chapter. Let's make it the odd problems. When you're finished, we'll go over it and see how you've done. Let's make it Thursday midmorning."

Felix made another note and nodded. "What about the science and history?"

Emily grinned. "Just skim your way through the first two chapters in the general science and the same in microelectronics and processors. No written work this time, but be prepared to discuss those passages by midweek, next.

"Oh!" She lifted a finger for emphasis. "Things are about to get hectic. It appears we've made better time than estimated originally. We're due to drop out of MS Sunday evening or Monday morning."

Felix' eyes widened. "That's almost a week early!"

Emily grinned. "Yep! Then we're going to have a wedding the following weekend. If all goes well, we'll be headed for the inner system about three weeks later."

Felix was excited. Something was going to go right this time!

Emily smiled. "Because of the insanity that's about to take place, I'll not require anything more till after the wedding. After Thursday you have a week and a half before we crack the books again."

Felix glanced at the time on his power-tab: '0950.' "Well, I'd better get cracking. I've been using the research and study hall. I hope you don't mind."

"Not at all, Felix. That's what it's for."

Felix got up and nodded before leaving the room.

PREPARATION — 6
WED 03.24.2094
ECS Destiny, Deck 2, 1220 Hrs

Tolya and Tanya made their way against the flow of lunch goers to present themselves at the Perlman residence.

Saul opened up. "Come on in. I've got lunch. It's not much, just some sandwiches and coffee."

Tanya smiled. "I've no problem with sandwiches and coffee."

Saul grinned. "I'm so relieved."

Samuel entered the room in the middle of friendly laughter. The men shook hands and Tanya was greeted with hugs.

Samuel started for the kitchen. "Let's eat. Then I have something to show you."

Samuel had a mysterious expression on his face as they arranged themselves at the table and Saul started handing out sandwiches, which vanished quickly enough.

After lunch, Samuel headed for his workshop, motioning his guests to follow. There, he picked up one of two small, velvet boxes and turned to Tolya. "Take a look."

He picked up the other, slightly larger box and turned to Tanya. He gently took her arm and led her to a table nearby. "While he's busy, why don't you have a look at this?"

Curious, Tanya took the box and carefully pried it open. Inside was the pendant of their drawings, but it was much more than she'd imagined. Everything they'd discussed was there.

Tanya noticed the dusted centerlines around the three rings. There was a shimmering iridescence that ran the circumference, constantly changing its pattern. It had a life of its own.

"Samuel, Saul. This is absolutely wonderful!"

She picked the pendant up from its velvet bed and carefully looked it over. The birthstones were richly colored, not dull like commercial stones she'd seen before...and the diamond; it seemed alive. The room was dimly lit and the inner glow caused by the nannites was visible. On the back were two sets of loops, giving multiple options for mounting it. Careful not to get fingerprints on the front, she placed it reverently back in its bed and closed the box.

Meanwhile Tolya had been examining the engagement ring. It was exquisite; white gold with gentle slashes of yellow gold worked from about a third of the way around the band to the base of the crown. In the slashes was a fine dust of diamond, treated with the nannite paint. The diamond in the crown had a natural fire, also enhanced by the nannite treatment. He carefully placed it back in its box.

Samuel smiled. "That will ultimately nestle in the wedding band which will be of yellow gold with a dusting of treated diamond dust. Tolya nodded his understanding. "Thank you. I believe you are a master magician extraordinaire."

Samuel shrugged. "I do what I love." He waved in Tanya's direction. "Go on now, give it to her!"

Tanya looked up from the pendant box as she handed it to Saul. Tolya was approaching with the tiny velvet box. "Tanya, this is a little something I owe you; a little something to remind you it's for real; not just a dream."

Her heart trembled all over again as she took the box and opened it. She just stood for a few moments, dazzled by the awesome fire shining from the box.

Tolya gently took the ring with one hand and her left hand with the other. He looked into her eyes and then gently slipped the ring over her wedding finger. Tanya stared at it for a moment and then, oblivious to the presence of anyone else, threw herself into Tolya's arms and buried her face in his chest.

"Thank you." She whispered, "I love you, ring or no ring, but this is beautiful."

They stood there in a prolonged embrace. Finally, they parted and Tanya brushed happy tears from her face; the flash of the ring tracing brief rainbow arcs in the air.

* * * *

ECS Destiny, Quarterdeck, Open Gym, 1530 Hr

Sherry and Felix emerged from the locker rooms and moved to stand together, quietly chatting until Tolya and Tanya entered from the port side entrance.

As they approached, the two turned and offered well-rehearsed bows. Tolya and Tanya stopped, returning the gesture with grins.

It took a second for Sherry to identify the odd flash she'd seen during Tanya's bow. Then she zeroed in on the beautiful ring on her left hand.

She ran forward and gasped as she got a closer look. "Oh, Tahnie! Its beautiful!"

Tanya pulled her into a hug. "Yes, but let's talk after. OK?"

Sherry remembered the circumstance. "Of course." She grinned and rejoined Felix on the matted floor.

Felix glanced at the glitter on Tanya's hand. *Very impressive.* In another time he'd have already calculated the odds of acquiring the prize. He realized the prospect held no interest. He had other purposes now.

An hour and a half later, flushed with exertion, the four headed for the locker rooms; Sherry already angling for another look at Tanya's ring.

The guys reveled in the soothing, hot shower. The fine, needle sharp spray working over sore muscles was therapeutic. When they had finished dressing Felix finally worked up nerve to ask his question. "Captain?"

Tolya looked up from fastening his shoes. "What's up Felix?"

"Dr. Strauss says we're going to drop out of MS a week early; that we made better time than expected."

Tolya finished and sat on the bench. "Yeah?"

Felix looked nervous. "I thought another week would've been better before making special requests, but...I'd really like to witness it on the bridge. I've never been up there and...well, the curiosity's killin' me."

Tolya suppressed a grin. "So, what do you suppose you'll see from the bridge?"

"Honestly, I don't really know, but if I'm supposed to be learning new things, this would be a good opportunity. Besides, it's an historic event. I want to see what you all really had in mind."

Tolya sat looking at Felix for a few moments, weighing things over. "Well, Felix. I'm not sure exactly what you're looking for, but I don't think the experience would hurt...

"I'll tell you what. My niece did this on her own initiative and I think you're quite capable of duplicating it. Go on ShipNet and find the pages on *Destiny's* bridge. Read up on what happens on the bridge of a starship. Then, you and Sherry will have dinner with us Saturday evening around 1900 hrs."

Tolya stood from his place on the bench. "Then, over dinner, I want you to tell me everything you've learned. If you're interested enough to go to that much trouble, I'll authorize a bridge visit and have Tanya update your bracelet. That doesn't mean you have perpetual access, but we'll discuss that later."

Felix remembered to breath. "Thank you sir. I look forward to dinner on Saturday."

Tolya met Tanya as she and Sherry came out of the locker room. "My favorite duo. Tahnie, we need to hurry if we don't want to keep Pastor Brad waiting."

Tanya nodded. "Oh, right! I'm sorry, Sherry. Later?"

"That's OK." She waved. "See you tomorrow." She caught up to Felix who was waiting by the starboard exit.

Tolya and Tanya headed off and he shook his head. "Poor Felix. He's hooked, netted and in the bottom of the boat. He just doesn't know it yet."

Tanya laughed as they hurried for the aft lift well. She pressed the call tab and he told her about his conversation with Felix.

"Well, I told him he couldn't go there without your invitation. So, that's up to you." She grinned, "But, why Sherry too?" The doors snapped open and they boarded.

Tolya tapped Deck 3 and answered. "Extra bait!"

Tanya laughed. "You're positively evil, you know."

He responded. "Yeah and you love it!"

That got him an elbow in the ribs.

PREPARATION — 7

ECS Destiny, Quarterdeck, Felix' Cabin, 1750 Hrs

Felix sat, searching ShipNet. The COMM chimed and he flicked the icon. Sherry's face popped up and Felix smiled. "Hey there. What's up?"

She grinned, "You asked me about Tolya's niece. I got permission to have a three-way conversation. Interested?"

Felix brightened. "Sure. I do have some questions for her."

"OK. She's on the other channel. Just a minute."

"OK."

Sherry's picture remained, but she was busily waving at her office computer.

Soon another window opened to display a bright young lady of thirteen. Felix saw the resemblance to the captain.

Her eyes widened when she saw Felix on her screen. She bit down slightly on her lip and seemed to steel herself.

Sherry's window highlighted and the audio returned. "Can you hear me, Felix?"

"Yeah, I hear you just fine."

Sherry's gaze shifted to one side. "And you?"

Lyuba spoke up. "Got it."

Sherry grinned. "OK, Lyuba, meet Felix."

Lyuba's eyes darted to connect with Felix.

"Hello, Lyuba, pleased to meet you."

She hesitated. "Hello, Felix…You're the other guy who caused all that trouble for my Uncle."

Felix wanted to sink into the floor. He looked down for a moment. "Yes, yes I am. I want you to know I'm very sorry for all that stuff. I was being stupid and listening to the wrong people."

Lyuba regarded him sternly. Then she looked over at Sherry's window. Sherry smiled and answered the unasked question. "It's true Lyuba. He's been trying to make up for all that. Your dad, I mean your uncle and Tanya are teaching us karate."

Lyuba puffed up for just a second at the reference to Tolya as her dad. "He's teaching you guys karate? He never taught anybody that stuff before."

She appeared to be thinking on the phenomenon. "Well, if my dad…he'll be my dad pretty soon. If he's doing that, I guess he trusts you. Kaitlyn…she's kinda like my foster mom…she said if Sherry was on, I could talk to you. So, what do you want?"

Felix grinned. Kids could be so direct; no small talk here. "Captain…your uncle…they're really adopting you?"

The idea distracted him. He'd not heard that twist in the story.

"Yes, it's going to happen at their wedding. I'm going to be part of it and then we'll have an adoption ceremony at the end."

"That's cool! Really. Congratulations."

Lyuba grinned. "Thanks."

Felix said. "OK. I'm just going to call him your dad. All this 'uncle or dad' stuff's driving me crazy."

Lyuba laughed. "I know. I get frustrated when I talk to my friends about it. To me, he's my dad already."

Sherry grinned as she watched the exchange.

Felix returned to his question. "Anyway, I asked your dad if I could visit the bridge when we drop out of MS this weekend. He said something I didn't quite understand. He said you did something about the bridge on ShipNet and if I could go to that kind of trouble he'd grant my request."

Lyuba laughed. "Oh that. It's nothing. I just went on ShipNet and dug up all the information I could find about the bridge. There's all kinds of information available if you know where to look. I wanted to understand why my…dad was always busy up there."

Felix shook his head. "OK. I guess I could figure it out, but if I knew where to go, I'd be able to get all the information faster and have more time to study it."

Lyuba got a sly look. "You're looking for a short cut."

Felix grinned. "You got me. Do you mind?"

She grinned. "No problem. It's easy, really. Are you familiar with ShipNet?"

Felix shrugged. "A little. I didn't need it much before...you know...Anyways I'm learning quick."

"OK. Listen. Go to the main index and look up the *Destiny* pages. There's all kinds of stuff there. There's this really cool section with plans and drawings of every part of the ship.

"One of those pages has a deck plan drawing with interactive icons that take you to a full description of the area you select. You can select the bridge on that page and another page comes up. There's a plan of the bridge there. Each of the stations has a link you can select that gives you all kinds of information."

Felix grinned. "You're right. That does sound easy. Thanks."

"No problem. So, are you going to the wedding?"

Felix sat stunned at the question. He'd sort of assumed he'd attend, but it was going to be held down on Promenade Deck, far out of reach for his confinement restrictions.

"I want to, but...well, do you know what house arrest is?"

Lyuba nodded. "That's where the prisoner's allowed to live in his home instead of in jail. Right?"

Felix nodded. "Yeah. Well, that's me. I'm still doing time, but I live in a cabin opposite Tanya. I have a bracelet that won't let me go anywhere but Quarterdeck. That makes it kind of tough to get down to where the wedding will be."

Lyuba looked thoughtful. She glanced over at Sherry's image. "What do you think, Sherry? You think we could talk to my...dad and...mom?"

Sherry grinned. "Sure. I'll talk to Tanya and you talk to your...to Tolya."

Lyuba had a mischievous look. "Kinda like getting them from both sides; I like it."

She looked at Felix again. "So, Sherry said you didn't kill anybody. Right?"

Felix flushed. "No, I didn't. I thought I did when I knocked Sherry down and she passed out. I didn't mean to do that. I was just too scared, but..." He glanced at the image of Sherry smiling from the other window. "I'm very glad I was wrong."

Lyuba smiled. "I just wanted to be sure. Before the trial, I thought you were another murderer. When Sherry asked about talking to you I was a little scared..."

She looked at Felix. "I'm glad I was wrong about you. I'll talk to my dad. The wedding will be the greatest thing that's happened here in a long time. "My new dad and mom are going to be in it. Sherry is going to be in it. I'm going to be in it…"

She looked at Sherry. "He's got to go. It'll be good for him!"

Sherry grinned and Felix sat trying to understand the female of the species.

Felix noted the time and realized he still had studies to complete. "Um, thanks, you two, but I have a bunch of assignments to finish. I gotta get busy."

Sherry glanced at the time. "Wow! You're right. Will I see you at breakfast?"

Felix grinned. "Sure. Sounds great."

Lyuba watched the conversation and another sly look crossed her face as pieces of a puzzle suddenly slipped into place. "Well, I better go. It's almost time to go for Wednesday night service. Bye."

Her window blanked and vanished from the screen.

Sherry looked at Felix. "Well, I guess I'll let you get back to work. See ya tomorrow. Bye."

Felix responded. "Ok. Thanks. Bye."

Sherry vanished and Felix quit the COMM.

PREPARATION — 8
ECS Destiny, Promenade Deck, 2030 Hrs

Daryl and Naomi walked slowly along the stone path in companionable silence.

"So how are our famous lovebirds?"

Naomi grinned. "Well, they're doing just fine." She looked thoughtful before continuing. "You know, I had my doubts about your approach, back when you gave them your little lecture. Now I'm glad you did it. Both of them have taken on a stronger character. They present a unified front. Their strengths tend to cancel out their weaknesses. They benefit from a loving relationship and the colony benefits from stronger, unified leadership."

Daryl thought about her comments. "We don't do so badly ourselves. That's one thing I told Tanya. She was struggling with what I was telling her and I pointed out how our own relationship was similar. We do tend to balance each other."

Naomi smiled, hugging his arm. "I'm glad you think so."

Daryl put his arm around her shoulders as they continued. "How are the wedding plans going?"

Naomi smiled. "Things are going well. The gowns should be ready by Tuesday. Tanya got her ring and Lyuba's pendant early this afternoon."

She looked up at his face. "They have a minister; you know, the one who presided at the trials?"

Daryl looked down at her. "He seems like a great guy. Most of the ministers I've ever met seemed...I don't know...they were less than they claimed."

Naomi stopped and turned to face him. Daryl stopped, curious. "Daryl, have you thought about giving faith another try? I have."

Daryl shrugged. "I don't usually think about stuff like that very often. Yet...in the last several weeks, I've been wondering about a lot of things."

Naomi looked thoughtful. "You know, we've moved far from our foundations. I'm wondering if it isn't time for us to reinvest our lives in God."

Daryl got a far away look in his eye. "I got so disgusted with church, I didn't want to ever go back to one. That horrible man destroyed everything." He sighed, "Now I'm not so sure. Maybe it's time to put all that behind me. Is that what you're thinking?"

"Yeah, something like that..."

She turned and looked at some beautiful flowers next to her. "When he counseled us before the wedding, I thought he was great. Then he ran off with that singer..." She looked back at Daryl, trying for positive territory. "The judge wasn't so bad." She smiled. "I got you. That's the best part."

"I think Tolya and Tanya are having their own reunion with faith," Daryl commented. "This Brad Hill seems to be the real deal. Maybe we should check out his little church."

Naomi considered. "Sure. Why not?"

Daryl grinned, "It couldn't hurt. I'll ask Tolya about time and place. They attended last weekend."

Naomi's brows arched. "Really? OK."

They stopped near the fountain pool and watched the ongoing work of transformation. Naomi had a wistful look on her face. "It's going to be one of the most beautiful weddings I've seen."

Daryl pulled her in close, pressing her head against the side of his chest, burying his face in her hair. "I'm so sorry."

She tilted her head up so she could see his face. "It's not your fault that man made such a mess of our wedding plans. I'm VERY happy with you."

* * * *

THU 03.25.2094
ECS Destiny, Quarterdeck, 0730 Hrs

Felix stood in the open lobby area of the Event Center. He was reading through his texts on his power-tab. A light trickle of foot traffic came and went between the lifts and the dining area. He was just starting to get restless when the lift doors snapped open and Sherry stepped out.

He bookmarked his place and shut down.

"Hey Felix. I hope I didn't keep you long. I got stuck talking with a friend and I couldn't get away." She came up to stand in front of him.

He smiled at her. "Good morning. And no, I've only been a couple of minutes."

He nodded towards the front. "Ready for breakfast?"

She grinned. "You bet."

She turned and fell in step with him. "So, how are things going with your classes?"

Felix shrugged. "OK, I guess. I sent in an assignment last night. So, this morning, I get to find out just how I did."

He glanced at her, "It wasn't hard really. It's kinda fun trying to figure out what an author really means. You'd think what they wrote was what they meant."

They found a table in a corner of the dining room. Sherry laughed. "Yeah, I know. I remember a professor once said, 'If the plain sense makes sense, seek no other sense.' I figure if you can't understand what an author's trying to say, either the author didn't say it very well, or the reader is way out of his or her depth."

They gave their orders and waited.

* * * *

ECS Destiny, Command Deck, Emily' Offices, 0840 Hrs

Emily looked up as her office door snapped open. Felix stepped in and waved. "Good morning."

Emily smiled and indicated a seat. "Good morning, Felix. I was just reviewing your work again. I like your analysis. If we were back on Earth, I'd make noises about your form, but you were very clear about what you had to say."

Felix sat down and placed his power-tab on the backside of her desk. "Thanks. Sherry and I talked this morning over breakfast. I told her a little about this assignment. We talked about how much digging a reader should have to do to get the whole meaning the author had in mind."

Emily nodded, "Go on."

"Well, she quoted some professor she had in college...it went something like... 'If the plain sense makes sense...'"

Emily grinned and finished the quote, "'...seek no other sense.' Yes, I've heard that one. Frankly, I believe that myself. I've seen more strange twists of philosophical fluff torn from the words of some author than I care to count."

She leaned forward and said. "That's how we should communicate. So, I plan to make it my department theme: 'Say what you mean, mean what you say.'"

Felix grinned. "I like it."

Emily sat back in her seat and flipped and swished her way through the files. "Well, let's have a look at your math. Could I see your board?"

Felix picked up his power-tab, turned it on and handed it across the desk. Emily keyed up the math assignment. She beamed the file to her computer and handed it back.

After going over the assignment, Emily looked up. "So, tell me. When you worked these problems, what was it like? How long did it take? Did you have any struggles? How did you get through them?

Felix grinned. "Which question first?"

"Yeah, I guess one at a time would be easier." She waited.

Felix considered the questions. They were all part of the first one. "Well, it didn't take all that long. I didn't really time it. I'd say maybe forty minutes or so. There were a couple of spots where I had to go back to the text. It's been a long time since I did problems like that. Some of it was new, but after a while it made sense."

He paused, "How did I deal with the tough ones? I don't know, I just reread the text, compared the examples to the problems, and reasoned it out."

Emily tapped a pencil on the pad on her desk. Her eyebrows settled back from the arch they'd achieved moments before. "Well, after the break we'll step up the pace on the math a bit. You did very well." She waved the pencil at her screen. "You've got tomorrow and next week off. Let's meet a week from Monday, first thing."

She stood and he followed suit. "Have fun. Good job."

Felix grinned, "Thank you."

He didn't see Emily's grin as he headed for the door. She wondered how long it would take for him to make his way to Sherry's office.

* * * *

ECS Destiny, Quarterdeck, Captain's Cabin, 1830 Hrs

Tolya tapped the COMM icon and Shane popped up in a window. "Hey Shane. What's up?"

"Hey yourself. You know, I was thinking. Before you go off and get yourself all married, it'd be kind of fun to get together over some coffee and a good chess game. You remember the all-nighters we used to pull out at Io base?"

Tolya grinned. "Yeah. Those were crazy days."

He drummed his fingers on the desk. "You know, it sounds like a great idea. It's been way too long."

Shane grinned. "You're not kidding. There are some of Kaitlyn's awesome muffins here, just waitin' for someone to polish 'em off. If you don't have any other plans, why not come on down this evening? The ladies are going to be out doing whatever they do and Owen's at a friend's place doing the usual ShipNet adventure game. So, there won't be any interruptions for a while."

Tolya grinned. "Sure. Why not? I seem to have been abandoned for the evening. Tanya has something going on with the ladies; it's a girl thing, you know?"

Shane laughed. "Great! Come on down. We'll just tell 'em it's a guy thing."

They laughed and Tolya reached to disconnect. "I'll be down in about a half hour."

* * * *

ECS Destiny, Promenade Deck, O'Connor Residence, 1900 Hrs

Shane answered the door announcer and admitted Tolya. The place was dimly lit and Tolya was about to ask why when the front room erupted with light and the throaty roar of men yelling like a bunch of fools.

Startled, Tolya looked around. His one step into the front room had left him surrounded by a small crowd of men. Daryl, Frank, Vince, Ichirou and Shane of course. Saul and Samuel were there also. Everyone crowded around, offering handshakes, backslaps and general congratulations on the up coming wedding.

Shane called everyone to come to the dining room. Coffee cups and desert plates waited on the table.

Shane waved to the table. "Kaitlyn took care of us before she went off on her business. So, let's grab some goodies."

Favorable comments rattled around the table as everyone sat down. Tolya was waved to the head of the table.

When everyone got seated, Shane placed a decanter of coffee on the table. It immediately began its trip around the group. He disappeared into the kitchen and returned with a plate of Kaitlyn's famous muffins.

He set it down and got everyone's attention. "Guys. As you all know, this is a little party to commemorate..." Chuckles. "Uh... celebrate the ending of a bachelorhood and the beginning of wedded bliss. Tolya. Friend, it couldn't have happened to a nicer guy!" More chuckles.

He picked up his coffee and held it aloft. "To Tolya, you lucky son of a gun...may your union be long and happy!"

Coffee cups rose in the air and a hearty shout of 'Yeah!' rattled the china hutch.

Tolya finished his sip and put the cup down. "Ok, Shane, you said it was a guy thing...but this..." He grinned. "I guess it really is a guy thing..."

He looked around the table. "All I can say is 'thank you.' It's gratifying to know I have friends on this venture. I feel I'm the luckiest guy in the...well, I was about to say, 'in the world'...but I guess that's a little odd out here."

That brought several chuckles.

"Anyway, I'm lucky to have friends who encourage me, and I'm lucky to have the most beautiful bride there ever was..." more chuckles... "I get a wife and a daughter. All things considered, a man could ask for nothing more."

He took up his cup again and hoisted it. "To friends and family." Another shout resounded and another long sip of coffee went down.

"Now, let's get to work on these muffins!"

* * * *

After Friday morning's staff meeting, Tolya turned to Tanya. "In a hurry?"

She grinned. "For you? Never!" She gave him a quick kiss. "So, what's up?"

He grabbed his pocket-tab and went for the door. "Let's grab breakfast and talk."

Tanya looked concerned. "Is everything OK?"

Tolya smiled. "Of course. It's just there's a little problem we need to address. It's about Felix."

Her eyes flashed. "Felix?"

"Yeah, I've come under bombardment from an unforeseen direction. Come on, let's eat and talk about it."

They walked briskly around the lift well and into the dining room. After picking a table and placing orders, Tanya poured two coffees and asked. "So, what's the problem with Felix?"

Tolya sighed. "Lyuba's pestering me about letting Felix come to the wedding."

Tanya's eyebrows arched. "Lyuba?" A sudden recollection hit her. "Wait. I forgot. Sherry appealed to me on just the same topic late last night"

She took a sip of coffee. "Now, Sherry, I can understand. She barely contains herself over him." She grinned, "Not that she doesn't try."

She looked up at Tolya. "But Lyuba? Has she ever even spoken to Felix?"

Tolya shook his head. "I had thought not, but Kaitlyn called me last night to inform me that Sherry had requested and received permission to have a conference call between her, Lyuba and Felix earlier in the evening. She said Sherry had promised to make sure everything was proper." He sighed, taking another sip of his coffee.

Just then their orders came and they set to eating. He continued, "I had a chat with Lyuba. She admitted she'd had a talk with them. She insists Felix was the perfect gentleman."

Tanya swallowed and took another sip of coffee. "I detect an orchestrated assault."

She was barely suppressing a mischievous grin. "I wouldn't worry a lot about Lyuba and contact with Felix. He's got it almost as bad for Sherry as she does for him. He just hasn't connected the dots yet. Lyuba's bright enough to see it and is having a little fun. She really likes Sherry."

Tolya shook his head. "So, it begins; playing both ends against the middle."

Tanya chuckled softly. "Yeah. In a way it's a good sign. She's treating you like a real dad. She sent Sherry to me because she's still not totally sure about me yet."

He put his cup down. "So, what are we going to do? The Felix question's a sticky one."

Tanya grinned. "You invited Felix and Sherry to dine with us tomorrow evening. Why not include Lyuba? We could deal with the Bridge Pass issue and sort of work our way from there. Let's find out whose idea this was."

Tolya grinned. "That just might be fun. Maybe we can get a few squirms out of a certain young lady."

* * * *

ECS Destiny, Quarterdeck, Felix' Cabin, 1445 Hrs

Felix reviewed his information. Life on the bridge of a starship was a strange blend of sheer boredom mixed with occasional bouts of screaming lunacy. Usually, the latter was blessedly rare. The trick was to know enough, and be disciplined enough, to be ready for the screaming moments.

He had a fair understanding of the basics of the various stations on the bridge. It occurred to him that much more of the functions might be done under AI supervision. However, there was sound reasoning pointing out the need for the 'human factor.' People were capable of making intuitive leaps that baffled the most advanced AI man could devise.

He'd looked into a little of what navigation was about. He'd learned that navigating in three dimensions across unimaginable distances was a complex science. To add to the problem, everything in space was constantly moving. So, calculations had to be updated regularly to keep on a course that would truly get you where you wanted to go.

Felix had a whole new perspective on the scope of the problem the crew of *Destiny* had had to contend with. This, of course made him realize the depth of the complications his participation with Ted's insanity had produced.

He pondered the current situation. *Destiny* was about to drop into normal space on the fringes of a star system that appeared to contain an earth compatible planet. Once they got there, the Multi-

Space drive would have reached the outer limits of its useful life expectancy. There was the real fear that if this system didn't work out, there was nowhere else close enough that would have any better chances of having a habitable planet.

What was life going to be like trying to carve out an existence on a world that hadn't been explored? What unknown dangers would imperil their efforts?

Then Felix considered another question; one he'd never honestly considered before. What could he do to contribute to the solutions? He spent a long time on that one.

PREPARATION — 9
ECS Destiny, Quarterdeck, MedCentral, 1630 Hrs

Vince entered the lobby of MedCentral. Brianna, in the middle of closing up for the day, greeted him. "Hello Vince. Dannie's in her office."

"Hi. Bri. How's it going?"

She smiled, "Wonderful. My shift is done."

"I know the feeling." He said, grinning. He walked on by and peeked in the door to find Daniela working on some report, her back to the door. He quietly entered the room and stepped behind her. For a few moments he watched her type. Finally, he couldn't resist any longer and began to message her shoulders.

Daniela practically jumped out of her skin at the surprise, turning to see who was there. With a grin she turned back and said. "Ooh! You startled me."

"Sorry, I couldn't resist."

"Who told you to stop?" She grinned. Vince grinned back and then went to work. She tried valiantly to get the system shut down in a masterful show of concentration. Finally she finished and sat back to relax.

After he was finished, Vince turned her around in her chair. "Let's take a walk."

Daniela shot a questioning look at him. "A walk?"

He grinned. "Sure. Why not?"

She shrugged, taking his proffered hand. Vince pulled and she got up. "I'd love to go for a walk with you. Where?"

Vince shrugged. "You pick."

Daniela looked questioningly at him. "I'd suggest we go to the Staff Lounge and enjoy a nice snuggle with a view, but there's no view in Multi-Space." She thought for a moment. "So, how about we go for a walk on the Promenade?"

They left MedCentral and headed for the lift well. Vince tapped the call tab. Daniela prodded, "So, what's this about anyway?"

The doors snapped open and Daniela punched Promenade.

"Oh…there's something I've been thinking about for some time and I decided we should talk about it."

The lift came to a stop and the doors snapped open. They were in luck. The usual crowd was quite small. After they'd walked a pace in silence, Daniela started getting impatient. "Vince. Why are you being so mysterious? We talk about everything. So, why wait?"

Vince picked a bench and sat, motioning Daniela to join him.

"Dannie. You remember the first staff meeting we had after we entered MS for this final leg?"

She nodded, "Yeah."

"There was an announcement about Frank and Emily deciding to marry. Then everyone asked about us, and when we were going to get down to business. Remember?"

Daniela nodded. "Sure I remember. We explained we'd just drifted into the idea; no muss no fuss."

Vince looked into her eyes. "Do you really think that's all just muss and fuss?"

Daniela sat there, all her vocabulary momentarily forgotten. Finally she shrugged. "No, I didn't mean it like that. What are you going on about?"

Vince looked down at the earth that had been so carefully laid out along the sides of the path. Then he looked up with determination in his eyes. "What I'm getting at is, Yes, we've made certain assumptions and we seem content with them, but the more I think about it, the more it seems that assumptions are not very sure things sometimes."

Daniela watched as he fished for something in his pocket. Her radar went up and her pulse quickened.

"Dannie. I don't want it to be an assumption any more. I want it to be a promise." He produced a small velvet box. "I want it to be official. Will you be my wife, for sure?"

Apparently it was Daniela's turn for the emotional roller coaster ride. Deep down she'd hoped something like this would happen. She'd decided the assumptions were adequate, but she'd hoped for something a little more romantic. Vince was a fun guy with serious undertones, but he seemed a bit too practical to be very romantic.

This was a pleasant surprise. "Oh, Vince…You know I want to be your wife." She opened the box to find a simple but very beautiful ring. It had a single, fiery diamond. It was set at a medium height; not too high that it would interfere with her medical work, but not so low it was buried.

Daniela grinned and cried all at the same time as Vince took the ring from its resting place and gently put it on her left ring finger. "This is my promise to you that at the very first opportunity, once everything else is taken care of and we're safely in orbit, we will marry. Large or small, we're going to have a wedding."

He stood and pulled her up. They joined in a long embrace. "I love you, Dannie."

* * * *

SAT 03.27.2094
ECS Destiny, Quarterdeck, SecCentral, Tanya's Office, 1030 Hrs

Kaitlyn smiled when she saw Tanya on the screen. "Hi Tanya. What can I do for you?"

"Good morning, Kaitlyn. I wanted to ask if you had plans for Lyuba this evening. We'd like to have her up for dinner."

Kaitlyn smiled. "You know you don't have to ask, but thanks for the thought. I'm sure she'd be delighted to have dinner with you."

Tanya grinned. "Yeah, well, it's going to be an interesting dinner. Can you tell me anything about the little COMM chat she had between Sherry and Felix the other day?"

Kaitlyn got serious. "I was reluctant to allow it, but Sherry promised to keep a reign on things.

She looked pointedly at Tanya. "From what I hear, everyone has a surprisingly high opinion of the young man. If everything I hear is true, he promises to become a remarkable person." She shrugged. "I thought Sherry had your trust in the matter."

"Well," Tanya replied. "For the most part she does. I don't know if you've figured it out, but she's pretty hung up on Felix."

Kaitlyn nodded. "I got that impression. So, did something happen? I hope everything is OK"

Tanya shrugged. "No, nothing happened, but somehow, our little princess and Sherry have elected to gang up on us. Sherry is working on me, and Lyuba on Tolya. The issue… whether we're going to allow Felix access to attend the wedding."

Kaitlyn laughed. "Wow! I know Lyuba's grown attached to Sherry, but that's funny. Welcome to parenthood, honey. Believe me. It's part of the territory."

She paused for a moment and then asked, "Tanya. Are you opposed to Felix attending your wedding?"

Tanya sat back in her chair and shook her head. "No. Not really. I really hadn't thought about it until Sherry mentioned it. I've grown to like Felix. He's polite, reliable, and respectful; heck he's working so hard to get his act together it's amazing. The problem is how people will take his presence at the wedding. Tolya is mystified over why Lyuba is so interested in Felix' participation."

Kaitlyn nodded. "I don't envy your problem. One thing I do know. Lyuba has shown a knack for assessing character. I don't know how she does it, but she has this sixth sense about people.

"I mean, look how she took to you. She decided quickly that she could trust you. Yet, she's shown an uncanny sense of caution with others who proved to be just what she feared. If she's allowed Felix into her circle of people, I'm willing to give him a shot."

Tanya nodded. "Well, I'm always amazed at Sherry. Anybody else would've rejected Felix forever, after what he did to her when he invaded my offices. Yet, she was the one who pushed for leniency in his case. She kept saying, 'There's somebody better hiding in there.' So far, I've come to agree with her assessment." She shrugged. "That doesn't help me handle the appearances issues I have to deal with. What will people say?"

Kaitlyn shook her head. "That's a tough one, Tahnie. One thing to your advantage is, we'll be in celebration mode. We'll have safely arrived in a promising system after a whole lot of fearful troubles.

"There'll be a festive atmosphere. Your wedding and Lyuba's adoption will create a sense of family. Maybe that would be the best time to let Felix be seen in some light besides a negative one."

Tanya grinned. "Thanks. I need some positive talk. Well, I need to check on a few things. So, I'd better get going. Would you send Lyuba to my place at 1800?"

Kaitlyn nodded. "Sure. She'll be there. I'll talk to you soon."

"Thanks Kait.' Have a great weekend."

About then there was a tap on the doorway. Tanya looked to see Daniela standing there, grinning. "Dannie, come on in." Tanya stood and gave Daniela a quick hug. "What brings you over? You don't usually visit much."

Daniela seemed much more animated than usual. "I know, I guess I'm not much of a social person."

Tanya sat down in her desk chair and waved a hand at another chair in the corner. "Please. Drag up a chair and sit. You should know you're welcome to visit any time. You know, you don't have to be social, just friendly."

Daniela smiled, brushing a lock of hair. A bright flash caught Tanya's eye and her mouth dropped open. "Dannie! Don't move!"

Daniela froze and Tanya reached out and gently grasped her guest's left hand. Daniela grinned and let Tanya examine her prize. "What have we here? If I didn't know better I'd say you had a new ring on your finger."

Tanya reached for her tissues and handed over a liberal supply as Daniela replied. "Last night he said he 'didn't want it to be an assumption anymore.' He said it was his 'promise that when everything was done and we were safely in orbit, we'd marry.'"

Daniela dabbed at her eyes and grinned again. "I'd given up on anything special. He's so casual about everything I just figured that's the way it'd be. He surprised the heck out of me."

Tanya reached out to take a closer look. "It's beautiful. I'm so happy for you."

She squeezed her hand gently and let go. "I wondered about those assumptions. I guess it can work that way, but I don't know… assumptions aren't much to go on."

Daniela replied. "Well, as far as it goes, it's true. We just wound up talking about, 'what ifs'. What if we got married and started a family? How would we go about it? Until last night it was… someday we'll get around to doing this thing we've talked about. Now, it's a destination; something to anticipate with joy."

She leaned forward and caught Tanya's hand fingering her own recent prize. "Now I know how you feel."

Tanya grinned and snagged a tissue for herself. They chatted on for a while when Tanya decided to pick Daniela's brain about her most recent problem.

"Dannie, I could really use some advice."

Daniela smiled. "Of course. What about?"

"Well, it's been brought to my attention that I haven't made plans to invite Felix to our wedding. I'd invite him in a second under other circumstances, but in the current situation, I don't know how to arrange it in a way that doesn't get people upset."

Daniela frowned in thought. "Wow! What prompted…wait…it was Sherry, right?"

Tanya grinned. "Bingo! You won't believe this, but I have another source. Lyuba!"

Daniela's eyebrows reached for her hairline. "Lyuba? What's she got to do with this whole mess?"

Tanya shrugged. "I'm not sure. I mean...it's going to be her ceremony too, so I guess she has a right to an opinion. I do know she's taken quite a liking to Sherry. She looks up to her for some reason and Sherry treats her like a surrogate little sister."

Daniela grinned. "You have your hands full, I can see. You know, I've been watching Felix. He strikes me as much more mature somehow. He's not the same fellow that came within a micron of following his peers out the airlock."

Tanya shuddered. That was one piece of history she'd just as soon forget. "You're right about that. I am so glad we didn't have to go that far with him. I still have nightmares about the other two."

Daniela grimaced. "Sorry. I know it's a touchy subject. What I'm saying is, he's grown up somehow in the last few weeks."

She thought for a moment or two. "As I recall the trial and the sentencing, it seems to me you were just a bit vague about the nature of Felix' treatment. For instance Tahnie, who was the court you referred to when you said, '...a period of time deemed appropriate by the court?' I remember that trial very clearly. You referred to the court as an entity, which was appropriate, but think about it. Who was the court in that trial?"

Tanya considered the question. "I guess Tolya and the rest who sat on the panel."

Daniela smiled. "Yes, Tolya presided. He's already made executive decisions about the method of incarceration. As long as the court doesn't act in a manner detrimental to the good of the colony, the court, which Tolya represents, and the governor, who happens to be?"

Tanya grinned, "Tolya. I get it!"

"You better get it, girl." Daniela laughed. "You put yourself directly in the middle of determining the fate of the entire colony when you signed on as first lady."

Tanya was a little numb. Every time someone reminded her of the change of status her engagement and coming marriage gave her, she felt guilty. "Dannie, that's not what I was after. I fell in love with the man not the station!"

Daniela reached out and grabbed her hand. "Tahnie. I don't think anyone thinks otherwise, certainly not any of us, but you need to remember to take advantage of your position."

She let go and waved a dismissive hand. "I don't mean get all power crazy or something, but don't be afraid to be who you're becoming. You're going to have to match and compliment your husband's ability to command to balance the tender heartedness you both possess.

"In that light, I'd have to say, if you're willing to have Felix attend the wedding and adoption, then get together with Tolya and make it happen. If it's public approval you're worried about, you'll know soon enough if there's going to be a problem. Frankly, I doubt many will care. Felix screwed up, but he didn't personally harm anyone but Sherry, and we all know what Sherry thinks about him."

Tanya grinned. "Yes, we certainly do...Thanks Dannie. I keep forgetting the fact I'm not just marrying a wonderful man. I guess in a way, I'm marrying a whole colony. They're his people. I reminded him of that when he sought my advice before that first ship-wide meeting. I guess that makes them mine too."

She sat there thinking. "You know. I think that scares me more than anything else about this whole thing. I'm nothing special. Why should I be elevated just because it's him?"

Daniela smiled fondly. "That's another thing I think Tolya loves about you. You aren't pretentious. The negative side of that is the tendency to denigrate yourself. You're special or Tolya would never have given himself to you so thoroughly. Even Lyuba can see that."

CELEBRATION — 1
SAT, 03.27.2094
ECS Destiny, Quarterdeck, 1955 Hrs

Saturday had been a slow day and Felix was going stir crazy. He'd spent the day reading through various texts, trying out different problems in the chapters to come, and of course, touching up on his knowledge of life on the bridge of a starship.

Sherry had the day off and was busy at home on Deck 1. He couldn't go see her because of his restrictions and she seemed too busy to do more than talk on the COMM a couple of times.

Felix had been issued several uniform outfits. They didn't have any of the crew insignia on them, but they still looked better than most the things he used to wear. Still, he wanted to look sharp for his dinner date with the captain and his lady...and, well, Sherry too.

He'd spoken with Daryl sometime during the day. Daryl was fun to talk with. Felix was fascinated with the technologies Daryl described. His wife, Naomi told him about some of the cool things going on in her own department.

He was particularly intrigued with the whole idea of tiny machines the size of a chain of molecules that could be programmed to do amazing things. They got his imagination going as nothing else had. Daryl had promised to introduce him to a guy named Saul. He was supposed to be a wizard with the little things.

Daryl sent Felix to see Vince about borrowing something sharp to wear. Vince was closer to his size. As it turned out, Vince had a couple of casual evening things he no longer wore, which he gave to Felix. "You'll impress her a lot more in these." He said with a wink.

Felix felt his face flush. *Is that what everybody thinks? It's not like I'm dating Sherry. We're just friends.* He let the comment go, thanked Vince for his generosity and took his new threads back to his cabin.

Now he stood next to the forward lift well, waiting for Sherry to appear. It was nearly 1900 and he was getting nervous. He woke his power-tab and started to read, but he couldn't concentrate. He decided to go over his notes about the bridge.

Finally the lift doors snapped open and Sherry stepped out. She was dressed up for the evening as well. They traded surprised looks as they appraised each other.

"You look nice." Felix said.

Sherry blushed lightly. "You don't look too bad yourself."

They turned and headed for the dining room when a teen-aged girls voice carried down the hall from behind them. They turned to see Lyuba running to meet them. Tolya and Tanya were walking behind, hand in hand.

Sherry and Lyuba exchanged sisterly hugs and then Lyuba turned to appraise Felix. "You don't look so bad." She stated, as if that settled some private argument.

Felix laughed and responded. "Hi, yourself! You look better in person too."

Lyuba grinned and held out her hand. Felix took it and shook it gently. "Good evening Ms. Lyuba. I'm Felix, at your service."

That got a chuckle out of everyone.

Tolya turned for the lift well. "OK, everyone. We're going to have dinner in my standby cabin. Let's hit the lift."

Felix was a bit confused and approached Tolya. "Um, pardon me Sir, but my bracelet doesn't permit me to go in that part of the ship."

The lift doors snapped open and everyone crowded on. "Yes, but you forget. Since I'm the captain and your favorite jailer is soon to be my wife, I have powers to cancel those restrictions as I see fit."

Tolya smiled at Felix' embarrassment. "It's ok, Felix. I appreciate your concern."

They stepped off the lift on Command Deck. Tolya headed for the standby cabin. The door recognized his patch and granted them all admittance.

* * * *

ECS Destiny, Command Deck, Captains Standby Cabin, 2000 Hrs

This was one of the few rooms Felix had never been in. He liked the spacious feel. There was a sizable conference table, which had doubled on numerous occasions as a dining table. On the inboard wall were a long couch and a couple of smaller tables. On the port side outboard wall were a cupboard and counter arrangement that contained a small sink, a snack, and a coffee dispenser. Forward of these was the captain's desk.

Felix wandered past the desk and noticed a small couch facing a blank wall with a heavy curtain stretched across it.

"Come on, Felix. We're going to order."

Felix rejoined the party around the captain's desk as Tolya scrolled through the menu items. It suddenly dawned on him his bracelet hadn't even twitched.

After placing their orders, Tolya arranged seating. He sat at the head of the table with Tanya closest to him along the right side and Lyuba opposite her. He placed Felix next to Tanya, and Sherry next to Lyuba.

"OK. I want this to be a pleasant meal among family and friends, but we have a number of things to talk about. I suggest we get down to business and get things said and done so the rest of the evening CAN be pleasant."

Lyuba gave Tolya a curious look before glancing at Sherry. Sherry shrugged and looked at Tanya, who just smiled and watched. Felix was lost to all of this, wondering what the captain was talking about.

Finally, when the silence had drawn itself out sufficiently, Tolya continued. "Initially, the primary business was going to be about Felix' desire to witness the drop from the bridge, but before we can go there, we must discuss something else."

The silence was deafening. "Tanya has been approached about this topic by Sherry, and I, by Lyuba."

The two glanced at each other with significant looks of 'uh-oh' on their faces. "It was recently brought to our attention that our friend Felix hasn't been invited to our wedding and adoption ceremony. Now, I don't mind the question. I don't mind who asked what. I do mind that no one asked me or Tanya for permission to permit Lyuba to have contact with an inmate."

He looked at the two on his left. "Lyuba. Tanya is officially going to be your mother in about a week. So, even if you thought you were doing right by asking Kaitlyn, you should have asked Tanya.

"Sherry. You know who your boss is. You also know who will be Lyuba's parents. So, I know you know better than to keep us out of the loop."

The ladies, young and younger, began contemplating the wood grain tabletop.

Felix spoke up. "Um...Excuse me, captain?"

Tolya turned to look at him. "Yes, Felix?"

Felix tensed up a little to hide his nerves. "Sir, I think this is all probably my fault."

Tolya sat back and did his best to suppress a smile. "And just how would this be your fault?"

Felix licked his lips. "Well, sir, I umm...I asked Sherry if there was a way I could talk to Lyuba. See...when you gave me the assignment about the bridge you said that your...dau...niece... Lyuba here, had managed to find all the information on her own.

"I uh...well...I was trying to save a little time by asking her where I might look. I wasn't very familiar with the ShipNet system and I wanted to get the information quickly and get down to studying it. I guess I've gotten Sherry in trouble by involving her in my short cut. I wasn't trying to cause any trouble." He shot Sherry an apologetic look that she graciously accepted with a sweet smile.

Tolya looked at him for a couple of moments. Then he got up and gathered up five coffee cups from a cupboard and set them on the counter. "Lyuba, a hand please?" Lyuba jumped up and darted over. Tolya filled cups from the dispenser and she passed them around the table.

After everyone was settled, Tolya took a sip and then spoke. "Felix. While I appreciate your concern and your loyalty to your new friends, you must understand this is not about them helping you get to the information. I expected you to be resourceful. That's why I left you that clue to begin with."

He turned back to the ladies. "What I'm concerned about is that the ladies didn't talk to Tanya or me about permission for Lyuba, a minor, to communicate with a convicted prisoner."

He looked back at Felix, who now found great interest in the wood grain patterns where he sat.

"Ladies. I understand you were led with your hearts more than your brains. I'm not really angry with anyone. I'm just asking you both to never again try to go around our authority. Sherry, I know you meant no harm. Lyuba, I know you were just trying to be a help to your friend. I hope you both understand, if it had been someone other than Felix, I'd scream and yell."

He took another sip from his coffee and looked over at Tanya. "Any comments sweetheart?"

Tanya put her cup down and glanced at the very nervous trio. "Tolya and I have talked this over. I've decided to let Felix come to the wedding."

Excitement started bubbling between the two young ladies. "Wait. My decision was not made because you two decided to do an end run. We think Felix has earned a certain amount of trust."

Felix looked up sharply, surprise in his eyes.

"Yes, Felix. So far, you've proven to be an honorable person after all. You go out of your way to be polite and helpful. You work incredibly hard at everything you're asked to accomplish, and you've remained a gentleman with a certain friend of mine." She saw the darting look he sent Sherry.

"So, in exchange for such good behavior thus far, I am allowing you access to two more area's of the ship. You will be permitted to ride the forward lift down to Promenade Deck. You have access to that entire deck. You'll be permitted…in fact, you're included on the list for the close seating at the wedding."

Felix was smiling at the small victory. The ladies were practically bursting with suppressed excitement.

Tanya held up a hand before either of the girls could interject a comment. "Felix. Now, I'm taking a risk. Tolya and I have decided you are trustworthy enough to be trusted with certain friends that don't live on the same deck as we do. For now, you have access to Deck 1." Both Felix and Sherry went still as stone as what that meant dawned on them.

"Don't disappoint me with this one in particular. If you fail to maintain an honorable rapport with this young lady here…" She nodded towards Sherry. "Believe me, I will become very disappointed with you. You don't want that. Frankly, I don't think I'm going to have to worry about it. Do you?"

Felix shook his head. "No ma'am. I'd never dishonor her or any of you."

Tanya smiled. "I'm glad to hear it." She turned to Lyuba and Sherry. "Sherry. Like Tolya said. I expect you to come to Tolya or me with anything that has to do with Lyuba. Lyuba honey? I know you're trying to be helpful to your friends. I'm happy you've given Felix a chance. Kaitlyn says you have a pretty good head about people's character; but honey, it's because we care about you that you must be open and honest with us. Let's not have any more secrets from each other. OK?"

Lyuba nodded her head seriously. "I'm sorry."

Tolya pushed back his chair and opened his arms. Lyuba came around the table and gave a big hug. Then she offered one to Tanya, who returned it with change.

Tanya looked over at Tolya. "Shouldn't we be seeing dinner about now?"

Tolya grinned. "Yes, you're right." He squeezed a tab on his shirt collar and spoke into his personal COMM device.

"Yes, this is the captain. Yes…Sorry to keep you waiting…Five minutes? That's fine, thank you."

He squeezed the collar tab again and smiled around the table. "You heard it. Five minutes. More coffee, anyone?"

Lyuba asked. "Poppa, do you have any green tea?"

Poppa... I love it. "Well, let's have a look." They got up and went rummaging through the cupboards. Felix just sat, toying with his cup. Sherry watched him, wondering what he was thinking.

Tanya got up and came around the table to sit next to Sherry. "You OK kiddo?"

Sherry looked at her. "Sure. Sorry, I guess I got a little carried away. Thanks for including Felix. And...well," She lowered her voice to almost a whisper. "I thought you didn't approve of my interest in Felix."

Tanya shrugged and spoke just as softly. "I didn't really, but I've come to realize I'm trying to keep the stars from shining."

Sherry reached out and squeezed Tanya's hand. She looked at Tanya's ring again and then back into her face. "Thanks for your trust. I think it'll be fine."

The door chime sounded and Tanya went for it. Much to Lyuba's delight Tolya pulled out a brand new box of green tea and handed it to her.

He turned to look at Felix who sat watching everything and feeling just a bit lost. He sat in Tanya's chair while the meal cart was rolled in. "Doing some thinking, Felix?"

"Well, sir, I'm just trying to figure things out. I've gone from convicted prisoner to trusted...I don't know what, in the course of, oh, half an hour. I appreciate the trust and...the leash extension. I'm really surprised about the last part."

Tolya shrugged. "We'll talk more about that later."

He got up and offered the chair back to Tanya. He thanked the kitchen helper, slipping him a credit token for the extra trouble. "Thanks, Henry. Have a great weekend." The door snapped shut and he returned to his place.

The meal indeed went quite pleasantly. Small talk was the unspoken rule around the table. Once dessert had vanished Tolya sat back and looked at Felix. "So Felix. Let's hear just what you learned from your greatly assisted research."

"Well, sir. I've become familiar with the various stations on the bridge. I could recite them in my sleep by now."

Tolya held up a hand. "We can hear about the bridge in a few minutes. First, I want to hear what impressions and understandings you've come to."

Felix nodded, looking thoughtful. "I see. I guess one of the first things I came to realize, is that life on the bridge is not the fantasized vision that's always on the vids. There are hours of bone weary boredom sometimes punctuated with moments of gibbering terror. I can begin to understand the concern and even fear that might have prevailed when the faulty NAV system blew us off course. I realize with fresh eyes just how damaging the things Ted got us to do must have been."

He took a sip of his coffee and put it down. "I wish I'd known all this before…"

He stared at the cup for a moment. "Anyway, all that fresh insight made me start asking other questions. I came on this trip, mostly to get away from trouble. I had no serious thought about my own contribution to the colony's future. I was just too busy thinking what advantages I could gain.

"My grand idea of staying out of trouble didn't last long. I have a small box of useless items that…well, when I acquired them, seemed worthy targets; you know, polishing my skills.

"From the time I started lifting, maybe a couple weeks after we left Earth orbit until the NAV system failure, I only lifted about a quarter of what I might have back home in that same time frame.

"I got involved with Ted and he started focusing me on…" He raised his hands and made quotation signs with his fingers. "…greater opportunities, is the way he put it. I was set up to listen to him and ignored my usual warning flags."

He sat back in his chair, looking frustrated with himself. "Everybody knows the rest of the story. What I'm trying to say is, my grand idea of staying out of trouble didn't last very long. Now I see it's because I didn't have another direction of focus."

He took another sip of his cooling coffee. "I survived this mess, thanks to Sherry and the rest of you, but it's taken this little exposure to your reality, Captain, to get me to see I need to find a purpose. I'm here. I'm alive. Whether people like it or not, I'm a part of this colony…

"I started asking myself new questions; questions like, 'What was it going to be like, starting from scratch on a world that has never been studied and catalogued and parceled out?' 'What kind of dangers are there that would set us back seriously?' 'What was I going to do to make things easier?' Finally, I asked, 'what kind of future I want for me and my…" He looked around, "My friends?"

He took another sip of his coffee to discover it was cold. Sherry reached across, took the cup and went to refill it.

Tolya looked at Felix thoughtfully for several moments. "Felix. I'd hoped this little exercise would shake you awake the rest of the way. It didn't occur to me just how much shaking it would cause. So, what conclusions have you made about these new questions?"

Sherry handed Felix the cup and stood with her hands on the back of his chair. Felix thanked her and took a sip. "Partially. I've a long way to go in my education, but I know I want to do something in the sciences. I've got this thing about those...nano-bug things Naomi and Daryl talk about. It doesn't sound like much I guess, but I can imagine some pretty cool things we might do with them once we figure out how."

Tolya raised an eyebrow. "Well, that's going to take a great deal of study. What are your plans, if you have any?"

Felix grinned. "Daryl wants to take me to meet Saul Perlman next week, but...well..." He held up his bracelet and shrugged. "I can't go there right now."

Tolya and Tanya exchanged glances. "Saul Perlman? I can't think of a better person to talk to about nano-tech."

He leaned over and whispered in Tanya's ear. She grinned and nodded before getting up and heading for Tolya's desk. She sailed through his security screens and pulled up her own system in SecCentral. After pulling up a utility window, she tapped in a few commands, swiped a couple of icons and blanked out the screen. Turning she nodded to Tolya. "All done." She smiled.

Tolya smiled and got up. "I think it's time for Felix to give us a short bridge tour."

Tanya tossed a small device which Tolya caught deftly with his left hand.

"Felix." He tapped a button on the device and Felix's bracelet buzzed on his wrist. Felix reflexively grabbed at the bracelet and looked incredulously at Tolya. "I just wanted you to see that the bracelet has truly been operational. If you'll recall, it didn't do that when you got here."

Felix nodded.

"It didn't because the proscriptions for this room and the bridge were removed." He handed the device back to Tanya, who'd moved up next to him. She clipped it on her belt and gave Felix a smile.

Tolya approached the port bridge door. It snapped open and he strode onto the bridge, his entourage in tow. The officer of the watch announced 'captain on the bridge,' and the skeleton crew snapped to a semblance of attention.

Tolya grinned. "As you were. We're just having a brief tour." They moved up to the command chair that presided over the room. Felix stood transfixed. Sherry also stood, staring about her. As promised, Felix' bracelet remained quiet.

Tolya stood next to the command chair, not making any move to take the seat. "Well, Felix. We're ready for that tour."

Felix glanced at him and nodded. Then, much as Lyuba had done three weeks earlier, Felix led them from station to station around the room in a clockwise path. Each station received a concise, but detailed description. They ended up back at the port side entrance and Tolya turned to face the crew. "Thanks, people. Good work."

He turned and led everyone back into the lounge. He seemed lost in thought as he watched everyone file back into the room.

As if he'd finally won a wrestling match, Tolya crossed the room to sit at his desk and awaken the screen. He glanced at Tanya's work and then opened another window. The colony logo was prominently emblazoned on the top of the window. Tolya logged onto the governors system and selected from the pull down menu. He went through a multiple answer questionnaire. His hands flew through the process and soon the document was submitted.

Another page popped open and Tolya typed for a couple of minutes. Then he pulled up his signature glyph and applied it to the bottom of the document. He saved the file and then sent a print command. Nine pages shot out of the printer to cool on the tray.

He fished in a drawer and pulled out three old-fashioned file folders. He put three pages in each folder. Then he got up and placed one of the folders in a file drawer in his desk.

He turned and handed one folder to Tanya. She opened it and glanced through the pages. Her eyes widened noticeably and she shot him a questioning look. She reread the page and after a moment, a slow smile lit her face.

Felix had joined Sherry and Lyuba at the table.

Tolya took the third folder and turned to approach Felix. "Felix. Are your quarters adequate for you?"

Felix looked confused. "Adequate? Compared to what I had before, I'd say they're like a room in a palace."

Tolya grinned in spite of himself. He turned and held out a hand to Tanya. She hesitated a moment before comprehending. Unclipping the remote, she handed it over to him.

"Felix Xavier Hernandez. In consideration of the tremendous improvement in character you've displayed, and by the evidence of actions witnessed by me and those I consider reliable; by my authority as Governor of this colony, I hereby grant a pardon for your role in the recent unpleasantness which landed you in your current circumstances."

He held out his hand. "Let me see your arm."

Dumfounded, Felix held out his arm.

Tolya held his hand under Felix' wrist and pressed a stud on the remote. The bracelet clasp snapped open and it dropped into Tolya's waiting hand.

Sherry, her eyes wide in excitement, put a hand over her mouth to smother the shout she almost made. Lyuba was grinning like a Cheshire cat.

Tolya turned and handed the small bundle to Tanya. "Obviously," he turned back to face Felix, who was still trying to digest things. "...you have access to the entire ship.

"I strongly suggest you stay in your current quarters. This change of status will be formally announced during the course of our wedding reception.

"You have friends up here now. And...there should be no more difficulty meeting Saul Perlman."

Tolya handed the third folder to Felix and then held out his hand. Felix stopped staring at his own hand and gripped back. They shook firmly.

Felix finally overcame his shock and replied. "Captain... Governor...I don't know what to say."

Tolya grinned. "Well, you could start with 'thank you.' I really want to see you keep up your work with Dr. Strauss. Emily is very excited about your potential. I want to continue training you in the gym on a regular basis, and I expect you to spend some time helping Daryl and Naomi in their departments. You might as well get to know that area if that's where your interests lie."

He released Felix' hand and smiled. "Unofficially, when I'm not on duty or in my public capacity as Governor, my friends call me Tolya. I'm extending that to you."

"Whoo-Hooo!"

He turned at the exuberant exclamation of a thirteen-year-old. "Oh Poppa, you're awesome!"

He grinned as she rushed over to give him a big bear hug. He hugged her close.

Sherry walked up and put a hand on his arm. "Thanks Tolya. I'm blown away."

Tolya reached out and brushed her cheek with the back of his hand. "You seem to know how to pick 'em Sherry."

Sherry blushed.

Tanya deposited the gear on Tolya's desk and joined the group. She shook Felix' hand and roughed his hair. "Way to go Felix. You've made us proud."

She turned away, and Sherry hurried over and gave Felix a warm hug. "I'm so happy for you!"

She backed up, feeling her ears getting warm.

Felix stepped forward, took her hand and looked into her eyes. He cleared his throat which threatened to betray his emotions. "Thank you," he said simply.

CELEBRATION — 2

ECS Destiny, Quarterdeck, Captain's Cabin, 2230 Hrs

"Tolya, is everything OK?"

Tolya grinned. "Hello, Brad. Thing's are just fine. I'm sorry to call you so late, but I wanted to tell you something. We're bringing a couple of guests with us in the morning."

Brad beamed. "That's great! You know we love guests."

Tolya replied. "Yeah, I know. Thing is, one of 'em you'll probably find very familiar. Do you remember the three defendants at the trial?"

Brad grew serious. "How could I forget? You must mean the young fellow that received the merciful sentence."

Tolya nodded. "Yes, exactly. He's been in Tanya's clutches since the trial, and about a week ago, I authorized a change from confinement in the lock up, to house arrest."

Brad's eyebrows darted upward in surprise. "Wow! I'd say that was kinda quick."

Tolya shrugged. "Yeah, that it was. Felix has been the model of what you would call repentant. He's gone out of his way to shine in every way possible.

"Anyway. He's been restricted to Quarterdeck for the last week or so. I've grown certain his determination to be a new person is a genuine and permanent one. So, tonight, you could say I did something rash...I issued an official pardon."

Brad's eyebrows had no place else to go. "OK...Tolya, you strike me as a good judge of character. I trust your decision's the right one. So, Felix is your Sunday guest?"

Tolya smiled. "Yes, I thought it would be good for him to make your acquaintance."

Brad grinned. "Thank you Tolya, but more than mine, that young man needs to be introduced to God."

Tolya nodded. "I know. I thought, 'who better to make the introduction?' I'm not really that tuned in just yet."

Brad shrugged, "That's OK. You'll get there. It's just a matter of time. Felix is welcome of course, but you said there were a couple of visitors."

Tolya nodded. "Yes, I did. Tanya has an associate named Sherry. She was the young lady Felix injured during his little rampage through Tanya's offices. Brad, if there's anyone who could model complete forgiveness like you've been talking about, it's her."

Brad replied. "Really!"

Tolya shrugged. "That's part of the whole story you never heard. When Felix stormed Tanya's office to spring the other guy she'd locked up, Sherry was on duty, but Tanya was elsewhere

"Sherry valiantly tried to stop Felix and he scuffled with her. In the scuffle, he swung the door to the key cabinet sharply and it hit her in the head. She fell and struck her head against a counter and was knocked unconscious. When she hit the floor, her arm was turned wrong and broke.

Brad winced. "That had to hurt."

Tolya nodded. "I'm sure it did. At any rate, when Felix was arrested, he was under the mistaken notion that he'd killed her.

He smiled grimly. "We let him stew on that for a little while. Then when he was confronted with a vibrantly alive victim, the floodgates opened. He confessed to his part and gave us the last information necessary to close the case."

He shook his head. "What we didn't expect was to hear Sherry forgive him there on the spot. We all witnessed it. She told him she understood he didn't really mean to kill her or hurt her. Then she announced that she forgave him. She begged him to tell us everything, hoping to save him from a severe punishment.

When Tanya questioned her about it later and told her she would have to press charges for the assault, she got very angry and said if she could forgive him, then Tanya should as well."

Brad sat forward and looked thoughtful. "Wow! You're right. That's a powerful example of forgiveness if I've ever seen one."

Brad got a glint in his eye. "Let me guess. They've become friends; maybe more than friends."

Tolya grinned. "Yes, they're friends indeed. I suspect she holds other hopes, but Felix is a little slower on the whole deal. It won't be long before he finally figures it out."

Brad shook his head. "I've heard of rare occasions where this type of thing happened, but I've never seen it in real life. It's going to be an interesting conversation to say the least."

He thought for a minute. "Tolya could you hold for just a minute? I want to ask Jodi something."

"Sure, no problem."

Brad stepped away from the pickup and was gone for a couple of minutes. When he returned, Jodi was with him.

"Tolya? I'm back. Sorry about that. Why don't you bring your friends with you and have lunch at our place after the service?"

Tolya considered the plan for the day. "Yeah, I think we could squeeze it in. We're due to drop into our destination tomorrow evening. So, we shouldn't be too long. There's a lot of last minute prep work to do before the drop."

Brad smiled. "I understand. We'll see you all tomorrow."

Tolya nodded. "Thanks Brad. I'll see you tomorrow. Thanks, Jodi for the hospitality."

He saw Jodi grin in the background. She leaned forward. "You're welcome Tolya. Say hi to Tanya for me."

"OK, I will. Good night."

* * * *

SUN 03.28.2094
ECS Destiny, Deck 3, New Destiny Church, 0930 Hrs

Tolya was ushering them into the lift when he heard a voice call. He looked up to see Daryl and Naomi hurrying for the lift.

Tanya saw and tapped the hold tab. "You two are up early."

Daryl grinned. "Yeah, we decided to check out this little church of yours."

Everybody made room and the two squeezed in.

Tolya tapped Deck 3 and resume. The doors snapped shut and they dropped a level. As they all piled out, Daryl took Tolya aside and nodded his head towards Felix. "I thought Felix couldn't leave the Quarterdeck."

Tolya shrugged. "I haven't had a chance to pass the word. I uh... I issued an official pardon last night." Daryl raised an eyebrow and Tolya grinned. "He's demonstrated rehabilitation in so many ways it's not funny. Besides, how else is he going to visit Saul with you?"

Daryl chuckled. "You're getting sly on me." Then he cleared his throat. "Seriously, do you really think this is wise?"

Tolya shrugged. "In the long run? Yes. It may be a bit bumpy at first, but Tahnie and I have been watching him like a hawk. He's just not the same guy we put on trial."

As they stood in the lobby of the Forward Public Commons, Naomi caught up and nudged Daryl, nodding in Felix' direction.

Daryl grinned. "Tolya pardoned him last night."

She glanced at Tolya. "Really?"

Tolya shrugged. "Yep. After much deliberation and discussion, and after a long talk with Felix, I decided it was the best course. You're going to see a lot more of him."

Her eyebrows rose. "Why?"

"What, the pardon or the seeing more of him part?"

Tanya was grinning at Naomi's confusion.

"Well...both I guess."

Tolya stopped. "Ok, I'll hit the last part for now. He's expressed a deep fascination with your nano-tech research. He's convinced somehow he can eventually dream up ways of helping the colony, using your little bugs. I know it'll take a while before he has the technical skill, but with Emily's accelerated plan and his determined enthusiasm, I think he might just accomplish something. That's just a teeny, tiny part of why I did what I did. I'll have to explain the rest later; perhaps a staff meeting midweek."

Naomi nodded and he turned to Daryl. "Since when were you two church goers?"

Daryl shrugged. "It's a long story. We used to attend a church a few years before we signed on. Something went wrong just as we were getting married and we both swore off church...We recently decided we shouldn't throw the baby out with the bath, so to speak. Besides, this guy, Brad, seems to be authentic. That's more than I can say for the last guy we called pastor."

They entered the main meeting room to a lively crowd. They were greeted by many people; all genuinely glad to see them. Even Felix was welcome. Most didn't seem to recognize him.

The pre-service music was ramping up and they found a seat. The music guy came out and welcomed the group. They prayed and the music began in earnest. There was such an air of joy in the room it was contagious. This was to be the last Sunday service in Multi-Space.

* * * *

Everyone participated in the breakdown process. The chairs went in one closet. The minimal furniture and sound system went in another, along with the drums and the electronic instruments. They were finished in record time according to many. Brad and Jodi stood around chatting with congregants as they drifted off for lunch.

The last of the crowd waved their way out the doors and Brad focused on Tolya and friends. He approached Felix holding out his hand. "Hello, Felix. It's good to see you. The last time I saw you things were much less pleasant."

Felix nodded and shook the proffered hand. "Yes, sir. I'm happy to say those days are behind me."

Brad smiled. "So I hear. Congratulations on your change of status. How does it feel to suddenly be a free man again?"

Felix smiled. "Thank you, sir. I'm still trying to get used to it."

Brad chuckled. "So serious and proper. I'm not going to bite, you know. Just call me Brad. When people are trying to sound official they say Pastor Brad, but I'm not so big on titles. Did Tolya mention lunch at my place?"

Felix nodded. "Yeah, he said we were having a talk with you over lunch."

Brad grinned. "I don't think this is nearly the sort of talk you might have experienced with Tolya. Think of it more like a lunch time chat with old friends."

He turned to Sherry. "And this must be the beautiful young lady I've heard so much about. Sherry, is it?"

Sherry blushed at the compliment. "Yes, Sherry Petrakis."

Brad grinned and offered his hand. She shook it and he looked over at Felix. "See, I don't bite." Felix grinned self-consciously and Sherry chuckled.

Brad turned to her. "Petrakis. That's Greek."

"Yes," she smiled. "My dad was Greek and my mom was from the States. They met in college. I was born in Greece where we lived for several years."

"Do you know what your last name means?"

Sherry looked curious. "I never really thought about it."

Brad smiled. "Well, Petrakis is a form of the word 'Petros' which is translated in English to 'Peter.' It's a namesake of one of Jesus' disciples. His Jewish name was Simon. Jesus gave him the nickname 'Petros' because it means 'rock.' Jesus said Peter's confession that

Jesus was the Messiah would be the rock, or foundation stone on which He'd build His church."

"Wow!" Sherry said. "That's cool."

Brad grinned and patted her on the shoulder. He turned and spotted Daryl and Naomi heading out the door. He moved to intercept them.

This almost turned into a traffic accident as a three-year-old Evan chose that moment to run between them. Daryl grinned as Brad did a spectacular dodge that almost lost him his balance. Brad approached and Tolya made introductions. "Pastor Brad, this is my good friend and Chief Engineer Daryl McIntyre and his wife Naomi. They surprised me this morning and joined us for the service."

Brad shook hands with Daryl and Naomi. "I'm pleased to meet you. Friends of Tolya must be good friends indeed."

Naomi grinned.

"So, what brings you two to our little church?"

Daryl shrugged. "Well," He looked over at Naomi.

She nodded and he continued. "We were once involved in a church back home. We were about to marry when things went into total melt down. We soured on church and, long story short, this is the first time we've attended in about four years."

Brad grew serious immediately. "I'm so sorry. It grieves me to hear such stories. Too many people have been turned away from salvation by poor treatment in the churches they attended." He gave a reassuring smile. "But, I'm encouraged to see you've considered a second visit."

Naomi responded. "Thank you, Brad. I've heard a lot about you from Tolya and Tanya, as well as from a number of people who work for me down on industrial deck. Both of us were impressed with your apparent sincerity at The Trial."

Nobody ever asked what trial. The Trial would have a permanent place in the history books.

Brad looked almost shy. "Thank you for that, but it's not me, really. I just try to be obedient and care for my people. God gets all the kudos."

Naomi smiled. "Daryl and I hoped that, maybe after the big wedding…" She grinned and squeezed Tanya's arm. "We could sit down with you and talk…maybe get some clear perspective."

Brad took both their hands in his. "I'd be delighted to. Let's make it the Monday after their wedding. I think that's a week from tomorrow. Sound good?"

Daryl nodded. "That would be fine. Thanks."

Brad looked over at his wife, Jodi. "How about dinner, say 1900 or so?"

Daryl looked over at Naomi. "Wonderful."

Brad smiled. "I'd invite you to lunch but...I have a lunch chat with a small crowd." He grinned and indicated Tolya's group.

Daryl nodded. "No problem." He took Naomi by the hand. "We're going home to enjoy a nice, peaceful lunch. We'll see you at the wedding."

"OK. Take care."

Daryl and Naomi headed for home.

Brad turned to the rest of the group. "I don't know about anyone else, but I'm ready for lunch."

They enthusiastically started for the Hill residence.

CELEBRATION — 3

ECS Destiny, Deck 3, Hill Residence, 1200 Hrs

Lunch was quick and tasty. It consisted of cold cut, do it yourself sandwiches, iced tea, and something Jodi called Lamingtons. They were simple squares of sponge cake smothered in chocolate frosting, sprinkled with sugar and shaved coconut. Evan managed to monopolize much of the lunchtime conversation with his antics. Finally, appetite sated, the little guy nodded off in his highchair.

Jodi, with a look of pure relief, carefully wiped off the little face and carried him off for a nap. When she returned, the conversation began in earnest.

Brad started off with a set of questions for Felix. "Felix, Tolya tells me he's pardoned you. I'd imagine that's quite a relief."

Felix, who'd become more comfortable with the pastor and his wife, shrugged. "Yeah. Cap...uh, Tolya and...well, everybody that hangs with him... They've treated me differently than anybody I've met before. Usually, the authorities I met on Earth were indifferent and...well, mostly just doing their jobs."

He looked over at Tanya. "Tanya treated me like I was a real person, not just another case."

Then he turned his look on Sherry, "But I think it was Sherry who really messed with my head." He shook his head. "I always thought I was really good at my skills. I was cocky and...well, stupid. When I knocked Sherry down and she stayed down, I thought I'd killed her. That scared me to death."

Sherry smiled encouragement. "Anyway, I didn't know she was in the med-center just a few cubicles away. I was in pretty bad shape from my short experience with breathing vacuum, and I was torn up about the real mess I'd made."

Felix took a sip of his iced tea and then continued. "When Tanya brought Sherry in to confront me, I was so shocked. I thought she was dead and it was me that did it."

He shook his head. "I'll never forget it. She just said, 'I forgive you, Felix.' Something made me want to earn that forgiveness. The way everyone went out of their way to help was amazing."

Brad smiled and watched the look Sherry was sending Felix' way. "Felix, I hope you understand the forgiveness Sherry gave you was just that…a gift. You can't earn a gift. Out of the graciousness of her heart, she gave you forgiveness for a serious offense to her personal safety and even her life. That's a precious gift."

While Felix pondered that one, Brad turned to Sherry. "So, Sherry. Tell me, if you don't mind, how does a person decide to go against the natural tendency to condemn and even hate the offender? You did something very unusual."

Sherry fidgeted as she thought of what to say. "I can't explain why, really. I was very angry when I woke up with a headache and a painful arm in a cast. Then, while I was lying there in my cubicle, they wheeled Felix into the next one. I wasn't sure who it was, but somehow I guessed.

"Every once in a while, I could hear him…" she glanced apologetically at Felix, "…well…quietly sobbing. He tried to hold it back, I could tell. Something made me realize how dreadfully sorry he was for everything." She shrugged.

"Then Tanya and Tolya came to accompany me back to my cabin. She confirmed my guess that it was Felix next door, and suddenly I knew I had to let it go. I just knew that somewhere behind all that trouble was a decent person."

Brad sat back, looking thoughtful. "So Sherry, do you know what motivates that kind of forgiveness?"

Sherry shook her head.

"Love."

Sherry blushed furiously, looking down at her plate.

Brad chuckled. "No, I don't mean romantic love. You showed a moment of pure, unreserved compassion. You did something almost as fantastic as what God did for us. Only, where you gave up your right to be angry and vengeful, God did even more. He gave his own son, who willingly gave up his life, to pay the price of mankind's rebellion."

He focused on Felix. "That kind of love is very powerful. You can't pay for it, or make up for it. All you can do is accept it with real gratitude."

He looked over at Tanya and Tolya. "Your governor and his lady followed Sherry's lead and afforded you forgiveness too."

He looked back to Felix. "It took them a little longer because of their concern for the greater good of the colony."

Jodi passed around a pitcher for tea refills. Brad excused himself and stepped into his tiny office. He returned with a small box. Opening it, he pulled one of several tiny folded pouches, each containing an L-ROM chip. "Felix, do you have access to a power-tab or pocket-tab?"

Felix grinned. "Yes, Dr. Strauss gave me one for classes."

Brad smiled. "Good." He handed the little folder to Felix. "This is the whole Bible. Just slip it in the external L-ROM slot on your board just like any other book chip."

He slid one of the little folders to each of the others. Lyuba picked hers up with a smile. Tolya looked it over and carefully slipped it in a pocket.

Tanya and Sherry picked up the last two.

Tanya commented. "Thank you. I don't think I've read this in a very long time. I don't even have it on my cabin computer."

Felix took his and turned it over in his fingers for a few moments. "I don't think I've ever read it. Religion wasn't very important in my world."

Brad smiled. "Really, religion, for the sake of religion isn't all that important. It's all about how you stand personally before God. I suggest you start by reading the gospels. Those are at the beginning of the second half of the book. Then work your way through some of the letters. If you're really interested in the history of it all, go back to the beginning and read through."

They chatted over their iced teas for a while longer when Tolya noted the time. "Brad. Jodi. I really appreciate your hospitality. Lunch was amazing and the discussion was, as always, thought provoking, but we're going to be dropping into Normal Space this evening. That means I must get to work."

Brad grinned. "Well, we enjoyed having you. Don't forget we have one more session Wednesday, before the wedding. We'll need Lyuba there as well.

Jodi grinned, patting Lyuba's arm. "We always need Lyuba."

Everyone got up and started bustling around in preparation to leave. Felix shook Brad's hand and thanked him for the lunch and the Bible.

Sherry held up her Bible chip. "I've never read this before, but I'll check it out. Thanks."

Brad smiled and squeezed her shoulder. "You won't regret it." He tapped Felix' shoulder and motioned him to join them. "Felix, Sherry. I'd like your permission to use your stories for a sermon. If you're willing, you could tell them. We'll leave out some of the detail if you like, but I think it would be a wonderful way to teach about forgiveness."

Sherry looked nervous. She glanced at Felix who was pondering the question. He glanced at her. She seemed to be waiting for him to speak.

"Well, Brad. I've never gotten up and talked to people before, but I don't mind if Sherry doesn't."

Sherry seemed to relax and turned to Brad. "If you think it would help someone…yeah, I guess it would be OK."

"Great!" Brad shook Felix' hand again and gave Sherry a brotherly hug. "Maybe we could get together next week and talk it over. I'll call and we'll pick a time that works for everybody." They agreed and made their farewells.

CELEBRATION — 4
ECS Destiny, Command Deck, Bridge, 2150 Hrs

"Attention Please. This is the Captain. All personnel should begin moving to transition stations. All crew on duty, man your stations. All who are not on official business should move to a secure location and prepare for turbulence. *Destiny* will drop from Multi-Space in thirty minutes. I repeat. All personnel should begin moving to transition stations. *Destiny* will drop from Multi-Space in thirty minutes."

Tolya tapped the icon, closing the connection and sat back in his chair. He looked up to his right and smiled at Tanya. Vince stood to his left. Three extra seats had been added to the back of the bridge. Lyuba, Felix, and Sherry occupied them as observers.

The final preparations kept the room buzzing with murmured communication. All things were green and the clock was slowly counting down. At the fifteen-minute mark the lift doors snapped open and Emily Strauss stepped onto the bridge.

Tolya turned his seat and looked to see who had entered. He grinned a welcome and waved a hand towards NavCom.

Frank glanced up to see Emily approaching. He grinned broadly, scooting his chair aside to give her room. She took the spot and placed a hand on his shoulder, watching the screen.

The screen was currently showing a computer-extrapolated view of space as it might look if they could actually see it. Multi-Space had different physical laws than Normal Space. If there was anything to see, it was not available to the human senses. This view wasn't nearly as inspiring as the one in Normal Space.

Down in MedCentral, Daniela Jacobs waved at the answer icon on her COMM. Tolya's face filled her screen. She could see Vince, just barely in the pickup to his left.

"Everything ready doctor?" Tolya grinned at her.

"Things are secure, stations are manned. All is well."

"Thank you Doctor."

She saw him reach for the monitor and the view rotated slightly to center on Vince. He leaned forward and smiled. "I'll see you in Normal Space."

"You bet you will, mister." Daniela grinned back.

The screen blanked and she sat back to admire the new ring on her finger.

Back on the bridge, Tolya turned the little monitor back to its proper position and tapped another icon. The screen revealed Daryl, down in the MS drive interface. "How's everything, Chief?"

Daryl grinned. "Purring like a kitten; there should be no trouble this time."

Tolya's smile deepened. "I like that phrase. 'No Trouble,' such a rare commodity."

He saw Naomi in the background. "Well, I'll see you two in Normal Space."

Naomi grinned and waved. Daryl nodded. "Yes sir."

The screen blanked. Tolya glanced at the count down clock. "I need a report."

The stations responded. All was ready, all lights were green. "We're at the five minute mark."

He tapped the all ship COMM. "Attention. Attention, please. This is the captain. We are now at five minutes till transition. Please secure yourselves."

The clock clicked to four minutes, fifty-eight seconds. There was always a little tension on the bridge during transition. This time the levels were a little higher. The guests on the bridge were seeing the process up close and personal. Tolya glanced around to see all was in order.

Finally the clock flipped to three minutes. Tolya stabbed the ship COMM once more. "Attention, Attention. This is the last call, we will transit in three minutes; secure yourselves now."

He tapped the icon, closing the all ship's channel and glanced at the clock. Two minutes. "Stand by, people. We have two minutes." Tension on the bridge ratcheted up another notch.

Emily stepped behind Frank's seat and gripped his shoulders with both hands. Frank grinned and reached up to pat a hand in reassurance. The clock hit one minute. "We have one minute. Final countdown has commenced."

Tolya grinned around the room. "We have transition in forty five seconds…thirty…fifteen…"

Sherry snatched Felix' hand and gripped hard. He glanced at her with a grin. "Ten…nine…"

Lyuba grabbed Felix other hand, eyes as big as saucers. "Five…four…three…two…one…"

There was a gentle surging tremor through the ship, followed by a hollow, pit of the stomach sense of falling. Almost before the feelings registered, they vanished to be replaced by a momentary sense of spinning. The main display flickered and a wash of color scanned from the center and out to the edges in a radial pattern.

Before their eyes was their first view of the system they'd fought so hard to reach.

Emily stepped away from behind Frank's seat and moved to the science station next to Tanya.

Destiny had dropped into the system high and at an acute angle. Low and to the left of center was the parent star. It was a discernible disk that seemed to be nestled in a thin haze. Lower and far to the left, was the barely discernible crescent of a large gas giant giving back the light from its sun. High and to either side of the target star was a string of distant stars arcing out and upward. The view was indeed like a gigantic jeweled tiara. The central gem was the parent star for this system.

Emily looked at Tolya. "It's the gem in the tiara. Gem is the star in the constellation, Tiara."

Tolya smiled. "Any objections?" he asked the room. There seemed to be none. "Status everyone."

Eyes quickly dropped to consoles and reports began to flow.

Vince announced. "Status, excellent. All systems, green."

Lyuba hopped up and ran to join her uncle.

Sherry was staring in rapt attention at the view on the screen. She'd forgot to let go of Felix' hand.

"We're here." He announced as he stood.

Sherry smiled. Squeezing his hand as she followed suite. "Yes, we are," she breathed.

CELEBRATION — 5

SUN 03.28 — WED 03.31.2094
Outer Fringes; Gem System
ECS Destiny

Life on board *Destiny* became much more animated with their safe arrival in Gem system. Life on Quarterdeck suddenly became hectic. It had been decided the captain's quarters would be expanded and turned into a living space large enough for the new first family.

This meant Tolya had to move out of his cabin for the duration. Some of his things got stuffed in odd corners of Tanya's cabin and some wound up stored in Vince's. Key items that were needed for use wound up in Tolya's standby cabin where he made great use of the couch for the better part of a week. In spite of the chaos that prevailed during construction, the mood of the staff was buoyant.

On the residential decks there was excitement and enthusiasm. The week was quickly becoming one long celebration with community parties all over the ship.

Tanya elected to cancel karate lessons for the week. With the wedding coming up Saturday, there was a flood of last minute details that threatened to overwhelm her. The wedding bands were finished and picked up by Shane. He wasn't chancing them getting lost in the construction madness. The ladies were working on the final outfitting and decorations. The Promenade Deck was steadily being transformed into a palatial garden.

* * * *

WED 03.31.2094
ECS Destiny, Deck 3, Hill Residence, 1725 Hrs

Tolya, Tanya and Lyuba arrived at the Hill residence with a few minutes to spare. Jodi invited them in and soon they were seated around the kitchen table. Brad came out of his study and joined them at the table where Jodi handed coffee and two cups of green tea around.

Lyuba grinned at the tea. "You remembered."

Jodi grinned, "That's right, sweetie." She held up the second cup. "Green tea's my favorite too."

Jodi turned to Tolya. "I heard we've named the system, Gem."

Tolya grinned. "Yes, I'll have to show you the view; maybe the night of the rehearsal, we'll have a look from the Officer's lounge."

Jodi smiled. "That would be nice."

Tanya spoke up. "Believe me, the view is way more than nice, it's breathtaking."

Brad spoke up. "I look forward to seeing it." He reached for a pastry. "Is everyone ready?"

They all nodded. With a short prayer, the meeting began. "We've discussed the gift of love God gave us; the different varieties of love that create a homogenous whole. There's the love siblings and friends have for each other, a love built around companionship.

"We talked about romantic love. That's the one that puts the icing on the cake in marriage." All the adults grinned. "All these types of love are connected to each other. Some people don't think romantic love is truly connected, but I think the Bible makes it clear that, practiced as God intended it, romantic love is a vital part of the love continuum."

"We also talked about the perfect love of God; a selfless, giving sort of love that's only concerned with the good of the beloved."

He turned to Lyuba and smiled. "Tonight we're going to talk a little about another kind of love. That's the one that grows between parents and their children."

Jodi brought a decanter of coffee and poured refills.

Pastor Brad continued. "When we talk about the love between parents and their children, we look at something similar to God's perfect love. The love between parents and children is a very sacrificial kind of love. Parents give up many of their personal freedoms and activities to make sure all is well with their children. Children give up some of their desires and preferences to do what's right by their parents."

The pastries soon disappeared as the discussion continued. Lyuba learned that the love that existed between parents and an adopted child was special because they were giving love to someone who started out a complete stranger.

Brad pointed out one difference. "Obviously, you and your uncle aren't strangers, but you and Tanya did start out that way."

Lyuba nodded in rapt attention.

"Before you were ready to accept Tanya as your new mom, you had to find a place were you trusted her. All the kinds of love are attached to trust."

Lyuba smiled. "I decided to trust her because Uncle Toly trusted her. Now I can trust her because I know she's keeping her promises.

Brad smiled. "Yes, and if you think about it for a while you'll understand that that was a very sacrificial act. She has given up private time with her new husband to share him with you from the very beginning. Most young couples need time to get acquainted with their new relationship as husband and wife before they decide to include kids."

Lyuba got a concerned look on her face. Tanya reached over and squeezed her hand. "Don't worry. I'm very happy to have you around." Lyuba smiled, squeezing back.

Brad took a sip of his coffee. "Love's about giving up the notion of always having things our own way. Lyuba must obey her parents. That means she can't always have her own way. God says we show our love by obeying Him. Children show they love their parents by obeying them. Parents can't always have their own way. Sometimes they have to understand that their child must have or do something they don't want. So, everyone has to be willing to give up having their own way about something if it will help make the relationship better."

The time quickly wound down and they had to part. The Wednesday service had been turned into a church dinner to celebrate the arrival in Gem system.

The meeting hall had a growing crowd of people in it. Daryl and Naomi were chatting with a couple of members. Felix and Sherry were talking to a couple of other youths. Tolya's eyebrows arched when Vince and Daniela turned up. The time passed with great food and great companionship.

The next day, Thursday afternoon, Felix and Sherry met with Brad to discuss their story and how it would tie into his next sermon. They explored more of the connections between human love and forgiveness and God's model of those qualities.

Through these discussions, Felix and Sherry soon understood their own individual need to accept God's love and forgiveness.

They talked about how they'd present their stories. A special celebration was planned to welcome each of them, based on their newfound faith, as new members of *New Destiny Church*.

While Felix and Sherry were busy with the Hill's, Tolya and Tanya began the process of moving all his things back into the newly completed Chernov residence. Some of her things wound up getting moved as well. So, Thursday and Friday evenings Tolya found himself rattling around in a place big enough for three people. It felt strange having so much room to himself.

Friday was the final day of insanity before the wedding. Announcements had been posted on ShipNet early in the week. The flood of happy responses and notes of congratulations nearly swamped both Tolya and Tanya's ShipNet mailboxes. Finally, it was time for the rehearsal.

* * * *

FRI 04.02.2094
ECS Destiny, Promenade Deck, Central Garden & Fountains, 1725 Hrs

The wedding party assembled on the marble tiled floor out in front of the Port Side lift well. Behind them were also the Port Side, medical and security stations and Education wing. In front of them was the edge of the grassy park center. There were ranks of folding chairs facing the central pool and fountain, which had been transformed to a stage with strategically, placed fountains.

Down the center of the seating area was a stone pathway that matched the existing Promenade walkways that ran nearly the length of the park. This stone path intersected the central walk to end in the middle of the temporary platform.

Brad Hill presided. "Tonight, we're simply walking through the various segments of the ceremony. For most of us, it'll be fairly simple. Simple's always good at weddings."

That brought laughter.

"Many of you have some level of religious background. Others have elected not to. That's ok, but it's the bride and groom's wish that this ceremony be religious in nature. That means we'll be honoring God in every aspect. I hope everyone here can, at the very least, show respect for the religious aspects you might be uncomfortable with."

He scanned the group before him, "That's probably the last stern thing you'll hear from me tonight."

"I'd like the bride and groom to stand here next to me." He stepped to one side to give them room, "Then we'll have the groomsmen and bridesmaids pair off and line up."

There was a general bustling about as they sorted themselves out. Soon, there was a double line stretching down the central path. Tolya and Tanya stood next to Pastor Brad. First in line were Sherry and Shane. Next were Vince and Daniela. Then, came Frank and

Emily, Ichirou and Midori, and finally Daryl and Naomi completed the lineup.

Brad grinned. "Very good. Basically, this is the way it's going to go. We'll have a live band. They're practicing elsewhere tonight so, don't worry. When everyone is ready and it's time to begin, the band will play a selection. Each of the couples…"

* * * *

Frank had co-opted Felix to take photos of the rehearsal. Felix jumped up on a chair and got a good shot of everyone in position. He zoomed in and got a close up of each couple in the party and then of the bride and groom. Then, on impulse, he swept the camera back to Sherry and zoomed in to take a solo shot of her.

The walk through went well. No difficulties emerged. When all was done, everyone headed for the lift wells and started the migration up to Quarterdeck and the Event Center Diner. It was late and the food service crew had volunteered to work the rehearsal dinner.

Dinner was a simple affair. The wedding party and a few close friends comprised the attendees. It was a fun time to hang out, tell stories and eat good food. Tolya and Tanya took turns thanking people by name for their various contributions to the work of making their wedding a success.

* * * *

Most of the party filtered out leaving Tolya, Tanya and Lyuba, Pastor Brad and Jodi, and finally, Sherry and Felix.

"Brad. Jodi. I promised to show you the view from the front row." Tolya grinned as he bade the group follow him.

The Lounge partitions had sunk into the floor, making the dining and lounge area one huge room. A platform for the wedding party was set up at the back of the room. Tolya led them around the back of the platform. There a comfortable space was left for the access of the wait staff.

"If everyone will back up against the platform, I'll open the curtains and you can see what will be our new home system." Everyone moved back and Tolya waved his hand in grand fashion. The massive curtains slowly parted causing the room lights to dim.

It was as if they were standing on a ledge at the edge of the universe. The floor to ceiling pane of transparent armoplast revealed the vast panorama of space. Stars abounded and blended in a multihued dusting of light. That alone was worth the thrilling sense of vertigo that tugged on the mind. Closer in to their field of view was the system's sun. It was a distant, but discernible disk. It appeared to be set in a thin, translucent cloud of fine dust that glowed, giving the star a diffused halo.

Tolya pointed out the other stars in the cluster outlining a circlet. The effect was what looked like a vast jewel studded tiara with a bright gem gracing the front.

Tanya stepped forward and pointed out a couple of the large gas giants. One was larger than Sol's Jupiter while the other was probably close to the size of Neptune. From their vantage point the two looked like glowing crescents, tiny and alone. It took a little searching to make them out from this distance.

Brad breathed a sincere "My God."

He turned to Jodi who was holding a half sleeping Evan. "It's the art work of the Almighty." He said.

Jodi nodded, just staring in awe at the sight. Felix stepped forward till he was almost touching the ice-cold armoplast. Wonder transfixed his face. He'd seen this from the bridge but this view was absolutely breathtaking. Sherry tentatively stepped up next to him and whispered something. Felix glanced down at her and smiled.

Jodi turned to Tanya. In hushed tones she complimented the choice of names. Tanya replied, "Oh, I agree, but it wasn't me. You'll have to talk to Emily Strauss. She's our science officer and Director of Education."

Jodi grinned. "Emily? We met her last Christmas when the children did their musical production. We have a couple more years before we have to get Evan started. Did she ever get someone to head up the young children's program?"

Tanya smiled. "I'm surprised you didn't go for it."
Jodi laughed lightly. "I've got my hands full as a mom and a pastor's wife."

Tanya grinned. "Yeah, your little guy's a hand full. He's pretty cute though."

"Thanks." Jodi replied with a grin.

Tanya watched Felix and Sherry standing together against the observation window. "Emily just filled that position recently. Tolya and I met this gal who seemed to fit the bill perfectly. So we introduced them."

Jodi shifted Evan slightly. Just three years old, he was a heavy handful. "Really? Who is it?"

Tanya grinned, "Francine Douglas."

"Francine? She and Dennis periodically visit our services. Her husband is a little unsure of the whole church thing, so it's difficult for her to attend more regularly."

Tanya smiled, thinking of little Dennis on the bridge. "Well, I can tell you it won't be too long before there'll be a class ready for your little Evan."

Tolya noted the time. "I truly hate to break this up folks, but tomorrow's going to be absolutely crazy. I think we all need to get some rest."

He waved his hand and the curtains began their long trip back across the universe. Felix and Sherry backed away and the room lights slowly faded up to previous settings.

Brad and Jodi volunteered to escort Lyuba back to the O'Connors' residence. Shane and Kaitlyn had left soon after dinner, leaving Lyuba with Tanya and Tolya. Tolya thanked the food services crew for the extra work and then ushered Tanya, Felix and Sherry out the door.

Felix and Sherry went ahead to stop and chat in front of his cabin. Sherry explained, "I'm staying with Tanya tonight, so I can help her in the morning. So, I'll see you tomorrow, right?"

Felix grinned, "Of course. I wouldn't miss it for anything...Good night." He squeezed her shoulder and let himself into his cabin. Sherry watched him go and then crossed towards Tanya's cabin. This was to be Tanya's last night in her old cabin. Tomorrow night she'd be across the corridor, married and a mom, all in one busy day."

She felt a twinge of envy and stole a fleeting glance towards Felix' cabin. *Someday*, she thought wistfully.

Tolya and Tanya enjoyed their last embrace for the night and Tanya warned, "I can't see you, you know; not until the ceremony tomorrow. It's a tradition."

Tolya gave his most convincing pitiful look. "I don't know if I can wait that long."

She poked playfully at his ribs. "I promise to make it well worth the wait."

Tolya's eyebrows reached for the ceiling. "Then I'll just have to hang in there with great expectations."

Tanya shook her head with a giggle. "You're a monster, you know that?"

"I do the best I can." He said innocently.

CELEBRATION — 6

SAT 04.03.2094
ECS Destiny, Quarterdeck, Chernov Residence, 0630 Hrs

Tolya woke early. He was too keyed up to sleep. Besides, the new arrangements in the newly enlarged residence left him off balance. He'd gotten used to the cramped cabin he had used for the last two years or so. The new bed was huge. *That'll change soon enough*, he thought with a grin.

Finally, he decided he needed to work off some stress. He quietly padded down the corridor. On impulse he stopped at Felix' door, tapping the page.

The door snapped open almost immediately.

Felix prompted, "What's up?"

Tolya grinned. "I can't get back to sleep. I thought if you were awake we could go spar in the gym for a little while."

Felix feigned a look of sheer panic. "Oh, sure. I'm not much of a match for you, but I might learn a thing or two if you clean my clock often enough." He grinned. "Give me a minute to grab my gear. I'll meet you there."

"Great. Thanks Felix."

Tolya turned and realized he'd forgotten his own gear. Quickly he returned to his place and changed into his gi. He grabbed, a set of sweats and headed for the gym. As the door to the gym snapped open, he saw Felix, in his new gi, white belt cinched proudly, carrying his own sweats, loping down the corridor towards him.

The work out felt good...Mostly.

Felix did get his clock cleaned a number of times, but he did manage to land a few hits that earned him words of praise. They hit the showers and then, each carrying a gi and wearing sweats, strolled down the corridor.

"You're nervous, aren't you?"

Tolya glanced at Felix, surprised. "Yeah, I guess. I don't know why. I've no doubts about Tanya and I'm excited about adopting Lyuba, but...I'm about as nervous as a mouse at a cat convention."

They stopped in the corridor between Felix' cabin and Tolya's new digs.

"I'm afraid I don't have any advice to offer." Felix said. " I've never had a girlfriend, much less thought of getting married. I think I'd be nervous as heck."

Tolya laughed. "Felix, Felix. If you only knew. I think you're in for a surprise."

Felix felt his face flush. "Why? What...you think...you think Sherry and I are... Oh no, no. We're just friends."

Tolya raised an eyebrow. "Is that what you think?"

Felix shrugged. "She's just...I mean, after what I did...that would just be weird."

"I don't think she finds it weird at all, Felix."

Felix looked like an ox that had just been hit over the head with a two-by-four.

Tolya chuckled merrily. "Don't worry about it. Things like this have a way of working themselves out. Listen, why don't you toss your stuff. I'll go do the same and we'll have an early breakfast."

Felix grinned. "Sure, I'll be right out."

* * * *

ECS Destiny, Quarterdeck, Tanya's Cabin, 0630 Hrs

They woke early. Sherry was serene and calm and Tanya a bundle of nerves. They had toast and tea in Tanya's cabin for breakfast and in a moment of calm, Tanya thought of something.

"Hey Sherry. I just realized something. I won't be needing this cabin anymore. I want you to have this space for yourself. You'd be just down the hall from the office. It'd make it easier for us to do stuff together besides work."

Sherry's eyes got big. "Oh Tahnie, that's...oh, thank you. I don't have to put up with my crazy room mates anymore!"

She came around the little fold up kitchen table and gave Tanya a hug. "Privacy! My realm for privacy!"

The laughter released some of Tanya's tension. The morning went much faster than expected. There was so much to do it felt like riding a whirlwind.

When Kaitlyn showed up with Lyuba, she and Sherry got busy. Kaitlyn started with Lyuba's hair and Sherry got busy with Tanya's, the process long and arduous. The guys gathered across the corridor in the Chernov residence.

Finally, it was time to head down to the gardens. Sherry went across the hall and instructed the men to get their ornery hides down to the Promenade so the bride could emerge, safe from the eyes of her beloved.

The guys finished the last bit of tucking and tightening and trooped aft to the port side lift well. Eight guys crowded into one lift and, using the captain's override, took an express trip down to Promenade Deck.

Shane hurried them all into the security station next to the lift. Once the way was clear, he gave Sherry a call and then instructed the guys to stay put. Brad took over while Shane went out to check on the band.

The ladies scurried from the lift to the med-station opposite the guys. Sherry and Jodi kept things organized. Final preparations were accomplished in frantic haste.

At last, all was as ready as anyone could ever hope.

* * * *

ECS Destiny, Promenade Deck, 1200 Hrs

To everyone's amazement, there was seating for nearly two thousand people. In Tolya's estimation, Ichirou and Midori had outdone themselves. The seats were full and people were standing. Along each balcony corridor on decks 1 and 2 above, people sat or stood against the railings with a wonderful view.

Suspended from beneath the Mezzanine on Deck 3 was a set of jumbo monitors that allowed the people on the balconies close ups of the event. There were four stationary digicams and one remote aerial vid platform. Two stationary cams were situated to either side of the path where the open area began. Two more were up on the terraces covering long shots. The remote aerial cam darted around, seeking out opportune close ups.

The platform had been built over the central pool and fountain. The cylindrical rain curtain had been temporarily modified to look like four arced, lighted columns of water enclosing the central area where the actual ceremony would take place. To either end of the platform, graceful fountains played.

Felix served as the lone still photographer. He'd discovered, much to Frank's pleasure, that he was very good at getting still shots. Frank reminded Felix these were for the historical record.

Felix was having the time of his life, doing something useful for the colony and giving back a little to his friends who'd helped him straighten out.

The band was surprisingly good. They'd congealed from the various residential decks over the course of the twenty-seven months in space. Some of them were also members of the church band that served *New Destiny*.

They played a wide variety of music, music that was as new as the songs they'd grown up with on Earth, to songs eighty to a hundred years from the past. All had something to do with love, of course. In the last fifteen minutes of the pre-service time, the band switched to contemporary gospel songs that spoke of love and trust.

Finally, the magic hour of 1200 arrived. The band paused for a couple of moments and then struck up an anthem that signaled the beginning of the ceremonies.

Shane and Sherry joined arms and started forward along the central path at a stately gait to the front.

Felix was there, snapping photos of the couple. He saw Sherry in her rich leaf green 'A line' gown, pale green sash and shawl, and his heart almost skipped a beat. It occurred to him that he'd never thought of her as beautiful before. He was revising his opinions as rapidly as he clicked the shutter.

As they passed the front row of chairs, Shane split right and Sherry left. They approached the platform along a line of rose bushes, stopping on the first step to either side of the path, each in front of one of the two closer rain columns. Felix got a great shot of them and turned to get the next couple.

Vince and Daniela made a dashing pair. The men wore a three-piece suit of deep, dark green. Ruffled shirts had come back into fashion in the decade before the flight, so they were a part of the outfit. They were a pale green with a darker green trim. Bow ties the color of their suits finished out the ensemble elegantly.

As Vince and Daniela split, Felix lowered his camera to spare another look at Sherry, who was watching him. He broke his appreciative stare and turned to shoot the next couple.

Frank and Emily came next. Felix noted that Emily looked mighty fine in her outfit, but Sherry really was…he got busy snapping those pictures.

Ichirou and Midori Akari were as stately as Felix had ever seen them. The younger married couple on the staff; they seemed almost regal in their demeanor.

Daryl and Naomi came last. They were the second and slightly older married couple in the lineup. They too were a stunning pair. Daryl and Naomi stopped in their places, creating the open end of a wide 'V.'

Pastor Brad and Tolya stepped onto the platform from behind. Tolya stood at the leading edge, next to Shane's rain column. Pastor Brad stood in the centerline, just in front of the unity candle stand. He looked over at the lead singer in the band and nodded. The music faded and after a pause, the synth player started up an excellent rendition of the traditional bridal processional. The audience stood as one and turned to face the center path.

Felix was ready. He was very impressed with the vision coming down the aisle. Tanya wore a pristine white, 'A line' tank with a ruched V-neck, bridged with a fine net mesh to match her veil. Her train was of medium length. She approached in regal stride, truly the Queen of the day.

Following closely behind Tanya came Lyuba. She was dressed in a youthful version of Tanya's dress. It was ivory, trimmed in a green that matched the color of the bridesmaids' gowns. A beautiful green sash completed her outfit. For a thirteen year old, Lyuba was very pretty indeed.

Felix finished his shooting for the moment and stood near the front, ready for shots of opportunity.

Tanya stopped several feet from the platform looking beautiful, eyes only for Tolya.

Lyuba moved to stand in front of Shane, facing the audience.

The music ended and a lingering silence, graced by the soothing sounds of softly falling water, washed unhindered over the crowd.

Brad Hill took a step forward and addressed the crowd. "It is my privilege to bring before you, two wonderful people who have quickly become my friends. They're here before God to join in one of His most holy and meaningful unions."

His voice, amplified across the deck, carried crystal clear. "Let's begin this occasion with a word of prayer."

A sea of heads bowed. As far as he could see, not a head remained unbent.

"Lord God, Master of the universe, and Maker of all, we call on you to witness today the binding of these two in the precious union which you ordained from the beginning. Bless this marriage as it is bound and protect it from anything or anyone who would seek to break it. I ask this in the powerful name of Christ Jesus, Amen."

Brad continued with the introduction of the couple. "Standing next to me is Captain and Governor Anatoli Gavriil Chernov." He addressed Tolya. "Anatoli, a young maiden by the name of Tanya Marie Nydel stands before you, offering her hand. Will you claim her hand?"

Tolya regained his breath, momentarily stolen by the vision of beauty before him.

He nodded, "I will." They stepped towards each other and grasped hands. Tolya assisted her up the steps.

As their hands touched the lighting on the entire deck began to fade slowly leaving a pool of light between four faintly glowing columns of water, shining softly on the platform and the solemn event. The new couple stood side by side before Brad who now stood on a small box, to see over their heads.

Brad began the short message he'd prepared. "Since the beginning of time, when our first parents, Adam and Eve, first met, God determined the union between a man and a woman would be a holy thing. There are many reasons for this, but I'll stay with just one of the primary ones.

"God chose to make marriage between a man and a woman holy because it paints a picture of the union God intended to keep with his most awesome creation; the creatures he called man. Tragically, that union was violated and broken by the sin the man and the woman committed, the sin of rebellion.

"The entire Jewish and Christian religions are about the great lengths God went through, to cleanse and heal that broken union. That effort culminated in the life, death, burial and resurrection of God's only human born son, Yeshua, or Jesus, as we've come to know him.

"That story, painful, but true, demonstrates the tremendous love God had for his creation, a love willing to sacrifice himself to heal the relationship.

"Today, this lovely couple is playing out a symbolic scene commemorating the relationship God intended to keep with us, his best creation."

He stepped back and pushed the box to one. "We will now exchange vows and rings. Anatoli, do you have the ring?"

Shane handed Tanya's wedding band to Tolya who then collected the engagement ring from Tanya. He deftly snapped the two rings together and held the set at the ready. "I have the ring."

Brad smiled and then continued. "Anatoli Gavriil Chernov, do you take Tanya Marie Nydel to be your one and only wife, sealed to you for your entire life?"

Tolya's voice had a slight tremor in it as he replied, "I do."

Brad continued. "Do you promise before God and everyone that you will love, honor, and care for her, accepting and overcoming whatever troubles may assail you, not regarding the cost?"

"I do."

Brad nodded. "Please place the ring on her finger and repeat after me...I, Anatoli Gavriil Chernov...offer this ring...as a promise...that I take you...Tanya Marie Nydel...and welcome you...as my one and only wife...And as Christ promised us...I will never leave you...nor forsake you...so help me, God."

Brad turned. "Tanya, do you have his ring?"

Sherry handed Tolya's ring to Tanya, taking the bouquet of white roses for her.

Tanya faced Brad again. "I have the ring."

Brad smiled and indicated she should face Tolya.

"Tanya Marie Nydel, do you take Anatoli Gavriil Chernov as your one and only husband, sealed to you to the very end? If so, please say, 'I do.'"

Tanya took an iron grip on her emotions and managed an unbroken reply. "I do."

"And, do you promise before God and everyone that you will love, honor, and support him, accepting and overcoming whatever troubles may assail the two of you, not regarding the cost?"

"I do."

Brad smiled. "Please place the ring on his finger and repeat after me...I, Tanya Marie Nydel...offer this ring...as a promise...that I take you, Anatoli Gavriil Chernov...and welcome you...as my one and only husband...And as Christ promised us...I will never leave you nor forsake you...so help me, God."

Brad moved to stand to one side, next to the unity candle display. He motioned the two to approach.

The lights dimmed further and the spots dimmed enough for the crowd to see the lighted flames. Brad took a lighter and lit the left and the right tapers while leaving the middle one alone. Tanya took the left and Tolya took the right.

Brad recited from the Bible; "And he said, 'this explains why a man leaves his father and mother and is joined to his wife, and the two are united into one.' Since they are no longer two but one, let no one split apart what God has joined together."

Tolya and Tanya lit the larger candle on the top, using the flames from their individual tapers. Then blowing them out, they returned them to the stand and turned, facing each other.

Brad turned them, urging them to the front of the platform. The main lights came up again and Brad announced. "By the authority granted me by God and by the charter of this colony, I declare you, husband and wife."

The crowd erupted in applause that went on for some time. As the applause faded, Brad looked at Tolya and grinned. "And now for the part everybody's been waiting for; Anatoli, you may kiss your bride."

Tolya gently folded the veil back from Tanya's face, letting it fall over her back. Then they met for the greatest kiss on record.

"My friends, let me introduce you to Mr. and Mrs. Anatoli and Tanya Chernov." The crowd was on its feet again with applause and howls of approval.

Brad waved to Tolya to take charge.

Finally the tumult began to fade and Tolya stepped forward, the pin mike carrying his voice firmly.

"Friends, normally, this would end the ceremony and we could all go eat."

There was more applause and hoots of laughter.

"But...there's an important ceremony we wish to share with you." He held out his hand and Lyuba took it, gracefully stepping onto the platform to stand next to him. Murmurs of curiosity whispered through the crowd.

"Thirteen years ago, Lyubova was born to my brother and sister in law. 'Lyubova' is Russian for 'Love.' We soon called her 'Lyuba.'

"My brother was in the rim wars as was I in my turn. Unlike me, my brother did not survive the war, dying in a flash as his fighter was destroyed. Within a year of this, his wife, drowning in grief, died, leaving Lyuba alone.

"I took my niece and attempted to care for her while still in the military. Though the Earth courts made Lyuba my ward, I was unable to be there for her as much as I had hoped, so, as a favor, friends of mine took her and cared for her as their own.

Tolya took a deep breath, working on his emotions. "God blessed me with friends who elected to follow me out to the stars with you, and brought my niece with them."

He looked over at Tanya, standing next to him, smiling broadly and blotting her eyes with a handkerchief Sherry had spirited to her. "When Tanya and I agreed to marry, she asked why we couldn't adopt Lyuba. Again, God blessed me with a woman who also fell in love with my niece."

Tolya pulled a kerchief from a pocket and dabbed his own eyes. "Today, to conclude this joyous event, we chose a formal adoption ceremony for Lyuba."

He squeezed her hand and got a squeeze back with change. "So please, hold on for a few more moments and then we can all go invade the banquet hall."

He turned to Brad. "Pastor, if you would?"

Brad stepped forward and took a breath. "As everyone knows, the natural method of acquiring children has been designed into God's creation. However, sometimes other means are necessary.

"The act of adopting another is a singularly sacrificial act. It is a demonstration of love that is subtly different from that which occurs when the child comes naturally.

"Please attend as Lyuba is joined to this new couple."

"Tolya, do you have a token to give?"

Tolya fished out the little box with the pendant and choker. "Yes, I do."

Brad smiled as he looked at the pendant. His eyes widened in appreciation and he handed it back to Tolya. "Tolya please put this on Lyuba and then repeat after me."

Tolya opened the choker and gently placed it around Lyuba's neck. As the ever-present hover cam zoomed in for a close up, he showed her the pendant. Her eyes grew round. Then he clipped the pendant onto the choker."

Brad began, "I, Anatoli Gavriil Chernov…welcome…Lyubova Anastasia Chernov…as the daughter of my heart…to cherish and protect…with God's help."

Tolya gave his kerchief to Lyuba who quickly applied it to her own eyes.

Brad motioned Tanya closer. "Tanya, do you also have a similar token to give?"

Tanya turned to Sherry, who handed her a rich green shawl that matched the outfit Lyuba was wearing. She turned to Lyuba. "I do."

Brad nodded and then continued. "Tanya, please place the shawl over Lyuba's shoulders and repeat after me.

The hover-cam zoomed closer as Tanya draped the shawl over Lyuba's shoulders. "I, Tanya Marie Chernov…welcome…Lyubova Anastasia Chernov…as the daughter of my heart…to cherish and protect…with God's help."

The shawl settled nicely over Lyuba's shoulders and Tanya knelt to give her a fierce hug. Lyuba returned it with change as well.

Brad called for the lights to dim. The three turned to face the unity candle stand. Tanya took the right hand taper, Tolya took the left and Lyuba took the untouched middle taper, turning to face the audience. Tanya and Tolya re-lit their tapers from the unity candle and then lit Lyuba's candle. Brad called out. "To the one that came from two, another has come to create a new family. May God bless this union!"

After replacing their tapers, they turned to face the audience.

Brad then prompted Lyuba.

Lyuba stood between Tolya and Tanya holding both their hands. "I, Lyubova Anastasia Chernov…do gratefully accept…the love and shelter...of my new parents...Anatoli and Tanya Chernov...I accept the privileges and responsibilities...of a real and true daughter... with God's help." The three stepped to the edge of the platform.

Brad finished the ceremony. "Ladies and gentlemen, I'm delighted to present to you Mr. and Mrs. Chernov, and their new daughter, Lyuba."

The crowd was on its feet. The applause thundered and not a few napkins, tissues, and kerchiefs were applied to teary eyes.

The music resumed and the newly completed family filed down the center path followed by the rest of the party.

Brad made an announcement. "I have it on good authority, there is good food to be had for all. The main banquet will be in the Event Center Banquet Hall on Quarterdeck. Due to the inevitable overflow, the same courses are also available at both the lecture halls next door and down on the Mezzanine. During the celebration, the first family will visit each of the overflow venues. Let's celebrate!"

CELEBRATION — 7
ECS Destiny, Quarterdeck, Event Center Banquet Hall, 1315

It took forever getting into the banquet hall. Everyone wanted to shake hands or hug or chat. Shane attempted to gently clear a path. He soon gave up. Tolya shrugged and grinned. "Don't worry, we'll get there eventually."

Felix sat at the front, left of center table closest to the platform along with other friends of the party. He sat facing the head table with Kaitlyn O'Connor to his left. Brianna, Daniela's aid sat on his right. Across from him, sat Jeryk, one of Daryl's guys from Drive Section. Four others shared the table; Robin, a tech from Drive Section, Saul and Samuel Perlman who made the jewelry for the wedding, and Jeffrey the bright lab tech who'd assisted Tanya with running the tests for the poison that nearly took her future husband.

Tolya, Lyuba and Tanya sat in the center three seats at the head table. To his right ranged the groomsmen. To Tanya's left sat the bridesmaids. Sherry sat immediately to her left. She kept glancing in Felix' direction. He knew because he couldn't keep his eyes from regularly straying to her place.

Felix excused himself. Taking his camera equipment, he began wandering the room taking photos of everything.

About midway through the reception, the tables were scrunched closely to either side of center. This helped enlarge the dance area.

There was little room for a band, so it had been decided to have a tunes-man handle the music. Somewhere in almost a hundred years, the old term, DJ, or disk jockey had finally gone the way of all extinct creatures to be replaced by a tunes-man. It turned out this tunes-man was the drummer for the band that had played for the wedding. He was quite a showman.

Tolya and Tanya broke the ice on the impromptu dance floor. Daryl and Naomi were first to join them. Not to be out done, Vince pulled Daniela along. After some coaxing, Emily persuaded Frank to come dance. Finally, Ichirou and Midori made a quick appearance on the floor.

Sherry leaned over and had a quick word with Shane, who seemed undecided. She motioned towards Kaitlyn and he nodded. He replied and she shook her head no. Shane grinned and hopped down to whirl Kaitlyn onto the floor.

The tunes cycled through a few fast and medium songs. Felix resumed his seat and sat alternately watching the dancers and Sherry, seated alone at the head table. Their eyes locked and he motioned to her, inviting her to come sit with him. Everyone at his table had gone to dance or mingle.

Sherry managed to hurry gracefully. "Felix. I was beginning to think you weren't paying attention."

Felix smiled. "Sherry, I've noticed almost no one else. I'd ask you to dance, but I can't. It would be a disaster."

They tried conversation, a feat made nearly impossible with the sound levels in the room.

The tunes-man announced the next song and Sherry perked up noticeably. "Come on, Felix. It's a slow one. It'll be easy. Just do everything I do."

Felix looked frustrated. "I can't."

Sherry got up from her seat, reaching for his hand. "Come on. You'll do just fine. I've seen you on the gym floor. You're a quick study. Come on!"

Felix shrugged and got up. Hand in hand they moved out onto the dance floor. He felt like a fool. The song started and he realized the rhythm was slow and easy. *Maybe I can get through this.*

Sherry turned to face him. Felix glanced around to see what others were doing and decided he could do that. She slid into his awkwardly open arms and took his hand. She began; step, sway and step.

"Just mirror my moves." She whispered. Felix felt slightly embarrassed, *but this is really nice*! *Me, on the dance floor…with the most beautiful girl in the room in my arms…and she wants to be here.*

His steps slowly became more natural as he got into sync. Sherry looked up in his face and smiled. Then she relaxed, resting her head on his chest as they danced through the song.

It seemed the song was much shorter than it should've been. The tempo suddenly picked up and a fast selection immediately broke the spell.

Felix was quickly out of his depth and reluctantly led Sherry back to the table. "I really enjoyed that, Sherry…" He hesitated. "I… have I been missing something?"

She gave him a mysterious smile. The sound levels were quite high and it was hard to talk.

"Let's go out in the lobby."

Sherry nodded and they wound their way through the crowd towards the doors.

Tolya nudged Tanya and pointed in their direction. From the dance floor, they watched the two heading for the door. Tolya half yelled over the music. "I think young Felix just discovered he's been caught." Tanya was on a joy high. She laughed and Tolya grinned as they moved out of the milling crowd and returned to the head table.

* * * *

Chairs had been placed about the extra wide lobby area in front of the lift well, but all were taken.

Felix turned to Sherry. "Let's walk, OK?"

She smiled sweetly and nodded. "Sure."

They strolled slowly, side by side, down the port side central corridor as Felix tried to work out his feelings. They passed several staterooms and stopped next to the new Chernov place. Felix looked at Sherry, trying to hide a sudden case of nerves.

"Tolya and I got up early this morning and worked out in the gym. He couldn't get back to sleep because of nerves, I guess. Anyway, he admitted he was nervous but he didn't know why."

Sherry was glued to his every word.

"I was trying to be helpful, I guess. I told him I wasn't the best one to confide in since I didn't have a girlfriend let alone any experience with weddings."

Sherry clamped down on a treasonous grin that might have spoiled the moment.

He looked into her face. *Damn, she's pretty.* "You know? Tolya busted a gut, laughing at me. He implied I had a girlfriend and didn't know it. I know he and some of others have been thinking that we're...you know, romantically attached. I tried to explain we were just friends."

Sherry's face fell and something warned him he was on very shaky ground.

He reached out and gently laid a hand on her shoulder. "Look, Sherry. I really like you a lot. I like hanging around with you. I just...well...don't you think a serious relationship with a looser like me would be kind of weird? I mean...after how I hurt you and all?"

Sherry considered his question. She realized it was how they'd met that was causing the problem. She reached up and took his hand from her shoulder and looked him full in the face. "Felix, don't say that! You're not a looser. You're just not the same guy who hurt me that afternoon. Somehow, I knew the guy I see now was just waiting to come out, and I've been waiting."

She gave his hand a squeeze. "I don't think a relationship with you is weird, even if everybody else does."

Felix put his other hand over hers. It seemed strange holding the delicate hand he often watched flashing over her computer station. "I never thought...I never dreamed you'd...you know, be interested in me as more than a weird kind of friend."

Sherry squeezed his hand again. "Well Felix, I most certainly am interested. There's nothing weird about you. Even Tolya and Tanya admit that."

Someone strode quickly past, headed for the reception. They moved on, stopping again near MedCentral. They stood looking into the sky-view at the party on the Mezzanine below.

Felix turned and gazed at her for several moments. "Did I ever tell you you're beautiful? I never thought about it, but seeing you in that gown today...I realized you're beautiful."

Sherry blushed. Felix reached for her and hesitated. "May I?"

She smiled and stepped freely into his embrace. "I thought you'd never ask."

He held her for a moment and considered his good fortune. After a while he released her gently and looked her full in the face. "Do you want to see where we go from here?"

Sherry nodded. "Absolutely!"

They continued, hand in hand, down to the aft lift well in companionable silence. Then they slowly walked back towards the Event Center.

As they passed Tanya's cabin Sherry remembered something. "Felix. Tanya's no longer using her cabin. This morning she told me she wanted me to have it."

Felix raised an eyebrow. "Um...You'll be right across that mini-park from me."

Sherry grinned. "I thought the same thing." She stopped and turned to him. "I could use your help moving my things."

Felix grinned. "No problem, how about I help you after church tomorrow?"

Sherry grinned. "That's perfect. Thanks."

* * * *

Tolya and Tanya watched Felix and Sherry make their way back to his table. Tanya got a face splitting grin. She leaned over to Tolya. "It's over. You were right. He's gone!"

Tolya laughed out loud, checking the time. "Come on sugar, we need to get to the fun stuff. We still need to visit the other venues."

Tanya grinned. "Speaking of Mr. Felix, aren't we forgetting a little something?"

Tolya slapped his forehead. "Wow! Of Course."

As it turned out, Emily won the bouquet toss and Frank won the garter toss. The rest of the staff found this hilarious.

Tolya tapped his pin mic to see if it was on. He signaled the tunes-man who faded the music and gave Tolya a thumbs up.

"Friends. I have an announcement to make."

The room quieted somewhat. Tolya looked pointedly at Felix' table. "I'd like to ask Felix Hernandez to come up here."

Curiosity coursed through the crowd.

Felix stood at his table and looked around, embarrassed to have the attention shifted to him. Sherry got up and moved next to him. She took his hand, looking into his face. "You'll be fine, Felix. This is a good thing!"

Felix smiled and squeezed her hand. He turned and mounted the steps to the platform and joined Tolya and Tanya. Many in the crowd finally recognized Felix. There were a few murmurs, but most people just waited to see what was going to happen.

Tolya took Tanya's hand and drew her next to him so they stood unified. "Not too long ago, we had a series of unfortunate incidents that culminated in the loss of three citizens and the incarceration of a fourth."

The crowd shuffled nervously. "I know everyone wants to put that part of our adventure as far behind us as possible." He smiled broadly. "Believe me, so do I."

Tolya turned to look at Felix, who was trying to look insignificant. "Mr. Hernandez here, has been on an odd roller coaster ride ever since he got involved in that unfortunate mess. I am proud to say the results of his experience has netted a significant and, I believe, permanent transformation in character.

"Some of you know that early, during our MS hop to this system, Felix was upgraded from living in a cell, to operating under house arrest. He has lived the better part of the last three weeks up here on Quarterdeck. The education department next door has become convinced Felix is a permanent fixture." A few brief chuckles brought reassurance.

"Last weekend I took further steps to upgrade Felix' status. After demonstrating to my satisfaction that he has learned some powerful lessons, and after noting his personal goals have altered to make the success of this colony his top priority, I made a decision some may think controversial.

"In the spirit of joy and celebration of our wedding, and our adoption of Lyuba, and the celebration of the successful transition to this beautiful star system we hope to call home, I am taking a privilege that the charter says, belongs exclusively to the Governor."

You could hear a pin drop as the crowd listened.

Tolya pulled a small case from under his chair and popped it open. He unrolled an official document that had the colony logo and the Governor's seal affixed. He held the document up so everyone could see it. Then he read from it.

"In acknowledgment of his true contrition and repentance for the crimes committed as noted in the record, and acknowledging that he has credibly expressed the desire and ability to contribute greatly to the establishment and strengthening of the colony, I, Anatoli Gavriil Chernov, Governor, do hereby grant a full and unreserved pardon to Felix Xavier Hernandez for his ill advised role in the criminal activity that placed him in confinement."

Tolya looked around the room. There was shocked silence. Then slowly at first, a couple of people started clapping. More joined in, and little by little, the applause became heart felt. Tolya allowed it to continue for a few moments before holding up a hand for silence.

"I am convinced that Felix, who is starting to become a friend to a number of us up here, is truly not the same person who was tried before the court not so long ago. He has a long way to go, and he's working furiously to catch up his education. He constantly looks for opportunity to be of assistance. It's as if we've gained a brand new member of the colony."

He turned to face Felix and held out his hand. Felix took it in a firm handshake. "Felix, I just want to say, 'welcome home. We've missed you.'" Tolya pulled Felix into a fatherly hug and then released him. Another round of applause erupted.

Felix looked around and then waved to the tune's-man, signaling for a mic. The tunes-man passed a mic up and Felix held it in front of his face. The crowd sensed more to come and settled down to hear what he might have to say.

Felix cleared his throat and started. "I ah...I just want to say that, um...from the bottom of my heart, I want everyone to know I'm truly sorry for my participation in the stupidity we recently experienced. I make no excuses.

"Also, I want everybody to know I am forever indebted to just about everybody on the command staff. From the Captain...ah Governor, to his new wife, Tanya...to the various members of the staff who have encouraged me on my path to rehabilitation. Most of all, I owe a great big thank you to Sherry Petrakis..." He waved her up to join him.

Sherry hurried up the steps and came to stand by his side, beaming like a brand new star in the sky.

"It was Sherry, the one person I directly and personally injured, who started the ball rolling to get the rest of the staff to see something promising in me. I owe her a tremendous debt of gratitude for her forgiveness, understanding and encouragement." He took her hand and gave a big squeeze.

The applause came up again and lingered long. Felix handed the mic back down to the tunes-man.

Tolya signaled for quiet. "I want to thank everyone for the wonderful time. My bride and I need to visit the other venues, but we'll be back soon. Please feel free to continue the celebration. Thank you."

Tolya grabbed Felix by the arm. "Hey. Grab that camera and the two of you follow me. We need to go visit the other venues before they think we've forgotten them." He waved Shane over. "Grab your sweetheart and let's go visiting."

The newlyweds and their thirteen year old daughter, accompanied by Felix and Sherry, Shane and Kaitlyn, made their appearances at each of the overflow venues. Everywhere they went they found people of good will. Well-wishers seemed to come from everywhere.

Before moving on to another venue, Tolya would repeat the announcement about Felix and Felix would repeat a version of his public apology. When they'd completed their tour and returned to the main dining commons, the party was clearly winding down.

The newlyweds and their new daughter bid everyone a fond farewell and made their way to the their new home. Sherry and Felix followed.

Sherry took Tanya aside. "Tahnie. I think almost everything was transferred to your new place. We're going to grab the last of your things to bring over if that's OK."

Tanya grinned. "Thanks, Sherry. You finally reeled him in."

Sherry blushed. "Yeah. He finally figured it out."

Tanya gave her a hug. "Thanks Sherry, for all your help. I'm happy for you. I think you'll do just fine."

She turned to go. "Oh. Just drop everything in the entryway. You can use my spare passkey this weekend. Monday we'll get all the patches updated."

"Ok. Thanks, Tahnie."

Felix stepped up as Tanya went inside. Sherry turned, grabbed his arm and headed for Tanya's old cabin. "Come on, help me get the last of Tanya's things so I can start moving in tonight."

Felix grinned and followed.

CELEBRATION — 8

ECS Destiny, Quarterdeck, Chernov Residence, 1620 Hrs

Lyuba finished changing. She wandered around her room musing. She'd checked the closet to find a single change of clothes, something to wear for the evening. She was having a slumber party with friends down on Deck 3 and then tomorrow, the rest of her things would be brought up to her new home.

Tanya came out of the bedroom wearing casual clothes, face flushed and smiling a wistful smile. It felt good to get out of all that formal fluff. She'd loved every minute of it, but it was definitely possible to have too much of a good thing; particularly stiff, fancy clothes.

Tolya came right behind, in casual clothes as well. With company still coming and going, they were forced to postpone anything special for later, but the preview had been quite delightful.

Lyuba came out in her one change of clothes and ran to the kitchen, where Tolya was starting a pot of coffee. She ran up to Tanya, who sat at the table, combing her hair.

"Hi, mom." She was trying to get used to saying mom. She liked it, but it was kinda weird too.

"Hi, sweetie." Tanya put the brush down and bundled Lyuba in her arms. "Welcome home."

Lyuba grinned. "I'm ready to go."

Tanya looked her over. "What about PJ's?"

Lyuba laughed. "I'll get some from my...from aunt Kaitlyn's place on the way."

"OK. Better give your dad a hug before you go."

Lyuba hurried to the kitchen where Tolya had just finished starting coffee.

"Hey princess, you ready to go?"

Lyuba grinned. "Yes, dad."

Tolya grinned back. "OK. Give me a hug."

The hug was brief but strong. "I'll see you at church tomorrow." She said.

"Yes, you will."

"OK. Bye!" Lyuba turned and hurried out the door, bound for an all night adventure with friends.

Tolya brought two cups and placed them on the table. He looked around as if to find spy eyes somewhere before taking Tanya by the arm and pulling her into a hug. They embraced, poking and kissing. Tanya giggled and the door chime sounded.

Tolya rolled his eyes and went for the door while Tanya went to the kitchen to collect the carafe of coffee.

Sherry and Felix stood there, looking apologetic. Stacked around them was the remainder of Tanya's personal effects.

Sherry smiled up at Tolya. "Sorry? Tanya said to set her things in the entryway. We got it all together so we could do it in one trip."

Tolya smiled tiredly. "That's OK. Thanks for making it quick. Let me help."

He dug in and they lined the entryway with Tanya's things.

Sherry smiled. "I checked thoroughly. There's nothing else, so we'll not bother you again."

Tolya grinned. "Thanks. You two made this go a lot faster."

Felix grinned. "You know, about this morning?"

Tolya nodded.

"You were right. Thanks!"

Tolya grinned as he took in their confident posture.

"Congratulations," He said quietly.

Sherry blushed and Felix grinned.

"I'll see you...in the morning." He said, pointedly.

Sherry and Felix hurried off to collect her things.

Tolya punched the 'Do Not Disturb' tab on the door controls. Now, if someone came to the door the chime wouldn't sound. Instead, a quiet voice would announce the party did not wish to be disturbed, suggesting the caller return at another time.

Satisfied, Tolya marched back to the dining room table. Tanya sat there sipping her coffee, looking beautiful. She watched him with a saucy little smile. Tolya sat next to her with a goofy grin. "What are you thinking about, delicious?"

She handed him his coffee and purred her answer. "Drink up, tiger. You're going to need your stamina."

Tolya laughed. "Am I? That sounds promising."

Tanya arched a delicate eyebrow. "Oh, it is! I told you I'd make it worth the wait."

Tolya gave a mock groan. "Yes, and I've been waiting a very long time."

Tanya got up, setting her coffee down.

She started around the table and Tolya stood up too. "My poor captain has suffered deprivation for soooo long."

She moved up close and started working on his shirt fasteners. "I think…" she pulled the shirt open, "I have just the medicine to make him feel all better."

Tolya lost all interest in his coffee. He started to return the favor and she backed away teasingly. "I think you should go straight to bed. The treatments will be more effective there."

He tried for her shirt again and she darted for the bedroom, laughing. Tolya chased her down the hall and tackled her, dumping her playfully on the bed. Tanya gave a delighted little laugh as the treatments began.

* * * *

SUN 04.04.2094
ECS Destiny, Quarterdeck, Mini-Park, 0930 Hrs

Felix left his cabin and went across the mini-park to Sherry's. He tapped the announcer and waited. The door snapped open and Sherry smiled.

"Good morning." Felix offered.

"Good morning to you," Sherry grinned giving him a lightning quick hug. "Are you ready for today?"

Felix shrugged and they started for the lift well. "I guess so. I'm a little nervous, but if it'll help Pastor Brad, I can get through it."

Felix called the lift. "How about you?"

Sherry gave it a little thought. "It's kinda like you said. Telling strangers all about myself feels a little weird. Besides, I'm not much of a public speaker." The lift arrived and they selected Deck 3.

As Tolya and Tanya started out for the lift well, Tanya nudged him and pointed down the corridor. Sherry and Felix were just turning the corner on their way to the lift.

Tanya grinned and grabbed Tolya's hand. "Body language tells the whole story."

Tolya nodded. "Yeah. I think seeing her in that gown of hers did something to him. He suddenly saw a woman in the friend."

Tanya shook her head. "She's not complaining."

Tolya laughed. They took the next lift, catching up with the subjects of their fond amusement.

"Good morning, you two." Tanya called.

Felix and Sherry turned and waited. The new Mr. and Mrs. Chernov caught up.

Sherry gave Tanya a big grin. "So, how are we doing this wonderfully fine morning?"

Tanya returned the grin. "Awesome, thank you."

They continued into the lobby where folks were gathering for the morning service.

* * * *

ECS Destiny, Deck 3, New Destiny Church, 0930 Hrs

"I'd like to introduce Felix Hernandez. Some of you may recognize Felix from a series of unfortunate events a few months ago. Most of you will also recall that Governor Chernov just gave him a full pardon this weekend. Felix is here this morning to tell his story. I would ask people to reserve judgment till you've heard what he has to say." Pastor Brad stepped aside and motioned Felix to approach the podium. "Come, Felix. Tell us what God has done for you."

Felix was very nervous as he came to the podium. "Good Morning. My name is Felix. Some of you recognize me from my time in the maintenance department. Other's of you are more likely to pin my face to the near disaster I was unfortunately involved with a couple of months ago." Most faces were simply curious. There was no hostility present.

"I freely admit my own stupidity, and yes, I guess you could say greed, that got me involved in assisting the late Ted Jackson in his personal campaign of rebellion. If I had known then, what I know now, I'd have never even spoken to him, but that's not my lot."

Felix told his story, his youth in the streets of old Chicago, hustling to keep food and drugs in supply for his addicted mother. He described his participation in the Jackson rebellion, as the incident had become known. He got to the part where he forced his way into security central at the insistence of the late Ted Jackson.

"I tried to get the card keys to the detention center." He glanced at Sherry in the front row. She gave him a smile of encouragement.

"I got desperate because it was taking so long, and flung the little cabinet door open just as she got up to stop me. The door hit her on the side of her head and she fell, striking her head on the desk/counter. Her arm broke in the fall.

He remembered vividly the horror of that scene. "Her face was bleeding badly and she was like a rag doll on the floor. In the confusion and the heat of the moment, I thought I'd killed her."

He described releasing Jake Townsend from his cell and then having to duck into the armory to hide when the security chief and the captain came running in. He told of lifting the gun from the armory and rushing out when the coast was clear.

The shooting murder of Jake by Ted brought a tremor to his voice and misty tears to his eyes as he described the scene. The final scene in the hanger bay brought gasps from his listeners.

"When I was recovering from breathing vacuum, Tanya," he waved at her, "brought the girl I'd injured into my cubicle to identify me. It was there I experienced my first taste of compassion and forgiveness. I've never met anyone who could forgive so thoroughly as Sherry Petrakis."

He looked over at her again and smiled. "Long story short, I've been forgiven by my victim, and restored to social life by my governor and new friend. Since last week, I've received forgiveness and restoration from God as well." He looked around and grinned nervously. "Thank you."

The congregation was quiet for a few seconds. A couple of people began clapping. Soon all were applauding.

Pastor Brad stepped up and put his arm around Felix' shoulders. "People, that's a testimony of God's grace if I've ever heard one. Thank you, Felix."

Felix returned to his seat. Sherry leaned over and whispered, "You did great."

Pastor Brad continued. "Now, we're going to hear another story from a young lady you've already heard a little about. Her story is very different from Felix,' yet they've unavoidably had their lives mutually impacted. Sherry Petrakis is the associate of Tanya

Chernov, our ship's Chief of Security. It was Sherry who had the unfortunate encounter with Felix. Please welcome Sherry as she tells her story."

Polite applause sounded as Sherry made her way nervously to the podium. She had a self-conscious flush on the face. "Good morning. I'm Sherry Petrakis. I was born and raised for a number of years in Greece, back on Earth…"

She told of the move to California, of her love for the coastal community she'd grown up in, and the heart breaking loss when, while the family was away on vacation, the entire community had been destroyed by a terrorist mini-nuke.

When she got to the part about the assault on the security offices, she looked at Felix who gave her a 'thumbs up' sign.

"I'd never met Felix before. He was just a familiar face that came and went, cleaning and fixing things on the ship. He ran into the room and started demanding the card key for the detention section…" She described the struggle and the blow that knocked her down. "When I finally woke up, I had a terrible headache and a cast on my arm. I was lying there thinking all kinds of nasty, angry things about Felix. I wanted to hurt him like he hurt me…Then I heard someone quietly weeping a few spaces over and wondered who it was. Whoever it was, they were pretty broken up about something. "Later, I heard Tanya talking with someone and heard the name Felix. When she got to my cubicle to walk me back to my quarters, I asked if the other person was the guy who'd hurt me. She nodded and everything snapped into place."

She talked about how Tanya wanted her to talk to him, show that she was still alive and identify him as the assailant. "I realized right then, this guy was convinced he'd killed me and his own life was in ruins as well. I suddenly knew it couldn't go on. I agreed to talk to him and, just like that, I just let it go. I couldn't be angry anymore." She paused and gave Felix another glance. "All I could do was forgive him and hope it did some good. Last week I discovered that, a long time ago, God did the same thing for me. It's like He was trying to tell me through the way things happened."

Sherry looked over at Pastor Brad. She'd run out of words and was working valiantly to not make an emotional scene.

Brad came up and placed his arm around her and addressed the congregation. "God does things in unique ways. This is something Sherry's not likely to ever forget."

He gave her shoulders a squeeze. "Thank you, Sherry, for your story." She hurried back to her seat as the crowd applauded.

After she settled in her seat, Felix put his arm around her and gave her an encouraging hug. That's when she lost it and leaned over to cry quietly into his chest. Totally at a loss, Felix sat there stroking her hair, listening to the rest of the sermon.

Pastor Brad noted the exchange and quietly said to his people. "I can see God's the master of irony as well." He finished his message and the people began filing out. That evening, the congregation had a special gathering to welcome two brand new members to their number.

Tolya and Tanya collected Lyuba at the O'Connor residence. With Felix and Sherry there, gathering and transporting Lyuba's things went quickly.

CELEBRATION — 9
MON 04.04.2094
ECS Destiny, Quarterdeck, McIntyre Residence, 1830 Hrs

Daryl threw his shirt on and fastened it up. Naomi came out of the restroom ready to go. "You ready?"

Daryl smiled. "Yeah. I guess." He gazed at her a moment. "Do you think we're doing the right thing? I mean, we really don't know this guy. He seems like a descent sort, but so did that liar we had before."

Naomi drew close and put a gentle hand on his chest. "You know Tolya and Tanya, and you're getting to know the O'Connors. Do you really think they're totally clueless about character judgment?"

He held her hand where it was. "I know. I'm just not sure I'm all that ready to trust another preacher."

"I know honey. I have my own doubts, but we've left Earth behind. Shouldn't we leave the garbage behind too?"

Daryl pulled her head to his chest and gave her a gentle hug. "You're right. I do sorta like this guy. He's got a fine little family, and he seems genuine." He released her and stepped back. "Let's go. We don't want to keep them waiting."

* * * *

They arrived at the Hill residence with time to spare. Brad answered the door and ushered them in. "Daryl. Naomi. It's good to see you. Come on in."

They sat in the front room and chatted with Brad for a few moments. Evan came flying from the back and stopped dead in his tracks upon sight of the visitors. He gave a shy look and then charged across the room to tackle his daddy.

Brad scooped him up and put him on his lap. From his new secure vantage point, Evan peered around at the visitors with curiosity burning brightly.

Brad's wife, Jodi entered the room from the kitchen. "Naomi, good to see you."

The two ladies hugged.

"Daryl. How are you doing?"

Daryl stood and gave her a polite embrace. "I'm doing just fine. Thank you."

Not to be outdone, Evan immediately squirmed his way down and demanded a lift to mommy's arms. Jodi grinned and picked him up. "Brad, dinner's ready. Why don't we head for the dining room?"

Brad grinned. "That sounds great. Shall we?"

The process of installing Evan in his booster seat was mildly entertaining, but once he got there, he was quite ready to get down to eating. The dinner was wonderful. The chatter was pleasant. Naomi was particularly delighted with the ambrosia fruit salad.

Finally it was time to put things away. Daryl and Naomi insisted on helping, so the after dinner clean up went swiftly. Evan managed to fall asleep during the meal, so Jodi carefully washed him clean and carried him off to bed. Brad started coffee and they trooped back to the family room.

They were getting settled when Jodi returned from the bedroom. She brought the coffee out placing it on the coffee table. She poured for everyone and then sat next to Brad on the couch. Daryl and Naomi sat on the couch opposite.

"So," Brad began. "If I recall correctly, the two of you were struggling with a severe case of disappointment stemming from a nasty experience in a church back home."

Daryl nodded. "I'd say a 'severe case of disappointment' doesn't come close."

Naomi nodded. "Total despair might suffice."

Brad sat back and put an arm around Jodi. "Is it something you can tell us about? What's said here stays here."

Daryl looked at his hands. He'd started picking his fingernails and forced himself to stop. "Yeah, I guess it could use tellin.'"

"About four years before *Destiny* shipped out, I got involved in this church. I'd made a friend on the job who was always going on about religion and the church and after a while, I began to connect with what he was telling me. I started attending the services and going to the class he was in. I committed and joined the church after about six months. Then, my friend was shipped out to another part of the country.

"A little later I met Naomi. We hit it off almost immediately and after a short whirlwind courtship, we decided we wanted to marry."

He looked over at Naomi who gripped his arm in support. She took up the story. "We were actively involved in the church. So, we approached the head pastor about marrying us. He was agreeable, so we began taking his pre-marriage counseling. Our dreams were bright and coming true; life couldn't get much better. Then…"

She stopped for a moment to clear her throat. She looked at Daryl and shook her head, trying to keep her composure.

While she took another sip from her coffee Daryl took up the story. "Well, the Sunday before the wedding date, we arrived for the service to find everything in turmoil. As the time for the service came, there was no sign of the pastor. The service started, but it just didn't feel right. The music pastor seemed distracted and worried. Finally, he just stopped and in a sad voice announced the chairman of the board wished to address us.

"The guy stepped up and addressed the congregation…Long story short, the pastor had taken a large amount of money and fled the country with one of the singers, a wife of one of the musicians.

"Just like that. One day we had a 'man of God' who was counseling us for a successful marriage. The next, we had nothing. It was too late to make other arrangements. So, the big wedding plans died and we went to a justice of the peace."

Naomi set her coffee cup down and took a deep breath. "We were so angry and devastated we swore off going to any church again. That was about two years before we boarded *Destiny*. It's been that long since we darkened the doorway of any church."

Jodi reached over and took a couple of tissues from the box on the coffee table between her and Naomi. Then after dabbing her own eyes, looked into Naomi's. "I'm sorry for your loss, but I'm happy you two stayed together in spite of it all."

Brad was silent for a couple of moments. "I can't begin to express how sad this makes me. I've heard these horror stories from preacher friends over the years, but I've never met someone who was directly affected like you two."

He poured himself another cup of coffee. "I truly sympathize with the feelings that led you to flee that church. I understand the anger and the loss of trust in the church, but I have to address something that many people tend to forget when they've been hurt by someone in church." He sat back, took a sip and then continued.

"We have a tendency to get our focus shifted. We get so busy being involved in the activities and enjoying the personalities of the leaders we've come to love, we forget whom we're really supposed to be following. While finding a good pastor who will truly care about your maturity in the Lord is extremely important, there's a danger of becoming more attached to the pastor than to the Lord he serves. That's the little trap you both fell into."

He held a hand up as Daryl began to protest. "Wait. I don't mean to criticize. This is a common problem in the church. It's not a personal attack."

"Yes, but what about the preacher? He's the one at fault here."

Brad smiled. "Daryl. You're right as far as you've taken it. Trust me. The Lord holds his shepherds accountable for the sheep. He takes it very seriously. Truly, I fear for the man who did this evil thing. You don't play at being a preacher without paying a very high price."

Naomi's eyebrows rose. "I never thought about that. It's hard to remember the pastor's not the top of the food chain."

Brad grinned. "That's one of the more interesting descriptions I've heard. What I was trying to say Daryl, is that we have to put our faith entirely in God. If you trust in other people rather than the Lord, you set yourself up for disappointment.

"Think about it. God is perfect. He can't be tempted to fail in some way like this pastor who failed you. Pastors are not perfect. Just ask Jodi, here. I'm definitely not perfect. We're subject to temptation, just like you or anyone else. Our job is to stay tuned to God so we can resist the temptations. In so doing, we are then able to lead and encourage the people God gives us to care for.

"Don't trust me as if I were God. Trust God to keep me in line. Trust God to take care of you even if I fail. Then, if and when I do fail, you can remain strong, knowing He's dependable."

He smiled and shrugged his shoulders. "That's the lesson I hope you will take away from your experience. You belong to God. He just entrusts me with your care."

Daryl digested Brad's words. "Ok, that makes sense. You're saying our expectations were in the wrong place. So, why even be involved in a church?"

Brad grinned. "Touché! Actually, besides the fact the scriptures warn us not to abandon the practice of assembling together, there's a very practical reason. We're all together for mutual support. Have you ever sat near a campfire?"

Daryl nodded. "As a kid I went camping with my dad a lot."

Brad looked at Naomi. "And you?"

"Sure. I particularly love beach bonfires."

Brad grinned. "Me too. Anyway, if you were to get a fork or a couple of sticks and roll a glowing coal out of the fire so it sets by itself, what happens?"

Daryl grinned. "I used to do that. The lone coal stops glowing after a while and goes cold and dark."

Brad nodded. "What happened when you tossed it back with the rest?" Daryl responded. "Why, it re-lights and…"

He slapped his knee and chuckled. "Brad, that's pretty slick, and I get the point."

Brad smiled as he glanced at Naomi. She grinned as she made the connection. "God is all about community. His very nature reflects a sense of community. We've been designed to function best in community. And…our faith grows strongest when we remain in community. If you're in a church that doesn't function as a close knit community, you're in a church that has become unhealthy."

Naomi sat forward and said with a smile, "Well, your church seems pretty healthy then, if yesterday was typical."

Jodi smiled. "Thank you, Naomi. We don't claim to be better, but I'd like to think we're a healthy church."

WET RECEPTION — 1
MON 04.20 — SUN 05.02.2094
Outer Fringes; Gem System
ECS Destiny

At over three quarters-c, *Destiny* took about three weeks to approach the asteroid cloud, a whirling torus of rock and ice around the outer edge of the system. Initial scans indicated a rich field of mineral and metal deposits and frozen hydrogen.

The system was very dusty, as evidenced by the glowing halo they'd witnessed upon entry. By staying above the upper edges of the asteroid cloud while crossing that sector, there were fewer collision hazards.

Since Normal Space fuel supplies were still plentiful, it was decided to get in system right away and begin studying the world they hoped to call home.

A couple of short-range probes were launched. They'd hang around the outer system and pick up a wide variety of information to relay back to *Destiny*.

Felix found himself doing plenty of astronomical research along with his regular load of class work. Emily kept him busy with her research team as the remote survey was taken. The primary task was to learn all they could of the workings of Gem system. *Destiny* had a very good suite of observational equipment running at maximum capacity.

* * * *

MON 05.03.2094
ECS Destiny, Quarterdeck, Staff Conference Room, 0930 Hrs

Six weeks after system insertion *Destiny* was approaching the orbit of the small Jovian gas giant that had been barely visible in the first observations.

The staff meeting started promptly, coffee in hand. "Good morning gang. I'm going to make the topic primarily on the things we're learning about Gem System, but before I give the floor to Emily, I want to give everyone time to report." Tolya looked around the table. "Frank, how are things on our progress in system?"

Frank shrugged. "We're making great time. I expect we'll begin a course correction event sometime tomorrow afternoon. Other than that, I have nothing to report."

"OK. Vince? Dannie?"

Vince grinned. "Things are going well. The civilian sector is jazzed about the trip now that we're in the system. I've been fielding many questions and suggestions; nothing spectacular, but they're thinking and working on little problems they perceive."

Daniela smiled and shook her head. "Everything is under control. I've had a slight rash of minor injuries. I attribute that to a lot more activity in the population. Things are just fine, otherwise."

Tolya glanced at Daryl and Naomi. "You two?"

"The drives are functioning at peek performance." Daryl offered. "The MS-drive section has been policed and is about to be put on long-term sleep. In about two days we'll be ready to de-interface on a moments notice.

"Also, the shuttles and work bees have been fully checked out. Sitting for a couple of years or so tends to allow things to deteriorate. I'm pleased to report all systems are in excellent shape...Honey?"

Naomi grinned and parked her coffee cup. "Things are going at full speed. We're geared up to clear the hanger bay and assemble our mining equipment should we get the opportunity. Our research in nano-tech is going strong. I hope I can get Felix on loan soon. I want to see what he thinks about it. We need more sharp minds in there. I've got Saul, but he could use some help."

Tolya nodded. "I think Emily's the one to talk to about that. About Felix, as I'd hoped, since his pardon, he seems to have redoubled efforts to make something of himself."

An amused look flickered on his face. "I'd lay odds his attachment to my wife's assistant, Sherry, has gone a long ways towards enhancing his motivation."

There were chuckles all around. Felix and Sherry had become the pair to watch. They were quite a team when it came to getting things done.

Tanya put her own two cents in. "I'd not like to bet you on that one. I'll save the numbers for Emily, but Felix is quite motivated. Sometimes I worry he's trying too hard."

Tolya grinned and turned to Ichirou. "Ichi, how are things on the farm?"

Ichirou grinned and shrugged. "Due to a certain deviation from normal work routines, production's still not quite back to its peak for this time as established last year. We may need to postpone our farmer's market for a few weeks till we get caught up. I'm pleased to note that Midori has good things to report."

All eyes switched to Midori. She had a self-satisfied grin on her face. "Yes, in deed. I do have something good to report. In Hydroponics, we have successfully reproduce a strong, quick growing grain that produces twice a year. It's nutritionally quite rich and responds well to the liquid growth chemicals."

Tolya smiled. "Excellent! Congratulations! Thank you both for your hard work. Do you think this grain can be adapted to standard planting techniques?"

Midori shrugged. "It's possible, I think. We'll probably have to make a genetic adjustment when the time comes."

Tolya nodded. "Understood. Well, Thanks again."

He turned to Emily. "Well, Emily. I think that brings it down to you, so I'll give you the floor. I know you have all kinds of exciting things to report."

Emily stood and offered a smile. "Thanks, Tolya. I do have a lot to talk about. So, I'll try to get through it quickly." She tapped an icon on her power-tab and glanced down at her notes.

"I guess I'll start with Felix since we've already segued in that direction. As Tolya commented, Felix has made amazing progress in the last several weeks. His math scores are nearly genius levels. His sense of space and of how things interact with each other is almost like a sixth sense. He probably could have been a fantastic fighter pilot if he'd been in the right place at the right time."

She looked around the table. "Naomi, I'm sure Felix will be a marvelous asset. I'd like to have him switch to helping out your man, Saul. He's good at observation and recording information. His aptitude for mechanical things and enthusiasm for new technologies points to a very promising path in that department."

She grinned at Naomi's smile of satisfaction. "But I can't let him get so bogged down with doing things that he looses track on his academics, so I'd like to ask you to be satisfied with part time participation for a while. Maybe in a few months we can slow his pace in the academics area. He's almost ready to start on a standard college level course set."

Naomi nodded. "That's fine, Emily. I can certainly understand your position."

"How about this?" Emily offered. "Let's get together after and work out a mutual schedule."

Naomi brightened. "That would be great."

Emily returned to her report. "We have a fairly complete sketch of the basic make-up of this system."

She tapped a couple of icons on her power-tab and the display was transferred to the tabletop. As the room lights dimmed, everyone sat back to get their elbows out of the way of heavenly bodies in flight.

"As you can see from the diagram, Gem has seven children. There's also the Debris Cloud we passed over on the way in. There's a very dense belt of rock and ice similar to the asteroid belt in our former home system, much denser than we'd expect.

"The outer two planets are typical gas giants. The outer one..." she leaned over the table and swirled a finger around the image on the screen. It brightened perceptibly for better viewing, "...is roughly the size of Jupiter."

She selected the next one and the previous selection dimmed in favor of the new one, "The next one in is a super-jovian." It's about three times the size of Jupiter. It's mildly disappointing both of these giants are currently on the far side of Gem. I'm itching to get a closer look."

Emily's curiosity was quite famous. She grinned at the chuckles as she moved around the table. "The asteroid belt I mentioned earlier comes next. As much as I'd like to stop and have a look, I recommend we keep some of our elevation above the plain of the ecliptic until we safely cross this region. It's quite dense compared to the one back home."

Frank grinned. "Let me just add that I've already taken it into account in our approach. It comes in handy being teacher's pet."

That got a new set of chuckles going. It was still a novel idea that they were engaged. Emily reached a spot just beside Frank and nodded. "Yes, Frank is becoming a quick learner." That earned some genuine laughter.

"Anyway, while the outer two planets and the asteroid belt itself described nice oval orbits, the next one is unusual."

She leaned over and tousled Frank's hair as she reached to swish the next planet. As before, the previous planet faded in favor of the one she selected.

"As you can see, this planet is traveling in an almost perfect circle compared with the outer ones. The entire orbit is off center from Gem. This gives it rather extreme temperature swings.

"This is also an interesting planet in that, while it is nearly the size of Neptune, it's not a gas giant. Rather it's a giant rocky planet. We're not entirely sure about its make-up, but we're giving it some study. This one is on our side of Gem and will be visible during our entire approach to the next planet on our list."

She moved around to lean over Ichirou's shoulder. "Pardon me," she whispered.

Ichirou smiled and leaned to one side.

Almost reverently, she swirled her finger around the reason they had come. "Here is the world that offers the most hope. It is indeed an earth type world. It's a bit bigger than Earth. This probably means the gravity will be slightly higher, but we'll know more, as we get closer. There appear to be two small moons and, oddly for this type of world, there appears to be evidence of a ring system."

"The last three inner planets are small and mostly barren. One, the one just in from our target is somewhere between Mars and Venus in size with a less than favorable atmosphere."

Emily moved to her seat next to Frank. She took her hands and swished them together over the table display. The entire image shrank to nothing. The screen blanked and the lights slowly brightened. "That's about what we know at this point.

Naomi spoke up. "You know, since we'll be passing just over this asteroid belt, I wonder if it would be possible to drop a couple more survey probes. I think it would be helpful if we didn't have to go all the way out to the periphery for resources."

Tolya nodded. "Great idea; Frank, would you handle it?"

Frank nodded. "No problem."

Tolya turned back to Emily. "Were you able to get any good visuals of our target?"

Emily shrugged. "We're still a ways out. Given our angle of attack and the planet's position in orbit, only a moderate crescent is visible. It looks like there's plenty of cloud cover, so I think it's safe to say there's evidence for decent sized oceans."

* * * *

TUE 05.04.2094
Gem Outer System;
ECS Destiny, 0840 Hrs

As Frank had predicted, *Destiny* began her first deceleration burn as she reached the orbit of the smaller-jovian planet. At the same time, he shallowed the angle of descent to skim over the asteroid belt before leveling up on the plain of the ecliptic.

After completing his morning academic routines, Felix would collect Sherry and the two would have lunch. Then he'd spend three hours of every day observing Saul Perlman and his team.

Felix found the world of nano-tech to be an all-consuming passion. It amazed him how such tiny objects could contain the circuitry necessary to store and manipulate data and effect work.

The weeks dragged on. The ship's population was keyed up, a sense of anticipation simmering just under the surface.

Destiny crossed the asteroid belt about eight weeks in. Another set of course correction burns put her in a level path to the plain of the ecliptic and started her on a sharper arc towards their long awaited goal. They were in the inner system now.

WET RECEPTION — 2
WED 05.19.2094
Gem Inner System
ECS Destiny, Deck 3, New Discovery Church, 2000 Hrs

The Wednesday evening prayer and Bible study was coming to a close. Pastor Brad got up after they'd sung the final song and made an announcement. "I'd like everyone to follow me over to the other side of the partition." He waved a hand at the partitioned off area of the hall where something mysterious had been going.

He continued. "Lyuba, would you come with me? I'll need a little help here."

Lyuba smiled, hopped up from her seat and hurried forward to join him and Jodi.

The others got up and chit chatted their way to the partition. Jodi gave Lyuba a friendly hug. "Hey, Lyuba. After everyone else gets in there, I'd like your help making an announcement."

Lyuba smiled. "OK. What are we announcing?"

Brad grinned. "Oh, something very special; you'll see."

Someone turned off the lights in the main part of the hall they'd just vacated. The lights in the partitioned area were dim. Lyuba was really curious.

After everyone had time to get settled Brad motioned them forward. As they stepped around the partition, the lights came up and everyone yelled, "Happy Birthday, Lyuba!"

Lyuba clapped a hand to her face and looked embarrassed. "Oh! You guys!" She laughed. "Thank you!"

Jodi stepped up next to her. "We couldn't resist."

The kitchen staff had supplied a marvelous cake and a couple of the ladies rolled it up to the front of the room. It was a large sheet cake with fourteen candles around the edges. Across the middle in fancy script it said, 'Happy Birthday, we Love You!'

Brad called out. "Hey, Devin. Come lead us in a round of Happy Birthday."

Devin, a youth of about sixteen came to the front with his ever-present guitar. As he came forward, Brad lit all the candles on the cake. Devin gave Lyuba a special smile before turning to the waiting group.

He struck up the appropriate chords and led off... "Happy Birthday to You..." There was plenty of laughter, and with another grin for Lyuba, Devin rejoined his parents.

Jodi handed Lyuba a cake cutter and waved at the cake. "Make your wish, blow the candles, and make the first cut."

Lyuba had been surreptitiously watching Devin through the birthday song. She accepted the knife and approached the cake. She closed her eyes in thought. Then blew all the candles out.

She looked the cake over and finally decided on her first cut. With great precision, she cut down the center of the cake. Everyone applauded as pictures were taken from several angles.

As the cake was being cut and distributed, Lyuba went to join her parents. Tolya grinned and gave her a quick hug. Containers of ice cream made their way down the tables and Tolya stood up.

Everyone quieted down to hear what he had to say. "I just wanted to thank everyone for the fine surprise birthday party. Tanya and I are very proud of our new daughter...Fourteen years old. It's hard to believe."

He sat down and dug into his cake. Lyuba, not to be outdone, stood up as well. "I want to thank everyone for this party. I was truly surprised and I really love all you guys for being there for me these last couple of years." She sat down and applied herself to her cake and ice cream.

Before the evening was over, everyone took turns passing by her table to wish a personal happy birthday. A number of small gifts piled up on the table in front of her.

The last person to pass was Devin. He seemed nervous for some reason Lyuba couldn't figure out.

"Uh...well... Happy Birthday, Lyuba." He placed a small package among the other gifts.

"See ya." He hurried away and she puzzled at his odd behavior.

* * * *

The stroll back to their new home was quiet and pleasant. Lyuba had a small bag of gifts to go through when she got to her room. She couldn't wait to open Devin's gift.

She saved his gift for last, carefully opening it to find a little box. A carefully written note said, 'I really hope you like this.'

Lyuba's face colored a bit and she opened the box. After unwrapping the tissue paper, she found a hand woven leather thong bracelet. Two rough-cut obsidian stones were woven into the leather braid bracketing a larger piece of obsidian with a cross, carved in and inlaid with chips of abalone shell.

Lyuba was intrigued by the gift. She was just a little surprised at his interest. Many of the other girls in the youth group were quite taken with Devin. Lyuba was also taken with him, but she didn't act silly about it like they did.

Devin was always helping around the church. He played guitar well and seemed like a sincere guy. She carefully put the bracelet on and looked it over. The more she looked at it the more she liked it.

* * * *

ECS Destiny, Quarterdeck, Chernov Residence, 2230 Hrs

Tanya came out of the bath cubicle and, shrugging out of her robe, tossed it on the chair next to the bed. She climbed into bed and snuggled up next to Tolya.

Her mind was almost as busy as his hands. "Did you notice anything unusual about Lyuba at the party tonight?"

Tolya looked up from his nibbling. "Different?"

"Yes, different. Didn't you notice the fascinating little signs of interest from a certain young man?"

Tolya sat up on one elbow to look at her while they talked. "You mean Devin?"

"Yeah. I thought maybe you hadn't noticed."

"Oh, I noticed all right. It's not surprising, really. What do you know about him?"

It was Tanya's turn to sigh. She put her arms up over her forehead and looked off into the ceiling tiles. "Not much really. He seems to be a decent fellow. I know most of the girls in the youth group are smitten by him. I think Lyuba is too, but she doesn't act all silly and crazy like the rest of them."

Tolya smiled and started his hands to work.

Tanya tried vainly to ignore his antics as she listened to his response. "His parents seem pleasant. I do know Devin's a very bright fellow. Emily has placed him in a special program for gifted students. Among other things, he's been recommended to Naomi for the Nano department."

Tanya's efforts at ignoring Tolya were failing fast. "Nano department? Wow, that's impressive for a sixteen year old."

Tolya nodded. "Yes, and he'll be seventeen in a few months."

He looked into her eyes. "Do you think Lyuba's truly interested in him?"

Tanya brought her hands down and stopped the way too pleasant distractions so she could think enough to reply. "I don't know. I think she's mildly interested, but she's not sure about him."

Tolya lay back on the pillows and considered the situation. "We'll just have to wait and see. It would be interesting to find out what that gift was he gave her tonight."

He looked over at Tanya. "Don't worry. I'm not blind. I'm just not worried just yet. She could find worse guys to be interested in, and he is in the Church. Surely that has to count for something."

Tanya smiled. "I'm glad you're paying attention." She rolled over facing him. She snuggled close and he responded in kind.

Tolya grinned wickedly and started smothering her with kisses. "Oh, I'm paying attention all right."

Tanya chuckled as her hand slid down his chest.

* * * *

Destiny shed momentum, so their rate of progress dropped noticeably, adding time to the wait for their arrival in orbit.

At the three-month mark, data from the probes dropped into the asteroid field, began to come in. The asteroids were nearly as rich as the fields out at the periphery. There were significant quantities of most of the metals needed for industrial purposes. There were also significant icy bodies with measurable amounts of hydrogen slush. They'd be well set for keeping the shuttles and work bees fueled.

The four-month mark brought a flood of data on the giant rocky planet. The viewing angles had become favorable for better direct observation. It was shrouded in clouds similar in color to those of Jupiter, but they were thinner and the surface of the planet was periodically visible. It was a beautiful planet in its own way, but definitely not a people friendly world.

The flood of info coming in on their target world was promising, but puzzling. The spectrograms of the atmosphere made it clear people would be very welcome there. There was a rich wealth of cloud cover, promising an active weather system.

What was puzzling was the difficulty getting a view of the land-masses. The ring system was clearly visible now. It was a bit thinner then those around Saturn. The two moons whirled quickly around each other as they tumbled around their parent just outside the ring system, locked on a common plane.

One constant as they progressed in-system was the seemingly cluttered nature of their surroundings. The closer they came to the inner planets, the more bits of rocky and icy debris they encountered.

WET RECEPTION — 3

WED 07.14.2094
ECS Destiny, Quarterdeck, Chernov Residence, 1530 Hrs

"Dad? What's a water world?"

Tolya looked up from his reading. "Sorry, princess, I didn't hear your question."

Lyuba sat down on the couch next to his recliner. "I said, 'what's a water world?'"

Tolya sat up in the recliner and placed the power-tab he'd been reading from, on the coffee table.

"A water world?"

Lyuba nodded her head. She seemed serious.

"Well, honey, I don't think anyone's ever seen a true water world. Free flowing water is quite rare in the universe. They've found two or three worlds that had small oceans, like the world we were going to colonize, but, so far, a water world is the subject of a few science fiction novels."

"Yeah, but what is it?"

"Sorry. I didn't answer that very well did I?"

He leaned forward and explained. "In theory, a water world is a world that has no land masses above the surface of the oceans. Some people speculate that a water world might have a few tiny islands on it, but most of those would be so small no one could live there for very long."

Lyuba got a serious, thoughtful look on her face.

"Lyuba, what made you think about something like that? Have you been reading science fiction?"

"No, dad I never tried science fiction. Is it bad?"

Tolya chuckled, "No princess. Good science fiction is great for your imagination. As long as you keep the perspective that the stories are just for entertainment, they're fun to read."

Lyuba nodded. "I've been helping Emily in the science lab in my free time. We get to see all kinds of pictures of the planet we're headed for. "I keep looking at those pictures, and the new ones that keep coming in."

She shrugged. "More and more, I hear the question, 'where are the land masses?' One of the techs was discussing it with Ms. Emily and I heard him ask if she thought the planet might be a water world. Emily got all worried and said he shouldn't spread unhealthy rumors."

Tolya sat back in his chair and looked thoughtful. "Are you sure about that?"

Lyuba nodded. "Yes, I am. Dad, what if it's true?"

Tolya looked at her and realized his silence was starting to frighten her. "Honestly honey, I don't know, but we'll think of something. You keep on listening and let me know about any other interesting bits of conversation. Ok?"

Lyuba got up and came around the chair to give Tolya a hug. "Sure, Dad. We'll figure it out."

"Yes, we will, Princess."

She went off to her room to get busy on her homework and Tolya glanced at the clock by the COMM station. Tanya was late. He wondered what was keeping her.

He got up to see about putting something together for dinner when the front door snapped open.

Tanya came in and he turned to greet her. They embraced before he noticed she wasn't alone. "Hi Emily. Come on in."

Emily looked frightened and he suspected she might have been crying recently. He looked at Tanya.

She crooked a finger and headed for the kitchen.

Tolya turned to Emily. "Please, have a seat. You want something? A coffee?"

Emily smiled and nodded. "Coffee, thanks."

"I'll be right back." Tolya turned and hurried into the kitchen to find Tanya rummaging for the coffee.

"What's going on?" Tolya whispered.

Tanya shook her head, "You'd better hear if from her. She's discovered something that's scared her badly. Something about that planet has her worked up."

She handed him a carafe of fresh coffee and snagged three cups. They returned to the front room. Tolya poured the coffee and handed it out.

Emily accepted her cup. "Thank you, Tolya. I'm sorry. This should have been a professional briefing, but what I have to tell you scares the hell out of me."

"Easy, Em. We're here to help, not to criticize. Would this, by chance have something to do with a water world?"

Emily sat stunned to silence by his question. "How...how did you know?"

Tolya gave his famous lopsided grin. "I have ears on your team. She has very good ears, by the way."

Emily's eyes grew round. "Lyuba..."

"Yes, about twenty minutes ago, she asked me what a water world was. She said she heard you and a tech discussing it."

Emily felt horrible. "I'm so sorry. She shouldn't have to worry about that. I didn't know she heard."

"It's OK, Emily. Tell me what's going on."

She accepted the tissue Tanya handed her and shook her head.

She began bravely. "I've been suspicious for a couple of days now, but I didn't want to believe my own observations. We're approaching the first example of a true water world mankind has ever encountered."

Tolya sat and pondered the implications.

Emily forged ahead. "All our observations have failed to turn up any significant land masses. The day night cycle is a few hours off from Earth's, but it was hard to determine because there's blessed little in the way of landmarks to time it.

"We've had weeks of observation now. We've seen virtually every inch of the planet as it's turned different faces to us...

"Tolya, what are we going to do? We can't leave this system. You know we don't have enough drive life or fuel for another jaunt. Besides, there's nothing remotely close enough in any of the local systems...all these people, the children...How long can we survive on a ship with no place to go?"

She broke down and Tolya looked lost. He looked at Tanya, who motioned towards her. "I'll get Frank."

She turned to go and Tolya sat next to Emily and hugged her to his side. "Hey. Come on. We don't have all the facts. You can't give up yet."

He sat that way for perhaps five minutes before the front door snapped open and Frank hurried into the room. Tolya waved him over and gently moved away from Emily. "She could use your help about now."

Frank nodded and sat next to her. "Hey, Em. I'm here. You're going to be fine."

He held her close, stroking her hair. He looked questioningly up at Tanya and Tolya who stood close, looking concerned.

Tanya offered. "Frank. She's been working herself ragged on this project. She just discovered very disturbing news she wasn't prepared to accept."

"What news?" He asked.

Tolya spoke up. "It seems our promising new world turns out to be a water world. This would be the very first one mankind's ever discovered. The irony is priceless."

Emily struggled to sit up and Frank released her. She looked in his eyes and said a silent "...thank you."

Then she looked at Tolya and Tanya. "I'm sorry. I don't know what's come over me..." She snagged another tissue and dabbed her eyes. "I'm not usually like this."

Tanya smiled. "I know Em. You're usually the stable bastion of intellectual detachment when it comes to science, but it's OK to have feelings about it. No one's gonna fault you."

Tolya heard a sound and turned to find Lyuba standing in the entryway to the family room, looking worried. She moved up close. "It's OK, Ms. Emily. We'll figure out something."

She patted Emily on the shoulder. Emily returned the affection with a big hug. "Thank you sweetie. You're right. Somehow, we'll figure out what to do."

Tolya scrubbed his face with his hands and Tanya rested a hand on his shoulder. "Lyuba, honey. Would you be a sweetheart and get Frank a coffee cup?"

She brightened. "Sure, dad."

She stepped off purposefully and he returned to the problem at hand. "Frank, what's our ETA to orbital insertion?"

Frank frowned in thought. "I'd say about three months, give or take a few days."

"OK, Emily do you think we're close enough to try a remote planetary probe?"

She sat up straighter and put her mind to work. "I'd say, give it about a week. We could probably do it now, but I'm worried about the lag time.

Tolya stood up. "I'm going next door to see if Daryl or Naomi are home. We need to include them on this. I'll be right back"

He squeezed Tanya's arm and headed out the door.

Lyuba returned with more coffee and they waited.

Less than five minutes of chat time elapsed when Tolya and the McIntyres arrived. Daryl sat on a chair and Naomi took the end of the couch closest to him.

Tolya quickly filled them in on the problem. Daryl and Naomi looked at each other as if to say, 'here we go again.'

Tolya posed his question. "Do you think one of our MK-VII probes can be programmed to do an unguided search pattern and then return? If so, what time advantage would we gain in knowing what to expect when we get there?"

Daryl ran a hand through his spiky hair and got that far way look. "Well, the MK-VII is a variable speed probe. It's built on the chassis of the MK-II strike missile. It's capable of speeds up to point eight two-c, but with speed comes shorter life."

He thought some more. "We could mate it to a booster. That would boost its longevity, but even after completing its mission, it'll, most likely, only be able to climb out of the gravity well and coast. Retrieving it might be problematic."

Tolya nodded. "How about the programming issue? Can we make it run autonomously rather than pilot it remotely?"

"That depends on what tasks you want it to perform. I would recommend something simple like way-point navigation, recording and data transfer routines. The probe looks big, but it has blessed little AI capabilities. There was no space left after the modifications to make it an RPV."

Tolya pondered the information and Tanya came back from the kitchen with two extra coffees. She refilled the empties and sat next to Tolya.

"OK Emily. Here's what I suggest. Set up a large-scale grid search pattern. Program the probe to do a surface hugging run, say about a hundred square miles. We should get a good idea of what's down there before we arrive. Then we can better assess what we're going to do."

Emily smiled. "That should be helpful. I'm sorry I fell apart like that. It's just that we've had so many set backs and life threatening hurdles, I just got a little overwhelmed there."

Naomi smiled. "It's OK, Emily. I know just how you feel, but we'll make it. We've overcome the odds so far."

Tolya stood and looked at the clock on the COMM station. "The dinner hour has just started. Why don't we go to the Diner and grab a bite? I don't think anyone's interested in cooking tonight."

* * * *

Thursday morning after breakfast, almost every spare tech and helper could be found in the Sciences Lab. Daryl and company had successfully mated a spare booster pack with one of a dozen MK-VII probes. The combined contraption was about twenty-three feet long. About half that length was the booster. The rest looked like a short, deadly missile. It had a set of short flight control surfaces that would deploy once the probe reached an optimal altitude.

One of the EVA certified crewmen piloted a work bee from its parking place on the floor of the hanger deck, situating it precisely over the probe. The bee's grapples clamped onto the probe and the pair of vehicles lifted from the deck, seeming to drift out the yawning doors into *Destiny's* wake.

The combined vehicles settled low, finally clearing the bottom of the great MS drive rings that circled the ships waist. After releasing the grapples, the work bee drifted upward and to one side to stand clear of the probe's drive.

Emily, in charge in the Sciences lab, heard the chatter between the bridge and the bee pilot over the room speakers. Phil announced he was clear of the probe and Frank, on the bridge confirmed the status before swishing open a lock on the remote ignition controls. A small display within the monitoring window showed the probe coming to life, systems coming on line. Finally it signaled a successful primary system boot.

Frank asked over the COMM. "Are you ready, Em?"

She smiled. "We're ready."

"OK!" he announced. "Phil, we are launching in ten…nine…" At zero he drew a finger down a graphic of a lever channel.

Small NAV lights started flashing on the probe and a faint wisp of exhaust burst from the drives tubes. The probe seemed to hang there for a moment and then slowly began moving forward. Within a few seconds it was a receding speck, only visible because of the flashing NAV lights.

Emily watched the tracking data. She was pleased it was functioning perfectly. The probe would enter orbit in about a month, while *Destiny* still had about three months of travel time ahead of her.

WET RECEPTION — 4

MON 08.09.2094
ECS Destiny, Quarterdeck, Staff Conference Room, 0930 Hrs

The special staff meeting started promptly. Everyone knew they were approaching another crisis. Tolya sat, sipping his coffee, as Emily hurried in, completing the count.

"Ok. As most of you know, we're about to face yet another major challenge. I'll have Emily fill us in on the facts as we know them and then we're going to have to put our heads together and come up with a plan. Emily?"

Emily grinned and took a sip of coffee. "We've found another major complication to our plans. Put simply, we're less than two months from a true water world."

A couple of eyebrows shot up. Daniela seemed to be digesting something that didn't settle well. "A water world? I thought a water world was just theoretical. No one's ever seen one."

Emily smiled grimly. "Believe me. The last thing I wanted to believe was the data that's been flooding in for the last two and a half weeks. The irony of it all is, even though we're the first humans to ever to see a water world, no one will ever know about it but us.

"Let me show you what we are seeing thanks to a powerful probe we've had surveying the planet."

She tapped her power-tab and the table display lit up. A thumbnail image of the probe lit in one corner and Emily tapped it, dragging her finger diagonally across her screen. The little square of light swelled.

The table flashed briefly and there was a window on space. A feeling of vertigo took hold as the star field suddenly swept to one side and a close up of their target swung into view.

"The time index is set to five times normal. Once the probe dives into the atmosphere, the index will switch to real time."

The ring system came at them like a knife-edge. Then things shifted upwards and the rings flashed overhead.

The planet swung to the left and they found themselves watching the limb of the planet on their left and the rings to their right. The planet loomed from the left and they were darting at unreal speeds into a vast sheet of white veined marble. The screen went dark as the probe shut its 'eyes' for reentry.

The time index indicator shifted to 'normal' and the 'eyes' snapped open. The dive was still a dive but the flying digital count down showed it was slowly shallowing up. The probe was traveling at about mach four point three. So, the cloud cover flashed past at incredible speed.

The dive had been converted to a shallow descent, more horizontal than vertical. As far as the eye could see was a brilliant azure blue. The probe hurtled north, light, choppy waves flashing below in almost a blur. A quick flash of green and beige passed directly below. To one side they could see a huge group of tiny islets that ringed an area of darker blue. The far end of the ring flashed below and the probe continued over the mottled azure waterscape.

The view blurred as the probe banked almost ninety degrees to start a run to the East. The same scene was visible for two or three minutes. A ragged arc of tiny, low-lying islets passed off to the South. These islands were somewhat rocky with hints of vegetation of some kind.

The playback ended and Emily tapped an icon, bringing the lights up.

"As you can see, there's very little land to speak of. This was the first of a long series of runs that covered about 25 percent of the globe. The probe should be coasting back out over the top of the ring system. If it doesn't get caught up by one of the moons that are due near it's trajectory, we'll be able to retrieve it as we approach orbital insertion."

Daniela spoke up. "Emily, a question. If the vid we just saw is consistent with the rest of the samples taken, it would appear there is a vast network of those tiny islands. That first one we saw looked like a coral atoll. The last one was rocky. Just how big are those islands anyway?"

Emily smiled. "Yeah, we've been examining that very closely. Unfortunately, the probe passed so quickly we didn't get very good close ups. Besides, we had no way, this far out, of controlling the thing and bringing it around for a better view. I don't have any numbers, but you're right. It looks like a series of these islands are scattered about the globe in what seems like a random fashion. If there are enough of them to give us good landmarks, we might be able to map the globe."

Daniela looked thoughtful. "What's your take on the depths? Is the water deep? I noticed quite a bit of variation in shades of blue. Back on Earth, darker water seemed to indicate deeper water."

Emily nodded. "You're absolutely right. Our best estimation is that the bulk of the planet is cloaked in one huge, shallow body of water. We don't yet know how deep. Unfortunately many of our questions are going to have to wait till we're in orbit." She held up a hand to forestall another question. "I'm very intrigued by the island rings. Especially the fact that the water depth inside the rings appears to be significantly greater than outside."

She pointed to Tanya. "I'm sorry, you had a question."

"That's fine, Em. You touched on it just now. Those deep waters surrounded by islands fascinated me as well, but another question comes to mind. What about weather? Large bodies of water often breed stormy weather. What about that?"

Emily grinned. "Wow! I wish some of my students asked such great questions. Weather is going to be one of the chief issues. I have footage of major storm cells from the probe, but it never got close enough to get a good look. What little we saw suggests they were very, very large storms. Also, the tiny islands, rocky or coral, all seem to be low lying. There was some evidence of vegetation, but again, the probe was traveling at about mach three during that survey. My guess is a major storm over these islands would tend to wash them pretty clean."

There was moody silence in the room. Tolya sat forward. "Thanks Em. That was very informative."

He glanced at the time. "OK. We know a lot more than we did. We know we have a challenge ahead of us, but we don't know enough by half, so let's keep on working on the problem. We don't really have to make any announcements just yet. I'd rather have some useful answers before we have to face handling another major disappointment." He looked around the table. "If there are no other questions or comments, let's get to work."

The meeting broke up and Tolya asked Daryl to hang around. Tanya cleared up the coffee cups and put them in the recycle bin. "Daryl. I'm concerned about the shuttles. How are they going to fare in that kind of environment? They can't be converted for aquatic work can they?"

Daryl ran a hand through his hair. "I don't know about that."

Naomi approached. "Tolya, if I may…"

Tolya grinned, "Of course."

"To the best of my knowledge, those shuttles are capable of a lot, but I'm not sure about what you're asking. Once we get them down to the surface, assuming we can land them, maybe on one of those islands, I'd say it's possible to convert them to a combination of atmospheric flight and aquatic work, but I don't know about their ability to make repeated re-entries as well.

"I would suggest, unless we can come up with a technological miracle, we find a way to base them on one of those islands and convert one or two of them to permanent planetary duty."

Tolya nodded. "OK. It was a thought."

Daryl grinned. "That doesn't mean she won't start racking her brains over the problem, but don't get your hopes up!"

Tolya chuckled. "Thanks. Keep me posted, will you?"

Naomi smiled and took Daryl's arm. "Absolutely."

Tolya and Tanya walked hand in hand back to the lift well.

"Were almost there." She said.

"Yes." Tolya stopped and searched her face. "Are we going to have another disaster like the last time things went wrong?"

Tanya rolled her eyes. "God, I hope not."

They walked into the lobby of SecCentral where Sherry was busily sorting reports. She smiled brightly. "Good morning!"

Tanya stopped at the counter. "Good morning. How are things?"

"All's quiet. No excitement anywhere."

Tanya grinned. "No excitement, I like the sound of that. Are you and Felix ready for workouts this afternoon?"

Sherry grinned back. "Yep! We've been practicing together almost everyday."

Tolya leaned on the counter. "Very good. I should see lots of improvement then."

Sherry replied, "Felix is really good at those katas. It's funny. He can't dance; except for the slow songs." She smiled to herself, "but he can do those katas better than me." She focused on her visitors. "Did you know he's been helping me with them?"

Tolya grinned. "It's not surprising. He seems motivated."

Tanya dug him in the ribs as Sherry's face flushed. "Don't mind my husband. He can be incorrigible at times. Why don't you two join us for lunch at our place?"

"Sure. I'll call Felix. Noon then?"

Tanya looked at Tolya. "How about 1230?" Tolya nodded.

"Sounds good." Sherry replied.

Tolya turned to go. "I'll be home then."

He gave Tanya a quick kiss and hurried out.

Tanya turned for her office and caught Sherry's big grin. "I see things are still hot!"

Tanya's face flushed a little. "And why not?"

Sherry shrugged. "Some of my old friends back home used to say things cooled off fast enough after the wedding was over."

Tanya sniffed. "Obviously, your friends didn't know what they were talking about."

Sherry grinned. "I'm glad. The way they talked, it was over after the first few weeks. Then, boredom."

Tanya shrugged. "If you're really in love, there's nothing boring about it. There are difficult times. We've had a couple of minor disagreements already, but..." She winked, "The best part about that was making up after!"

She blushed and turned for her office. "I'd better get busy. We can chat later."

* * * *

ECS Destiny, Quarterdeck, SecCentral, 1220 Hrs

Felix dropped by. "Sherry. It's 1220. We'd better get going."

Sherry glanced up from her project and saw the time. "Wow! I lost track of time...again." She got up and turned to look at him.

"What?" He asked.

"Oh, nothing." He saw the slight flush in her face. "I ah...just had a stray thought." She explained lamely.

Felix grinned. "Stray thought, huh?" He took her hand. "Let's go, then. As we've noted before, Tanya doesn't like to be kept waiting."

They started down the corridor, "So Felix, how'd it go this morning?"

* * * *

Tolya stopped by the classrooms in the starboard side education wing. It was placement testing day. Each student had two hours of private testing as part of a program to place them into the new educational model they would be using in the future.

He glanced in through the door's window. She looked like she was finishing up. They'd thoroughly gone over her study materials last night. She'd been worried she wouldn't do well.

Lyuba tapped submit and put her stylus in the slot in her power-tab. Francine was going over assignments on her own power-tab. "Ms. Douglas. I'm finished."

Francine looked up, glanced at the time display and grinned. "My Lyuba, that was fast. So, how do you feel about this last test?"

Lyuba gave a big grin. "I was worried about it last night, but dad helped me study. I feel great."

Francine caught motion at the window. Tolya was patiently waiting in the corridor.

"I'm glad to hear it. You've been doing well." She walked over and waved the door open. "Tolya. You don't have to lurk out here. Come on in."

Tolya grinned and entered the room.

Lyuba hopped up. "Papa!" She hurried to meet him as he crossed to her.

They hugged and Tolya backed away. "You ready for lunch?"

She looked up at him. It didn't seem as far to look as it might have been just a year or so ago. She was growing so fast. "I'm starved after all that thinking."

Francine laughed. "She's been working hard this morning. Lyuba. Why don't you report to Dr. Strauss after lunch? I bet she could use your help over there."

"OK. Thanks. Ms. Douglas."

Francine chuckled and turned to Tolya. "She's getting more about scientific observation just doing the work, than I could give her talking about it."

He squeezed Lyuba's arm. "Well, I guess we better get to lunch. Mom's got sandwiches going and Felix and Sherry are coming."

Lyuba brightened. "Sherry's coming? Cool!"

Tolya steered Lyuba toward the door. "Thanks for the extra effort Francine."

Francine smiled. "That's OK. As long as she continues to work at it, I'm happy to handle it. I've got six new elementary school instructors now. I've scheduled a conference with Tanya in a couple of weeks. If you could come it would be helpful. There are a number of adjustments we need to discuss."

She saw the beginnings of alarm on his face. "Oh. It's nothing to be concerned about, just a question of where to go from here."

Tolya relaxed. "Oh. That's fine. I'll be there."

They left the classroom and headed down the corridor. "Dad, I love helping Dr. Strauss in the lab. It's cool learning about a brand new planet, all about the weather and the magnetic fields and the ice caps. I wonder what kind of animals live there."

Felix and Sherry came up the corridor.

Lyuba called and they stopped to wait. "Hi, guys!"

Felix grinned, "Hey kiddo. How's school?"

Lyuba grinned. "School's great. I think I just aced my math test. I get to go help Dr. Strauss in the lab."

"Great!" He looked at Tolya and gave a slight bow. "Sensei."

Tolya grinned returning the gesture. "I see you two are doing just fine." Tolya had a teasing gleam in his eye.

Sherry flushed and grinned. "Yes, of course."

"Come on. Let's grab lunch." They trooped in to find Tanya setting a plate, piled high with tuna fish sandwiches, on the table.

She looked up and grinned. "Tuna! I thought we should celebrate our homecoming. We'll have to get used to lots of fish!"

Felix raised an eyebrow and Sherry turned to Lyuba. They'd both been very busy on other projects and done little of the research on the planet. So, they were unaware of another problem bearing down on them.

"What's this about getting used to fish?"

Lyuba looked pained. She'd been asked to keep the story quiet for a while.

"It's OK honey, I'll explain. Sit down everybody." They said grace and began devouring sandwiches.

Felix looked up in surprise. "Hey. These are really good."

Sherry grinned at him. "New to tuna?" She teased.

He shrugged. "I never considered them the most exciting choice, personally, but these are great!"

Tanya chuckled. "I'll take that as a compliment, young man. Honey, do you want to explain?"

Tolya swallowed. "You're doing just fine, dear."

"OK." Tanya smiled and turned to Sherry and Felix. "We've been trying to keep this quiet for now; no point announcing trouble before we have answers. "Here's the deal. Our would be home is classified as a water world…" She explained what they knew.

Felix was stunned, but after some thought, he decided this was more a challenge to be met and overcome, rather than a disaster in the making.

"I'm confident we'll work something out. In spite of every roadblock we've hit, we've still managed to get this far. We'll get through this. I just know it."

Sherry grinned. "There's got to be a way. Besides…" she waved the last bit of her sandwich, "fish ain't so bad."

Tanya looked at Tolya. "I think we should arrange a brainstorming session with the entire staff."

Tolya nodded. "I think that's a great idea. I'll call for a special meeting in the lab."

He tossed his coffee down. "Well, let's get back to work."

He pointed at Sherry and Felix. "I'm expecting good things this after noon. A little mouse told me you've been practicing regularly."

They grinned. "Yes, Tolya, Sensei," they choroused.

* * * *

ECS Destiny, Quarterdeck, on the way to Sciences Lab, 1305 Hrs

Tolya walked Lyuba aft to the sciences lab.

"Dad?"

"Yes, princess."

"Why can't I learn karate?"

"I didn't know you were interested." He brushed some hair from her face.

"Well, you and Mom are teaching Sherry and Felix."

They stopped. "I'll tell you what…we'll bring you with us this evening. You can watch us practice and then you can decide if you're still interested."

They reached the Sciences lab. The large room was lined about the perimeter with dedicated stations linked to the ships computer core. A large percentage of *Destiny's* computational power was available to this room. Two huge conference tables bracketed the room with research terminals at each place.

Affixed dead center was a heavy looking hexagonal table with seats around it. Mankind's first true holo-vision display had been duplicated and sent on this mission. This was the cutting edge in viewing technology. It was so cutting edge, it was still in the experimental stages.

Many of the workstations were occupied. A number of people were gathered around the holo-viewer where an azure blue globe floated in the air above the table. Periodically, flickers would ripple through the display as the computer struggled to keep up with the data flow.

Emily spotted them and quietly came to greet them. "Hi Tolya. Hi there, Lyuba. Have a good lunch?"

Lyuba grinned. "Great. We had tuna fish sandwiches."

Emily grinned. "Tuna fish sandwiches?"

It was Tolya's turn to grin. "Yeah. I think Tanya's in a peculiar mood today.

Emily grinned. "Shocking news can do that."

Tolya noticed the time and grimaced. "I'm running late. I've got to get going."

He turned to go and then a thought struck him. He turned back. "I promised to take Lyuba with us to the gym this afternoon before thinking about the time. Do you mind if I come by at around 1530 to pick her up?"

Emily smiled. "I don't mind. Lyuba has been working her little heart out in here. Officially, she's free at 1500. She usually stays longer than required. I think she's just having the time of her life."

"I see." Tolya looked down at Lyuba. "I don't mind you hanging around here if you want, but I think Mom and Dad need to know about it. Otherwise, it makes it more difficult to make plans."

Lyuba looked down at the deck plates. "Sorry, I get so busy here I forget the time."

Tolya reached over and brushed her cheek. "It's ok, honey. Just remember, we need to know what's going on. Why don't you be home by 1530 today? Then you'll have time to change into some exercise clothes and you can warm up with us."

Lyuba looked up. "OK. I'd like that."

Tolya gripped her shoulder and gave her a wink. "OK, I'm off to work. I'll see you around 1530."

He smiled at Emily. "Thanks. I'll see you tomorrow." He cast a glance at the azure blue globe suspended over the table before turning and heading for the bridge.

* * * *

ECS Destiny, Quarterdeck, Chernov Residence, 1545 Hrs

Tanya entered the family room, suited up for practice. "Hey, I hear you want to learn karate. That's great!"

She crossed to Tolya as he stood. She gave him a kiss, "I'm ready when you are."

Tolya raised an eyebrow that earned him a poke in the ribs. She turned and put an arm about Lyuba's shoulders.

"Men!" she uttered. Lyuba grinned, and together, they headed out the door.

They arrived at the gym to find Sherry and Felix doing unofficial warm-ups. The two young people stopped and bowed. Lyuba thought it was kinda weird, but she filed it away for future consideration. Tolya waved them to the middle of the room and they formed up.

Tanya began. "Lyuba has expressed an interest in learning karate. So, we're going to let her warm up with us. Then she'll sit to the side and watch. Let's show her what she's getting into."

There were grins all around. Tolya began… "Ready…"

Lyuba enjoyed the exertion. This was more fun than P.E. She watched the advanced practice with avid interest. Felix and Sherry were getting really good. Felix was going to test for his yellow belt in a couple of weeks. Sherry wasn't very far behind.

On the way home Tanya asked, "So. What do you think?"

Lyuba smiled. "I like it."

"You know it requires dedication and hard work?"

"I know. Dad's done it for years. You too. Why not me?"

Tolya chuckled and Tanya grinned. "Well, OK. You can start practicing with us regularly. If you hang in there for a month, we'll order a gi made for you."

"Cool!" She intoned.

WET RECEPTION — 5

TUE 08.10.2094
ECS Destiny, Quarterdeck, Felix' Cabin, 0445 Hrs

Felix spent most of the evening thinking about the new challenge of conquering a water world. He'd talked for a long time with Sherry during dinner. They'd agreed, if worse came to worse, and if they could find adequate resources of food and materials in the oceans of this world, the colony could live indefinitely in space aboard *Destiny*. It was not a great option, but a possibility.

That night, he tried to sleep, tossing and turning for hours before finally drifting off sometime after midnight. He dreamed. Whatever he'd started to dream ended with startling abruptness. A new dream took over. It was an odd sort of dream; He was fully aware. It seamed so real.

Felix found himself moving across an azure blue ocean. He wasn't exactly swimming. He just willed himself in a direction and he would go. There was no land anywhere in sight. It seemed to him he'd been traveling this way for hours. Yet, he didn't feel tired.

Sometime or other, he'd had the sensation of someone yelling at him, as if to get his attention. It wasn't a sound really, just a strong sense that his attention was needed. Sudden motion in the water drew his attention from his search for a seashore. An odd-looking creature surfaced near him and started moving in anxious circles around him. It was nothing like any sea creatures he'd every seen, not that he'd seen many, growing up in Chicago. It seemed to him, though, that any self respecting sea creature should at least have fins for swimming. This guy didn't.

His guest had a longish torso with short, powerful hind legs ending in thickly webbed digits. Slender upper limbs had trailing fringes of fin type material and the muscled portion of the limbs ended in hands with long webbed digits. The head appeared vaguely humanoid in a disturbing sort of way. Its mouth made it look vaguely like an elephant seal and the creature was covered with some sort of fine pelt. The eyes were double lidded with nictitating membranes.

Unlike any seal he'd ever seen, it propelled itself through the water using some kind of water jet mechanism similar to that found in squid on Earth. Obviously, his visitor could breath air because it was purposefully staying above the water's surface.

There was a sense of increased agitation. It accelerated its circular patrol adding little, halfhearted leaps from the water. Felix stopped. The creature came just out of arms length and stopped. It rose up so both its upper limbs were visible and started gesticulating, periodically looking up into the sky. Obviously the creature wanted him to look up.

Felix looked up to see a scattered cloud of objects falling from a great height. After a few moments, people he recognized from Destiny *began cannoning into the sea around him.*

The creature suddenly darted forward and attempted to grasp Felix' arm. He reflexively fended off the limb and the creature dove deep.

It surfaced quickly, jumping clear over him, diving again. A webbed hand attempted to grasp his ankle. Felix kicked at it and the creature surfaced to stare into his face.

It's mouth, or snout, lifted like a very stubby elephant's trunk and a chatter of high-pitched squeals painfully assaulted his ears.

The creature gestured to the Northwest and chattered some more. Felix looked in the desired direction and saw a massive wall of gray and black. Flashes of lightning could be seen, even from this great distance. The creature gestured at the water, uttered one more squeal and dove.

Clearly there was a sense of urgency. Felix obliged and, taking a deep, deep breath, flipped over and dove under the increasing chop. The creature was at least thirty feet below him. He began pulling hard to catch up.

Felix was surprised to see he was near the center of a ring of sea-mounts that were chopped off a few feet below the surface. If there'd been no water, he would have been flying across the middle of a valley or maybe a canyon.

Felix began to see the flash and swirl as people hit the water, breaking through around him. There were violent gouts of air bubbles as each person hit, like upside down explosions. An inverted fount of water and bubbles violently pressed down just next to him. Felix turned to look at the source and found himself face to face with Sherry, struggling in the water.

Without thought Felix lunged toward her, grabbing her tightly around the waist. He struggled valiantly to get back to the surface. Sherry hugged him desperately and as he broke the surface…

Felix picked himself up from the floor next to the door to his bedroom. His head hurt and he found a bump on his forehead where he'd hit the closed door. He struggled out of his bed sheets that were wound around him in a hopeless tangle. He was dripping wet from sweat.

Deep in his mind, Felix sensed Sherry was wide-awake. She was physically unharmed, but she was scared to the point of trembling. He briefly wondered at his certainty about what she was feeling.

He checked the clock. It was 0500. Another half an hour and he'd have to wake up to the alarm. There was no point in trying to get more sleep.

He shrugged. Grabbing the clothes he'd set out for the day, he headed for the tiny shower cubicle. He'd take a quick shower and go check on Sherry.

* * * *

ECS Destiny, Quarterdeck, Sherry's Cabin, 0445 Hrs

Sherry lay tossing in bed. Her discussion with Felix about the new, daunting challenge of this water world had disturbed her. She hoped to God it would all work out.

Finally, very, very late, she drifted off to sleep. A very disturbing and frequent dream intruded. She hated this dream, but figured she was stuck with it.

This time, there was a major change.

Felix was being bound and taken down to the aft airlocks for execution. She ran with all her might to catch up and stop them.

Like every time before, the corridor kept growing longer and longer. The harder she ran, the closer the executioner got to the airlocks and the further she had yet to run. There was a yell as if someone were trying to get her attention. Just as they shoved Felix into the airlock she let out the scream!

Unlike all the other times, she tripped over a door-frame marking the edge of a precipice that yawned over the top of the world. Below was an endless ocean and her scream continued unaltered as she fell, and fell.

The sheer, raw terror of her situation was overpowering. She begged to wake up, to stop this endless fall, but there was no hope of that. She barely had the presence of mind to pull a deep, ragged breath as she hit the water feet first.

She sank deeply, a cloudy swirl of bubbles enveloping her. She had no control over her limbs, totally unable to swim.

Suddenly, Felix was there. His face loomed rapidly toward her. He grabbed her tightly about the waist. She clung to him desperately as he struggled valiantly to get her back to the surface.

*As they broke the surface...*Sherry sat up in bed with a stifled yelp that expressed her fear, shock and relief in one short syllable. In the back of her mind she knew without question that Felix was wide-awake. His forehead hurt from where he'd bumped it...against the door? He was otherwise OK, but very shook up.

Sherry got up and noticed the time. It was 0500. She realized she was soaking wet with sweat, so she decided on a quick shower. Then she'd check on Felix. She fought her way from the hopeless tangle of sheets.

* * * *

ECS Destiny, Quarterdeck, Chernov Residence, 0445 Hrs

The rings of Aambü *were beautiful. The rocks and ice crystals, glittering brilliantly in the distance from the light of Gem, called her onward. She skimmed past the smaller of the two moons and soared a slalom course through the rings, dodging the particles and rocks playfully. She knew she was traveling at incredible speeds.*

The rings receded behind her and she reached the edge of the atmosphere of this, their new home. As she dove into the atmosphere there was a sudden sensation. It was familiar; yet odd for the fact it didn't belong here.

Lyuba never really heard anything. Not with her ears, anyway. Yet, she was startled by what she could only describe as a yell. It was the kind of yell her parents and her two best friends made occasionally when they were practicing karate, or maybe, it seemed like the kind of yell a PE coach would use to put a stop to some horseplay going on between two misbehaving students.

Whatever it was, it startled her so badly she forgot momentarily how to fly. She plummeted, tumbling like a rock. She was suddenly afraid.

"Wait! This is a dream, darn it! I know it's a dream and its mine. So, I'm just going to have to start flying again!"

She spread out her arms and legs and slowly stopped her tumbling. Then she aimed to the right and swooped around, leveling off her fall into flight! She forced her heart back down from her throat to where it belonged. She'd fallen far and could see the worldwide ocean below her.

There were many weather systems she could see below her. The clouds were beautiful way down there. To the South and east of her position was a huge, nasty looking storm front.

On impulse, she dove purposefully towards the storm. Soon the intense buffeting of the wind flailed about her but didn't bother her.

A powerful updraft threw her thousands of feet. Lightning crackled and thunder boomed all around her. She could smell the strong, heady tang of the fresh ozone in the air. The sense of limitless raw power thrilled her to her toes.

Finally she burst through the leading edge of the storm front and the sudden tailwind catapulted her like an arrow to the Southeast, angling sharply downward. She pulled up and slowed to a glide.

In the distance, off to the East, southeast, was a large oblong circle of shallow spots in the water. It seemed to invite her attention, so she banked gently in that direction and leveled off.

In the deeper water that was surrounded by the shallower places, Lyuba could see two tiny dots moving about. "Wow! Someone's swimming. I wonder who it is?"

She started to descend at a shallow angle, trying to get closer to find out who else was here. Something hurtled downward, just past her right shoulder. At first she thought, rocks falling? *Then she realized it was a person flailing wildly in terror.*

Another person flashed downwards a little farther along. She realized she was flying into a mass of falling people; all people she recognized from Destiny. Oh, my God! Help! What do I do?

Farther out and at a much higher altitude, Lyuba saw someone that struck her as really familiar. She arrowed towards the person and suddenly realized it was Sherry.

Sherry hurtled past her and Lyuba immediately dove hard and fast.

As she followed Sherry down, she saw the two individuals in the water. One suddenly submerged and then the second one followed. She was hurtling at the water and watched in dismay as Sherry knifed into the chop feet first.

Lyuba veered right and skewered the waves, boring deep. She flipped end to end and raced upwards.

She suddenly recognized Felix as he grabbed Sherry by the waist and hurried to the surface. Lyuba redoubled her efforts towards the surface and...sat upright in her bed with a startled yell.

* * * *

ECS Destiny, Quarterdeck, Chernov Residence, 0500 Hrs

Tanya jerked awake, scared to death.

Tolya rolled over to face her. "What's wrong sweet?" He sat up next to her and she threw her arms around him. She was trembling. Tolya stroked her hair from her face. It was wet with perspiration.

"Honey, you had a nightmare. You're shaking like a leaf!"

Tanya slowly regained her composure. "It's really weird. I know I had a really strong dream, but I can't remember a thing...except..."

She turned to look at Tolya. She realized the main room lights were off and only a dim night-light was on. She looked up towards the ceiling, "Lights, up one quarter..." The room lights faded up so there was just enough light to see Tolya's features.

Tolya prompted, "Except?"

"Falling!" She shuddered. "Falling from an incredible height and then drowning."

"Drowning? What do you mean?"

Tanya shuddered. "I don't know. I fell for what seemed like miles and then I was drowning."

Frantic slapping sounded at the door. "Mom! Dad!"

Tanya threw the covers the rest of the way off and hopped out of the bed. She welcomed the action. She needed the action. Tolya pulled the covers around himself, making himself somewhat more presentable than he had been. He watched appreciatively as Tanya threw a robe around her athletic body.
"I'm coming, sweet heart."

Tanya tapped the door release and Lyuba rushed into her arms. "They were all falling! I tried, but I couldn't save them! They just kept falling!" She was nearly hysterical.

Tanya gently tipped her head up so she could look her in the eyes. "Lyuba, honey. Slow down."

Lyuba stopped. Tanya turned and escorted her to the bed. "Come on. Sit down and tell us about it."

Tanya sat on the edge of her side of the bed. Lyuba sat cross-legged in the middle of the bed next to Tolya's feet.

"You had a nightmare too, Princess?"

Lyuba frowned. "It was beautiful except for the end."

Tanya smiled. "Do you remember it? Can you tell us?"

Lyuba sat thinking for a moment. "I remember the whole thing!" She told her story. Tolya and Tanya exchanged glances.

When Lyuba got to the part about the cloud of people falling into the sea Tanya's face paled and she turned, grabbing Tolya's arm in a vice like grip."

Lyuba stopped. "What, mom?"

Tanya stared at nothing. "I remember. I was falling from the sky and there was a vast ocean below me. Then I was drowning in the ocean and I woke up."

"Mom, you must have been one of the people I saw falling. I didn't see you, but it was all kinds of people from the ship. I even saw Sherry...and Felix!

Tanya was confused. "Wait a minute! How can I remember part of your dream?"

She stopped as something Lyuba had said registered. "You said you saw Sherry...and Felix?"

Lyuba was puzzling something out. "Yeah, but Felix wasn't falling. I think he was one of the two people I saw first. They dove under the water."

"They dove?" Tolya prodded. "Is there more to the dream you haven't told us?"

Lyuba nodded. "Yeah. Sherry fell right past my shoulder and when I realized it was her, I dove like a hawk, trying to stop her. I saw Felix and someone else dive under the water just before Sherry hit. Then she went down and I dove after her to help. When I got turned around in the water, I saw Felix holding Sherry and swimming really hard for the surface. I chased after them and when we came out of the water, I woke up."

Tanya was thinking. "Did you see the other person who was with Felix?"

Lyuba stopped, perplexed. "No. When I was in the water I only saw Felix."

* * * *

ECS Destiny, Quarterdeck, Felix' Cabin, 0545 Hrs

Felix realized he was aware of Sherry's shower. It was strange. He wasn't imagining her taking a shower. No. He was aware of her pleasure in the warm relaxing shower. It was separate somehow from his own experience, yet he knew her sensations as surely as he knew his own. On one level, it was quite pleasant. On another level, it was profoundly disturbing. It felt like he was peeking at something he didn't have permission to look at.

He stepped out of the shower, toweled off and started to get dressed. He was aware, in ways he was embarrassed to admit, that Sherry was working a towel over her own body.

"Stop it!" He yelled at himself.

He knew exactly when she was ready to leave her cabin and stepped out of his own door at nearly the same time.

They both crossed the mini-park that separated their line of cabins. When their eyes met, she blushed deeply. Then she hurried to him. "You hurt your head. Are you OK?"

They both stopped and stared. Felix reached up. "It's not bleeding is it?"

"No, silly. You bumped it on your door. Why were you by the door anyway?"

Felix was trying to piece things together and finding missing pieces. "Sherry, how do you know I hit my head?"

She stopped. "I…I don't…When we came out of the water…"

Felix echoed, "Out of the water…"

Sherry put a hand to her waist where he had wrapped his arms so tightly. She stepped forward and said, "In my dream…you saved me."

"Your dream? I…"

Sherry reached to touch the nasty bump on his forehead.

A brilliant flash and a flood of sensory information hit both of them like a massive avalanche…

* * * *

ECS Destiny, Quarterdeck, Micro-Park, 0550 Hrs

They left with the intention of going to the Diner for breakfast. Those plans evaporated when they found Sherry and Felix in the middle of the small park, slumped together on the grass, unconscious.

Tolya checked their pulses while Tanya quickly checked for any evidence of physical trauma. There was nothing except a bump on Felix' head. "Pumpkin? Please run down to MedCentral and get some help."

Lyuba was already on he way, "Sure Mom!"

Just then, Daniela came reluctantly out of her own cabin. She looked tired and shook up.

When she saw the tableau in the park she hurried over. "What in the world…"

Tanya replied, "I don't have the slightest idea. We came out to go to breakfast and found them like this."

Daniela finished checking vitals and then Lyuba returned. "They're coming."

Tolya turned to her. "Thanks, Princess."

Daniela rubbed her eyes. "I want to get them hooked up. It's almost like they're just peacefully asleep. Their signs are normal for a sleeping person."

She stopped to rubbed her eyes again. "It looks like they met out here, spoke to one another and then just collapsed."

Two male nurses hurried up with a pair of ELU's. Tolya motioned for Felix. He moved to Felix' feet. "One of you help me with him. The other, help the Chief with the girl."

The guys hesitated.

Daniela waved them to it. "It's OK. They just collapsed."

As they moved Sherry from off of Felix, a strong tremor pulsed through both of them at the same time. It was strong enough to startle those doing the lifting. Tolya glanced at Tanya. She had a bemused expression on her face.

Daniela asked, "Why's everyone up so early?"

* * * *

ECS Destiny, Everywhere, 0615 Hrs

As if the mystery of Felix and Sherry's mutual collapse weren't enough, calls began flooding every med station on every deck. Literally hundreds of people were complaining of falling dreams. All culminated in a drowning sensation. There were five people who'd been found in a catatonic state similar to what seemed to be afflicting Felix and Sherry.

MedCentral soon had seven unconscious people taking up much of the emergency section. The lobbies of all the medical facilities were seething with agitated people.

* * * *

The staff meeting was somewhat more tense than usual. There was much murmuring, muttering and quiet discussion going on as they waited. The door snapped open and Vince and Daniela hurried in.

"Sorry." Daniela offered. "It's absolutely insane for my medical staff today."

Tolya sympathized with her sentiment. "I can imagine."

He leaned forward as the two took their seats. "OK. Before we get Dannie's report, I want to poll the group. How many present experienced a significant dream; specifically a falling dream?"

Daniela, Tanya, Emily and Frank raised their hands looking around self-consciously. Ichirou shrugged and lifted a finger. After some hesitation Daryl raised his hand. "I don't know about a dream, but I woke up scared to death."

Tolya looked at Daniela. "I'd say it counts."

"OK" Tolya nodded. "Hands down. Do any of you who raised your hands remember the dream?"

There were confused looks on most of the faces. Tanya ventured a comment. "I only remember part of it. Lyuba says it's the very last part."

There were puzzled faces around the table.

Emily raised an eyebrow. "Lyuba had this same dream too?"

Tanya nodded. "She had a really strange dream." She shrugged her shoulders. "I would've brought her along to tell it but she's sound asleep. She was really tired, like she'd been working out."

Daniela spoke up. "I heard her tell it when you brought Sherry and Felix into emergency. It was really weird, that's for sure."

She looked at Tanya. "Why don't you tell us what you remember of it?"

Tanya nodded. "OK. Lyuba said that…"

Lyuba's original telling had been quite detailed. So, Tanya's report of the events was reasonably accurate.

There was a long silence in the room. Emily and Frank had both tensed and shared a glance, shock on their faces. Frank spoke up. "I remember mine better, now." Emily nodded grimly. "Me too."

She looked across at Tanya. "I believe your little lady was doing something they call lucid dreaming. She had a fair level of control in her dream. Did you say she saw Felix and Sherry in her dream?"

Tanya replied. "Absolutely. In fact, Lyuba thinks they're somehow a key pivotal point in the dream. Also, there's this mystery person nobody's actually seen yet."

Daniela spoke up. "I think you're right about the lucid dreaming, Em. I wish to heaven Felix and Sherry would wake up. I can't help but think they hold a major part of the puzzle locked up in their heads."

She looked at Emily. "I looked briefly at dreaming in med-school, but I'm baffled about this…well, what amounts to a mass dream sharing. Any thoughts?"

Emily pondered the question. "Dannie, I'm really stumped. You've heard of mass hallucinations. There is usually a common stimulus, but people in a dream state? I've never heard a clear case of it."

Tolya took charge of the meeting. "I think we're stuck until we can get something out of Felix and Sherry. I agree with Dannie. When we separated them, out in the corridor this morning, there was a strong tremor that hit them both at the same time. Something very odd is going on there."

FUNDAMENTAL CHANGES — 1

WED 08.11.2094-Earth / TRN 16.03.6998-Aambü
2.75 months from orbital insertion; Aambü, Gem System
Ruling Clan Caverns, Entry Chamber and Pool, 0915 Hrs / 0683 Slashes

AgraVadin Adhiraj signaled a change of topic. *We will now hear from AnalaRaksa.* The meeting cavern was lit with the phosphorescent glow of hundreds of glow globes; weed bulbs filled with tiny glow swimmers suspended in warm sea-water. In the cool unwavering light, some thirty-two individuals lounged on the moist, sandy cavern floor around the entry pool.

AnalaRaksa made a complex gesture and expanded his reach to make his thoughts brighter. *AgraVadin Adhiraj, you honor me. I have learned a thing, which concerns us all. If you please, a question. Has anyone reconsidered the new presence beyond the rings?*

MahAsthavira of the southern clan responded. *If you refer to the light growing beyond the moons, take no concern. We sense no evil there.*

AnalaRaksa signed his respect. *I do not yet weigh evil or good, wise one. I but report a most illuminating observation. Permit me to explain.*

Two turns ago, during my watch, I considered the coming great storm, which just passed on. As is my duty as Third Watcher, I scanned for wayward youngsters or travelers to warn them and guide them to safety with us.

I sensed a brightening of light out in the deep that made me suspect a youngster out and about. I sounded the call, as is my duty. As I sounded the call, I realized it was not a youngster I had sensed.

The light was shining out from an individual in dream form. This individual was exploring over the deep. The source of the dreamer was from the growing presence beyond the moons.

A ripple of curiosity and perplexing wonder flowed around the chamber. *My friends, I followed my call to see where it would be received. What I found both disturbed and excited in the same instant.*

The new presence we have been watching from beyond the rings is not just a single individual. It appears to be the light from a large clan of individuals traveling in a vessel that can move itself across the stars.

AnalaVadin offered objection. *Perhaps AnalaRaksa has watched too long. He now sees ghosts of things from tales of fantasy.*

Humor echoed off the stone walls of the cavern.

AnalaRaksa rebutted Third Speaker's statement. *My friend, the honored AnalaVadin, doubts my report. Allow me to continue.*

I went to investigate. The dreamer was strange in appearance. It has naked flesh with no covering pelt. It has no swim organ and its arms and hands have no web structures to pull the water.

Great curiosity colored with doubt radiated from his hearers. He continued. *Apparently, this people does not have the same facility to touch the mind, as we. I sensed the one creature had the rudiments of mind speak ability, so I attempted to make conscious contact. It would appear my call was far stronger than anything these creatures are used to. This one seems to have the facility but is like an infant, being not yet awakened. The call awakened him and possibly a few others in his clan.*

Doubt was winning over and the younger ones were becoming more restless. AnalaRaksa expressed regret but did what was necessary. *Friends, I sense great doubt. To gain unity in dealing with what I perceive to be either a potential problem or benefit to our world, I offer the Viewing. I am willing to endure the pain.*

AgraVadin Adhiraj expressed dismay and respect. *AnalaRaksa, you have offered the Viewing, being aware of the personal discomfort this will bring?*

AnalaRaksa waved a web hand in a nervous gesture of resignation. *It seems the best way to get past the posturing and on to the truth. I can hide nothing in the Viewing for the Viewing is true.*

AgraVadin Adhiraj expressed reluctant acceptance. *I call on all present to witness, the honored AnalaRaksa offers the Viewing. I accept this offer. We shall all participate now.*

Nervous assent flooded the chamber. Suddenly motivated, all the members of the council hurried into the entry pool.

A close packed sphere of his fellow council members surrounded him. Bracing himself for the intense pain, he dropped his shields, opening his mind. He focused on the events that transpired during the approach of the great storm and flooded them with light.

* * * *

AnalaRaksa returned to consciousness to find he'd been respectfully returned to the meeting cavern. The rest of the council reclined, patiently awaiting his recovery. The pain when his shields had come down and all present were in his mind together, was a memory he would not soon forget.

AgraVadin Adhiraj noted his condition and announced. *AnalaRaksa is revived. As is proper, there will be no more talk of doubt regarding his report.*

He addressed AnalaRaksa. *We discussed your experience as you recovered. We regret the necessity of the Viewing. We have decided you are to pursue productive contact with this people, for they are indeed a new kind of people. We would know the purpose of their presence here. We must learn so we may determine the welcome they should receive.*

AnalaRaksa, you are assigned a new name to fit a new task. You, AgradUtya, are instructed to seek out this individual who was awakened by your call. You are now AgradUtya, first ambassador of your people to these strangers. This is a singular honor and great responsibility.

AgraVadin Adhiraj signaled the end of the meeting. *AgradUtya, please accompany me for food and refreshment. Your personal sacrifice shall be rewarded in my chambers.*

FUNDAMENTAL CHANGES — 2
THU 08.12.2094-Earth / TRN 17.03.6998-Aambü
Aambü, in a dream state, 1115 Hrs / 0843 Slashes

Felix drifted quietly in a calm sea. The water was warm and there was almost no breeze to stir the surface. The gentle swells were nearly imperceptible. The storms of the last few months had passed and he was at peace. He could sense Sherry nearby. She was asleep and he thought not to awaken her yet.

He considered the most recent events. He'd had the most peculiar dream and Sherry had been in it. It seemed important to remember the dream, so he focused on it. After a time he began to recall parts of it. Then suddenly, like a storm, the whole thing came flooding back: the strange creature, the approaching storm, the cloud of falling people, the dive to follow the creature and rescuing Sherry.

The breeze began to pick up and turn mildly uncomfortable with its chill. The smoothness of the water was replaced by a bit of chop and the gentle swells were getting stronger, more insistent. There was a sense of urgency, of something he had to do, but he couldn't think what. Yep! It was definitely time to... Wake up!

* * * *

THU 08.12.2094-Earth / TRN 17.03.6998-Aambü
Aambü, in a dream state, 1115 Hrs / 0843 Slashes

Sherry floated peacefully in the quiet swells, the tentative breeze cooling her skin. She knew Felix was nearby. She was content to let him sleep as she pondered the events of the last few days.

The swells got a little stronger. The breeze picked up and became uncomfortably chilling. The smooth water was starting to get choppy. Suddenly, Felix was gone. One moment he'd been there, just out of sight. The next he was nowhere she could sense. She rolled up into an upright position and, treading water, began casting about trying to see him. "Felix! Felix, don't leave me!"

The peaceful scene had become one of oppressive loneliness. She had no idea where she was and there were no landmarks anywhere to be seen. She was alone in the middle of a worldwide ocean. Frantically, she picked a direction and began swimming.

* * * *

THU 08.12.2094-Earth / TRN 17.03.6998-Aambü
ECS Destiny, Quarterdeck, MedCentral, 1120 Hrs / 0859 Slashes

The ambient sound of ships' systems, the familiar smell of a medical clinic and the sound of voices murmuring told Felix he was back home.

"Doctor. Doctor? He's awake."

"Are you sure?" That was Daniela. He was certain.

"Yes, I saw his vitals pick up and suddenly he was awake."

"Felix... Felix... Can you hear me?" A cool comforting gloved hand touched his brow. Felix opened his eyes and looked around without turning his head. He was back in MedCentral. Felix turned his head to find Daniela and a nurse looking worried.

"Hello, Doctor."

Felix tried to sit up and Daniela placed a gentle restraining hand on his chest. "Not just yet, Mister. You have so many patch links on you, you'd think you were part of the ship."

Felix looked around more carefully. True enough, there were tiny versions of the patch on his hand attached to his head, his chest, and his arms; just about everywhere.

He was just a little confused. "Why am I here?"

Dr. Jacobs frowned just a little. "You don't remember? We found you out in the mini-park in front of your cabin with Sherry on top of you. Both of you were out cold."

Felix pictured what that must have looked like. Then suddenly he remembered.

It hit him like a slap. He couldn't tell where Sherry was. She'd touched his forehead where he'd bumped it during his dream…He reached up and fingered the spot on his forehead. It wasn't even tender and there was almost no swelling left. "Where's Sherry?"

"Sherry's just fine. She's still out, though."

Daniela moved towards the foot of his bed. "Look to your right."

She checked a couple of readings on the monitors that ranged the length of the bed before stripping the gloves off her hands.

There she was. Sherry was indeed out cold. It was coming back to him, how, strangely, he'd been able to *know* where she was and somewhat what she was feeling. He was concerned he couldn't sense her at all now.

He remembered the flash and the sensory burst when she'd touched his forehead.

Felix was tired of the little patches everywhere. He was aware of each patch's location and he wanted them gone. He wanted to get up and check on Sherry, so he sat up.

It tingled and felt strange under every patch. He thought about how they held themselves there and wished they'd just go away. The tingling increased and slowly, one by one the patches seemed to suddenly come unglued and drop from his body. It was like the patches suddenly didn't like the taste of his skin. They fell onto the bed, some onto the floor. Most of the monitors started complaining.

Daniela turned in irritation. Felix was sitting up in spite of her warning. She dropped the gloves on the end of his bed and stood watching in fascination as the monitor connections began literally shedding from his body. The spots where they'd been affixed were wet with sweat while the rest of the skin looked normal.

Felix looked at his arms where some of the patches had been. The tingling sensation was gone. He stood up and wiped the dampness from his arms. He found he was wearing pajama style pants and shirt.

Felix crossed to Sherry's bed and stood watching her sleep. He was having difficulty understanding his perceptions. His eyes told him Sherry was alive. She was simply in a deep sleep.

The problem was that since waking from THE DREAM, he'd been able to feel her presence. It was as real as seeing her. Now, he felt nothing, just an empty void where she should be.

"Felix… Felix…? Felix!"

He finally heard his name and turned to look at Dr. Jacob. "Felix, she's unconscious, but she's not in any immediate danger. It's like she's in a deep sleep."

Felix was distressed. Intellectually, he knew Daniela was probably right, but deep down inside, he knew he had to do something; that he was the only one who could get her back.

"You can believe things are fine if you like. She's not here. I can't feel her!"

Daniela was getting worried about Felix. "What do you mean, you can't feel her?"

Felix looked around feeling trapped. "I just can't. She's not here!" He tapped the side of his head.

"Felix. I want to help, but I don't understand." Daniela looked around. "Look, can we talk? Come, sit with me in my office and explain it to me." Daniela placed a gentle hand on his elbow coaxing him to come with her.

It was almost electric. Suddenly he could sense worry and dread coming from her. He looked at her and saw a bright glow clinging like a second skin about her features. Her eyes glowed with a brilliant inner fire.

Felix thought he was loosing it. He didn't understand the situation much himself. Finally he gave her a jerky nod and allowed himself to be steered to Daniela's office.

Daniela offered him the seat in front of her desk and then poured a glass of cold water from the small water cooler she kept in a corner. She sat down at her desk and handed him the glass. "Now, tell me all about it. Start with your dream and tell me everything you can remember."

Felix gulped down the water and suddenly realized how thirsty he was.

He handed the glass back. "More, please?"

Daniela smiled and refilled his glass. This one went down at a more reasonable rate.

"Thanks." He said.

Since she'd let go of his elbow he could no longer sense her feelings. The glow had faded.

He told the story. It was very similar in some respects to Lyuba's except he had found himself in the water and interacting with the missing individual in her story. She was not surprised about the shower of people or the scene of him saving Sherry. It was only a difference of perspective. Everyone had had the same dream, but from his or her own point of view. Hearing all the tellings was a bit disconcerting, but what worried her more was what seemed to be happening to them in the waking world.

"I can't explain it." Felix continued. "It's like we know exactly where the other is, whether the other is asleep or awake. Sherry knew I'd bumped my head before I ever told her. I felt emotions and sensations that should have been hers privately. I think the same is true for her because when we came out of our cabins, we did it almost exactly at the same time. When she looked me in the eye, she blushed deeply like I'd embarrassed her."

"Felix. What happened out in the corridor this morning?" Daniela was seriously perplexed.

Felix shrugged. "I don't remember much. We puzzled over how she knew about my bump. She got confused about things and started talking about when I saved her from drowning in THE DREAM. It's like she was aware of how my dream went. Our dreams were linked somehow."

Felix thought for a moment. "The only thing that seems important is that we touched in the dream. I wrapped my arm around her waist and held on hard while I dragged her back to the surface. She hugged me tightly, terrified. When we broke the surface…we just woke up; in our separate cabins, naturally."

Daniela prompted. "But what happened in the corridor? We had to carry both of you to MedCentral."

Felix blushed, thinking of the scene it must have been, Sherry laying across him on the deck. "I'm not sure. She was so worried about the bump on my head. She touched it and…"

Felix eyes widened as he remembered. "There was this blinding white flash, and this incredible rush of sensory information hit me like a hammer. It was like a sudden dump of all data from one computer to another. I can remember things that happened to Sherry…that I know I wasn't there to see."

Daniela sat stone still, staring at him.

"Daniela? Dr. Jacobs? Hey!"

Daniela blinked and shook her head. "I've never ever heard of this kind of thing. It's like some kind of science fiction fantasy." She pondered. "All this resulting from some very odd dream."

She looked up at Felix. "To be honest. You're starting to frighten me just a little bit. I shouldn't be saying that to you. It's not very good behavior for a doctor, but I have to be honest.

"I'm very far out of my depth with this one. If everything you're telling me is accurate, something strange has happened in your brain, and maybe in Sherry's too."

Felix looked worried. "I'm just telling you what I know. It's a bit scary for me too."

He shrugged. "We must bring her back. I think she's lost."

Daniela blinked. "Lost?"

"I can't explain it. All I know is, she isn't where she's supposed to be and that's why she's still unconscious."

"Felix. Can you tell me what happened when you got up?"

Felix frowned. "What do you mean?"

Daniela looked grim. "I was going to detach those monitor links in a few minutes. You got this look on your face and sat up. Those links began falling off so fast you'd think they were jumping off."

She gently slapped a palm on the desk. "Those patches are very good. They're designed just like the one on the back of your hand. I notice that one's happy to stay."

Daniela shrugged. "Occasionally, one will be defective somehow and it won't stay put, but I've never seen all of them come off the way those did in there. Your skin was sweaty wherever those pads had been. You noticed it yourself, because you wiped the sweat from your arms before crossing to Sherry."

It was Felix' turn to sit, stunned. "I...All I could think was, I couldn't hear Sherry. Now that I think about it, I remember feeling every one of those little pads and wishing they'd go away. I wanted to rip them off, but you said to wait."

He remembered the strange tingling sensation where each of the pads had been. He realized he'd not been surprised when they fell off, as if he'd expected that result. "I just don't know."

Daniela shrugged. "OK, Felix. We're doing everything we can to help Sherry. The best thing you can do right now is get some rest. I'd send you back to your cubicle, but something tells me I'd never keep you there for long. Can I trust you to go to your cabin and get some sleep?"

Felix realized she was doing her best, and he realized at the moment there was nothing he knew how to do. *Maybe some uninterrupted sleep will clear my mind enough to solve the problem.*

He nodded. "Yes, Doctor. I promise, I'll go straight to my cabin and try to get some sleep, but I need your promise that if Sherry wakes on her own while I'm asleep, please let me know right away."

Daniela grinned. "You've got yourself a deal, Mister."

He reached to shake on it. When they touched, Felix again sensed her surface emotions. It wasn't very clear. It was like the whisper of someone present. He looked in her eyes. The glow had returned along with the glow over her features.

He released her hand as if shocked. The emotional link was silenced but the glow simply faded to a hint of its former state. The glow outlining her face was just a faint sheen in her skin.

Felix shook his head. "Well, I'm going to bed."

Daniela sat staring into the space he'd been for several minutes.

* * * *

THU 08.12.2094-Earth / TRN 17.03.6998-Aambü
Ruling Clan Caverns, Questing Chamber, 1320 Hrs / 1000 Slashes

AnalaRaksa, now AgradUtya floated quietly in the questing chamber. He closed his eyes and cast outward. *It was a long journey to the strange light beyond the rings, but he had time. The vessel was such an odd shape. He passed through its skin and flowed through the halls. He saw these people as almost translucent; their minds not tuned to his wavelength enough to be fully discernible. He finally found the one he was searching for. He'd become more solid to his sight.*

AgradUtya entered the private space where this one individual rested. He was not yet in slumber. This was a good thing. His new friend needed to know this was no dream, as he understood them.

FUNDAMENTAL CHANGES — 3

THU 08.12.2094-Earth / TRN 17.03.6998-Aambü
ECS Destiny, Quarterdeck, Felix' Cabin, 1320 Hrs / 1000 Slashes

Felix couldn't sleep. He wasn't terribly surprised. He gave up and was about to turn the lights on when he noticed a glowing shape forming in the air by his door. It was fairly shapeless, but it was slowly taking on a discernible form. It didn't take long for the form to become familiar. It finally struck him that it was a shadow image of the sea creature from his dream.

I'm not dreaming. That's for sure. So, am I going crazy? Felix sat up on his bunk and watched the apparition. The thing in his room took on more detail until it was clearly visible.

"Who are you? What do you want?"

Excellent! My new friend has noticed and yet he doesn't respond in fear. AgradUtya applied more effort to his likeness. *He fears, but not the vision. He fears for his mind. I must find something that proves my reality. Ah, the young female he saved in his dream. She is still lost in the sea.* AgradUtya projected an image of the young woman.

Felix watched the creature watching him. It made a gesture to one side as if Felix should notice something. Slowly a small likeness of Sherry congealed out of the air. Felix realized the creature was trying to say something to him. The image of Sherry drifted away like smoke on a breeze. The creature approached slowly. It's webbed hands outstretched in what seemed a peaceful gesture.

Tentatively, Felix leaned closer. The hands rose slowly and moved to either side of his head. They came together slowly and stopped where they'd be if they were touching his temples.

Memories of his dream played back as if on a recording. Felix realized the viewpoint of the vision was different. It was from the viewpoint of someone much deeper in the water, looking up.

He saw himself begin to descend and Sherry's plunge into the water next to him. He saw another person shoot into the water behind him and penetrate almost to the depth of the watcher. From the watcher's perspective, he realized the second person was Lyuba Chernov. She was almost transparent, but it was truly her. She chased him and Sherry back to the surface and the watcher saw all three vanish as they broke the surface.

"You're the creature of my dream, but you're real, not a dream." The realization amazed and frightened him a little.

One of the hands next to his head came around and with fingers held together like a shield, paused in front of his lips. The other hand pointed to the creatures' own head.

"Head, mind…you…you speak using the mind?"

He could sense pleasure from the creature. The hands found their way back to the sides of his head. *I am called AgradUtya. Who are you?*

Felix was shocked. "I am Felix Hernandez." This was an actual first contact. He wondered, *Why me?*

You were awakened when I called during your dream visit.

"Awakened?" Felix said aloud.

The fingers returned to his lips. *No need for vocalization.*

AgradUtya continued. He'd found the tuning of *Felix Hernandez* mind. He removed his web hands from the vicinity of this *Felix Hernandez'* head.

It appears you're one of a very few individuals of your species that has the latent ability to mind speak. When I saw you on the sea, I mistook you for a youngster and sent out a warning call. Your potential was activated. We would say, you were 'awakened.'

AgradUtya had the notion that while this creature was an adult, it was a fairly young adult. *Felix Hernandez, I would ask you, who is the young female you rescued in the dream vision?*

His new friend's face shifted in odd patterns. *You're speaking of the girl in the image you showed?*

AgradUtya found pleasure and amusement in the tone of Felix' response. *Indeed. She is special to you?*

Again, Felix Hernandez' face colored, this time to an alarming shade of red.

It soon faded to its usual hue. *Yes, she is my closest companion.*

AgradUtya understood. *You intend to take her to mate.*

Again the face changed colors. AgradUtya wondered if this was a physiological response to some emotion? Felix Hernandez only did this when discussing his favorite female.

What of Sherry? I fear she's in danger. She has yet to recover.

AgradUtya considered. *Have you touched since waking?*

Felix Hernandez seemed uncertain. *She was concerned for an injury I received. My dream ended suddenly and my body leaped in response to the change. She touched the injury to see if it was severe. There was a sudden burst of sensory information and then we fell asleep. What was that?*

AgradUtya understood the problem. *Sherry is also a latent mind speaker. She's not quite as strong as you but she has the potential. She was also awakened when I called you. My call was very strong, I regret.*

When, in your dream, the two of you touched, you created a bond that is likely unheard of in your species. For us, this is normal.

The irony of the situation was amusing. *You probably noticed strange new sensations of awareness of each other. When she touched you in the physical world, the bond was made permanent. We have special ceremonies to prepare young couples that wish to mate.*

AgradUtya allowed himself a small chuckle. *It is most fortunate for both of you that mating was a desired outcome. Because you are untrained in the use of mind speak you were not prepared for the sensation of bonding. It probably flooded the two of you, causing your minds to flee, to seek refuge.*

Felix Hernandez expressed concern in the tone of his response. *She hasn't revived. I don't know why, but I fear for her.*

This was serious. *You fear, as you should, my young friend. I told you that you're the stronger one. She'll rely on you for strength from time to time. This is such a time.*

AgradUtya put his most stern form of voice into the next statement. *Attend me carefully, young friend. Go to where her body rests. Hold her and use your mind to find her. It'll be as if you were again dreaming. However, you will be awake. I have seen her on the sea, but she's lost and doesn't know how to get home. You must help her find the way, and soon. It would be most unfortunate if you waited too long and she could no longer return.*

The situation would to be a touchy one, but if his new friend was successful, there would be a foundation of trust on which to build.

Felix Hernandez, I wish you well. I shall make appeal to the Maker to aid you. We have much to discuss and little time before your vessel arrives over my world. Go. Rescue your life mate again. I'll come speak with you at this time, next turn. Go. Quickly.

The strange vision began to loose cohesion and then vanished from sight. Felix sat for a moment, exhausted. Then he bounded from his bunk.

* * * *

THU 08.12.2094-Earth / TRN 17.03.6998-Aambü
ECS Destiny, Quarterdeck, MedCentral, 1350 Hrs / 1050 Slashes

It had been nearly three hours since Felix left MedCentral. Daniela felt like the walking dead. Almost everyone was taken care of and the worst was over. She still had six unconscious people in her emergency cubicles, but there seemed nothing she could do but keep them comfortable.

Felix came into the office like a whirlwind looking for a place to strike. "Doctor. I know what to do. We have to do it now!"

Daniela looked up from the never-ending reports she had to complete. "Felix. You promised to go to sleep. This doesn't look like sleep to me!"

Felix was beside himself with desperation. "I know! I tried! Really, I did! I couldn't sleep, but I just found out how to bring Sherry back. She's lost and can't find her way. I have to help her get back."

Daniela stood up from her desk and came up to Felix. "Felix. You're not sounding very rational right now. I think I might need to readmit you."

"I don't care. Readmit me if you must, but help me bring her back before it's too late!"

Daniela paled. "What do you mean, too late?"

"I can't explain it very well. AgradUtya told me if I didn't follow his instructions quickly, Sherry could become permanently lost."

"Agra...who? I've never heard such a name."

"Doctor. Right now, if I told you all about AgradUtya you'd slap a straight jacket on me so tight it would hurt. I'll even put up with that if necessary."

He assumed an unusually commanding tone to his voice. "But first, we save Sherry. Now!"

Daniela searched his eyes for an answer she couldn't see. "I don't know why I'm doing this. Go! Show me."

Felix didn't need to be told twice, he turned and hurried to Sherry's cubicle. Daniela was hard pressed to keep up.

"OK. Sit her up for a moment until I get situated." Daniela shrugged and waved a male nurse over. They carefully sat the unconscious Sherry up.

Felix hopped up on the bed and adjusted himself. "Now lay her head on my lap."

The male nurse looked at him and then at Daniela as if to say. *Is this guy for real?* Daniela wondered the same thing.

Felix sensed resistance and spoke up. "Dannie. Remember the discussion we had in your office just hours ago? It's more of that kind of stuff. I'll explain later. Now please, lay her on my lap." Daniela raised an eloquent eyebrow, then motioned to the nurse.

Felix looked relieved. "OK, look. If you want, wire my head and take notes, but please, don't disturb us for however long this takes."

He raised his hands and carefully placed one on her forehead. He took her hand with the other. Then, leaning back against the wall behind him, he closed his eyes.

Daniela and team placed monitor pads on both their foreheads and temples and waited.

* * * *

THU 08.12.2094-Earth / TRN 17.03.6998-Aambü
ECS Destiny, Quarterdeck, MedCentral, 1420 Hrs / 1066 Slashes

It looked as if Felix had fallen asleep with Sherry resting her head contentedly on his lap.

Half an hour had passed and neither of them had so much as twitched. The monitors showed lots of brain wave activity coming from Felix, but Sherry's monitor remained unchanged. Another half an hour passed and there was still no change.

As long as it takes, huh? Daniela stood and watched for several more minutes and decided to go work on her reports. Just as she turned to go, Sherry's monitor registered a small spike. "Brianna!"

Brianna came running from the lobby. "Yeah, Dannie?"

Daniela nodded at the monitor. Bri looked and took a sharp intake of breath.

* * * *

THU 08.12.2094-Earth / TRN 17.03.6998-Aambü
Aambü, in a dream state, 1420 Hrs / 1066 Slashes

It took a long frustrating search to find what he was looking for. There'd been no instructions on how to search for her. He considered treating it like another dream. He gently sought to find a way into her mind. There was no resistance. It was like passing through a flimsy curtain. In the darkened room he could see no clear features. A thin thread led in a straight line from the room into a darker passage. He followed it.

He finally broke out of the long featureless passage and found himself approaching the rings of the new world. He accelerated, hurtling just above the ring plane. He was an arrow darting for its target. The thread had become thicker, brighter, easier to see.

He followed it diving into the atmosphere, hurtling towards the worldwide ocean. The trail touched the water and ended. Felix stopped, hovering just above the water, and looked around. Sherry was nowhere to be seen.

He concentrated; focusing on the sense of her he'd felt when they'd awakened from the dream. He suppressed a surge of panic. Panic would only doom the mission. He prayed, something he was trying to get in the habit of doing regularly. He prayed for strength to continue the search and to find her.

A brilliant flicker of light came from far to the South. Felix hurtled in that direction, hope bursting in his chest, and there she was. She was turning in circles, panic etched on her features. Felix sent a prayer of thanks and dove. Just above her he stopped and called her name.
She looked up and saw him. "Felix! You left me!" She cried out. "I couldn't find you. I was so scared."

She seemed small and helpless. It hurt, but it was true; he had left her. He hadn't imagined she'd have any difficulty. "I'm so sorry, love. I didn't want to wake you, and I thought you knew the way. Forgive me. Please, come with me. I'll take you home."
She reached up and Felix took her hand pulling her out of the water. She hugged him close and started to cry. "Felix, please, don't ever leave me again. It's horrible without you."

Felix stroked her hair. "I know how it feels, love. I'll never leave you again. Let's go home."

He turned and, holding her close to his chest, arrowed into the sky, aiming for the rings of Aambü.

FUNDAMENTAL CHANGES — 4

THU 08.12.2094-Earth / TRN 17.03.6998-Aambü
ECS Destiny, Quarterdeck, MedCentral, 1455 Hrs / 1116 Slashes

Sherry's monitor started showing repeated spikes as if something were trying to get started. The furious activity on Felix' monitor had settled down to a calmer level. Sherry suddenly stirred slightly as if disturbed in sleep. Felix' began stroking her hair. Tears began streaming down both their faces and the monitor activity for both of them seemed to sync. Sherry's monitor took on a normal pattern as did Felix'. The monitors virtually synced with each other.

Felix abruptly hugged Sherry close and a sharp gasp came from both of them. Their eyes opened simultaneously. Sherry looked up at him and smiled her brightest smile. "We're home!"

Felix grinned and looked up. Daniela and Brianna were staring at them, totally lost.

* * * *

Daniela shook her head. The readings on Sherry's vitals were perfect. There was no sign of damage. The brain scans were normal; well, almost normal. There was some new activity in a region that normally displayed none. These areas were thought by many neurologists to be dormant. The same was true of Felix' scans. Something odd was going on in that area of the brain.

She had no real reason to keep either of them, but asked them to stay over night for observation.

It was strange. When she'd asked, they'd glanced at each other and then said, 'yes'…in perfect unison.

* * * *

THU 08.12.2094-Earth / TRN 17.03.6998-Aambü
ECS Destiny, Quarterdeck, SecCentral, 1615 Hrs / 1209 Slashes

Tanya looked up from her reports. Daniela stood tiredly at her office door. "Hey Dannie. Come on in. Sit down."

Daniela smiled. "I can't sit right now. I just came to tell you. Sherry's awake."

Tanya got up and came around the desk. "She's awake? Wonderful! I've been so worried about her."

Daniela pushed off the door jam with her shoulder. "Yeah, I know. I thought you might want to see her."

"Absolutely! Thanks, Dannie."

"Tahnie, there's something you should know."

Tanya's face visibly sagged. "What's wrong?"

Daniela shrugged. "I don't know if you can call it 'wrong' so much as different. Don't worry. She's fine. There was no damage."

She frowned. "It's just that there's a new facet to her...and Felix, for that matter, that may take getting used to."

Tanya searched her face. "Getting used to?"

Daniela was struggling for words. "Something about the dream and...someone Felix claims to have met; has given them...expanded brain function is the best I can describe. Come on, they'll be really glad to see you."

Daniela turned to lead the way and Tanya followed. "Felix met someone? What do you mean?"

"Tahnie, I don't know. I am as mystified as you are. He mentioned a name and said this person had given him instructions on how to revive Sherry." They cut through the morgue to MedCentral.

* * * *

Sherry turned her head and looked at Felix, resting in a chair next to her bed. *Tahnie's coming.*

He opened his eyes and smiled at her. *You hear others?*

She smiled and nodded. *A little. It's not like us. Just a sense of 'who.' I think it's when the person is close enough and is thinking about me, like she is right now.*

She looked toward the entry a moment before Daniela parted the curtain and invited Tanya to enter.

Tanya stepped in and took in the scene. "Hey Sherry, Felix. I see you're awake."

She came up to the bed where Sherry was sitting in a partially elevated posture. She gave her a hug.

Sherry tensed for just an instant as a strange sensation came over her. When Tanya touched her, she could suddenly hear a kind of whispery sound, kind of like the ambient sound in a crowded room that one took for granted till it was pointed out.

She quickly returned the hug. When Tanya turned away, the sensation passed. She could still see a faint glow outlining Tanya's features. "Yeah. Felix brought me back."

Tanya raised an eyebrow and glanced over at Felix, who sat with a pleasant smile on his face, regarding her with frank curiosity. "What Felix?"

Felix grinned, "Sorry. Since this thing started, we've been learning a whole new way of perceiving things. I'm trying to get used to how you look."

Tanya was confused. She glanced across the room at Daniela, who was lingering at the entry.

"Don't ask me." She responded.

Sherry spoke up. "What Felix is trying to say is, something has happened to us that makes us see everything, especially people, differently. You look subtly different to us than before. It's not you. It's our new way of seeing things."

"OK, Sherry. This is starting to sound a bit weird." Tanya was feeling nervous.

Felix and Sherry exchanged glances. She nodded.

He got up and offered his chair. Tanya thought to decline, but Sherry had shifted her position on the bed and Felix hopped up to sit next to her.

"Please, Tanya. Sit down. This is going to take some time to explain and you might need to sit down to hear it anyway."

Tanya shrugged, hooked the chair over with her foot and sat. "So, what's this grand mystery?"

She was really curious now. Felix tilted his head slightly towards Sherry as if listening. He looked at her, nodded and turned to face Tanya. It was like they'd just had a quick conversation.

"I don't know really which part to tell you first." Felix began. "I guess the best thing is to start from the beginning and go from there. In a way, we're afraid to explain because we don't want to scare away a friend."

Tanya was really worried now. "I don't know what's happened to you guys, but I think by now you should know we're quite faithful to our friends." The notion that they doubted hurt a little.

Sherry spoke up. "We don't doubt you, Tahnie."

Tanya blinked. She hadn't said anything about doubt.

"What's happened to us will be thought of as freakish when it gets out. Felix is right. We desperately need to maintain our friendships especially with what's happened."

Felix nodded and began. "I believe we've had a severe dose of mass dreaming here on *Destiny*."

Tanya nodded. "Unless you've been talking to someone since you woke up, I'm surprised you know that much."

Felix grinned. "No, I've only talked to Dannie and Sherry. We know because we're sort of responsible."

Tanya dropped her jaw and stared at Felix as if he'd transformed into a toad. "How can anyone claim to be responsible for a bizarre dream that managed to affect almost the entire population?"

Sherry smiled. "It was an accident."

She glanced at Felix. He flushed a little and grinned. "Let me get on with the explanation. You'll have a lot more questions later."

Sherry sat up and leaned on Felix' shoulder. "It's because of that dream that everything changed."

Felix nodded and then asked, "When Lyuba told you her dream, did she mention me or Sherry?"

Tanya started. These two were full of surprising insights. "Yes, actually. She had a very vivid dream, apparently the same dream from her point of view that everyone else seems to have had. Including me, by the way."

Felix winced. "Let me guess. She saw me rescue Sherry from drowning in an ocean."

Tanya grinned. "So your dream was similar?"

The two nodded in unison.

"Did Lyuba mention a stranger in her dream?"

Tanya raised an eyebrow. "Yes, she didn't get to see the person, but she mentioned that while she was flying high over a worldwide ocean, I'm assuming this is someplace on our target planet, she saw two individuals swimming.

"When everyone began falling from the sky, she dove to try to save Sherry. She saw both of you dive under the water just before Sherry hit. Lyuba dove in, hoping to save Sherry and saw you drag her back to the surface. She never saw the unknown person after she hit the water."

Felix nodded. "I have something to tell you. It needs to be reported to Tolya soon, but I'll explain it to you so you'll be able to back me up."

Tanya looked curious.

"The odd, unknown person has a name. He's called AgradUtya. I don't know much about him except that he's a responsible individual in a community of people who live on the planet. They're indigenous, and they are definitely not human."

Daniela dropped a pen she'd been toying with.

Sherry looked over. "Dannie, please come on in. There are no secrets here."

She smiled and looked over at Felix. "We don't have many secrets anymore."

Tanya closed her mouth. She was wondering if a bit of tape to hold it shut might be useful. She was glad she was sitting, Felix had been right about that.

"Felix. How could you meet anyone on the planet? There's still weeks before we enter orbit, let alone land!"

Felix shrugged. "The dream. These people are telepathic. They communicate mind to mind. I don't know anything else about them. AgradUtya's going to have a chat with me...us," he glanced at Sherry who grinned back at him, "...tomorrow afternoon. I suspect he'll tell us more then."

He wrapped an arm around Sherry's shoulders. "Evidently, I was having a dream I don't even remember. I'd been worrying over the problems of taking a water world and I guess it had something to do with my dream. AgradUtya says that while he was watching, he saw me and thought I was a youngster in the path of a coming storm. He sent out some sort of call. I guess it was some kind of warning call.

"Anyway, he says we are among a small number of humans with a latent ability to, as he puts it, mind speak. He said the ability hadn't awakened in us. I don't think it ever would have under normal circumstances, but...He was kind of apologetic. He said his call triggered an awakening in me. It was such a strong call, it surged through the whole ship.

"Anyway, as I said, Sherry was also triggered. Somehow, the call coupled with our awakening, pulled anyone who was dreaming at the time, into my own dream. My dream was changed from whatever it was to something different. I found myself swimming on the surface of Aambü.

"These people are able to send themselves in something like a dream state to other places. AgradUtya went out to see who I was. He warned me of a coming storm and then pointed out the cloud of falling people. Then he urged me in a game of charades to dive out of the danger of the storm.

"In my dream, I decided to follow him and that's when Sherry fell in the water next to me. From there, you know the the story from Lyuba's perspective."

Tanya shook her head. "OK, you had a weird dream and met a weird character. That doesn't make him real."

She seemed almost eager for such an explanation.

Felix shrugged. "I thought the same thing, but after I revived from the corridor episode, he came to visit me while I was awake. He instructed me on how to rescue Sherry, and Daniela knows most of the rest of that story.

Daniela spoke for the first time. "You never really explained the whole corridor episode fully."

Sherry spoke up. "Felix didn't fully understand what had happened when you asked him about it. Yes, I know about your question. If Felix knows something, so do I. It's the same for him. Let me explain, as I understand it now.

"In Felix' dream…in our dreams, Felix came to my rescue. He grabbed me around the waist and I grabbed on tight to him in fear when he saved me from drowning. Evidently when we touched each other in the dream, we were somehow linked to each other.

"When we woke up…in our separate cabins, we became aware that even though we were wide awake, we could still sense one another. We knew exactly where we were, that we were both awake, that…" She blushed deeply, "…we knew what we were doing, what we were feeling, things we shouldn't have been aware of…private feelings.

"After cleaning up from a very sweaty dream," she grimaced, "we met out in the mini-park in front of your place. We were going to discuss the dream over breakfast. I knew about the bump on his head. He got when he threw himself from his bed trying to rescue me in the dream.

"We were very surprised that I knew about his bump when he hadn't said anything about it. I reached up to touch his forehead and we were both hit by a blinding flash and what amounts to a sensory data dump."

She looked at Felix. He nodded and faced Tanya and Daniela.

"This is kind of embarrassing. Everybody knows we had become close friends, that we were seriously dating and all that. AgradUtya asked about it because the incident in the park concerned him. I didn't know it then, but both of us harbored secret hopes of marriage one day…well, guess what?"

Daniela got a strange look and Tanya bit her lip.

"AgradUtya said what happened to us in the park would have been preceded by special ceremonies and careful preparation in his culture. From their point of view, the first form of mating has taken place. It's a mind bonding, and it's very permanent."

Sherry grinned. "Tahnie, I got him for good. We need a long talk with Pastor Brad."

Tanya stared. She didn't know whether to laugh, cry, or go screaming from the room, drooling.

"I…ah…are you OK with this…this arrangement?"

"Yes!" It was a chorus in duet.

Felix laughed and, with a grin, Sherry continued. "We've been in love for quite some time. We just thought it was important to wait till a more appropriate time.

"This...you were going to say, 'weird' or 'odd' arrangement is permanent. AgradUtya said it was fortunate that, mating was a desired outcome."

Daniela grinned. "I've heard some pretty wild marriage proposals in my time, but this has got to take the cake!"

She turned to Tanya. "Something fundamentally more important is at stake here."

Tanya sobered and after a quick thought realized where Daniela was going. "You're right. This is clearly a first contact situation. It's not like anything we had in the scenarios, but there' no mistake."

She looked at her friends, friends who had been fundamentally changed. "I hope you know the two of you have just been bumped up to de facto xeno-ambassadors. We must tell Tolya."

She looked at Daniela. "Can I steal them? We can meet with Tolya in my offices."

Daniela shrugged. "Sure, why not? Everything just got turned on its ear."

Tanya reached for the tab on her collar when Felix and Sherry got up from the hospital bed and headed for the entry.

"Where are you going?" Tanya and Daniela grinned at their well-timed duet.

Felix smiled. "Sorry. We'd like to change into something fresh before we have this meeting, and we're starving to death! We promise to be back in your office in about an hour."

Daniela shrugged. "It's a reasonable request."

Tanya realized how really worn out they must be from their ordeal. "I'm sorry. We'll see you in my office in an hour then.

"Oh, please don't tell anyone about this till we can sort it out."

Felix grinned mischievously. "Don't worry. We won't say a single word."

The two young ambassadors laughed together as they left.

FUNDAMENTAL CHANGES — 5

THU 08.12.2094-Earth / TRN 17.03.6998-Aambü
ECS Destiny, Quarterdeck, SecCentral, 1650 Hrs / 1266 Slashes

"Why don't we meet at home then? It's more comfortable and just as private." Tolya spoke into the link on his collar.

Tanya seemed a bit agitated. "I guess you're right. So, what about Lyuba?"

Tolya grinned to himself. "I suspect Lyuba has some of this figured out already. If she hasn't, she'll probably figure it out. It would be better to let her hear it completely and have some control over who gets to hear it next."

Tanya nodded. "Ok. It's time we thought about dinner anyway. I'll tell them."

"Good. I'll sign off here and come on down. Love ya."

Tanya grinned. "Back at ya!"

She closed the connection and gave Felix a call.

"Hi, Tanya. What's up?"

"Well, Tolya said it might be more relaxing to meet at our place."

Felix hesitated. "Well, I..."

He stopped and halfway cocked his head. He grinned and amended his reply. "Sherry says that would be fine."

Tanya hesitated. It was going to take some getting used to, this odd communication. "Have you had anything to eat?"

"No. I just cleaned up and changed. Sherry's...ah...finishing up her shower." He blushed.

Tanya thought Felix' discomfort over aspects of their new connection charming. He tried so hard to be the gentleman.

"Well, why don't you two come right over and have dinner with us? We have plenty to snack on while you wait, and we'll have time to catch up."

"OK." He paused; then shrugged, "Sherry says that would be fun. We'll be over when she's ready."

* * * *

THU 08.12.2094-Earth / TRN 17.03.6998-Aambü
ECS Destiny, Quarterdeck, Chernov Residence, 1710 Hrs / 1300 Slashes

"These brownies are fantastic!" Sherry picked a final crumb from her napkin. "Brownies and coffee; Tahnie you're a genius."

Tanya grinned as she set the kitchen timer and hit start. Sherry seemed ravenous. She'd never seen her so eager to eat. "I'm so glad you approve."

The front door snapped open for Tolya and Lyuba.

"Sherry! You're better!" She hurried over and gave Sherry a sisterly hug.

Sherry tried not to wince at the sense of presence Lyuba possessed. She and Felix could sense the mental or emotional strength of a person by touch. She remembered Daniela's as being a pleasant whisper. Tanya was a strong firm whisper. Lyuba was very loud, almost a hum.

She knew Felix on a different level. There was no 'sound' as she described the sense of others. His was just a strong overlay of presence that comforted and reinforced her.

She glanced at Felix. *Wow! She's a strong one. Do you think she might awaken?*

Felix shrugged. *I don't know. I think we've a lot to learn.*

Lyuba was watching them. It was a little weird. They sort of looked at each other and used subtle facial expressions and body language as if they were talking, but they weren't talking. "Sherry. What's all that? Is it a new kind of game?"

Sherry darted a look at Felix. Then she focused on Lyuba. "No honey…it's kinda hard to explain. We…something happened to us. It's why we were unconscious today."

She struggled for words. She looked at Felix and then said. "Yeah. Felix is right. We've been changed because of the dream and what happened to us this morning."

Felix chuckled. "Kiddo, we don't have to talk to each other out loud anymore. Something happened and now we can hear each other in our minds. It's a lot quicker once you're used to it. We'll tell all about it in a little while."

Lyuba looked at them, eyes round. "You mean like telepathy?"

Sherry grinned. "Yeah, something like that. It's a long story, so you better listen good when we tell it."

Lyuba smiled. "Don't worry. I'll be all ears."

Tolya wandered into the dining area and snatched a brownie. "Hey you two. It's good to see you awake and getting around. We can't have too much lazing around on this ship, you know." His eyes twinkled as he looked at them. "You look pretty good for having been unconscious for half the day."

Felix smiled. He stood and shook hands with the captain. Tolya was a strong whisper, firm and confident.

"Well, some of the side benefits make it more tolerable." He threw Sherry a grin.

He looked back at Tolya. "You're pretty tired, aren't you?"

Tolya was startled by the change of topic.

"Sherry just mentioned it."

Tolya glanced at Sherry and then back at Felix. "I didn't hear her say anything, and I know I didn't mention it."

Felix shrugged. "I'm sorry. I guess Tanya hasn't explained everything to you yet. I guess I'd be a little reluctant to admit believing what she's heard from us."

Tanya came in from the kitchen. She was about to deny her doubts when Sherry spoke up.

"It's OK, Tahnie. I know you worry whether we might be missing a couple of cards in the deck. I would be too, if our roles were reversed. Please don't be hurt. Felix meant no criticism."

Tolya was getting confused. "Will somebody please tell me what's going on?"

Tanya looked down. "I'm sorry honey. They've had a new life thrust at them and it must be really tough to adjust...It's true. I just don't know how to explain it."

She glanced at the timer in the kitchen. "Dinner's almost ready. Let's eat. Then we can sort this whole thing out."

She looked at Tolya. "They're right, you know. You're pretty tired. I know I am."

Tolya shrugged and took his seat. "Yeah. You could say I'm tired. I've been running on worry since 0530."

Sherry got up and moved around the table to stand behind Tolya. She put her hands over his shoulders as if to give a massage. Then she stood, eyes closed in concentration. Her face paled a little, and she started looking as if she might wilt, but she stayed put.

Tolya's expression changed. He looked more alert.

Felix watched. *What are you doing? It's like you're infusing energy or something.*

Sherry kept her eyes closed, but he could feel her smile. *I don't know. He felt so weary I couldn't stand it. Besides, I've had nothing but rest today.*

Tolya worked his shoulders as if he'd just had a major massage. "I don't know what you did, but I feel like I just got a second wind."

She stepped away and almost stumbled. Felix hurried over and took Sherry by the shoulders, escorting her back to her seat.

Tolya noticed that Sherry looked pale and unsteady on her feet as Felix helped her into her seat. They gazed at each other, looking, for all the world like they were in private conversation.

That was very sweet love, but whatever you did took something out of you. Are you OK?

She squeezed the hand he had on her shoulder. *I know, but you're here. I'm feeling stronger already.*

It was true. He could sense a slow trickle of energy welling up in her like water in a fresh dug hole on the shore of a lake.

He suddenly felt just how tired he was. He sat in the seat next to her, wondering if he would be able to stay awake.

Tolya was more than curious. Tanya went to answer the beep of the timer. Lyuba gave another round-eyed look and hurried after.

Felix? Are you OK?

Felix nodded. *It's my turn to be tired. I love you and I recognize the need to fix everybody, but I think there's more work to this mental stuff than it seems. It takes energy and you don't have unlimited reserves. You must be strong before you can make others strong. If you're too tired, you endanger yourself. I don't want you to go missing on me ever again.*

Sherry was apologetic. *I'm sorry. I had to do something.*

Felix nodded. *I know.*

* * * *

THU 08.12.2094-Earth / TRN 17.03.6998-Aambü
ECS Destiny, Quarterdeck, Chernov Residence, 1850 Hrs / 1400 Slashes

Dinner must have been good. Felix felt stronger for the energy the meal provided, but he'd been so weary he wasn't sure he remembered much of the table conversation.

They retired to the living room and had coffee and brownies. "So, Felix. Tanya says you have things to say I need to hear. Why don't you start with this morning and catch me up?"

Felix smiled. The sugar and caffeine were working their temporary magic. He told the story from the beginning: the dream, their partial bonding through the dream, and the completion of the bonding that knocked them for a loop out in the park. When he got to his conversation with a dream character while awake, Tolya turned very still.

"That other person, the one Lyuba saw from a distance but never met; the same individual?"

Felix nodded. Sherry piped up. "I get to meet him tomorrow."

Tolya remembered another question. "You know, something about you two has changed. You tend to complete each other's statements. You act like you know what the other is thinking. What's that all about?"

Felix glanced at Sherry and nodded. He sat back with his coffee and let her talk.

"You're right. We have changed...a lot. I don't know if we're done changing yet. We'll just have to wait and see."

She sipped her coffee. "Felix mentioned the bond that resulted from the dream and from our subsequent physical contact out in the park. He didn't mention exactly what the results of all that was, or what the bond really means."

She looked over at Felix. He smiled and nodded. *Go ahead. It's nothing to be ashamed of.*

She grinned self-consciously and continued. "This guy, AgradUtya is a native of Aambü."

Tolya interrupted. "Aambü? What's that?"

"Sorry, that's where we're going; the planet that we've been fretting over. That's what they call it."

Tolya sat up. "They? Wait a minute. Are you saying what I think you're saying?"

Felix grinned. "Yes, she is. AgradUtya is a member of the dominant sentient species on this planet. I don't know much about them yet. We just met, but I do know they're powerful telepaths."

Tolya looked over at Tanya. "You said something about first contact. I didn't understand the reference at the time."

He looked at Felix and Sherry. "You've met an alien species? How? We're not even in orbit yet."

Sherry grinned. "Tolya, I think it only fair to point out that in this case, WE are the alien species. This is their world." She took another sip. "How did we meet, or more accurately, how did they meet," she nodded towards Felix, "I was getting to that."

She set her coffee cup on the coffee table. "As I said, AgradUtya is a member of a race of people who communicate telepathically.

"He explained in his waking visit that his mistaken notion that Felix, in his dream, was a youngster gone astray, caused him to sound some kind of warning cry. He did this not by voice but by mental broadcast.

"That call intersected our dreams. In our cases," she pointed at Felix and then herself, "it woke something that would have remained dormant forever if we hadn't been in range of it. He was very apologetic, by the way.

"AgradUtya says Felix and I are among a small percentage of our population who possess latent telepathic ability. His call awakened that ability in both of us."

Tolya sat staring, trying to digest what sounded like something from a B-rated sci-fi movie. "Telepathy?"

Felix sat up and placed his cup on the table. "So it would seem. Apparently it also included Empathy in Sherry's case. There may be other 'symptoms?' that'll pop up later, but that's the size of it." *Go ahead, love.*

Sherry continued. "In our dreams, in the process of Felix rescuing me from drowning, we touched.

"When we surfaced the dream ended and we woke in our separate places."

She looked shyly at Felix. "It seems that our touching, in the dream created some kind of link between us. We sensed it right away when we woke."

She looked back at Tolya, "In Felix' dream, when he lunged to catch me, he actually leaped from his bed and hit his forehead on the door."

Tolya laughed, in spite of himself. "Wow Felix, you sure get into your dreams."

Felix grinned and said. "Don't worry, it gets better."

Sherry blushed and continued. "We met in the park with plans to go to the dining commons for breakfast. I was aware of his bump through this new link we have and was concerned about it. I reached up to touch his forehead where the bump was and something happened."

She looked at Felix and blushed again. *You tell it.*

"OK." Felix smiled at her and took up the narrative. "When she touched me, there was some kind of massive energy transfer, or something. We received a full sensory dump of each other's… memories, I guess. That kicked us into some other place…I can't explain it, but to everyone else, we were unconscious."

Tolya and Tanya exchanged glances.

Lyuba, who'd been sitting in rapt attention, suddenly spoke up. "Is that why you guys keep looking at each other and making all those faces?"

Sherry laughed. "Yeah, honey, we're always talking to each other in our minds. We hear each other think."

Lyuba's eyes were quite round. "Weird…" She breathed it, almost reverently.

Tanya chuckled. "Lyuba, that's not very polite, you know."

Sherry grinned and waved Lyuba over. She gave her a big hug. "It's OK, Tanya. She meant no harm."

She paused a moment in thought and then looked at Lyuba. "But I guess your mom's right. Usually, that's not the most polite way to express things."

Lyuba nodded. "I'm sorry."

"Don't worry about it. I like you just the way you are." She hugged Lyuba again and patted the seat next to her.

Lyuba sat between Sherry and Felix.

Sherry resumed the story. "It gets better." She grinned and looked at Felix.

"Yes, it does," he quipped.

"Felix woke from the corridor episode first..." *You tell this part.*

Felix took up the story. "Well, I was in this other place...a very calm relaxing place. While I was there I knew Sherry was close by. I started thinking about things and felt there was something important I had to do. So, I decided I should wake up."

"Yeah, and he left without me." Sherry sniffed and gave a pretend pout. *Sorry love, I couldn't resist.*

Felix grinned. *I know.* "I woke up and Dannie and a nurse were watching me. We talked and I asked where Sherry was. I couldn't sense her anymore. They said she was fine, but unconscious and they didn't know why.

"I guess I got a little upset. I got up and went to see her. Dannie took me to her office and gave me a talking to. She agreed to release me if I'd go to my quarters and get some sleep. I tried; no luck. That's when I met AgradUtya while awake.

"He somehow sent himself, I guess kind of like how we moved about in the dream. He came out to the ship and looked for me. He showed himself in my cabin. Since the lights were off, I could see him quite well. We talked for a while and I told him I was worried about Sherry.

"Long story short, he told me how to bring her back from where she was. I went back to MedCentral and persuaded Dannie to help me get Sherry back. I followed AgradUtya's instructions and, thank God, Sherry's back with us."

You forgot to tell him the good part. Sherry had a mischievous grin on her face.

Felix blushed and continued. "Sherry says I forgot a part. It's not that I forgot. It's just it's a little embarrassing. You see. When we touched out in the park, we evidently completed something that got started when we touched in our dreams. AgradUtya said it was something that, in his culture, would have been preceded by counseling and ceremonial preparation. To their way of thinking, Sherry and I are not just linked. We're married, bonded for life."

They looked at each other and blushed in unison. Felix commented. "All that's missing now is the formal wedding and... what comes after."

Tolya glanced at Tanya and a big grin split his face.

"Oh, stop it you monster." She playfully punched his arm.

Tolya turned serious. "We've got a lot to work out here, but Felix is almost asleep. Sherry, you're not looking too chipper yourself."

Tanya smiled. "I don't want to find you two on the deck out in the park again. Why don't you just crash where you are? We can go to breakfast in the morning and discuss what's next."

Felix was too tired to object. Lyuba stretched.

Tanya stood. It was 2000. They'd talked long and the day had been a long one with little sleep preceding it. "Lyuba honey, I think you should get some sleep. You have classes tomorrow."

Lyuba yawned. "OK. See you at breakfast."

She turned and trooped off for bed.

"Thanks Tahnie. You're right. I don't think he'd make it across the hall." Sherry shifted to cuddle up against Felix.

Tanya smiled back. "No problem, honey...if you want, you can use the other couch."

Sherry grinned a mischievous little grin. "That's OK. We're both too wiped out to get naughty."

She tucked in close and the two were asleep before Tanya could turn out the light. She got a thin blanket and covered them for the night.

HEALER BY DEFAULT — 1

FRI 08.13.2094-Earth / TRN 17.03.6998-Aambü
2.75 months from orbital insertion; Aambü, Gem System
ECS Destiny, Quarterdeck, Daniela's Cabin, 0530 Hrs / 2208 Slashes

Daniela closed the connection and went to the kitchenette to start some coffee. The clock on the coffee maker said 0530. It was early, but she was concerned about the five who hadn't awakened from their dream adventures.

She'd been hesitant. Near closing time yesterday, she'd actually considered consulting Felix. *Imagine that!* She thought. She felt it was an awful lot to ask so soon after his recovery from his own bizarre bouts of unconsciousness.

Then there was that really weird thing he did getting Sherry to snap out of it. *We're home?* All the explanations in the world were not much to go on, at this point.

But today...today was a different animal. Her five charges had not recovered over night and they showed no signs of change or improvement of any sort. She routed a call to Felix. The insistent COMM chime produced no satisfactory results. She hesitated and then called Sherry's number. Same results! At least there was a kind of consistency here. Then it struck her. *They're both not answering. Is something wrong? Don't panic!* She told herself.

* * * *

Tanya reached over with a groan and slapped the bedside COMM link. "Yeah."

She knew she sounded horrid, but it had been a great dream.

"Tahnie. I'm sorry to wake you. I was trying to get a hold of Felix, but neither he nor Sherry are answering their COMM. I'm worried about them."

Tanya groaned and sat up. Tolya turned over and opened his eyes. "It's OK, Dannie. They were over for dinner last night and literally fell asleep on the couch. They're fine."

"Oh. I'm sorry Tahnie. When you're up and about, could you have him call me?"

Tanya was awake now. "Sure...Hey, you're awake kinda early. Have you had breakfast yet?"

"No. I just got off the COMM with Melanie. She says there's been no change whatsoever in the comatose five."

Tanya nodded absently. The screens were asleep just then. "I see. Why don't you come on over? We'd planned to go to the Diner for breakfast. I'll release the door. Just come on in. Your favorite curiosities are snoring on the couch."

"Tahnie are you sure?"

"It's fine. What are friends for? Once I can get my hunk out of bed we'll head on over for breakfast."

Tanya heard amusement in Daniela's voice. "Don't get to involved in that little project or we'll not be going anywhere soon. I'll be over in a few minutes."

Tolya chuckled as Tanya slapped the COMM to sleep. She turned to find him eyeing her hungrily.

"Ah. You're awake. Sorry, Mr. Hunk. You're on short rations this morning. I don't think you really want to entertain company at the same time."

Tolya faked a pout. "But…"

Tanya pounced on him and smothered him in kisses. "But nothing. You'll just have to hang on till this evening. I think you're man enough to do that." She squeezed where it counted. Tolya laughed heartily returning kisses gleefully.

"OK, but you know you're in for it tonight, don't you?"

"Oh, you insatiable beast! We'd better get up and presentable."

She flounced out of bed and took the morning's sunshine with her into the restroom.

HEALER BY DEFAULT — 2

FRI 08.13.2094-Earth / TRN 17.03.6998-Aambü
ECS Destiny, Quarterdeck, Chernov Residence, 0545 Hrs / 2233 Slashes

Felix. Wake up. Daniela's here. Oh, this is embarrassing.

Felix' eyes popped open and he turned his head to see Daniela standing in the entryway, watching them with a trace of humor in her eyes. *Why be embarrassed? We just slept.*

Sherry struggled to sit up. *With our bodies, but…*

Felix sat up. *Yeah, I know. The mind is ever active.*

Sherry blushed, which made Felix grin all the more. *I love it when you do that.*

"Good morning, Daniela. What brings you here all bright eyes at 0545 in the morning?"

Daniela grinned and came into the room, selecting a recliner to park in. "Sorry to disturb quality time…"

They blushed in unison and she relented. "Really, I'm sorry I woke you. I'm here for two reasons. The first is, I think I'm going to need some help with the five people who haven't regained consciousness from their dream…"

"Five?" Felix came fully awake. "You have five unconscious people? Why?"

"I never got a chance to tell you yesterday. Hundreds of people on board were directly affected by that dream. Some nearly went hysterical. Five were found in a catatonic state. They look almost like you did. It's been more than twenty-four hours since they locked up and I'm worried they might be in trouble, like the way you said Sherry was."

Felix was thinking. "OK…" he prompted. "You said there were two reasons."

"Oh. Yeah. When I called this morning and told Tanya I couldn't get an answer from either of you, she said you were here and not to worry. She invited me to join you guys for breakfast. So, here I am."

Felix relaxed and Sherry chuckled. "He thought you had more disturbing news. Maybe we should go see your five first." *Felix? What do you think?*

Felix smiled at her. *Remember last night? You have to be strong to give your kind of help. We both need to be strong.*

Sherry nodded. "He's right. We should eat breakfast first, unless it's an emergency."

Daniela shook her head. "I don't think so."

Felix hadn't said a thing about eating breakfast first. *Oh, well.* She shrugged.

Felix saw the confusion in her eyes. Pointing to his temple, he replied, "Don't forget, we're always together up here. It appears the use of some of our gifts require significant amounts of energy. We need to be charged up before we do anything as intensive as what I did for Sherry, or what she did to Tolya."

"Tolya?" Daniela was lost.

"Yeah, my big hunk was wiped out around dinner time." Tanya entered the room and gave Daniela a quick hug. "Sherry did something. I don't know, but whatever it was boosted his stamina so he was less tired. Unfortunately, it turned on them and they practically fell asleep at the table."

Daniela looked at Sherry. "No, Dannie. I don't know what I did exactly. I just felt compelled to help. He was really tired."

Daniela shook her head. "That's all well and good, but even if you ARE gaining unusual abilities, you can't go beyond your endurance. Our bodies are designed to use only so much energy before they need fuel and rest."

Felix grinned. "Yeah, I sort of told her that last night. It seems that because of our bond, we tend to draw on each other's abilities and energy. AgradUtya said I was the stronger and she would 'depend on me from time to time.' That's exactly what happened last night. After she handled Tolya's weariness, she almost collapsed. I helped her to her seat and I could feel her pulling strength from me. It's not conscious really. It just happens."

Daniela looked thoughtful. "So, somehow you two team up as needed…stranger and stranger."

She got up, came over and gave Sherry a hug and one to Felix. "Don't worry. I like you guys anyway."

Tolya had quietly entered the room watching and listening, Lyuba next to him. "I second the notion."

Everyone turned and laughed.

"Do you want to go change first?"

Felix grinned. "I'm starved. I vote we go eat and then freshen up. Then we'll see Dannie's five problem people."

"We must be ready for Mr. A's return visit." Sherry interjected.

"Yes, and sometime we need to make an appointment with Pastor Brad."

HEALER BY DEFAULT — 3

FRI 08.13.2094-Earth / TRN 17.03.6998-Aambü
ECS Destiny, Quarterdeck, Event Center Diner, 0700 Hrs / 2328 Slashes

Breakfast was most fulfilling. Felix announced, with a grin, that their batteries were fully charged. They freshened up quickly and accompanied Daniela to MedCentral. Lyuba wanted to go with them to see what they would do, but Tanya prevailed, pointing out that her teachers were awaiting her presence.

* * * *

The five patients were all located in adjacent cubicles. Daniela escorted them to the first cubicle, Recovery-1. The display read, 'Kevin De Silva.'

"He was the first one we found." Daniela said in a quiet voice. "He's married with two kids."

Felix nodded. "I don't know much. I took Mr. A's advice and muddled through till I found a way." He shrugged. "We'll do what we can."

Daniela smiled. "That's all anyone can do."

Sherry, you know what I did to find you. Let's take a look. They stood, one on either side of the bed. Sherry placed a hand on Kevin's forehead and Felix placed his over hers. They closed their eyes and... *{Let's see if he left a trail.}*

It was dim, as if the lights had been turned down for the evening. That would be a sign he'd gone to bed comfortable and happy, everything at peace. There was a sense of neatness, order. He was a bit of a neat freak.

They went from room to room. He had plenty of wonderful childhood stories. They didn't stop to watch. He had a happy marriage. His two kids, a son and a daughter, were doing well. He was proud of them.

They came to a darkened room. Sherry hesitated. {{Why's it so dark?}}

They carefully stepped in. The light from their presence cast a dim glow. There in the middle of the room was a door in the ceiling going up into an attic crawl space. There was a flickering light coming from up there. {{He's up there. He's freezing cold and he's scared to death.}}

Felix nodded. {I know. Let's go slowly.}

They rose through the opening in the ceiling; Sherry first.

Kevin sat huddled in a corner, his light flickering, his cold breath throwing foggy clouds. Sherry approached first while Felix hung back, trying not to appear too threatening.

Kevin's eyes darted towards them, his terror was evident. [Who are you? Go away! Leave me alone!]

Slowly, Sherry sat down on the floor in front of him. {{It's OK, Kevin. I won't hurt you. My name is Sherry. I work for Tanya Chernov in security. Do you remember the big wedding; the captain and his lady got married and adopted his niece?}}

Kevin looked doubtful, but she could see a flicker of hope in his eyes. [I remember. That was before...] The hope began to fade.

Sherry continued, {{This is my...fiancé, Felix. He came to help.}}

Kevin's eyes darted to Felix who was just a few steps from the opening in the floor. [I remember him. He was one of the guys in that trial we had.]

Sherry smiled. {{Yes, you're right, but he's changed his ways and lives to serve the colony. We're going to be married. Do you think I'd trust him if I didn't believe he was different? Better?}}

Kevin gave that a moments thought. [I guess I can see that. Yeah.]

Felix slowly stepped forward and sat next to Sherry. {So, what happened? You've been up here for almost two days. Your family's worried about you.}

Kevin glanced at Felix. [My family's dead. They died drowning, calling my name.]

Sherry looked at Felix, sorrow written on her face. {{I'm sorry, Kevin. Can I hold your hand?}}

Kevin hesitated. Then he slowly slid his hand out for her to grasp. She took it gently and poured a bit of peace into him. {{Kevin. You hid yourself up here too soon. That was a dream. Your family didn't die. You thought they were gone, so in your grief, and terror from the falling…yes, I know about the falling. We had the same dream. Hundreds of people had the same dream, even your family.}}

Kevin seemed calmer. [They're alive? It was so real.]

Felix dared to speak again. {Yes, they're alive. What Sherry said was true. They're worried about you because you've been gone a long time.}

Sherry nodded. {They love you Kevin. They need you. Nobody drowned to death. It was all a dream.]

Kevin uncurled from his original position. [I feel so dumb. A dream? I was scared of a stupid dream?]

Felix responded. {Don't feel bad Kevin. I saw Sherry drowning and I was scared to death. It was hard, but I had to save her.}

[I should have saved them…]

{There was no need to save them. The dream ended just after you came up here. Everyone came back to their beds and woke up.}

Sherry spoke. {{Kevin. We're sorry we had to enter your place without permission, but we told Doctor Jacobs we'd go see what was wrong. Would you lead us back? Your family misses you.}}

Kevin let go of Sherry's hand and stood up. [Out? Sure, it's easy. Just go back the way you came.]

Sherry grinned. {{I'm sure you're right, but we don't want to damage anything on the way out. We were so careful coming in. Please, would you lead us out?}}

Kevin shrugged. [Sure. Why not? Let's go.]

Kevin led them to the opening and down to the floor of the room below. Sherry and Felix followed.

{{You have a wonderful place.}} Sherry ventured.

Kevin glanced at her. [You think so? Thanks. I try to keep it neat.]

They passed the collection of childhood memories. [These are all my favorites. You want to watch?]

Felix smiled and shook his head. {Thanks, but those are your private memories. Maybe you can tell us the short version sometime.}

Kevin shrugged. [OK. Here we are. That's the door. Come. I'll introduce you to my family.]

* * * *

The monitors above Kevin's bed began registering normal activity. Felix and Sherry opened their eyes and took their hands from his forehead.

Daniela stepped up to Sherry. "Are you OK?"

Sherry nodded. "Just a little weary. He thought he'd let his family drown. He went to a private little place to grieve."

Felix asked, "Is his family here? He'll be looking for them anytime now."

Daniela smiled and sent a nurse to collect them from the waiting room. "They just arrived to check up on him."

Felix breathed a sigh. "I'm glad. We told him they were here, looking for him."

Just then, Kevin's eyes popped open and he started looking around. He saw Sherry and relaxed. "See? That wasn't so bad. It was easy. Just like I told you."

Sherry gave him a beautiful smile. "Thanks Kevin. I appreciate your help."

Kevin looked over at Felix. "I think she's right. You're gonna be OK after all."

Felix flushed a little and grinned. "Thanks Kevin. That was one crazy dream. Wasn't it?"

Kevin nodded. "It sure was. Where..." Just then a woman and two teens entered the room. "Kevin. You're awake! Thank God. We've been so worried."

Felix and Sherry quietly left the room and went out into the aisle next to the examination room. They leaned against the wall and took a few deep breaths.

Wow. That was interesting. Felix commented.

Sherry nodded. *It wasn't too bad. He wanted to believe they were OK. I hope the rest go that well.*

Daniela came out of the recovery area. "Come to my office. You can sit down, get a drink of water and recover. That must take a lot out of you, Sherry."

Sherry nodded. "I had to calm him, lend him a little peace. He thought his family had drowned and he'd failed to save them."

"How long were we in there?" Felix asked.

Daniela glanced at the clock. "Oh, about twenty minutes or so. I was starting to get a little worried. Once, Sherry swayed briefly, but then she was fine."

Felix nodded. "I think her...specialty...takes a lot of energy. I feel a little tired. She was drawing on me some near the end."

* * * *

FRI 08.13.2094-Earth / TRN 18.03.6998-Aambü
ECS Destiny, Quarterdeck, Event Center Diner, 0850 Hrs / 2462 Slashes

The next two were quite similar to the first one. In both cases they were able to convince the individual the danger was past and it was all a dream.

Unfortunately, Sherry was starting to look like death warmed over and Felix wasn't far behind.

Daniela sat them down in her office and gave them another glass of water. They'd had coffee and tons of sweets. She thought they were running on sugar and caffeine alone by now. "I can't let you do the last two; not today. You're both done in. You don't know how much you've helped already."

"Dannie there are only two more." Sherry pleaded.

No, Sherry. "No, Sherry." Felix' reaction came at the very same time as Daniela's.

Sherry thought it surreal. "That was just weird."

Sherry. We can try again tomorrow, when we've gotten stronger. What'd happen if we collapsed in there? It would be bad enough to loose each other, but what about the person we're trying to save?

That brought Sherry up short. Concern for another seemed to get her attention if nothing else did. She looked from Daniela to Felix. *I'm loosing it, aren't I?*

Felix shook his head. *I think it's a part of your specialty. You seem to be driven by the need to fix others. That's a beautiful thing, but it looks like it could be a deadly thing if you don't learn to take control of it. You can't save everyone, all the time.*

Daniela was getting a little nervous. All of this silent face making was going to drive her nuts. "Um, hello? I think you should go take a nap or something. I know I'm asking a lot, but I do want you to survive this new development."

The young couple nodded in unison. Felix helped Sherry up. "Sorry, Dannie. You're right. I think she'll see it more clearly after she gets some rest. I'll call you later."

HEALER BY DEFAULT — 4

FRI 08.13.2094-Earth / TRN 18.03.6998-Aambü
ECS Destiny, Quarterdeck, Felix' cabin, 0900 Hrs / 2472 Slashes

Felix locked the entry door open; no need starting juicy gossip. He helped Sherry onto his bed and then grabbed his office chair and got settled with his feet up on his desk. He'd slept like this many times during long nights studying.

Just as he was about to nod off, there was a knock and Tolya peeked in. "Sorry to disturb you. Sometime this afternoon you're supposed to meet with your new friend. We haven't discussed what to say."

Felix shrugged. "That's OK. As long as I'm relaxing and not doing mental calisthenics, I'll be fine. I guess we should consider what to say."

Tolya smiled. "Exactly. I ah...I think we need to make sure they understand we're not here to invade or harm them. We just need some place to settle.

We're out of options and I'd like to work out some sort of sharing arrangement. Right now we won't take much space, but our species is notorious for 'being fruitful and multiplying,' to borrow an old, famous phrase."

Felix grinned at the reference to the biblical command given to Adam and Eve. Sherry was asleep, but there was a hint of a grin that crept across her face.

Felix replied. "I'm not sure how much practical negotiating we'll get done this visit. There's still some getting acquainted to do. We need advice on all this mind stuff. It looks like it can be dangerous if we don't know what we're doing."

Tolya nodded. "I understand. You've been made to jump through too many hoops so soon after coming into this new mode of yours. We need time to get used to it."

He shrugged. "If you get that far, tell him what we just talked about, our situation, our peaceful intentions, all that."

He paused. "If nothing else, try to send this message."

Felix pulled out his power-tab, palming the stylus.

Felix prompted, "Ready."

"OK. My name is Anatoli Chernov. I am the leader of this people. I wish to establish peaceful dialogue with you, and hope to establish a mutually equitable arrangement. I respectfully await your response."

Tolya made a chopping gesture. "Let's see how they respond."

He frowned a little. "You realize this really complicates our situation. We're not just dealing with how to colonize a water world, now we're dealing with whether we can colonize without destroying them. We truly have no place to go except to stay in orbit; maybe develop a ring of space habitats over the years, but that would be a really tough sell to people who had their hopes set on a new world."

He sighed and got up from the chair. "I hope and pray we can work out a mutually acceptable arrangement. Our people need some hope."

Felix got up and put a hand on Tolya's shoulder. "I think they're reasonable. We'll certainly do our best.

He considered the irony if his situation. "I know we're young and have no training about negotiations and politics, but since we don't have all that professional baggage to haul around, maybe we can present a truly sincere case that's more open and honest than things our species have done in the past."

Tolya smiled. "I like your spirit anyway. Being able to communicate is a great big plus, and I like the notion I can trust my chief negotiators."

Felix face turned serious. "Thank you for that, Tolya. You don't know how much that means to me."

Tolya turned and headed for the door. He looked at the two he'd come to like so much. "Let me know what happens."

Felix nodded. "We will."

Tolya left the room and Felix resumed his seat.

He's a really nice person. Tanya struck gold there.

Felix glanced up. *Yeah, but I think I got pretty lucky, myself.*

She sat up and patted the bed beside her. *I've known for a long time; long before this new thing we're getting into.*

Felix shrugged his shoulders and got up. He sat on the bed and leaned his back against the bulkhead. Sherry turned and lay down, placing her head on his lap for a pillow. *Isn't that more comfortable?*

Felix grinned. *Yeah. It's a good thing we're really tired.*

He spoke the words aloud for the first time. "I love you, Sherry."

Sherry looked up into his face. "I love you too, Felix. It means a lot to hear you say it out loud. Thank you."

She readjusted her head, closed her eyes and let out a deep sigh. *Now sweetheart, let's get some sleep.*

HEALER BY DEFAULT — 5

FRI 08.13.2094-Earth / TRN 17.03.6998-Aambü
ECS Destiny, In Questing Mode, 0700 Hrs / 2328 Slashes

AgradUtya was curious. He decided it would be helpful to go early to Felix Hernandez' vessel and observe. He wanted to see first hand how these people lived. It was so odd to think an entire race could live their lives out of the sea's embrace.

He quested outward. When he entered their vessel, he just flowed from one end to the other. Passing from level to level. He could see the vessel was craftily designed to resemble the warrens of a clan cave. Most levels were dedicated to living arrangements for the population.

There were a number of levels. Those closest to the outer boundaries of the vessel had functions he barely understood. Some seemed to harness massive energies bottled up in mysterious ways.

One level he saw intrigued him. On that level, almost the whole length of the vessel was dedicated to the care of plant life. The variety of plant life was amazing.

In the very core of the vessel was another place where plant life was plentiful and water everywhere. These people literally used water to decorate their home. Here was a place where his kind might maintain reasonable comfort for a short physical visit. Even the air was just moist enough; certainly it would be adequate.

All this, AgradUtya observed as through a foggy lens from the distance of his questing. He wondered what it would feel like to truly walk there and breath the air. He supposed it would not be very comfortable in other parts of the vessel. It was probably like staying too long on one of the dry, exposed tips of sea-mounts scattered across his world. Any visit here would have to be brief.

AgradUtya was most curious about the people themselves. Most of them were difficult to observe in the questing mode. They didn't have the capacity in most cases to communicate from the mind. He wondered at that; to be crippled so.

Because of this trait, they appeared almost transparent. They were best seen while moving. If they stood still, they could be lost in the background.

It intrigued him that this trait seemed to vary in intensity between individuals. So far, he'd only seen two people who were clearly visible, Felix Hernandez and his mate. He would not name her until they were formally introduced. There was another who was visible enough to see even standing still. This was another female, a very young one who seemed oddly familiar. Perhaps she might soon awaken.

After some thought, he realized this was the one who'd deliberately dived after Felix Hernandez' mate. She'd almost seen him then.

It was still a significant amount of time before he would again speak to Felix Hernandez. A light pulse of energy attracted his attention and he ascended through the levels till he was near the top of the vessel. There was a chamber here where mental energy was being put to work.

AgradUtya cautiously entered the chamber and followed his senses. He was surprised to see that the source of the energy pulses came from his new friend and his mate.

How odd. There were several subdivided chambers where some of these people reclined in postures that didn't look healthy. Felix Hernandez and his mate were standing over one of these, hands joined over the creature's head. They glowed brilliantly from the energy they were using.

A thin thread passed from the hand of each of them and entered the creature. AgradUtya summoned the extra energy resource available to him in his questing chamber and came close to have a look. He was shocked. They were attempting something normally done by a trained healer.

AgradUtya realized what was wrong with the creature. These people would have described him as unconscious. He was locked into crisis fugue that prevented him from interacting in the physical world. His friend and his mate were attempting to release him.

What to do, he pondered. They are novices. Look at the wasted energy. They'll tire themselves out in a fraction of the time even he would take, and he was no healer. It was frustrating. He was so limited by the distances involved and the fact that his physical presence was back in that chamber.

He couldn't come to their aid. He couldn't even advise them.

It dawned on him that Felix Hernandez' mate was very powerful in her gift. She was going to make a fantastic healer eventually; if, he reminded himself, she doesn't burn herself out in the first turn.

He was surprised when they succeeded and made a safe exit. It was a tricky thing to enter another's mind unbidden. The dynamic between them was very powerful. He'd been right. She drew on Felix Hernandez strength. Otherwise she would have tired more quickly. She was attempting a difficult and power sapping exercise.

They moved away from the creature. It had resumed what passed for a normal appearance amongst his kind. His friends interacted with another. This one was somewhat more visible than most. She was not likely to awaken, he surmised, but she had many of the attributes that marked her as a healer.

The human healer urged his friends out into another chamber where they sat and conversed vocally. The healer provided them with a small quantity of nourishment. His friends recovered their strength fairly quickly for newly awakened novices.

He noticed though, that they didn't reach the peek he'd seen when he first discovered them over the ailing creature.

They interacted with the healer for a time and then the three rose and returned to the chambers of the ailing. They entered a neighboring chamber where another creature suffered from the same condition.

AgradUtya considered this situation. Clearly the healer was not able to do anything for them but keep their bodies alive and nourished. Insight flashed. This was a new ailment the healer was unfamiliar with. A hunch tickled the back of his mind. He quickly explored the chambers nearby.

There had been five of these individuals with this ailment. He wondered why so many should have the same new ailment. He'd have to ask them.

AgradUtya returned to the chamber where his friends were already busy working on the second creature. The results were pleasantly the same.

They repeated the process of rest and discussion. He noticed the two were more worn this time than the last. They were pouring excess energy into their task and not allowing themselves to fully recuperate.

Oh, no, not another so soon. They trooped back to the next station and went through the process again. Again they were successful, but had grown dimmer and physically displayed extreme weariness.

Even the human healer was concerned for them. She surely could not see their mental weariness. Their physical signs must be alarming indeed.

She encouraged them to return to their meeting chamber were an animated discussion was held. He could hear the whispers of conversation between his friends, but he hesitated to listen closer. Such uninvited scrutiny would be highly impolite.

AgradUtya had the feeling his friend's mate wished to proceed yet again, but the healer and his friend were strongly opposed. Good for them.

Finally his friends agreed with the healer and wearily made their way to Felix Hernandez' sleeping chamber. All praise to the Maker! He'd feared they might try again, unsure that would have ended so happily.

AgradUtya watched them for a while. Another creature, one who seemed to command some authority, came and talked with Felix Hernandez. His friend's mate was already in slumber. The elder left the chamber and the disturbance stirred the female.

Warm whispers passed between them and Felix Hernandez joined her on the resting platform. He sat awkwardly and his mate lay down. Warmer whispers passed for a moment and then they both entered a deep restful slumber.

AgradUtya sensed his own fatigue. It would be wise to retreat and rest before they met again. He dove from the vessel, letting himself fall back to his chamber where he sought his own rest.

* * * *

FRI 08.13.2094-Earth / TRN 18.03.6998-Aambü
ECS Destiny, Quarterdeck, Felix' cabin, 1238 Hrs / 0342 Slashes

Felix woke with a start. He was sitting crossways on his bed, leaning up against the bulkhead and Sherry was asleep with her head on his lap. He remembered the events of the morning and realized he felt really good. It was 1238, lunchtime. He considered getting up and fetching something for lunch, but wound up sitting, gazing at Sherry, fingers brushing the hair sweeping across his leg.

She stirred and opened her eyes and gave a wonderful smile. *That's a great idea! I'm starved.*

Felix grinned. *I bet you are. What would you like, or would you rather come along and eat there?*

Sherry sat up. *I'd like to come along.*

Felix scooted forward and stood, reaching out to help her. *OK. We'd better be quick. It's almost time to meet Mr. A, as you so charmingly call him.*

Sherry gave him a quick little kiss on the cheek. *It's a lot easier to say than 'AgradUtya' now isn't it?*

Felix chuckled. *Yeah, I guess it is. Let's not call him that in person though. That might be rude.*

She gave him a mischievous grin and started pulling him towards the door. *OK. You're probably right. It'll be our little secret. Come on, I'm starving.*

* * * *

Lunch was quiet. People were a bit withdrawn after the dream the morning before. It took a while to realize why they got curious looks from people from time to time. He and Sherry were eating in total silence, looking up from time to time and making facial expressions consistent with earnest mealtime conversation. It probably looked strange.

He decided to vocalize for a while, but Sherry spoke up first. "You're right. We must make people nervous when we don't talk out loud." They ate ravenously.

Felix looked at the time. *We'd better hurry back. I want to call Pastor Brad before Mr. A shows up.*

Sherry grinned. *Great idea. This keeping up appearances is wearying. We need to finish what's been started.*

Felix took her hand and they strolled out of the dining commons. *I agree. We're already married in more ways than people could imagine. We should finish the process and...celebrate.*

Sherry gave him a knowing look. *The celebrating part sounds really good to me.*

Felix gave her a kiss. *Seriously, what's happened was mostly out of our control. I want to do something we choose to do, something to show we really do want this bond.*

Sherry stopped and looked into his eyes. *I couldn't agree more...I love you.*

They went back to his cabin and he put in the call to Pastor Brad while Sherry straightened up the bed.

HEALER BY DEFAULT — 6

FRI 08.13.2094-Earth / TRN 18.03.6998-Aambü
ECS Destiny, Quarterdeck, Felix' cabin, 1345 Hrs / 0433 Slashes

Jodi's face lit up when she recognized Felix. "Hi. What can I do for you?"

Felix grinned. "I was wondering if I could talk to Brad. Things have changed suddenly and Sherry and I want to marry...soon."

Jodi looked surprised. "Wow! That's sudden. Are you guys... you know..."

Felix laughed and Sherry echoed it from across the room. "No, nothing like that. Honestly. Everything is fine. There are a number of reasons for this sudden request. Can we come over and talk?"

Jodi was madly curious. "Sure. How about tonight?"

Sherry called from across the room. "Sounds great."

Felix shrugged. "As you can hear, Sherry's definitely part of this conversation..." *If you're going to talk, come over and join me in front of the pickup.* "Tonight would be fine."

Sherry came over and looked over Felix shoulder. "Hi, Jodi."

Jodi grinned. "Hi. So you guys decided to marry. That's wonderful. Brad and I've been wondering when, but we expected a little longer wait."

Sherry shrugged. "You wouldn't believe the things that have happened to us in the last couple of days. We'll tell you about it tonight. What time?"

Jodi thought for a moment. "How about 1800? You must have dinner before the serious talk."

Felix nodded. "That's fine, we'll be there. We have another appointment any minute now, so we'd better sign off. See ya' tonight."

Jodi grinned. "OK. Bye now."

The connection broke and Felix turned. He was drawn to a familiar apparition forming near the door. *Sherry...*

She turned to face the doorway. The lights were still dim from their lengthy nap.

* * * *

AgradUtya tightened the focus on his form. He hoped it was easier for them to see than last time. *Greetings, Felix Hernandez. Is this your new mate?*

Felix smiled. *You're almost correct friend. From your perspective, we're indeed mates, but we have yet to complete the appropriate ceremonies. We're arranging things now.*

AgradUtya seemed happy at the news. *You're proceeding with the mating. That is excellent.*

He waved a web hand in Sherry's direction. *Would you mind formally introducing your bond mate?*

Felix winced. *My apologies, AgradUtya. In my culture this is a lapse of polite behavior, not to introduce someone. Please meet my...bond mate and...as we would say, wife. Well, she will be my wife soon. Her name is Sherry Petrakis. Once the ceremonies have taken place she will assume part of my name. She will become Sherry Hernandez.*

AgradUtya performed a complex, formal gesture in her direction. *To save confusion, I shall address you as Sherry Hernandez. I hope you don't mind?*

Sherry was charmed. He was so clearly not human, yet he seemed almost human in his own way. *AgradUtya, I'm happy to meet you at last. I've learned about you from Felix, but it's much better making your acquaintance.*

I would be most pleased with you calling me after my bond mate. In our culture, we use the first half of our names for personal address among friends. I would consider you a friend, so please call me Sherry.

AgradUtya exuded pleasure and approval. *Felix Hernandez. You have excellent taste in your choice of mates. This one is exquisite.*

Felix grinned. *Thank you. I'd also like to extend the offer of friendship. Please feel free to call me Felix. It would please me.*

AgradUtya made a formal hand gesture. *As you wish. I am pleased to call both of you my friends.*

He assumed a serious mental posture. *However, we have much to talk about, and I regret I must begin our discussion with a mild rebuke. Please be comfortable.*

Felix and Sherry settled on the edge of the bed and waited for him to continue.

The image of their guest moved forward to rest before them as if he were physically seated. *As I said, I must begin our discussion with a mild rebuke. My concern is with the activities that occupied you earlier this turn.*

Felix and Sherry looked startled, glancing at each other. *What of this morning? I was unaware of your presence.* Felix was a little put off.

Their guest continued. *I must apologize. I was curious, so I came earlier and took a tour of your vessel. You have a very impressive arrangement here.* He almost seemed embarrassed. *I really should have let you know of my intentions.*

He paused a moment and then his 'voice' became a bit stern. *A friend is more than a pleasant person to keep company with. A friend also speaks boldly when his friends are being foolish or placing themselves in danger. I found you doing both.*

Felix and Sherry looked at one another. He could only be referring to their efforts in MedCentral.

Yes, that is my concern. First, allow me to offer compliments. Sherry. I am amazed at your heart. You are emotionally a perfect match for the role of healer amongst my people.

You give of yourself as few healers I have ever met. You'll one day become a master healer, perhaps for both our peoples; that is of course, if you don't burn yourself out before the next few turns have passed.

Felix gave Sherry an, 'I told you so' look.

She stuck her tongue out, but then blushed. *I admit my eagerness may have been excessive, but something had to be done.*

AgradUtya was touched, but he kept at it. *That's true, Sherry, but you've just barely awakened and you were attempting feats difficult for trained healers. That you were successful is a testimony to the strength you will one day have, but you have much to learn before you should fearlessly endanger yourself.*

You were able to deal with all three 'crisis fugue' victims because you had your bond mate with you. He afforded you the necessary strength to complete each attempt.

Had he not been there, you very well could have gotten lost inside the afflicted person's mind. That's such a horrible way to go mad and eventually die. Sherry's face paled, as did Felix'.

But there are two more who need help. Sherry pleaded. *I can't just ignore that.*

AgradUtya signed great sympathy. *That's the curse of your gift. You're one who finds it nearly impossible to say no to the call to heal.*

I'm aware of the last two victims. One will be much as the other three were, a little more stubborn, but you'll probably succeed. It's the second one that worries me greatly.

At this point in the relations of our two peoples, neither race knows anything useful about the other, mentally or physiologically. This burdens you with being the only person with a hope of succeeding.

AgradUtya went still, sorting options. *One problem for you, for both of you, is you're so new to your skills, you waste enormous amounts of energy doing anything. Another is, neither of you have more than the faintest of rudimentary shields. You've developed just enough shielding to create the necessary buffer between you so there is room for fleeting privacy. Even bond mates need brief moments of privacy to meditate, for personal growth.*

I believe in this environment, he indicated the space about him; *those shields are adequate, but the second victim is going to present a problem. She'll be flooding you with terror and anger as she lashes out at her perceived fate. You need those shields to protect yourselves, and those shields take energy away from what else you must do.*

Felix felt helpless. *You make it seem so hopeless. Neither of us has the slightest clue about shields, nor how to manage our energy.*

AgradUtya agreed sadly. *I know, but Sherry is right. She's particularly correct about the second and most difficult victim. That one's a different case. Rather than being closeted in a hiding place, unable to come out, she's stuck in a cycle, repeating a portion of the dream over and over. You'll have to break the cycle to bring her back.*

He emanated a sense of worry and reluctance. *Under the circumstances, we must take the risk. It's unlikely that I can help or advise you in there, but at some cost, I can supply extra energy reserves to keep you through the ordeal.*

I don't care for this situation, but we're forced by circumstances to act. It's the right thing to do, even if it is costly...So, here's what you'll do.

You will do nothing more, but wait until next turn. I'll return as we are visiting now and together, we'll go to the healing chambers where I will observe you handle the first of the two victims.

If needed, I'll lend energy so that one will not be too taxing. Afterwards, you will rest for half a turn. Then, we'll deal with the last and most difficult one.

I'll have some help from a few of my friends. Together, We'll lend a large quantity of energy to sustain you through the trial.

He looked straight at Sherry and added emphasis to the next statement. *You however, must pledge to me, that after this crisis, you'll resist any further ventures of this type of healing until we can train you in the basics.*

You're like younglings in a predator's nest. If not for the extreme circumstances, I'd forbid you making this attempt."

Sherry was fearful and looked to Felix, eyes wide. *I'm going to need your help. It's so hard to ignore it when someone's suffering.*

Felix hugged her close. *Don't worry. I have no intention of loosing you. I'll do anything it takes to keep you honest.* He kissed her forehead.

Sherry looked at AgradUtya. *I pledge to you that I'll abide by your requirements, but please help me learn what's necessary, soon.*

AgradUtya radiated pleasure and respect. *I'll do all I can to assure your success. I sense the touch of the Maker on both of you. Do not hesitate to seek his strength in this struggle. You've a similar heart, Sherry. It's not nearly as great or powerful, but He also yearns to make people whole.*

AgradUtya's image began to fade. *Until the dawn of next turn, rest. Enjoy each other's company, and appeal to the Maker for His aid. I must go and prepare my part. Until then, farewell.*

His image continued to fade as he soared through the ceiling and back towards the rings of Aambü.

RITE OF PASSAGE — 1

FRI 08.13.2094-Earth / TRN 18.03.6998-Aambü
2.75 months from orbital insertion, Aambü, Gem System
ECS Destiny, Deck 3, Hill Residence, 1753 Hrs / 0670 Slashes

Jodi answered the door. "Hey! Come on in."

Sherry gave Jodi a hug and Felix followed her in. Sherry was learning that everyone had a different signature 'sound.' Jodi's persona produced a quiet whisper. Brad came out of his study and shook Felix' hand heartily. "Hey, Felix." Brad's sound was a low driving hum.

Jodi urged them to the dining room. The heavenly smells from the kitchen were all the urging they needed. They missed a little of the usual dinnertime entertainment because little Evan had eaten early and was fast asleep in the back.

Dinnertime conversation covered all the usual topics, lingering on how things were going in their little church.

Afterward, they retired to the front room with coffee and muffins and Brad brought them around to the purpose of the evening's gathering. "So, Jodi tells me you've decided to marry and want to talk about it. The impression I got was, there were unusual circumstances involved in your decision."

He smiled. "I get a little nervous when I hear 'unusual circumstances' and 'sudden decisions to marry' in the same paragraph. Would you like to fill me in?"

Brad and Jodi were curious. Something was definitely different about their guests, besides the fact they looked incredibly tired. Brad couldn't put his finger on the problem. If he'd had to choose a word, it might have been maturity. They seemed to have matured in some way.

Felix began. "I'm sure you've heard a lot about the strange dream that afflicted most of us recently."

Brad rolled his eyes. "Afflicted is the perfect word. Jodi had it worse than I did; falling forever, then drowning in an endless ocean, but what's that got to do with you?"

Felix shrugged. "Well, you're not going to believe two-thirds of what we're about to tell you, but I ask you to try."

Sherry added. "What you're about to hear, explains that dream."

Felix nodded. "First, I should probably apologize. In a way, that dream was caused by something that interrupted a dream I was having, and everyone got sucked into it."

Brad looked perplexed. "Felix. Dreams are very strange things, but I've never heard of hundreds of people having the same one. I don't understand."

"What Felix is saying is, this dream was not a natural dream. It was caused by someone."

Sherry seemed rather emphatic. "Something happened while Felix was dreaming. He doesn't even remember what the original dream was, but the dream he was drawn into also grabbed anyone else on board who was dreaming. That something is the foundation of our sudden decision to marry. It sounds weird, but there it is."

Jodi frowned. "OK, but how can you pull other people into your own dream?"

Felix grinned. "That's the problem in a nut shell."

He looked at Brad. "I trust that everything we tell you tonight stays here."

Brad nodded. "Absolutely."

"OK..." Felix glanced at Sherry.

She prompted. *Well, you've primed the pump. You can't stop now.*

Felix nodded. "You're right, honey." He returned his attention to his pastor.

"Um, Felix. Sherry didn't say anything."

Felix flushed. "I, ah...well, we're getting to that." Sherry grinned and squeezed Felix' arm.

"To start with, you need to know a couple of things most of the rest of the population doesn't know yet. The first is, the world we're approaching, that we're putting our hopes in, has been classified as a water world. It is virtually all ocean."

Brad sat taller. Jodi looked stunned.

"How can we settle in such a place?" She asked.

Sherry replied. "Emily and team are madly studying the problem, trying to come up with solutions, while Daryl and Naomi are analyzing *Destiny* for alternative arrangements."

Felix leaned forward. "Brad. Have you ever wondered what would happen if we met another intelligent race out here?"

Brad was startled by the question. It seemed so incongruous to the conversation. "Hmm...well...it's been a while since I gave that much thought. It seems unlikely from our experience so far."

He thought for a moment. "I guess it would blow most pet theories right out of the water... no pun intended." He smiled wryly. "We have no frame of reference to help us think about the idea. From a biblical standpoint, there's basically, silence.

"The scriptures speak of a variety of what we've come to call angels; intelligent creatures God made before us. They serve Him in a variety of capacities and several classes of angel have been assigned to assist the human race in mostly non-overt ways, but I doubt they'd qualify for the scientific notion of 'ET'."

Felix nodded. "OK, but you're not ready to deny the notion out right? You're willing to entertain the possibility?"

Brad shrugged. "I've no reason to be closed minded about it. Like I said. It's not something I think about often. We've enough problems without looking for alien ones."

He looked over at Sherry. "What's this about? You didn't bring this up just for idle conversation."

Sherry smiled self-consciously, "Our new world has thrown us another curve ball. It's the second 'something' the rest of the population is unaware of. We've met an indigenous, sentient species on our target planet."

She hugged Felix close and said, "Felix and I have become mankind's very first unofficial 'xeno-ambassadors'."

Brad and Jodi were dumbfounded.

Finally, Brad found his tongue. "Felix...Sherry. I'm sorry, but that's a really big bite to chew. Are you for real? This isn't some elaborate gag?"

"This is for real." Felix responded. "I wouldn't play cruel games about things that have greatly changed our lives. It's one of the reasons we've rushed our decision to marry."

Sherry squeezed Felix' shoulder. "Felix, you need to tell them the whole story."

Sherry looked at Jodi. "You see, in one strange way, we're already married."

She saw Jodi's eyes widen, "No, not like that just yet. It's a much deeper tie than the physical. That'll be the final consummation, as it should be."

She looked at Felix. "Tell them. Start from the dream and help them understand."

Felix nodded. "Right. Let's go to the beginning."

He recounted the whole story, starting with the dream and ending with the last healing session they'd completed.

"So, we decided that since we're already bonded irreversibly up here," Felix tapped his temple, "we'd best make it official in the sight of God and our own people..."

Felix stopped and grinned at Sherry who blushed profusely, "...before we're overcome by the physical drives boiling up."

Brad raised an eyebrow. "Wow. You're seldom so...frank about personal matters."

Felix colored. "I'm not usually. We're serious. We want to start our marriage honorably before God. That's all."

Brad nodded. "I can't fault you for that. Assuming everything about this incredibly fantastic story is true, I commend you for staying conscious of the need to keep God central in all this."

Sherry brightened. "By the way. I'm not sure what he meant, but AgradUtya made comment just before he left this morning. He said he sensed the touch of 'the Maker' on both of us. He said we should appeal to Him for aid in tomorrow's trials."

Felix nodded. "He's made a couple references to someone called 'the Maker.' He said Sherry had a heart that was like 'the Maker's' heart, but not as great and powerful. He said, 'the Maker' also yearned to make people whole."

Brad looked thoughtful. "The Maker? Intriguing."

He shook his head. "We don't know enough. We don't know who or what this refers to. I'll have to reserve judgment till I can learn more. In the mean time, you can certainly appeal to your Maker. I suspect that's their way of describing prayer."

He looked at his guests. "To the immediate issue, we can have a wedding ceremony on short notice. It won't be a coronation like Tolya and Tanya, but..."

"I don't want a coronation," Sherry interjected. "As far as we're concerned our unique bonding is a form of marriage. We just want to do what's right before the Lord and our community. Nobody's going to understand our situation."

She colored slightly, "Sorry. I interrupted you."

Brad grinned. "That's OK. The bride's the boss...mostly."

"Seriously, what I was saying was, the quicker we move, the simpler we'll have to make the wedding. Exactly how fast do we need to move, realistically?"

Felix glanced over at Sherry. There was a short pause. They were just looking at one another. Yet it was more than just looking. Jodi was intrigued.

Felix nodded and returned his attention to Brad. "Sorry. We've not had time to really discuss much. Is this weekend too soon? It's Friday now."

Brad looked at Jodi.

She asked, "What about Sunday evening? That would give everyone two whole days to prepare."

Brad considered, shaking his head.

Felix remembered something. "What about rings. We don't have any and there's no time to get them made."

Brad stopped him. "Felix, wait. First, I think I know you and Sherry well enough to say you both have some strength of character. You love the Lord, and you want to do what's right. I don't think you're looking at all the angles."

Felix and Sherry looked at him. "You have a better idea?"

Brad grinned. "I think I do, but I need a few moments to discuss it with the boss." He grinned at Jodi. "If you'll excuse us, we'll have a little huddle."

Brad and Jodi stood. "Have some more coffee and muffins. Relax, chat...or...well, whatever you do. We'll be back in about five minutes. All right?"

Jodi was giving him questioning looks. Felix and Sherry were looking at each other in that odd way. Sherry spoke for both of them. "OK, Pastor. We'd appreciate any suggestions you can come up with."

Jodi followed Brad to the back rooms.

Sherry took another muffin. *What was that all about? How are we not seeing the bigger picture?*

Felix shrugged. *I don't know, but maybe he has a point. We're so emotionally tangled in this; maybe we're just not thinking clearly.*

Sherry smiled. *I just want to do things right. You heard what Pastor Brad said about marriage at Tanya's wedding. Even for us, it should be holy as well as pleasant.*

Felix gave her a hug. *I know, sweet. So do I.*

They were making headway on their second muffins when their hosts returned. Jodi had a satisfied expression on her face, and Brad looked pleased with himself.

They sat down. "OK. Here it is. You're focusing on the shortest rout to a solution before you buckle under the load of temptation. I'm certain God recognizes this new relationship of yours. He wouldn't have permitted it unless He had a reason."

Jodi poured more coffee and Brad took a sip. "First, a question. Is this communication you have dependent on line of sight, or a certain distance?"

Felix blinked. He looked at Sherry who smiled and shook her head. "No. We don't know what the range is, but we don't have to be in the same room."

Brad grinned. "I'm so glad to hear it. I think we have the perfect solution. If this whole first contact situation had never come up, and if you two had decided to marry, wouldn't you have wanted to take at least a little time to have a wonderful wedding rather than a rushed one?"

Felix and Sherry answered as one, "Of course."

That got all four of them laughing. "OK. I think we can at least extend the preparation time so it doesn't have to be a rushed thing both of you will regret later.

"We wish to offer Sherry the use of the extra bedroom for a couple of weeks. During that time, you'll be able to have normal, daily routines, see each other and all that, but during the tough times, like bed time when you're so close together, you'll have a little more distance between you. You can still communicate to your heart's content, but the temptations will be greatly minimized."

Sherry shook her head, "That would be an awful burden to put on your family. You need someplace for little Evan."

Jodi reached over and took Sherry's hand. "No, Sherry. It's OK. He spends most nights in our room anyway. These shipboard bunks weren't made for little toddlers. They're just too big for the little guy.

"Besides, I'd like to get to know you better. What would be better than to spend some time together?"

"I ah...That's so kind." Sherry finished lamely.

Felix smiled at her discomfort. *Nice save, honey. It's not bad, really. Wouldn't it be wonderful to make our wedding something you can remember fondly?*

She smiled self-consciously. *You're right.* "Thank you Jodi, Brad. I know it's a big sacrifice."

Brad grinned, "Not at all. We want to help, and we want you to have a wedding you'll want to remember. After all, it is to be a once in a lifetime thing."

He looked directly at Felix. "Another advantage is, your husband needs time to come up with a cabin built for two. If I was him, I'd be over to Tolya's place requesting a new nest."

Felix' mouth came open to protest and stopped short. "I could kick myself. I never thought of it."

Brad chuckled. "See? What are friends and pastors for? I like what Tanya always says, 'We take care of our friends.'"

"OK." Felix shook his head with a wry grin. "Thank you. You don't know how much this means."

Brad got a mildly stern look on his face. "However, just because you have this ultra super hyper bond, or whatever you call it, doesn't mean you get off without marriage counseling. I think we can do it in two sessions instead of three. The Chernovs had the adoption thing to cover while you don't. I want you both here on Tuesday and Thursday evening for dinner and counseling. Got it?"

Felix and Sherry nodded seriously. "Thank you," they chorused.

That set off another round of laughter.

They got up and hugged all around. Jodi turned to Felix. "Why don't you go with Sherry and bundle up some things for tonight? Tomorrow you can help her bring the rest she'll need"

Felix nodded. "No problem. We'll be back in, oh, a half our?"

Brad shrugged. "No matter. Just keep it quiet if you're much later. We don't want to wake Even; believe me."

They turned to go and Brad tapped Felix on the shoulder. He crooked his finger and Felix followed him a few steps away from the ladies. "Listen Felix. Don't forget about those rings. I know you mentioned it earlier, but there seem to be a lot changes going on right now."

He grinned at Felix face. "I'd forgotten all about it. Thanks."

Brad smiled. "Talk to Samuel Perlman; the sooner the better. You better talk to Tolya first. You'll need his authorization to order the materials."

Felix grinned, "Good point."

"OK." Brad steered Felix back to Sherry's side. "You should get going. See you in a little while."

They hugged around again.

I heard that little 'secret' conversation Pastor Brad had with you. I do want three rings, one for you, and two for me. Got it mister?

Sherry grinned and hugged his' arm as they walked.

What kind of rings would you like?

Sherry pondered while the lift took its time arriving. *I don't know. Why don't you surprise me?*

Felix laughed out loud. He looked around to see who might have seen the crazy guy laugh at nothing. *Me, surprise you? You're kidding, right? I've almost given up on keeping secrets from you.*

They boarded the lift. *Seriously, I don't want to keep secrets from you. I love you and I trust you. Why would I want to keep secrets?*

Sherry hugged him harder. *The same goes for me, as I'm sure you already know, but sometimes, temporary secrets are useful to spice things up. We should ask Mr. 'A' about that. Occasional privacy's not a bad thing, you know.*

The lift opened on Quarterdeck and they headed for Sherry's cabin. The work of gathering clothes for the evening and tomorrow was simple enough. The few ladies specialty items, he left for her.

Back at the Hill residence Felix said his goodbyes. *I'll be back for you in the morning just after dawn. I may have to have a chat with Mr. 'A' before I come. I'll tell you what's going on when I know.* They kissed goodnight and Felix hurried back to his cabin. He was very tired after such a crazy day.

RITE OF PASSAGE — 2

FRI 08.13.2094-Earth / TRN 18.03.6998-Aambü
ECS Destiny, Quarterdeck, Felix' Cabin, 2000 Hrs / 0900 Slashes

Felix arrived at his cabin to find Tolya just leaving. "Hey. There you are. I just stopped by to see that everything was OK. I hear today was pretty rough."

Felix waved his door open. He went inside and sat on the edge of his bed waving towards his office chair. "Have a seat. We're fine, but thanks for checking. Tomorrow's going to be crazy...Do you have any idea the correlation between ships time and dawn on that planet?"

Tolya shook his head. "Wow. Dawn? Dawn where? Dawn's a relative thing. It depends on were you are on the planet. Why?"

Felix sighed. "Of course, I knew that...I'm supposed to meet our new friend at 'the dawn of next turn.' That would be dawn, as he knows it at home, I guess. Aambü's a bit larger than Earth. So their day must be a different length."

Tolya frowned. "You're right. The problem is, we don't even know where your friend lives."

Felix winced. "Well, I hope he'll try waking me. I don't know if he can from that distance. Well, it'll be interesting."

He looked up. "Speaking of interesting. I have a couple of requests. You know about our unique relationship, right?"

Tolya nodded. "You tried to explain that. Have you talked with Pastor Brad?"

Felix smiled. "Yes. The result is, Sherry's spending the next two weeks with the Hills. We'll be formally married then."

Tolya smiled. "Congratulations, Felix. You're great together. I'd never have said that a few months ago, but I'm happy for you."

He grinned. "Which leads to your requests?"

Felix grinned. "Yeah. Pastor Brad reminded me we're going to need larger accommodations like what Daryl and Naomi are in."

Tolya nodded. "I'll put in the order tonight. Next?"

"I ah...I'm going to need a little gold for Sam Perlman to make some rings for us."

Tolya smiled. "Of course. Why didn't I think of that? I'll leave a note for Sam tomorrow authorizing him to requisition what he needs. Call him and arrange for a sitting."

Felix was pleased. "Thanks Tolya. You're too kind, you know that don't you?"

Tolya gave one of his famous lopsided grins. "I've been told."

Felix got serious. "Tolya, tomorrow, we're going to finish what we started today in MedCentral. Mr. 'A' told us the last one's going to be extremely dangerous, especially for Sherry, but he agrees there's no other way. He's promised to lend energy for both attempts. He intends to have a team reinforce his efforts for the last and most difficult patient."

He gave a worried look. "I'm just a little worried for Sherry...and myself, to be honest. Mr. 'A' instructed us to include appealing to 'the Maker' for His aid. Until Pastor Brad tells me different, I'm going to assume he's referring to the same God we have. The way he talks makes me think I'm right."

Tolya was equally serious. "I know Tanya will be unhappy with Sherry putting herself in more danger. You should have seen her when she found out what you guys did today. She was proud as punch, but I think she paced a hole in the deck plates of her office.

He smiled reassuringly. "I do want to hear from you when it's over. Understood?"

Felix nodded. "Certainly. I hate to seem rude, but I'm going to hit the sack. Thanks again."

Tolya nodded and clapped Felix' shoulder. "Sleep well."

RITE OF PASSAGE — 3

SAT 08.14.2094-Earth / TRN 18.03.6998-Aambü
Ruling Clan Caverns, Questing Chamber, 0820 Hrs / 1828 Slashes

AgradUtya entered the questing chamber and tested the waters. They'd been heated to his specifications. This turn would be very trying indeed.

He decided to handle this initial rescue himself. Later, the real test would come. This would be Sherry's rite of passage as a healer. She had no idea. It seemed a kindness not to add to her pressure the knowledge she would soon be evaluated in this final event.

The council had been surprised and pleased at the speed with which Felix' new mate was growing into her gift, though she had far to go. Given her alien origin, there was some concern she'd harm herself irreversibly. So far, she'd proven surprisingly resilient.

AgradUtya stepped into the water and dove to the deeper half of the pool. He surfaced, took a deep cleansing breath, uttered a word of praise to the Maker and then submerged himself, curling into a water sleep posture. A set of gills between his ribs would extract the life gasses his body needed until he ended his questing.

He quested outward, soaring to the ever growing light that was a vessel filled with a species from beyond the stars. He knew exactly where to go now. Quickly he began focusing on his likeness.

Felix was still in slumber. AgradUtya waited for a time and decided he had best act. He came forward and placed a web hand near Felix' head. *{Felix Hernandez. It is time to wake.}*

* * * *

Felix' eyes snapped open. In the darkened room he saw the web hand hovering over his face. He glanced to his right and saw the face of his new friend. The projection was much sharper this time. It wasn't quite solid, but definitely a clearer view.

The web hand retreated. Felix sat up and brushed a hand through his hair.

AgradUtya regarded him. *Awake at last.*

Felix nodded. *Yes, I'm awake. Our days...turns... differ significantly from yours. Since we didn't know when dawn would be in your part of the world, we were unable to calculate when that time would match our own.*

AgradUtya made a small gesture. *It is of no importance. You are...awake... We will explore the diverse aspects of culture at a less pressing time.*

AgradUtya glanced about. *I don't see Sherry. Where is she?*

Felix grinned. *From your point of view, Sherry and I are bonded. My culture requires proper ceremonies and blessings from our God, our Maker. This was thought to be an event far enough in the future and not of immediate concern. Since we've bonded, we've initiated preparations for our own ceremonies. Before that's accomplished we may not physically consummate our bonding.*

Sherry shares temporary sleeping chambers with our spiritual leader and his mate to minimize temptation. Our spiritual leader teaches about our Maker and helps us to remain true to Him.

AgradUtya was fascinated by the differences in their relationship to the Maker. *We're taught that the Maker is one. There is no other but Him. We have obscure teachings that suggest He has other children we don't know who are far away. This would be an interesting discussion, but it must wait for another time. Please tell Sherry we must meet.*

Felix stood up. *We arranged to meet after waking. You may come with me, or, since you've become familiar with the ship's layout, you're welcome to go directly to her. I must take physical conveyance to travel from deck to deck.*

AgradUtya acknowledged the choices. *I shall precede you then. Your physical movement would be slow for me.*

He faded and flowed out through the wall. *Sherry, wake up. Mr. 'A' is coming. I'll be there in a few minutes.*

Sherry was half awake. Felix finished the process.

The familiar glittering cloud appeared and quickly took shape. *AgradUtya. Welcome.*

AgradUtya regarded her. *I'm pleased to see you're awake. Your life mate comes by more conventional means.*

Sherry grinned. *Yes, he told me. It must be interesting to pass through solid objects and go wherever you wish.*

AgradUtya signed amusement. *I suppose, to a novice, this method of travel would have a certain charm. However, once it is a familiar thing it is no more charming than walking down one of your passages might be.*

* * * *

Felix entered at Brad's invitation. "Our guest is chatting with Sherry right now. I don't know if you can see him or not. You're welcome to come and...Uh...just a minute." *Sherry, I'm bringing Pastor Brad in.*

Sherry grinned. *That's fine. You know I'm dressed.*

Felix blushed. *Yes, of course.*

He turned to Brad. "OK. Let's go."

Sherry released the lock and it snapped open. She was standing near her bed, facing to one side. Brad looked in and stood stock-still. He saw what looked like a faint glittery cloud of light hovering near Sherry. There was definitely something in the room. He just couldn't see it very clearly.

Felix crossed the room and made a small hand gesture. *I brought our spiritual leader. He bears the title 'Pastor.'*

AgradUtya turned to include Felix and the other human in his field of view. This human was slightly more visible than most. This one might barely discern his presence.

Tell him I am honored to meet him. Also convey my apologies that I cannot communicate directly.

Felix turned. "His name is AgradUtya. He says he's honored to meet you and apologizes that he can't speak to you directly."

Felix added. "His physical body is located somewhere on the planet. I don't know how it works, but it must be similar to how we might move about in a dream."

Brad smiled in spite of himself. He was meeting an alien species and he was just fine with it. "Please tell...Agrad...Utya?"

Felix nodded.

"Tell him I'm pleased to meet him as well. I'm not offended at his inability to communicate directly. Maybe in time we can meet face to face."

Felix relayed the message. AgradUtya was pleased. This human was polite. He sensed no fear in him. *Please inform your...'pastor' that we are preparing for the recovery of the final two afflicted humans in the healing place.*

Felix turned to Brad. "I told you of the five people trapped in their minds and unable to wake from the dream?"

Brad nodded.

"Yesterday, Sherry and I were able to successfully release three of them. They woke and will be released from MedCentral today. If you noticed how tired we were last night, that's why. The process is very taxing and consumes a lot of energy."

Brad thought Felix seemed a little nervous.

Felix continued. "We're preparing to attempt the release of the last two. AgradUtya says these two are going to be more difficult with the last one being especially trying. We'd appreciate your prayers for successful completion. These rescues have been exceptionally hard on Sherry. This last one, so I'm told, may be dangerous for her...and me I guess."

Brad was very concerned. "If it's so dangerous, why take it on by yourselves? Why can't your new friend help?"

Sherry replied. "He will be helping today. The problem is, he's not here physically. He's projecting himself here from the planet and we're not even in orbit yet.

"I'm learning that the things we can do pull energy from our bodies. He's using a tremendous amount of energy just to be here. Besides, we have to physically touch the patient to gain access.

AgradUtya was listening through Felix' link. *Your mate is very astute. Her intuition will serve her well. Tell your friend that I confirm her assessment. I have taken steps at home to supply reserve energy that I can tap from. I'll be lending as much energy as I can spare to the struggle.*

Felix passed it on and Sherry colored at the praise.

Brad nodded. "I think I understand. I'm still concerned about the danger. We're on the edge of delving the border between mind and spirit, so I suspect we don't know the perils by half."

Felix got that detached look again and then refocused. "AgradUtya appreciates your concern. He's impressed with your insight. He means no disrespect, but we must prepare."

Brad smiled. "I understand."

He turned to leave the room. "Jodi and I will be praying. I assume you've told Tolya and Tanya?"

Sherry nodded.

"Good. God grant you success." He stepped back and the door snapped shut.

Now, let me give you some instruction on conserving your energy. Your display of last turn was dazzling for its wastefulness...

RITE OF PASSAGE — 4

SAT 08.14.2094-Earth / TRN 18.03.6998-Aambü
ECS Destiny, Quarterdeck, MedCentral, 0900 Hrs / 1870 Slashes

Felix and Sherry stood in the lobby area near Daniela's office. "Well, if you're ready, we'd better get started. You said your friend would be here to assist?"

Sherry nodded. "He's here right now, but it's not a physical presence. That's not possible at these distances. When we get in the dimmer light of the recovery area you may be able to barely discern his presence. Pastor Brad was able to see a vague luminescent cloud in my room this morning. My lights were dimmed at the time."

Daniela looked skeptical. "I can't deny the results of whatever you did yesterday, so I guess I'll just have to accept it for now."

She saw Sherry's look and smiled. Putting her hand on Sherry's shoulder she said, "I'm sorry Sherry. I didn't mean an insult. This whole thing is turning many assumptions on their heads. Don't worry, I'll get there."

Sherry smiled and gave Daniela a sisterly hug.

"Well, let's get cracking." Daniela led the way to the first patient. Felix and Sherry assumed their positions at either side of the bed. The dim light was comforting. Daniela was about to give them information about the patient when she saw a stream of glittering light enter through the curtain wall and coalesce at the foot of the bed. It was faint, but visible, a vague column of glowing cloud.

She looked over at Sherry who grinned. Felix smiled as well. *AgradUtya, I'd like to introduce our ship's doctor. You would probably say, our chief healer. Her name is Daniela Jacobs.*

AgradUtya made a gesture of respect, which Daniela could not have seen. *Tell her I'm honored. Her vocation is highly respected among our people.*

Felix relayed the comment.

Daniela stood staring for a moment. "Uh...sorry. Tell him I'm pleased to meet him. I'm grateful for his assistance."

AgradUtya projected mild humor as well as respect. *I offer assistance freely. My hope is to develop friendly relations with your people. I cannot allow my new friends to come to harm for my inadvertent triggering of the dream you all experienced. Why should I not help?*

"He...?" Daniella stammered.

Felix nodded. "When he mistook me for a youngling out in the path of a dangerous storm he sent a warning call. It triggered my awakening while in my dream. That pulled everyone else who was dreaming into the same dream world."

Daniela shook her head. "I think I'm getting a headache. My gratitude remains."

Sherry smiled. "Shouldn't we get started?"

Daniela nodded. "Of course. This is Leena Sullivan. She lives on Deck 1. Her husband found her unconscious. "While we were examining her we found what we're pretty sure is a cancerous tumor on her left lung. I've postponed dealing with it till we deal with this post dream syndrome thing."

She grinned. "That's what one of my staff's been calling it. It's not bad, really."

Sherry grinned. "It's kind of catchy."

Felix chuckled. *Let's get to it.* "Dannie, we're going to begin the procedure. I don't know how long it'll take. AgradUtya seemed to think this one would be a bit more difficult than the last three."

Daniela got a worried look. "Are you sure you're going to be OK? I saw how wiped out you two were yesterday."

Sherry shook her head and gestured in the direction of the thin glowing cloud at the end of the bed. "Don't worry Dannie. He's lending support today."

She placed a slim hand on Leena's forehead and Felix placed his gently over hers.

* * * *

ECS Destiny, Quarterdeck, MedCentral, 0930 Hrs / 1916 Slashes

As with the previous three, Leena's place was dimly lit, as if darkened for the night. They moved quietly through the main room. A picture of her husband and a small child hung on the wall. They were in a park, back on Earth. He was pushing her on a swing.

There were other photos of the child on end tables and mantle. There was a sense of sadness about the quantity of them. Sherry got the sense this woman's place was becoming a shrine to the little girl. There were two pictures of the couple hidden amongst the other photos.

They passed various rooms. It seemed impolite to investigate them. They checked for Leena's presence and moved on. They searched everywhere, becoming worried that maybe Leena was no longer present.

{This doesn't look good.} Felix remarked.

Sherry shrugged. {I know, but I think we missed something obvious.}

They'd glanced into the kitchen and then moved on. As they passed by again Sherry decided to look in.

Leena's place was a small country house in the foothills of a mountain range. The kitchen windows looked out on the backyard. The sky was dark, but the yard was dimly lit by a single lamp high above the door leading from the kitchen onto the back porch.

Sherry ventured out and Felix followed. The porch light was not adequate to reveal the whole yard. A waning moon was reflected off a body of water out in the yard.

Felix moved to the railing around the perimeter of the porch. {If I don't miss my bet, that's a swimming pool.}

Sherry joined him. {You're right...Listen. Do you hear something?}

Felix listened carefully. {Yes, I think...}

Sherry became agitated. {Honey, it's crying. No, weeping.}

She hurried to a set of steps down to the yard.

Felix followed. {Wait Sherry. Be careful.}

She slowed, but not by much. They reached the pool, as it proved to be. It was beautiful. Even in the dark it looked like an elegant piece of work.

Sherry followed the sound. She circled around the far side of the pool, Felix hurrying to keep up. There, in the darkest corner, was a woman in her mid thirties. She was kneeling on the deck at the edge of the pool rocking back and forth and weeping in deepest agony.

Felix had an idea. {We need a little light.}

In his hurry he'd almost tripped over the base of a torch style lamp. He moved back and examined it. It was a decorative patio torch with a container of oil with a wick poking out of it. {If this is like a dream, maybe I can get this to light.}

He thought for a moment. He imagined his finger was a lighter. All he needed was a small flame to light the wick. He focused on lighting a flame on the tip of his finger.

He was about to abandon the plan as preposterous when a sudden sensation of warmth welled up and a small flame flashed into being. He touched it to the wick and immediately the flame left his finger and caught in the wick. The torch soon lent a bit of visibility to the scene.

Sherry approached the woman with the broken heart. {Leena?}

{{Go away! Can't you see this is a private place?}} She shuffled away from Sherry, still weeping.

Felix approached carefully. (We need her to accept our presence.)

Sherry nodded. She moved around so she was facing the woman from the other side. {Leena, we're here to help. Dr. Jacobs is worried about you.}

{{I don't deserve anyone's worry.}}

Sherry looked up at Felix, deep sorrow glinted off her eyes in the torchlight. {What do you mean? Everyone needs the concern of others.}

The tortured woman looked up at Sherry. {{Who are you to doubt me in my own home? You don't even know me.}}

Sherry knelt down on the deck. {You're right. I don't know you, but I still care. My name is Sherry. I work for Tanya Chernov. You remember the big wedding? I was the maid of honor.}

Leena looked at her. {{I...remember. You're... Why are you here? H-how did you get here?}}

Sherry smiled. {How I got here is quite complicated. Why I'm here is much easier.}

Felix moved around so he wouldn't be behind the woman where he might make her nervous.

Leena looked. {{Who's he? Can't I have any privacy?}}

Sherry held out a hand. {Leena, this is my fiancé, Felix. He came along to help.}

{{You think I need help? Can't a woman grieve in peace?}}

Sherry kept her hand out. {Many people think you need some help. You've been gone nearly three days.}

Leena broke down and began crying again. {{I got what I deserved. I know how she felt now.}}

Felix suddenly knew what this was all about; the pool, the little girl in all those pictures, the reference to knowing how someone felt. It painted a sad picture.

Sherry tried again. {Leena, your husband's the most worried. He told Dr. Jacobs you were gone.}

Leena wiped her eyes of the tears still streaming down her face. {{Jimmy doesn't know it was my fault. He'd be so devastated. I can't loose him too.}}

Sherry moved closer and placed her hand on the woman's shoulder. Leena clung to Sherry in a crushing hug. {{I can't stand this.}}

Sherry poured a liberal flow of peace into the distraught woman. Felix could feel the flow of energy and pressed hard in support.

Sherry returned the hug. {Tell me about it? It helps to tell it. I'm a good listener.}

Leena seemed calmer. She dried here eyes and sat back, her feet curled under her to one side. Sherry followed suit as Felix joined the circle.

{{It was before we signed up with the Foundation. My husband and I had this beautiful little place and a beautiful little girl. She was the jewel of our lives. Jimmy went down to the village for supplies for the picnic we were planning the next day. I sat next to the pool and watched little Jenny playing in the water.}}

Tears started running down Leena's face again and Sherry reached out and took one of her hands. {It's OK. Let it out.} She added another portion of peace.

Leena continued. {{I wasn't expecting any calls, so I didn't bring the remote COMM out to the deck. I was always forgetting and leaving it outside...The COMM chimed and I was going to ignore it, but it was very insistent. Jenny was having so much fun, I didn't want to interrupt her...I should have ignored it, but like a fool, I hurried in to answer. I was going to tell them I'd call back.}}

She gripped Sherry's hand and another gush of anguish flooded down her face. {{They'd given up. The line was dead. I turned to go back and it sounded again. I answered. It was a sales call. I told them 'no' and they persisted. I heard a shriek and little Jenny's voice crying 'Mommy!'

I thought she was just playing, but I told them I wasn't interested and they'd better remove me from their list. I started back to the kitchen and realized it was way too quiet. I ran like the wind out the kitchen door and tripped, falling down the steps. It hurt like heck, but I got up and ran.}}

Her shoulders shook with the weeping that ensued and Sherry added more peace. Felix was feeling a little shaky when a sudden influx of energy seemed to flow through him like a warm river.

Sherry looked up at Felix, glowing with gratitude.

Leena gathered herself. {{She was out in the middle of the deep end; face down. She wasn't moving. I dove in and grabbed her and dragged her to the edge of the pool. I pressed the water out and began CPR.}}

She looked at Felix. Lips quivering. {{Jimmy said, when he got home he had to stop me. I must've been working on her for twenty minutes. I...I lied to my Jimmy. I said I didn't know Jenny had gotten into the pool...I couldn't tell him it was my fault.}}

She turned her gaze back to Sherry. {{But Jenny's been avenged in a small way. I got to find out what she must have felt like when she was drowning and nobody, not even her mommy would come to save her. That dream...that horrible, horrible dream...was one way for Jenny to tell me how bad it was.}}

Sherry looked at Felix. Tears were streaming down her own face. He put one arm around her and one around the profoundly grieving woman..

Felix ventured a comment. (Leena. There was no connection between your loss and the horrid dream you had. That dream was repeated in hundreds of people all over the ship. Sherry and I had much more vivid versions of it. It's a terrible shame it awakened your grief.)

He looked into Leena's eyes. (I don't believe for a minute your husband, Jimmy, will stop loving you because of a horrible mistake you've paid for daily ever since. If there were a way I could bring Jenny back, I'd do it in a flash, but God has her now. She's much better off in His hands than anything even you and Jimmy could provide. All you'll do, by blaming yourself to your grave, is hurt Jimmy more.)

Sherry added a pinch of hope to the flow.

Felix broke the circle and took Leena's free hand. (I can't help but think Jimmy figured out what really happened. I think he just wants to have his lover and friend, his wife and confidant back. With every day you hold onto the lie, and every day you beat yourself up again, you prolong his agony at having lost two people he loved. Jimmy needs you and you need him. We're out here to create a new start. So, we need to leave the old things behind.)

Felix looked at Sherry. Sherry took over. {Leena, please forgive yourself and come back to your man. I know he's worried about you. Everyone else is worried too. You need to give all this misery to God and let Him heal you. Make Him your source of peace and who knows? Perhaps in another time and place you'll get to see Jenny again and tell her you love her.}

Leena sat for a moment, considering. She stood and they followed suit. {{Thank you. I miss Jenny so much.}}

She wiped the tears from her face. {{You're right. I've been so unfair to Jimmy. I want to talk to him. I want to tell him everything. I want to beg his forgiveness and feel good in his arms again.}}

Felix hugged Leena and then took Sherry's hand. (Why not come with us and tell Dr. Jacobs you're OK? The dream's over. It's time to wake up.)

They turned to retrace steps back to the house. Sherry stopped them and approached Leena. {Leena? Forgive me. I need to check on something. It's not personal. Think of me like a nurse or a doctor. I'm going to touch you as a doctor would. Do you understand?}

Leena hesitated and then nodded. Sherry gently placed her left hand flat against Leena's chest, between her breasts. She pressed firmly and got a far away look on her face.

* * * *

ECS Destiny, Quarterdeck, MedCentral, 1015 Hrs / 1966 Slashes

Daniela was getting a little worried. This was taking much longer then the last three had. The monitors for Leena were steady and unchanging. The only sign that anything was going on was that there were tears coursing down both Leena's and Sherry's faces. Now, just as she considered trying to get Sherry's attention, two things happened. First, there was a subtly brighter pulse of light in the cloudy form at the foot of the bed. Sherry and Felix seemed to firm up their sagging posture as if they were getting a second wind. Second, Leena's monitors suddenly registered new activity. Brain wave activity was ramping back up to normal.

Sherry adjusted her stance. Leaving her right hand on Leena's forehead, she placed her left hand gently on Leena's chest right between her breasts. After a few moments Felix right hand came over and covered Sherry's. The monitors started showing a wide range of changes.

* * * *

Felix knew what Sherry was after and felt certain he needed to help. He placed his right hand over her left, careful to only touch her hand. (Easy, Leena. I'm only helping Sherry. We won't hurt you.)

He saw the spot that Sherry pointed out. A dark, nasty lump grew even as he watched. {What should we do?}

Sherry smiled. {We're going to get that thing out of there. I have the empathy. I have a limited amount of healing ability. I sense something very special in you that you haven't had a chance to explore. We're going to put our gifts together and heal Leena right here and now.}

Felix ventured. {We should really be praying right about now, don't you think?}

Sherry smiled. {Oh, yeah. You got that right.} They prayed for strength and skill.

A peculiar feeling began in Felix' right arm. It reminded him of the sensation he'd experienced when he'd somehow gotten the monitor leads to fall off his body. His hand seemed to pass through hers and into Leena's chest. He touched the nasty mass, grasping it with thumb and forefinger. The tingling sensation intensified and he concentrated on making it go away. He could see the base of the mass slowly separate from the rest of the good tissue, little by little. It came off in his hand and he watched in fascination as Sherry poured energy into the good tissue, accelerating the healing and growth of replacement tissue. In moments, the only evidence of the event was the lighter color of newly grown cells.

They retreated, taking their hands from her chest.

Sherry smiled. {It's as I thought. There was a little problem, but it's all better now. I want you to have a long happy life with Jimmy. Let's tell Dr. Jacobs you're OK.}

Leena smiled and led them through the house. The lights were brightening as life returned for another day. They stepped out on the front porch and...

* * * *

ECS Destiny, Quarterdeck, MedCentral, 1045 Hrs / 2000 Slashes

Sherry and Felix inhaled deeply and removed their hands from Leena's chest. Moments later they opened their eyes and removed their hands from her forehead. Felix' right hand looked bloody.

"Dannie, do you have a place for this?" He opened his hand and presented her with the tumor.

Daniela stood numbly and then signaled the nurse to handle it. The nurse pulled a small jar from a cupboard and held it out to Felix. He dropped the offending chunk inside and looked around. "I wouldn't mind washing up."

Daniela was catching up. "Of course. Right across the hall in O/R there's a washing station."

Felix smiled and headed that way.

He and Sherry were feeling utterly exhausted, but they also felt very good. They'd done well.

"Doctor, she's coming to." Daniela whirled to look at Leena. Leena's eyes opened, noted the doctor and moved on. Her gaze locked on Sherry.

"Sherry! I'm in the clinic?" She seemed confused.

Sherry nodded. "Yes, you've been out for almost three days. When Jimmy found you after the dream was over, he couldn't wake you, so he brought you here for help."

"Jimmy. Where is he?"

Daniela approached the bed as Sherry moved aside. "Your husband's on the way. He went for a bite to eat. He's been sitting in the waiting room for almost the whole time you've been here. I had to shoo him out to get sleep or food. I'm so glad you're awake. He needs taking care of." Daniela grinned.

Leena smiled and looked at Sherry. "Thank you. I'll always remember your gentle help."

She looked at the doctor. "Did you know? When they were visiting, they checked on my chest. They said they wanted to check on something. I guess thing's are OK."

Daniela smiled tentatively. "Yes, I think you're right." She glanced at the jar with the tumor in it. "You'll be...just fine."

Felix returned and took Sherry by the arm. AgradUtya had quietly left the room. They waved at the doctor. "We're going to take a nap. I'll call you when we're ready for the last one."

Daniela nodded and they left MedCentral.

* * * *

ECS Destiny, Quarterdeck, Felix' Cabin, 1100 Hrs / 2016 Slashes

AgradUtya was waiting in Felix' cabin. *I'm glad you're back. I want to lend a small amount of energy. Then I want you both to get some sleep. I'll come back for you after I take some rest.*

He motioned them closer and held a web hand over each of their faces. *When I've finished, I'll leave rather abruptly. Do not fear. I must conserve energy.*

The light of his image grew almost painfully bright. A surge of energy pulsed through them and then he vanished.

Let's get something to eat. Felix prompted.

Sherry grinned. *You read my mind.*

She leaned into Felix and they hugged earnestly and long. After a time they left his cabin and headed for the diner.

* * * *

AgradUtya opened his eyes and flexed his muscles, stretching them, awakening them. He moved to the edge of the questing chamber pool and climbed out.

Two anupadin (his current assistants) rested in the moist sands. *Thank you for your vigilance. This one was more demanding, but they performed very well.*

AgraAnupadin expressed relief and satisfaction. *You were out for an unusually long time. We became concerned.*

AgradUtya signed his gratitude. *Yes, this rescue was very demanding. I am impressed with this couple. The male is surprisingly strong for one newly awakened. His mate is not quite as strong, but still, stronger than expected. It appears she'll become one of the more powerful healers we've seen in at least two generations.*

ApraAnupadin inquired. *AgradUtya, a question. Who are these foreigners? Where do they come from? What does this mean?*

AgradUtya allowed humor to color his response. *So many questions. One at a time allows for easier responding.*

ApraAnupadin's arm fins drooped. *I sound like a youth. Forgive my impatience.*

AgradUtya kept the humor in his tone. *No harm done; this is a unique episode in our history. I cannot fully answer your questions yet. The difficulties I've caused them have been very time consuming to correct. I can tell you, they're a race from beyond the stars we see. Imagine, if you can, a world where the people live on islands so large you cannot see the opposite shore.*

The two questers expressed awe mixed with doubt.

AgradUtya explained. I *wouldn't have believed it had I not witnessed these people unable to breath in water. They must surface regularly to breath, else they would die. That's why dreams of falling into the ocean brought such terror for them.*

AgradUtya finished his thought. *Once the final individual has been returned to a normal condition, we'll have time to properly discuss the details. Then, maybe we'll know what this means.*

AgradUtya started for the passage marked by an opening in the living stone. *Please, have two more questers ready in two slashes. The final effort will be very difficult on these two. It will tax all of us to keep them safe.*

* * * *

SAT 08.14.2094-Earth / TRN 18.03.6998 - Aambü
Ruling Clan Caverns, Council Chamber 1230 Hrs / 2133 Slashes

AgradUtya had the floor. *These two are going to be very powerful. Together, they've handled the healing of mind fugue. This is shocking given they're so recently awakened.*

There was some agitation amongst the council members. The rapid development of power witnessed in the two alien people was amazing. It was also mildly disturbing.

The questions were many. Who were these people? Where did they come from? Why were they here? More important was the question, 'What plans did they have for dealing with the Aambüka, the Water People?'

Factions were developing. Some were willing to welcome these strangers with open arms. Some felt a little more cautious. All the questions and concerns should be answered satisfactorily. Then decide what to do. Still others wanted to forbid contact. Maybe, if the people stayed out of sight long enough, the interlopers would go away.

It had been a very long time since one single event had generated so much angst among the Water People. This one was unprecedented in all the histories. No one knew what to make of people from another world entirely. They were still coming to grips with the notion of another world but Aambü.

AgraVadin Adhiraj assumed the floor. *I believe all agree there are pressing questions that need asking. We must face the reality that these people are approaching and we cannot change that without becoming what some of you fear they might be. I'll not countenance overt hostility towards strangers who have, as yet, made no threats.*

There was a strong sense of approval from the council. The few dissenters relaxed their postures of challenge. The First Speaker had spoken. They would watch and wait.

AgraVadin Adhiraj addressed AgradUtya. *We will lend all the power and support you and your friends require to finish dealing with their crisis. Once the immediate crisis is resolved, we need those answers. All the concerns of the people need to be addressed along with any others you may think to add.*

AgradUtya gestured gratitude and acceptance. *First Speaker again honors me with the continuation of this task. I shall do my best to obtain clear answers.*

* * * *

SAT 08.14.2094-Earth / TRN 18.03.6998 - Aambü
ECS Destiny, Quarterdeck, MedCentral, 1356 Hrs / 2246 Slashes

Felix woke with a start. He was half sitting, half reclining on the end of a sofa in the Officer's Lounge. Sherry was resting against the hollow of his side, legs tucked behind her on the sofa. She sat up part way. *It's OK, Felix.*

Few people were in the lounge. Most were in the diner finishing lunch. The lights were dim and the curtain was still drawn revealing the glorious star spangled depths.

They'd snuggled on the couch, unable to sleep. Finally, while trying to see the world that held so much dread and promise, they'd nodded off.

Sherry snuggled back into the hollow of his side and Felix held her gently. He felt good. *How long have we slept?*

Sherry was simply enjoying the quality time with him. *We've been out for almost three hours. That last episode with Leena was really draining.*

Now she felt ready to take on the world.

Felix temporized her growing enthusiasm. *I wish I knew what it is about this last one that worries Mr. 'A' so much.*

Sherry gave a one-shoulder shrug. *He said Leena would be more difficult, too. She had a bit more of a complicated tangle, but it didn't seem as difficult as all that.*

Felix tilted her head up enough to kiss her forehead. *It might not have been harder to solve, but it was much more draining on your empathic abilities, a lot more than any of the others.*

She looked into his eyes. *I guess you're right. I get so involved with the patient that I forget to pay attention to what it's doing to me.*

Felix smiled and kissed her upturned lips. *That's why we're doing this together. Let's eat and go see Daniela.*

* * * *

They finished eating. They were alert, well fed and full of confidence. As they were prepared to get up from the table, the now familiar glow of AgradUtya coalesced before them. The room was still dimmed for the star field dominating the room.

Two or three diners stopped in mid bite, trying to decide if they'd really seen a glittering glow form near the table across the way. The odd young couple there seemed aware of something.

Felix and Sherry. I found you. You both seem refreshed from your rest. Do you feel ready for the final struggle?

Felix grinned; *we're feeling well indeed.*

Sherry also smiled at the apparition of their guest. *I'm eager to get to work on the last challenge.*

AgradUtya waved his arms in a pattern that accompanied a sense of satisfaction. *I am pleased to see you recovered. I propose we meet again in the healing chambers. I remind you, the others were truly easy compared with this last one.*

Felix stood projecting respect and acceptance. *Thank you for your concern. We'll meet you in the healing chamber.*

AgradUtya allowed his likeness to fade and moved on. As Felix and Sherry headed for MedCentral, the curious diners continued their meal, recalling the oddly glowing form fading from sight. Something strange was going on. They'd not just imagined what they'd seen.

* * * *

Daniela pulled the curtain back and waved them in.

She followed, but froze for a moment. There at the foot of the bed hung a faintly glowing cloud, the barely visible sight of AgradUtya.

AgradUtya projected respect, welcome and calm at the barely visible form that comprised the physical doctor for these people.

Felix and Sherry exchanged glances.

Daniela seemed to relax, a look of wonder crossed her features. "Sherry. Did he just...say something?"

Sherry grinned. "Yes, he gave you a sign of respect and indicated you should be calm and welcome."

Daniela smiled tentatively. "I felt this sudden warmth and calm flow through me."

Felix nodded, "I think he would love to talk with you, but he can barely see you."

Daniela grinned. "Well, you can tell him it's mutual. I can hardly see him either."

Felix turned towards AgradUtya's likeness. *The healer appreciates your gesture. She regrets she can't hear you; she can barely see you.*

AgradUtya projected pleased humor. *Tell her it's only a matter of time and we may meet face to face. Tell her that, for your kind, she does well to sense my presence at all.*

Felix relayed the comment and Daniela grinned more broadly. "I look forward to meeting him face to face..." She remembered where she was. "Perhaps we should get this over with?"

AgradUtya agreed. *Indeed we should begin.*

Felix and Sherry arranged themselves on either side of the patient. Daniela drifted to one side of the curtain to keep watch on the monitors.

RITE OF PASSAGE — 5

SAT 08.14.2094-Earth / TRN 18.03.6998-Aambü
ECS Destiny, Quarterdeck, MedCentral, 1400 Hrs / 2248 Slashes

Janelle Ferrin was single. She was an independent sort with few friends. The only close people she had in her life were her teammates. They were a team of deep-sea divers specializing in underwater survey, mining and construction. They'd come for the ride hoping to make a go in the oceans of *Nova Terra*.

Daniela was worried about Janelle. "I don't like some of her brain scans. Whatever is going on in there is wearing on her terribly. I don't know how long it can go on. It's like she tries to come out of REM, then sinks back again. That can't be good."

Felix kept a running translation for AgradUtya.

Felix, I am concerned for you and Sherry as well. If this individual expires suddenly while you're in there...I don't know how to get you back when your bodies are physically so far away. You should discuss this with your healer.

Sherry was looking stubborn.

Felix soothed. *Don't worry. We just need a back up plan.*

"Dannie. AgradUtya's concerned...He says, if Janelle...expires while we're in there, well...He says because we're physically so far away, he doesn't know whether he can get us back."

Daniela's face turned white as a sheet. "OH NO! I'm sorry, but this is just way too dangerous for you."

Sherry faced her. "We HAVE TOO! I WON'T LOOSE her!" Sherry pleaded, eyes glistening. "We haven't even tried yet."

Daniela hesitated and Sherry pressed on. "Dannie, we've rested. We're ready."

Daniela felt frantic. "You're making me to choose between her or both of you!"

"Dannie." Felix spoke up. "We don't even know it'll come to that. What can we do to minimize the danger?

Daniela stood rooted to the spot, thinking desperately. Sherry's eyes kept pleading. "I don't even know if this will work. I could hook her up to a portable LSU. It'll keep the chemlectric signals of her nervous system going for a while after...well, you know.

"It keeps the heart and lungs on automatic and stimulates the nervous system. The problem is, the average body usually stops responding after a few days, max.

Felix felt Sherry's angst. He hesitated a moment. "Does it kick in when the body quits, or is it running all the time?"

Daniela was clearly unhappy. "It monitors the patient and the moment it detects failure, it kicks in."

She wanted to object, but Felix was somehow suddenly in control. "OK. Let's do it. I'm sorry Dannie. This has to be done. Hook her up and pray...really hard."

Daniela gave a jerky nod. She didn't like it, but he was right. She looked briefly at Sherry and tried to smile before turning her attention to business.

She called for a nurse and together they hooked Janelle up to a portable LSU.

When that was done, Daniela insisted on running monitors for Felix and Sherry. She deftly placed the little patches on their foreheads and tuned a couple spare monitors to them. She got their scans going and nodded at Sherry.

Sherry turned to face Janelle. She looked at Felix. *Well, sweet heart. Let's get going. No matter what, you know I love you.*

Felix poured all the love and yearning he had in her direction. *Count on it, honey. We'll win. We have to.*

The Life Support Unit was now in standby. Daniela tried to watch everything.

Sherry and Felix assumed their usual stances on either side of the bed. Sherry's right hand gently rested across Janelle's forehead, careful not to disturb the monitor patches. Felix placed his left hand over Sherry's. They closed their eyes and a few moments passed.

Suddenly they tensed, as if caught by some surprise. The faintly glowing nimbus cloud that was their strange guest, flowed up the length of the bed to hover above Janelle's head between them...

* * * *

They swam frantically for the surface of a deep pool. The surface was barely discernible as an eerily glowing set of ripples just out of reach. It was terribly far to struggle without warning to take a breath.

They broke the surface gasping and swam the icy water to the nearest edge, crawling out onto solid ground. After a moment they stood looking around, clinging to each other for warmth.

They were in a rocky cavern, apparently deep inside a mountain. A faint phosphorescent glow in the walls offered scant illumination.

{It's so dark. I wish I had a torch.} Felix heard the sound of a piece of wood falling to the stone floor. He turned and peered around till he found a wooden torch, right out of some ancient castle dungeon.

Sherry looked at him. She could barely see him in the dim blue-green glow. {{What happened? That thing just popped into thin air and fell to the floor.}}

{All I said was I wished I had a torch.}

Sherry giggled. {{Now all you need is some fire.}}

Felix laughed. {Yeah, like I could just snap my fingers and light a flame.} He snapped his fingers to illustrate and a brilliant flash that lit the cavern dazzled their eyes. A small, bright flame danced in his hand.

Sherry's eyes got round, {{This is getting weird.}}

{You're telling me.} Felix responded as he reached down and picked up the wooden torch. He held the flame up to the windings of old rag and it transferred to the torch, quickly taking hold.

{O...K...} Felix said as he held the torch aloft. {Let's worry about that later. Now, where do we go from here?}

Sherry looked and then pointed. {{Is that a passage over there?}}

They headed that direction and, yes, there was a passage that slowly wound its way upward. They followed the passage for a long while. Then they heard a terror filled scream from somewhere up ahead. A long run brought them to a chamber that opened out into the mouth of a cave.

The ceiling was low overhead but sloped upward quickly as they slowly walked towards the opening. There was a large, ragged hole torn from the edge of the cave entrance and the wind was howling across the opening, blowing bitter cold gusts into the opening on one side that swirled around angrily across their faces. The wind blew the torch out the moment they stepped into the chamber.

Felix and Sherry cautiously approached the ragged hole in the floor. Felix looked over the edge and backed away quickly. They were in a cave entrance that thrust out over a sheer drop so high, the clouds were an angry grey black carpet below them.

Sherry inched forward and looked over the edge and froze in place. She suddenly pointed frantically at something down below.

Felix knelt and looked down again. Far below, a tiny human figure was flailing in free fall, surrounded by a cloud of rocky debris from the edge of where they stood. The horrifying scene vanished into the evil looking blanket of storm cloud below.

Sherry let out a short little scream and jumped back from the hole. Felix also felt the tremor and scuttled back. He stood and moved near Sherry, holding her close against the bitter cold wind.

They watched in fascination as the ragged hole in the floor slowly, stone by stone, began to repair itself. In a moment, there was no sign of a break.

{Was that...her?} Felix looked at Sherry.

She nodded, but she seemed confused. {{Yes, but...}}

[Who are you? What are you doing here?]

Sherry's jaw dropped and Felix whirled to see who it was. {{Janelle?}}

The athletic woman with the attitude stepped forward and looked Sherry up and down. [Yeah. Who's askin'?]

{{I'm here on behalf of Dr. Jacobs. She's very concerned about you. You've been...missing for several days.}}

Janelle was definitely perturbed. [Since when does anyone care about me? I can't even find my crew. They all left without me.]

Janelle turned and moved towards the cave opening, examining the stones in the floor and along the sides. [There's something strange about this stone, but I can't figure it out. I should know something about it, but...I don't know.]

She returned to the center of the opening and peered over the edge. The wind whipped her short hair wildly about.

There was a sudden jolt and a loud cracking sound. The edge of the cave opening where Janelle stood suddenly sloughed off. With a wild shriek Janelle seemed to hang suspended for a tiniest fraction of a second before plunging after the fall of rock, gravel and dirt, into the roiling storm below.

Sherry let out a short scream of her own.

She would have run to the cave opening had Felix not stopped her. {Wait! Wait. She'll be back.}

Sherry was incredulous. {{What? Are you sure?}}

{Yes, Daniela said there was a strange repeating cycle to her brain waves. This little scenario is happening repeatedly.}

They felt a lurch and turned to watch the ragged break repair itself.

They moved back near the entrance to the inner passage. Soon, Janelle came marching into the chamber. She didn't see them on either side as she approached the cave opening. She began examining the stones of the floor and walls in the opening.

{You'll find nothing.} Felix announced.

[What?] Janelle was startled. She didn't expect his voice. [Man! You scared the crap out of me.]

She studied them, her expression puzzled. She pointed tentatively at Sherry and then Felix. [Have we...met? Are you supposed to be here?]

Sherry stepped forward and held out her hand. {{My name's Sherry.}}

Janelle automatically took her hand in a tentative handshake. Sherry pointed towards Felix. {{This is my fiancé, Felix.}}

Janelle frowned. [I should know you, but I just can't remember.]

Sherry smiled, adding a little reassurance to the flow that had begun between them. {{Maybe you remember that big wedding we had a little while ago. You know, the one for Anatoli and Tanya Chernov?}}

Janelle let go of Sherry's hand and started pacing the cave floor. [It seems I remember something about a wedding...I keep forgetting stuff.] She paced more quickly; agitated she didn't even remember a wedding.

She stepped to the edge of the entry and looked down. {Hey Janelle. You might not want to...}

The predictable lurch and cracking sound struck again and Janelle went screaming after the rubble of the freshly torn rock face.

{That does it. We can't let this go on. Whatever is happening to her is slowly screwing with her memory.} Felix thought for a moment. It occurred to him he'd defied physical laws a number of times.

This environment was a lot like a waking dream. He had a sudden idea. With a little concentration, he slowly rose off the rocky floor to hover suspended in the air. He experimented with floating about the chamber. Then he started for the opening.

Sherry came unglued. *{{Felix! Don't! What if you don't come back?}}* He stopped. *{I won't fall.}* He turned and floated back to her and settled to the floor of the cave. *{It's just like a dream. Remember the torch? Remember when I lit my hand? It's like a dream. When we were in Leena's...place, I lit my finger like a lighter and lit the patio torch nearby. We can manipulate things here. Come on, now. Try floating in the air.}*

Sherry giggled. *{{Don't be silly...You're serious.}}* She considered it. *{{Yeah like, 'think happy thoughts' or something?}}* Slowly, she rose from the stone floor. *{{Wow! You're right.}}*

She floated about the chamber and then came to rest in front of Felix. *{{So, how does this help us?}}*

Felix grinned. *{We catch her as she starts to fall and we ride down with her, but we stop it before she gets to the bottom; wherever that is.}*

Sherry looked uncertain. *{{How does that help?}}*

Felix lost the grin. *{You had to ask. I don't know yet. We're making this up as we go, but I think we have to stop the cycle.}*

Janelle strode into the cavern and stopped when she saw Felix and Sherry. *[Didn't I...You...We just talked right?]*

Felix nodded. *{Yeah. We just talked a few minutes ago. How many times have you fallen from there?}* He pointed at the healed rock face.

[What do you mean?] She seemed confused. *[I think this spot is important...]* She walked to the edge again. *[...but I don't know why.]*

Felix moved up to one side of her and motioned for Sherry to take the other side. *{Janelle, you'll fall. Step back from the edge, please.}*

[Oh don't worry. I'm an adventurer. A little danger doesn't bother me. Though, I do prefer water adventures.]

Sherry spoke up. *{{Janelle, you've fallen from here more times than we can count. We've witnessed at least three times ourselves.}}*

Janelle was incredulous. *[Nonsense! If I actually fell from this height, I'd be dead the first time.]*

The cave lurched again and the lip of the cave broke away as before. Janelle screamed as before and started down, but this time, Felix and Sherry jumped at her, grabbing her by both arms.

The wind was biting. The air was thin. They seemed to fall forever.

{Sherry!} She looked up into his face. He was hugging Janelle from behind and Sherry was hugging her from the front. Janelle reflexively wrapped her arms around Sherry.

{Let's stop the fall. Let's do it together. We'll just stop in mid air.}

Sherry hesitated and then nodded. {On the count of three; one...two...three.}

Their plunge slowed and finally came to a dead stop. They hung there, a bundle of terrified and desperate hugs.

[What the heck's going on? How'd we just stop?] Janelle was almost as terrified of hanging in thin air as of the fall.

Sherry spoke loudly. {{We stopped it.}}

Felix added, {Janelle. This is all a dream. You've been dreaming the same part of a dream for the last several days.}

[That's not true. We just got here. My whole crew disappeared and I'm going to look for them.]

Sherry looked at Felix. {{We changed something.}}

Felix nodded. He looked around. The sheer rock face was out of reach several feet to his left. Far below, was a ledge jutting out.

He looked at Sherry. {Let's try for that ledge. We can rest there and figure out what's next.}

* * * *

Daniela was fascinated. The monitors for Felix and Sherry might as well have been repeating each other's data. Except for a few minor variations, the two seemed totally synced with each other.

Janelle's monitors had done some odd fluctuations. The strange recycling of the REM and deep sleep modes had changed pace. Her periodic spasms, short little jerks that came at regular intervals, had reoccurred three times in more rapid succession and then stopped.

Even the wild gyrating of the brain scans had settled down to more of an agitation associated with fear. Daniela murmured to the room at large. "They're doing something, but I don't know what."

After a time, the fear traces settled down to a mild series of peaks associated with nervous apprehension.

RITE OF PASSAGE — 6

They landed on the ledge. It was wide enough for them to sit together comfortably without fear of falling off.

Felix was deep in thought. Sherry was listening and trying to keep Janelle occupied at the same time. {I wish I could talk with Daniela...Wait!

She's watching all those monitors. I need to get her attention.} He considered certain possibilities.

He warned Sherry, {OK. I need to communicate with Daniela. I'm going to be very still for a while. I have to concentrate on those patches she has stuck to my forehead.}

Felix closed his eyes and thought about how all that medical stuff worked. Sherry watched. {Yes, the signals leap from the patch to receptors that go into computer controlled machinery...If I could...no not there...ah...almost...umm...yeah. Follow this path. Yes, there's the matrix. OK...how can I...ummmm...Yeah. How about this?}

* * * *

Daniela stopped with a jerk. She'd been about to turn away from Felix' monitor when one of the trace lines began to gyrate strangely. She watched, wondering if the monitor was choosing now to go bad. Oddly, the single trace no longer drew the jagged lines across the screen. Instead, it broke up into tiny, gyrating segments. Fascinated, she watched the odd display. Slowly, in fits and starts, the tiny segments began sorting themselves out into recognizable shapes. "D....O..C..T..OR.....J...A...C..O..BS"

Daniela stood, transfixed. "This can't be happening."
She looked at Felix. He was sweating. She looked back at the monitor. A sentence finally formed. "IF YOU CAN READ THIS AND YOU CAN INPUT DATA TO THIS SCREEN INDICATE IT SOMEHOW."

Daniela thought for a moment. "Computer. Enable voice to text on this terminal."

"WORKING" After a moment, "READY."

Daniela thought for another moment. "Felix. I got your message. Do you understand me?"

* * * *

Felix grinned. He had to fiddle with the receiving side of the connection. This was not what the system was designed to do. "I'm receiving your message. This is really weird. Do you have scans that show any physical damage to Janelle's brain?"

His request startled her. Daniela thought a moment. "I'd have to look up her files. It may take a while, so please be patient."

"OK. I'M NOT GOING ANYWHERE, ANY TIME SOON."

Daniela grinned, relieved. That was Felix' humor. "Great, I'll be right back."

* * * *

{Sherry. Daniela's checking Janelle's files.}
Sherry gave him a sidelong look. {{That's what I thought. You've found part of your own specialty, haven't you?}}

Felix grinned. *{I think so. I don't understand what it is, or how it works. Somehow I was able to reach through my monitor patches and put a message up on my monitor.}*

Sherry raised a delicate eyebrow. *{{So, how was she able to respond?}}*

Felix shrugged. *{I guess she found a way to hook up a text input. Her typing was crazy fast...I bet she used VTT. That would have been the fastest way.}*

Janelle had been watching. *[What's going on with you two? You stand there looking at each other, making faces like you're talking, and while we're at it, if this is supposed to be a dream, how are you two here in the first place?]*

Felix looked at her. *{Janelle, if you knew all that's gone on since you started dreaming, you'd think we'd gone loony.}*

He looked at Sherry, then shrugged and started telling an edited version. *{A bunch of stuff has happened, but right now I'm going to explain your part in it. The rest will have to wait till we're done.}*

He gathered his thoughts. *{A few nights ago, something very odd happened that interfered with a dream I was having. People who were dreaming at the time, had their dreams interfered with as a result. For lack of a better explanation, let me just say that what happened was accidental, not intentional. For most people, the interference jerked them from their own dreams and deposited them into mine.}*

Janelle looked at him like he was no longer human.

Felix shrugged. *{Don't look at me like that. I'll explain more thoroughly later. Everybody who was dreaming wound up in my dream, but from their own perspective. Most people simply experienced a long terrible fall from an incredible height into a vast worldwide ocean, followed by the sensation of drowning, which woke most people up.}*

He continued. *{Apparently, you were also dragged from some dream where you were with your diving crew. You were yanked into my dream where you were falling, much as you just experienced. But, for some reason, you've been living part of the dream over and over again.}*

Janelle didn't look like she was buying it all that well. *[Let's pretend I believe all this dream mumbo-jumbo. That doesn't explain how you two can come in and do what you're doing. We're sitting here talking on a ledge a million miles in the sky of some strange place that doesn't look very friendly. You and your girlfriend are flying around like Peter Pan and Wendy...I'm just a little confused.]*

Sherry spoke up. *{{Janelle, we're still trying to understand what's happened. When all this started, Felix and I were somehow changed.}}* She tapped the side of her head. *{{We communicate without needing to speak. I found out I can heal people's emotions. Felix. I don't know everything he* *can do. I guess he can do things to physical objects somehow. All I know is, we've spent the last three days rescuing five people who were adversely affected by this dream thing and didn't wake up on their own. You're number five.}}*

Janelle sat staring at them. She looked over the edge of the ledge. Whatever thought she had was still born. She pulled back from the edge quickly enough. [So, what now? Do we just sit here and hope the dream ends? Can't you stop it since you seem to be able to do everything else?]

Felix shook his head. {Janelle, your situation is entirely different from the others. They were emotionally traumatized in some way that made them hide in a little corner within themselves. We had to go in and coax them out. You're totally different, and, I might add, you're belligerence isn't making things any easier.}

Janelle was not happy with that comment. [My belligerence? Just whose 'dream' is this anyways?]

Felix winced. {OK...OK. Look. I'm sorry. Really. You can't imagine how draining this business is. We only just discovered we could do anything like this, what...maybe three days ago? We have limited energy to do what we do and I can tell you that running into major resistance is very draining. I'm sorry. I didn't mean to offend.}

Janelle stopped and pondered the situation. If everything she was being told was remotely true, these two might be taking some risk. She didn't know anything about this kind of stuff. Heck, did anybody? The only 'authorities' on this kind of 'mind stuff' were self made psychics, spiritual quacks, and their ilk. As far as she knew, none of those folk were present on the ship...'The ship.'

There was a ship. They were going to a new planet they hoped would be a new home for them. Why was she in some bizarre place like this when they had so much at stake?

Janelle held up her hands to ward off further argument. [OK. Skip it. My main question still stands. What's next?]

Felix replied. {I'm waiting for...} *He seemed to lose concentration.* {Wait. Dr. Jacobs is back...}

* * * *

Daniela approached the monitor. "Felix, I'm back..."

The flash of text startled Felix. He focused on it. "I'M HERE. I WAS TALKING TO JANELLE."

Daniela shook her head. "OK. Apparently, a couple of years before she signed on with the foundation, Janelle and her crew were on a deep sea project and there was some kind of incident. She was forced to surface from depth too quickly and developed arterial air embolisms. She was treated for those using a hyperbaric chamber; that's standard procedure in that business."

Felix sent back, "OK. HOW DOES THAT AFFECT US? THERE'S SOMETHING GOING ON THAT CAUSES HER TO LOOP THROUGH ONE PORTION OF HER DREAM REPEATEDLY. WE'VE BEEN ABLE TO BREAK THAT CYCLE, BUT NOW WE NEED TO FIND THE CAUSE AND THEN FIND A WAY OUT OF HERE. WE CAN'T GO BACK THE WAY WE CAME. I'M CONCERNED THAT IF WE GO BACK TO THAT LOCATION, WE'LL REACTIVATE THE LOOP."

"Well, Felix, I don't know anything about what you're doing, or how, or anything like that. So, I cant' give advice there. As to Janelle's condition, she had some MRI's done on her skull."

She paused as she scanned through the volumes of information. "Um...yeah, here it is. Apparently during the re-compression procedure she lapsed into unconsciousness. They were concerned about a stroke. If an embolism blocked a small blood vessel somewhere it could have caused a mini-stroke. By the way, an embolism is a small object...in this case a tiny bubble of gas... caught in the circulatory system.

"They did a series of MRI's. While they were studying the results, she regained consciousness with no apparent ill affects. They found nothing of consequence in the MRI's...except...for a tiny, little spot deep in the front of the Occipital lobes. It says here that no known function is associated with this area, but some speculate...whoa! Some think there might be some correlation with dream function."

Felix expressed surprise. "REALLY! MAYBE IT EXPLAINS WHY SHE HAD NO SYMPTOMS. I BET NO ONE CHECKED ON HOW SHE HANDLES DREAMS... DANNIE. DOES SHE HAVE A HISTORY OF SLEEP PROBLEMS?"

Daniela scrolled through the files she'd uploaded to her power-tab. "It notes here that she doesn't sleep very deeply any more. She seems to skim through REM very quickly and then the deeper sleep states are short lived. She borders on insomnia.

"I've been noticing that, on her monitor scans, she doesn't make it past REM, but I thought it had to do with this whole thing we're dealing with."

Felix nodded at nobody. "IT PROBABLY DOES. I'D BET SCANS FROM BEFORE WOULD SHOW A NORMAL SLEEP PATTERN. I'D ALSO BET THAT TINY SPOT ON HER...OCCIPITAL LOBE...IS THE CAUSE OF HER CURRENT SLEEP PROBLEMS."

Felix thought it over. Somehow they were going to have to take a closer look. He was very afraid of messing around with the brain.

He was still not sure what he'd done with Leena's lung. That made him nervous enough.

"OK. Thanks Dannie. At least I have an idea what we're up against. Sherry is getting worried. I'll be in touch. I don't know when. Later..."

RITE OF PASSAGE — 7

SAT 08.14.2094-Earth / TRN 18.03.6998-Aambü
ECS Destiny, Quarterdeck, MedCentral, 1445 Hrs / 2300 Slashes

Daniela backed away from Felix' monitor and Brianna cleared her throat. "Dannie, are you OK?"

Daniela jumped and turned to face her. "Sorry. You startled me...Yeah, I'm fine."

"So, um...what was all that? You don't usually talk with your medical equipment."

Daniela looked back at Felix' monitor and then at Brianna. She grinned. "Oh! I'm having a bizarre conversation with Felix."

Brianna came in and regarded the tableau. The patient was lying peacefully on the bed; Felix and Sherry were standing like breathing statues on either side, her hand on the patient's forehead and Felix hand over hers. "What are they doing?"

"Bri, I really don't know exactly what they're doing, but it's more of the stuff they've been doing for the last couple of days. They're trying to bring Janelle back from her unconscious state, and they're having more trouble with her than the last four."

Brianna processed the information. It was totally beyond anything she'd ever studied about in nursing school. She liked Sherry and Felix, but she was certain they didn't know a thing about medicine. How could they help? Daniela saw her confusion.

"Bri, something happened to them when that weird dream hit, but, well...it's stuff right out of some science fiction movie. They discovered they could talk to each other with their minds."

Brianna quirked an eyebrow. "Well, why not. Everything has been totally weird since that dream."

Daniela nodded. "Yeah, they discovered some other things about themselves."

Brianna looked up. "Other things?"

Daniela smiled. "Yeah, all kinds of other things. Imagine knowing your boyfriend's every thought. Imagine being able to finish each other's sentences without discussing what you were going to say first. They know more about each other now than most married couples learn in years."

Brianna's eyes grew round. "Wow. Wouldn't that make it kinda, you know, hard on the privacy thing?"

Daniela grinned. "Yeah. They've talked with Pastor Brad. They're going to be married soon."

Brianna smiled. "Oh...that's wonderful."

Daniela replied. "I agree. They're already as good as married in many ways. I'm glad it worked out for them.

"There are some other things."

Brianna grinned, "More?"

"Yes, because of this weird thing that happened to them, because of the dream, Sherry has found a way to touch other people where they hurt; I mean emotionally. She senses their hurt and then she's driven to deal with it.

"I've been reading. If we all believed in that weird psychic mumbo-jumbo you find in *The Daily Star* and tabloids like that, she'd be called an 'Empath.' In fact, because she can influence other's emotions she'd be called a 'Broadcast Empath.'"

Daniela shook her head in bemusement. "I'm beginning to think that while the stuff in the tabloids was pretty far out there, there must be something to all this telepathy stuff, or we wouldn't have Felix and Sherry the way they are now."

"So, what about Felix? What does he do?"

"Well, I'm not sure. Besides, his mental link with Sherry, he has something I don't know how to describe. It's like he can make physical objects do things. I don't mean pick things up and throw them around. I mean...I don't know. It's something on the cellular or microscopic level."

Brianna was still feeling a bit skeptical. "So, what does it look like? Have you seen him do stuff?"

"Well, its on a microscopic level...like when he woke from his near coma. Remember when they were found unconscious?"

Brianna nodded her head. "Is that when they...you know..." She tapped her head and Daniela chuckled.

"Yeah, that's part of what changed them. Anyway, when Felix woke up, he was worried about Sherry. He kept saying 'she's not here,' and he'd point to his head. I didn't understand anything about their link. "He tried to get up and I told him he had to wait till I removed the monitor patches. I showed him that Sherry was right across the aisle from him.

"I guess it was really bothering him. She was still unconscious and he couldn't sense her. He got very insistent and then he got this look in his eyes. All of a sudden, the monitor pads started falling off like hair from a haircut. Everywhere a patch had been, his skin was shiny with sweat, but everywhere else was dry."

Brianna's eyes went round again. "That's it?"

Daniela laughed. "Oh there's more. I don't know how he did this but well...remember when Leena was in here. She was number four. Remember?

"She went home yesterday, right?"

"Yep. Do you remember when we discovered the tumor on her lung while we were working her up?"

Brianna nodded. "You hesitated to do anything while she was still unconscious."

"That's right. Guess what? It's gone. Felix handed it to me when they were finished bringing her back. I guess they decided to look since I'd mentioned it."

Daniela gave an eloquent shrug. "It wasn't cut. It wasn't torn. It's almost like it...grew itself off..."

Brianna looked askance at Daniela. "Yeah, right."

"OK, my favorite skeptic. Go look at it yourself. It's in a jar on my desk."

Brianna got an odd expression. "On your desk?"

Daniela grinned. "On my desk. Oh, would you be a sweetie and get me a stool to sit on? My legs are starting to kill me..."

"Sure, Dannie."

Brianna wandered out to find a stool. Daniela went back to stand next to Felix. She considered their postures. They'd been at this for some time.

* * * *

{So, Janelle. Can you tell me about the diving accident you had before signing on?}

Felix grinned at the consternation on Janelle's face. [How did you...you talked to the doctor?]

{Yes, she says you had a close brush with death.}

[I don't know. I think they exaggerated it somewhat.]

Sherry looked at Felix, then at Janelle. {{You don't sleep very well?}}

[What...did she talk to you too?]

{{No. I know because Felix knows. See, we're linked somehow. We know each other's thoughts. We communicate without words, like he said. It makes it easier to work together, like we are now.}}

Janelle looked at her hands. She was starting to like these two in spite of herself. [I...I'm sorry. It's really kinda weird hearing things about myself from strangers.]

{{It's OK. We're only trying to help...Your file says you had a very mild mini-stroke while you were in the re-compression chamber. Did they tell you that?}}

Janelle was incredulous. [They did not. If The Foundation had known, I'd have been rejected for this trip. I never felt any different when I recovered from the accident.]

Felix entered the discussion. {Apparently a tiny bubble of air made its way to just the right capillary and lodged there, cutting off blood to a tiny area deep in your brain. The specialists all say there are no known functions in that area. It's one of those supposedly unused segments of our brain, but some think it might have something to do with dreaming.}

Janelle looked worried. Sherry rejoined the conversation. {{They say you don't sleep well. Dr. Jacob said you're a borderline Insomniac.}}

Janelle shook her head. [I don't sleep much. I wake up often and I never dream.]

She looked up at Sherry. [That's why I don't understand what this is all about. I never dream. So why, as you say, am I stuck in a dream?]

Felix smiled, as did Sherry. {It's not that you don't dream. You don't stay in REM long enough to keep a dream going.}

Sherry nodded. {{We think this mass dream we had hit just as you were entering REM sleep. You wound up locked here. Your body tries to move on, but it's stuck in a sort of feedback loop. We just broke the loop by stopping you from finishing your fall, but you're still stuck.}}

Janelle looked at Felix. [So how do I get unstuck?]

Felix shrugged. {That's what I'm trying to figure out. I think that tiny spot of damage in the front of your Occipital lobes has something to do with just about everything; your lack of dreaming, your sleep difficulties, your...sorry...consequent nasty moods.}

Janelle gave a grim smile. [Am I that nasty?]

Sherry grinned, {{only if you don't get enough sleep.}}

Janelle rolled her eyes. [Very funny.]

Felix stood up. {First, I think we need to get away from this place. I think that storm down there is something we want to avoid.}

He'd been looking around, examining the horizon for any sign of a break in the greasy grey nastiness below. {I don't even know where this place is supposed to be. I'd say we were on Aambü except there's no way this cliff should exist.}

{{But, Felix. We've never seen the entire planet.}} Sherry countered. {{Come to think of it, we've only ever seen it from a dream perspective, and you know, that even from the dreams there are some pretty nasty storms.}}

Janelle was looking confused. [Amboo? Planet? What are you babbling about?]

Sherry looked chagrined. {{We haven't told the whole story, I'm afraid, but I promise, once we get this all straightened out, we'll fill in all the gaps. I'll just say that Aambü is the name of the planet Destiny's approaching. The reason Felix feels this cliff we're on shouldn't exist is that Aambü's a water world. There are only tiny islands and atolls; no land masses big enough to matter.}}

Janelle's mouth dropped. [A water world?] Anticipation lit her face. [How cool!]

Felix smiled, shaking his head. {I'm glad someone thinks so. I'm going to have a look around. You two stay here. I'll be right back.}

Before either woman could object, he launched himself straight up. He flew, just like Lyuba said she had. {{Felix. You can't get away from me that easily, honey.}}

Felix grinned as he arrowed upward, seeking the top of the cliff. {I'd never try to get away from you, love. It's just that Janelle doesn't know she can fly yet. So, one of us has to stay with her.}

{{I was teasing, you silly. I love it that we can communicate in situations like this.}}

Felix shot above the top of the mountain peak. He brought himself to a stop and turned in mid air. As far as he could see in almost every direction he saw the ugly storm clouds stretched out.

Off to the...South (?) He felt sure it was south; there was a brilliant break just calling for his attention. {{Felix. That's beautiful. How far do you think it is?}}

{Normally, too far, but if we can get Janelle airborne we might be able to get there easily enough. Should I go take a look?}

He sensed her nervousness. {{No, let's get Janelle adjusted and go together. There's nothing good here right now.}}

Janelle watched Sherry's facial expressions. Sherry had gotten up to watch Felix. He'd all but vanished, just a spot against the bright sky. Sherry was quiet, looking up and making subtle facial motions as if she were having a silent conversation with someone.

Janelle remembered Sherry's description: "See, we're linked somehow. We know each other's thoughts. We communicate without words, like he said. It makes working together easier, like we are right now." [You two were talking just now, weren't you?]

Sherry turned to look at her. {Yes.}

[But doesn't that get...I don't know, invasive after a while? I mean...no private thoughts?]

Sherry smiled. {I don't know. It feels natural now. It was sort of awkward at first. We hadn't decided we were ready to consider marriage yet. Then this happened and private feelings and thoughts...even the embarrassing ones, were common knowledge. We discovered we really did want to be a part of each other. We kind of got married by accident, at least from everyone else's point of view. We've arranged for a wedding. We should enjoy the other benefits.}

She blushed brightly and Janelle laughed lustily. [Wow. I think that'd take a lot of getting used to.]

Felix landed behind her. {Not if you're really in love.}

Janelle whirled around with a start. [Don't do that! You scared the crap out of me...again!]

Felix grinned. {Sorry.} He didn't look terribly repentant. {Janelle, you saw what I just did. I flew up there and found out which way to go. Watch Sherry.}

Sherry slowly lifted off the ledge and drifted in a circle around Felix and Janelle. Felix pointed his chin skyward and Sherry grinned. She shot like an arrow into the air just like Felix had. She zoomed about and then settled at her starting point.

{This is a dream; not just any dream. For you it's a lucid dream. That means we can control things that happen in it. The natural laws don't apply here if you don't want them to. I can make a fireball in my hand.} He demonstrated. {We can fly as you've already witnessed. In fact, you can do everything we can except, of course, communicate the way we do. That we have in the waking world too.}

He looked at Janelle. {You can fly just like us. I know it sounds totally stupid, but this is a dream. We can make it up as we go. We need you to fly. We can't carry you very far. It takes too much energy.}

Janelle was giving what Felix was coming to think of as her mulish look. She had a stubbornness that was very annoying. [I think you're nuts. You two obviously have something weird going on, but me? I'm just a normal girl with normal abilities, like walking, climbing, swimming...normal stuff.]

Felix opened his mouth to sling a barb and Sherry smoothly stepped in. {{Come on, Janelle. You're not curious about all this flying stuff? I mean, you, the adventurous one, not interested in a new adventure?}}

She took Janelle gently by the shoulder and guided her over to the comfort of the cliff face behind them, effectively removing her from further confrontation with Felix.

Felix grinned to himself. {You know me too well, Love.} She grinned at him. While guiding Janelle, she gently infused a little gush of confidence. She gave Janelle's natural curiosity a gentle nudge.

[It's not that I don't want to try new things. It's just...well, he makes me so irritated.]

Sherry nodded, {{I know. He's just trying to get things going. He's impatient to be off to the South where there's a big gap in the clouds.}}

Janelle's eyes brightened. [Really? I'm so tired of those nasty things down there.]

Sherry nodded agreement. {{I know what you mean. Look. I want you to just think about it. Think of yourself being light as a feather. You can just float right off the ground if you want to.}}

Janelle gave her a look, but she stood still and got quiet. Sherry removed her hand from her shoulder and watched.

Janelle was quiet for several moments. Then she simply rose off the stone to hover about a foot in the air. She started laughing and slowly settled back to the ledge. [I can't believe it. It's that easy?]

She rose more quickly. Feeling unsteady, she grabbed the cliff face.

Sherry grinned. {See? Just like I told you. Now just decide you want to move in one direction or another and you'll move.}

Janelle leaned a little and then started moving towards Felix. She got going faster than expected and Felix had to catch her or be run over.

{Just a little work on control and you'll have it.} He grinned as she touched down. {Now. It's time for us to head south. Which is...} he turned and pointed off the edge of the ledge behind Sherry...{off that way. We have a long way to go, but I think you'll find it's not too tiring.}

Janelle looked a little doubtful. [I just barely found out I can fly, and you want me to go for a long flight right off the bat?]

Felix grinned. {Well, I'd rather not leave you here all alone. It would be kinda counter productive.}

Sherry shook her head at him and then turned to Janelle. {{Don't mind him. He can't resist the occasional tease...You'll be fine, really.}}

She looked at Felix. {{Come on, take her hand. We'll go slowly for a while till she feels confident.}}

Felix winked. {Yes, Dear.} He held out a hand. Janelle hesitated and then took Sherry's hand, then Felix's.

Together they rose to disappear into the South.

[Are you sure it was south?] She asked plaintively.

* * * *

They reached incredible speeds once Janelle got comfortable with the whole idea of flying. Even at those speeds, it took quite a while for them to notice any progress. The break in the storm below became more clearly *discernible. It turned out to be the edge of the storm front. Finally they passed over the edge of the storm and, far below, they could see the azure blue of the worldwide ocean.*

They flew on for maybe another ten minutes before spotting a small ring of atolls. Sherry looked over at Felix, who nodded. They went into a shallow dive and approached one of the nearest atolls.

They landed on a crushed shell beach with clear water lapping at the shore. The sky was bright and the rings were barely visible; a white arc rising from the Northeast and setting in the West. To the North they could see a long thick band of dark grey.

[This is beautiful.] *Janelle was looking around.*

Sherry grinned and pointed inland. The crunchy beach sloped slightly upwards and ended in a fine sandy soil. Odd-looking plants had sprouted and thickened as they moved inland. Eventually, they became a rich green ground cover.

From the top of the slope, which was no more than ten feet above the water, they could see inland. There was another shore that was sort of marshy in nature.

{Emily's going to be like a kid in a candy store when she sees this,} *Felix commented as he scanned the area.*

Sherry smiled. {{Oh, yes.}}

Janelle quipped. [This is great, but how does it help us?]

Felix turned to regard Janelle. {Here we can concentrate. We don't have to worry about a storm, or falling off a ledge a couple miles up a cliff. I need to have a look at you.}

[Excuse me!] *Janelle took a step back from Felix.*

Sherry giggled. {{He didn't mean it the way it sounded. He gets ahead of himself sometimes.}} *She turned and put a hand on Janelle's shoulder.* {Janelle, Felix needs to take a look at your brain.}}

Janelle blanched, [Wait just a minute. What do you mean? I'm not sure that's much better!]

Felix looked her in the eye. {It's true, Janelle. We think that mini-stroke you had a few years ago may have done something to hinder your dreaming. I need your permission to go in there and look. I won't touch anything. I won't do anything. You probably won't feel anything, but I need to take a look.)

Janelle was justifiably nervous. [I ah...I really don't like this...It's too freaky, and I think, way too dangerous. Can't we just let the Doctor do it?]

Felix shook his head. {I'd love to. I'm not any happier about this than you, but I don't see another way. I'll just look. If it's what I think it is, maybe I can help. If not, we'll have to hope and pray for something else.}

Sherry was still holding Janelle's shoulder. {{Janelle. I trust Felix with my life. He won't do anything to hurt you, and if he finds something he thinks he can do, he'll tell you first.}}

Janelle was worried. [I ah...I...I'm scared, but you've been honest with me so far. I...I guess you can have a look...I don't even know how you think you're going to do that. You don't have any knives.]

Felix shook his head with a lopsided smile. {I wouldn't dream of using knives. I'm going to have a look the same way we've done everything else so far. In here.} He tapped his forehead.

Felix looked around. The ground was reasonably flat where they stood. {I need a hospital bed like the one she's on in the waking world.}

A hospital bed shimmered into existence next to him. He motioned Janelle to lie down. Then he signaled Sherry to stand in her accustomed place. He assumed his on the opposite side of the bed. {OK, Janelle. We're going to assume the same postures we're in, in the waking world.}

Sherry placed her right hand over Janelle's forehead and Felix placed his left. {Now, I'm placing my other hand behind your head where your scull meets your neck. I need you to relax. Just pretend you're tanning yourself on the beach. In a way, you are.}

Felix placed his right hand under her head at the base of her scull. Sherry placed her left hand under his.

He glanced at Sherry. {Now this is the weird part. We're inside her dream right?}

{{Of course. Why...Oh.}}

{Yeah. We're coming from inside to work our way out to the physical brain, so we'll be kind of folding back on ourselves. First, I need to ask Daniela some questions.}

RITE OF PASSAGE — 8

SAT 08.14.2094-Earth / TRN 18.03.6998-Aambü
ECS Destiny, Quarterdeck, MedCentral, 1530 Hrs / 2366 Slashes

Daniela sat upright. She'd been fighting the urge to doze off. Felix and Sherry had adjusted their stance a bit. They were placing their free hands under the back of Janelle's head. She got up and moved closer.

"What are you two up to?" She whispered to no one. She hadn't heard from Felix for some time now.

Brianna came into the cubical and handed Daniela a sandwich and a coffee. "What are they doing now?"

Daniela absently took the snack and continued to watch. "I don't know, but I'm a little worried."

She glanced at Brianna and then at the sandwich and coffee. "I'm sorry. Thanks for the food."

"No problem. You look like you need some sleep."

"I probably do, but I have to see this through. This is a weird one and I'm worried about all three."

Daniela glanced again at the various monitors. There was little change. She was about to look a way when Felix' monitor jittered again. She nudged Brianna, pointing. The tracer line broke up and text began forming.

"DANNIE. ARE YOU THERE?" Daniela approached and spoke to the pickup. "I'm right here, Felix."

The monitor faithfully printed her response. A ghost of a smile graced Felix' face. "I KNOW BY NOW YOU'RE GETTING NERVOUS. I NEED TO SEE A DETAILED GRAPHIC FILE ON THE HUMAN BRAIN. I HOPE I CAN MANAGE GRAPHICS. WE'RE GOING TO NEED TO GO IN AND TAKE A LOOK, JUST A LOOK. I WON'T DO ANYTHING UNLESS WE AGREE TO IT."

Brianna looked worried and Daniela bit her lip before replying. "Felix, this is not a lung here. You can't just make things go away."

"I'M VERY AWARE OF THAT, DANNIE. I WANT TO SEE THE DAMAGE UP CLOSE. I'LL COMPARE THE DAMAGE TO WHAT IT SHOULD LOOK LIKE. THEN WE'LL DISCUSS OPTIONS. I HAVE JANELLE WILLING TO SUBMIT TO A SIMPLE PROBE. I PROMISED HER I WOULDN'T DO ANYTHING WITHOUT HER OK.

"I DON'T KNOW IF THERE'S ANYTHING I CAN DO, BUT I DO KNOW WE CAN'T DO MUCH MORE THE WAY THINGS ARE. WE CERTAINLY CAN'T STAY HERE FOREVER."

Felix thought for a moment. "BY THE WAY, DANNIE. HOW ARE HER PROSPECTS OF NEEDING THAT MACHINE YOU SET UP?"

Dannie smiled, "Whatever you did to stop that cycling seems to have reduced the danger of loosing her so easily. Many of her signs have partially stabilized."

Another ghost of a smile flickered across Felix face. "DANNIE, SHERRY'S BEEN TRYING TO FOLLOW OUR CONVERSATION. SHE'S STARTING TO FOLLOW MY PATHWAY AND PICKING UP THINGS. SHE SAYS SHE'S HAPPY TO HEAR THERE'S SOME IMPROVEMENT."

Daniela grinned. It felt good to hear from Sherry, even if it was through Felix.

Daniela turned to Brianna. "Bri. I need a graphic scan of the human brain. I want a 3-D movable model and I'll need scans of the internal layout. Can you fish those out for me so we can send them to the station here? I'll set up a repeater to place the graphics on Felix' monitor." She sighed. "How much crazier can things get?"

Brianna grinned. "You took the words right out of my mouth. I'll send the files to your station here; be right back…"

Daniela patted her arm. "Thanks Bri." She moved into pickup range of Felix' altered monitor. "OK, FELIX. BRI IS GOING AFTER THE FILES YOU REQUESTED."

* * * *

Sherry commented, {{Felix, I'm going to chat with Janelle while we're waiting. By now she probably thinks we've forgotten her.}}

{You're right. Tell her I'm in conference with Dr. Jacobs, and ask her to please be patient.}

Sherry turned to regard Janelle. {{Hey Janelle. I'm sorry this has taken longer than we thought. Felix decided to have a discussion with Dr. Jacobs before going in for a look-see. He asked for your patience.}}

Janelle's eyes popped open. She'd been quietly trying to relax. [You haven't done anything?]

Sherry smiled and shook her head. {{No, we haven't. We want to make sure we do things right. Don't you think that's a good idea?}}

It didn't take Janelle long to consider that question. [You bet. Who's idea was it? Yours, I bet.]

Sherry chuckled. Janelle was still not too sure about Felix. {{Honestly, it was Felix. I would have suggested it, but he thought of it first.}}

That took the wind out of Janelle's 'let's be nasty' sails. [I'm sorry, Sherry. I'm not good at this stuff. I think maybe Felix isn't so bad. He just pushes my buttons some times.]

{{I know.}} Sherry responded. {{He loves to have fun with people. I know he doesn't mean any harm, but I guess you don't have any way of being sure of that.}}

Janelle considered that. [I suppose if you're engaged to him, there must be something pretty good there. I like you. You're so patient. I guess if he's won your heart, I could try harder to give him a break.]

* * * *

Felix sensed his monitor going active. He'd discovered he could tell when something was going to happen on the monitor. There was a sort of tiny surge just before text appeared. He'd learned quickly to recognize the characters from their feel. His ability to manipulate the pixels on the screen had improved.

Finally the message began. "Felix. I have almost all the data. I was just thinking. You two have been standing in that one position for a long time. It's not going to be good news for those muscles when you return to us. I brought in a couple of tall stools. I'm going to place them near each of you and guide you to sit down. Don't remove your hands. I'll do as much as I can to help you get situated. I'll start with you and then I'll get Sherry settled as well."

"THANKS DANNIE. I'M SURE YOU'RE RIGHT. I NEVER DREAMED THIS WOULD TAKE SO LONG. I BET WE'RE SORE FOR A WEEK."

There was a short pause and then, "I WARNED SHERRY. LET ME KNOW WHEN YOU'RE READY FOR HER."

Daniela grinned. "OK. Hang on, I'm going to start moving you about. Just keep those hands where they are."

With that, she and Brianna began gently moving Felix bodily onto the medium height swivel stool. After a few adjustments she moved to his pickup. "OK, one down, one to go. You'll thank me later.

Daniela and Brianna moved over to Sherry's side. "Felix. Tell Sherry we're ready to get her seated."

* * * *

On the MEDCOM terminal, Daniela scanned the files Brianna had collected. She set the order of availability and was about to send the batch over to the limited memory available on Felix' monitor. Then it occurred to her, if Felix could get into the monitor of the diagnostics console, he might be able to go another step and get to the actual computer source. She sent a repeater signal from his monitor over to MEDCOM, leaving the channels open.

"OK, Felix. I have the files. I've gotten the diagnostics monitor to connect to MEDCOM. If you can navigate farther you have access to the entire computer library."

* * * *

Felix' dream eyebrow shot its way up his forehead. He explored the channels that came and went from his monitor. There was one channel that was like a thick, fat, red carpet, begging him to follow.

With a grin, he accepted the invitation and flowed quickly down the line. He found himself in a vast field of information that stunned him.

He backed into the familiar area of his monitor and considered what he had available to him. He decided to select needed files from the library and pull them into his monitor area rather than getting lost in the main library.

He noticed a large packet of information and considered it. It turned out to be a combination of text and graphics. He finally found his away through the graphics representations and watched as a 3-D model of the human brain slowly rotated in front of him. He considered the occipital lobes. Two sections of the upper back portion of the brain lit up to get his attention. {Cool!}

After a bit of searching, he discovered something really interesting. Suddenly the model exploded in slow motion so the internal sections could be seen. There was a small section right in the middle of the brain that looked almost like a human tongue. It clearly connected with the front portions of both Occipital lobes. In fact, it seemed to be a part of the Occipital Lobes. If you couldn't see inside, one would never know that part was there.

He considered the functions attributed to the Occipital lobes. Management of human vision was handled here. Right near the front where this part merged, the Lingua something; he looked for a name. {Ah...Lingual gyrus}. This area was supposed to have something to do with dreaming, particularly the visual aspects.

It was amazing. A network of tiny blood vessels served every area of the brain. It was like a fine cloud or net of tiny capillaries that spidered all over the place. Carefully, Felix zoomed in on the target area. Then he began searching for images of Janelle's MRI scans.

He found them and took a long look. {Yep. There's the damaged segment.} It looked like about the size of the head of a pin. Could that little thing cause all this trouble?

He took another look at the reference graphic. He wondered whether it might be possible to coax those cells to grow back. He thought about his experience with Leena's lung earlier that day. Somehow he'd gotten the cells of the lung to respond. The cancerous cells had died back from the healthy cells and the healthy cells had grown in to replace the damaged cells. Could he get that to happen here? The thought was daunting. This was the brain after all. {Sherry. Are you seeing this?}

{{I'm here honey. You get to some of the strangest places these days. I take it we're somehow in the med-computer?}}

{Yeah. That's exactly where we are...well...almost. We're looking at stuff from MEDCOM on my monitor. I decided it was quicker to do that than to try to find my way around in the computer. I mean, we've a brain to navigate.}

{{Felix, I know you'll do the right thing. I know you'll succeed. I think right now would be a great time to do some serious praying.}}

Felix smiled. {You got that right.}

They prayed for wisdom to know where to go and what to do or not to do. They prayed for strength to complete the work and safely get out of the maze they were in. They also prayed for Janelle's survival and sound mental faculties when this was over.

{Sherry. Get a good look at these graphics. We need to remember what things look like when we go looking around in Janelle's brain.} Felix began a retreat from the computer system. {It's time to go.}

They left the computer system and returned to the atoll where Janelle patiently waited on an out of place hospital bed near the surf of the worldwide ocean.

{Here we go.} Felix focused on the base of Janelle's skull. He felt the area under his hand get mildly warm. He imagined shrinking himself down to a tiny bunch of cells and then passed through the skin, muscle and bone. He realized it was a much more deliberate and detailed version of what he'd done to locate that lump of cancer before.

Felix and Sherry worked their way up between the brain and the boney wall. Felix wondered about the fluid they were passing through.

{{Felix. I remember reading about a fluid inside the skull that helps cushion the brain from injury from bumping against the skull wall.}}

Felix grinned. {You're right. I forgot about that.} They continued upwards along the skull wall.

{Sherry. See that cleft just ahead? That's the division between left and right halves of the brain. We should head in between the halves about here. This puts us near the bottom parts of the Occipital lobes.}

{{OK. I'm just following you.}}

Felix moved into the canyon, looking for a way in. {We're going to have to pass through the surface material. I don't see any...Wait. Those blood vessels pass through easily enough. We'll squeeze in near one of those.}

{{I'm right with you.}}

Felix could see the bottom of the canyon, as it were. He moved to the right and approached one of many veins that dove through the surface of the right Occipital lobe. With the slightest sense of resistance, he passed through between the vein and the surface membrane and looked in wonder at the goings on inside the brain.

It was fascinating to watch the constant pulse and flicker of electric blue light. It was like watching low voltage lightning coursing along a million distinct pathways.

He could see where tiny blood vessels passed along among the countless bundles of nerves. There were little nodules everywhere the various nerve bundles sent small branches.

They passed between the nodules and the bundles and worked their way lower and deeper into the center through a 3-D latticework.

As they broke through to what appeared to be a new level Felix realized they'd entered what had to be the Lingual gyrus of the Occipital lobe.

Of the many small blood vessels passing through the gap to join the maze of nerve bundles and nodules below, for some reason one vein drew their attention.

It hit Sherry first. {{Felix. It's like its calling to me. Look at that vein on your left.}}

Felix immediately knew which one.

Sherry was agitated. {{Isn't that damaged? Look at it!}}

The vessel arced down into the maze below, but about midway through the gap, there was a misshapen spot of damage...a 'stretch mark' was what came to mind.

A very thin spot had signs of tearing that had self-repaired. {Sherry. What are the odds we'd come out exactly where the damage was without having to make an exhaustive search?}

Sherry sounded like she was grinning. {{We did pray, Felix. Why act so surprised?}}

{You're right.} Felix angled for a closer look, and then followed the vein down to where it vanished into the maze. He stopped and looked around carefully. {Sherry. What do you feel?}

She looked around and then pointed. {{Something feels wrong over there.}} She darted off and Felix hurried after.

One of the millions of nodules loomed up as they came close and Felix could see a large, discolored portion. He saw a branching of nerve cells and a feeder vessel spiraling into the nodule. {Here's the damage. I'm going for a closer look. Keep in touch.}

He seemed to grow smaller still and then passed into the nodule itself. He was surrounded by a forest of nerve fibers that shot up from the floor to branch out into a latticework of filaments. Many of them were flickering with the electric blue flashes that had become a common feature of their surroundings, but a number of them seemed unresponsive, even wilted.

He followed one of the dead branches up and watched the smaller branches weaving in and about the living ones. {Sherry, can you hear me?}

{{Yeah. You're a little faint but you're there.}}

Felix considered the situation. {{If you went straight back to the monitor room and then out to Janelle, could you make your way back?}}

Sherry thought about it. She sounded a bit worried, but there was determination in her response. {{Truthfully, I'm a little nervous about it, but I don't see why I couldn't go directly back and then return. I think we'll loose contact for a little while. That's what makes me nervous.}}

Felix wasn't happy about that either. {I know, but I think there's a way to regenerate these dark branches. Give me a moment; I want a look at the condition of the DNA inside the nerve cells. I suspect that some of the bonds have been broken and need to be repaired. If I can get that to happen, maybe they will restart.}

Felix was nervous about that as well. He selected a darkened nerve cell and looked deep inside. The interior was not very active. It appeared to be alive, just not doing its job.

He found what he was looking for. The nucleus seemed to be almost paralyzed. The DNA masters were in tact. No damage seemed to be present. Then he found it, nestled against the outside of the nucleus. The replication process seemed to be shut down.

Felix explained the situation. {I need you to tell Janelle what we've found and what I propose. I think if I can restart the replication system, the nerve cells can effect repair. My guess is, somehow, when the influx of oxygen and nutrients was shut down for too long, the system locked up. I think it might be like a fail safe to prevent serious deformity and deviation from the pattern. I need her permission to try and restart the system.}

Felix considered further. {Before you talk to Janelle, get together with Dannie and explain it to her. See what she has to say. Then explain it to Janelle. Get her permission and then come back to me. I'll wait. Please don't take too long. You know how it feels to be separated.}

Sherry remembered their earlier separation when they first discovered the depth of their bonding. {{I'll be back as quickly as I can. I love you!}} Suddenly, she was gone.

RITE OF PASSAGE — 9

SAT 08.14.2094-Earth / TRN 19.03.6998-Aambü
ECS Destiny, Quarterdeck, MedCentral, 1600 Hrs / 2400 Slashes

Daniela was startled to see Sherry's monitor switch from diagnostic to text mode. "DANNIE. IT'S SHERRY. ARE YOU THERE?"

Daniela moved closer. She quickly activated the voice to text function. "I'm right here, Sherry."

She glanced at Felix' monitor. All seemed normal, whatever that was anymore. "Is everything OK? Where's Felix?"

Sherry grinned to herself. "FELIX IS FINE. I SUSPECT HE'S GETTING LONELY ALREADY. HE SENT ME TO TALK WITH YOU AND JANELLE."

"I assume Felix thinks he's found something?"

"YES, HE'S INSIDE A NODULE THAT LOOKS LIKE WHERE THE STROKE HAPPENED. SOME OF IT IS DARK INSTEAD OF ALL LIT UP LIKE EVERYTHING ELSE. OH DANNIE, YOU SHOULD SEE IT IN HERE. IT'S JUST AWESOME!"

Daniela grinned. "I'm just a little jealous. If this all works out, I'd love to get together with you guys and find a way of recording some video of things like this. So, what's up?"

Sherry smiled. "WELL, FELIX GOT A LOOK AT THE INSIDE OF ONE OF THE DARKENED NERVE CELLS. HE SAID THE DNA MASTERS WERE INTACT. HE SAID SOMETHING ABOUT THE SYSTEM THAT REQUESTS

REPLICATION HAVING SHUT DOWN. HE THINKS IT MAY HAVE BEEN A FAIL SAFE EVENT."

Daniela considered. "OK. That kinda makes sense. No-one's ever looked at this from his perspective. I'm glad he remembers his cellular biology so well. So what does he think can be done?"

Sherry replied, "HE SAID HE THOUGHT HE MIGHT BE ABLE TO GET THE SYSTEM TO RESTART NOW THAT THE NUTRIENTS ARE FLOWING AGAIN. HE SAID THE CELL WAS STILL ALIVE, JUST KIND OF PARALYZED."

Daniela hesitated. Then, "Sherry. This is way beyond my expertise. I understand the concepts, but no one's ever delved this deeply into a stroke-damaged cell and seen damage like this.

"I suppose if he can wake up the system, it may be able to self repair. He better have a closer look at that master DNA chain. If there's the slightest chance of screwing up the replication, it could cause greater problems than we could possibly imagine."

She hesitated again and then continued. "There aren't a whole lot of choices here. We need to get you two out of there safely."

Sherry was getting nervous about her time away from Felix. She was starting to feel it and she knew he was also. "I'LL WARN HIM. SHOULD I TELL JANELLE YOU'RE APPROVING THIS ATTEMPT?"

Daniela stepped back and thought long and hard.

"DANNIE. ARE YOU STILL THERE?"

Daniela stepped forward again. "Sorry, Sherry. I was just taking a moment to think this out. I'm really nervous. We're dealing with a human life here..."

She took a deep breath. "OK, I'll approve the attempt. We've no other options. We're going to do lots of praying out here."

"THANKS FOR THAT, DANNIE. YOU MIGHT WANT TO CALL PASTOR BRAD AND GET HIM AND JODI TO START PRAYING RIGHT NOW. THIS IS GETTING REALLY INTENSE."

Daniela smiled. "You got it. I'll call him when we're through here. You two be careful in there. Your friend, out here, has been very quiet. He's been hovering above Janelle's head the whole time. I hope he's aware of what's about to take place."

Sherry was clueless. "I DON'T KNOW HOW ANY OF THIS STUFF WORKS. WE HAVE A LOT TO LEARN AND ALL THIS STUFF WE'RE DOING IS MAKING IT DIFFICULT TO LEARN IT."

She was feeling time pressure. "DANNIE, I'VE GOT TO GO TALK TO JANELLE. WE'LL BE IN TOUCH SOON. SEE YA."

Just like that she was gone and the monitor switched back to tracing diagnostics.

* * * *

Sherry flashed back to the atoll. She was standing with her hands on Janelle's head and neck. {{Janelle, I'm back. How are you doing?}}

Janelle opened her eyes and glanced at Sherry. [I'm feeling just fine. What's going on?]

Sherry explained the situation.

Janelle bit her lip. [Dr. Jacobs approved?]

Sherry nodded. {{Yeah. She's as nervous as we are, but she says there are no other choices that bring success for all of us.}}

Janelle took a deep breath. [You two are in some kind of danger doing all this aren't you?]

Sherry winced. She'd tried to minimize that aspect of the relationship for Janelle's sake, but Janelle was no fool. She'd figured out there were dangers for them as well. {{Janelle, I won't lie to you. Yes, we took on a certain amount of risk in attempting this whole venture. We're very new to these mind gymnastics, and this business we're up to right now has never been done by a human being before. I know that doesn't give you a whole lot of confidence, but I want you to know, that while this is our best chance of recovering from the attempt, it's far from our only consideration. We want you to recover, or we'd have never made the attempt at all.}}

Janelle could see that right away. This new couple had something strange thrust on them and then had volunteered on a life-threatening mission to save her.

They were her best chance of living through this. [Sherry...I don't admit things like this to anyone, but...I'm scared as hell. I understand and respect the danger you two have placed yourselves in. Tell Felix to do what he has to. I'm totally in your hands.]

Sherry smiled. {{Thanks, Janelle. I'll never say a word to anyone about the 'scared as hell' part. By the way, there are at least two other sets of hands involved in this. There's the native of our new home who's lending mental energy to keep us strong, and we've been doing a lot of praying. There are a number of people on board Destiny who are also praying for you and us. God's already assisted in finding the problem's source. Otherwise we'd still be searching.}}

She gave Janelle a conspiratorial wink. {{My man's waiting for me. I'd better get back. I know you're in good hands. I'll see you after.}}

Janelle saw Sherry's eyes loose focus as she delved back to wherever Felix was.

She closed her eyes and prayed for the first time in her life. [God. If you're really there, I really hope you can help us here. At least, don't let them be hurt or killed. Right now, I'd kind of like to think you were really out there.]

* * * *

Felix was getting a restless feeling. It had been a while since Sherry left. The discomfort of not having her right there in a corner of his mind was intense. He was also getting impatient because he was sure he knew what to do.

He just needed confirmation that he could begin. {God, please bring Sherry back to me safely. I really need her right now. I need you desperately now as well, more so, to be honest. You designed all this stuff and I'm just muddling through. Help!}

Suddenly Sherry was flooding his mind, joyful at finding him. {{Felix! Are you OK?}}

Felix smiled. {With you back, I've never been better. So, what's the official verdict?}

{{Dannie agrees with you. She says she's way out of here depth here. She also said no one's ever come at this kind of problem from this angle before. No-one's ever dealt with the brain at this level of detail before.}}

Sherry expressed wry humor. {{Janelle has come to some conclusions about you. She gave her blessing to go ahead. She's scared, but for us too; if that's any consolation.}}

Felix felt her smile. Sherry added. {{By now, just about everyone's busy praying.}}

Felix replied. {That's what we need right now. OK. I'm going to go in and try reactivating the replication system. Hang on.}

He delved back into the cell he'd been studying. Considering how to give it a mild jump-start, he held out his hands and imagined generating an electrical charge within. He felt a welling of power. When it felt like he'd burst, he let it go. A flare of electrical energy, similar to the flashing going on throughout the brain, leaped from his finger tips and danced all about the inside of the cell.

There was a shudder like something suddenly waking up. Then there was movement all over the place.

The nucleus began to pulse slightly. A current began to flow through the cell, sweeping minute particles past him. A tiny object sailed past and headed straight for the nucleus. It paused at the membrane and then dove into the center. Felix watched as flickerings began to take place inside. After a moment, the object popped back out, a flickering object somehow attached to it.

The object sailed past in the other direction and darted into a maze like structure. Another object dove for the nucleus and the process repeated itself. Another object emerged from the maze like structure and darted off in another direction.

{Sherry! I think it's working! Look!}
{{I see, love, but there are so many!}}

{Yes, but there's two of us. Did you see what I did?}

{{I think so, but I'm out here and you're in there.}}

Felix smiled. *{Sorry. I forgot. Just having you back was such a relief. Can you get in here? You just have to make yourself smaller. I'll wait.}*

Sherry thought about it a moment and then concentrated on getting smaller. She entered the nodule and found Felix standing at the base of a partially lit strand.

{Hey, love. Welcome. If you can do what I just did, we could each take a strand and halve the time it takes to clear this up.}

RITE OF PASSAGE — 10
SAT 08.14.2094-Earth / TRN 19.03.6998-Aambü
ECS Destiny, Quarterdeck, MedCentral, 1615 Hrs / 2416 Slashes

The first indication Daniela had that something crazy was happening was when the ghostly cloud that represented their alien visitor began pulsing and brightening. It was no longer so difficult to see.

AgradUtya gathered himself close to the head of the ailing creature and attempted to get a picture of what his obviously crazy charges were up to. *They truly are crazy,* he thought to himself.

The sudden pulse of power confirmed his fear. Felix was doing something rash. Another pulse coursed over him. *That was Sherry, rushing in where the holy messengers hesitated to go.* He sent a call for aid back to the questing chamber at home.

* * * *

First Quester got the call and immediately sent for a third Quester. <<ApraAnupadin. You are to take charge here. I must go to AgradUtya's aid. His students are doing something rash. He fears they'll deplete their energy too quickly. Keep the energy flow going as strong as you can. I'll be in touch from time to time.>>

AgraAnupadin dove into the questing pool and took a place next to the body of AgradUtya. He composed himself and quested outward.

* * * *

Daniela was trying to see what this AgradUtya was up to. He suddenly rose and flowed down the length of Janelle's body. He veered towards her and stopped inches from her face.

Daniela stood stock still, wondering what was going to happen next. The cloudy shape grew a couple of wispy appendages. They slowly extended to either side of her head and stopped.

Daniela was frozen in place and closed her eyes, trying not to be afraid. Slowly, pictures began to form like a dreamscape.

It showed Felix and Sherry reaching up and out into a dark background. Then nearly simultaneous flashes, like lightning flared in her vision. The background began to glow and a pulsing light could be discerned. Felix and Sherry moved on and the picture faded away.

Another picture showed Felix and Sherry sitting back to back against a glowing column, looking like a pair of dilapidated Raggedy Ann and Raggedy Andy dolls. They were unable to go on and there was a sense of fear pulsing from the picture.

The picture changed again. It showed one of the creatures, an Aambüka as Felix had described them to her. The creature lifted its short trunk like mouth and keened an ear-piercing screech that seemed to echo forever across space.

The picture changed again and a second creature could be seen arrowing from the ocean up past the rings of the planet. Clearly it was coming to *Destiny*.

The picture show ended and Daniela blinked. "Felix and Sherry are doing something dangerous to save Janelle and they're likely to wear themselves to dangerous levels. Agr...you've called for help and it's on the way."

She realized that AgradUtya had just done the best he could to communicate the situation to her.

Daniela wished she could communicate like Felix and Sherry did. She tried to project her gratitude as she spoke out loud. "Thank you so much for your thoughts. I hope someday I can make you understand that."

The apparition that was AgradUtya pulled back and flowed over to Felix' stationary form. Suddenly another, slightly smaller apparition arrowed into the cubicle. The two came together and remained for several moments. Then the newcomer flowed over to wrap itself around Sherry's head. AgradUtya assumed his place about Felix. They visibly glowed, casting an eerie radiance that bathed the whole room in a cool blue-white hue.

"Bri! Come quick!"

Brianna hurried into the cubical and stopped dead in her tracks. The room glowed a cool blue-white. There were two brilliant, flickering clouds, one over Felix and one over Sherry.

She looked at Daniela. "What's going on? What are those cloudy things?"

Daniela glanced over from her study of the monitors. "Those, Bri, are the only visible aspects we can see of the natives of Aambü right now. These two have come to give aid to Felix and Sherry. They're doing something dangerous to save Janelle."

Daniela watched as the diagnostics monitor for Janelle began to show minute spikes in the electrical energy bands. She moved to the computer and instructed it to perform a brain scan. Slowly, a blue green colored, 3-D image of Janelle's brain began to assemble. She focused in on the area where the older MRI scans had shown the site of the mini-stroke. There were pulses of energy coming from the region of damage. They were tiny to be sure, but there should have been nothing happening there.

Slowly, the discolored spot where the stroke had occurred began to shrink. The red of damaged cells were transforming to the blue green of healthy ones. "Felix. I don't know what you're doing, but it looks good from here."

She knew he couldn't hear her, but she had to say something. This was an impossibility happening right before her eyes.

* * * *

After a few times of pulsing subsequent cells, Felix was starting to feel the stress. Even with Sherry doing half the work, this was going to be a very draining task. He began to wonder if he had the strength.

There was a sudden surge of presence that hit Felix like a slap. ***Ah, my friend. You seem to have decided on a path of destruction.***

Felix saw no one, yet he knew AgradUtya was nearby.

Yes. It is I. You're spending energy so lavishly it was no trouble finding you. Do you truly wish to survive this little adventure?

{*Of course I do. I'm trying to finish the restoration of these cells so we can get out of this place and save Janelle at the same time.*}

Ah. Do you think that even with both of you doing this rash thing, you'll be able to repair all the cells and still have energy to escape?

Felix felt the chagrin he was meant to feel. {*I'm doing the only thing I know, and that incompletely.*}

{{*Felix! Someone's trying to talk to me. It's similar to Mr. 'A', but yet different. What do I do?*}}

{*Just a minute, sweet. You've been so busy you didn't notice the conversation I was having with Mr. 'A'.*}

{{*Sorry, but what about the stranger?*}}

{*AgradUtya, can you explain this extra presence?*}

Ah yes. That would be AgraAnupadin. He came at my summons to help me keep you from burning yourselves out. He's assigned to work with* *your mate as I am trying to work with you. I would advise Sherry to open communication with him. He will not harm her.

{Sherry. Did you hear that?}

Sherry seemed more relaxed. {{Yeah honey, I heard. It just surprised the daylights out of me. I'll allow contact.}}

Felix felt her retreat to a small corner of his mind. {OK, AgradUtya, you said you couldn't communicate with us while we were deep in another mind like this.}

Yes, well, it is a very, very difficult thing to achieve. However, with you two trying to kill yourselves, it seemed to be the best course to take. This is costing much personal energy from a great, many individuals.

Felix pondered this. {I'm truly sorry we've caused such trouble, but I can think of no other way to resolve the problem. I've discovered that the area of Janelle's mind that has been damaged may be repaired by jolting each individual affected nerve cell with a bolt of energy.}

Yes, Felix. The whole jolting thing was apparent to all, including your healer. Might I suggest that the amount of energy you're using for each...jolt, as you call it...is somewhat excessive? I suspect that a much smaller...jolt...perhaps a tiny squirt of energy will suffice nicely. The result should be the same and perhaps we'll get you both back in the bargain.

{I...I'm sorry. I never considered that a smaller amount of energy would suffice. I feel stupid.}

I might be tempted to say, 'as you should'. However, we must make allowances for your inexperience when it comes to these matters. You two are, after all, operating far beyond what you should be able to at this level of your development.

Felix felt thoroughly chastised. {Thanks for your patience. I'll explain it to Sherry.}

**No need my friend. AgraAnupadin has already communicated the information. What I need both of you to do is to continue what you're doing, but at a much lower level of energy. This may take just a little longer, but you and your mate will more likely survive the experience.

You'll be...bone weary...I think that would be a good description. You'll be bone weary when this is over. We'll talk more then. Oh. On your way out, you might want to go over that damaged blood vessel and see if you can encourage those cells to complete repairs. Your memories of that view trouble me. We don't want that to rupture in the future and render everything done here useless.

Felix would have nodded, but he wasn't sure the gesture would be seen or understood. {OK. We'll begin again. May I presume you and your friends will continue to supply backup energy?}

He could sense a ghost of humor in Mr. A's response. **Yes, you may rest assured we will continue support. Though from the point of view of most of my people, this is only the right thing to do, our chief-king, AgraVadin Adhiraj has commanded that this support be rendered without hesitation. You'll have no trouble in that regard.**

Felix pondered the implications of such an edict. He'd have to explore those implications later. Right now he had work to do. {I thank you and extend my thanks to your leader. We'll always remember the willing help of friends.}

Felix turned and moved upward to the next cell. {Sherry, we've a long way to go. Did you get the part about less energy per burst?}

{{Yes, dear. I wish we'd thought of that sooner.}}

{So do I. I feel like I just got smacked.}

{{I'm on it honey, things will be fine.}} She moved up the strand she was working on as Felix did on his.

* * * *

Daniela watched the monitor. The changes on the screen had stopped when the two aliens had settled over the heads of Felix and Sherry. Now she could see that activity had resumed. The little spikes on the EM band were much smaller. The color shift in Janelle's progressive brain scan resumed more slowly.

"Computer. Zoom to maximum on the area of damage." The computer calculated the various angles and expanded the view. The area of damage was now the size of a child's fist. The color shifts were more visible, but were taking an agonizingly long time. Since the computer didn't 'know' what the interior structure looked like it could not simulate the actual activity. The best Daniela would see was this slow changing of colors.

* * * *

Brianna shook Daniela's arm. "Dannie. Wake up!"

Daniela jerked awake and mentally began kicking herself for falling asleep. "How long was I out?"

She looked back at the screen. The red had been reduced to just a tiny spot. She checked the zoom index. The view was still at maximum magnification.

She looked over at the two guests wrapped around Felix and Sherry's heads. They seemed dimmer. When the last spot of red vanished the visitors flared brightly for a few moments.

* * * *

Felix wasn't sure he could move. He felt like jelly. He looked around. The nodule they'd been working in was significantly brighter. The show was spectacular.

He could barely sense Sherry. {Sherry honey, are you OK?}   The long pause worried him.

Then, {{Felix? I'm so tired. Are we done?}}

{Yeah. I think we've done it. Now we need to see the results. Come on. Let's get back to the Atoll.}

They slowly came together and supported each other as they made their way out of the nodule into the larger world of the Lingual gyrus.

{{Felix. Don't forget about that vein.}}

Felix groaned. {You're right. God, I hope I can do something in my condition.} They located the vein again and summoned all their strength to fly upward.

Suddenly there was a massive surge of energy that infused both of them. It was like a surge of adrenalin. Felix reached out and put a hand on the surface near the damage.

He could feel the slight rhythmic flexing as the blood flowed on the other side of the membrane. He examined the cells that were damaged. Placing his hand on the good cell at the end of the stretched area, Felix concentrated on getting it to divide. As the division began, he touched the next cell and concentrated on getting it to self-destruct.

The result was almost like closing a zipper. The damaged cell dissolved and the new cell moved in to take its place. Felix moved to the opposite end of the damage, repeating the process. This way, he figured he'd give each new cell time to recover from the division process before being asked to do it again. The process took time but the result was a normal looking vein, no sign of damage.

A few stray red blood cells floated around. Felix tapped each one with a self-destruct command and then headed up the vein with Sherry, back the way they'd come. Sherry noted the blood cells had dissolved.

* * * *

Daniela watched as Felix and Sherry physically removed their hands from under Janelle's neck. They attempted to stand, but were having trouble.

"Bri. Get Sherry. I'll get Felix. They need to stand for some reason, but they're too weak. I wish I knew what was going on."

They took up positions and guided their friends up from their stools and helped to support them as they stood, trembling. Brianna looked across the bed at Daniela. "I'd say they're done messing around in her head. What's next?"

* * * *

{{Janelle. How are you feeling?}} Janelle opened her eyes, glancing to left and right.

Felix and Sherry were there, but they didn't look so good. It looked like they'd fall over any moment. [I'm OK. Did you do anything?]

Felix looked over at Sherry and laughed.

Sherry grinned and looked back down at Janelle. {{Yeah, I guess you could say we did something. Everything looks like it should now. We just have to wait for the results.}}

Felix commented. {In the mean time, before we collapse and become a part of the scenery, I suggest we head home.}

He backed away from the hospital bed on the shore of a small atoll. {Go ahead, see if you can get up and move around. How do you feel.}

Janelle got up from the bed. [I don't feel any different. Are you sure you guys did anything?]

Felix grinned. {Believe me. We did enough. If I see another neuron any time soon, it will be too soon.}

He waved a hand at the bed and Janelle watched as it wavered and then faded from view.

Janelle shook her head. [I'm sorry, but that's so weird.]

Sherry grinned. {{It's a dream remember?}}

Janelle nodded. [Yeah. You're right. So, what now?]

Felix looked up at the rings. {Let's go home before I can't fly.]

The three linked hands. [You mean we're flying back to the ship? What about space? We're not suited up for that.]

Felix shook his head. {You forgot already. This is like a dream. We're not physically here. We can do anything we want. Come on. You'll love the view.}

The three of them lifted shakily off of the beach and slowly began to rise. They gained speed till they were a streak in the evening sky. They soared clear of the atmosphere and headed for the rings. Felix took them on a slalom coarse among the ring particles till they broke free. Janelle gave a 'whoop' of surprise and glee at the awesome view.

Sherry pointed out the small moon far to their right. Janelle laughed. [This is just too much!]

Felix looked about and then angled their flight off to one side before accelerating to unbelievable speeds as they hurtled for Destiny *and home.*

Soon they passed through the hull plates of the ship and settled slowly through the decks till they got back to the cubicle. They came back to Janelle's mind and stopped.

RITE OF PASSAGE — 11

SAT 08.14.2094-Earth / TRN 19.03.6998-Aambü
ECS Destiny, Quarterdeck, MedCentral, 1730 Hrs / 2416 Slashes

Janelle's place was small and tidy. There was little in the way of decoration. Little that is but for the books on deep sea diving and mining. There were pictures of her and her team gathered about the stern of a boat, working on their diving gear.

Felix commented. {You've a nice place here.}

Janelle smiled. [Thanks. It's home.]

She stumbled, but caught herself.

Sherry was worried. {{Are you OK?}} She searched Janelle through her empathic link. There was no serious trouble. Janelle was feeling sleepy. {{You're tired aren't you?}}

Janelle nodded and then yawned. [Wow. I'm so sleepy.]

Felix looked at Sherry. {{That's good. I think. Why don't we go and get some rest of our own?}}

He addressed Janelle; {We should meet when we're all awake. OK?}

Janelle yawned again. [Sure. I'm sorry guys; I'm practically asleep on my feet.]

Sherry guided her over to the couch. {{It's OK. You've had a hard time. Get some sleep. We'll talk in the morning.}}

Janelle nodded as Felix and Sherry helped her down on the couch. She no sooner lay down than she was asleep.

* * * *

SAT 08.14.2094-Earth / TRN 19.03.6998-Aambü
ECS Destiny, Quarterdeck, MedCentral, 1740 Hrs / 0133 Slashes

Felix and Sherry removed their hands from Janelle's forehead and jerked awake at the same time. The two nurses Daniela had summoned were all that kept the two from collapsing to the floor. They returned the weary couple to their stools where they could sit and recover.

Daniela rechecked the monitors. Janelle's signs were showing a normal REM state, but she was drifting towards deep sleep.

Felix and Sherry's vitals were low and slow. They were beat beyond endurance.

Suddenly Janelle twitched and then let out a monstrous yawn. Daniela glanced at her monitor. All the vitals were returning to normal and she was almost into the deep sleep she needed so badly. Janelle let out another cavernous yawn and dropped quietly into a deep sleep.

"I need a couple of large glasses of water in here right now." Daniela called.

Brianna dashed from the room. She returned in record time as Daniela continued to look over her two patients.

"Felix. Can you hear me?" Felix tried to reply, but only emitted a dry croak.

Brianna pressed a glass of water in his hand and Daniela guided it to his lips.

Brianna hurried around and helped Sherry down hers.

Felix finished his glass. "Thanks. I think I'll be OK. I'm just..."

He laughed quietly to himself. "Mr. 'A' was right. I'm 'bone weary.' That's what he said we'd be."

Sherry cleared her throat and spoke up. "I feel like melting right where I sit."

"OK." Daniela broke in. "It's off to bed with both of you."

She addressed the male nurses. "Guys. Let's get them next door. There are two beds there. I'll be there in a minute."

As the two weary people were half carried, half escorted to their beds, Daniela double-checked the data she'd collected. This whole thing was beyond crazy. She glanced at Janelle's monitor. She was stable. The monitor reported she was comfortably in deep sleep. Only time would tell what was to happen next. Hopefully, she'd wake normally in a few hours, none the worse for wear.

No one noticed when the two alien guests had departed, but there was no sign of them in the room. Daniela was almost disappointed. She still hoped to be able to communicate with them someday. She was just bubbling with questions.

* * * *

SAT 08.14.2094-Earth / TRN 19.03.6998-Aambü
ECS Destiny, Quarterdeck, MedCentral, 1750 Hrs / 0133 Slashes

Felix and Sherry were deeply asleep. Their monitors showed little time spent in REM sleep.

Two cloudy shapes emerged through the bulkhead and hovered in the room between the two beds. AgradUtya moved slowly over to where Felix was sleeping. AgraAnupadin moved to Sherry's side.

They reached over and placed cloudy appendages over both forms. ***Rest well. You've done the impossible. I don't know what this bodes for our races, but besides the wastefulness of inexperience, you have done as well, if not better than any healer my people has known in several generations. We'll talk next turn. I appeal to the Maker you stay out of any more trouble till you can be properly trained.***

AgraAnupadin sent his thoughts to Sherry. *++I must concur with AgradUtya. You have done amazingly for ones so newly awakened. I'm grateful to the Maker that we were able to keep you through the trial. I trust we find common purpose somehow. You've done honorably by your new mate. Felix couldn't ask for anyone better to complete him and I feel for any who stand in your path. We'll speak again I am sure. Rest well.++*

The two apparitions turned to face one another, made complex gestures and then winked out of sight.

Stars In The Deep
~Destiny~

Book 3

Destiny Redefined

By

David F. Snider

Stars in the Deep
Volume 1: Book 3

Table of Contents

Chapter Sections	Starting Page
Coming Out 1 - 6	481
Made Official 1 - 10	530
Arrival 1 - 8	592

COMING OUT — 1

SUN 08.15.2094-Earth / TRN 19.03.6998-Aambü
2.50 Months from orbital insertion; Aambü, Gem System
ECS Destiny, Quarterdeck, MedCentral, 0840 Hrs / 1250 Slashes

Felix woke feeling like he'd rolled down a flight of stairs. He looked across to see Sherry laying in quiet slumber, but he already knew she was asleep. Something nagged at the back of his mind. He sat on the edge of the bed and wondered what it was. Then it came to him. There was a message. He'd never experienced something like this before, but what was new these days? Apparently Mr. 'A' had somehow left a parting message.

Felix experienced something like a brief waking dream. He could see Mr. 'A' hovering over him. It was probably while they'd slept after their adventure with Janelle's dream. **Rest well. You've done the impossible. I don't know what this bodes for our races, but besides the wastefulness of inexperience, you have done as well, if not better than any healer my people has known in several generations. We'll talk next turn. I appeal to the Maker that you stay out of trouble till you can be properly trained.**

Felix smiled. It was kind of amusing when Mr. 'A' combined criticism and praise in the same sentence. He was looking forward to the next meeting with him. At the very least, it was going to be quite instructive.

He sensed Sherry waking and glanced up as she slowly turned on her side to look at him. *You're awake. I feel...terrible. All my muscles are rebelling.*

Felix grinned. *Yeah, I have the same problem. Do you think you can make it to the diner?*

Sherry sat up, groaning over unhappy muscles. *I...think so.*

She stood up unsteadily and Felix got up to help her. They stood that way half hugging, half holding each other up. Just then the curtain parted and Daniela came in. Her casual clothes said she wasn't really on duty. One look at them and she assumed her lecture posture.

Felix and Sherry burst out laughing at the comic picture they must have presented.

"Where do you think you're going?" She tried hard to keep the smirk off her face. It was funny, but it wasn't. "As you can tell, you can barely stand, let alone traipse all over the ship."

Sherry masterfully brought her laughter under control and tried to look repentant. It wasn't working very well. "I'm sorry Dannie, but we're famished. We wanted to get something to eat. "What time is it, anyways?"

"It's about 0850." Vince came through the curtain.

Daniela grinned at him and then turned her attention back to her wayward patients. "We were headed off for church and I thought I'd drop in and check on you. I figured you'd be out for another couple of hours."

Daniela smiled. "I'll tell you what. You decide what you want. We'll send in an order and get it brought here. I'm serious. You need to stay quiet and rest. If you can't sleep, at least relax. Those muscles are not very happy right now."

Felix nodded. "You're right...Oh. I promised Janelle we'd talk this morning when she woke up."

Daniela smiled. "Well, that'll just have to wait. We just stopped by her cubicle and she's still asleep. She doesn't usually sleep very long, according to her records. I think she probably just set a record, a personal best, for length of sleep onboard ship."

Felix looked at Sherry who'd settled back on the edge of her bed. *Well, something seems to be going right. She's sleeping better.*

Sherry smiled. *Isn't that wonderful? Maybe she'll be a little less...prickly.*

They both laughed.

Daniela turned for the curtained entryway. "I'll get a pocket-tab so you can order. Stay put!" She marched out of the room. Vince rolled his eyes and shrugged before following her. Sherry and Felix looked at each, and then broke into peals of laughter.

Felix sat next to Sherry since he was already half way there. *What? I was facing this way anyways.*

Sherry gave him a coy little look. *Oh, it's not that I mind. I just thought it so convenient.*

Felix gave her a quick hug. *Felix. Something's bugging me. I keep feeling like there's something I've forgotten and I can't think for the life of me what it could be.*

Felix smiled knowingly. *You too? Take a moment and think about how you want to remember. I think you have a message.*

Sherry blinked. *A message? Oh, you too. Ok, Oh! Wow! How'd they do that?*

Felix grinned. *I don't know, but it's kinda cool.*

Sherry went over the message again. *I must concur with AgradUtya. You have done amazingly for ones so newly awakened. I'm grateful to the Maker that we were able to keep you through the trial. I trust we find common purpose somehow. You've done honorably by your new mate. Felix couldn't ask for anyone better to complete him and I feel for any who stand in your path. We'll speak again I am sure. Rest well.*

Sherry pondered the message, comparing hers with Felix'. *So, they think we did a good job, but Mr. 'A' was mildly critical at the same time. I wonder what they mean by finding common purpose, 'somehow.'*

Felix shrugged. *I have a hunch they're having debates about what to do about us. Our people are going to present a sizable challenge for theirs. Mr. 'A' seems to think our performance might somehow influence the outcome of the public debate.*

Daniela came back with the pocket-tab. "Ok. Let's order some breakfast. I'll get them to bring it here." She handed the pocket-tab to Felix. "You two seem to be turning into minor celebrities."

Sherry frowned, "Oh? How's that?"

"Well, the news has gotten around through the ever present grapevine, that you two are responsible for saving five people from becoming 'mindless vegetables.' I've had a few requests for your attentions for various minor ailments."

Felix shook his head. "We don't need this. We've no desire to become curiosities. Besides, Mr. 'A' instructed us strictly to 'stay out of any more trouble' till we've had proper training.

Daniela grinned. "Don't worry. I told them the stories are greatly exaggerated, but I warn you, sooner or later people are going to start asking all kinds of tough questions. I suggest you tell Tolya another ship-wide meeting's in order; the sooner, the better."

She accepted the pocket-tab back and turned for the curtain. "Vince and I are headed off to your little church. Afterward, we'll bring the gang up to see you." She cast them a stern glance. "Rest. That's doctor's orders." She showed the slightest little smile and left the room.

COMING OUT — 2
SUN 08.15.2094-Earth / TRN 19.03.6998-Aambü
ECS Destiny, Quarterdeck, MedCentral, 1045 Hrs / 1400 Slashes

With breakfast finished, Felix transferred back to his bed. The staff helped adjust them so they could sit partially reclining.

One of the weekend nurses came to the curtained entry and poked her head in. "Someone's here to see you two."

Sherry grinned. "A visitor. Great!"

The nurse came in and placed a chair in the room between the beds so that someone could see either occupant comfortably. She left and a moment later returned, ushering Janelle into the room.

Janelle seemed uncertain. She approached Sherry. "Sherry?"

"Yes, it's good to see you."

Janelle smiled. "You look just like you did in the...dream. I thought it was all a dream till I woke up in MedCentral."

Sherry grinned. "It was a dream; a very long, troublesome dream. Sometimes, dreams can have connection to the real world as you've discovered. I take it you slept well?"

Janelle nodded. "I slept better than I have in years."

She turned to Felix. "And you're Felix. You look the same too. I...I'm not sure what you did, but thank you. Dr. Jacobs says I owe you big time."

Felix grinned. "No sweat. I'd hope you'd hear Captain Chernov out when he calls for you and your team. I have a hunch we'll need your expertise on this new world."

Janelle sat down and considered her two new friends. "Sherry, you told me, back in...there, that I was in good hands; many good hands. You said you'd been praying...in there...and that there were a lot of people here that were praying for us as well.

"I...ah...well, when you left to rejoin Felix, I...ah...oh, this is kind of embarrassing." She looked down at her fidgeting hands. "You got me to thinking and, well...I prayed, I think, for the first time in my life. I told God that if he was really there, I needed him to help us. Even if he didn't help me, I wanted him to help you guys. I...I've never been much for religion and stuff, but...well, I guess God did what I asked him."

Sherry smiled. "Yes, He did. We'd never have made it if He hadn't helped us find the damaged spot, or if He hadn't motivated our friend to call for help and lend us more energy. So, what do you think about God now?"

Janelle seemed almost shy, a response neither Sherry nor Felix would have expected from her. "I...ah...I want to find out more about him...I've heard so many confusing things."

Felix spoke up. "Janelle. The first step is recognizing He's real and that He's truly interested in us. We have a couple of good friends. He's pastor of a small church meeting down on Deck 3. He and his wife are putting Sherry up for a couple of weeks while I get our housing arranged for when we're married. I think Pastor Brad would love to meet you and have a heart to heart talk."

Janelle looked over at him. "I think I'd like that. You know. I figured out where I've seen you before." Felix flushed. "You're the one guy who didn't get executed after that sabotage thing a few months ago."

Felix nodded and looked away. After a moment he looked back at her. "Yes, Janelle. That was me. I was a stupid fool who got in with the wrong people. I spent my time thinking of just myself, and what I could get.

"Sherry's the one I injured when I broke into SecCentral to spring the man who tried to kill the captain. She chose to forgive me; for what reason I still don't understand. That act of kindness made me want to truly change...that and the trial and the realization that I'd come very close to ending my life for nothing."

Sherry spoke up. "During his time in confinement, we got to know each other and became good friends." She smiled. "See, I work for Chief Tanya in SecCentral. So I had many opportunities to talk to Felix. Captain, and Governor Chernov, pardoned Felix partially because of good behavior and because he showed signs of becoming an asset to the colony.

Sherry looked over at Felix. "When Captain Chernov and Chief Tanya were married, Felix and I discovered we wanted to be more than just friends."

She waved a hand about. "Then all this other stuff happened. We discovered God during all of that and had our own heart to heart talk with Pastor Brad."

Janelle sat and pondered the story. "Well, I have to say the way he...the way both of you were so self giving in trying to save me, I wouldn't have guessed he was the same person that was on trial."

Sherry grinned. "That's because he's not! He's changed since our rude introduction. Like I told you last night, I trust him with my life. I'd have never imagined saying that the day we met." *And you know I mean that, sir.*

Felix glanced at Sherry. *I know love. You probably saved my life with that decision to forgive me that day.*

Sherry looked down. *I know. That's what my original dream was, you know.*

Felix knew because of the mutual memory dump they'd experienced. *I know. You've got to find a way to get over that dream. That chapter is over.*

Janelle was watching them. The room had gotten quiet during their silent exchange.

She smiled, "You're doing it, aren't you?"

Felix looked at her.

"You're talking to each other up here." She tapped her temple.

Sherry smiled. "Yeah. It's just so easy to slip into. Is it really that obvious?"

Janelle nodded. "You look at each other and use some of the visual cues that normally come with a spoken conversation. Frankly it's a little spooky to watch; especially if you don't know what's going on."

Felix shrugged. "It's just a part of us now. I don't know how we can make it less...overt."

Janelle shook her head. "Don't. It may be unusual for the rest of us, but it's what you're becoming. I understand it from first hand observation. I've come to expect it. The people that matter will be the same."

* * * *

SUN 08.15.2094-Earth / TRN 19.03.6998-Aambü
ECS Destiny, Quarterdeck, MedCentral, 1115 Hrs / 1438 Slashes

The weekend nurse, Connie, stuck her head in and announced. "Janelle. You have company."

Janelle grinned. "Ah! That would be my team."

Connie smiled. "You want to meet somewhere else?"

Janelle shook her head. "Send them on in..." she looked over at Felix and Sherry, "I'm sorry, that's if Sherry and Felix don't mind."

The two chorused. "No." Sherry continued with a grin, "We'd love to meet your team mates."

Connie shrugged and ducked out. In a few moments Janelle's team trooped into the slowly shrinking room.

There were two guys. One was Japanese. He went by the name, Kiyoshi. He was quite the character and probably the life of the party. He sure laughed a lot.

The other was from France. His name was Corin. He was quiet and carried himself with a certain grace.

Then, there was Marva. She was from Israel. She seemed to be the listener of the group. All of them were excited to see Janelle up and around. When they learned it was Felix and Sherry who brought her out of her near coma, they gathered around to express their appreciation.

Some curiosity over the methods caused much speculation. Felix and Sherry tried to keep much of the detail quiet. It was going to be tough getting past the celebrity status once it began.

Janelle sensed Felix and Sherry were tiring and suggested it would be delightful if they would go grab some lunch and bring something back for her when they were done. They took the hint good-naturedly.

COMING OUT — 3

SUN 08.15.2094-Earth / TRN 19.03.6998-Aambü
ECS Destiny, Quarterdeck, MedCentral, 1230 Hrs / 1533 Slashes

Janelle was considering leaving to let her new friends sleep when Daniela poked her head into the room. "You have several visitors and I don't think I can keep them out much longer." She gave them a big grin.

Felix grinned back and waved an arm as if to say bring them on. "It's OK. Send them in."

It's Tahnie and the others isn't it?

Felix grinned. *Yes, they're a bit impatient.*

Daniela pulled back the curtain to admit the Chernov Family and Pastor Brad and Jodi Hill.

Tanya made a beeline to Sherry's side and gave her a fierce hug. "You keep putting my friend in danger, young lady. You keep scaring me."

Sherry grinned and hugged back. "I'm OK really. Dannie won't let us out till we're fully rested and we can walk on our own. We abused our muscles, standing in one position forever. Then they got us seated and we sat on stools in awkward postures for another couple of hours. Our backs, legs, just about all our muscles are sore and rebellious."

Daniela grinned. "That's right. Maybe this evening they can go home; we'll have to see."

She whispered something in Sherry's ear before leaving the room. Apparently, she and Vince were off to have their own private lunch date.

Tolya approached Felix and gripped his shoulder. "I never thought I'd care so much what happened to you, mister, but I'm glad you're back in the real world. Life would be so much more boring without you."

Felix felt embarrassed. "Thanks Tolya. I'll be fine in a few hours. How was the service?"

Tolya grinned. "The service went well. We had a good time offering thanks and praise for everyone's' safe return from wherever you went. You'll have to tell me about it some time."

Felix glanced over at Pastor Brad and Jodi. She'd joined Tanya at Sherry's bed and Brad started his way.

"So, Felix, I see God brought you through, mostly unscathed."

Felix grinned. "That He did."

Felix raised his voice a little to be heard above the heavy murmur of all the voices at once. "Hey everyone. I'd like to introduce Janelle, here. She's the one that gave us the opportunity for so much fun!"

Lyuba had already been eying Janelle. She beat everyone else to the punch and introduced herself. "Hi. I'm Lyuba. That's my Dad and Mom."

She was still very proud about those facts.

Janelle smiled. "They're wonderful, Lyuba."

Tolya and Tanya moved to say hello, and Sherry called to Lyuba. "Hey kiddo. I didn't get a hug yet."

Lyuba hurried over and threw her all into a big hug for Sherry. "Are you really OK?"

Sherry nodded. "Yeah, I'll be just fine. I think Daniela might let us go tonight."

"Oh...that's great!"

"Hey Lyuba." Felix called. "You didn't even say, 'HI.' What's up with that?"

Lyuba walked over to his side of the room. "Hi, Felix. I didn't mean to ignore you."

She patted his arm and turned serious. "So, what's it like in somebody else's head?"

Felix laughed. "Well, it's kinda hard to explain. It depends on the situation. Most of the time, we found ourselves in a place, like a home where the person lived. Each person's 'place' is unique. It says something about their personality. Why do you ask?"

Lyuba got a thoughtful look on her face. "Lately, I've been seeing weird things like people turning sorta shiny."

Sherry's head snapped over to where Felix and Lyuba were chatting. *Did she just say what I thought she said?*

Felix glanced back. *Yes, she did. We'd better have a talk with Mr. 'A' really soon.* "Hey kiddo. Are there any other kind of weird things you can remember?"

"Well, sometimes I know when Dad's going to get home before the door opens...Mom too. And Friday, I was working in the lab and Ms. Emily came to my station. She put her hand on my shoulder and I started hearing this weird humming noise. It stopped when she let go and walked away."

Felix touched Lyuba's arm. *Can you hear me, Lyuba?*

Lyuba's eyes got round and darted to Felix' face.

She pulled from his touch, looking worried. "What did you do? There was this sound like when the air systems come on all at once. I thought I could hear the room get echoey...there was a voice, but I couldn't hear it very well."

Felix. Is she awakening?

Felix looked at Sherry. *I don't know, but I think it's possible. I heard Mr. 'A' say something about how she might awaken soon.*

He glanced at Lyuba. *Kiddo. Can you hear me?*

Lyuba looked up at him. "Did you just talk to me?" She pointed to the side of her head.

Felix smiled. "Yes, I did."

"I heard it, but it was really quiet."

Felix nodded. "We need to talk. I have a little theory. Why don't you go to Sherry and touch her arm? She'll say something to you. I think there has to be touch first. Then later, you can hear if you want to. I don't really know because I'm new to all this."

Lyuba nodded, "OK. This is weird." She headed over to Sherry who was ready for her.

Felix glanced up and thought about talking to Tolya. Tolya frowned slightly in a pause in his conversation and glanced sharply over at Felix. Felix grinned and signaled him over.

Tolya excused himself and joined Felix. "Did you just do something?" He waved a hand at his head.

Felix shrugged. "I just wished to talk to you and you looked up."

Tolya shook his head. "It's weird, because I just had the notion you wanted to talk to me."

"I did, uh, do. Mr. 'A'...ah, sorry, that's our private pet name for AgradUtya. Anyways, he warned that Lyuba's dream experience was strong enough, and she had enough potential, that she could 'awaken' soon."

Tolya frowned. "You never mentioned this before."

Felix felt defensive. "How could I? It's been nonstop since we regained consciousness!"

Tolya relented. "I know, I know. I just get a little touchy where Lyuba's concerned."

Felix smiled. "...I know... I'm sorry this slipped through the cracks. The reason I brought it up is, I think she's starting to 'awaken' now. We've got to get a meeting with Mr. 'A' soon."

Tolya looked over at Lyuba, who was hugging Sherry again. "Will she...you know, get linked...like you two?"

Felix shrugged. "I really don't know anything about all this stuff. She hasn't met anyone but us who've been awakened. I think once a bond like ours takes place, no one else can bond with either party.

"There'd have to be another guy somewhere on board who has the potential and is awakening. If so, we'll just have to make sure we're ready to deal with the possibilities."

Felix took Tolya's arm. "Tolya. Sherry and I think of Lyuba like a little sister. We love her and we'll do whatever we need to, to protect her and make sure this experience is a positive one."

His glance darted to Sherry, who was looking at him earnestly and holding Lyuba's hand. *That's right love. Tell him I'm listening and I totally agree.*

Felix grinned and relayed her message.

Tolya seemed to relax. "OK. It's an awful lot to chew on. Does Lyuba know?"

Felix nodded. "She's been having twinges of telepathic...oh, I don't know, call it 'whispers' for lack of a better word. For example, she senses your presence just as you're about to come in the door. The same goes for Tanya. She's sensing the ambient undercurrent each person has that we hear when we touch someone. It happened with Emily, Friday. Lyuba didn't know what it was.

"She's also starting to perceive people differently. Like us, she now sees a slight glow or sheen in people's faces, and, just now, she was able to hear me calling her. It's still not clear, and she doesn't know how to send yet; but it's just a matter of time."

Tolya shook his head. "Tanya needs to hear about this. Maybe we can have dinner tonight and discuss it."

He looked over at Tanya and Janelle. "So, what do you think of this gal, Janelle?"

Felix shrugged. "I think she's pretty sharp. Did she tell you her profession yet?"

Tolya shook his head. "We were talking about the dream thing. She was going on and on about how you two took control of her dream and made it different."

Felix grinned. "Janelle and her three friends are a team. They're professional deep sea divers who specialize in construction for mining operations."

Tolya's eyebrow shot up. "Really!" He shook his head. "I'm convinced God has this incredible sense of humor. He keeps doing things full of twists of irony. I mean, look at our situation. Who could we use more than people who know something about working in the ocean? It's just amazing."

He pondered the information for a moment. "We need to have a heart to heart talk. Who's the leader?"

Felix shrugged. "I'm not sure. They seem to share a common bond, but they tend to defer to Janelle."

A thought struck Felix. "Speaking of heart to heart talks. During the more tense moments of our adventure with her, she felt compelled to pray for the first time in her life. When it was all over, she commented that God must have been listening because he did what she'd asked. She wants to know more about Him. I told her she needed a nice heart to heart chat with Pastor Brad."

"Ah!" Tolya smiled. "An excellent idea."

He turned to Brad who was coincidentally headed his way. "Brad. Felix has something interesting to tell you about our new friend, Janelle."

Brad smiled and looked at Felix. "Well, sir. As I said earlier, I'm happy you're doing well. Now, what's this interesting tidbit?"

Felix grinned. "Janelle's close brush with disaster compelled her to try prayer for the first time in her life. She was quite surprised at the result and wants to know more about God. She says she's heard so many confusing things she doesn't know what to believe."

Brad's face glowed and it wasn't just because of Felix' new way of perceiving people. "Is that right? You know I always say, 'God sometimes does drastic things to get our attention.' I think we could classify her ordeal as rather drastic. Don't you?"

Tolya and Felix chuckled and then he got serious. "I'm delighted to hear she's decided to honor her notion that God was truly involved. That's an important first step. Thank you Felix. I certainly agree, we could surely use a heart to heart talk..."

He glanced at Jodi who was showing off Evan to Janelle. "I'll arrange things with Jodi and we'll have a meal and then a nice chat. I'd like you and Sherry to be there if you don't mind. I'll let you know when."

He started to turn away and then remembered something. "Now don't you forget; you're due for counseling on Wednesday before Bible Study."

Felix slapped his head with the palm of his hand. "Thank you, Brad. With all that's been going on, I'd completely forgotten. We'll be there, sorry we missed the service."

Brad grinned. "Apology accepted. You had a very good reason. Well, I guess I'd best go talk with Jodi." With that, he returned to join Jodi and Janelle.

Tolya signaled Tanya to join them. He filled her in about Lyuba. Tanya pulled Lyuba into a hug. "What's going on, honey?"

Lyuba looked serious. "I've been having all kinds of weird experiences lately and Felix and Sherry say I'm going to be kinda like they are. I thought it would be cool, but now I'm kinda scared."

Tanya smiled and hugged her again. She looked at her and then said quietly so the guys wouldn't hear. "Remember when we talked about the...those monthly times, a little while ago?"

Lyuba looked around. She said, in a hoarse whisper, "Mom...That's embarrassing."

"I know honey, but think about it. What's going on now is just as natural for you as the other thing is. Once you get used to it, you'll be just fine with it." She gave her a wink, "Mostly."

"But Mom. It's not normal. I'll be weird."

"Honey. Are Felix and Sherry really that weird?"

Lyuba looked down and shook her head. "No, they're as nice as ever, but that's different."

Tanya hooked Lyuba's chin with a finger and gently tipped her head up to look at her. "Is it really, sweet heart? Felix and Sherry are way different from other people their age now. They can do things that other people their age can't do. They just find ways to use their new abilities to help people. That makes them see that they're still useful and welcome.

"It's going to be difficult when other kids find out, but you'll just have to find a way to use the new abilities you gain to your best advantage. They'll eventually learn to respect you."

She hugged Lyuba again and then looked up at Sherry. "So, what's next?"

"Honestly Tahnie, I don't know. We think she needs to meet with Mr. 'A' and hear what he has to say about this."

Tanya blinked. "Mr. 'A'?"

Sherry grinned and shook her head. "Sorry, it's our nickname for AgradUtya. We don't call him that in person. We don't want to insult him, but you have to admit it's a lot easier to say."

It was Tanya's turn to grin. "I suppose you're right. I understand this alien ambassador's hard to see."

Felix nodded. "That's because most people can't see with their mental eyes. When he comes to the ship right now, he comes in a mental, or dream state...they call it questing...he's not physically here at all. So, only someone like Sherry and I can see him clearly. I think Lyuba will have no trouble seeing him when he arrives."

Tanya sighed. "How are the rest of us supposed to interact with these...people."

Both Sherry and Felix shrugged in unison.

"That," Felix said, "is the big prize question. They can speak vocally, but the sound range of their voices is up towards the ultrasonic end of the audio spectrum. That could get pretty painful after a while."

Sherry smiled. "I'm sure we'll figure something out. By the way, Dannie warned us that bits and pieces of this whole adventure are starting to get around in the general population. She suggested we get busy and have another ship wide meeting...soon. Otherwise, the rumor mill is going to start making things dicey."

Tanya nodded and looked at Tolya. He'd heard the comment and was looking thoughtful. "I'd like to wait till we get a proper introduction to this ambassador person. Now that this dream fallout is behind us. Maybe we can get to the nuts and bolts of diplomacy. Felix. We need an official meeting."

Felix shrugged. I think we're supposed to meet him again sometime today. He said he'd talk to us 'next turn' when he left us last night. Did he mean our 'next turn' or theirs?"

"The time differences are significant if you think about it. When he gets here, I'll let you know. That's the best I can do right now."

Tolya nodded. "OK, but we need to get busy."

Felix. Behind Janelle...I think the problem just solved itself.

Felix nodded at Sherry and looked where she'd indicated. He could see AgradUtya coalescing behind Janelle. Felix raised his voice to carry above the ambient sounds of conversation.

COMING OUT — 4

SUN 08.15.2094-Earth / TRN 19.03.6998-Aambü
ECS Destiny, Quarterdeck, MedCentral, 1400 Hrs / 1650 Slashes

"Computer. Dim light to one quarter." Felix announced to the air around him. The room dimmed significantly and everyone looked at Felix expectantly.

"For some of you this may seem very mysterious. To others, you'll catch on soon enough. We're being graced with a visit from our friend AgradUtya, from Aambü.

"Janelle, don't move. He's behind you and will pass by you into the middle of the room."

Ah, my friend AgradUtya, welcome. As you can see we have a room full of visitors.

The apparition that represented AgradUtya passed near Janelle. She saw a thin vaguely cloudy form. Brad saw him a little more brightly. Jody, like Janelle barely saw the cloud. To Tolya, it was like seeing a ghostly shape that had little distinct form. Tanya saw a little more clearly, while Lyuba was rooted to the spot. She saw, like Felix and Sherry, a reasonable likeness of the physical form of the person that sent it.

I fear I have interrupted some meeting. My apologies.

Sherry smiled. *No apologies needed. These are friends who've come to wish us well after our ordeal.*

AgradUtya regarded Lyuba and moved towards her. Lyuba stood her ground with round-eyed wonder. *Felix, Sherry. It appears our young friend is awakening sooner than expected. Please tell her I will not harm her. I need to help open her mind so she can converse.*

Sherry called to Lyuba. "Lyuba, it's OK. This is how our friend looks when he's questing. He's really somewhere on his planet.

"He says he needs to help you hear him better. He's going to place his hands on either side of your head just like if he was going to touch your ears. It won't hurt. So, just let him do it. OK?"

Lyuba never took her eyes off AgradUtya, but she nodded and swallowed her nervousness down. Everyone watched the cloud move towards the young girl and after a moment a look of wonder passed over her face.

Little one, I welcome you to a very small collection of humans who are able to mind speak. You are gaining a new set of abilities. Try to talk to me, but don't open your mouth.

Lyuba was dumb struck. She couldn't have spoken with her mouth if she'd wanted to. Finally she worked up the courage. *Uh...Hello? Can you hear me?*

AgradUtya radiated approval. *Yes, you're doing just fine. That was easy wasn't it?*

Lyuba's eyes were wide with surprise and excitement. *Yes, it was. This is cool!*

AgradUtya smiled in the questing chamber. This one was full of enthusiasm. He considered the comment. *Cool? Sherry. What does the child mean, 'cool?'"*

Sherry grinned. *It's an old expression. I truly don't know where it came from, but it expresses positive enthusiasm for a new experience. Lyuba is thrilled.*

AgradUtya expressed humor. *I suspected. Her emotions seemed to be on that current. Little one. May I have the pleasure of knowing your full name?*

Lyuba smiled. *It's Lyubova Anastasia Chernov.*

AgradUtya made a set of gestures of respect. *Lyubova Anastasia Chernov. I am known simply as AgradUtya. I've heard your friends address you as Lyuba. May I call you this?*

Lyuba smiled. *Sure. All my friends call me Lyuba.*

AgradUtya expressed mild humor. *I'd be honored to be one of your friends, Lyuba. Which of these people are your parents?*

Lyuba pointed towards Tolya and Tanya. *That's Anatoli Chernov. He's captain of this ship, and Governor of our people. He's my new father. That's Tanya Chernov. She's Chief of security and the First Lady of our colony. She's my new mother.*

AgradUtya queried. *Felix. Why does Lyuba refer to her parents as her 'new' parent?*

Felix grinned. *Captain and Mrs. Chernov were recently married and they adopted Lyuba as their daughter. Her original parents died when she was an infant. Captain Chernov has cared for her in her father's place. Now he's her new father.*

AgradUtya was intrigued. At home, an orphaned child became a child of the whole clan. These children were cared for by whoever was able at any given time. It certainly appeared that humans had a unique relationship with their young. There was a certain appeal to the practice.

Lyuba must be trained, as must you two. Unfortunately, you are too old to have parents to take the responsibility, and Lyuba's parents aren't sufficiently gifted in this area. So, in keeping with your practice, as you describe it, I think it would be interesting to have you and Sherry be responsible for Lyuba's training in her parent's stead. They would still have parental authority, but you would represent them when it comes to her training. In turn, I will personally see to training both of you.

AgradUtya considered options. Then an idea struck him. *Felix. Would you please summon your healer? I need her as official witness. I've had limited success communicating with her.*

Felix raised an eyebrow. *Of course, it may take some time. She's off duty now.*

AgradUtya signed acquiescence.

Felix turned to Tolya. "Tolya. Could you please call Dannie? AgradUtya's asking for her; something about an official witness."

Tolya quirked an eyebrow. "Yeah, sure. Hang on."

He pinched his COMM tab. "Doctor Jacobs."

After a moment, "Yeah, Dannie. I hate to bother you, but a significant development has happened with Lyuba, of all people. That guy, AgradUtya is here, asking for you...

"Yes, you...I don't quite understand; something about an official witness...OK. Sure, I'll tell 'em."

Tolya turned to Felix. "They're on the way. Fortunately, they finished their lunch."

Felix smiled. "Thanks."

He addressed AgradUtya. *Friend. The healer is on her way. It will be a few moments.*

AgradUtya signed understanding. *Thank you.*

While they were waiting, Felix thought it might be a good idea to fill everyone in on what was going on.

"OK. Can I have everyone's attention?"

All eyes in the room focused on Felix. Janelle got up from her chair and moved where she could see the goings on better. "I just want to explain some things. "Most of you are aware of the presence of our friend, AgradUtya. You saw him interact with Lyuba. He requested me to call Daniela for a special purpose I am still waiting to discover."

Daniela pushed the curtain aside and stepped into the rather cozy environs of the cubicle. "Why are the lights dimmed?" She stopped in her tracks as she saw the glittering cloud that floated in front of Lyuba. "What's going on?"

Felix smiled. "It's OK, Dannie. You remember AgradUtya from yesterday, don't you?"

Daniela hadn't taken her eyes off of the cloudy form. It seemed a bit more distinct than yesterday. "Yes, I...would you tell him I'm very grateful for his assistance...and that of his associate?"

Felix smiled. "Sure, but let me reintroduce you. Maybe he can find a way you can tell him yourself."

Dannie's eyes got round. "How?"

Felix shrugged. "I don't know, but he specifically asked for you."

AgradUtya moved away from Lyuba and approached Daniela. *Now, Felix. Before I begin, It might good to complete your explanations.*

Felix grinned. *You're right. Thank you.*

AgradUtya signed acceptance and mild humor.

Felix raised his voice again. "I'm sorry, everyone. Let me finish my explanation.

"I believe, by now, everyone in the room is aware that we're in contact with a new species, indigenous to our target planet; a world they call Aambü. Most of you know at least peripherally that Sherry and I have been changed in a way that makes us able to communicate mind to mind, telepathy if you like. For now, suffice to say, The Dream we recently experienced is the primary cause of those changes.

"Something we were not aware of happened, however. While Sherry and I were 'awakened,' as our friend would say, Lyuba here, was also affected. She has taken a little longer, but she is currently in process of awakening.

"Our friend AgradUtya sensed this when he arrived and saw to the successful completion of that event. Lyuba, is now able to speak mind to mind with anyone able to reciprocate.

He glanced over at AgradUtya's form. Then he concluded his little talk. "AgradUtya requested that Daniela be present for some special ceremony, I believe. So, we will proceed, and I will explain as I am able."

My friend. I believe we are now ready to continue. Felix waited to see what AgradUtya would do next.

AgradUtya acknowledged Felix comment and took over. *That was well said, Felix. Until I have made contact, I would like you to translate for your healer.*

AgradUtya gave his full attention to Daniela. *Would you please introduce her to me?*

Felix replied. *Certainly.* "Dannie. AgradUtya is going to attempt to devise a means to communicate with you. To begin with, he'd appreciate your full name."

Daniela was a bit nervous. Just then, Vince, who'd been standing just in the entryway, slipped up and placed his arm around her waist. Dannie glanced at him and gave him a welcoming smile. She turned to face the glittering luminescent cloud. "My name is Dr. Daniela Renee Jacobs."

Felix passed along the information.

AgradUtya signed understanding. *Lyuba. Please explain that I am about to show her some images similarly to when I did so during the ordeal, last turn.*

Lyuba went to Daniela's side and explained. "AgradUtya is going to place his web-hands near your head and give you some images. He says he did something like this yesterday."

Dannie smiled. "I remember. I guess It's OK."

Vince was just staring at the faint luminous cloud, trying to get an idea what this character was supposed to look like.

Lyuba faithfully repeated Daniela's response and AgradUtya signed understanding.

The incandescent cloud grew a pair of appendages about where arms would be. The arms reached out and stopped inches to either side of Daniela's head.   She felt a slight sense of nerves, but yesterday's experience left her less fearful.

Daniela found herself floating in space to one side of the ship. The view was impressive. She seemed to rotate and found herself facing the ringed planet far ahead. Suddenly she was hurtling at incredible speed towards the beautiful, blue, ring-girdled globe. The rings flowed rapidly beneath her and the planet surged towards her.

She dove into the atmosphere and then straight for the worldwide ocean. This is just like The Dream, *she thought.*

She noticed a group of islands arranged in a tight circle with an area cut away. The vision sent her deep into the water and then straight towards the side of a sheer sea-mount.

Just when she thought she would collide with the rocky surface, her view swept upward. She realized part of the wall of the sea-mount curved inward sharply, leaving an opening directly above her. She could see the underside of the surface of the water, strangely close to her.

Rising through the surface she found herself in a rocky cavern lit by clusters of glowing globes. The entry she had just used was at the bottom of a large pool.

The view rolled through various passageways and chambers, finally ending in a smaller cavern with another pool of water. The vision dove into the pool and came to a stop before a creature, loosely curled in an almost fetal position. An odd ribbon of light originated from the chest of the creature, arrowing through the rocky ceiling at what seemed to be a random angle. Daniela realized this was the physical form of their guest.

Felix was right. They look almost like elephant seals. *She considered the description and decided though it was truly far from accurate, it was a reasonable comparison.*

Motion resumed and she found herself hurtling along the ribbon of light, right through solid rock, out into the ocean and then up into the sky. The light ribbon arced gracefully out of sight over the rings. She followed it at unbelievable speeds. Destiny *seemed to race up on her and she was sure she'd crash right into the front.*

Daniela was suddenly back in the recovery cubicle. She experienced a moment of vertigo. Vince grabbed her elbow to steady her. She opened her eyes, though she didn't remember closing them.

AgradUtya's web-hands settled back to his sides. *Lyuba. Please take the healer's hand.*

Lyuba reached out and took Daniela's hand. *OK.*

Daniela was amazed. Though the cloud that represented their guest was still a cloud, she could see more clearly a form reminiscent of the creature she saw in her vision.

Lyuba. I want you to speak to your healer with your mind. Don't let go of her hand. After you speak to her, I want you to remember how that feels and then keep that feeling as you listen to me. This way you will keep the connection open so she can hear me through you.

Lyuba nodded and faced Dannie. *Dr. Jacobs. Can you hear me?*

Daniela looked down at Lyuba in surprise. "Lyuba, honey. Did you just say something?"

Lyuba smiled. *Yes, in a way. I'm speaking to you with just my mind. AgradUtya says you can hear me because we're touching. He's going to talk to you through me."*

Daniela was feeling seriously out of her depth. "OK... This is, well...kinda strange." She turned to face AgradUtya. "I'm ready."

AgradUtya signed respect. *Dr. Daniela Renee Jacobs. I am pleased to finally be able to speak with you. Do you hear me?*

Daniela was amazed. She looked at Lyuba and then back at the apparition of the Aambüka Ambassador. His 'voice' was surprisingly pleasant, a rich, low tenor, smooth and soothing. "I... I hear you very well. Can you hear me?"

AgradUtya colored his reply with amusement. *Yes, I can hear you just fine.*

Daniela was excited. "Mr. Agrad...U..tya, I just realized I can express my deepest, heart felt gratitude for the assistance you and your friend afforded Felix and Sherry."

AgradUtya signed humble acceptance. *Dr. Daniela Renee Jacobs. It was the least I could do. While it was supremely important that Felix and Sherry survive the experience, I confess I am developing a certain fondness for them.*

Daniela smiled. "Yes, well, it's the same with us. They've become close friends we would dearly be sorry to lose." She was feeling a bit awkward hearing her full name and title every time this fellow addressed her. "Mr. AgradUtya. It would please me if you would address me simply as Daniela. Among friends, we simply use first names."

AgradUtya signed respect. *I would be pleased to call you a friend, Daniela. In my culture our names reflect our occupations. Since I have become my people's First Ambassador to what many are calling The Star People, I am known as AgradUtya. It is the only name I need now.*

AgradUtya moved to place himself near Felix. *Daniela. I would be delighted to carry on a longer conversation, but right now, I need your help in a little ceremony I must conduct. Then we should let everyone get back to what they were doing.*

AgradUtya addressed Lyuba. *Lyuba. You may let go of Daniela's hand for now. We are going to have a little ceremony. Then you will resume contact with her.*

Felix. Would you summon Tolya? Sherry. Please summon Tanya.

They complied. Tolya and Tanya seemed unsure, but moved to join them.

AgradUtya explained. *Felix, Sherry. I must do the same procedure for Lyuba's parents. Please, explain what I'm about to do.*

Felix signed understanding and explained things to Tolya as Sherry did for Tanya.

AgradUtya moved towards Tolya. *Felix. It might be a good time to explain what's going on to the rest.*

Felix grinned. *Right. Give me a moment.* "OK, everyone. This is probably getting just a little confusing. So, I'm going to explain what has just happened. AgradUtya did something to assist Dannie so she can hear what he says. As long as she has physical contact with someone who can mind speak, she can hear and understand. Now, he's going to do the same thing for Tolya and Tanya. When he's finished he'll conduct his ceremony.

Thank you, Felix. AgradUtya reached out with his web-hands. *Please explain as Lyuba did for Daniela.*

Felix acknowledged the request. "Tolya. AgradUtya will show you a series of images. When your tour is done, you'll be able to hear AgradUtya through touch, just like Dannie."

Tolya nodded. "I guess I'm ready."

AgradUtya asked for Tolya's full name and then began. After a time, Tolya's eyes flew open as a look of amazement crossed his features. "That was amazing. That's where you live? I saw no one else there."

AgradUtya expressed amusement at the comment. It wasn't doubt at the reality but rather, curiosity at what he perceived to be missing. This human was a thinker, similar to their healer, Daniela.

Felix, please make physical contact with Tolya.

Felix took Tolya's wrist. "AgradUtya wants to speak to you."

Captain, and Governor Anatoli Gavriil Chernov, what you experienced was a limited view of the reality. I couldn't possibly project where all the people would be, so I left them out. It would've taken too much energy to make the attempt. Now, I'll bring your mate into the circle.

AgradUtya moved over to Sherry's side of the room. He approached Tanya. *Sherry. Please explain what I will do.*

Sherry acknowledged the request and then explained to Tanya something of what AgradUtya would be doing for her. After hearing Tanya's full name AgradUtya placed his web-hands on either side of her head and repeated the process for her.

Tanya's mouth went round in wonder as she started her virtual tour. She closed her eyes and watched.

Sherry was ready, her hand gently clasping Tanya's wrist. Tanya opened her eyes, swaying as she returned to the physical reality.

AgradUtya addressed her. *Tanya Marie Chernov. Do you hear me?*

Tanya grinned. "Yes, I do! This is really strange, but I could get used to it."

AgradUtya expressed humor. *Tanya Marie Chernov, it's good to be able to converse with you more directly.*

He addressed his three prodigies. *I need all three of you to keep your perceptions open so your partner can hear and be heard.*

He got a chorus of agreement from the three. *Felix. You probably need to catch everyone else up.*

Felix grinned. *Right.* "OK. Now that we have the three principles tuned in, we can have a reasonable conversation. So, AgradUtya will conduct a brief ceremony."

Janelle, Brad and Jodie watched with a blend of curiosity and mild confusion with a hint of frustration thrown in. Everyone else in the room was involved in a complicated communication ring, so they appreciated the explanations.

David F. Snider

AgradUtya addressed Lyuba. *Since there are still three who cannot fully follow the communication, I would ask you to provide spoken translation of my part of the ceremony.*

She readily agreed. So began an odd little ceremony to provide Lyuba legally binding sponsorship for her training.

AgradUtya explained. *Daniela. Please attend as we begin. Anatoli and Tanya Chernov. The purpose for this ceremony is to ensure that Lyuba is sponsored for training. In our culture, the parents of a newly awakened child will sponsor their child for training. They make certain the child follows the instructions of the teacher.*

Since it is quite rare that the parents would be unable to mind speak, this process has become more of a formality than it should. Because you're not gifted with mind speak, it becomes necessary to find other means to gain sponsorship for Lyuba.

Felix and Sherry have described the practice your people call adoption. It so intrigued me that I thought to borrow the idea for our purposes. I propose that Felix and Sherry adopt Lyuba specifically to be responsible for her training. You two would remain her parents, of course. Felix and Sherry would simply cover those areas of Lyuba's new skills that you could never adequately teach her. Before we continue, I would like to secure your permission to do this.

Tanya looked over at Tolya. Felix, sensing their need for privacy, removed his hand from Tolya's wrist. Sherry, understanding immediately, released Tanya as well. Tolya and Tanya chatted quietly for a moment.

Tolya took Felix' wrist and spoke. "AgradUtya. We would be happy to share Lyuba with Felix and Sherry to assure her training. They have become almost family as it is."

AgradUtya signed understanding. *Felix and Sherry Hernandez. Do you promise to take Lyubova Anastasia Chernov under your guidance and protection during her training?*

Felix and Sherry responded together. *We do.*

AgradUtya continued. *Do you promise to respect her parent's wishes where her training is not at issue?*

Again the young couple responded affirmatively.

AgradUtya addressed Tolya and Tanya. *Anatoli and Tanya Chernov, do you grant permission for Felix and Sherry to take the role of adoptive parent regarding Lyuba's training?*

Tolya and Tanya exchanged glances and then looked over at Lyuba. Together they replied. "Yes, we do."

And do you promise to respect and support their authority regarding her training?

"Yes, we do."

AgradUtya addressed Sherry. *Now Sherry. If you would take Lyuba's place translating*

Lyuba, do you accept Felix and Sherry Hernandez as your adoptive parents regarding your training?

Lyuba looked over at Sherry and smiled. *I do.*

And do you promise to respect their authority and follow their instruction as they receive it from me?

Lyuba's face sobered as she considered the seriousness of his question. *I do.*

AgradUtya addressed Daniela. *Dr. Daniela Jacobs, You have witnessed this somewhat awkward, but binding ceremony. Lyuba's parents have freely given Felix and Sherry parental authority over Lyuba when it comes to her training in her new mind skills. Lyuba has agreed to accept the authority of Sherry and Felix in the area of mind training. Felix and Sherry have freely accepted the responsibility of mentoring Lyuba. Do you understand and will you bear witness to these facts should you be asked to do so?*

Daniela realized the gravity of this question, though she was unsure of the purpose of this whole exercise. She was beginning to wonder if this wasn't a kind of political sleight of hand to present to the governing body he served. "I certainly do understand, and I will bear witness to these facts if I am so asked."

AgradUtya expressed satisfaction. *Then it is finished. Before the Maker and before this official witness, a parental sponsor has been secured for Lyuba's training. The formal ceremony ends.*

Daniela couldn't stand it. The question gnawed at her. "AgradUtya. I apologize if my question seems uncomfortable, but what was the purpose of this? Do you anticipate difficulty back home getting training for Lyuba?

Sherry. Please continue to translate.

Daniela. No apology is needed. It is a wise question.

Sadly, it appears there are three main divisions amongst my people regarding your existence and imminent arrival.

Most are of the first persuasion; that is, to afford you welcome as visitors and learn what we can from each other. Many are of the second persuasion; that is, to be extremely cautious in approaching this pending meeting. These people are very nervous.

Finally, there is a small, but significant number who, frankly, wish you'd just disappear. These are divided up into two groups: Those that simply want us to ignore you in the hopes you'll go away, and those who advocate active efforts to make you choose to go away. Of those, I assure you, there are very few.

When it was discovered that Felix and Sherry were awakened and that both of them were able to function in useful and helpful ways, the debate grew heated again. Some are delighted. Some are cautiously optimistic, and a few are more fearful and unhappy with the situation.

Lyuba's awakening will send another ripple through my people's collective consideration. We don't know, besides her ability to mind speak, what other skills she may manifest. Some will accept the need to properly train her. Some will be nervous about it, and some will oppose the idea out of hand.

By performing this small ceremony, I have done what I can to ensure that no lawful objection can be made before the council. To us, she may be alien, but Lyuba has indeed awakened, and has been provided legal, parental sponsorship.

Daniela was satisfied with the answer. She was impressed with the frank answers. She sensed nothing was being hidden. "Thank you for your frank explanation. I appreciate the awkward circumstance that our presence must place on your people."

She glanced at Tolya and continued. "I think I speak for all present when I say we seek peaceful interaction and possibly cohabitation with your people. We're not here to take what's not rightly given."

Tolya nodded slightly and smiled.

AgradUtya moved towards Tolya. *Felix. If I recall you named Lyuba's father as something called captain or governor. I'm not familiar with those terms, but they feel like words of authority. Please properly introduce him and explain these titles.*

Felix sat up and put his legs over the side of the bed. Laying around was getting old, but getting up was not in the equation quite yet. He retrieved Tolya's wrist and explained. *AgradUtya. I would like to present to you, Captain and Governor Anatoli Chernov. Captain is a title given to a person assigned ultimate authority over a ship, this vessel for instance, and those who keep it running properly. He makes the final decisions, determines discipline and makes sure all the people who work on board are properly taken care of.*

Governor is a title given to a person who is called to lead a large community of people in all aspects of daily life. He's responsible for the well being of the entire colony. A colony is a large community of people who have volunteered to go to a far away place to build a new permanent community of human beings. I suspect he's similar to the one you refer to as First Speaker.

COMING OUT —5

SUN 08.15.2094-Earth / TRN 19.03.6998-Aambü
ECS Destiny, Quarterdeck, MedCentral, 1530 Hrs / 1766 Slashes

AgradUtya made a series of gestures that were meant to combine understanding, great respect, and great contrition all rolled into one. *I beg your forgiveness for my ignorance. I've been sadly unaware of your position and authority.*

Tolya looked slightly uncomfortable, maybe even a little embarrassed. "AgradUtya. Please, be at peace. I have authority, as described, but I'm not terribly concerned with formalities regarding address, particularly from my guests. You've done so much, from your limited circumstance, to help my people through this awkward beginning. I'm profoundly grateful for your assistance."

Cap....Gov...ah...Forgive me, but how should I address you?

Tolya grinned. "My friends call me Tolya. You've acted as a friend. I only need formal address if it's an official activity. For instance, when we meet face to face before your leaders, you might simply use Governor before my name. That will be my final responsibility once we leave the ship."

As you wish, Tolya. I want to thank you for your gracious treatment of my many errors. For, it is I who caused the whole cycle of events to take place. None of your people would have experienced the unhappiness they did, had I not been so impulsive with my initial call of alarm.

Tolya shook his head. "Nonsense. You had no way of knowing you would have any affect on us. You were simply doing what you knew to do with the information you had. I'd say the same to my own subordinates should they have committed a similar error. Besides, you've done more than anyone could expect to correct the problems that occurred.

I thank you for that.

AgradUtya turned to Tanya. *Lady Tanya Chernov. I'm honored to know you. I presume, as the Governor's mate, you are due similar respect.*

Tanya smiled and shook her head. Being called, Lady Tanya felt extremely odd. "No, while it's true that I share his authority in our culture. I do not expect great acts of obeisance. I agree with my husband. You've acted as a friend. In private, or among friends, you should simply call me Tanya."

As you wish, Tanya. I am delighted to meet Lyuba's adoptive mother. As I understand it, you certainly seem more the proper mother than simply a replacement.

Tanya blushed. "I...Thank you."

AgradUtya addressed Lyuba. *Lyuba, little one, you've proven a very cooperative and helpful person. It should be very interesting watching your training.*

You have very loving parents. You must be very proud of them. I also begin to see why you seem a little more mature than I might have expected. After all, you're the daughter of the Governor and Governor's mate of this entire group of people. That's a great responsibility and I see you also appreciate responsibility. Keep that perspective and you'll do well. We'll talk again later.

Lyuba smiled and moved to stand before AgradUtya's image. *Thank you for your help, AgradUtya. I will do my best.* She curtsied formally and then moved to stand with Tanya.

AgradUtya addressed all those who were linked. *As I said, we've taken everyone else's time for far too long. I'd like to have a private meeting. Tolya, if you don't mind, I'd like to have you, Tanya, Felix and Sherry there. It's only a short time before your vessel...your ship, arrives over my world. I need to take answers and communications back to my own...leader.*

Tanya considered. "We must allow Felix and Sherry to complete their rest. Perhaps there's a way Felix or Sherry might contact you? One of them could tell you when they're released from the medical center. Then we could meet directly after."

AgradUtya considered the possibility.

He turned to Felix. *Do you recall when you went to find Sherry while she was trapped in the sea?*

Felix remembered. *How could I forget?*

AgradUtya signaled agreement. *Indeed. You are capable of traveling like that without going into another's mind first. You simply have to compose yourself as if to sleep. Then, like a dream, you choose to move outward.*

I want you to try this. Lie down and compose yourself. Then I want you to move yourself out and over next to Sherry. It's a short distance, but it will prove to you that it can be done.

Tanya, before we answer, we must test something. Please be patient.

Sherry. While Felix attempts this exercise, you should monitor his energy. If it ebbs, you must carefully infuse small, metered amounts.

Sherry nodded. *No problem. I think we're starting to unconsciously monitor that some.*

AgradUtya registered mild surprise. *That's an interesting development. I suppose given the kind of advanced activities you've been up to, it's no surprise.*

Felix composed himself. He tried an exercise that seemed to help him when he had trouble sleeping. He began to consciously isolate muscle groups in his body and relax them. After a while he was so incredibly relaxed, he appeared almost unconscious.

He began to think of himself as standing next to Sherry's bed. It was a strange feeling. He had no understanding of what he did. Just like when they had entered each of the five dreams, he just seemed to find the way.

He was next to Sherry. He could move about freely. He saw AgradUtya clearly.

Very well done, Felix. You're catching on well. You can move around. How do you feel? Is it tiring? Felix shook his head and then realized that was not truly necessary. It was a surreal experience looking at his own body. *I don't feel the least bit of exertion.*

AgradUtya addressed Sherry. *What do you sense?*

Sherry replied. *I can feel his use of energy, but it doesn't seem to be too taxing.*

AgradUtya was pleased. *Felix. You're learning to conserve your energy. This is very good.*

Felix noticed something. *AgradUtya. What's this line or ribbon running between me and my body?*

AgradUtya expressed humor leavened with seriousness. *Be glad you see the tether. It's a natural part of your questing mode. The day you are out and you see no tether will be the day you can no longer return to your body since it will have expired.*

Felix was sobered by that declaration. *Won't it get tangled in the moving about one does while questing?*

No, Felix. The tether is as immaterial as you are in questing mode. It simply supplies a reference for you to know where your corporeal body is located. Even if, Maker forbid, someone were to relocate your body, you'd be able to find your way back. Also, another quester can trace your tether in an emergency.

Felix started to ask another question, but AgradUtya motioned him to stop. *No more questions now. We'll have time for questions during formal training.*

Now. I want you to go to your sleeping quarters and then come right back. Don't linger, I just want you to get the feel of traveling. Don't worry about physical objects. They do not exist on the mental plane. Simply aim yourself at your target and go.

* * * *

Everyone in the room saw the little cloud of light emerge from Felix and coast over to hover next to Sherry. After a few moments, it moved back towards the bed before coming to stop next to their guest. After a few moments, the oddly human shaped cloud oriented itself and zipped from the room, right through a bulkhead.

Lyuba and Sherry saw things much more clearly. They saw and recognized Felix in that cloudy shape. *AgradUtya, Felix has arrived in his quarters. He's on his way back.* Sherry was excited. Here was some progress for Felix. She clearly understood what to do because of her link to him. Though Lyuba could see and recognize Felix, she could not sense him the way Sherry could.

Felix returned abruptly.

Very good, Felix, in an emergency, or if you're loosing too much energy, you'll trigger a reflexive return. Wherever you are, you'll snap back to your physical body. The sensation is very uncomfortable. So, I suggest you keep tabs on your energy.

Your advantage is you have your bond with Sherry to pull from. Be careful how deeply you pull from her reserves. You can deplete her to dangerous levels if you don't keep her needs in mind.

Now. Please return to your body and awaken to the physical reality. We must conclude this meeting.

All watched as the faint cloud that hovered near AgradUtya's apparition darted back to Felix' bed and settled into his body. With a quick gulp of air, Felix came too and sat up.

Honey are you all right. I think you sat up too quickly. You're all dizzy and disoriented.

Felix shook his head like a he'd taken a sudden chill. *I'm fine, love, but I think you're right.*

AgradUtya had Felix resume holding Tolya's arm.

Tanya. To answer your question, Felix is now able to travel without associating himself to the dream of another. So, to the question of Felix coming for me, yes, it is possible. It will be a bit of a challenge for him, but it is possible.

AgradUtya signed dry humor. *Challenge is good. Felix needs a good challenge. Felix. Do you recall the vision image I gave Tolya?*

Felix smiled. *Yes, I do.*

Very good, simply recall that motion image and you should be able to find my home. When your healer releases you, come to me. When you arrive in the first chamber, coming up from the water, you'll have to deviate from the routing at that point. I'll warn the watchers and questers that you are expected. This will make your access easier.

Ask. Use the hands next to the head to strengthen your projection if necessary. Ask one of them to show you to my chambers. If you tell them you're expected they'll bring you. Do you have any questions?

Felix shook his head. *Just a word of explanation. We have a way of naming everything. This ship was named* Destiny. *For the last nearly three years, we've lived aboard this vessel. For us it has become home, at least temporarily.*

AgradUtya was intrigued. *That's an interesting piece of information. It does help me to have a name to call your ship. Thank you. I don't anticipate any trouble with your first questing. You have instructions, and the vision images I provided.*

Now, I thank you for your friendly communication. I look forward to a productive session of discussion as we explore the possibilities that exist for both our races. Until then, I will leave you in peace.

With that, AgradUtya's form began to dissolve like a wisp of fog as it rose and darted out through a bulkhead.

Felix dropped his hand from Tolya's arm.

Tolya relaxed and looked around. "Well, to tweak Tahnie just a little, that was interesting."

She rolled her eyes and grinned, shaking her head. "You and your understatements." The mild tension that had developed in the room evaporated in chuckles.

Janelle, who had seemed almost forgotten, piped up. "I wish I knew what was going on."

Tolya looked at her. "We just established a beachhead on the shores of diplomacy. When Felix and Sherry are released from MedCentral, Felix is going to go ahead of us and bring AgradUtya back for a diplomatic meeting to decide how best to communicate with his leaders."

"Felix is going ahead of us? How...oh you mean he's going to take one of the shuttles?" Janelle seemed more than satisfied with that explanation.

Felix disabused her of the notion. "No, Janelle. I'm going ahead of the ship in a similar fashion to how we came back from your dream. I'll just do it without being in a dream."

Everyone looked at him like he was a little bit nuts.

Sherry spoke up. "Did everyone see the cloudy object that moved from Felix and hovered next to me?

All heads nodded. Faces were a bit perplexed. "That was Felix in a mental state these people call questing. In this state, one can travel far and fast.

"When the time comes, Felix will enter questing mode and go to collect AgradUtya. Together they'll return. Then, using the techniques they came up with today, we'll have a meeting to begin the process of gaining the support of these people in sharing a portion of their world with them."

She paused and looked around, making eye contact. "It is, after all, their world. We're the aliens in this little adventure. I'd appreciate everyone's help in making sure our people remember that fact."

Tolya nodded. "Thank you Sherry. She's right. We must be on our best behavior and sincerely work for coexistence with them. Frankly, we're somewhat at their mercy. We're in need of their friendship and hospitality. Let's all pray often that we find favor with their leaders. Otherwise, we'll be spending LOTS of time on this ship, figuring out how to become a race of space monkeys."

That brought a few nervous chuckles.

Pastor Brad spoke up. "I fully appreciate the sentiment that's been expressed here. If we maintain this attitude, I can feel comfortable in supporting a move to find a means to settle here.

"I've been most concerned that we not do what so many of our ancestors did back home. They had this bad habit of simply taking what they needed when they discovered someone who'd been there first. I won't support such a spirit, but this spirit of humility I embrace with a will."

He turned and took Jodi's arm. "We should be getting home. Tolya, I would be interested to hear what comes of this meeting."

Tolya smiled and clapped Brad on the shoulder. "Brad. Besides my staff, you'll be the first one to know what was said. I appreciate your insights."

Felix spoke up. "Actually. Once we're in orbit, there should be opportunity to meet physically in person. There, I think the process we used today would be less awkward. I think physical contact with them will allow those touching to hear what's being said."

He looked over at Janelle. "Janelle, would you come over here for a moment?"

Janelle approached his bed and he took her hand. "I can sense your mental activity. It has gotten stronger since we finished bringing you home. I'm going to say something to you. Close your eyes and listen for my voice." Janelle nodded and closed her eyes.

Janelle's mind was a strong hum. Felix focused on the hum, getting a feel for the pitch. *Janelle. Can you hear me?*

Janelle's eyes flew open and she darted a look at Felix.

Well, I guess something happened. Sherry grinned.

Janelle answered, "Yes. It sounded just like in my dream."

Very good. Thanks for your help. He let go of her hand. As she stepped back, he looked around. "Jodi, would you mind trying this? You're not familiar with my 'voice'." He tapped his forehead.

Jodi seemed a little shy, but nodded and approached. Felix looked at Brad. He nodded and Felix took her free hand.

Hers was a strong hum of a different pitch. He focused again. *Hi, Jodi. Do you hear me?* Jodi had a similar reaction.

Her eyes got wide and she reflexively pulled her hand back. "Sorry. You startled me."

"That's OK. I think I've made my point."

Evan looked at him, frank curiosity on his little face.

Felix glanced at Jodi. "Jodi, I can't resist. Do you mind?"

She seemed uncertain and then shrugged. "Why not?"

She came closer. Felix looked at Evan. "Hey Buddy. How's it going?"

Evan had finally gotten used to him and Sherry. He liked to play simple games with them when they came to visit. He gave one of his big grins.

"I have a new game. Give me your hand. OK?"

Evan threw out his hand, eager for the sudden attention. Felix took the hand and patted it.

Evan was a tiny, little buzz. *Hey Buddy. Tell me if you can hear me.*

Evan gave a little jerk and looked around.

Was that fun?

Evan went from uncertainty to giggles. Evidently he could hear well enough.

Felix let go and Jodi backed away. "I guess the physical contact theory works just fine. Perhaps AgradUtya needed the extra tuning process because he wasn't here physically."

He looked at Brad and grinned. "The next trick will be, once we get there and come face to face with these people, how will we manage the physical contact? Will some of us wind up with an aversion to physical contact with them? Will some of them have the same reaction towards us? It sounds silly now, but how'd you feel about walking up to a bull elephant seal in his prime and shaking flippers with him? It's a thought anyway."

Brad got a thoughtful look on his face. "I never gave much thought to that possibility. Hopefully, I won't have any difficulty."

He looked over at Tolya. "It's something we should all come to grips with. If we look at them as people God made, regardless of where they call home or how they look, maybe we'll be just fine."

COMING OUT — 6

SUN 08.15.2094-Earth / TRN 19.03.6998-Aambii
ECS Destiny, Quarterdeck, Chernov Residence, 1720 Hrs / 1900 Slashes

"Dad, Sherry says they'll be released in about forty minutes." Tolya was in his favorite chair, unwinding from another odd day. He looked up from his reading. "Sherry? But you...She just told you that?"

"Yeah. She said she's so bored in that room she's ready to climb the walls."

Tolya grinned. "I'm not surprised. Thanks for the warning. So, what do you think about all of this?"

Lyuba came over and sat on the ottoman in front of him. "You mean all this mind stuff?"

Tolya grinned. "Yeah, all that mind stuff."

Lyuba got serious. "I was scared at first. I started seeing people's faces glow and I knew things like when you were going to come in the front door, or when mom was going to call me to dinner. When Ms. Emily put her hand on my shoulder in the lab Friday, I heard this kind of humming sound. When she moved on, it went away.

She grew slightly more animated. "Then AgradUtya showed up out of thin air and came right to me...I never saw something like that before. When he spoke to me in here..." she tapped her temple, "I was so surprised!"

She shrugged, a slow contentment coloring her features. "Then I could hear Sherry and Felix when they talked to him. It was really weird, but now that I know what's going on, I think it's kinda cool."

Tolya gazed into her eyes. "As long as you're OK with it, I guess I don't mind. You're still my princess?"

"Of course, Poppa."

Tolya gave her a big hug that she returned with enthusiasm. She flinched when he first touched her though. She could hear the hum in his mind. *I love you Dad.*

Tolya stiffened a moment and then pulled back to look in her face. "I...I love you too, Princess. I heard you just now."

She grinned. "I was watching what Felix was doing. I guess if we touch someone, they can hear us talk to them."

Tolya smiled. "I kinda like that part. You better tell mom. I think she'd appreciate the warning."

"OK." She hopped up and hurried off to find Tanya. That wasn't too difficult. She sensed her in the bedroom.

* * * *

SUN 08.15.2094-Earth / TRN 19.03.6998-Aambü
ECS Destiny, Quarterdeck, Chernov Residence, 1815 Hrs / 1966 Slashes

Lyuba opened the door before Felix hit the announcer tab. *Hi Felix, Sherry, come on in!*

OK, Show off, Sherry grinned. "We better hold off on too much mind talk in front of your folks. I think it makes them feel left out."

Lyuba looked thoughtful. *I guess you're right.* "I never thought about that."

Felix smiled as they trooped into the family room. "Don't worry about it, kiddo. We're still trying to figure out what polite manners should be in this whole thing."

Tolya came out of his study area and greeted them. Tanya came out from the kitchen were mouthwatering scents were making everyone a little more hungry. "Hey you two. They finally let you out. I suppose it was for good behavior; typical story."

Everyone laughed and Sherry went over to give Tanya a hug. The men shook hands and then Tanya commented. "Lyuba, if you would get some coffee going, we can sit and chat for a while. Dinner should be done in about a half hour." She turned to her guests. "So, how are you feeling?"

Felix winced and glanced at Sherry. She grinned and answered. "We're doing well except for being sore all over. I think we'll be stiff for a few of days."

The conversation quickly gravitated to the whole process of awakening. Felix and Sherry could tell nothing they hadn't seen first hand with Lyuba.

"Our awakening came suddenly because of the dream. One minute we were normal, the next we had awakened. Then we were bonded and everything went nuts."

Sherry nodded. "We need training too."

Lyuba came back from the kitchen with coffee and cups. She set them down and started to pour. She handed them out one at a time. As she was carrying the last cup to Tolya, her foot hit the coffee table and the coffee cup she was carrying went flying. She barely kept from falling as she cried out, "NNNEU!!!!"

* * * *

There was dead silence. The coffee cup, with coffee in mid spill, hung in place a couple of feet above Tolya's lap. Everyone sat staring. Lyuba stood in shock.

Felix got up stiffly and went for a better look. "Tolya. See if you can slide out of the chair without touching anything." Tolya nodded and carefully slipped out of the chair.

Felix stooped down and looked at the strange sight. Curious, he touched the liquid. It was solid, like ice, but it wasn't cold.

It didn't feel like anything, really. He could feel the pressure of his finger pushing on it, but like touching something with a numb hand, he didn't feel hot, cold, soft, hard, smooth, rough...none of the usual cues.

He looked at Lyuba. "Hey kiddo. What did you do?"

Lyuba moved up for a closer look. "I didn't do anything...did I? I mean...I didn't want the hot coffee to hit Dad. I just wanted the whole thing to stop, but how can that do anything?"

"How indeed?" Felix replied.

He looked at Sherry. *Is she manifesting?*

Sherry shrugged. *How else do you explain this?*

Felix shrugged. He took the cup by the handle and tried to move it. It refused to budge. "Kiddo. I think you're still holding on to it."

"But I'm not doooing anything!"

He looked at her. Tanya came over and gave Lyuba a gentle hug. "It's OK sweetheart. Nobody's mad at you. I don't know what's going on, but it's OK."

Felix looked at Sherry. *What do you think? If she stopped it somehow, could she still be holding it?*

Sherry was as mystified as everyone else. *I don't know.*

Sherry looked at Lyuba. *Honey, I want you to relax. Tolya's not going to get burned now. The worse that can happen is it lands on the chair and things get wet. No harm, no foul. When you're calmed down, just try to think about letting go of everything there.* She pointed at the bizarre tableau.

Lyuba wiped her eyes. This thing had really upset her. She hugged Tanya back and took a couple deep breaths. *You're right, Sherry. Dad can't get burned now. He's out of the way.* She looked at the cup and liquid. Not knowing what else to do, she made a motion as if dropping something.

There was a crack and tinkling sound like thin glass Christmas ornaments breaking.

Everything: the coffee, the cup, the wisps of frozen steam surrounding the liquid...everything shattered into tiny shards and started to fall. They crumbled further into a fine powder before they hit Tolya's chair. The dust rattled around on the surface of the chair seat before sliding off onto the floor.

Tolya's face paled. He tried to lighten the serious mood. "I don't think they meant pulverize it, Princess."

Lyuba moaned. "I just let go, like they said."

She started crying and Tolya took her by the shoulder and pulled her to him. "There, there, I was just kidding. We don't know what happened, but you did just fine."

Felix knelt down and had a look at the dusty mess. There were streaks of moisture down the seat front, and the tight weave carpet was wet. All the surfaces he touched were so cold they might have been stored in a refrigeration unit. He sat back on his heels and looked at Lyuba. She was starting to calm down.

He got up and walked over to her. Holding out his hands he invited a hug. Lyuba responded and Felix quietly held her. *Kiddo. It's going to be OK. You're developing some kind of ability to manipulate objects. I can make objects do things at the molecular level. I don't know what all I can do yet, but that part I've figured out.*

You have a different approach. You literally stopped all motion. I think it may have gone even further.

He gently pressed her back so he could see her face. *You just made it all stop. Then when you let go, everything went extremely cold. That's why I think what you did might have gone down to the atomic level. Everything just fell apart.*

He shook his head. *Maybe it has something to do with energy states. I'm just not sure. At least that's my guess, anyway.*

Felix gave her an encouraging smile. *Now that we've seen it, we'll have to figure out what it is and how you can control it better.*

Lyuba stepped back and looked thoughtful. *Would AgradUtya know what to do? I don't think he does that kind of thing, does he?*

Sherry entered the conversation. *I don't think anyone knows what he can do. We haven't met him in his physical form yet, but I think if he can't help you figure it out, nobody can.*

Tanya made her way to the kitchen and Tolya headed for a utility closet to get something to clean up the chilly mess. Lyuba followed Tanya to see if she could help.

Felix looked at Sherry and shrugged. *That was really weird. I can't think of anything else. She didn't just grab it. She clamped down on the motion. It was like the cup was firmly wedged in concrete. If it were simple telekinesis I'd think she'd have been able to drop it, or move it. Instead, everything disintegrated.*

Sherry grinned. *One thing's for sure. Don't ever get her mad at you!*

Felix got a funny look on his face. *You know, that little talent she displayed could be extremely dangerous without skilled control. It's a good thing all she grabbed was the cup. What if, in a different situation, she'd grabbed someone's hand; say to stop a blow or something. That person might have lost the hand.*

* * * *

Dinner conversation was subdued. There were many things to think about, not the least of them, the strange developments regarding Lyuba's talents.

They adjourned to the family room and got comfortable. Tolya ceded his armchair to Felix, allowing him a safe, comfortable posture for questing. Sherry sat on the couch directly next to Felix' chair. She would be watching him like a hawk.

Lyuba got to stick around unless AgradUtya said otherwise. They all wanted to hear what he had to say about her manifestation.

Soon it was time. Conversation fell to hushed tones and Felix composed himself, finding a quiet center. His physical perceptions faded. Then he was free.

Felix drifted from his body. It felt as weird as the first time when AgradUtya had tutored him through the process. He turned to observe each of the people in the room. Tolya and Tanya were translucent. Lyuba and Sherry were nearly solid. He came close to Lyuba and whispered a quiet good bye.

He lingered a little longer over Sherry. {Love, I'll be back before you know it. Don't worry.}

Sherry nodded. She was trying not to worry. {Ok, honey. I'll just pray instead.}

Felix sent her a big smile. He checked for his tether, relieved to find it properly in place. Then, he arrowed off into the night.

The sense of passing through solid objects was disconcerting, but he tried to ignore it and made his way quickly out into the vacuum of space.

He arrowed for the planet that was now a visible ring encircled disk, tiny and inviting. He sailed through the ring system. Rock and ice in all forms and sizes whizzed past him. He still wondered how this ring system could have developed around a rocky world like Aambü.

Pausing in mid flight, he played back the vision AgradUtya had provided. He tried to memorize the view of the planet as AgradUtya had depicted it. As he worked on this, he stayed just above the plane of the rings and quickly began an orbit of the planet. He searched for the view that would match the scene. It took him a while, but then, there it was. The lighting was quite different, but features of the surface were too similar to reject.

He dove. The atmosphere whipped around him. He felt nothing, of course. He was not physically present. He'd be dead otherwise.

There was the small semicircular chain of islands and there was the blue lagoon that was partially open on one side. He dove deep into the water. After casting about, he found the odd shaped side of a sea-mount where it curved inwards under itself. There. He saw the entry.

He rose through the rippling surface to find himself surrounded by five large specimens of the Aambüka people. They didn't move towards him, but neither did they move to let him pass.

Somehow, he sensed that, unlike everywhere else, he would not be able to just simply pass through them. He hung there over the entry pool and turned in a slow circle taking the measure of each of the huge individuals he faced.

Who enters a clan cavern, not his own?

Felix felt totally out of his depth. {I am Felix Hernandez of the colony ship Destiny. *I come at the invitation of AgradUtya.}*

He sensed the agitation as the creatures digested this information. **You speak boldly, Child of the Stars. It is true. You are expected.**

The largest of the five moved aside to open a path to dry...well, comparatively dry land.

Felix wondered at the gesture considering he had no use for solid ground at this point. He tentatively moved to fill the gap, but didn't venture any further.

He sensed a hint of approval from the big guy next to him. **I am AradevArin, Alina Adhas Kambu. I shall escort you to AgradUtya. Come, I have told him of your presence.** AradevArin turned and headed down a passageway that led slightly upward.

Felix' sense of direction was all but useless. Between the fact that he was questing rather than physically present, and that he was deep in the heart of a mountain, deep under an ocean, it was hopeless to try to keep a sense of direction.

AradevArin walked, if you could call it walking, with an odd shuffling motion. His legs were fairly short and articulated oddly. Rather than knees that let the leg bend back, the joint was turned slightly and the stubby legs had a bowed shape that reminded him vaguely of a frog or toad. His escort had long arms. Occasionally, he would use one web hand or the other as an extra walking limb. It seemed to be more for aid in balance than actual support or locomotion.

They crossed a couple of major cross-corridors. People shuffled back and forth along these passages more often than they did down the one Felix was traversing at present.

AradevArin responded to a wave from a smaller individual. He sensed an exchange, but didn't understand the conversation. It was muffled, meaningless. The smaller creature kept glancing at Felix' apparition.

AradevArin reached out a web hand and gently touched the face of the smaller person. Then they resumed their journey.

{Was that a friend of yours?} Felix asked. He couldn't understand why his escort wasn't talkative.

AradevArin glanced at him. **That was my bond mate. She is curious. Most of our people are curious about you and your people. They wish to know what it all means.**

Felix nodded. {You're the third of your people I've met. Your mate would be the first female I've met, even at a distance. The news of our encounter has yet to reach the rest of our population. We're waiting until we can discuss any mutual benefits our two peoples can agree on.}

AradevArin seemed mildly interested. **I presume you have a mate. She's with you?**

Felix thought to correct the observation. {She stayed to watch over my physical body.}

AradevArin made a gesture Felix wasn't familiar with. **If she's not here, then she is not truly a bond mate.**

Felix realized the misunderstanding. In the back of his mind he could hear Sherry chuckling.

{AradevArin, forgive me, I misspoke. I'm still unaccustomed to the changes that have come over me in the last week or so. I meant that my mate hadn't quested with me. She is with me in my mind, of course.}

AradevArin glanced back at him and signed what seemed to be humor. **I believe you still have much to learn. I will admit you do reasonably well for one newly awakened...Here are AgradUtya's chambers.**

Sherry murmured in her little corner of his mind. Felix passed it on. {Thank you AradevArin. My mate wishes to offer her thanks for helping me safely reach my goal.}

AradevArin looked at him. It was a long considering look. **Tell your mate it was my duty and my pleasure. One day we should meet face to face; you, your mate with me and mine. Till then, fare well.** With that he turned and quickly shuffled back down the passage.

A curtain of some kind of plant matter, possibly a sort of seaweed, parted. AgradUtya regarded him. **Well my friend, I see you've caused quite a stir. You'd not believe the reports and rumors flying about this very moment.** He stepped into the passage. **You've come for our meeting?**

Felix affirmed. {Correct. I think we'll have a more productive discussion this time.}

AgradUtya turned and started further along the passage. **Come, we'll go to the questing chamber. What do you think of our home?**

Felix considered. It was hard to truly appreciate all of it without the full benefits of his physical senses. The place seemed to be fairly compact, not all that spacious.

{It's very interesting. I've not had opportunity to truly get to know it. Is the entire place this compact?}

AgradUtya signed a smile. **No. In fact, when you arrive physically, you'll see the grand hall, and have an audience with AgraVadin Adhiraj.**

Shortly, they reached a small chamber with a pool in the center, similar in some ways to the entry chamber but for its size and lack of a guard detail. A person was presiding over a small desk type surface situated in a corner. The quester stepped from the desk and signed welcome, respect and readiness in a few hand gestures.

AgradUtya motioned towards Felix and the quester turned and approached. <It is a pleasure to make your acquaintance, Child of the Stars. I am eager to meet you in your corporeal form.>

He indicated the pool. <I offer you safe and pleasant questing.>

He stepped aside and AgradUtya slipped into the water. Felix moved out over the water and allowed himself to sink till he could see what AgradUtya was up to. His new friend composed himself in what looked almost like a fetal posture. After a few moments, AgradUtya's mind image detached itself from the body and looked over at Felix pointing upwards before darting upward at an angle. Felix followed.

COMING OUT —7

SUN 08.15.2094-Earth / TRN 19.03.6998-Aambü
ECS Destiny, Quarterdeck, Chernov Residence, 1940 Hrs / 2082 Slashes

Sherry was starting to nod off when she felt Felix presence begin to strengthen. They'd not yet discovered the limits of their range, but she'd sensed him as he moved about the cavern system that comprised AgradUtya's home. Their short conversations felt distant, but contact remained strong.

"Hey, everyone. Felix is almost back."

Tolya and Tanya sat up a bit straighter and Lyuba put away the pocket-tab she'd been playing on.

Tanya poured more coffee around. She was about to put the pot down when Felix and AgradUtya appeared in the dimmed light of the family room. She poured another cup for Felix.

It was tough for Tolya and Tanya to decide which of the two apparitions was Felix until one of them darted into Felix' body.

Felix body trembled throughout for just a second and then his eyes snapped open. He looked around, moved his hands and feet and decided everything was as at should be.

Sherry moved over and touched his hand. *It's good to have you back.* Felix smiled and looked her over. *It's good to be back. What a vision to wake to!*

Sherry blushed, but the room was dim enough she thought probably nobody noticed. Felix sat up carefully.

There was AgradUtya floating in the middle of the room. *AgradUtya. We hope to have a good discussion this time.*

AgradUtya replied. *Little could please me more. I see our newest member is here.*

He focused his attention on Lyuba. *Hello, little one. You seem a bit stronger than when we first met.*

Lyuba smiled and replied *I feel great, but I do have some questions.*

AgradUtya expressed good humor. *In good time Lyuba. First I should properly greet your parents and see to some discussion about the future of our peoples. We'll talk soon.*

Felix, Sherry, by placing yourselves where you can touch Tolya and Tanya, we can begin.

They rearranged themselves on the long couch as Lyuba snagged the vacated recliner. Everyone seemed to like that chair. Well, it was her turn. She grinned smugly to herself.

Felix commented. *Hey Kiddo. Let's try to skip the dramatic events for now. They're a bit distracting.* Lyuba stuck her tongue out at him.

AgradUtya was determined to have a productive meeting, so he ignored the exchange, not realizing it was an oblique reference to Lyuba's manifestation.

* * * *

SUN 08.15.2094-Earth / TRN 19.03.6998-Aambü
ECS Destiny, Quarterdeck, Chernov Residence, 1945 Hrs / 2090 Slashes

Everyone was settled and comfortable. AgradUtya hovered at one end of the coffee table opposite Lyuba. Tolya offered AgradUtya the floor since he represented the host species in this strange twist of circumstances. AgradUtya made no comment at the potential advantage this arrangement gave him at the table.

Two things I should say before we begin.

First, thank you for your hospitality. Since I'm not present in corporeal form, you can do nothing for my creature comforts. However, you've consistently acted cordial and considerate. Also, I wish to acknowledge that I'm here at your pleasure. If it had come to you requiring me to leave, I surely would have acquiesced.

Second, as I said earlier, one could say we originally met by accident, but I'm convinced The Maker has arranged this meeting for His own purposes. Though, through an error of judgment, I forever changed the life courses of Felix and Sherry...and the young one, Lyuba, not for a moment do I regret having come to know any of you. It would not be an exaggeration to say I've grown fond of my three prodigies.

Now, I truly must get down to the purpose of this meeting. I have been commissioned to learn all I can of your people before we meet face to face. My leader...I believe you might equate him with what you call a chief or king...requires answers to many questions. I believe the safest way to begin is to ask the primary questions.

They are, "Who are you? Where do you come from? And, why did you come here?"

Tolya leaned forward and considered his words. "First, I'd like to welcome you as the representative of your race. You've been gracious in the face of personal frustration.

"Your unintentional triggering of Felix, Sherry and now my daughter might have been taken less happily, had you chosen to ignore the difficulties those events presented us. However, your efforts to be helpful in solving the problems caused by the unusual contact have done much to reassure us of the general kindness of your people.

"Second, I tend to agree with you. The entire set of circumstances that brought us together cannot simply be attributed to coincidence or chance. We have a Maker as well. Perhaps he is the same, perhaps not. It's a question we must answer in due time.

"As to your first set of questions, I'll answer as best I can.

"The first two questions are best treated as one. We are a group of some nearly two thousand five hundred individuals of our species who volunteered to band together, leave our world, which we call Earth, and sail across the sea of stars to find a new world around another star to make our home. We call such a group of people a colony.

"Now, this is an important part of the answer. We didn't originally set out for your world. We had no idea this world existed.

We were traveling to a world in a totally different part of space from this one, one that circled yet another star.

"Through a series of most unhappy events, our ship went far off course. When we discovered the fault, we immediately tried to correct the error and resume our journey. However, because of a limited amount of fuel, and because of a drive system designed to only go so far, we could not complete the trip safely.

"This brings us to your third question. While we sought desperately to continue our journey, it became obvious this was out of the question.

"My Science Officer, a woman who would dearly love to meet you, discovered your star while searching for local stars with desirable planets. Your star was the only one with a potentially habitable world we could find within reach.

"Of course, we had absolutely no idea there could possibly be another intelligent, sentient race on your world. It was the last thing on our minds. You see, in the hundred plus years we have been learning to operate in space, we've never come across the slightest credible proof of the existence of other races out here.

"We made the jump into your system and started in-system to have a look. The first notion we had that we would be having trouble was when we discovered your world is what we'd classify as a water world."

AgradUtya considered the information he'd learned. *I'm not sure I fully understand some of the terms you use. We've never felt the need to visit the stars.*

Somehow, in our ancient past, we learned how to study the stars and gain helpful information about our surroundings, but no one has ever seriously considered leaving our world...Tell me, if you will, do you truly live exclusively on dry land on your world?

Tolya nodded. "Yes, we are a land species, but we've been gifted with a marvelous ability to adapt to less hospitable circumstances.

"Our people live in a wide variety of climates. We live in swamp lands where it is very moist and hot, in mountainous regions where the climate changes through the seasons from temperate one season to hot the next, ice cold the next, and temperate again. Some live in desert regions so dry we've devised ways of leaching moisture from the air.

"We've learned, with the use of devices we've created, how to make artificial environments where we can control the climate we live in. This ship is an example of that knowledge put to the purpose of keeping us alive while traveling across the dead reaches between stars."

AgradUtya was amazed at the audacity and skill this species had to defy their natural limits by taking their environment with them. They were truly a determined people. This was good, but it could also be very bad for his own people.

How did you plan to overcome the paucity of land on Aambü? It seems clear you cannot survive long under water. So far as I can observe in my state, you have no air exchange systems to gain the riches from the water.

Tolya shifted. "Honestly, that was still an issue of study when we discovered your people. There are numerous possibilities that require designing and building means to control our environment."

Felix offered a comment. *Over the thousands and thousands of generations of our existence on Earth, we've developed many ways of coexisting with the oceans there. Our world is a bit smaller than yours. It has no rings, as does yours. Its axis of rotation is not so acute. Yet, nearly three quarters of our world's surface is covered with water, vast oceans to us, but probably puddles compared to your worldwide ocean.*

Like this ship we live in, we have devices on Earth that allow us to travel through and across the oceans. We have artificial habitats built entirely underwater, but they require much care in design and upkeep. This is because, if something were to go wrong with the systems in such places, the occupants would be surely lost to the crushing pressure of the depths.

AgradUtya was again amazed at how these people risked so much to go places they were not created to inhabit; that they could successfully challenge the environs that were so harsh to them.

So, now that you're here, and you know we're here, what are your intentions regarding us?

Tanya had been quiet so far. "We simply need a place to live, and grow. Truly, had we found your world uninhabited, we would've found a way to fully adapt to it, and make it our own.

"However, under the circumstances, our situation has been complicated further. As has already been said, we have no desire to force our way where someone else is rightly in place. We can only hope there can be sufficient good will between our peoples, and enough space for us to grow without putting too much pressure on you. Coexistence is the goal.

AgradUtya considered his next question. *Tell me, why you must settle on Aambü at all. Why not use your skills and knowledge to expand the habitat you already have?* He indicated the ship with a wave of an ethereal web hand.

Sherry spoke up for the first time. *AgradUtya, you clearly make a logical point. It's true; potentially, we could find a way of living indefinitely in space. It's not, however, the type of solution our people were equipped to pursue.*

It takes vast resources and much specialized equipment to accomplish what you suggest. If our colony had been organized for that purpose, those resources and devices would have been equipped and sent along with us.

Unfortunately, we were sent to an existing world with no native peoples. Therefore, we were not so equipped. To accomplish what you suggest, we would have to locate raw materials and design and build equipment. We would then have to combine the equipment and the raw materials to build the various parts that would then be assembled into the whole. We could accomplish these things given enough time, enough people with the necessary skills and the will to do it.

We don't necessarily have the time, however. Under the current circumstances, this ship was not designed to be used indefinitely in the environs of space. It was built to deliver us to a preselected world, there to be dismantled, and brought down out of the sky to be disassembled further and the materials used to build our first settlement. Redesigning her while occupied in space would be very hazardous to the people inside.

AgradUtya considered the reply. He didn't fully understand all the concepts. This people had chosen a path utilizing physical tools to a fine degree. His people had gone the rout of using the mind to accomplish great things in a different way.

Please understand, the question was not a reflection of a preference of mine or of anyone I know. It was meant simply to understand the circumstances you face. I think the idea of living permanently in the closed environment your people share would be unappealing to most of my people.

AgradUtya seemed to be out of questions, at least for the moment. *Now, I believe I've hoarded the questioning thus far. I imagine you, in turn, have many questions to ask about us.*

Tolya looked at Felix. Then he sat forward. "I'm curious about a great number of things. When we first dropped into this system, we noticed an unusually dense cloud of rubble spread across nearly the entire system. We've come to believe it's fairly unusual for rocky core planets such as our home world, Earth, or your own Aambü, to have ring systems. Also, the rotational axis of Aambü is unusually great for a habitable planet. My science officer is wondering whether your people have any ancient stories or legends of world shaking events that nearly destroyed everything."

AgradUtya seemed surprised by the question. *Truly, they are much more than legends. We have recorded history of a time such as you describe. We're an ancient people. We have records of events that date back nearly seven thousand ring cycles. Very little is known of the times before.*

The records state that an event on the scale of your surmise did take place. This event we have come to mark as the beginning of the civilization we have now. We call it 'The Remaking'

I'd be interested to know how you came to such a singular conclusion when you haven't even arrived on our world yet. It's as if you had read the story from the stars themselves. Seven thousand cycles is a very long time. Most people don't even know the story as anything but an abstract legend.

Tolya smiled. "As I said, my science officer, Emily Strauss has been very curious about the condition of this system. She says it's most unusual. Her opinion is that something very large, something the size of a small planet perhaps, hurtled through the system, broke up and parts of it nearly collided with your world. There is debris consistent with such a notion all over this system.

"Your ring system is particularly dense. It's density compares to the rings around a large gas giant planet in our home system. Yet, our understanding is, most rocky core planets, have no ring system at all.

"Also, your moons are unusual. They appear, at least with our instruments from this distance, to be badly damaged. Emily thinks they may be two pieces of a much larger moon that existed before the catastrophe."

AgradUtya was again amazed at their ability to learn so much with complex instruments. *I must get to know this person, Emily, you speak of.*

The legends, passed down for nearly seven thousand cycles, say that before the beginning of our records, our world was more like the one you describe as your home. It was still larger, of course, but it had several sizable land-masses. This is something my people can't conceive, dry land so vast you can't see the far shore.

The legends say that before the catastrophe, as you call it, Aambü had one large moon. There was no ring in the sky, and we had seasons much different from the ones we know now. There is, however something you could never know from your observations, so far. Before the Remaking there were two races of sentient peoples on Aambü.

Great surprise registered around the room.

We were here long before the Remaking, but before the Remaking, there was another people, another race; land people like you. I'm not sure what they looked like. We'd have to search the records to find descriptions. They lived on the land and built wonderful things. Thus, we called them

Bhumika. There was peace and harmony between our races. We maintained trade and cultural exchange.

The record says that a large object was seen among the stars. Our land bound neighbors, who had more sophisticated devices, such as your people use, studied the object and reported it was approaching our world.

There were raging debates among the Land People about whether this object would truly collide with our world or just miss.

Apparently, they were neither right nor wrong. The object came close enough that it broke into many large pieces. The records say the great moon was hit by one of those large pieces and broke in two. Other pieces broke up further. This happened after the world was shaken by the power of its passage. As noted earlier, the axis of our world is severe. We might not have been aware of it save for our access to knowledge of the Land People.

When the axis tilted, the oceans swept the land-masses, killing nearly all the Bhumika. The fragments from the intruding object broke up further. Large pieces fell near the poles, which in those times, were covered with thick ice sheets through entire cycles.

Afterwards, the ice quickly broke up and melted. The rising oceans destroyed the remainder of the Bhumika. In less than two cycles, there was no more land except the islands you observe with your instruments.

When the Remaking took place, an entire race was swept from the face of our world. They couldn't live in the oceans, so they perished.

There was a long moment of silence in the room. All present felt the horror of an entire race destroyed.

Finally, Felix spoke. "It would have been interesting to have been able to meet them too."

Tolya nodded. "AgradUtya, if you don't mind my asking, what is the extent of the population on your world?"

AgradUtya considered the question. *I am trying to think of a meaningful term. We still have a long way to go in learning each other's languages. Our brains, and yours, supply the language as necessary, but we don't project language. Rather, we project ideas.*

You said there are two thousand, five hundred individuals on this vessel. In my own clan caverns, we have less than half that number, perhaps, one thousand, two hundred individuals. Among the islands for my clan, we have probably three thousand, three hundred people. My clan is considered the largest clan. It's the ruling clan, so more people wish to associate with it.

There are eighteen clans directly under the authority of AgraVadin Adhiraj. They are further divided into sub-clans. Most of those clans cannot boast one thousand individuals.

Tanya did a quick estimation of the total population of the clans under AgradUtya's clan. "That's slightly over nineteen thousand people; nineteen thousand for the entire world? Are there any independent clans?"

AgradUtya hesitated. *There are a few clans who remain independent. I cannot give reasonable figures for their people. They tend to live a harsher life. They have greater exposure to Bhairava and other dangers. One I'm aware of, numbers two hundred individuals.*

Tanya pressed, "Yes, but do you have an idea how many of these clans there might be? Frankly I'm shocked at the low total population. This cataclysm must have taken a great toll on your own people."

AgradUtya seemed mildly agitated. *This is information I probably shouldn't be telling to total strangers, but yes. Our numbers were greatly reduced by The Remaking.*

Even though we live most of our lives in the depths, there were tremendous tidal disturbances that caused much death and injury. It's rare for one of us to drown, something your kind fears greatly.

The conditions caused by The Remaking killed many of our people. Rock formations collapsed, huge chunks of the offending space object fell in the northern reaches, killing more.

I understand your life spans are somewhat shorter than ours. We're slow to reproduce, though we live longer. Then, we have the constant battle with Bhairava. He's an insatiable destroyer of our people. He's one reason I was on watch when we first met.

Tolya stepped in. "You've never mentioned a natural enemy. What is this *Bhairava*? How prevalent is it?"

AgradUtya was unhappy. *Bhairava is a creature that preys voraciously on our people. We've tried to understand where it came from. Before The Remaking there was nothing like Bhairava in the records. We had the usual predators, but not this evil.*

We're always on guard for Bhairava. It seems to always accompany the worst storms. That's why I called to Felix when he appeared in his dream.

I knew of the approaching storm and I mistook him for a young one playing in the waves. We loose more people to Bhairava when they're too slow to retreat from the storms. For some reason, Bhairava doesn't go very deep. We retreat to the greater depths, or better yet, to our caverns till a major storm passes.

Tolya was incredulous. "You've been tormented by this thing for nearly seven thousand ye...cycles? Don't you fight this thing? Can't you drive it away, or, better yet, kill it?"

AgradUtya was frustrated. *We've tried to fight Bhairava. All our best efforts seem to do little. He has his way during the worst storms. On the rare occasions when he ventures out in lesser storms, or simply cloudy weather, he's more easily driven away. No one has come close to killing him. Anyone who has seen Bhairava clearly has never survived to tell of it.*

* * * *

Lyuba was getting bored. The discussion was sort of interesting. This story of *Bhairava*, whoever that was, was better, but she was frustrated that no one wanted to discuss what was happening to her.

She wanted some tea, but no one was paying any attention. She didn't want to interrupt, but she couldn't reach the box of tea bags. Her frustration peaked and she wished she could just grab the stupid box and have done with it.

As if sensing her wishes, the box suddenly darted down the length of the table to leap the gap into her hands. Only her newly trained reflexes prevent the box from painfully striking her chest.

All conversation stopped. Even AgradUtya stared at her.

Lyuba was staring at the box of tea, trying to push it away with her hands. It wanted to continue its flight.

Little one. Use your mind. You must let go of the box. You're still pulling it.

Lyuba looked up at AgradUtya, who was moving, with no regard for the table's presence, towards her. Lyuba thought about letting go. Suddenly, there was a release and the box lay harmlessly in her hands.

AgradUtya kept his gaze on Lyuba as he asked, *Felix. Is this her first manifestation?*

Felix grinned. *No, she's had one that was much more spectacular before I came for you.*

AgradUtya turned towards Felix. *And you didn't tell me?*

Felix felt like an irate PE coach was chewing him out. *There hasn't been sufficient opportunity. She tried to talk to you about it before our meeting began. If you recall, you told her you'd talk after.*

AgradUtya lost his bluster. *I apologize. It is as you've said.*

He returned his attention to Lyuba. *You, young one, are going faster than I can keep up. It appears your species adjusts to your abilities a bit differently than mine. So, I apologize for delaying our conversation. What was the earlier manifestation?*

Lyuba suddenly felt self-conscious. *I did something really weird. I was carrying a hot cup of coffee when I tripped and almost fell. I saw the*

528

cup and the hot coffee fly and I knew it would land on my Dad. I don't know what I did. I guess I just made it stop.

AgradUtya was suddenly very attentive. *You just made it stop? How do you mean stop?*

Lyuba fidgeted. *I don't know. Everything stopped.*

AgradUtya gestured confusion, *Felix, describe, please, the event she has referenced.*

Felix shrugged, keeping his hand on Tolya's arm. *It's just as she told it. She just missed a few details. The cup and the hot liquid and the steam from the hot liquid simply froze in midair.*

When I tried to touch it, it was solid as a rock. There was no sensation to my hand except the pressure of poking at it. It took us a few moments to figure out it had to be Lyuba. We talked her into calming down and encouraged her to release things.

When she finally let go, the cup, the liquid, and the steam from the liquid shattered and then crumbled into dust as it fell from the place it hung. I touched the powdered remains and found them to be extremely cold, as if they had been deep-frozen.

AgradUtya's image darted away from Lyuba as if she'd physically thrown him.

His state of agitation was intense. *Lyuba! I insist you not do that thing again before we can learn more! I must have your promise you will not do this again until I permit it!*

Lyuba was very confused. *I...Sure, if you wish. I'll try not to do that again till you're ready, but...why?*

AgradUtya's agitation was only slightly reduced. *I'll explain later. The other thing you just did, that's fine. Practice it, but leave the other alone. I apologize, but I must go.*

With that, he vanished.

MADE OFFICIAL — 1
SUN 08.15.2094-Earth / TRN 19.03.6998-Aambü
2.5 Months to orbital insertion; Aambü, Gem System
ECS Destiny, Quarterdeck, Chernov Residence, 2053 Hrs / 2166 Slashes

AgradUtya jerked awake and rose abruptly from the pool. The quester on duty shuffled to his aid. *<Do you require assistance?>*

No, thank you all the same. I've just had a very disturbing experience, which will require some meditation to come to grips with. Please pardon my abruptness, but I must see AgraVadin Adhiraj now.

AgradUtya shuffled urgently from the questing chamber, leaving the quester mildly distressed and exceedingly curious. AgradUtya sent ahead a request to meet with the first speaker. His status as first ambassador granted him immediate access.

AgraVadin leaned comfortably at his work desk, going over reports of the turn. Things were blessedly quiet. When his aid reported that an agitated AgradUtya was on his way for an urgent discussion, he almost welcomed the distraction from the mundane pieces of evidence of the usual routine.

AgradUtya was ushered in with all due protocol. He signed an abbreviated gesture of respect.

{Ah, AgradUtya. Please dispense with formalities. Make yourself comfortable. You look like you've seen Bhairava himself.} AgradUtya froze in mid-shuffle. His agitation spiked to an alarming degree.

AgraVadin hurried over and took AgradUtya by the arm and urged him to lean on a mound of moist sand. *{Come friend. That was a jest. Surely you've not truly seen our enemy, else sadly, we'd not be having this friendly conversation.}*

AgradUtya settled himself on the sand and gestured profound thanks. **I'm afraid you startled me with your jest. It is possibly about our enemy that I have come to commune with you. I just returned from a questing to the Star People's vessel* Destiny.***

AgraVadin settled himself on another mound. He sent a summons for some refreshment and then returned to the discussion that was about to ensue. *{Friend. You've been singing glowing praises of your accidental students from the stars. What could have stricken you with such fear?}*

AgradUtya glanced at the First Speaker. A simple fact of birth had snatched his best friend from his youth and placed him in the seat of greatest honor. He was pleased their friendship continued. It wasn't as light hearted as before, but a richer, more mature friendship had resulted.

Remember when I warned you their youngling might awaken soon?

AgraVadin signed his recollection.

Did I tell you she was the daughter of their leader; someone who has equivalent rank to yours?

AgraVadin sat up a little straighter. {Truth? This child is the daughter of their Adhiraj?}

AgradUtya signed affirmative. *She is.*

AgradUtya looked up at Agravadin. *Well, she awakened. That would not be such a problem. I arranged for proper sponsorship to train her, but she has begun to manifest.*

AgraVadin sensed that his old friend was having trouble getting to the point. {That should hardly come as a surprise, my friend. It may be a little soon from our perspective, but it's hardly surprising that a newly awakened youngling should begin to manifest. Tell me about this manifestation that has you so terribly worried.}

AgradUtya paused, realizing he wasn't getting to the point. Friends or not, AgraVadin was indeed a very busy person. {The youngling is called Lyuba. They have different traditions for naming than we. At this early stage, she has shown a definite ability to move objects with her mind. It was her first time, but she did it with little difficulty. I only had to encourage her to release the object after it landed in her hands.}

At that moment, hired servants entered and presented a tray of delightful treats; various morsels of flitterings dipped in a tangy sauce, nectar from the bulbs of the ameerta plant, fresh cesta baked in madhu sauce...they were wondrously inviting.

The servants left quietly and AgraVadin blessed the meal. {Now, I can't imagine this young child's moving of objects is what has brought you to such an agitated state. There must be something else.}

AgradUtya popped a slice of cesta in his mouth and selected a bulb of ameerta nectar. *She has another ability. It'll prove to be one of the most powerful abilities we've ever seen. In living memory, I've only ever known of one creature that has it.*

AgradUtya leaned forward making a gesture promising something of profound importance. *I've not seen the child do this, but I trust Felix' ability to describe it...She can change energy states of matter.* He described the cup of coffee event as Felix had told it.

AgraVadin heaved himself up from his sand mound and shuffled about the room. {*That's exactly what happens to those who get too close to Bhairava. Are you certain, my friend?*}

AgradUtya signed absolute surety. *She doesn't yet understand what she did. I forbad her to practice it until I know what it means.*

AgraVadin calmed himself, returning to his mound. {*We have no one with such power. The ancient records tell of one of our own who had this ability. One! Over the course of thousands of cycles, we've only ever heard of one! Do you realize how rare this talent is?*}

AgradUtya commented, *I sense Lyuba will be very powerful when she finally understands what she's doing. It frightened me when I realized what she might become. As much as I like these people, are we certain they're not more dangerous than we thought? What if I'm training a new mortal enemy?*

AgraVadin took a pull from his nectar bulb. His thoughts raced as he considered the situation. {*AgradUtya. We have no one who could possibly train her in this ability. We can explain to her what she's doing when she uses it, but we don't have anyone who can show her...Do you truly think the same people willing to endanger themselves to save another, could choose to become mortal enemies?*}

AgradUtya gestured mild shame at thinking such a thing. *So far, they've shown themselves to be honorable. Their Adhiraj and his mate said they do not wish to take what's not rightly theirs. They wish to find a means of peaceful coexistence. It's just...this development with the youngling brought back the horrors we've witnessed when our people see Bhairava. She could very well become quite formidable...Imagine, a formidable child.*

AgraVadin Adhiraj suddenly had a gleam in his eyes. He was thinking in new directions. {*Friend. Imagine a formidable child who is our friend, who is the daughter of a people who would be our friends.*}

MADE OFFICIAL — 2

MON 08.23.2094-Earth / TRN 25.03.6998-Aambü
ECS Destiny, Quarterdeck, Felix' Cabin, 1515 Hrs / 1140 Slashes

Felix spent the day running errands. The morning started out nicely. He'd gone down to Pastor Brad's place and had breakfast with Sherry and her gracious hosts. Then Jodi and Sherry went off to begin working out details about the coming wedding.

They'd agreed on Saturday, September 4. It would be a small, friends and family wedding. Their closest friends, members of *New*

Destiny Church and...well, they certainly considered the Chernovs to be almost family.

Sherry wanted only one bridesmaid and had chosen Lyuba for the honor. Lyuba, now fourteen, would be really jazzed when she found out about it.

Felix was at a loss to come up with someone for groomsman. He didn't know anyone near Lyuba's age. For that matter, he didn't yet know anyone in his own age range that qualified as a close friend.

"Wait!" He said it aloud, responding to sudden inspiration. He knew Devin. Devin was probably the oldest member of the youth group at *New Destiny*. He was in Emily's growing program of accelerated learning for gifted students. He and Devin saw each other at church, but he also saw Devin in the Nano-lab. Felix was periodically allowed to spend a few hours getting a look at how the whole nano project worked. Devin had recently been recommended to Naomi and was placed in the same program as Felix.

The lift stopped and Felix stepped off on Quarterdeck. He headed down the starboard side and noted that the workers were already busily transforming a double stateroom into a unit like Daryl's or Ichirou's.

They were large one-bedroom units with a micro-kitchen in place of the second bedroom. He watched for a few moments and then crossed the park to his cabin.

His session with Samuel Perlman had gone well. The rings would be ready in about a week and a half. That was plenty of time before the wedding.

He sat down at his desk and tapped the COMM icon. He thought for another couple moments. He liked Devin. He was responsible, bright and witty. What couldn't be liked about him? He and Lyuba would look good together at the wedding. Felix nodded to himself and selected the code.

A face came into view. "Hello?"

It was Devin's mom. She was really friendly with the most dazzling smile he'd seen except the one on Sherry. She was dark, a rich caramel color.

"Hi. Mrs. Hawkins? It's Felix, from church."

She gave a big grin. "Hi, Felix. I remember you. So, what brings the pleasure of your call?"

Felix smiled. "I was wondering if Devin was in. You do know Sherry and I are getting married on the fourth, right?"

"Yes! I'm so excited. You're perfect together."

"Thanks, Mrs. Hawkins. I..."

"Now, now, Felix. I've told you before, you must call me Sally. My man says you can be way too polite sometimes."

Felix felt embarrassed. "Sorry, Sally. I'll try to remember."

"That's better honey. Now, Devin's in, but he's occupied, if you know what I mean."

Felix grinned. "OK, I don't need too much info."

"I didn't think so. What do you want with Devin?"

"Well, I was going to ask him if he'd like to be my groomsman."

Sally beamed her biggest smile. "Oh, Felix! That's wonderful. And who's to be the bridesmaid?"

"Sherry's going to ask Lyuba Chernov."

"Lyuba; such a darling girl! She and Sherry are pretty close, aren't they?"

"Yes. Lyuba's kinda like an adopted sister."

Sally glanced off the screen. "I think Devin's available now. Wow! I'm so excited. Yeah, here he comes. Hey Devin! Get over here. Felix wants to talk to you!"

Devin stepped into view. "Hey, Felix. What's up?"

Sally grinned, gave a big thumbs-up and hurried off, probably to tell her husband.

"Well, you know Sherry and I are getting married in a couple of weeks right?"

"Yeah. I think it's great."

Well...I was wondering whether you'd like to be my groomsman. We're only having one couple."

"Your groomsman? Sure! I've never done that before. What do you do?"

Felix grinned. "It's pretty easy, really. I've never done it myself, but I did get to help a little with the Chernov wedding. The head groomsman took care of the details. He held the ring during the ceremony, and, of course, he escorted Tanya's maid of honor."

Devin grinned. "Sounds easy. So, who's the bridesmaid?"

Felix smiled. "Sherry's asking Lyuba Chernov."

"Lyuba? Really! Hmmm..."

A fleeting look crossed Devin's face; a look Felix thoughtfully filed for future consideration.

"Yeah...she seems like a really nice girl."

Felix raised an eyebrow. "Yes, she's a very nice girl. We look at her kinda like a little sister."

Devin shrugged. "Sure, I know. I'd love to do it."

Felix grinned. "Thanks, Devin. We'll talk soon. I'll see you at the bot factory."

Devin grinned. "Sure thing. Catch ya later."

He backed away and Felix cut the connection.

* * * *

MON 08.23.2094-Earth / TRN 25.03.6998-Aambü
ECS Destiny, Deck 3, Hill Residence, 1530 Hrs / 1166 Slashes

Sherry and Jodi trooped back, flushed with satisfaction at a job well done. They'd gotten dresses selected and handled many other wedding necessities.

Sherry tapped Jodi on the arm. "I'm going to have a chat with Felix and Lyuba. Give me a few minutes, then I'll help you get ready for dinner."

"Sure. No problem, and thanks, I could use the help." Jodi took young Evan off to the back to put him down for a short nap. He was all tuckered out after all the running around.

Felix. Devin?

She felt Felix grin. *Sure, why not? He's a decent kid. He's close enough to our age and still young enough not to look like Lyuba's dad.*

Sherry grinned in spite of herself. *I guess he's OK. I'm wondering about his reaction to escorting Lyuba.*

Felix' shrugs could almost be heard. *Yeah, I was a little surprised by that, but heck, Lyuba's kinda cute. I'd be surprised if guys didn't notice. It'll be OK. We're both on it. Right?*

Sherry grinned. *You got that right, honey. I'm going to ask Lyuba now. Catch you at dinner?*

I wouldn't miss it for the world; love you.

Sherry smiled. *I love you. Later.*

She let Felix fade to his little corner of her mind. Then, she composed herself for her chat with Lyuba. She thought of Lyuba's face and sent out a call. *Lyuba, honey. Lyuba, can you hear me?*

Lyuba was on the way home from the science lab. *Hey, Sherry. What's up?*

Sherry took a deep breath. *I need to ask you a big favor. I couldn't think of anyone else to ask.*

She heard the brightening of Lyuba's 'voice' in her response. *Of course, Sherry, all you have to do is ask; anything for my favorite big sis!*

Sherry grinned. She loved the relationship she had with Lyuba. *I really need someone to help with my wedding. I was wondering whether you'd be interested in being my bridesmaid?*

There was a long moment of silence. Sherry wondered if something was wrong. Then, *Sherry! You mean it? Oh! I'd love to! This is way cool!*

Sherry could feel the raw excitement that coursed along Lyuba's 'voice.' *I'm so glad you like the idea. We'll get together and go over details tonight after dinner. OK?*

Lyuba responded. *Sure! Oh, who's going to be the groomsman?*

Sherry thought of putting off the answer, but that wasn't fair to Lyuba. *You know Devin Hawkins from church, right?*

There was another long silence. Lyuba unconsciously fingered the bracelet she always wore. *Devin? Devin...um...yeah. You mean that nice, tall guy who helps out at church, right?*

Sherry sighed. She could hear that special, wistful tone in Lyuba's response. *Yeah. That's him. Are you OK with that?*

The response was almost immediate. *Is he OK? Uh yeah, he's fine.*

Sherry's eyebrows arched. *OK, honey. I'm gonna go now. We'll get together tonight. Bye.*

Sherry released her concentration, allowing Lyuba to fade.

Felix quipped from his little corner. *Fine?*

Sherry grinned. *My thoughts exactly...*

MADE OFFICIAL —3

WED 09.01.2094-Earth / TRN 32.03.6998-Aambü
7 weeks, 5 days to orbital insertion; Aambü, Gem System
ECS Destiny, Deck 3, Hill Residence, 1715 Hrs / 0700 Slashes

Sherry hurried to the door. Felix was crossing the mezzanine and she wanted to be the one to answer it. She stepped out in time to meet him as he reached the door.

They stood and embraced for a lingering moment. Then he stepped back and fished in his pocket for a little something he'd brought with him. *You know what this is, but I wanted you to see it with your own eyes before I put it on your hand.*

He handed her the tiny box. She knew what was there. She even knew what it looked like from Felix' eyes, but it just wasn't the same as when she opened the box. The fiery solitaire was exquisite. The white gold shone brightly in the ship's lights.

Felix spoke out loud. "It's hardly a surprise, but I want you to know that if we didn't have this mental bond. I'd still love you very much. I'd still want you to marry me."

Sherry's eyes glistened. "Thank you, Felix. You know I feel the same way."

He gently took the ring from the box and placed it on her wedding finger. "Forever..." He whispered.

The tears flowed and she hugged him fiercely again. "Forever..." She echoed.

They went back inside. *I truly don't regret this bond.*

Sherry chuckled quietly. *Nor I.*

Pastor Brad came out of his study. Felix and Sherry were just entering the room. He could see traces of tears on her face. Then he caught the flash of light from the new ring on her finger. "Ah, you have a prize."

Sherry grinned and held out her new possession.

"Yes, indeed. It's quite beautiful." He looked into her eyes. "And I see joy and contentment in there. I'm happy for you."

He turned and motioned for them to be seated. "Let's sit and talk. Jodi's bringing the coffee."

He picked his favorite chair and Felix and Sherry settled on the couch. "So, Felix. How's it going?"

Felix sat back. "Preparations are going quite well. As you can see," he patted Sherry's hand, "the rings are ready."

"I just reorganized things in our new place. My groomsman's pretty jazzed. I think we've done well for such short notice."

Pastor Brad grinned. "I wish all weddings went so much according to plan. I've found that even simple weddings have their perilous dalliances with disaster. Yours seems to be an exception."

Sherry grinned. "Oh, I don't think it would have been so seamless if it hadn't been for the awesome help of Jodi and Tanya. Lyuba's been quite the trooper too."

Jodi set the coffee on the table. "Oh, Sherry. It was my pleasure. I've had so much fun. Tanya's so much fun to work with, and you're right about Lyuba. She's getting pretty sharp about practical things. She's going to be a challenge for someone one day."

Felix grinned. "Uh, yeah. Is it my imagination, or does Lyuba have a 'thing' for Devin Hawkins?"

Sherry laughed along with Jodi.

Jodi took a sip of her coffee. "Felix. I think almost all the young ladies in the youth group are swooning over Devin. He's a sharp looking lad. Plus, he's bright, witty, and mature for his age. He's got the 'older guy' bug running through the ladies ranks. We'll keep an eye out, of course, but I wouldn't be too concerned."

Brad chuckled. "I think I'd be more concerned if she didn't show any interest. She's a normal, healthy, and cute young lady."

Sherry nodded. "Yeah, I think Devin's noticed the cute part. He's behaving, I'll hand him that, but I see those eyes. They're innocent, but this association with the wedding has certainly piqued his interest."

Brad chuckled again. "Well, we certainly didn't get together to talk about Devin. I believe we have our last session to go over."

Sherry smiled. "Of course."

They sat around the coffee table while Jodi went back to bring out some muffins.

The session went well. Near the end, Pastor Brad concluded with some comments about the unique nature of their relationship. "So, if I understand the way your bond works, you're always aware of each others thoughts and experiences. Is that right?"

Felix put his cup down on the coffee table. "I think that's mostly true. We haven't really tested the limits. I think we're learning to better separate our personal thoughts from our shared ones. There aren't too many areas where we need much separation."

Sherry nodded. "I've noticed we're starting to set aside a tiny partition that has the other constantly present. I know it would be the most desperate sense of loss, to have him missing from there."

Brad nodded. "I can't imagine what that would be like. I'd venture to say that even with this bond, your continued health in your relationship depends on honest effort on both your parts. Even more important. Never, ever forget that keeping God at the heart of your marriage will guard and protect that relationship from any harm."

He took a sip of his coffee. "I don't know how this whole enhanced mind state works, but I can say this. It doesn't surprise God in the slightest. I think He has some unrevealed reason for allowing us to be detoured to this region of space, to be in the right place at the right time to place you two in the path of that whole dream thing. There must be some reason you've been inextricably pulled into a relationship with a people that has never seen the light of our sun.

He put his cup on the coffee table. "I think He's allowed this bonding thing to take place because you'll need the extra strength it'll give you to accomplish some task only you two, and perhaps Lyuba, are equipped to complete.

"Right now, literally, God alone knows what that task might be. You'll need the strength this bond adds. If Lyuba's involved, which seems likely, she'll need the unified strength you two possess to bolster her in her task; whatever that is."

Pastor Brad stood and Felix and Sherry joined him. "Bottom line? God's fully aware of what's happening. He's allowed you two to be equipped as no other young couple has ever been equipped. He has powerfully special plans.

MADE OFFICIAL —4
FRI 09.03.2094-Earth / TRN 33.03.6998-Aambü
ECS Destiny, Deck 3, Forward Public Commons, New Destiny Church, 1800 Hrs /
0742 Slashes

Pastor Brad looked about at the small group gathered in the forward public commons where *New Destiny Church* met. The bridal party was small, but fun. The newest addition, a little girl named Tiffany had been selected to strew rose petals down the aisle ahead of the bride during the processional.

"So, I think this rehearsal will be rather short. It's pretty straightforward. As you can see, we have a swath of seats, two wide, straddling the aisle. Tomorrow it'll be fully set up like it is for our Sunday services. We'll practice coming down the aisle so everyone knows their exact places, and we'll talk through the order of service. Then, we can go over there," he pointed out a partitioned off area of the hall, "to enjoy a nice little meal some of the ladies worked up for us."

All could smell the promise of a tasty good time. Mouths watered at the thought.

"The *New Destiny* band was jazzed about playing for the wedding; pun intended. They'll be here tomorrow. I'm told the music's ready, and they'll not disappoint. For now, we'll just pretend we have music...Any questions?"

There were none, so he had everyone go to their places. Lyuba stood nervously next to Devin and cast surreptitious glances at him. He was almost a head taller. *He looks nice.* She thought to herself.

Devin was trying hard to be aloof. It wasn't coming off very well. He watched Lyuba whenever he thought she didn't notice. He noticed she was wearing the bracelet he'd given her for her birthday. He was glad she liked it.

"OK." Brad began. "After the second musical selection, I want the bridesmaid and the groomsman to link arms. When the next song starts, you'll walk at a slow casual pace down the aisle, separate at the first row of chairs and stand opposite each other on the tape marks in front of the platform. Let's try it, shall we?"

Devin hooked his arm as he'd been instructed. Lyuba placed her right arm through the crook of his arm and then he placed his right hand on top of hers.

The moment they touched they knew something was odd. Devin was nervous, but that didn't explain the odd sensation he had as if he'd stepped into a room with a massive power generator, complete with a strong background hum.

Lyuba was instantly aware of Devin's situation. His background sound was like a huge fan winding up. She wondered if maybe, he was about to awaken. *That would be weird.* She thought to herself.

They stepped out for their short march to the front of the room. Lyuba had an idea she couldn't wait to try. She glanced over at Devin who was trying not to be obvious about watching her. She decided to try a little experiment. *Hi Devin.*

Devin's head snapped her direction with a strange look of surprise on his face. His feet tangled up at that moment, causing him to trip. He managed to save himself from falling, but Lyuba had to tug on his arm to help. Lyuba couldn't help it. She laughed.

Devin looked embarrassed. He'd just made a total fool of himself in front of her and everyone else.

Lyuba got herself under control as they reached the final row of chairs where they were to separate.

"Sorry." She offered as they parted to either side of the platform as instructed.

Devin looked at her as if she'd just danced a jig. "Sorry? I'm the one who tripped."

His response was almost as funny as his reaction to her little greeting. She managed to keep from breaking out into gales of laughter. *I gotta do something about you.* She thought.

Devin's eyes darted back to her face. She couldn't hear him anymore because they were no longer touching, but she could see the sheen of mental energy that was present on every face she looked at. His was fluctuating in odd patterns rather than just glowing. Lyuba called back to him. "We have to talk after. It's really important!"

Devin shrugged. There was something weird going on. He was certain he'd heard her voice, but she hadn't been speaking. Then she'd laughed at his stupid clumsy feet.

That was humiliating, but then she spoke without speaking again. He was certain she said something about 'doing something about him.' That had really been weird.

He couldn't figure her out. First she'd laughed at his clumsiness. Then she'd apologized for it as if it had been her fault. Now she wanted to talk about something important; whatever that was. He figured he'd find out soon enough.

Pastor Brad was talking. "...good. When Devin and Lyuba reach their assigned places, I want Tiffany to start down the aisle. Tiffany, I want you to go nice and slow. You'll have a basket of rose petals. As you go, you want to just toss a few petals in the air behind you so they make a pretty path for Sherry to walk down. Got it?"

Tiffany, all concentration, nodded her head.

Finally, the rehearsal was over. Everyone was eager to move on with the next part of the evening; good food. "OK, gang. As I said earlier, the ladies, under the watchful eyes of Kaitlyn O'Connor, have prepared a wonderful dinner to help us celebrate. So, if we all want to move around to the other side of the partitions, we can eat."

That got enthusiastic acclaim as the group flowed into the partitioned area. Tables had been set out and there was a place for everyone according to their part in the wedding party. The scene behind the partition reminded Lyuba of her birthday party not so long ago.

Devin sat next to Felix on one side of the table, and Lyuba sat next to Sherry on the other. Soon everyone was at his or her place.

Tolya was trying to figure out why Lyuba was so animated and jittery. And, as if he were a study in contrasts, Devin, who was usually fairly lively himself, was rather quiet and introspective. He looked around the table a lot. Tolya thought there was an almost haunted look to his eyes. Except for Devin's curious demeanor the dinner was lively.

As the dinner dishes were being removed and fresh cups of coffee were being distributed around, Tanya stood and tapped her cup for attention. All eyes looked expectantly. "In the excitement this evening, something important was nearly forgotten."

Surprise registered on many faces. What could have been forgotten for this darling couple's beautiful wedding?

Tanya moved around the table to stand behind Sherry. "Our beloved Sherry. I've known Sherry since the fourth day of our voyage. She started out as a new and welcome face to serve in my office. The 'gentleman' who was supposed to be running the post before me, made the mistake of ignoring Sherry's application and I am so incredibly happy I was able to rectify that situation.

"Sherry has become someone who I'd be sorely lost without. I found in Sherry, not just someone who worked for me, but someone who wound up being my first real friend on board *Destiny*.

"Since those early months, she's nearly become the little sister I never had, so I thought, who better to handle this little task than her honorary big sister?

"Today's the day before Sherry's wedding; a moment she's dreamed of for a long time, I'm sure. Today is also something more. Today is Sherry's birthday. I just couldn't let that go by without a little extra celebration."

Everyone applauded the announcement as Sherry blushed at all the extra attention.

"I know almost everyone has benefited from the artistry of our sister Kaitlyn, so I thought, who better to make a fabulous cake?"

There was a sudden bustling as the ladies rolled out a wonderful cake. It was a work of art; two layers of sixteen-inch diameter chocolate fudge cake, with a filling of raspberry and blackberry, were covered with a delicate white whipped cream frosting. The whole thing was decorated with fresh raspberries and blackberries from the gardens on Ag-Deck. 'Happy Birthday & Best Wishes' was written in careful calligraphy. It seemed almost a sin to cut it.

The whole room erupted in a hilarious caterwauling of 'Happy Birthday.' With backslapping, hugs and kisses going around, the evening wound out happily.

Finally, Pastor Brad announced it would be a good idea for everyone to get some rest for the big day tomorrow.

As some people began to make their exits, Lyuba headed over and got Devin's attention. "Devin. Come on. We need to talk."

He looked at her for a moment, and then shrugged his shoulders. He tossed down the punch that was left in his cup and followed her past the partitions to the other end of the hall.

Lyuba sat on the edge of the low platform used for the church services and, after some hesitation; Devin joined her.

"Devin. I...Look at me."

He looked up from his feigned fascination with his shoes. He looked into her face.

"That's better. This is really important. I know what's happening to you."

Devin tried to act like he didn't understand.

"Devin, look. I'm sorry I laughed at you during the practice. It was really my fault you tripped. What you heard from me earlier this evening was real."

He looked at her squarely this time, finally ready to listen. "Now, you've known the rest of us kids for nearly the whole trip. Right?"

Devin nodded. "Of course."

Lyuba persisted. "Do we...do I look entirely the same as a few months ago?"

Devin frowned. "What do you mean?"

"How long has it been since you started seeing that odd shine in people's faces?"

Devin's eyes widened. "H...how do you know?"

Lyuba gave him a grim smile. "I know. It happened to me...How about the weird background noise you hear when you shake someone's hand, or, like this evening, when we touched at the practice? When did that start happening?"

Devin looked around, feeling trapped. "There's nothing wrong. I'm not crazy."

"No! You're not. Look, Devin. Hold out your hand." After a moment's hesitation, Devin complied. Lyuba took his hand and then projected. *You can hear me now, can't you?*

He looked at her with haunted eyes. "What did you do?"

I spoke to you with my mind instead of my voice.

"You're kidding, right? I mean, nobody does that except in science fiction stories."

"No. I'm not kidding. Tell me. Does my face shine just like everybody else's?"

Devin was caught off guard by the change of tack. "Uh...Well, yeah...I mean, no. Yours is brighter."

"Ah! Is there anyone else in this crowd tonight that seems brighter than the rest?"

Devin thought about it. It dawned on him that, yes, everyone seemed to have a faint sheen about them, but now that he thought about it, there were two others who were bright, just like Lyuba. "I'd say Felix and Sherry are almost as bright as you are."

Lyuba grinned. "Devin. I'm going to let you in on a little secret. It won't be secret much longer, but you're going to have to know about it now.

"First, I'm going to tell you something about yourself. You are among a rare few people on board *Destiny* who has a latent ability to mind speak. It is latent and would have been latent for the rest of your life except for one very huge event that happened just a few weeks ago."

"The Dream." Devin breathed. "That's what you're talking about isn't it?"

"Yes, Devin. It was after The Dream that you started seeing and hearing things about other people that you'd never seen or heard before. Right?"

"Yeah. You're right."

"OK, Devin. Because you are a latent telepath...don't look at me like that. It's true. You just can't imagine it because everybody says it can't be true. Let me finish.

"Because you're latent, The Dream triggered something that would have remained dormant. For some reason, it has taken longer to show up for you than for me, but it's true. I think it really bumped up a notch when we linked our arms this evening."

Devin considered. "Something happened there, I'll admit that."

"OK. There is someone who helped me break through the final barrier. You'll meet him later, but for now, I'm going to try to do for you, what he did for me. I need you to trust me. I'm not making fun of you. I'm not trying to trick you, or make you look stupid. If you cooperate..." she let go of his hand and projected again. *You'll be able to do this too.*

Devin's eyes reflected awe. "You...I heard you..." He tapped his head. "Inside...I heard your voice."

"Yes, you did. When we're done, you'll hear much better and you'll be able to speak as well."

She stood up and motioned for him to do the same.

* * * *

Sherry sensed strong emotions emanating from somewhere. *Felix. Do you feel it?*

Felix moved over to join her. She was slowly walking towards the partitions.

Nearly everyone else was on their way to bed. Just a few remained, helping to clean up. Sherry looked around the edge of the partition and watched the most interesting tableau she'd seen in some time.

There was Lyuba, near the platform, motioning Devin to stand in front of her.

What are they doing?

Sherry shook her head. *I've noticed something strange about Devin all evening. Lyuba seems to be onto it too.*

They slowly, quietly, walked further across the room towards the scene unfolding before them. They stopped and listened quietly.

Lyuba was saying... "I'm going to place the tips of my fingers on your temples. Then I'm going to talk to you just with my mind. OK? Are you ready?"

Devin nodded.

Felix looked at Sherry. *Have you seen this before?*

Sherry nodded. *What should we do?*

Felix shrugged. *I think we'll just have to watch for now.*

Lyuba carefully raised her arms and gently placed the tips of her fingers against Devin's temples. "I want you to look in my eyes. Don't look away. This won't hurt."

She took a slow breath and projected gently. *Hello, Devin. You're awakening into a whole new world of possibilities. What began with The Dream is about to break open like a flower in the morning sun. Welcome to a brother and sisterhood of human mind speakers. With you, we are now four strong.*

Devin took a deep breath and the look of distress that had been with him the whole evening simply evaporated.

Lyuba slowly let her hands drop back to her side. *Thanks for waiting, you two.*

She regarded Felix and Sherry. *I was afraid you'd try to stop me.*

She returned her attention to Devin. *Can you hear me?*

Devin smiled. "Yes, I hear you fine."

Lyuba raised a hand and gently placed her fingers over his mouth. *I want you to talk to me, but you must not use your voice. I know you can. You just have to want to say something.*

Devin looked slightly frustrated for a moment and then, *Uh...how about this?*

Lyuba grinned. *That's great. It takes practice like anything else, but you can do it.*

She turned to Felix and Sherry. *So, are you two going to come over here and greet the newest member of our little club?*

Felix felt silly. *Sure thing, kiddo, I wish you'd warned us.*

Lyuba sniffed. *And would you have been all that eager to let me meddle in this kind of 'dangerous' stuff?*

Sherry chuckled. *You know she has a point, honey.*

Felix shrugged and walked up to join the two younger kids. Sherry was right beside him and linked her arm around his as they came to a stop.

Hi, Devin. I didn't know you were about to awaken. If I had, I think we all would have tried to help.

Devin smiled. *Truthfully, I didn't know what was happening. I was afraid I was going nuts. How did you manage to get through this with so little trouble?*

Felix and Sherry burst out laughing. Felix laughed till his eyes watered. Lyuba grinned.

Devin looked confused. *What did I say?*

Sherry calmed herself enough to come to his rescue. *Oh, Devin. If you only knew the trouble we've been through. Lyuba's had the least amount of trouble with this because she had us to help her and we had someone else to help us who understood it better than we did.*

Devin nodded. *Of course, The Lord would know all about it.*

Felix grinned, having gotten himself mostly under control. *The Lord surely protected and guided us, but the one Sherry's referring to lives on the world we're so quickly approaching.*

Devin looked at him sharply. *Wait. How can anyone...you're kidding, right?*

Sherry shook her head. *No, we're not kidding. His name is AgradUtya. The best I can do right now is tell you there's an entire race of people living on the world we thought we'd have to ourselves. They're mind speakers, one and all.*

Lyuba put in her two cents. *It was AgradUtya who did something that accidentally triggered The Dream.*

Devin was amazed. *How do you know so much about it?*

Sherry gave the short explanation. *We were the first to meet him. He explained all of this to us. Felix and I have kinda fallen into the unofficial role of Xeno-Ambassadors to the Aambüka, the Water People.*

There's a whole lot more to the story, but for now, I think we should leave it at that. Don't forget, we have a wedding tomorrow. After that's over, there'll be meetings, and announcements. For now, for the sake of sanity, we're keeping this quiet till we've had a chance to talk with these people and see what chance there is for coexistence. We really don't have any place else to go.

Felix ushered them all back to the exit door. *Devin, it's good to have you on board. We'll catch you up on all the facts whenever things get back to normal. I need your promise, for now, that you won't talk to anyone else about what you've learned tonight.*

Devin sensed the seriousness of the request. *OK. I promise I'll keep quiet until you tell me it's safe to talk. I guess I'd better get some rest.*

He glanced at Lyuba. *I'll see you in the morning. Thanks for your help. Really!*

Lyuba smiled back at him. *That's OK. What are friends for? Oh, by the way. If anything really weird starts happening, like you do strange things you couldn't normally do, call for me right away. You have the tuning of my mind. The range on this is long. I don't know how far, but inside the ship, no distance is too great. Just call for me.*

MADE OFFICIAL — 5

FRI 09.04.2094-Earth / TRN 34.03.6998-Aambü
ECS Destiny, Deck 3, Hill Residence, 0800 Hrs / 1800 Slashes

Tanya and Lyuba left home early, their arms full of items of clothes and make up and such. They arrived at the Hill's place ready to do battle with the elements, if necessary, to wrest beauty from the ravages of sleep.

Sherry was up. The shower had seen much use. Jodi was putting coffee and pastries on the table to fortify the troops for battle.

Meanwhile, Brad somehow managed to gather little Evan's things and beat a hasty retreat out the door. He and Evan met Devin at the lift well and wound up at Tolya's door. The guys sat down to coffee and doughnuts pilfered from the diner. Tolya told Brad about the early morning sparring match he'd had with Felix on his own wedding day.

Felix was surprised. He remembered that morning telling Tolya he'd probably be scared to death. In fact, he was more impatient than anything. He intimately knew where he stood with Sherry.

They were inextricably twined into a unit already. This was the beautiful wrapping on the gift. This was to put the responsibility into the relationship. It was a promise to God and each other that mental bond or no mental bond, they meant to honor each other to the very end. Felix wanted to get to the doing of it.

The morning sped by much more quickly than it felt. They were madly throwing the last elements of formal civilization onto their shoulders and scurrying out the door when Sherry called to Felix. *Hey love, you guys better get down here and ready to go. It's 1130 already.*

Felix grinned as he tossed Devin the box with the rings in it. *You caught us headed out the door, but you knew that already.*

He could hear the grin on her face. *Yeah, but I couldn't resist. See ya soon.*

The public commons had been set up for the usual church service. It was decorated with beautiful blue and white banners on either side of the platform. A dusty blue runner had been rolled down the center aisle. Slender rods were fastened to the aisle chair of every other row on both sides of the aisle. Candles in beautiful glass globes were fastened to the top of each rod. They alternated between a frosty white globe and a frosty blue one.

Pastor Brad and Felix made their way to the front of the hall. They found seats at the back of the platform and sat to wait. Tolya headed back out the entryway to watch and wait for the ladies.

At 1148 they could be seen, hurrying gracefully along the port side balcony from the Mezzanine. They arrived looking very self satisfied and Tolya thought they had every reason to feel that way. They looked beautiful.

Tanya was wearing a beautiful gold colored gown. She wasn't in the line up, but she looked like she would have belonged there. Lyuba wore a graceful gown of azure blue to which Tolya was assigned the honor of pinning a beautiful lavender corsage.

Then there was Sherry. She was resplendent in a full white dress. She looked like she was ready for a formal ball. Her train was short but regal. The headpiece with veil thrown back revealed her beautiful medium blond hair touched ever so carefully with hints of azure blue highlights.

Tolya stepped forward and gave Sherry a gentle hug. "You look beautiful, young lady. Felix is a lucky man."

Sherry, all grace and poise, hugged back and replied. "Thank you, Tolya. You're not quite old enough to be my dad, but I wouldn't have complained if you really were. Lyuba's a lucky girl to have you."

Tolya squeezed her arms gently as he backed away. He turned and greeted Lyuba. "Ah. My little girl's not so little any more. You look every bit the princess today, sweet heart. Watch out for princes lurking at every turn. You're going to capture someone's heart."

He gave her a gentle hug. She hugged back and stood looking back into his eyes. "Have I said often enough that you're the best dad ever?"

Tolya smiled. "I don't think you can say it often enough. You're going to make me proud. I know it."

Tanya stepped up and took Tolya firmly by the shoulders, turning him for a great big hug and kiss. "We better get to it before things get any mushier."

Tolya gave one more squeeze and turned. He motioned Devin to join them. He'd been standing in the doorway, looking uncertain.

Lyuba swept up to him and gave him her most dazzling smile. *Good morning Devin. How are you doing so far?*

Devin smiled and gave her a nod. *I'm doing well, thank you. You look very nice.*

Lyuba blushed at the compliment. *Thank you.*

Devin noticed the birthday bracelet on her wrist. It seemed she wore it everywhere.

She glanced around at the rest of the group. It was clear they were curious. Not one word had transpired between the two. Yet, it was apparent to all that they'd just talked.

Tolya looked at Tanya with a look of confusion mixed with concern. Tanya shrugged and glanced at Sherry.

Sherry, in turn was watching the scene with a hint of a smile playing about the corners of her mouth.

"OK, Sherry. You're hiding something. I know that cute little smile lurking in there. Come on, what's up?"

Tanya was grinning, but Sherry sensed an underlay of concern.

She glanced at Devin. *Devin, would you come here, please?*

Devin looked up at Sherry, grinned and started their way. *Sure. The bride's wish is my command.*

Sherry grinned and rolled her eyes. "Tanya, do you remember last night, Devin seemed somewhat out of sorts?"

Tanya thought back. "As a matter of fact, yes. I remember commenting on it to Tolya. He usually seems so lively. We decided he must not have been feeling very well."

Sherry smiled. "I guess you could have said that."

Tolya had been listening in on the conversation. He approached to hear better.

Sherry continued. "We know, until last night, there were only three of us who had the talents of our new neighbors."

Tolya was about to stomp on the conversation. This was getting into territory he wasn't ready to divulge to the general population.

"Tolya. Please. No secrets have been told that were at all possible to avoid."

Tanya commented. "You said, 'until last night.'"

Sherry grinned. "Yes, I did. You see, last night it became obvious to Lyuba that Devin was awakening. So, as AgradUtya did for her, she helped usher Devin the rest of the way into this new little world of ours. "There are now four humans in the universe who can fully communicate with the Aambüka."

Tanya looked at Devin, then at Lyuba. "And you didn't tell me, Lyuba? You didn't warn me you were about to do something no human's ever done before without any regard for your own safety? What if..."

Lyuba turned to face Tanya. She stepped up and grasped her by the arm, gently but firmly. *There was no time mom. It started at the beginning of the rehearsal.*

AgradUtya did it for me. I saw it. I felt it. I just knew what to do. Shouldn't Devin have had the same courtesy AgradUtya showed me?

Tanya stared at her daughter. Then she hugged her close and whispered. "You keep scaring me."

She looked around at Sherry, Tolya and Devin. "I'm sorry. This is the wrong time to make a scene. Sherry. I understand there was no time. I understand with the wedding you didn't have time to talk to me afterwards. I just worry about what's happening to Lyuba. She's changing so fast."

Sherry stepped up and gave Tanya a quick hug.

"Tahnie. We wouldn't just let her do anything that seemed dangerous. We walked up on them as Lyuba was starting. It was too late to stop her. I don't know what would happen if the process were interrupted."

She stepped back. "But I promise you, whenever possible, we'll keep you informed on all aspects of her training and development in this new area of her life."

She gave Tanya a loving smile. "We love her too, you know."

Tanya smiled. "I know. Thanks. It's almost time."

Sherry nodded. "Yeah, let's do this!" They turned and headed for the entrance to the hall.

As if on cue, the band struck up the first song on their list. The seats were full of eager smiling faces. Tolya and Sherry stayed just outside the door where they couldn't be seen while Lyuba and Devin stepped to the back of the room, ready for their part.

Lyuba gave Devin a particularly dazzling smile. *Don't worry about Mom. She's been watching me develop this new mind thing since shortly after The Dream. She'll calm down. You'll see.*

Devin returned her smile. *It's OK. Moms are that way. She loves you very much. If I didn't know better, I'd think she was your bio-mom.*

Lyuba turned back to look at him. *That was so sweet.*

The song they had been waiting for began. Devin grinned, holding out his arm. *This is it.*

Lyuba took his arm as they'd practiced and he placed his other hand over hers. They walked confidently down the aisle, looking for all the world like they'd done this a dozen times before.

Tanya had Tiffany ready for her debut. Tiffany was in a smart little replica of Lyuba's outfit. Tanya handed her the basket containing the rose petals. "OK, honey. Are you ready?" Tiffany nodded her head; looking very serious. Tanya had to suppress the urge to giggle.

The music changed again and Tanya walked Tiffany to the center of the blue runner. "OK. Just walk slowly and throw handfuls of rose petals up in the air so they fall behind you. When you're done, I want you to go stand next to Lyuba. OK?"

Tiffany nodded again. "Ready...Go."

Frank was there with his camera. His extra help taking pictures had opted out to get married. Frank didn't mind. Felix had turned out to be a decent sort after all. Besides, this too was a chunk of the history of this colony. However things turned out, it looked like Felix and Sherry were going to be in the story.

The music changed again and the people rose as one to greet the bride as she came down the aisle.

Sherry was regally striding, holding onto Tolya's arm, truly the Queen for the day. The rose petals were a nice touch against the blue runner and the globed lanterns.

They reached the front row of chairs and stood, waiting for the last phrases of the song to end.

As the music ended, Pastor Brad stepped forward from the back of the platform to stand just above and to one side of Felix, who stood next to Devin.

After warm greetings to the people gathered there, Pastor Brad turned to face Sherry and Tolya. "Sherry Marie Petrakis has come to give her hand in marriage to Felix Xavier Hernandez. Who gives the bride?"

Tolya responded. "I do."

Pastor Brad nodded to Felix who stepped forward. Tolya turned slightly to meet him and as Felix offered his arm, Tolya handed Sherry off. "Go get her," he whispered with a grin.

Felix grinned and whispered back. "Thanks."

Felix and Sherry stepped forward to stand before Pastor Brad.

Though much smaller and a whole lot less dramatic than Tolya and Tanya's wedding just a few months ago, this one was every bit as beautiful and touching. The entire command staff could look back, knowing details about this couple, and see the amazing turn of events this represented. The irony was immense.

Pastor Brad gave another moving message. Then came the giving of the rings. Devin handed Felix the ring.

Pastor Brad began. "Do you, Felix Xavier Hernandez take Sherry Marie Petrakis as your lawfully wedded wife, to love and cherish, to honor and protect, all the days of your life?"

Felix voice rang strong and true. "I do."

He took Sherry's hand and, taking the engagement ring, twisted it and the wedding band together to form one ring. He slipped it lovingly on her hand.

Then he repeated the vow as Pastor Brad spoke it. "I, Felix Xavier Hernandez, give this ring as pledge and promise that I will love, honor and care for you as Christ cares for the church, that I will never leave you nor forsake you, as God is my witness."

Pastor Brad turned to Sherry. Lyuba swapped Felix' ring for Sherry's bouquet.

Sherry placed it on Felix' hand and repeated her vow. "I, Sherry Marie Petrakis, give this ring as pledge and promise that I will love, honor, and follow you as we are to follow Christ. I promise I will never leave you nor forsake you. As God is my witness."

After the beautiful unity candle ceremony Pastor Brad uttered the magic words. "By the authority given to me by Christ and the laws of this charter, I pronounce you husband and wife."

Pastor Brad had the two turn and face each other. Then, with a mischievous grin, paused, letting the moment linger. "Now for the moment you've been waiting for; Felix, you may kiss your bride."

Felix grinned back and then slowly, tenderly; he lifted the veil and folded it back over her head and they took their first truly masterful kiss. It seemed, at least for a moment, that they'd pass out for lack of air.

Daryl regretted not having thought to bring a stopwatch. Finally, when it seemed they would surly collapse, they parted and turned to face the congregation. Sherry had joyful tears streaming down her cheeks and a dazzling smile that could have competed with the stars.

They held hands and Pastor Brad stepped up next to Felix. "My friends, I would love to introduce to you for the first time, Felix Xavier and Sherry Marie...Mr. and Mrs. Hernandez. What God has united let no one split apart."

There was wild applause. Shane patted Tolya on the back and Kaitlyn dabbed happy tears from her face as she hugged Tanya across the back of the seats.

The music resumed and the new couple marched purposefully up the aisle to the back of the room. There, they were flooded with well-wishers as Devin and Lyuba escorted Tiffany after them.

A team began tearing down the chairs on the side of the hall nearest the kitchen. Soon that half of the hall was converted to a dining area. Food was quickly transported from the crowded kitchen to the serving tables along the wall. One table was set aside and reserved for the wedding party. Everyone not employed setting up the reception stood around the periphery speculating on the fortunes of the new couple.

Kaitlyn nudged Shane who stood up on a chair and called for everyone's attention. "Right. Now, we have a lot, and I mean a lot, of good food for everyone. We'll do this buffet style, so if everyone will form a line we'll get started. Oh! I believe it would only be proper for the bridal party to cut to the front. Never fear, there's plenty here."

That last got some hearty laughter as the miniature crowd sorted itself out. The prospects of getting food prepared under the watchful eye of Kaitlyn O'Connor was incentive enough for all to cooperate in an orderly assault on the food.

Felix and Sherry made their way down the table. Neither was all that hungry, really. They were much too excited about the events of the day. Truth be told, they were eager for the part of the event were they could quietly vanish into private anonymity.

The meal was as sumptuous as expected. The cake was beautiful. For the garter toss, Devin prevailed. The bouquet toss went to Brianna from MedCentral and the band stayed around and played through a number of songs for those who wished to dance.

The youth, under the Lyuba's instigation, dashed off, with permission from Jodi Hill, to collect Sherry's things and take them to the new Hernandez quarters.

When Felix and Sherry finally, gracefully bowed out, they were surprised to find a group of youth standing patiently outside their new cabin, watching a surprisingly large pile of Sherry's things. Felix waved the door open and the kids hurried to line the entryway. They finished in record time and Lyuba ushered them out. Sherry gave Lyuba a quick hug. *Thanks sweetie. That just saved us a whole lot of bother.*

She looked out in the hall and called. "Thanks everyone."

Felix waved and added his own thank you. Soon all the teens were hurrying back to find more to eat.

Felix and Sherry stepped back inside their new place. The door snapped shut and he tapped the 'do not disturb' tab.

He turned and grabbed Sherry about the waist and pulled her into a hefty hug. They worked their way around all her stuff and headed for the bedroom.

It's done! Felix exulted and Sherry grinned. *Finally.*

She looked at him appraisingly. *I think that monkey suit has been on you long enough, Mister.* She reached up and undid the bow tie and the first button at his collar. Felix decided it would only be polite to return the favor.

He reached behind her neck and undid the fasteners that kept the top of her gown firmly in place. *Isn't this a little confining?*

They continued the mutual unsheathing as they slowly inched their way to the bedroom. By the time they stumbled over the edge of the bed, the fun little chore was done.

They kissed long and hard. Then Sherry gave a little gasp...*Felix!*

MADE OFFICIAL — 6

THU 09.23.2094-Earth / TRN 08.04.6998-Aambü
4 weeks, 4 days to orbital insertion; Aambü, Gem System
ECS Destiny, Quarterdeck, Science Lab, 1515 Hrs / 0542 Slashes

The excitement seemed to have finally settled down. There were no more wild dreams, no more emergencies requiring Felix or Sherry's talents. Lyuba was back to classes, as was Felix.

Lyuba thought maybe it had gotten just a little boring. She'd been playing around with the whole TK thing, as it was being called. She really tried not to show off, but it was hard not to let it slip occasionally.

The first time Emily saw something sail across the lab into Lyuba's hands she'd come unglued. "Lyuba! What the heck was that? Who threw the pocket-tab?"

Lyuba looked slightly embarrassed. A couple of classmates who'd been invited to participate in the lab routines watched the confrontation with avid interest.

Lyuba was 'OK' as classmates went. She hadn't gotten too 'miss uppity up' after she'd became the daughter of the governor, but still...None of them were more than cordial acquaintances.

One girl had seen the pocket-tab leap from its place on the table and dart across the room into Lyuba's waiting hands. If her eyes had gotten any rounder, they would have probably bugged out.

Her name was Melissa. "Nobody did, Miss Strauss. It just flew to her. I swear it!"

The others laughed at what they thought was a joke. "It did. I saw it!"

Emily was starting to loose some of her seemingly endless patience. "That's not very funny, Melissa. We don't have time for silliness like this. If you don't..."

"Ms. Emily?" Lyuba's voice carried well.

Emily turned. "Ms. Emily. Look..."

Lyuba held the pocket-tab up as if for Emily to inspect it. It rose several inches from her hands and floated in Emily's direction.

When it was close to Emily, Lyuba stopped its progress and let it hang there. "Melissa's telling the truth. I guess my folks forgot to warn you."

Emily was staring at the pocket-tab. "It's OK, Ms. Emily. Just grab it like it was on a table or shelf."

Emily tentatively reached out. She passed her hands all around the pocket tab, searching for strings or wires. Finally she touched it. It dipped slightly but remained in place. She grabbed it and pulled.

Lyuba let it go and Emily held it gingerly, staring intently at Lyuba. "Warn me of what, honey?"

"Well, the same thing that happened to Felix and Sherry started happening to me almost a month ago. I've tried to keep it quiet, but I forgot. I needed to use the tab and I just reached for it before I remembered I wasn't at home."

Emily looked at her searchingly for a moment. "OK. I...I guess I'll have a chat with your folks."

She looked around. "All right everyone, back to your stations. We need data."

Melissa sidled up to Lyuba. "I thought she was going to yell at me. Thanks for taking the heat...Did...how'd you do that anyway?"

Lyuba shrugged. "I don't know. I decide I want something to move and it does."

She looked at Melissa's long ponytail. It whipped up like a real horses tail and draped over her shoulder.

Melissa's eyes widened. "That is soooo weird!"

"Lyuba! Enough with the demonstrations, already. How's your data coming?"

Lyuba winced. "Sorry. I'm right on it. Uh...can I have that pocket-tab back?" Emily, who'd walked away from Lyuba, turned. She held up the pocket-tab.

Lyuba reached out and deftly snatched it from her. "Thanks!" She turned back to her work.

* * * *

THU 09.23.2094-Earth / TRN 08.04.6998-Aambü
ECS Destiny, Quarterdeck, Chernov Residence, 1545 Hrs / 0572 Slashes

Lyuba darted in the door and headed for her room. "Hi, mom! Hi, Dad! I'm getting changed right now."

Tanya, preparing dinner for after karate practice, peeked out from the kitchen, "Hurry, honey. We're running late."

Tolya stepped out of his office area and wandered into the kitchen. "She's a bit late, herself. Isn't she?"

Tanya nodded, punching in instructions for the auto-chef. "Yeah. I got a call from Emily today. It appears Lyuba got in a little of her own practice while she was in the lab...Honey, we need to get those meetings going."

Tolya winced. "I know. Now that things are back to normal, we should get down to business."

She turned and put her arms around his neck. "When do you think that ambassador fellow will come back? Do you really think Lyuba's oddly forbidden talent has endangered our relations?"

Tolya kissed her forehead. "I really don't know. He was certainly very upset about what Felix told him. It's odd how that particular talent should be so disturbing."

He stepped back and smiled. "We're almost there. Maybe if we can meet face to face, we can figure it out."

Lyuba popped out of her room, suited up for practice. Her gi was just right; the white belt with the three black slashes on the ends was tied precisely. "I'm ready." She announced to the room at large.

"OK." Tolya said as he headed for the door. "Maybe you'd like to explain why you're so late."

Tanya followed them out. "Yeah, and you might add a little explanation about why Ms. Emily called me about a certain disturbance in her lab today."

"Oh, that."

Tanya raised an eloquent eyebrow as they walked forward to the gym. "Yeah...that."

Lyuba shrugged. It was hardly a repentant gesture. "I just forgot where I was. I wanted the pocket-tab I'd left on the table and I was clear across the room...I just reached out and took it."

They reached the gym and the doors snapped open.

Tanya shook her head. "Emily was totally weirded out." She addressed Tolya, "We have to talk, Tolya. This can't go on being our little secret. Eventually there'll be talk we can't contain."

Tolya sighed. "OK. Get them warmed up. I'll call a staff meeting for tomorrow and we'll get down to addressing a public statement followed by a ship wide meeting. I'll be back in ten minutes or so."

He turned and jogged back out the door.

Tanya and Lyuba continued onto the workout floor. Felix and Sherry were already doing stretches. Tanya led them through the warm-ups and the basics. It was quite disconcerting to see Felix and Sherry moving almost as one.

Tolya returned. He took Felix and Sherry to one end and began going over weapons training. Meanwhile Tanya took Lyuba through her katas.

Lyuba was learning fast. Tanya anticipated she'd test for yellow by the time they reached orbit. "OK, Lyuba. Let's try a tuck and roll technique. Watch me once and then I want you to try."

Lyuba watched as Tanya backed a little ways and then started to run. She leaped and as she flew forward, she tucked her shoulder so that she rolled on the mat and came up on her feet in a front stance, hands bladed.

"Now. I want you to try it." She picked up a short rod from the sidelines and held it across Lyuba's path. "Back up a little. Then run and jump over the rod. As you clear the rod, I want you to tuck your head and shoulders so you roll as you hit the mat. Then roll right up into *zenkutsu dachi*. Got it?"

Lyuba nodded. She backed up a ways and took off at a dead run. As she leaped and cleared the rod, she did as instructed and tucked her head and shoulders.

Instead of hitting the mat, with a short screech of surprise, she continued forward, somersaulting through the air.

The three at the other end of the room ducked in time to miss being bowled over. Lyuba flailed about and somehow managed to get her feet aimed at the bulkhead when she hit.

Accompanied by a cry of pain, her feet and legs absorbed most of the impact, but as she bounced off, she dropped face down.

Tanya was running before Lyuba hit the floor.

Felix and Sherry were closer and hurried to her side. Lyuba was trying to push herself up from the floor. "OW!!" She curled up reaching for her left ankle.

Sherry was on it. *Lyuba honey. You hurt your ankle. Let me look.*

She settled quickly to the floor, gently placing her hands around Lyuba's ankle. "Oh! Sherry, it hurts!"

I know kiddo. Let me see it.

Sherry could feel the pain. She delved deeply. There was swelling, a little tearing. She sent a flow of peace to relax her patient. She dampened the pain as best she could. Then she began going over damaged tissue.

Felix. See the tear? I think it's a muscle. I see no broken bones.

Felix was there. Yes, he saw the tear Sherry was seeing. Sherry did something. He could feel a flow of energy course through her and into Lyuba's ankle.

The swelling began to go down. The muscle tissue steadily began to mend. In moments the damage was reversed and the only evidence was a slight redness on the skin of her ankle.

Tanya knelt and took Lyuba in her arms. "Are you OK, honey? What happened?"

She looked up at Tolya who had hurried around to see how his little girl fared. "I'm OK, Mom. I hurt my foot. It hurt so much I couldn't stand up, but Sherry did something and it's better. It barely hurts now."

Tolya hurried over to the computer/COMM call box. "Computer. Report. Explain the gravitational anomaly that just occurred in the gym."

The briefest of moments passed. "No gravitational anomalies have been detected. All grav-plates report fully nominal function."

Tolya turned to regard the curious faces watching him. Lyuba was getting up on her feet with the assistance of Tanya and Sherry. She whipped her head about to look at Felix, who started laughing. Soon Sherry and Lyuba were laughing as well. Obviously a private joke had passed. Lyuba looked all the better for the laughter.

Tolya announced. "I think we'll call it an evening."

Tanya nodded grimly. "Yes, I want to get Lyuba over to MedCentral and look at that ankle."

She glanced over at Sherry. "No, Sherry. I don't doubt your ability. I'd just feel better double checking, that's all."

She motioned Sherry over to her side. Sherry came to her and Tanya gave her a grateful hug. "Honey, Thank you for taking care of her leg. I'm just not used to this mental powers thing. Someday, I'm sure I'll get used to it."

Sherry hugged back and then pulled Lyuba into the embrace. "It's OK, Tahnie. I'm not upset. I'm not used to being able to do this kind of thing yet, but I'm confident they'll find her ankle's fine.

Tolya spoke up. "OK, let's go." He started for the exit. "I'd still like to figure out what happened just now, but first let's get Lyuba looked at."

Lyuba walked gingerly on her left foot for a few moments, but as they progressed to MedCentral, her gait settled till there was no limp at all when they arrived.

* * * *

Lyuba's ankle turned out to be just fine. The evening staff was a little mystified by the story that she'd twisted it. They found no evidence of damage, save for a small residual amount of blood, essentially a minor bruise was quickly being absorbed into the surrounding tissue.

They all trooped back to the Chernov place. Tanya invited Sherry and Felix to stay and eat with them. The meal was ready in minutes after they arrived and everyone was happy to chow down.

Tolya pushed his plate away and took a grateful sip of his coffee. "So, Princess. Can you tell us what happened in the gym?"

Lyuba shrugged her shoulders. "I don't know. I was just following Mom's instructions. When I jumped, I wanted to get over the rod and do the tuck and roll perfect, but when I jumped, I suddenly felt really light. It felt like...well, like when I was flying in The Dream."

Felix looked over at Sherry. *Do you think?*

Sherry smiled. *It could be. We've no idea what all she can do yet. I want to ask her some questions. Do you remember when we convinced Janelle that she could fly in her dream? I remember telling her to just think about going up a little bit. She did and floated about two feet off that ledge.*

Felix grinned. *Yeah, I remember the look on her face.*

Sherry laughed out loud and looked guiltily around. "Sorry, we were just discussing something. Tahnie, do you mind? I'd like to try something with Lyuba."

Tanya glanced at Tolya. He nodded. "It's OK. If we can get to the bottom of this I'd be pleased."

Tanya shrugged. "I agree. What do you have in mind?"

Sherry stood. "I have a suspicion."

She waved for Lyuba to join her next to the table. "OK, kiddo. You said you felt the way you did when you were flying in your dream. Right?"

Lyuba nodded.

"OK. I have this weird feeling that somehow you're going to be able to fly for real. It sounds crazy, but that's what I think, so here's what I want you to do. I want you to imagine that you can float in the air. Just think about yourself going up a little bit. Don't go too far or you'll bump the ceiling."

Lyuba up. "That's weird. Nobody can fly except in dreams."

Sherry smiled. "Nobody except you."

Lyuba was intrigued. It would be kinda cool, she thought. She concentrated on going up just a little bit.

Nothing happened at first. Then, she suddenly felt light as a feather. She rose about eight inches off the deck. The motion startled her so much she grabbed hold of Sherry's shoulder to steady herself.

There was a gasp from Tanya and Tolya's jaw hung slack.

Felix grinned. *Just like in Janelle's dream.*

Sherry glanced at Felix and grinned back. Then she looked back at Lyuba. "OK, I'm going to step back where you can't reach me. You just stay right there."

Lyuba nodded. She let go of Sherry's shoulder and just hovered there. Sherry stepped back towards Tanya's end of the table. "OK, honey, now think about slowly moving towards me. Don't go fast, you don't have good control of this yet. Just a casual sort of move will do."

She held out her hand and Lyuba reached for it. She began floating towards Sherry. Sherry kept her hand just out of reach till Lyuba was very close. Then she took Lyuba's hand. "That's great. Can you let yourself come back down? Not too fast."

Lyuba glanced at the deck and slowly settled. "Awesome!"

Sherry laughed. "Yeah, I guess you could say that." She went back to her place at the table. "That's enough for now. Have a seat."

Lyuba walked carefully back to her seat.

It felt strange realizing what she could do. "Is that what happened in the gym? Did I start...flying?"

Sherry nodded. "That's what I think. You were thinking about getting up high enough so you could make the jump perfect. Somehow, that triggered your mind to go into...oh...flying mode?

"Anyway, the problem is, you didn't know you could do that. When you tried to tuck and roll, you didn't expect to stay in the air. You didn't even think about going down until you bounced off the bulkhead. Then you thought, 'down' so hard you fell all the way."

Tolya shook his head. "What's next? I have one friend who can manipulate objects at the molecular or cellular level, another who can heal emotions and even physical wounds and they talk to each other mind to mind. Oh, I forgot, you can 'quest?' out of your bodies. Now I have a daughter who can also talk mind to mind with other 'like minded' folk. She can stop objects so thoroughly that when she lets go, they shatter. Not only that, she can make things move by thinking about it. Now she can fly with her mind." He shook his head. "Did I miss anything?"

Felix grinned. "She'll probably be able to quest too. We don't know what else."

MADE OFFICIAL — 7

FRI 09.24.2094-Earth / TRN 09.04.6998-Aambü
ECS Destiny, Quarterdeck, Conference Room, 0930 Hrs / 1916 Slashes

The staff conference room filled up quickly. Extra chairs had been placed around the table, making for a cozy seating arrangement. This was the second meeting in little over a month. They were usually once a week. Most of the command staff only had a vague notion of what was going on since the whole dream thing worked itself out. There was much curiosity over the suddenness of the meeting.

The main door snapped open and Tolya and Tanya breezed in. Felix, Sherry and Lyuba followed. The curiosity gradient rose to new heights. Felix and Sherry had grown almost legendary over the whole dream episode. Though no one knew all the facts, the surprise at their presence in the meeting was slightly less than the fact that Tolya's daughter was also present. At least the extra chairs now had a practical explanation.

With everyone finally settled, Tolya began the meeting. "Good morning everyone."

He leaned over and whispered in Lyuba's ear. Lyuba nodded before tapping Sherry's arm. After a quick mutual glance, the two headed for the cupboards to put things together for coffee.

"Sorry." Tolya continued, "I thought everyone might appreciate some coffee. We have crucial things to discuss this morning, but before we do, I'd like an update from everyone about preparations."

He looked around the table and then pointed at Emily. "Emily, why don't you begin? We'll just go around the table. When all is finished, I'll bring up the main reason for this meeting.

"Oh, Emily, don't hesitate because two of your students are present. If you have something to say, they'll live, I'm sure."

He sat back and Emily looked around the table. "Well, now. I guess I'll start with our research on our target. It turns out there are a number of small islands that may be just large enough to hold all of us for a short time. We're considering setting up a temporary settlement while we work on a more permanent one.

"Our data regarding the surface of the planet has gotten more detailed as we've gotten closer. We've detected the presence of what might be a sizable land-mass at the northern pole. We have no detail because the place seems to be permanently shrouded in dense storm clouds and a marine layer type fog.

One of our first projects when we establish orbit,will be to run some RPV's under the cloud cover and have a look at what's there."

Emily glanced at her pocket-tab. "As far as education is concerned, my prize pupil," she glanced meaningfully at Felix, "is doing surprisingly well considering the distractions he's had.

"Naomi, I think I may just release him to you for a while once we get into orbit. I think the classroom activities will have to go on a short vacation till we get settled in."

She looked at Tolya. "I think that sums it up."

Tolya nodded. "Thanks. We may have some complications, which I'll discuss a bit later. Frank?"

"Yeah. Well, I've started a little project for the history files. I'm soliciting volunteers and collecting stories about life on board *Destiny* during our eventful voyage. I'll be compiling them and putting them into a file that will provide insightful reading (I hope) to the following generations."

He grinned. "I've had more time to do the history stuff since we've hit the last leg of our inbound trek. The computer's working phenomenally, so I won't be needed much till the orbit insertion."

Tolya grinned. "Don't worry Frank, I have some things for your history files that should keep you very busy. More later. Daryl?"

"Well, things are running beautifully. All is in readiness for the MS drive separation. Our shuttles are primed and eager to be off. The crews are brushing up in the sims. They're also eager to be off. Except that we're light years in another direction from our original destination, you'd never know we'd had problems."

Tolya grinned. "I love it when I hear good news. Naomi?"

She smiled. "All systems in the shops are up. Once we know what where making, we'll be rarin' to make it. I have the deep space mining prototypes stored for future use. With all the debris Emily claims is in this system, we should have little trouble collecting stray materials in orbit.

"In the nano lab, Saul continues to plug away at new applications for his little bugs. Felix should be having some fun there. I've noticed Devin Hawkins has taken a more serious attitude on work in the nano lab. Ever since Felix and Sherry's wedding, he's started acting a little more mature. I'm not sure what's going on, but I like the trend so far. I guess that's it for now."

Emily nodded. "I know what you mean. I'd forgotten till you mentioned it. Devin's really starting to shine."

Tolya grinned. "In a few minutes, I'll shed some light on that as well. Vince. Anything interesting?"

Vince was curious what Tolya had up his sleeve. "I've been helping Daryl, getting the pilots back in top shape. They've been letting their skills atrophy for the bulk of the trip. I'm delighted to say we're on track for one hundred percent readiness. By the way Tolya, there's a certain young man who's been approved as an apprentice pilot."

Tolya raised an eyebrow. "Oh? Anyone I know?"

Vince grinned. "Oh, Yes. Owen O'Connor."

Tolya was hardly surprised. "His folks were OK with that?"

Vince nodded. "Yep. Shane's proud as punch and Kaitlyn has something new to worry about."

Tolya grinned. "That she does. That she does. Well, I'm glad to hear we're on track for the sudden heavy use of shuttles I expect we'll need in another three weeks or so."

He turned to Daniela. "Now for my favorite doctor." That earned him a grin. "How are things in medicine?"

Daniela sat forward and considered her information. "Health remains good news. I'm a little concerned about the sense of cabin fever that's starting to show in little ways. People are ready for a break from ship life." She shrugged her shoulders, looking around as if something was missing.

"Oh, by the way, though most of our medical supplies are still in great shape, our supply of contraceptives is showing signs of imminent shortage. That was one of the items on the list scheduled to be phased out."

Odd looks resulted and Frank spoke the unspoken. "Phased out. Phased out? You're kidding right?"

Daniela grinned at his discomfort. "Yes, Frank. Once we landed, we were supposed to be good little colonists and be fruitful and multiply. It's kinda hard to do that if you have a seemingly endless supply of contraceptives."

Tolya came to Frank's aid. "Well, I'd suggest we begin to thin the use of the stuff. Don't eliminate it, but see if we can get a program going to make it stretch. We're getting uncomfortably close to my turn."

All eyes were on him now. Then Daniela finally realized what she'd been absently looking for. "What happened to the coffee?"

A plaintive chorus of, 'Yeah. Where's the coffee?' swelled around the table

Tolya grinned. "Sorry, I sort of asked the girls to take their time.

"Sherry? Go ahead."

Sherry got up from a desk chair that had escaped being co-opted into 'extra chair at the table' duty.

She went to the end of the table where Daryl and Naomi sat. "OK, Lyuba."

Lyuba poured a cup of coffee at the small food counter next to Tolya's desk. She placed the cup on a saucer and turned to hold it in the palm of her hand.

The curiosity of those at the table turned to consternation as the cup and saucer ensemble neatly rose from her hand and gracefully sailed across the room into Sherry's waiting hand. She placed it in front of Daryl and turned to receive the next one that was half way to her.

There was dead silence as the final cup settled in front of Tolya.

Daniela looked at Lyuba, then at Sherry. Sherry met her look and smiled at her expression. "When? I...I mean I know about the awakening thing, but...this?"

Sherry moved to her seat at the table next to Felix. "It was the day we convalesced from our work with Janelle. You remember our little encounter that day?"

Daniela nodded.

Sherry smiled. Well, that evening she started manifesting some new talents."

Frank put up his hands to form a 'T', the classic sign for 'time out.' "Wait a minute. I get this funny feeling we've been left way out of the loop here. I'd like to know why Lyuba's here doing parlor tricks, and what that has to do with anything."

Lyuba's face set in an angry frown. She marched around the table till she was standing on the same side as Frank.

His chair rocked back sharply and lifted into the air about four feet. "Mr. Frank. What I'm doing here is very important. It's not about me, but it is about what's really going on. Are you experiencing a parlor trick now, Mr. Frank?"

Tanya touched Lyuba's arm. "Lyuba! That's enough!"

Lyuba looked at Tanya and reluctantly set Frank and chair back down on the deck. "I'm sorry. He made me mad; talking about parlor tricks."

She turned to Frank. "How would you like to be the only person on the ship who can do something like this? I'm going to be a freak to most of my friends. I don't need to be thought a freak by everyone in here too."

Before Frank could recover his breath, Tolya stepped into the mix. "I'm afraid I owe everyone here an apology. There's a lot that needs to be said to catch you up. Ever since The Dream, things have been going so thick and fast, I've barely been able to catch up. I've been remiss in not keeping everyone up to speed.

"When events overran my own family, I was reluctant to talk about it till I could come to grips with reality."

He stood up and walked over to stand behind Lyuba, resting his hands on her shoulders. His forearms were almost horizontal, not angling downward like they might have a year or so ago.

"Until Felix and Sherry's wedding, she was the most recent person to have her life changed in ways most of us can't truly understand." His eyes roamed the room, making contact with each person there.

"The Dream was the catalyst for this entire chain of events. Unfortunately, only Daniela was fully aware of some of the details because she was dealing with the physical results. I assume everyone recalls there were five people who were rendered catatonic as a result of the dream."

Nods went around the table. Vince spoke up. "Shouldn't that be seven? Weren't Felix and Sherry also unconscious for a while?"

Tolya looked his way. "Yes, and No. Felix and Sherry were affected in other ways that resulted in a temporary bout of unconsciousness. I'll explain more in a moment."

He swept the room with his gaze again. "Does everyone know the involvement of Felix and Sherry in reviving those five?"

All except Daniela and Vince shook their heads. Tolya moved around to stand behind Felix. "Felix and Sherry were instrumental in bringing all five of the patients out of their comas."

Emily started to object but Daniela stopped her. "It's true, Em. Felix and Sherry have different talents from the one's Lyuba has. They woke up with them."

She turned to Tolya. "Would you mind getting to the point? I think everyone's convinced something strange and unbelievable is going on. It's high time for an explanation."

Tolya smiled and nodded. "You're right Dannie. This is kinda hard, but here it is..."

Sherry interrupted as she got up from her place at the table. "Tolya, I'm sorry. There's something that needs to be repaired before we go on."

She glanced over at Lyuba and everyone watched the obvious interaction that was going on, though not a sound was made. *Lyuba honey, I think that little deal with Frank was over the top, don't you?*

Lyuba's face colored a little. *I'm sorry, but he made me mad. I'm not some parlor trick freak.*

Sherry smiled and walked around the table to take Lyuba by the shoulder. *I understand honey. Frank was frustrated at the lack of information. I think it would be a good idea for you to apologize.*

She turned to Tolya. "Can we have a couple minutes?"

Tolya shrugged. "OK. If you think it's necessary." He looked around. "Let's take five minutes. Fix up your coffee and we'll get down to business."

* * * *

Sherry walked over to Frank and whispered in his ear. "Frank, could I have a word with you outside?"

He looked up and nodded. Sherry headed for the door and Frank followed. *Come on Lyuba. This way it won't be in front of everybody else.*

Lyuba nodded reluctantly and followed.

When the door closed, Sherry turned to face Frank. "Frank. I know you were frustrated in there, but honestly. That was a bit over the top calling Lyuba a parlor trickster. Don't you think?"

Frank started getting defensive. Sherry could feel it radiating from him. She reached out and gently touched his arm. She sent a light flow of peace through him. "You were frustrated, and I know you didn't mean any harm."

Frank seemed to calm a bit. "I guess I was a bit rude." He looked uncomfortable.

Sherry looked over at Lyuba. "Honey. I know you were very upset. I also know you used great restraint in there. We know what else you can do."

Frank darted a look at them and Lyuba dropped her head as she realized what could have happened if she'd really lost her temper.

Tears welled up in her eyes as she looked over at Frank. "I'm sorry, Frank. What I did was sort of like throwing a tantrum, I guess. I just can't stand thinking that all my favorite people think I'm a freak."

Frank sighed. Tears always hit hardest. "Look...Lyuba, you're not a freak. I don't understand all this stuff, but you're not a freak. I'm sorry I said that about parlor tricks."

He shrugged his shoulders. "I've always just 'known' that kind of thing was impossible. I guess I can't 'know' that any more."

He held out his hand. "Friends?"

Lyuba stepped in to give him a big hug. "Friends!"

He looked at Sherry.

Sherry smiled. "Frank. There's a lot more to this than her ability to move things with her mind. All three of us have very unusual abilities we didn't have before The Dream. We're all going to explain it when we get back in there."

He nodded and they returned to the meeting.

Frank, hand on Lyuba's back, approached Tolya. "Sorry about that. I guess I was out of line."

Tolya grinned. "That's all right. I suspect Lyuba's going to be quite capable of taking care of herself."

He headed for his seat and called the meeting back to order. "Everyone here knows we're approaching a water world. Right?"

There was unanimous agreement. "Well, it has a name. It's called Aambü."

He looked around. He could see the questions percolating. "No, we didn't just come up with it. It's a name this world has gone by for a very long time. Current history starts about seven thousand local years, ago. I think that would be closer to ten thousand years in our reckoning.

"Ladies and gentlemen, we're not alone." He looked around the table watching the dawn of recognition, of the turn of phrase, if not the reality.

He went on. "The reason Felix and Sherry are here in this meeting is that together, they are now humanity's very first unofficial xeno-ambassadors."

Daryl stood. "Are you saying we've found aliens?"

Before Tolya could answer, Sherry stood and looked down the table. "No, Daryl. He's not saying that at all. He's saying that the locals on this planet have found aliens. Friends, we're the aliens in this little adventure."

She sat and Tolya grinned at Daryl's slack jawed stare. "It's OK, Daryl. Have a seat. Believe me. When we figured it out, it was as much of a shock for us."

He waved a hand at Felix and Sherry. "These two have had personal contact with their ambassador, but before someone points out that impossibility, remember how your coffee was delivered."

Eyebrows twitched and a couple of chuckles leaked out. "So, I've asked Felix and Sherry to help with the explanation. Felix. Why don't you start with The Dream and work your way from there."

Felix smiled and stood at his place at the table. "Well, I never thought I'd be standing in front of you like this."

He glanced over at Sherry. He nodded and returned his gaze to those at the table. "As we've already surmised, it was The Dream that got this whole thing started. For the sake of time, I'll try to keep to the salient points."

He told the story from beginning to the end. Sherry often stepped in and continued when Felix paused. This went back and forth with no discernible break.

Emily signaled a question. "I'm sorry guys, but could you please explain why you do that?"

Sherry and Felix chorused. "Do what?"

Emily felt a little embarrassed. "I mean, you're both telling this, but it seems like you're telling the same story from the same perspective. You start and stop and take up for the other as if you knew intimately what the other would have said next."

There were several nods and curious looks.

Felix grinned. "I'm sorry, Em. I fear I forgot a very important point. Let me put it this way. Did you wonder why we suddenly decided to get married?"

Naomi nodded, "That question did come to mind. Honestly, I fear it might have been because of some, ah...indiscretions."

Felix grinned. "Well, no. That's not what happened. We've been mutually attracted, romantically, since Tolya and Tanya's wedding, but we hadn't come to the point of...indiscretions, as you put it."

Sherry continued. "No, when Felix and I touched each other in the dream, we experienced a mental link that would have faded over time, but when I touched his forehead out in the corridor we sealed the deal unwittingly. We have an unbreakable mental bond.

"Wherever I am, a part of Felix is with me. We converse all the time, regardless of distance. The same is true in reverse. Wherever Felix is, a part of me is with him."

Felix picked up the thought. "AgradUtya, their ambassador, explained that what happened to us was normally preceded by the equivalent of marriage counseling. In his people's eyes, we were half way through the process of marriage as they practice it."

He looked at Frank. "Imagine always being aware of Emily even when she's not near you. Imagine you know when she's taking a shower, you know how hot the water is, you know how it feels on her skin, you know...well, you get my meaning."

Frank shook his head trying not to grin. He got poked in the ribs for his troubles.

Frank whispered something in Emily's ear that produced a rich red blush.

"That could get...complicated." Frank ventured.

Sherry laughed out loud. "Complicated is a nice word for it. We decided that before we were driven to the indiscretions Naomi feared, we'd better marry. We were as good as married in every other way."

Felix stated. "AgradUtya said it was fortunate mating was a desired outcome. I can only surmise that occasionally, this can happen to two who are not anticipating mating..."

Sherry continued. "At any rate, we talk like this in public because, in fact, we are aware of what the other is going to say. I hope we don't spook you too badly."

Emily shook her head. "No, knowing why helps me understand. I don't have any trouble with it. I confess it's hard to imagine."

Sherry shrugged. "We never imagined it till it happened. It was very shocking to say the least."

Felix took up the account, finally ending with, "Since then, we've had several remote meetings with AgradUtya. He went back a few days before our wedding to report to his king or chief."

Daniela spoke up. "If anyone's still trying to resist these developments, I can verify almost everything he said. The parts I can't verify fit snugly into the parts I can, so I have no reason to deny the truth as I've observed it."

She managed one of Tolya's lopsided grins. "I even ran several scans and various tests while Sherry and Felix were at work on the five patients. They're quite normal except for some active places in their brains that are usually quiet. Something has indeed been awakened in them."

A thought struck her. "By the way, Vince and I were present when this ambassador fellow of theirs showed up for a visit. He approached me and, as Felix said, did something so I could understand him if one of these three were in physical contact."

She shrugged and looked at Felix, "But that doesn't explain Lyuba's awakening."

Felix smiled. "I beg to differ. We just didn't cover everything. The Dream is the reason for Lyuba as well. When AgradUtya called out to me in alarm, it was a very intense mental call, an alarm, if you will. That call was strong enough to sweep through *Destiny* while everyone was busily dreaming. Lyuba, was one of those who also had the latent ability. She took to the dream like a fish to water."

Sherry continued. "She had the same dream we did from her own perspective. You'll have to get her to tell it sometime. Anyway, she was also triggered to awaken. For some reason it took her a week or two longer than it did us."

Felix continued. "That's not all. Naomi, you were commenting on Devin Hawkins' much-improved attitude and maturity. Well, he was also awakened. He took even longer than Lyuba. Lyuba sensed it in him when they were linked arm in arm at our wedding rehearsal. After the rehearsal dinner, she helped usher him into his full awakening just as AgradUtya did for her."

Sherry finished the thought. "So, there are four of us who are now able to communicate with the Aambüka."

Tolya sat forward. "As you can see, things have gotten totally crazy around here this last month." He nodded at Felix and Sherry. "Thanks, you two.

"Now, we have many decisions to make and policies and rules of conduct to establish. If you think you've been out of the loop, the general population is clueless. Some are aware of the nature of the challenge regarding the water world issue, but no one is aware we've established first contact."

He grinned and looked around the table. "Dannie and now Tanya have been hounding me in the last few days to get busy and communicate. I confess to being reluctant. This is going to be a huge pill to swallow."

MADE OFFICIAL — 8

FRI 09.24.2094-Earth / TRN 09.04.6998-Aambü
ECS Destiny, Quarterdeck, Conference Room, 1050 Hrs / 2000 Slashes

Just then, Lyuba sat up straight and pointed at a spot directly behind Felix. *Guess who's here? It's good to see you again, AgradUtya.*

Everyone in the room looked at her and then at the spot she had pointed at. Felix stood and moved to stand next to the spot. "Tolya. AgradUtya has decided to join us."

Tolya grinned. "Computer, lights; twenty-five percent."

The room lights dimmed suddenly and everyone in the room could see the faintly glowing, slightly glittery cloud of smoky substance. Sherry stood and made a little bow. She smiled, *Good Day, AgradUtya.*

She turned to the table. "If you can see anything at all, you're looking at the representation of the individual known as

AgradUtya. He's the ambassador for the Aambüka, the Water People of Aambü.

Felix, Sherry, Lyuba. I greet you. It appears that again, I've come during some kind of gathering.

Felix moved next to Tolya and offered his arm. Tolya grinned and grabbed the bare part of his arm near the wrist. "Good morning AgradUtya. I am pleased to see you again. The last time we met you were abrupt in your departure."

Lyuba grabbed Tanya's hand so she could hear and Sherry stood next to Daniela, giving her the opportunity to hear.

AgradUtya gestured mild self-reproach and respect mixed together. *I truly regret my abruptness. The thing Lyuba manifested was a most disturbing development. I'll explain, but first, please, I have interrupted yet another meeting.*

Everyone in the room was stuck somewhere between great curiosity and mild irritation at the lack of understanding.

Sherry turned again to the table. "Everyone. The last time we met with AgradUtya, he became quiet agitated and left the meeting abruptly. We thought we had caused some insult. AgradUtya just tendered an apology for his abruptness and now apologizes for interrupting our meeting. Go ahead, Tolya."

Tolya nodded. "AgradUtya, please be at ease. There's no way you could have known when we might have a meeting. Actually, we just finished discussing the existence of your people. Please allow me to introduce my command staff. You're familiar with my wife, and chief of security, Tanya."

But of course. I greet you, Lady Tanya.

Tanya nodded and smiled. "I'm glad to see you again. I feared we might have scared you away."

Lady, I regret my precipitous actions. As I said, something about Lyuba's manifestation frightened me more than you could possibly know.

Sherry sensed the frustration of the group that had no way of hearing the whole conversation. She began a running explanation and translation.

Tolya took charge. "AgradUtya, to my left is Franklin Drake. He's the one responsible for guiding this vessel through the stars. He also manages the computer systems that control almost everything about this ship. Next to him is his intended mate, Emily Strauss. She's the Chief Science officer I told you of.

Emily Strauss. I would be delighted to speak with you once we meet face to face.

Sherry translated AgradUtya's comment for Emily.

Emily grinned. The avarice for new knowledge was clearly evident. "Tell him I eagerly look forward to it."

Tolya continued. "Next are Ichirou and his life mate, Midori Akari. They're responsible for keeping the agricultural aspects of ship life productive."

Sherry added. *Ag-Deck is the level you explored with the great variety of plant life.*

AgradUtya expressed some enthusiasm. *I am most excited to meet the persons responsible for the wonderful abundance of water and plant life. If there were a single place on this vessel that I could be nearly comfortable in my corporeal form it would be your...Ag-Deck or the water gardens on your Promenade.*

"Across the table from the Akari's are Daryl McIntyre and his life mate, Naomi. She is my Chief Mechanical Engineer. She specializes in building things we need. He is my Chief Engineer. He specializes in keeping the power systems and the drives that move this vessel, in good shape.

"Next to them, on my right side is Vincent Leoni, my first officer. He is the second in command aboard this vessel. He also is my back up in the governmental arena. He is what we call Lieutenant Governor. Assistant Governor, if you will. Of course you've met our Chief Medical Officer, our Doctor or Healer if you prefer, Daniela Jacobs. She is Vince's intended mate."

AgradUtya addressed Daniela. *I'm happy to see you again. I share your joy at gaining a life mate. May your union be long and full.*

AgradUtya turned to Tolya. *Thank you for your introductions. You have a strong group of assistants.*

He changed the subject. *I must explain my previous actions. You may recall our talk of Bhairava, in our initial interview?*

Tolya nodded, recalling the surprise that something had been trying to destroy them for generations.

When Felix described Lyuba's manifestation, the incident with the...coffee cup?

Tolya grinned. "Yes, the coffee cup. AgradUtya. Just for clarification, coffee is a substance derived from certain plants that we find pleasant to drink. It provides a minor stimulant which probably encourages the user to drink more." He held up his cup. "Please observe this coffee cup."

AgradUtya signed gratitude. *Thank you for the clarification, Tolya. When Felix described what Lyuba did to the coffee cup, it put me in mind of the primary method Bhairava uses to destroy his prey. Anyone who gets close enough to see the form of Bhairava is stilled in the way she stilled the cup. He then deliberately releases the victim without setting the motion to normal first. Thus, a living person is shattered and rendered to dust as you described the fate of the cup.*

Felix tuned to AgradUtya. *Friend, I apologize for the fright that caused for you. I assure you Lyuba did not deliberately destroy the cup. She'd never manifested in any way before and didn't know how to set things right.*

AgradUtya signed understanding and replied. *This I understand. AgraVadin Adhiraj reminded me of the lack of training Lyuba has had. The problem is, there is no known member of my race that has this ability. The last recorded user of the stilling ability is generations dead. We can advise Lyuba but none of us can show her.*

Tolya sat back in his chair considering while Sherry finished translating for the rest of the staff. "Are you sure she has this 'stilling' you speak of?"

If Felix' description is accurate, then yes. Has...

AgradUtya turned to Lyuba who was providing a link for Tanya. *Little one, have you had any more interesting adventures since I left?*

Lyuba shrugged and started to say no when she remembered the experience at the gym and later the assistance of Devin through the awakening. *Yes, there are two things. The first happened shortly after you left. I have discovered that I am not only able to lift other things. I am able to lift myself.*

AgradUtya showed signs of mild aggravation. He moved closer to her, *show me.*

Lyuba looked at Sherry who simply nodded. *It's OK. If he needs to see, then you should show him.*

Lyuba looked at Tanya. "I'll be right back, Mom." She let go of Tanya's hand and considered her move. She decided on a simple levitation, nothing too fancy. She concentrated and slowly rose from where she stood. When she cleared the table, she leaned slightly and drifted across to settle gently next to AgradUtya.

There was some consternation amongst the staff members. One thing was to see her float coffee cups about; another was to watch her literally glide through the air over the table.

Lyuba smiled shyly and then concentrated again. She turned to face the spot where she'd been standing.

She reminded Emily of nothing less than a cat considering a difficult leap. Emily was still quite surprised when her sense turned out to be correct.

Suddenly Lyuba crouched down slightly and leaped forward and up. She sailed through the air doing a summersault and a half spin to land just a little off balance next to Tanya.

AgradUtya stared at Lyuba. *It's true then. She is the first with this skill since Parzu a Raudra.*

Lyuba was feeling nervous. *What's this Parzu a Raudra?*

AgradUtya considered. *The best I could render it for the human speech would be something like 'Knife Woman the Wild.' Parzu is a curved knife for a warrior class female. Raudra means wild, dangerous, or fierce. She was a legendary warrior seven hundred cycles in the past.*

He looked at Tolya. *To the best of our understanding, the ability to move one's self about, like one does an object, is quite rare. It usually accompanies stilling.*

Lyuba spoke up again. *There was another thing that happened. It was someone else, but I was involved.*

AgradUtya faced her again. *And what was that, Lyuba?*

Lyuba seemed to brace herself and then answered. *I have a friend. During the rehearsal for Felix and Sherry's wedding, he started to awaken, so I helped him break through.*

AgradUtya signed nervous concern. *You helped him break through? How could you do that? You've never done it before! No one has taught you!*

Lyuba shrugged. *I watched when you did it for me. I just copied what you did. It worked well.*

AgradUtya looked over at Felix. *Tell me.*

It was Felix' turn to shrug. *It's true. Sherry and I weren't close enough to realize what was going on at first. We sensed energy flow and went to investigate. Lyuba was in the middle of the process and we were reluctant to stop it in the middle for fear of causing more harm than good.*

AgradUtya relaxed a little. *You did well. It is not good to stop a break through once it is initiated.*

Where is this person? Lyuba? Call him. I wish to meet him.

Lyuba shrugged. She let go of Tanya's hand and thought of Devin's face. Then she sent out the call. *Devin, can you hear me?*

The staff members were getting restless. This was turning out to be more a personal investigation rather than a profitable discussion.

Tolya, sensing their discomfort called for their attention. "I'm sorry this has become somewhat bogged down. I'd like to call an end to the formal meeting. We should meet again tomorrow at the same time. We need to determine what to say and begin preparations for another ship-wide meeting.

"If you need to leave, feel free. If you wish to stay, and observe the outcome of this little event, that's fine as well." He nodded towards their guest. "Thanks for your patience."

* * * *

Frank elected to stay. This was looking quite a bit like an important piece of colony history in the making. Emily gave him a quick kiss and headed for the door. She had students who would be showing up any minute.

Daniela made apologies and headed for MedCentral. As much as Vince wanted to stay, he decided to go check up on things on the bridge. Daryl and Naomi headed off for Industrial Deck. Ichirou and Midori seemed rooted to their seats. They were obviously fascinated with current events.

Sherry decided to have a seat while they waited for Devin.

Midori got up and approached Sherry. "Would you like some more coffee?"

"Why yes, thank you, Midori."

"That's OK. I thought I saw some green tea in the cupboard. I'll make a coffee for you and some green tea for me and my husband."

Sherry grinned. "Thank you. You want help?"

"No, thank you. I'll be fine."

* * * *

Devin was working on an assignment and was having a frustrating time of it. This advanced synthetic math was driving him nuts.

Suddenly a picture of Lyuba flashed into his mind...*{Devin, can you hear me?}*

Devin sat back in his chair and after a moment's thought, answered back. *Hey, Lyuba. It's good to hear from you.*

{Remember when we told you about the fellow from the planet? The ambassador from Aambü?}

Sure. What about him?

{Well, he's here and demands to meet you right away. Can you come up to the Staff Conference Room on Quarterdeck?}

This alien guy wants to see me?

{Careful, Devin. This is serious stuff, and we're technically the aliens here. Aambü's his world.}

Sorry. You're right. OK. I'll be right up. It'll be a few minutes.

{That's fine. Thanks, Dev.}

She let the image of his face fade and returned her attention to AgradUtya. *Dev's on his way. He'll be a few minutes.*

Tolya glanced at Lyuba and then at Tanya. "Dev?"

Lyuba blushed. "That's just a short way of saying Devin. It's no big deal."

Tanya suppressed a grin and looked at Sherry.

Sherry reached across and took Tanya's hand. *You don't mean to tell me you haven't noticed the non-removable bracelet?*

Tanya looked at Lyuba. She had the leather thong bracelet she always wore.

Tanya spoke quietly. "You mean..."

Do you recall her wearing that before her birthday party?

"I...no. I just assumed it was something she had from before we adopted her."

Oh, no. That's what Devin gave her at the party. She even wore it at my wedding.

Tanya smiled slowly and shook her head. "What do we do? She's too young to get too involved."

You're right, but I think it'll do more harm than good to make a big deal about it. Let's just pay a little closer attention. Besides. They have something in common none of the other kids their age have.

Lyuba came back over and hugged Tanya. "Mom, can we get something to eat? I'm starving."

Tanya raised an eyebrow. "You ate just a couple of hours ago didn't you?"

Sherry spoke up. "Yes, but I'd imagine that levitation consumes a great deal of energy; especially when she's still new to it."

Tanya looked stricken. "I'm so sorry. I forget the things you guys do are so draining. Lyuba, honey, of course you can have something to eat. I'll call the dining hall and see if we can get some cookies or something. OK?"

Lyuba grinned. "Sure Mom. That'd be great." Tanya reached for the little tab in her collar.

The doors snapped open and Devin stepped into the room. His eyes immediately found Lyuba, who'd already started for the door. Then he stopped dead in his tracks staring at AgradUtya. This was his first time seeing him.

AgradUtya immediately moved to stop in front of Devin.

Sherry took Tanya's hand and Felix grabbed Tolya's arm so they would hear.

AgradUtya motioned to Lyuba. *Little one. Would you please formally introduce your friend?*

Lyuba stepped forward and grabbed Devin's hand. *Don't worry Devin. He won't hurt you.*

Devin nodded as she turned to face AgradUtya. *I'd like to introduce my friend, and our newest mind speaker, Devin Hawkins.*

She turned to Devin. *Devin, this is AgradUtya, Ambassador for the Aambüka, the Water People of Aambü.*

AgradUtya signed a greeting and then took a long look at Devin. *Devin Hawkins. Can you hear and understand me?*

Devin licked his lips. He was a little nervous. This, after all, was a non-human intelligent species from a planet they'd not even reached yet.

Yes, I hear and understand you. AgradUtya...It's an honor to meet you. Lyuba speaks highly of you.

AgradUtya allowed a flow of humor to color his response. *Thank you Devin Hawkins. I'm sure you're a bit curious about my appearance and how I am present when you haven't yet arrived over my world.*

Devin grinned. *The question had crossed my mind. Lyuba tells me that somehow you're present without your physical body.*

AgradUtya signed approval. *That's true. We do something we call questing. You should ask Felix about it. He's had opportunity to try it. In questing, we place our physical bodies in a comfortable state and then, with our minds; we quest outwards to accomplish what we wish.*

Lyuba tells me she was present to assist in your break through. I'd like to take a look to see how things went. I need permission to scan your memories of that event.

Devin hesitated and looked over at Lyuba.

It's OK Dev. He won't hurt you. He just wants to see what I did because he didn't train me to do that. There wasn't time to get his help and I remembered what he did for me.

Devin shrugged. *OK. What do I do?*

AgradUtya allowed a smile to color his response. *You need do nothing. I'll simply place my hands on either side of your head and watch the memories of the event of your awakening.*

Devin braced himself and nodded.

AgradUtya's web hands slowly came up to hover at Devin's temples. He concentrated and watched a replay of the event.

AgradUtya lowered his web hands and considered.

Clearly Lyuba was in charge in that situation. She had definitely handled herself remarkably like an adult, and she'd deftly helped Devin Hawkins finish his awakening break through.

Lyuba. I am very impressed with your memory of what I did to help you. While I wouldn't have given permission, I commend you. Well done.

Devin Hawkins, you have been handily initiated into your awakening. Lyuba has served you well.

Devin smiled at Lyuba and then AgradUtya.

Devin Hawkins. I have observed that amongst your people, the second name is often omitted in normal conversation. Would that form of address be acceptable to you?

Devin nodded. *Of course. I was going to comment. Most of us don't use the last name except in formal address. Please, just call me Devin.*

AgradUtya accepted this. *Thank you Devin. Can you tell me whether you have experienced any other kinds of things you can't explain?*

Devin frowned and tried to figure out what this person meant. He looked at Lyuba.

Lyuba grinned. *I told you to tell me if something ever came up. He means other kinds of gifts besides mind-speak. Watch this.*

She reached out and took the cup of tea that was still at her place. It rose smoothly and sailed sedately into her hands.

She smiled and looked at AgradUtya. *AgradUtya. I have given much thought to the ability you were worried about last time we met. I have avoided its use as you commanded, but I think there is something else I can do with that ability. Would you permit my attempt? It should be safe enough.*

AgradUtya felt nervous, but he was also intrigued. *Exactly what do you have in mind?*

She smiled. *My tea is cold. I like it hot. If I am able to slow the motion of the atoms to the point they freeze, what's to stop me from speeding the motion to make something hot?*

AgradUtya was left with nothing to say for a moment. *You present a very interesting question. Use great care and try it. I trust your good intentions.*

Devin looked at her. *What are you talking about?*

She shook her head. *I'll explain later. First, I need to try this.*

She focused on her tea, ignoring the cup and saucer. In her science classes she'd learned that when things cooled, the energy states of the atoms in the molecules moved downward, or slowed. When things were heated, energy states raised a level, or sped up.

When she'd stopped all motion in the coffee cup that evening, she figured she'd somehow brought the energy states as far down as they could possibly go. Theory said you couldn't bring the electrons of an atom to a complete, absolute stop.

She imagined the molecules of the liquid. The pictures of them from her texts were vivid in her mind. She imagined the atoms that comprised the molecules. It was now possible to see the actual parts, well not the parts, but the orbits of the electrons clearly. The pictures in her texts were very detailed.

She considered the possibility of speeding up all that motion. Slowly, at first, then more noticeably, she sensed the liquid responding. After a few moments, Felix could see wisps of steam rise from her cup.

Devin's eyebrows rose. Finally, the speed seemed just right and Lyuba stopped. She tested the tea. It was warm; just right, even.

Sherry. Look. She floated the cup over to Sherry who took it carefully. She took a sip and her eyes got wide. "It's just hot enough to drink."

Sherry held the cup up in the palm of her hand and Lyuba snagged it and returned it to her own hands.

Suddenly, she felt dizzy and started to fall. Devin hurried to her side and caught her, helping her into a nearby chair. He took the tea and set it gently on the table. *Are you OK?*

She shook her head. *Yeah, I just feel really weak.*

AgradUtya seemed overwhelmed. *You used an amazing amount of energy, so I shouldn't be at all surprised you feel weak.*

Sherry came around the table and placed a hand on Lyuba's shoulder. Felix was ready. He felt Sherry infusing Lyuba with a little energy.

He also felt it slowly draining from himself. He carefully metered it so it wouldn't go too quickly.

Sherry stopped. *Better?*

Lyuba looked up at her. *Yes, thank you.*

AgradUtya looked from Sherry to Felix. *That was well done. Felix, you metered the energy well, and Sherry, you were more careful how much you pulled. You two have made progress.*

He looked at Lyuba. *Lyuba. You've done something new. I'm not sure what you did, but it's a new use of what we've come to call 'Stilling.'*

Lyuba smiled at AgradUtya. *Yes, but I didn't still anything. I accelerated it. I made the liquid hot by accelerating the energy states of the atoms. I guess it can work both ways.*

AgradUtya considered her statement. *If that's true, then the full potential of this talent has not been realized by anyone. You may have discovered new uses for it besides the obviously destructive aspects.*

Lyuba looked at AgradUtya. *I can't believe these abilities, including those we haven't seen yet, were intended as weapons. Like anything else, I think people learn to adapt them for destructive purposes.*

Felix interjected a comment; *I'd think The Maker had greater things in mind with his gifts.*

The doors snapped open and someone brought in a tray piled high with brownies. The mood turned festive as everyone considered the brownies. Lyuba got first shot at them, however.

Devin approached AgradUtya. *AgradUtya, I haven't found anything that I am able to do besides ah...mind speak.*

AgradUtya suppressed excess humor. *Don't be concerned Devin. Many times these giftings come later, often at unexpected times. Please tell me when something like this occurs.*

Devin nodded. *I will.*

Tolya leaned towards Felix. "Felix. We'll be in orbit in about three weeks. We need to find a place planet side where we may allow people to get down, breath fresh air and feel like they've actually arrived. Also, We need to discuss more long term arrangements for our people. This is going to be awkward. Ask where we can meet face to face."

Felix nodded. "OK. I'll grab your arm again."

Felix grabbed Tolya's arm and then addressed AgradUtya. *Friend, we have issues to settle. In about thirty days, our time...oh, bother.*

Let me quickly explain our system of time keeping. A day to us is like a turn for you, but your planet takes more time to complete one turn than ours by about a third. We have years. They are to us what your ring cycles are to you. We have months, which are different. Months are divisions of our year by the cycles of our moon. With a little mathematical juggling we have twelve months in a year. I've never heard of an analogous measure from you yet. A week is seven days with approximately four weeks in a month.

AgradUtya signed good humor. *I think I follow your system. Please continue.*

Felix grinned. *Well, thirty days, our time, comes out to about twenty-three turns. That means you have that long before we enter into orbit over your world.*

AgradUtya considered this information. *So, you're saying, we have that long to determine how we will receive you?*

Tolya shook his head. "No, that's how much time till we arrive. You take the time you need to determine how you'll receive us."

AgradUtya signed grateful understanding. *My Adhiraj and I discussed this need to meet on solid ground. We have a ring of islands that circle a generous lagoon. You could bring some of your people down to these islands as guests. We could meet and work out all the issues that need discussion.*

AgradUtya approached Felix. *Allow me to leave you with a memory of the exact location of these islands. You'll be welcomed there as guests.*

Once you get close enough to see the islands with your own eyes, you will see decorative arrangements that will help you find the exact location.

He placed a web hand near Felix' temple and stood for a moment. Felix felt a sense of vertigo and watched a quick flight that took him from *Destiny* to the surface of the planet. He recognized the islands from his questing trip. *You will keep this memory until you have personally made the trip.*

Tolya Chernov, Governor. I thank you for your hospitality. I must go and help my Adhiraj prepare. I look forward to meeting all of you face to face. I bid you a pleasant journey.

With that, he began to fade like a wisp of smoke and vanished through a bulkhead.

MADE OFFICIAL —9

FRI 09.24.2094-Earth / TRN 09.04.6998-Aambü
ECS Destiny, Quarterdeck, Conference Room, 1240 Hrs / 2156 Slashes

Frank caught up to Felix and Sherry as they left the conference room. Lyuba was with them, intent on a hefty lunch. Devin was along because...well, Lyuba was there, and he didn't want to go back to working on that math assignment just yet. He was too jazzed about the conversation with a genuine alien.

"Hey guys. Tolya told me you had coordinates for this island chain the Ambassador mentioned."

They turned to starboard to walk around the lift well. "I don't have coordinates, exactly. What I have is a motion image of the approach from space."

Frank looked frustrated. "How can we sync with that if I don't have coordinates?"

Felix grinned. "It's simple really. After you and Emily come with us to lunch, we can go to her fancy science lab and play with that new holographic projector of hers. We can look till I recognize the spot and then we can calculate the coordinates."

Frank grinned. "Why didn't I think of that? OK. I'll get Em. We'll meet you in a few minutes."

Sherry called after him, "We'll save places."

Frank waved as he started for Emily's offices.

* * * *

They wound their way through the tables and the crowd till they got to the officer's lounge where they found a large unoccupied table to commandeer.

So Lyuba. What do you want to eat?

Lyuba looked at Devin and grinned. *I could eat almost anything right now.* They tabbed through the offerings on the menu. After ordering, they sat back to wait. Felix and Sherry were obviously in a lengthy, but quiet conversation.

Devin smiled at Lyuba. *You said you'd tell me about the coffee cup incident later. Is this later enough?*

Lyuba grinned. *Sure. We'd just gotten back from visiting Sherry and Felix in MedCentral when they were recovering from their rescue efforts. That's when AgradUtya helped me break through. Anyway, I was getting coffee for everyone. I poured my dad's cup last and was carrying it around the coffee table when my toe hit the table leg. I almost fell...*

Lyuba finished her narrative. Devin's eyes got big. *Wow! I can see why that might upset AgradUtya.*

Lyuba nodded. *Yeah, he was really upset when he heard about it. He forbade me to practice doing that kind of thing until he gave permission. Then he just left...in a big hurry.*

She leaned closer to Devin. *I don't know if you heard this part, but there's some kind of monster or something that goes around killing people, using this same talent.*

Devin looked at her. *You mean they're in danger? Maybe we can help them.*

Lyuba shrugged. *Maybe we can, but we don't know enough yet. We'll have to see what Dad says about it.*

Devin decided to change the subject. He reached over and caught Lyuba's arm. He looked at the bracelet he'd given her for her birthday. *You like it? I see you wear it all the time.*

Lyuba colored, pulling her arm back. *Of course I do, did you make it yourself?*

Devin looked down at his hands. He suddenly felt nervous. *Yeah. I collected the stones and the shell and put it together. I wanted to give it to you right away, but...well, there was never a good time till your birthday came.*

It was Lyuba's turn to feel nervous. He'd been thinking about giving the bracelet to her for a while before her birthday. She wondered how long he'd been interested in her. Then she thought about all the other girls in the youth group. They'd be jealous if they knew where she'd gotten this bracelet. *Well, Devin. I never got a chance to tell you, but thank you. I like it a lot. You did a wonderful job making it.*

Devin was tongue-tied. It was a good thing he didn't always need his tongue to communicate. *I'm glad you like it.*

The awkward moment was saved by the arrival of Frank and Emily. "Hey everybody."

Emily was in great spirits. "I hear we've been invited to land. That's awesome!"

Felix shrugged and turned to Emily. "That's right. AgradUtya gave me directions to a ring of islands he said would serve as a place for us to stay as guests."

"Wow! I'm excited." She turned to Felix. "Frank says you want to play with my Holo-projector."

Felix grinned. "Well, I wouldn't necessarily say, 'play with it.' Frank needs coordinates, but AgradUtya didn't give coordinates. He gave me a visual guide on the rout to take to get there. I have to study the globe and see if I recognize the spot. Oh, were you able to get the complete data overlay into that thing? I'll need lots of detail."

Emily nodded. "Absolutely. We boosted the scan rate significantly too. The view is much more realistic. I believe we can actually see things in real-time now."

Felix response was profound, but brief. "Cool!"

Frank and Emily sent off their orders and then the earlier ones began to show up. The lunch gathering was fun. Lyuba stuffed herself to the gills and they had brownies and coffee for dessert.

* * * *

The lab was still a busy place. Data about Gem was perpetually being processed. Emily led them to the center of the room where the holo-table was located. Someone had just finished adding fresh data to the display.

"OK. Here's the beast. It may be huge and ungainly, but it's the best we have in real time, 3-D viewing."

She approached the control pad and deftly tapped in a series of commands. "Felix, you've used this a couple of times right?"

Felix nodded. "Yeah, but you've added features since then. I wouldn't mind a quick review."

The teacher in Emily exulted in the opportunity. "OK. We added real time updating. You'll see things change on the display when the computer gets the info and inserts it into the stream. Here's the interface. We redesigned it to allow for the new capabilities."

Felix watched her manipulate the control pad. The recessed center of the table started to glow with off-white, almost blue light.

The principal of the thing was based on an adaptation of field tech, similar to the technology that helped to protect the ship in space by sweeping away objects that might collide. Scientists had been looking for a way to reduce the size of the generators and create smaller fields for close in work.

The first side benefit of that was here in this room; an energy field developed in the shape of a large sphere. It wasn't visible usually, but by projecting certain frequencies of light on it, the field would contain an image and shine it out into the room.

This application; a globe representing a planet was particularly easy for the system because it was shaped similarly to the primary shape of the field.

The blue white light seemed to wash up and around the perimeter and over the top to completely cover the spherical space. The light show went through seemingly random flickers, and blocks of flashing color.

Finally, the planet Aambü resolved itself above the table, complete with rings and two ragged moons. Steadily, tiny points of light appeared, darkening into chunks of space junk as the computer calculated the presence of the larger pieces of rock and debris that remained unclaimed by the rings.

Emily noticed Felix interest in the extra objects. "You've probably guessed, there are a host of potentially dangerous objects hurtling about out there. Our probes are doing their best to, besides survive, map all the objects big enough to get through the ships deflection grid."

She grinned and squeezed Frank's shoulder. "Frank says, *Destiny* fired her DCPA's twice yesterday."

Felix looked up from his scan of the control console. "DCPA...aren't they particle accelerators?"

Emily smiled. "Very good. 'Directed-Charged Particle Accelerator' is the full name. They fire a massive stream of highly excited, positively charged particles at the target. The effect is to bust up the target into smaller pieces that can then be swept aside by the main deflector system."

"So, Felix, go ahead and do what you need to find that location. We'll get the computer to define the coordinates based on the system we've devised.

* * * *

Felix smiled. "Thanks, Em." He placed a hand on the panel, but didn't touch any of the control icons. Instead, he stood there and let his senses sink into the panel systems and started exploring. He found the interface matrix quickly enough. He studied the interface and found his way to where he could affect the matrix without touching the controls.

Felix sent a simple command to see if his guess was correct. A small rectangular window appeared, floating just outside the orbit of the larger moon.

Felix grinned. Sherry was watching of course. *Are you trying to get yourself in trouble, mister Felix?*

Felix grinned again. *No, just exploring.*

He made the little window glide higher and farther from the planet; adjusting the color to match the background.

Emily was looking on and trying to figure out what he was doing. Felix's hands weren't moving. In fact, they had drifted away from the control surfaces to rest on the wooden frame. Yet, the system was responding to something.

Felix created a little image of a shuttle. It was a fanciful one, but he just needed a placeholder from which he could observe. He allowed himself to sink into the image and sent it into the depths of the scene.

Emily saw a look on Felix' face like he was half asleep. "Sherry. What's he doing? Is he OK?"

Sherry reached over and squeezed Emily's shoulder, allowing a trickle of calm to transfer. "It's fine, Em. He's trying some of his own talents out. He's working the system from inside."

Emily looked at her. "He's what?"

Sherry grinned at the consternation in Emily's voice. "He's able to feel his way into the flow of data in a computer and manipulate it somehow. It's hard for me to follow. All I know is, right now, he's created an icon of a shuttle craft and has placed himself inside it so he can see the approach as he would if he were really there."

Emily was still confused. "Yes, but how is he doing that without using controls?"

Sherry grinned and tapped the side of her head. "It's his gift. I heal and deal with people's emotions; Lyuba moves things around with her mind. We don't know yet, what Devin can do, but Felix can work with things down at the molecular level. He can move things around. Apparently, he has some effect on electronics and optronics as well."

Emily was trying to absorb this. "You mean he doesn't need controls to operate a computer?"

Sherry shrugged and grinned. "Apparently not."

Felix was still getting the feel of things. The entire display went up in a brilliant flare of pyrotechnics. Then, all the broken bits of image seemed to suck back into their places and the image changed.

"Oops," came Felix' strained voice. Instead of seeing the globe as before, they were seeing things as if they were looking out the windows of a shuttle-craft in orbit.

The scene shifted with the stomach wrenching reality of 3-D vision. The little window he'd created before began to show a set of numbers that changed at blinding speeds. Frank was trying to appreciate the simulated view of flying in a shuttle while keeping track of the spinning numbers.

It seemed as if they were diving into the atmosphere. *Sherry, did Em get the data from all those probe passes?*

Sherry passed the question. *Honey. She said it's all in there.*

The dive continued. *Thanks. Stay tuned!*

She could sense humor in his 'voice.'

Clouds whipped by and they could see water forever in every direction. Felix leveled them off early and began cruising just under the highest of the clouds. An oddly colored scene popped up, overlaying the scene out the shuttle window. A small rectangle began scanning back and forth, up and down in the window.

Frank noticed the three sets of numbers had slowed their spin, but still counting down. One set had gotten very slow.

"There you are." They heard Felix voice, almost a whisper. Off to the Southwest, according to the instruments that had appeared in the display, was a series of islands.

This wasn't so spectacular considering there seemed to be tiny islands everywhere, but this set was large and had a semicircular shape to them.

They could see a shadow image superimpose itself on the scene and the little target box zipped triumphantly across the scene to bracket the islands.

The shuttle dove suddenly at incredible speeds. Quickly they found themselves hovering over a grand lagoon created by the entire island group.

The numbers in the little window froze and Felix stood up from his slight stoop. "There you go, Frank." Felix was pale. Perspiration glistened on his face.

Devin pulled up a chair and Sherry coaxed Felix to sit. *Oh, Honey. You look wiped out.* She fed a little energy into him.

Thanks Sweet. I guess I got carried away there. He looked over at Frank. "I used Em's coordinate system. We haven't sown geo-sats yet, have we?"

Frank had his pocket-tab out and was copying down the numbers that floated in the window next to the cockpit instruments. "No, we can't put the sats out until we get into a parking orbit."

Felix nodded wearily. "That's what I thought. Well, I hope those numbers help. I'm ninety eight percent certain that that," he pointed at the frozen scene in the 3D viewer, "is AgradUtya's home.

Frank tapped enter and turned to look at Felix, who continued. "I think one of those islands has a cave system that bores down into their living spaces. He's awfully trusting to let us set down there."

Frank grunted his understanding and clipped his pocket-tab to his belt. "I see what you mean. I think you should bring that up tomorrow when we reconvene our meeting.

MADE OFFICIAL —10

SAT 09.25.2094-Earth / TRN 10.04.6998-Aambü
ECS Destiny, Quarterdeck, Conference Room, 1000 Hrs / 1346 Slashes

The staff arrived promptly, even though it was Saturday morning. The events of yesterday made everyone all the more eager to get things done. Lyuba laid out the coffee cups in the normal way. Clearly everyone had gotten the point that things were far from normal these days.

Tolya got the ball rolling. "Let me fill you in on exactly what happened yesterday. There were enough confusing moments that clarification is in order."

Daryl piped up. "You got that straight."

Devin chuckled, looked around and decided perhaps now was not a good time for chuckles. Lyuba grinned as she handed him the plate of brownies. *Devin, here, have another brownie and drink your coffee.*

Devin self-consciously took a brownie. *Thanks.*

Tolya continued. "We were concerned that one of Lyuba's more spectacular gifts might have alienated, no pun intended... our friend, Mr. AgradUtya. I'm happy to report all is forgiven or set aside and Lyuba stays in his good graces. He gave her permission to 'carefully' practice the more dangerous skill she has.

"I know most of you don't understand, so let me put it this way. Lyuba can literally adjust the energy state of anything. She has quick-frozen and then literally destroyed a hot cup of coffee, liquid, steam and all...and she has since successfully and peacefully reheated her own cup of tea; all with just her mind."

Murmurs rustled around the room as the full implications settled on everyone.

"The result of yesterday's encounter is as follows." Tolya stood and paced the floor at his end of the table. "We're invited to bring people down to the surface at a prearranged location."

He turned and rested his hands on the tabletop and leaned forward for emphasis. "They're treating us as welcome guests, so I want our people to be on their absolute best behavior. We don't know what is unacceptable to these people. We know they look a lot different from us. That means we must resist the urge to stare and make comment."

He looked around the room to see if there were any concerns. Felix piped up. "Tolya, I'd like to make an important point here."

Tolya nodded. "Certainly, you and Sherry have become our experts on these people."

Felix nodded. He understood the scope of this responsibility.

"As you know, I took Frank to the lab and we managed to dig up coordinates to the area where we're instructed to land. While I was exploring, using Em's awesome 3D viewing machine, I found the island group we're headed for to be very familiar."

He stood so that he could be sure everyone was paying attention. "These are choice islands. They're unusually large when compared to the average islands across the globe, but there's something much more important. I'm very certain one of the islands has an outlet that comes up from their...village, if you will. "They live in vast under sea caverns. These are the islands I saw when I went to visit on my first questing. I entered from underneath the water; their front door.

"Folks. We're being allowed to camp in their back yard. That means we must be absolutely sure none of our people decides to go wandering about to stumble on the entrance to their living spaces."

He sat down and Sherry patted his arm. *Well said.*

Felix grabbed her hand and gently squeezed it.

Daniela spoke up, somewhat sobered. "I ah...Felix, thank you for that. You're absolutely right. I really want to encourage us to take his warning to heart. Possibly one of the most insulting things we could do would be to invade their homes uninvited."

She sat forward and looked all around the table. "And, we absolutely can't afford to alienate these people. Our very lives depend on developing deep, trusting relationships with them."

Tolya nodded and stepped back from the table where he'd been leaning throughout Felix' comments. "Thank you, Felix, and thank you, Dannie for backing him up."

Tolya paused and looked around the room as if he were taking the pulse of the people there. "I know it was announced jokingly yesterday, but I think it's important to officially acknowledge reality. It's my opinion that Felix and Sherry should be commissioned as our official Human Ambassadors to the planet Aambü."

He saw several looks of concern and held up a hand to forestall comment. "Yes, I know. There are any number of objections based on past indiscretions."

He walked around and stood behind Felix and Sherry, putting a hand on the backs of their chairs, "I believe however, that a number of you made comment in the last few weeks on just how far Felix has come. I believe all he really needed was the right people and the right motivation," he squeezed Sherry's shoulder a little, "to bring out the fellow we see today.

"All that aside, as I've told Felix recently, I'm very pleased to have someone I can trust, handling discussions with our neighbors. Felix is the first to have had contact with these people. He has, admittedly for only a short time, mingled successfully with them.

"Sherry, on a number of levels, has proven herself invaluable. I think Tanya would agree about that.

Tanya grinned, "Absolutely!"

Tolya continued. "Sherry's only slightly behind Felix in the amount of time spent with this race. Besides. As all of us should know by now, wherever one is, the other is unavoidably present."

Tolya looked about. "Questions? Comments?"

Ichirou startled everyone with a comment. He and his wife were the quiet ones. "I am aware, of course, of Felix' past...indiscretions, as you put it. However, I too have watched a young man take on an unasked for challenge, a daunting task, and see it through. He and Sherry are of like spirit. They take on a task and push to completion.

"Some might argue that a more mature, perhaps more experienced individual take on this role, but I say, who else would be more qualified? There's no one else on board this ship that has the experience these two have at this moment. They've successfully developed a friendly relationship with another race; an alien race. They've successfully gained for us a hearing in the halls of their highest leader. They've successfully gained us a cordial status that will permit us to breath the first fresh breezes of open air in over two and a half years."

Ichirou stood up, facing Felix and Sherry. "It's highly likely each one of us can think of some indiscretion in our younger years that we would rather not remember, but someone graciously forgave us those indiscretions or we wouldn't be where we are today."

He paused and then said. "I second Tolya's recommendation to place Felix and Sherry in the honorable role of humanity's very first official xeno-ambassadors to an alien culture." He gave a graceful little bow in their direction before sitting down.

There was a long silence. Then, Daryl slapped the tabletop with his palm. "Well said. I agree."

Naomi nodded her head. "Same here."

Midori reached over and squeezed Ichirou's arm. "I stand with my husband."

Frank grinned. "I'm in."

Emily considered for another moment and then nodded. "Ichirou, your argument has great merit. I just pray these two can keep it up under the pressure. I'm for it."

Vince and Daniela sat looking at each other. He shrugged and sat forward. "I find no credible argument against it. So, Yes."

Daniela looked about and nodded. "I'm one of those who recently noted the amount of maturing that has been evident in Felix' life. I worry these two have a talent for taking on more than they can handle. At the same time, I'm repeatedly amazed at the way they seem to snatch success from the thinnest cloth. I think I can support them as our official Ambassadors."

Tolya glanced at Tanya. "Well?"

Tanya realized she hadn't voted yet. "I've grown accustomed to having Felix and Sherry present me with odd, but pleasant surprises. I can't think of anyone else I'd rather have at this post."

Lyuba had been quietly drinking her tea. She knew she wasn't likely to get a vote. She was, after all, just a kid! Devin was watching the process, his eyes keenly filing away the things he saw for further consideration. He'd learned a lot this morning.

Tolya clapped Felix and Sherry on the shoulder. "I need you both to stand and face me." Tolya moved back to his place at the table, pushed his chair in and stood behind it. As Felix and Sherry sorted themselves out, he spoke quietly to Tanya.

Tolya turned to face the two young people. "Felix, Sherry. Both of you have continually surprised us and given us reason to be proud during events that have transpired since the night of The Dream. I'm very proud to be able to take this action this morning.

His smile was proud. "Please raise your right hands and respond appropriately.

"Felix? Sherry? Do you promise before God, that you will faithfully uphold the colony charter, so long as it does not violate the basic rights of intelligent beings, be they Human or Aambüka?"

Felix and Sherry chorused, "I do."

"Considering the previous promise, will you diligently seek to find fair but decisive advantage for this colony as we endeavor to fulfill our purpose?"

Felix and Sherry glanced at one another and then faced Tolya again. "As God is our witness, we do."

Tolya grinned and shook Felix' and then Sherry's hands. "All present have witnessed the installation of Felix and Sherry Hernandez as our first Xeno-ambassadors." He looked around the table. "An official document commissioning them to this title will be available for your signatures later today."

ARRIVAL — 1

SAT 09.25.2094-Earth / TRN 10.04.6998-Aambü
30 days to orbital insertion; Aambü, Gem System
ECS Destiny, Quarterdeck, Conference Room, 1040 Hrs / 1400 Slashes

Tolya sat down and made another quiet comment to Tanya. She nodded and stood, giving him a little peck on the cheek. She motioned to Felix and Sherry. "Come on, let's get you updated."

Tolya looked around the table. "Now then. We have a lot more to accomplish. Naomi. Please see about programming a progressive gradient in the gravity levels on board. Aambü has a one quarter higher gravity pull than we're accustomed to, so we need to start adjusting to the new conditions."

Naomi nodded. "Sure. I'll start this evening so it'll be less noticeable starting out. You'll probably want to let the people know what's going on."

Tolya grinned and shook his head. "This is one little secret we'll just overlook. If you don't know you're being stretched, you often overlook the process, only to discover that for some reason, you're suddenly taller."

Daniela looked grim. "I'd better gear up for more medical emergencies. There's likely to be an increase in accidents related to falls, pulled muscles and other adjustment problems due to the increasing gravity. The slow build up is a good idea. Thanks." She shrugged. "We probably should have done this a month or so ago."

Tolya smiled and nodded. "You're right, Dannie. I regret we weren't entirely sure, a couple of months ago, what was going to happen next."

He looked at Emily. "I think we must be close enough for some RPV drones to start recon trips."

Emily nodded. "Frank put Shane in charge of the pilots. The shuttle, work bee and RPV pilots are under his direction. By the way, his son, Owen has been working very hard and doing very well in the sims. He's going to be trying his hand on an RPV. He wants to pilot one of the shuttles, but now's not the time. He has a ways to go yet."

Tolya grinned. "I forgot Shane had taken command. I bet he's about to bust a button or two over Owen. Ok, tell Shane I've approved some RPV work in the region where we're going to be landing. Frank has the coordinates. Once we're in orbit, we can seed the geo-sats and get a GPS system on line. That'll make navigation easier.

"Frank. I guess you have little to do in navigation for another week or so. Right?"

Frank shook his head. "I don't know Tolya. We're coming up on a debris cluster. It's probably the source of a regular meteor shower spectacular for the locals, but right now, it's in our path. I think most of it will pass before we intersect, but we'll probably have the DCPA's firing a little more often from here on out. Em's right about the chunks out here."

Tolya frowned. "How about the sat-suite we'll be sowing? Will we have trouble keeping them up?"

Frank scratched his head. "I've been thinking on that. If Naomi could put together some modular frames, we could mount the sats along with point defense lasers to knock out the stuff that gets too close. The power reactors for the lasers could also power deflector fields. It may make coverage a bit thinner for a while, but if it works we could make more and eventually bring coverage up to specs."

Tolya nodded. "I like your thinking."

He turned to Naomi. "What do you think?"

She smiled. "I think my people have something to do! We're ready to work."

"Very Good. I'll let you get to it."

He turned to Daryl. "You said the MS drive section was ready to shut down. Do it. Make the resulting power surplus from the reactors available to Industrial Deck. She's about to go into full production to create satellite pods that can defend themselves from the trash that's hazarding space around here."

Daryl grinned. "It's as good as done."

"Thanks Daryl."

Finally he turned to Ichirou and Midori. "Thank you, Ichirou for your gracious support for Felix and Sherry."

He inclined his head slightly in a token bow. Ichirou returned the gesture. "I'd like you to keep up what you're currently doing. Once we get into orbit, I'll need you to get together with Emily. It'll be a little while before we can put spade to soil down there, but once we have permission, we need to know what'll be necessary to make things compatible with the echo system.

"We'll need to set up teams to explore the islands, collecting samples for analysis and that sort of thing. You two know what you'd be looking for. Emily knows how to get the data crunched."

Midori smiled and looked at Ichirou who gave a brief nod. "No problem, Tolya. That project will be guaranteed to keep us very busy. I look forward to my first look at the products of this world."

Tolya stood and picked up his power-tab. "I believe that leaves nothing further but to get to work. Thanks everybody. Please keep me informed."

The meeting broke up and people started for the doors. Tolya motioned for Lyuba to wait. "Devin, wait. I want to talk to you."

Devin stopped in his tracks and looked at Tolya. "Yes, sir."

Tolya smiled to take the sting out of his command. Then, he turned and answered a question Frank had.

* * * *

SAT 09.25.2094-Earth / TRN 10.04.6998-Aambü
ECS Destiny, Quarterdeck, Conference Room, 1115 Hrs / 1438 Slashes

The doors snapped shut and he was alone in the room with Lyuba and Devin. Tolya was quiet as he resumed is seat. Lyuba was at a loss and Devin was just nervous.

Tolya looked at Lyuba and then at Devin. "I'm not sure how to approach this. I never thought seriously about this situation until the last few days."

He bid them sit and tried to be less intense. "Devin. I'm not blind, and I'm not that far away from certain personal feelings I thought I'd never experience. If I'm not mistaken, you're about to turn seventeen. Lyuba has just hit fourteen. I'd be terribly remiss not to notice certain trends."

Devin fidgeted nervously.

Tolya looked at Devin. "Tell me. What goes through your mind when you regard Lyuba the way you do?"

Devin wanted to crawl through the deck plates and flee far from this moment.

He looked at Lyuba and then back at her father. "I ah...I confess I like her a lot. I have for more than a year now, but...well, I was afraid to try getting her attention until her birthday party."

He looked down, thinking hard. Then he looked up again. "We haven't even talked about this till now."

Tolya smiled. "OK. I wouldn't probably have said anything except I know what happened between Felix and Sherry when they

594

awakened and were not made aware of certain things that can happen between two mind speakers in your situation."

He turned to Lyuba. "You've heard Sherry's story. Heck you witnessed most of it. Do you fully understand what happened between them?"

Lyuba's face was crimson from embarrassment. "Dad, I...I kinda understand...a little, I guess."

Tolya nodded. "I must ask the questions, honey. What goes through your mind when you look at Devin the way you do?"

She looked at Devin and almost teared up. "I've always thought he was nice. I..."

She put her hands on the table, playing with the bracelet she always wore. "When Devin gave me this...I suddenly realized he liked me more than the other girls. I was surprised, happy, worried...I didn't want you and mom to get mad."

Tolya took her hand. "We're not mad at you, princess." He fingered the bracelet. "May I see it? I'll give it back."

Lyuba nodded and slipped it off, handing it to him. Tolya took it and leaned back in his chair, gazing at it. It was well made. Care had gone into the work. It was clear this guy thought enough of her to go to some effort. He sat forward, regarding Devin.

He'd done some homework and knew more about him. Devin was quite a catch. He was smart and intuitive. He was very creative. Even his music was pleasant. He was genuinely committed to his faith. Devin had a lot going for him.

Tolya held up the bracelet. "So, you made this?"

Devin nodded and then thought better. "Yes, sir. I wanted something really nice to give her."

Tolya gently handed it back to Lyuba. "It's very nicely done. You know she almost never takes it off."

Devin's eyes darted towards her. "Yes, sir. I noticed that."

Tolya shook his head. "You realize this awakening complicates things tremendously, don't you?"

Lyuba nodded. "I thought about it a couple nights ago. I guess I don't really know what happens."

Devin shrugged. "I never got the whole story. I guess something happens because of these talents that affects a relationship somehow."

Tolya grunted. "To be honest, I don't fully understand what happened to Felix and Sherry. I do know they adjusted to it quite well, but I doubt that's always true. Their bonding was accidental."

He looked at them. "I realize that right now, you're still trying to figure out what your relationship is and what it might become. If it wasn't for the bonding, I'd be content to sit back and watch, but I have to make sure you fully understand the possibilities."

Tolya shifted uncomfortably in his chair. "The way I understand it, if a couple reaches a certain level of certainty that they're completely comfortable with each other, it's possible, with physical contact, to create a permanent mental or spiritual bond.

"According to AgradUtya, that bond is unbreakable by anything but death. It's not like most people who can, unfortunately, decide things aren't going well and go their separate ways. The bond is like a physical chord tying two people together.

"Both of you are much too young to form such a bond at this point in your lives. So, I'm very concerned to see you're becoming more attracted to one another."

Tolya gave Devin a smile. "Frankly. So far, I think my daughter demonstrates good taste." Devin's embarrassment was clear.

Tolya continued. "The purpose for this conversation is to make sure you're both aware of the possibilities and potential dangers of allowing this to develop carelessly.

"I want both of you to sit down and talk with Felix and Sherry about this. I think a talk with AgradUtya would be a good idea, too. If, in a couple of years, you're still speaking to each other, and you're still interested. A deeper conversation might be appropriate.

"In the mean time, Devin. I welcome you as a family friend, but I expect you to be an honorable gentleman who treats the lady in his life with deep respect. The jury's still out, so it's up to you to acquit yourself well."

He stood and shook Devin's hand. He gave Lyuba a hug and then said. "I believe your mother is saving spots for us in the diner. Let's go have lunch."

ARRIVAL —2

MON 09.27.2094-Earth / TRN 11.04.6998-Aambü
28 days to orbital insertion; Aambü, Gem System
ECS Destiny, Quarterdeck, Event Center, 1900 Hrs / 1416 Slashes

The ship-wide meeting was reminiscent of the last one. There were some differences, though. There was no urgency because of life threatening circumstances. This time, the people wouldn't be facing the captain and his security chief. They'd hear from the governor and his first lady.

"Friends, I regret we haven't had this meeting a lot sooner, but much has happened that needed to be absorbed and understood. I have a number of astounding things to tell you." He looked around. All eyes were fixed expectantly.

"Some of you have heard through the grapevine, that the planet we found is uninhabitable after all. Not true. It's true we're looking at a water world, but a water world isn't necessarily such a bad thing. We have the ability and the technology to wrest victory from a world like this.

"There's something else far more momentous we must consider. I'm certain everyone within the sound of my voice has a story to tell about their experience with The Dream."

This brought quite a few murmurs. Nobody had any trouble knowing what dream he was talking about. "One of the things I am going to do tonight is clear up a number of questions about that dream and some of the stories that came out of it. Most of you are familiar with the term, mass hallucination. Now I'm bringing for your consideration, mass dreaming."

More anxious murmurs erupted. Tolya held up a hand. The room quieted down. "One of our people was having a dream. He'd been worrying over the whole problem of trying to settle a water world. He wound up dreaming about the problem when he finally got to sleep. The odd thing is, his dream shifted gears and took him to another place, one that actually exists on the planet we're approaching."

Someone piped up. "How can that be? You can't mix dreams and reality."

Tanya stood up and joined Tolya. "There's a lot about dreaming people don't understand. The study of dreaming is hardly an exact science. What my husband is trying to tell you is what happened; not the scientific explanation of how.

"Believe me. Many of the things we have to tell you were hard for us to swallow. I would simply ask you to trust that we're telling exactly what we've experienced."

She paused. The gentleman shrugged and resumed his seat. "I'd also like to remind everyone there'll be a question and answer period after all the information and reactions have been divulged. So please, try to hold your questions till then."

She smiled sweetly, "Thank you." and sat down.

Tolya continued. "As I said, this place where our friend found himself was on the planet we're approaching. It has been named, 'Aambü.'"

He saw the consternation on several faces. "Before someone complains that we've jumped the gun and haven't given others a chance at naming things, this name didn't come from anyone here on *Destiny*."

That got everyone's attention. Absolute, stone silence greeted him. "While our friend was swimming about in the ocean, he met someone. This person broadcast a mental alarm that was intended as a warning to what he mistook for a youngster in mortal danger."

Confusion was starting to make itself apparent. "Hang in there folks. This is where the explanation of The Dream comes in. This mental alarm was quite strong. It propagated through our friend's dream and echoed through the minds of everyone who happened to be dreaming aboard *Destiny*. Our friend was strongly affected by this alarm and anyone who was dreaming at the time was drawn into his dream."

He looked around the room. "Every one of you experienced, to some degree or another, a portion of the same dream."

The room started to buzz. "Every one of you who was dreaming woke suddenly at nearly the same time. Each of you could swear you'd fallen thousands of feet through the air, and then drowned in a vast ocean."

The buzz in the room started to sound like a hive of bees. Tanya decided she needed to make another appearance. She stood and rejoined Tolya. "People. Please!"

Slowly the room quieted. "The governor isn't telling stories to get everyone worked up. Please listen patiently and all will become clear."

She looked at Tolya and he nodded. She continued, "I think all of you can relate to the basics of the story so far. It brings deep emotional responses when we're reminded of that experience. Believe me. We had the same feelings you had. Let me continue where my husband left off.

"Everyone knows that five people were found in a comatose state after The Dream. Most of you have heard a variety of rumors about a couple that somehow 'magically' brought these five people out of their comas.

"While it was hardly magic in the traditional sense of the word, there is some truth to the rumors. The guy who originally started the dream met the one who sent that alarm.

"The fact is, there's a race of people who live on Aambü. The person who sounded the alarm was one of them. That alarm affected us the way it did because these people are telepathic."

That set off another mumbling session. A woman stood near the back. "Why the fairy tales? Telepathy's for science fiction and fantasy!"

Tanya held up a hand. The people slowly quiet. "Ma'am. All of us on the staff, all seasoned professionals, all with the same opinion as your own, have had to come to grips with the idea that sometimes, what we think we know for fact fails to match reality.

"The truth is, science has never proven that mental abilities of this sort don't exist. In fact, there were a few in the scientific community back home who were trying to revisit the question. Believe me! The last thing a command staff aboard a star ship needs is to entertain flights of fancy.

"I'm here to tell you, we have living proof that telepathy and a number of other related 'gifts' are possible. They're common to the native people on this new world.

"Now if you'll let us finish, we can get on with reality."

That brought a number of chuckles; nerves releasing the tension with light laughter. Tanya looked over at Tolya. He nodded and motioned for her to continue.

Tanya shrugged and turned back to the crowd. "Several people who were involved in the greater portion of The Dream have had their lives changed as a result. The fellow who's dream we wound up sharing is the first and primary example."

"In The Dream, he was witness to the vast cloud of people from *Destiny* who fell from the top of the sky to plunge into the ocean he was swimming in. The native individual who was trying to get our man's attention finally persuaded him to dive after him. When he did, our man saw a friend plunge into the water next to him. He saw her drowning and valiantly dragged her back to the surface to save her life. While saving her, the two were mentally linked by their physical touch during their mutual dream."

Tanya could see she had their undivided attention. "When they woke from the dream in their own separate quarters they found they were still aware of each other, though wide awake. They had chance to make physical contact that morning on the way to breakfast. That contact did something we have trouble understanding. They became permanently linked. This mental bond was, for the people on Aambü, a form of marriage. In accordance with our customs, these two were properly married under the hand of Reverend Brad Hill."

"Because of the tremendous changes this experience wrought on them, this couple was able, together, to bring all five comatose people back from their prolonged sleep."

Murmuring of a different sort rippled through the crowd. Tanya looked to Tolya. He grinned and stepped forward. Tanya remained this time, content to watch and wait.

Tolya picked up the narrative. "I think it only appropriate to have the rest of this story told by the principles themselves. I would like to call Felix and Sherry Hernandez up here to the stage."

Felix and Sherry, dressed in their new ambassador's uniforms, moved self consciously through the crowd and mounted the make shift platform. Recognition slowly made its way through the crowd. Tanya sensed mixed reactions.

Tolya sensed it too. "I'm sure most of us remember Felix. To a lesser degree, many of you probably also remember Sherry. I would just remind you of a decision that was made and announced at our own wedding just a few months ago. Considering the tremendous turn-around Felix made by that time, and still demonstrates today, he received a full pardon from my office. In my opinion, he has conquered his demons and become a better man. With that said, I wish to have him and his new bride tell you the rest of the story."

As the crowd murmured to itself, Felix and Sherry stepped forward. Felix nervously adjusted the pin mic that was stuck to the collar of his shirt. "Good evening folks. I, ah...I'm a bit nervous. I want to thank you for hearing us out.

"As Governor Chernov has pointed out, a number of changes have taken place in our lives that make us a lot different from how we were before The Dream."

He could feel the crowd. He'd never spoken to this many people at once, but somehow he felt a confidence he couldn't explain. "One of those things is the way we communicate between ourselves. If you find us speaking after and for each other, or finishing each other's sentences, it's because of how we were bonded as the Governor mentioned." Felix quickly hugged Sherry to his side and then started right in.

"The truth is clear. Both of us have had personal encounters with the individual who sounded the alarm, drastically altering all of our dreams and our very lives. Let's be clear; we were fully awake during all the encounters since The Dream."

Sherry picked up their train of thought. "These people are ocean going people. They breathe both from the water and from the air.

"They're highly intelligent. They were aware of our approach before we knew they existed. I can tell you that all the members of the council and command staff were highly skeptical when these events first began to unfold, but you will find them in full agreement now"

Felix stepped in, "because, everyone on the council and staff have personally met their ambassador."

The crowd stirred at that statement. That was a claim that would be hard to refute.

He continued. "This development has been forming ever since The Dream. There's a small percentage of our population that has a latent ability in the area of telepathy. Most of us have always thought of mental abilities like telepathy as simply fanciful stories."

Sherry continued. "The thing is, just because we don't understand something doesn't make it go away. There are currently four people on this ship capable of communicating directly with these people..."

Felix continued, "...who, by the way, call themselves Aambüka, which means 'water people.'"

Sherry grinned and squeezed his hand. "We are part of a small segment of our population with the ability necessary to connect with these people. These abilities surfaced because of what the Aambüka call the awakening."

Felix explained. "The awakening is what brought our latent abilities to the fore."

Tolya stood and moved to stand behind and between the two younger adults. "Folks. Standing before you are the two human experts on the Aambüka. Their continued successes in communicating with and befriending the people of this planet have been nothing short of exceptional."

He glanced at Tanya and then back out at the crowd. "Many of you are wondering how all this can take place before we've even entered into orbit. The answer is simple, yet complex. It's simple in that the ambassador from the Aambüka has repeatedly visited *Destiny*.

"The answer is complex because his visits, and one that Felix has made to his world, are done by a mode they call questing. They're able to range outward with their minds to places their bodies can't normally go.

"My reason for interrupting is to make it clear that my wife and I, and my staff hold Felix and Sherry in the highest regard. The council has officially and unanimously called them as humanity's first xeno-ambassadors to the people of Aambü. They've earned the respect of the leaders of both races, so hear them and realize this is for real. We're not alone in the universe after all."

Tolya returned to his seat leaving Felix and Sherry to face the people. There was a different feel to the personality of the crowd. They were seeing this couple in a new light.

"The people of Aambü are, in some ways a lot like us. They have similar fears as we would have."

Sherry stepped in. "I remind everyone that in this little adventure, we're the aliens.

"Imagine if you will, that you're back on Earth and you just found out that an alien race is approaching your world in a huge star ship. Now imagine the kind of responses that might come from people you know.

"Some of us would say, 'Great. Let's welcome them and make friends.' Others of us might say, 'Wait a minute. What do we know about these people? How do we know they're friendly? We should be careful.' Then, I'm sure you've run into the kind of people who would say, 'we don't need them. They must be up to no good. In fact, maybe we should do something to make them go away.'

"Our counterpart tells us that describes his people."

Felix continued. "There are numerous ways in which we're totally different. They can stay indefinitely under the water. We can only stay until we run out of air. Conversely, we can stay out of the water and breath the air, while they can come out of the water and breathe the air until they become dangerously dry. Then they must return to the water."

Sherry added, "They can move through the water quickly with elegance and grace. We can only slog through the water using our limbs to pull us along. We tire easily in the water while they exult in the freedom of the sea."

Felix concluded. "This is a small part of the richness we can expect from seeking their friendship."

"We could go on and on, but," Sherry grinned, "we'd cause mass boredom for sure."

Felix said, "Bottom line, we've been invited to camp on a series of small islands. This allows the majority of us to be off the ship and in fresh air. We'll be able to meet physically, face to face for the first time. And there, we can appeal to them for space and possibly help to settle in."

Sherry finished up. "There's more we could tell, but we'll save it for the Q and A."

Sherry and Felix stepped back and Tolya stood again. The room slowly filled with applause as people began to grasp the new reality.

Tanya and Tolya stepped forward. "Folks. We have a singular opportunity to represent humanity to a people that has never seen the light of our sun. I request the help of each and every one of you to make this initial contact something we can be proud of.

"To that end, we'll be issuing a report and a list of policies aimed at helping us show what we can do if we make an honest effort.

Tanya smiled. "Questions?"

ARRIVAL — 3

TUE 10.05.2094-Earth | TRN 17.04.6998-Aambü
20 days to orbital insertion; Aambü, Gem System
ECS Destiny, Industrial Deck-main, 1530 Hrs | 0564 Slashes

They assembled modular segments for the pods designed to protect the NAV-SATS. One platform was carefully stacked in the hanger bay; waiting to be towed piecemeal, out to its assigned location for assembly.

The overhead crane ran the first of the longitudinal support sections out over the main floor and lowered it. Felix and Devin had been co-opted from the nano lab to help supervise the grunt work. Naomi was in her office, making design updates.

Felix was in charge of the crew receiving the finished modules and getting them stacked in the queue for the short trip into the hanger bay.

The huge steel module settled massively towards the floor as the guys guided it into place. Felix gave the signal and the crane operator began to let it down the rest of the way.

This process had gone on for several hours. The crew had all agreed to skip lunch so they could finish early. The module settled on its side and as the massive grapples went slack, Devin ran the length of the piece tapping the release tab on each. *It's clear, Felix.*

Felix gave a thumbs-up and then signaled the crane operator to pull the grapple. The grapples swung clear of the work and started back up, people ducking the swing of the grapples automatically.

* * * *

Lyuba placed the pocket-tab carefully on the narrow counter and turned to check the fresh flood of data scrolling down the screen behind her. Since classes were on hold for the final run up to orbit, she spent the better part of each day in the lab.

Lyuba crossed to another station and entered a query on an odd fluctuation in the information. *Lyuba. Can you hear me?*

Lyuba grinned. It was Sherry. *Of course, big sis. What's up?*

She felt the grin in Sherry's reply. *Since the guys stood us up for lunch, I thought they might be pretty hungry. You wanna come with me and bring them a snack for when they get off?*

Lyuba exclaimed. *Oh, Sherry! You're a genius. I'd love to!*

Sherry was laughing, she could tell. *OK, kiddo. Meet me at the lift in Event Center lobby. We can pack some things and head on down.*

I'll be right there. Thanks, Sherry. Lyuba quickly closed up anything that wasn't in mid-run and headed for the door.

"Ms. Emily. I'm off to help Sherry take some snacks to the guys on Industrial."

Emily looked up from her own screen. "No problem. Thanks for your help. You coming tomorrow?" The door snapped open. "You bet! See yah!" The door snapped shut on empty air.

* * * *

The next section, a huge half circular shape was on its way down. It was half of a mount for one of those nasty high-powered pulsed lasers. Everyone moved aside to make a large clear area for the umpteen ton steel section to settle on. Felix noticed one side of the piece was off center and hanging slightly lower. He looked around to be sure no one was directly underneath the load. As the piece came within arms reach, Felix signaled a stop.

The odd angle had increased noticeably. It looked like it could tip out of the grapples at any moment. *Devin. This thing's dangerous the way it is. Let's see if we can find a way to adjust it before it crashes to the floor and damages the grav-plates.*

Devin came over to have a look. *How'd that happen? What can we do about it?*

Felix was unsure. They needed to get it down to make space for the final piece.

He reached out and rested a hand on the canted chunk of the steel. The thing barely moved at his touch. It was incredibly heavy.

He and Devin worked their way around the section that was in reach, trying to see what could be done. Foolishly, they crossed under the higher portion to get another look at the other side.

Someone yelled and Devin looked up. A loud report, like a stick of dynamite going off, reverberated all across the deck. The lower part of the piece smashed to the floor and two more mighty reports reemphasized their doom.

The rest of the piece inexorably began tilting their direction. Felix turned and tried to make a dash for safety with Devin right behind. At the last instant, Devin grabbed Felix and forced him to the floor.

I have to shield him, Devin thought as he landed on top of Felix, trying to cover him. He had no idea why he did that.

* * * *

Sherry had a platter piled high with finger sandwiches and Lyuba had a bag of cookies and a jug of punch. They figured the guys would be famished after their long shift and would like something to munch to hold them till dinner.

They were descending through Ag-Deck when Sherry's face contorted into a hideous mask of horror.

"Nooooo!"

Lyuba could feel the mental scream that came with it. *What Sherry? What's wrong?*

Sherry wanted to claw her way from the lift, but she couldn't. *Oh God! They're gonna...*Sherry was sobbing uncontrollably.

Lyuba was wild with frustration. "What! Sherry, tell me!"

She dropped the bag of cookies and grabbed Sherry by the arm. Sherry held back as best she could but she dumped the scene she'd seen from Felix' perspective straight to Lyuba.

The lift stopped and the doors snapped open on the balcony level of Industrial. Lyuba was out the door and leaping over the rails of the stair platform before Sherry could blink.

Lyuba hit the deck on her feet in the middle of a milling crowd of workers, some sixty feet aft of the stairs and fifteen feet below. She was totally unfazed by the impact that landing should have caused. Naomi was running from her office down the center lane of the deck, coming under the balcony area from which Lyuba had just descended like an avenging angel. She could see Sherry trying to run down the stairs from the forward lift well.

Lyuba dashed for the massive half circular chunk of steal. It was leaning over, resting on nothing, just inches from Devin's back. Devin was lying on top of Felix. They couldn't move for the pressure of the object above them. No one could figure out how they weren't smashed beyond hope of recognition.

Lyuba took hold of the piece and heaved upwards. The mass rose ponderously several feet into the air to hang suspended on nothing as she dove under to check on her men. *Devin, are you OK?*

Devin looked her way. *Lyuba? I guess I'm OK. I don't know what happened but that thing fell and stopped just inches over my back.*

He rolled off of Felix. *Felix, are you OK?*

Felix got up shakily and dusted off his pants. He flexed everything and looked up at the offending metal just hanging there. Devin sat on the floor, sweat pouring down his face as if he'd just spent a couple of hours in the gym.

"Don't just stand there, people! Somebody go turn off the gravity for this part of the deck!" Naomi bellowed angrily. "This could have been avoided if only the gravity had been turned off!"

She turned to Lyuba. "Honey. Why don't you put that thing down now? Everyone's OK."

Lyuba released Devin's arm where she'd clung when he'd rolled away from Felix. She looked over at the massive steel piece hanging in the air.

"OK Everybody. Please move. I need to put this down!"

Confused looks crossed face after face as people scurried away from the hanging mass of steel.

Lyuba concentrated and it slowly settled to the deck without so much as a sound. Only then did the confused looks turn to awe at what she'd just done.

Just then the warning sound came on and the gravity quit. People grabbed for anything to hold on to.

Naomi dove for the gravity control box. She deftly caught the chicken bar next to it and flipped over to place her boots on the deck. "Everyone, get your footing!" She waited for a few seconds and then tapped in a series of commands. The gravity came on gradually, winding back to its 1.25g setting.

Naomi walked back to the scene. "All right. Somebody tell me what the heck happened here!"

Felix stepped forward, looking sheepish. "Uh, I guess this is really my fault. I noticed the piece was hanging irregularly from the grapples. I had the operator stop and Dev and I did a quick inspection to see why. I darted underneath just as the grapple on that side gave way. We tried to run for it but it was too late. Devin tackled me and then the piece fell on top of us. The weird part is, for some reason, it stopped just inches from Devin's back. I think he was holding the entire weight somehow."

Naomi looked at Devin. He was still sitting on the deck, leaning on an elevated knee. She walked around him checking for injuries. Sherry darted in and hugged Felix hard. *You scared me to death, honey. We were on our way down with some munchies when I saw the whole thing.*

She relaxed her hold and began delving. Felix wasn't hurt. He was definitely shaken up, but he needed no healing. She looked deep in his eyes. *Don't scare me like that.*

She smiled and then turned to Devin. Lyuba had returned to Devin's side. She sat next to him on the deck, holding his arm as if she hadn't just lifted a twenty-three ton chunk of steel, kept it hovering in the air and then gently placed it down on the deck plates. *I saw you under that thing and I...I thought you were...were gone.*

Devin reached around and gave her an awkward hug. *I'm OK, Lyuba. I...you...thanks. Thanks for your help. I doubt I'd have held out much longer.*

Sherry approached, *Devin, let me have a look.*

Devin pulled gently from Lyuba's grasp and tried to stand and face Sherry.

Stay where you are. She knelt in front of him and placed a hand on his shoulder. She delved as she had with Felix.

The muscles in Devin's back were sore. She sensed swelling and minor tearing. He would be stiff and in pain in an hour or so if she didn't do something.

Sherry reached in and soothed the muscles. She applied energy to the torn tissues. They began to knit and after a moment she moved on. There was little else. The muscles in his arms were sore, but nothing was seriously damaged.

Devin. I don't know what you did, but you and Felix are the luckiest guys around. By all the laws of physics, the two of you should be...should...be dead.

Sherry turned, satisfied that Devin was OK. She went to be with Felix who was standing, looking blankly at the steel resting serenely on the deck.

Devin asked. *Was this the 'something weird, I can't explain' thing you mentioned?*

Lyuba had calmed down. She sat hugging her knees. *It must have been. Can you describe what happened? I don't mean with the steel. I mean with you...your mind, your feelings.*

Devin considered. *I don't know why I even tried to go for Felix. I knew we were done for, but I also knew I had to shield us.*

He paused and considered what he'd said. Lyuba's eyes got round. *Hey you two, you gotta hear this.*

Sherry and Felix looked her way. Felix sensed Lyuba's urgency and the two came over to join them. *Devin, tell that last part again.*

Devin shrugged. *I was convinced we were done for, but something told me I had to shield us. I knocked you down and jumped over you and thought about shielding us. I felt the weight of the metal hit, but something kept it from actually touching us. I didn't want that thing crushing us.*

He looked at Lyuba and then back at Felix. *If she hadn't come when she did, I think I wouldn't have been able to keep it up much longer.*

Felix considered. *Shielding? Huh!*

Devin looked around. *Did somebody say something about munchies? I sure could use something to eat!*

Felix offered a hand. Devin accepted it and received an assist back to his feet. *Thanks Sherry. I feel better.*

Lyuba hopped up and announced. "I'll get the munchies." She looked up at the railing of the stairway to the balcony level, bent her knees slightly and then leaped up, and up and up.

She cleared the railing and looked around. The tray of finger sandwiches had survived its hurried placement on the floor next to the lift. The bag of cookies was right where she'd dropped it

She didn't even remember dropping the jug of punch. It had burst open, leaking all over the deck. Lyuba grabbed all the remaining goodies and hopped back over the railing. She floated down to join the rest.

Naomi watched, shaking her head. Lyuba was just full of surprises. The entire crew gathered around and helped themselves to finger sandwiches and cookies. Devin and Lyuba were much the better for the quick infusion of energy.

ARRIVAL — 4

TUE 10.12.2094-Earth / TRN 23.04.6998-Aambü
13 days to orbital insertion; Aambü, Gem System
Ruling Clan Territory, Welcome Island, Aambü, 0940 Hrs / 0733 Slashes

The workers emerged from the caverns into the light of day. They stood inhaling the sweet smell of the flowering plants that grew along the ancient path down to the lagoon.

Avuka. Where are the new people going to be?

Madhura's father looked fondly at his daughter. *Adhiraj says they will arrive in great flying vehicles. They will arrive on the large flat area across the lagoon.* He pointed the place out with a web hand.

They can fly? Ha! I would see them fly!

Her father laughed. *No Madhura. They can't fly. They have machines that carry them through the air.*

Madhura bounced along the path in anticipation. *Ha! I will see these flying machines then.*

The party labored its way down to the beach. They were charged with beginning the preparations for the great Abhinand, the great welcome. Slowly, over the course of the turn, great open walled pavilions sprouted along the beach.

* * * *

TUE 10.12.2094-Earth / TRN 23.04.6998-Aambü
13 days to orbital insertion; Aambü, Gem System
ECS Destiny, Quarterdeck, RPV Flight Ctr, 1325 Hrs / 1000 Slashes

"All right. Today, I want a pattern flown over the target sight. Captain wants confirmation that we actually have the right spot."

Shane looked at his team. Five young men sat in the small ready room across from the RPV control center. One of them, Owen, was his son. He was incredibly proud of his rapid rise through the levels. He was exceptionally skilled for his age.

Shane glanced at the time. "Right. Let's go."

Owen found his cubicle, 'RPV-05.' It wasn't an inspiring name, but he was flying something real; not just another computer sim. He sat on the pilot's couch and strapped in. Technically, the strapping in might be considered superfluous. After all, they weren't really in the craft they were flying, so they couldn't be physically injured. However, good habits repeated regardless of need were bound to save a life someday. Besides, there was a certain amount of tactile feedback that helped sharpen the pilot's sense of the moment.

He slipped the finger pads on and checked that they were secure. His patch took on a slight glow as it assimilated its place in the network. The COMM came to life and his dad's voice sounded in five sets of ears. "OK, guys. On my mark we'll begin undocking your MIPOD. Once your MIPOD reaches orbit, you'll have three minutes before your craft are ejected. After that, you're on your own. When the mission is completed, regroup at the MIPOD. Your craft will be linked up and towed back to *Destiny*. Once you have the Link Successful light and AI confirmation, you may disconnect and leave your cubicle. Stand by."

After a few moments, "OK guys, on my mark...MARK." The AI simulated the sense of motion as the MIPOD pulled itself free of *Destiny's* hold.

When the thrusters of the MIPOD kicked in, Owen felt an insistent force pushing against his back. Since the craft were unmanned, the acceleration was incredibly high. Seasoned pilots called it brutal after a few less complimentary descriptives.

With *Destiny* just days away from Aambü, the trip in this express mode only took a couple of hours.

* * * *

The AI announced they were entering orbit. Owen keyed up the visual sensors and got his first orbital view of the planet Aambü. The AI interrupted his sight seeing. "Orbital insertion is now complete. You have exactly three minutes before ejection. Please stand by."

Owen watched the count down timer. He waved a hand and glanced at the tiny window that appeared in the canopy. He scanned the categories, double-checking that all was in good shape. He waved the window away and considered his situation. He decided the only thing he really hated about this was the waiting.

"You have exactly one minute. Please stand by."

Oh, the waiting and that prim irritating AI voice, he thought. The thirty-second count down began and he joined in quietly for the last five...four...three... two...one...

"OW!" It didn't seem right for the AI to kick the couch quit that hard. He knew he was on the way.

* * * *

TUE 10.12.2094-Earth / TRN 23.04.6998-Aambü
13 days to orbital insertion; Aambü, Gem System
Ruling Clan Territory, Welcome Island, Aambü, 1545 Hrs / 1180 Slashes

The first segment of the preparations was complete and the workers began the laborious walk back up the shallow rise to the cavern entrance. They'd gotten about half way when Madhura exclaimed. *Ha! Hanta!* Everyone turned to look in the direction she was pointing.

A dazzling point of light had appeared high and near the edge of the rings. It speared downward like the attack of Zagkunta, the spear-fisher. Suddenly it flashed and split into five independent sparks that soared at incredible speeds across the deep blue sky.

They watched as the five points of light spread further apart and made a sweeping turn off to the Northwest. They completed their turns, now forming a wide line of sparks in the deepening sky. They kept getting lower. Finally, they seemed to be hurtling straight at them. Moments before they might have passed right over, they split apart. Two angled farther to the West, two veered to the East and the fifth speared straight ahead across the beach the workers had just left. There was a tiny whining sound and the rush of air over tiny wings as they hurtled on.

The watching workers were feeling just a bit nervous. They'd never seen anything very pleasant come from the sky. Madhura, herself a study in contrasts, was ebullient. She bounced and waved as the five strange flying objects circled out at sea and made a wide turn to approach again.

The clearly artificial flying things came at a slower pace. They soared and wheeled like hunting flyers at sunset looking for the prey that massed at the surface of the water. One of them flew back over the beach right over their heads. As it approached, it spun on its axis like a child's spinning toy. It was almost as if it had waved at them.

The five flyers regrouped and hurtled southwards before racing back towards the rings that were starting to glow in their early evening brilliance.

* * * *

The five RPV's stayed in tight formation all the way down till the camera's resumed recording after reentry. Then they performed the first maneuver.

Owen stayed with the plan, keeping his craft dead center of the group. At the correct time he pulled up sharply and began his high speed run to the Northwest.

He allowed the altitude to slowly bleed off. The view was awesome. As far as the eye...well, camera...could see was nothing but azure blue ocean.

Their target was down there somewhere just to the southeast of his position. Their altitude was so high there was nothing to see but the targeting square pinned to the lower right corner of his canopy

They continued to bleed altitude, finally banking into a sweeping, miles wide turn. Now headed due south, they rapidly bled more altitude. The targeting square suddenly came alive and rose from its rest position to point at a spec in the ocean just on the edge of the Southeastern horizon.

Owen opened a ship-to-ship link. "Dart five, Dart one, copy?"

After a moment, "Dart One, Dart five, what's up?"

"I have a visual low and to the Southeast. Copy?"

The flight leader checked the readings and confirmed an identical sighting. "I have it Owen, thanks. OK, bank two degrees southeast and hold steady. Drop to one five zero and we'll buzz the beach."

All four pilots acknowledged the instructions and reoriented themselves. The altitude was now flashing downwards as they dove for a hundred fifty feet.

"Dart one, flight. When we reach my mark..." a green triangle lit near the growing island cluster... "I want us to perform maneuver fourteen. Owen, you'd better stay straight and true on this one."

Owen grinned. "Never fear, Owen's here."

That got one groan and two laughs.

"But that's exactly what I do fear." Flynn, in Dart One, laughed.

They reached the designated way-point and Owen aimed straight over the tiny beach. Two of his team banked left and two banked right. Owen laughed out loud. "Dart five, Dart one, we have an audience."

James came back. "I thought I caught motion on that little hill above the beach."

Owen was excited. He'd seen a handful of the most interesting creatures. "Yeah. They're standing on that hillside near some kind of cave opening."

Owen checked their formation status. "Dart Five requesting permission for a solo fly by."

Flynn replied. "OK. Lets get our milling around straightened out and you can do your fly by."

A few more moments of jockeying for positions brought them back in formation. "Dart One, Dart Five. Go with your fly by, then form up and we'll kick it in the pants."

Owen grinned and brought his Dart around for the pass. He slowed and approached the island so he was flying along what looked like a flower-lined walkway. He saw his audience. One of them, probably a youngster was bobbing up and down and pointing. Owen couldn't resist. He performed a single snap 360 roll before arrowing off to the Southwest to catch up with the flight.

"I'm right behind you, Dart one."

"Gotcha. OK gang, let's head upstairs."

The five Darts lunged heavenward straight for the thin glowing line that marked the rings of Aambü.

* * * *

TUE 10.12.2094-Earth / TRN 23.04.6998-Aambü
13 days to orbital insertion; Aambü, Gem System
ECS Destiny, Quarterdeck, RPV Flight Ctr, 1700 Hrs / 1272 Slashes

Owen's Dart was the last to link up to the MIPOD. The Link Successful light blinked on and that prim irritating voice confirmed the successful locking of his craft to the MIPOD tow links.

Owen signaled the end of his session. As the screens blanked out he stripped off the finger pads and stuck them in his belt pouch.

The rest of the team was already headed for the ready room when his dad approached. "Owen. Flynn says you got a close look at the natives."

Owen grinned. "Yeah, I gave 'em a good show."

Shane sighed. "Owen. I know you're having the time of your life. I was just as excited about this as you are, but you have to think. We don't know what these people are used to, or what they understand about our technology. We want to be very careful not to frighten them so badly that they stop trusting us."

Owen began examining a spot on the deck plates. "I guess I wasn't thinking."

Shane reached out and clapped Owen on the shoulder. "I checked the recordings. I don't think it was as bad as all that. In fact, that one character seemed to be quite excited, maybe even entertained by your little show."

Owen looked as his dad. "Don't think I don't know how it felt the first time I went out on a real mission, but remember. You're not out there to show off. You do your job well, and people will be impressed enough with your performance."

He glanced in the direction of the ready room. "Now, go report for debriefing. I'll be right with you."

He watched Owen turn and head across the corridor. "Owen."

Owen turned to look back at his dad. "Besides that little gratuitous exhibitionism, you did well. I'm proud of you."

Owen's face lit up. "Thanks, Dad."

* * * *

TUE 10.12.2094-Earth / TRN 23.04.6998-Aambü
13 days to orbital insertion; Aambü, Gem System
ECS Destiny, Quarterdeck, Forward Lift well, 1815 Hrs / 1366 Slashes

"...Anyway, I can confirm we have the correct location. It looks like the locals are setting up for some festivities. Owen saw what looked like the entrance to a cave on the rise where the locals were walking when our team flew by."

Shane handed Tolya a crystal. "Here's a composite of the fly-by. I think the kids did a great job."

Tolya put the crystal in the depression in the back of his pocket-tab. "I guess you're proud of Owen."

Shane grinned broadly. "Yes, I am. Thanks for letting him take a shot. I think he's a natural."

Tolya chuckled. "Of course. His dad was the best wing man I ever had, must be in the jeans."

Shane laughed and gave Tolya a friendly punch on the shoulder. "Thanks for that."

The two parted in the corridor. "Oh, Shane." Shane stopped and turned back to face his former flight leader. "Once we get the shuttle runs down to a routine, I just might let Owen give one of the smaller ones a spin...if and when you think he can handle it."

Shane grinned. "Owen will go nuts!"

Tolya returned the grin and waved for the lift.

ARRIVAL — 5
MON 10.25.2094-Earth / TRN 32.04.6998-Aambü
Commencing orbital insertion; Aambü, Gem System
ECS Destiny, Command Deck, Command Bridge, 0630 Hrs / 1670 Slashes

The last couple of days had given everyone a spectacular pyrotechnic show. The DCPA's were very active. If someone had been observing from farther out, they might have thought a minor battle was being fought in the path of the beautiful ringed planet.

Destiny was simply doing her very best to protect her precious cargo from the mountain-sized chunks of space rock that tumbled ceaselessly in her path. The partially vaporized, pulverized remains lent their own sparkle as they brushed *Destiny's* far-reaching deflection grid.

This morning was the moment everyone was really jazzed about. This moment signified what was hoped to be the end of a seriously altered journey to a destination that hadn't even been on the charts.

Frank sat at his station, looked around with a big grin and made a great theatrical point of cracking his knuckles and wiggling his fingers like a pianist working out the kinks before the concert.

Tolya rolled his eyes and glanced at Vince who was grinning at the show. "Ok, Frank. Are we there yet?"

Frank turned to regard Tolya. "But of course, sir."

"Then, Mr. Drake, would you be so kind as to park this baby?"

Frank made a showy salute. "Right away, sir."

He turned to his console and was suddenly all business and professionalism. "Sir, I guess you want a low orbit for unloading?"

Tolya shook his head. "You've probably noticed the ring system extends well into the mid-orbital bands. Given the greater diameter and the higher gravity gradient, I'd think we might want to stay in the middle."

Frank nodded. "Yes, I think lower orbits here would be less advantageous than back home. We'd have to maintain a reasonably fast pace due to the higher gravity...I could put her just above the inside rim of the rings; say, high enough to avoid larger clutter, low enough to maintain an equatorial stance. I'm assuming you want geo-sync with the target."

Tolya grinned. "You assume correctly, your plan sounds good. Let's do it."

Frank nodded and began playing his console like some musical instrument; occasionally murmuring commands.

Destiny had been firmly in the pull of Aambü for some time. She'd done the equivalent of a fly-by of the planet, but as she was pulling away from the backside of Aambü's path, she obeyed the laws of physics and began to fall towards the planet. It was a delicate, graceful dance. By the time Frank intervened, she was already committed to a very high, elliptical orbit.

For the next few hours, Frank orchestrated the dance, refining the physics. He located the coordinates of the proposed landing sight and set NavCom to pinpointing the exact altitude for the orbit.

He slowly spiraled *Destiny* into a tighter orbit, hugging the upper side of the rings. When all was finished, *Destiny* appeared to hover about two miles above the surface of the inner edge of the rings. The planet was visible to port and space, to starboard.

People were glued to external displays, drinking in the beautiful scene of the rings stretching out below on one side and the day-night line advancing slowly across the planet on the other.

* * * *

TUE 10.25.2094-Earth / TRN 32.04.6998-Aambü
Geo-sync parking orbit; Aambü, Gem System
ECS Destiny, Quarterdeck, Hernandez Residence, 0930 Hrs / 1915 Slashes

Landing rotation arrangements began shortly after Tolya announced their successful arrival in orbit. The process of organizing people for the trip planet side had its glitches. Getting over two thousand people to accomplish something in an organized manner invariably invited moments of drama. The initial landing was going to be tight.

Only so many people could fit on the small island that had been designated for the purpose. So, it had been decided that a steady rotation between *Destiny* and the island would give everyone an opportunity to stretch their legs and breath fresh air.

More importantly, they'd get their first look at the local population. There was still some concern about adverse reactions. The people of this planet didn't look terribly human, after all.

Felix considered trying to contact AgradUtya from orbit. It was about a local hour past sunset over Welcome Island. He sat quietly at the kitchen table in the new housing he and Sherry shared and began casting out a call for AgradUtya. *AgradUtya, it's Felix. Can you hear me?*

After a few moments, he thought to give up. *Hey, honey. Keep trying. I'll help push.*

Felix chuckled. *Push. That's interesting. OK.*

He could feel Sherry lending him just a little strength. He tried again, hopefully a little louder. *AgradUtya, it's Felix. Do you hear me?*

Friend, friend. You don't have to shout. I hear you very well...Ah. Sherry is helping you. Very good. This is quite a long distance for a chat. When are you two coming down to visit?

Felix grinned. *We're getting things organized. I just wanted to see if you and yours were ready for our friendly invasion.*

He could sense a bit of humor in AgradUtya's reply. **Friendly invasion indeed. We've been watching for several turns, so we saw your vessel stop in the rings.**

Felix replied. *I'm glad we can communicate from here. I'm not exactly sure about the timing. I suspect we'll try for sometime around dawn, next turn. I'll talk with Tolya and get back to you.*

Very good Felix. I'll await your call. Until then.

Felix sensed AgradUtya was gone.

Sherry placed a hot cup of coffee in front of him and then sat across from him. *I guess the rest of the day is going to be crazy busy.*

Felix took a grateful sip. *That's for sure.*

* * * *

TUE 10.25.2094-Earth / TRN 33.04.6998-Aambü
Geo-sync parking orbit; Aambü, Gem System
ECS Destiny, Quarterdeck, Hernandez Residence, 2200 Hrs / 0440 Slashes

Felix went to the small desk to answer the COMM. The screen lit up and Tolya's grin. "Hey Tolya. What's up?"

"Well, we're going to make a preliminary drop to put leadership faces together and break the ice. I'd like you and Sherry there. I have Lyuba, of course. Also, were bringing Devin along. I thought we might as well introduce all the compatible minds first."

"When?" Felix grinned at Sherry who was headed to the bedroom to get dressed.

"Well, I was just going to ask you about that. Do you think you can make contact now that we're in orbit?"

"It's funny you should ask. Sherry and I managed to make contact already. AgradUtya's wondering when we plan to arrive. I told him I'd let him know soon as I knew. Oh! He said they've been watching for several turns."

Tolya grinned. "That's what I like, efficiency and initiative. Very good. I checked out the time sync. It's 2200 now. If we can get down there by midnight our time, that'll be about 0600 their time. That would be about sunrise. Why don't you and Sherry meet us at the command shuttle bay in about an hour? I'll make a general announcement and then we'll make the drop."

Felix nodded "You've got it. We'll meet you then."

"OK, Felix. This is it. Let's do it right."

The *Destiny* logo was left glowing on the screen. Felix went to the bedroom. Sherry was pulling out her dress uniform. Felix appreciated his beautiful catch.

OK, tiger. We'll have to find another time for that.

Felix grinned. *I can't help it if you put it on display! Besides we have an hour.*

Sherry still blushed at the frank talk. *Just think of it as a sneak preview. We need time to get down there and checked in.*

Felix laughed and with a mock pout, pulled his own dress uniform out. After their swearing in, they'd had their patches completely replaced with fully updated ones. Felix had never had a proper ship's uniform, unless you called the maintenance and janitorial overalls a uniform. Now he and Sherry had brand new outfits, specifically designed for their new positions.

They helped each other get dressed, a moderately entertaining proposition in itself.

After checking that everything was as it should be, they stepped into the corridor and secured the door.

Together they made their way to the forward lift well and down to the main level of Industrial Deck. They arrived early at the Forward Shuttle Bay control room, so they left their carry-ons in the seating area and took a walk down the midway of Industrial Deck.

They strolled down the center where markings on the floor indicated the area covered by the crane mounted high above them. About two-thirds the way aft began the machinery that pumped the vital life of the ship from one end to the other. Air recirculation, water, heat, sewage; all these things were ultimately controlled here.

Hey Sherry. Where are you?

Sherry laughed. *Lyuba. We're down on Industrial Deck. What's up?*

Lyuba was excited. *I'm on Ag-Deck with Devin. We're headed down there. Mom and Dad got delayed. Dad decided he wanted Pastor Brad and Jodi to come along. So they're coming together whenever Evan's ready.*

Felix grinned. *That'll take a while. We're going to take a look at the preparations going on in the main shuttle bay. Why don't you guys come meet us? We can walk back to the Command Shuttle Bay together.* Sherry squeezed his hand. *See you soon.*

Lyuba's grin could be felt big and strong. *OK.* She was gone. Felix and Sherry kept their pace slow, just enjoying their limited time together. They'd be quite busy, he figured, once they touched down. He was excited and nervous at the same time.

Sherry was content to hold his hand. *Hey. Maybe we should let AgradUtya know we'll be leaving soon.*

Felix shrugged. *We'll call him on our way back.*

They cycled in to the interface room for the main shuttle bay and stood quietly at the thick windows looking out on the hanger. Felix considered the last time he'd been down here. It wasn't a fond memory. The scar from the bullet wound in his shoulder remained as a reminder. They'd done a good job of patching him up, but that was before he and Sherry had been changed. She'd have probably completely healed his shoulder if she'd had the ability then.

Sherry squeezed his hand, *you betcha!*

Felix grinned. *Sweetheart. I'm still amazed at how you treated me after that mess.*

Sherry pulled him close. *I'd do it again. I know I was right.*

Lyuba and Devin cycled into the room and they separated. *So, Felix. Are you ready to go impress their king?*

Felix shook Devin's hand. *Well, I don't know, but it ought to be an interesting meeting. It's not like we're putting on a show.*

Devin got a thoughtful look. *I guess you're right.*

Lyuba and Sherry exchanged sisterly hugs. *I guess we'd better head forward. Even Evan can't take much longer.*

They all laughed at Lyuba's comment and cycled back into the main portion of Industrial Deck. They were almost midway when

Felix' COM-Bud chirped in his ear. He still wasn't used to carrying such a thing.

These devices were reserved for officers, command staff and the captain. He and Sherry were suddenly included in that heady level of responsibility as official ambassadors. "Felix, here."

"Hey, Felix, Tolya. We're on the lift, headed down. I told the staff to begin processing you. Don't forget to let AgradUtya know we'll be there soon. I'd guess in about an hour or so."

"Got it. So, Evan grew tired of the entertainment industry?"

Tolya laughed. "No, he's discovered the joys of riding on Daddy's shoulders."

Felix and Sherry laughed. "Lyuba and Devin are with us. We'll start processing." There was the tiniest of clicks in his ear and the connection closed.

ARRIVAL — 6

TUE 10.26.2094-Earth / TRN 33.04.6998-Aambü
Geo-sync parking orbit; Aambü, Gem System
ECS Destiny, Industrial Deck, Cmd Shuttle Bay, 2315 Hrs / 00535 Slashes

The preflight crew took their carry-ons and began the process of logging, weighing and sending out to the waiting shuttle. Each person passed their patch over a reader and was logged as a passenger. A tech approached with a small case. "Excuse me, Sir."

Felix refrained from automatically correcting him. The whole deferential 'sir' thing was something else he had to get used to. "I need to add this to your COMM package. May I see your control module, please?"

Felix smiled and unclipped the tiny device from his collar, surrendering it to the technician. "So, what're you adding?"

The tech deftly snapped a tiny crystal into a similarly tiny slot. "This will enhance your coverage so you can contact the ship from shore. You'll be able to contact the shuttle in case of an emergency."

With a smile he handed the device back to Felix and did the same for Sherry. "Thank you, Sir, Ma'am. If you'll follow me, I'll direct you to the shuttle."

Felix nodded politely and indicated the technician to precede him. "Thank you, Li." He'd picked up the name off the guy's uniform patch.

They cycled through the airlock. Even though the pressure was equalized, the cycling process was strictly practiced. No amount of safety precautions was too much when it came to the possible exposure to the hard vacuum of space. Felix could readily appreciate the cautions, having given vacuum breathing a brief try. That was one thing he never wanted to experience again.

Even though this was the small shuttle bay at the front of the ship. It still seemed quite spacious as ship spaces went. The generous ten-foot ceiling clearance in most of the ship was still quite confining when that was almost all you ever saw for years on end. This room felt almost cavernous. The space was heated enough to take the worst of the chill out. Any colder, Felix thought, and he'd be able to see his breath.

It's a lot colder out there, Sherry commented.

Felix glanced at the clamshell doors. *You're right about that, Sweet.*

They mounted the boarding ramp and entered the shuttle. This was a very small version of the two monsters back in the main shuttle bay. She had three slightly larger sisters back there as well. They were designed for special assignments and to supplement lifting capacity.

The sleek, mirror finish gave the craft a look almost like a massive and eager drop of mercury. Once inside, and everything ready, the ramp would roll up and fold into the side of the ship. From the outside, there'd be little to indicate a door was ever there.

Like any other spacecraft in the emptiness of space, this one would maneuver somewhat like a graceful brick. After all, there was no air to bite into. Once they were in atmosphere however, these craft were suddenly very agile creatures, eager to soar.

Since this was the captain's personal shuttle, the cabin felt more like a small, comfortable lounge. There was plenty of room to get up and move about. The bulkheads and ceiling could, on a whim, become transparent, giving the passengers a full sweep of view from one side of the craft, to the other. This made for a very exhilarating experience.

Their carryons were already clipped firmly to the back, base of their seats. Clearly, seating assignments had been taken care of ahead of time. Felix found his on the forward port seat. Sherry sat on the port seat next to him. Lyuba sat next to Sherry and of course, Devin parked next to Lyuba.

After a few minutes, a preflight crew person boarded with carry-ons for the rest of their party. She murmured polite greeting before checking ID tags and deftly snapping them to their appropriate seats. She gave them a fleeting smile and hurried to carry out her next task.

Laughter could be heard echoing in the small cavern outside the craft. Pastor Brad and family trooped up the ramp and searched out their seats.

"Good morning, everyone." Brad was pleasant, if a little strained. It turned out Brad was across from Devin, while Jodi and Evan were across from Lyuba. Jodi whispered in Lyuba's ear. Lyuba grinned and mentally passed the comment on to Sherry and then Devin.

Pastor Brad looked around and then at Jodi. "Did you tell them?" he whispered.

Jodi grinned and nodded her head. Brad rolled his eyes and looked persecuted. Apparently, Brad was a bit claustrophobic. He hated shuttle rides.

More laughter came up the ramp. Tolya and Tanya followed, the leftovers of mirth still on their faces. The pilot came right behind.

Tolya patted his shoulder. "She'll get over it." The pilot grinned and headed forward.

There was a restraint system for each seat, but they were currently being ignored. They were rudimentary leftovers from the days of micro-gravity space flight. With variable gravity generators and inertial damping, the restraints were not as essential.

On a shuttle however, these technologies were limited in power. During reentry, they'd be required to hook them up. It was during reentry that they'd feel the greatest buffeting.

Tolya suddenly remembered something. "Oh, Felix. One of the other small shuttles will be following us down. Tahnie has a small security detail, about nine. Then, Daniela and a small team of specialists including genetics people need to check on things we eat.

"Also. We must have Frank along to keep a record. And...well, it didn't seem right to leave Emily out. She'll be a help for Dannie."

Felix grinned. "And Vince. Won't he miss Dannie?"

Tolya smiled. "Perhaps, but he's going to have his hands more than full coordinating and organizing the shore rotation. Everyone wants some dirt side time. So, there's going to be a continuous rotation of people between *Destiny* and the festivities."

Felix looked grim. "I don't envy him in the least."

Tolya chuckled. "Neither do I. I feel just a little bit guilty leaving him the chore, but..." he heaved a sigh, "...a man's gotta do what a man's gotta do."

Felix gave Tolya a sidelong look and then shook his head, grinning at the theatrics.

* * * *

David F. Snider

TUE 10.26.2094-Earth / TRN 33.04.6998-Aambü
Geo-sync parking orbit; Aambü, Gem System
CS1 Bound for Welcome Island; Aambü, 2345 Hrs / 0565 Slashes

Felix was eavesdropping through his COMM link to the pre-launch chatter, so he and Sherry were ready for the beginning of their flight. *Felix, we haven't called AgradUtya.*

Felix looked up, startled. *You're right. Let's do it now before they take off. We have...*

I know, three minutes. She grinned at him.

AgradUtya. It's Felix. Can you hear me? A couple of tries got their host's attention. *Yes, Felix. I hear you just fine.*

Felix passed his message; *we've boarded our shuttle and are beginning our trip. You can expect to see us in...about a half slash.*

AgradUtya was pleased. *Very good Felix. We await your arrival. Safe journey.*

Felix projected pleasure. *I look forward to our meeting. Until then...*he released his concentration.

Just then the lights in the ceiling went from normal hues to soft amber. "Attention, ladies and gentlemen. They are depressurizing the hanger at this time. We'll be lifting in about a minute.

Felix flexed his patched hand towards the wall to his right. An arc of the cabin flickered to transparent and they could see the insides of the shuttle bay. The lights out there had gone to flashing amber. He could hear, in his mind, the friendly voice warning of imminent depressurization.

He shook his head and blanked out that memory. Sherry squeezed his hand, knowing his discomfort. The clamshell doors slowly began to retract, exposing the forward part of *Destiny's* drive frame. The massive EM scoops loomed above the entrance. If you looked carefully, you could make out the DCPA's mounted in the frame, looking lethal. Felix reminded himself that *Destiny* knew her own fledglings.

There was the tiniest of lurches and the shuttle bay slowly spun around them as the pilot rotated the shuttle to point out the door. After a moment they started moving forward.

The doorway passed overhead and, looking back, they could see the huge brightly lit cavern already closing. Their home was falling behind quickly.

Sherry nudged Felix and nodded towards Brad. *I don't think you're helping very much, honey.*

Pastor Brad was wide eyed. He was doing masterfully well, considering the view. *I'm sorry. I didn't think.*

Felix waved the transparency off. They were, again, in a nice, comfortable lounge, no sense of motion left. Brad gave a profound look of gratitude without a word.

At the extreme opposite end of the ship, another small shuttle exited the aft shuttle bay and followed the captain's shuttle down to the planet.

ARRIVAL — 7

TUE 10.26.2094-Earth / TRN 33.04.6998-Aambü
Welcome Island; Aambü, Gem System, 0030 Hrs / 0630 Slashes

Madhura was bored. Everyone was waiting for the new people from the sky to make their appearance. She remembered the strange little artificial birds that flew so swiftly across the sky; and the one that swept right over her, waving at her with its tiny wings.

She wondered why it was taking so long for them to arrive. Those...machines, father called them, had been unnaturally fast.

Madhura. You're kicking up dust. Do you want to dirty the decorations so quickly?

Madhura looked guiltily down at the scuffing she'd been doing with her feet. She looked up at Ambi. Her mother was shuffling towards her. *Apologies, Ambi, when will the new people come? It takes so long.*

Her mother looked fondly at her daughter. *Madhura, my favorite, Adhiraj says their ship is parked up in the great ring. It takes a very long time to travel from the ring to the ocean, I should think.*

Madhura considered this information. Just the thought of someone living in a home that traveled with the great ring and the moons was awesome. *Ambi. You're right, of course. I grow impatient.*

Her mother colored her response with rich humor. *Of course you're impatient. This is a moment of great expectation and mystery. I'd be surprised if even the grownups were not just a little impatient.*

A ripple of excitement raced through the people scattered along the beach. AgradUtya had just passed the word. The first landing craft had started its journey.

Madhura gazed expectantly into the sky at the great ring. Even in the early morning the tiny bright spot that was their home was visible, a glittering jewel in the ring.

She waited and watched. Her jittery patience was finally rewarded by another bright light. It was just a flash, but she knew it had to be them.

Periodically, there was another flicker as the tiny object slowly traversed the arc of the great ring. *Ambi. Why do they have to go all the way to the sunrise to come here instead of coming straight down?*

Avuka, her father, came to her mother's rescue. *The craft they ride in is like a great bird. It must catch the wind. They're not yet familiar with the wind so they must hunt for the right one. See? Now they are turning to come back.*

Madhura gazed into the dawning light to the East. The light of the strange craft had suddenly flared brightly as if it had caught on fire. Now anyone could see the progress of these strange people.

Madhura was afraid for them. What if they burned up? What if they all died before they ever got here?

Another flash of light came from much higher in the sky. It looked like the second craft was also on its way. Madhura wondered why there were just two coming. The ones she'd seen that time several turns ago had been sort of small to have more than one person in it. She wondered how uncomfortable it would be to have several people in one.

The fiery trail suddenly winked out, leaving a single glowing dot that was now hurtling hard across the sky.

The craft did look a little like a bird as it arced over the island, still incredibly high. Sharply defined wisps of cloud shot out from around the craft; three distinct bursts that looked almost like the heads of fishing darts.

They were headed towards the sunset now. Suddenly three claps of thunder rolled across the lagoon, shaking her hearing organs to the bone. It felt really odd.

Little dart shaped clouds lingered high in the air, slowly spreading as the prevailing winds stirred them about. Madhura looked to the West, high. She couldn't see them. Then her gaze dropped lower and there they were, a larger spot in the sky slowly growing as it headed their way.

The appearance of the craft was a surprise for all the time the small crowd had watched its flight. It was indeed shaped a bit like a flying creature, but it was huge, and very bright. As it slowly sailed, like a wind driven cloud over the crowd and out over the lagoon, some swore they could see the ground and the crowd watching reflected on the bottom of the craft.

There was an open place prepared for the craft to land. Madhura could see the sky and the clouds clearly glinting off the top of the strange thing as it settled low over the lagoon, turning in place and slowly scooting forward. It extended graceful looking legs with flat surfaces that gently touched the hard packed sand. Slowly the craft settled and became still.

Another triple blast of thunder caused the crowd to look up quickly. The second craft was making its final turn. Agira had finally broken the horizon and was halfway out of the water.

A message quickly rippled through the crowd. *Don't touch the craft. It's hot enough to burn and cause damage to skin. It must cool.*

As the second craft sailed over their heads and rotated over the lagoon, Madhura glanced about, realizing she was not going to be able to see if she stayed where she was. She made her choice and, just as Ambi turned to look at her, vanished from sight.

Not again. Ambi looked around for her mate. *She's gone again. I think she's going for a closer look.*

Her mate signed humor. *She'll be fine, you'll see.*

* * * *

TUE 10.26.2094-Earth / TRN 33.04.6998-Aambü
Welcome Island; Aambü, Gem System, 0120 Hrs / 0700 Slashes

The door unsealed with a sound like a giant, vacuum-packed drink being opened. The smell of a sea breeze came through the seal and permeated the cabin. Everyone just sat, breathing it in.

Sherry looked over at Tolya. "Oh my! I haven't been near the ocean in so long. Let me at it!"

Hold on sweetheart. Let's let the hull cool first. Sherry looked mildly rebellious. Felix grinned. He could feel her barely contained eagerness to be out, playing along the shore.

Soon enough, everyone got up and stretched. The door finished opening and the ramp extended.

Tolya signaled Felix to join him. Tanya and Sherry came right behind followed by Lyuba, Devin and the Hill family.

As they started down from the top of the ramp they were surprised to find a reasonably large assembly of the locals fanned out across the beach and up the path.

Felix saw AgradUtya approach through the crowd, which quickly parted like the wake behind an ocean liner. Another male was with him. He wore some decorations hanging from small straps of some kind of leather. There was clearly a sense of authority about him. If the parting crowd hadn't been enough, his regal bearing would have suggested royalty of some kind.

As the second shuttle settled behind the first, AgradUtya stopped a respectful distance from the bottom of the ramp as the guests from the stars finished their descent. *Felix, welcome. It is good to see you face to face.*

Felix stepped forward to greet his counterpart.

A formal greeting goes like this: Place your right hand on my left shoulder and your left hand to the side of my head. He demonstrated and Felix copied smoothly.

There was a slapping sound all across the beach. Felix noticed the Aambüka were slapping the intake flaps of their swimming organs, causing the sound. It appeared to be a form of applause.

Felix asked, *we never got to protocol. What's next?*

Humor colored AgradUtya's response. *Protocol has as many variations as there are clans. Simply introduce your...ah, chief. That would be Tolya.*

By the way, to address a crowd, you must expand your sending to cover a wider range of individuals. It will take some practice. Go ahead, try it.

Felix felt like a child about to give his first class presentation. He warned Tolya as he took his arm. "OK. I have to introduce you. I've never addressed a crowd using mind speak so it ought to be very interesting."

Tolya grinned. "Good luck with that."

Felix rolled his eyes. Sherry encouraged him, offering her strength.

AgradUtya. I would like to introduce to you my Adhiraj, Governor Anatoli Chernov.

Sherry had taken Tanya's hand and Felix turned to wave a hand in her direction. *This is his bond mate, Tanya Chernov. I regret they do not possess the gift of mind speak.*

AgradUtya colored his personal response with approval. *Well done. I believe most heard you. Now I shall reply formally.*

AgradUtya turned to include the clan chief and chief of chiefs. *Governor, Adhiraj Anatoli Chernov, Lady Tanya Chernov, AgradUtya Felix Hernandez, AgradUtya Sherry Hernandez. I proudly present to you, AgraVadin Adhiraj.*

First Speaker, leader of the unified clans of Aambü stepped forward. *Governor, Adhiraj Anatoli Chernov and Lady Tanya Chernov, welcome. AgradUtya Felix Hernandez and AgradUtya Sherry Hernandez, I am pleased to finally meet you.*

He stepped closer and Felix realized a physical exchange like the one he and AgradUtya had had was expected. He instructed Tolya as Sherry did Tanya.

The physical greeting went smoothly enough. AgraVadin Adhiraj then approached Felix. He was ready and performed the ritual. Sherry followed.

More slapping sounds came from the crowd, louder and more enthusiastic than before.

* * * *

Madhura crept quietly from group to group. As long as she didn't bump into people, she could go unseen for quite a long time.

It surprised her that Ambi hadn't called out. She was nervous about sneaking past Agravadin Adhiraj, but his august presence was busy getting all that attention from the Star People.

These people from the stars were strange indeed. They had naked skin, covered by artificial coverings. The only pelt they had was a patch on their heads. Some had little bits of pelt on their...oh, those faces!

They were flat. She wondered how they could breath with those tiny beaks. She knew they couldn't breath the water.

She could tell that the males tended to be taller. The female, at least the one called 'Lady Tanya,' whatever a lady was, was only a little shorter than her mate. Their ambassador and his mate were almost the same height.

She could tell that of the eight, no, nine individuals, only four were truly awakened.

Madhura's attention was drawn to a smaller person still part way on the ramp. This one was somehow different from the rest. The pelt was quite long and blew about, lazily in the breeze. She had the sense that this one was also a female. She was standing at the base of the ramp, a male standing next to her.

What got Madhura's attention was that of the four mind speakers in the group, this one was somehow brighter. She sensed that the two ambassadors were very strong. They had a strong bond that would have made them stand out in the crowd even if they weren't alien, but this one had a strength that shone like a large cluster of glow globes.

Madhura concentrated on getting up next to the female on the ramp. She had to see what made her so different. It never occurred to her to take into account what abilities the visitors might possess.

* * * *

While the clan chief introduced another functionary, Sherry sensed something odd. She could feel someone who was being sneaky. She was about to let out a cry of dismay when she got the distinct sense this was more curiosity than aggression. *Lyuba, I think someone's sneaking up on you. I can't see them, but someone is almost to the ramp on your right.* Felix glanced over, as did Tolya.

AgradUtya sensed a sudden shift in the attentions of the visitors. He was worried about the loss of attention they were displaying. Adhiraj was just finishing his introduction and looking slightly confused at his guest's inattention. AgradUtya couldn't afford some accidental insult to happen now. He was wondering how to fix the problem when Lyuba struck.

A loud, ear splitting squeal, up on the edge of the ultrasonic range pierced the peaceful scene. Suddenly an adolescent Aambüka female could be seen flailing about in mid air, just out of reach of Lyuba's face.

There was stone silence across the beach, save for the waves and Madhura's keening protests. Lyuba slowly moved the young girl across in front of her, keeping her just out of arms reach. She had no idea what damage those fingers could do. *Stop it! I'll put you down if you stop.*

Adhiraj had started towards the tableau. Madhura stopped struggling and hung limply in the air.

Lyuba kept her promise and slowly let the girl down. *I won't hurt you. Stay with me and I'll see you don't get in trouble.*

Madhura darted a nervous look at her captor. She could sense the human's gentle hold on her, but she was free to stand.

AgraVadin Adhiraj reached the ramp as Tolya and the rest of the humans cleared a path for him. *What is this disgraceful interruption!*

Madhura knelt to the floor of the ramp trembling and Lyuba stepped forward. *Adhiraj. Please.*

Agravadin looked at the young human female. He could see in that instant; this was the one AgradUtya had so feared not so very long ago.

He stopped where he stood, waiting to see what she would do.

Lyuba reached down with her hand and touched the trembling girl on the shoulder. Madhura looked up at her. Lyuba offered her hand and after a moment's hesitation Madhura took it with her own web hand and Lyuba gently pulled her up, fully releasing any hold she had kept earlier.

AgraVadin Adhiraj. This one has done no harm. I was surprised and took hold of her because she was sneaking up close, but no harm was done.

She turned to Madhura. *I am Lyuba. What are you called?*

Madhura, trembling, could only play along. *I am called Madhura.*

Lyuba smiled and turned back to face Adhiraj. *I've just met Madhura and I'd like to get to know her. Would that be acceptable?*

AgraVadin was perplexed. The youngster clearly needed discipline, but this human youngster, the daughter of their Adhiraj, no less, was protecting her with offers of genuine companionship.

He considered quickly. To continue his course would be to cause a greater stir that could be very damaging. To let them 'visit?' would be a peaceful solution that could preserve the friendship between the races that was beginning to bud.

Young one. To honor your kindness and since there truly has been no harm done, I would be delighted to allow Madhura to visit with you for now. We shall see what her parents have to say.

As he turned to see about repairing the sense of ceremony that had just been shattered, the young girl's parents shuffled forward and prostrated themselves. *Adhiraj, this turn, our profound shame is displayed before the clan.*

He wanted to make sure they didn't forget the fact. Then it occurred to him that this whole situation could very well work to everyone's advantage. *Rise, AbhivazMaha;* he expanded his thoughts for all to hear.   *Let it be known that this minor incident was simply a misunderstanding. No harm has been done. In deed, the first childhood friendship between our races has taken its first steps.*

After several moments of confused silence, the odd slapping sound that signified applause began to sound across the beach.

Lyuba was trembling. She'd stood up to the chief of these people. She'd stuck her neck out for this 'girl' who had tried to sneak up on her. She realized they could have messed things up.

She regarded her new friend. *So, Madhura, let's try this again, this time without all the drama. My name is Lyuba, daughter of Governor and Lady Chernov. You are Madhura. That's all?*

Madhura was very confused. This girl was being nice to her even though she had embarrassed her in front of everyone. And to think she was the daughter of their Adhiraj, an alien princess, while she was just the daughter of the Festival Master.

I am Madhura. I am the daughter of the Festival Master and his mate. They are the ones who came before Adhiraj because...of me. Again, I have disgraced them.

Lyuba watched the proceedings while listening to Madhura. *You may have embarrassed them, but I doubt you truly disgraced them. Are they responsible for the decorations I see?*

Madhura waved her arms slightly in what could have been a shrug. *Yes, they plan all the festival events. In spite of my crazy antics, they are the favorites of Adhiraj.* Lyuba sensed pride in that.

Hey Lyuba. You need to pay attention. Sherry had a slightly stern tone of voice, but there was a giggle trying desperately to stay tucked away for later.

I'm sorry, Sherry. We were talking.

Sherry pointed towards the Hill family. *Pastor and Jodi are about to be introduced. Why don't you and Devin grab their hands or arms and get them ready?*

Lyuba nodded. *Sure.*

She turned to Madhura. *Come. Let me introduce you to some friends of ours. They're really nice.*

Lyuba turned and headed for Jodi. *Hey Devin. Come help me with Pastor. They need to hear what's going on.*

She grabbed Devin's arm. *Hey. Meet my new friend.*

She waved Madhura to come to her side. *Madhura, this is a very close friend. His name is Devin. He's going to help me with our friends here.* She indicated the Hill's. "Hi, Pastor. I'm sorry you've been kinda out of the loop. Sherry asked us to catch you up and get you ready for a formal introduction."

Brad shrugged. "It's been quite a show. Who's the creature next to you?"

Lyuba blushed. "I think we both got carried away a little." She turned to Devin. *Devin if you would take hold of Pastor's arm, I'll do the same for Jodi. Then we can catch up.*

She turned to Jodi and offered her hand. Jodi knew the drill and turned an elbow towards her. "This is exciting."

Lyuba grinned. She took Jodi's elbow and projected. *Jodi. Can you hear me?*

Jodi started. She was still not used to this kind of conversation. "Yeah. I hear you just fine."

Pastor Brad? He looked at Lyuba in surprise before realizing he was hearing through Devin. "Yes, I hear you quite nicely."

Lyuba grinned. She waved her free hand in her new friend's direction. *Jodi, Pastor. I want you to meet my new friend, Madhura.*

Jodi and Brad murmured greetings. Madhura made a series of gestures that must have been something like a curtsey or bow. *Madhura, this is Pastor Brad and his wife...ah...mate, Jodi. The youngster is their son, Evan.*

Madhura looked up at Lyuba. *Pastor?*

Lyuba grinned. *I'm sorry. Pastor is a title. He is our spiritual advisor, the one who helps us to grow closer to our Maker.*

Madhura seemed impressed. *I'm happy for you. It's always good to have a spiritual advisor about. Our spiritual advisor is here. I bet you get to meet him soon.*

Brad smiled. This young female was cute in her own way. "Tell her I'm most happy to meet her."

Lyuba grinned. "She can hear your speech through me as long as we're touching."

Madhura added. *I am honored to meet you...Pastor Brad, and your mate...*she turned to Jodi...*Jodi?*

Jodi smiled. "It's nice to meet you. I'd like to meet your parents some time."

Lyuba could feel Madhura's swell of pride. *I'll tell them.*

Just then, Sherry called for them to bring Brad and Jodi forward. Devin and Lyuba escorted Brad and Jodi to the front of the group. Madhura stuck like glue to Lyuba's side.

The greetings were formal and cordial. Adhiraj introduced his spiritual advisor. With the assistance of the four human mind speakers, the conversation went surprisingly well. They decided to set aside time in the very near future so the two spiritual leaders could compare notes and learn from each other.

The human guests were invited to join their counterparts under the large well-appointed pavilions. These were arrayed along the beach so close to the shore that half of each was carefully erected in the wet sand in the gentle surf and the other half over slightly dryer sand. Careful work had been done to divert the run in from the surf. Just enough water trickled in to keep the sand moist.

On the surf side of the pavilion, several carefully sculpted mounds of moist sand were arrayed before low tables. Opposite the tables, small couches of woven plant matter were mounded gracefully over dryer sand in deference to the humans who had dryer needs.

The locals flopped casually on the wet mounds looking quite blissfully comfortable.

Tolya and Tanya took their example and attempted to get settled on the mat covered mounds. They were surprised to find them reasonably comfortable.

"Dad. Could I go meet Madhura's parents? I want to get their permission for her to sit with us."

Tolya looked at the two youths, one his own, and one from a race that had never seen Earth. "Princess. I hope you know that little display was a bit over the top, yes?"

"I know Poppa, but she kinda took me by surprise."

Tolya sighed. "Fortunately, all is well. The result couldn't have worked out better...OK, but try to stay out of trouble."

He turned to Madhura who was looking downcast at the edge of the pavilion cover. He took a chance and motioned her over. "Lyuba." He held out his arm. Lyuba took his arm so Madhura could hear his thoughts. "Madhura?"

She signed yes.

"Don't look so downcast. I presume you meant no harm. Next time, the direct approach would be less embarrassing."

The young Aambüka female was in awe of being addressed personally by the human Adhiraj.

Thank you Adhiraj Chernov. You are very kind.

Tolya grinned. "Have fun. Come back soon." He turned to converse with AgraVadin.

ARRIVAL — 8

TUE 10.26.2094-Earth / TRN 33.04.6998-Aambü
Welcome Island; Aambü, 0200 Hrs / 0740 Slashes

AbhivazMaha and his mate were moving from pavilion to pavilion checking that all was well. Their close brush with disgrace was ever in the back of their minds. Ambi AbhivazMaha stopped dead in her tracks as she saw Madhura and her new friend trudging purposefully towards her. In the bright morning light, the young human's glow was clearly visible. The brilliant glow of her features was the brightest she'd ever seen.

Madhura's father, Avuka AbhivazMaha stepped up next to his mate as the two young people approached. They stopped before them in awkward silence. Then Lyuba addressed them. She tried miserably to imitate the motions Madhura had offered to Brad and Jodi. She finally gave up and did her best curtsey.

Ambi recognized the young human's attempt at the old polite greeting sign and warmed slightly to the child. *Ambi AbhivazMaha. I am called Lyuba. I wish to apologize for the unfortunate public display. I reacted in surprise, but I should have shown more restraint.*

Avuka AbhivazMaha tried to hide the humorous overtones that threatened to ruin such a serious moment. Ambi gave him a look. Then she turned to regard the youngsters.

The human female was clearly very powerful. It occurred to her it was possible the child wasn't fully aware of the potential she held within. *Lyuba...such a pleasant name. Thank you for your kindness toward our daughter. She would have deserved the discipline Adhiraj felt appropriate. We understand that Madhura took you by surprise.*

Avuka could no longer suppress his own curiosity. *Forgive my curiosity, child. How did you manage to spot our little pest? She's clever at staying unseen.*

Lyuba grinned. This, she noticed, seemed to leave these people with a sense of unease that puzzled her. *In truth, I didn't see her. My close friend...she's the mate of our ambassador...Sherry is a strong Empath. She sensed Madhura's presence and her approximate location and warned me. I...sort of scooped the area until I found her. Then I just picked her up.*

Avuka was impressed. *Ah! Teamwork. This I constantly emphasize to my workers. You say your AgradUtya's mate is an Empath?*

Lyuba nodded before realizing that might not mean anything to these people. *Yes, she not only receives, she broadcasts as well. She can also heal.*

The adults exchanged looks. Ambi refocused the conversation. *I think that's enough interrogation for now. I thank you for your kind treatment of Madhura.*

Assuming the conversation was ended, she turned to go when Lyuba spoke again. *Forgive me. I almost forgot the other reason for seeking you out.*

Ambi turned and inclined her head in a posture clearly suggesting, 'I'm listening.'

I would ask if Madhura might sit with me at our pavilion.

Avuka stood still, surprise was clear.

Ambi was startled. *Lyuba. Again you show kindness. It would be an honor for Madhura to sit at your side. Who are we to deny such an honor? Yet, you honor us by seeking permission.*

She looked over at her mate and then ended simply. *Madhura. You may go with our blessing, but please, please. Try to stay out of trouble.*

* * * *

By the time Lyuba and Madhura returned to the main pavilion, Dr. Jacobs and her team had arrived and were deep in discussion with Tolya and Tanya. Lyuba saw Frank and Emily seated on a matted sand mound, chatting with Felix and Sherry, getting introduced to some of the functionaries assigned to their pavilion.

Four of Tanya's nine security people were back at the shuttles, keeping the curious out. The team leader and the other security folk were waiting patiently at the edge of the pavilion, feeling a bit like extra set of thumbs.

Lyuba went around introducing Madhura to everyone. The security guys brightened a little at the sight of Lyuba running around with a native in tow. Perhaps they could take up escort duties to protect the Governors daughter, but no, the two were becoming fast friends and there was no hint any trouble would be in the offing.

Tanya took pity and called the Lieutenant to her side. "Lieutenant. I appreciate your vigilance, but I think everything is under control. Why don't you work out a rotation for the shuttle detail and have your people take turns at the festivities? When we hear from Dr. Jacobs we'll know whether it's safe to eat or not."

The lieutenant saluted crisply. "Thank you ma'am. It'll be good to relax a little and just see the sights."

Tanya smiled and nodded. "Keep in touch. If I need your expertise, I'll call you."

"Thank you, Ma'am." He turned to pass the word. "Oh, and Lieutenant." He turned back. "Why don't you tell the shuttle crews to close up and come on over? That way, the temptation will be reduced. You can step down from two to one person per ship; make the duty turns shorter."

The lieutenant grinned as he saluted again. "Yes, Ma'am. I'm sure you'll be more popular than ever with that one."

Tanya grinned. "I wouldn't be surprised, Lieutenant. Carry on."

Dannie heard Lyuba laughing and turned to see what she was up to. Her eyebrows arched as she watched her carousing with a native youth at the other end of the pavilion. She looked over at Sherry. "Is that the one?"

Sherry grinned. "Yes, they appear to get along well."

Dannie grinned, making a beeline for the youngsters. "Lyuba."

Lyuba saw Dr. Jacobs approaching. She smiled and waved.

Daniela slowed and watched the young Aambüka female as she turned to look. "Who's your friend?"

Lyuba grinned. "This is Madhura. We just met about an hour ago. Her Dad and Mom are the people who organized the festivities." Daniela looked around appreciatively. "Tell her that..."

Lyuba put up her hands in a time-out gesture. "If you put your hand on my arm, she'll be able to hear what you say through me."

Daniela remembered the whole convoluted procedure she'd experienced before.

She smiled and took Lyuba's arm. "Madhura. I'm pleased to meet you. Please tell your parents the decorations are wonderful."

Again, Lyuba sensed Madhura's pride. *Thank you Doctor Jacobs...*she looked at Lyuba. *Doctor?*

Lyuba explained. *'Doctor' is another title or position. You might call her our chief healer.*

Madhura reflected amazement and deep respect. *Healer Jacobs. I am honored to meet you. I'll tell my parents of your pleasure at their work.*

Daniela smiled sweetly and turned to Lyuba.

"Lyuba, honey. Do you think I could get her cooperation in getting a sample? We need to get busy and figure out what we can eat down here."

Lyuba shrugged. "I don't know. We could ask." *Madhura. The healer needs a special kind of help. You know we come from another star, far away from yours, right?"*

Madhura signed her understanding and Lyuba continued. *We've learned from long study that different species are made up of tiny things.*

Madhura showed her excitement. *We talked about that in our lessons. My teacher said there are tiny objects, so small that we cannot see them. They're like pieces of sand that make a rock.*

Daniela enjoyed the enthusiasm. "We call those tiny things, cells. We discovered that the cells are made of even smaller things. Some of them have just one purpose. That's to tell the cells what kind of cells to be. I'd like to look at some of your cells; just a few."

Madhura wasn't clear how that was done.

Lyuba had an idea. "Dr. Jacobs? I could show her so she'd feel better about it."

Daniela grinned. "Now why didn't I think of that? OK. Let me get the equipment over here. Let's use that small table over there."

They gathered around the low table, getting comfortable on the covered sand mounds. Daniela pinched her COMM tab. "Phil. Bring the genoscope over here to the South end of the main pavilion. I have a volunteer."

"Yes...well, hurry before she changes her mind."

"Great. Thank you."

A few moments later Phil and a couple of other team members came into the pavilion and spotted them. They brought the equipment over and started setting it up on the little table.

Lyuba pulled a single strand of hair. Madhura watched with interest. *Your pelt has a strange shape and texture. It's long and fine.*

One of the techs handed Lyuba a small case. *We don't really have pelts as you think of them.*

She popped the case open and dropped the strand of hair inside. *We call it hair. It's made of similar material to a pelt, but it has a very different shape.*

She closed it up and handed it back to the tech. The tech handed her another small case. "Honey, can you give me a mouth smear?"

Lyuba nodded and accepted a simple cotton swab. Some things just couldn't be improved upon.

Madhura was fascinated by the procedure.

Lyuba wiped the cotton swab around the inside of her mouth, dropping it into the second case.

What did you just do?

After closing the case, she handed it to the tech as well. *Well, our cells grow, reproduce and die. I believe it is the same with your people. The dead cells from the flesh inside my mouth eventually wash down and out normally. I just wiped a few of them on the swab, so the technician can study them.*

So, what are they going to do?

Lyuba pointed at the odd looking device that squatted on the table. *The samples I just gave them are going to go into that machine. It will study the samples and figure out what they're made of. You'll be able to see the images on this screen.* She gently tapped the display surface that glowed a gray-blue.

After a while, the screen flickered and images began to resolve. They were looking at the strand of hair. Madhura watched in amazement as the image of the hair grew and grew. Soon, only the hair's cellular structure was visible.

Madhura, look. My hair...and your pelt are made up of cells just like other parts of the body. Watch...

Madhura wouldn't have known she was still looking at the hair if she hadn't been watching what they were doing very closely.

A set of green lines framed one of the cells. The cell grew till it filled the screen. The green lines did a little dance as if trying to find something. They bracketed the nucleus of the cell, which zoomed to dominate the screen. *See? We're looking at the inside of one cell in that strand of hair.*

The lines danced some more. Soon a tiny strand was selected and the zooming process repeated. What they were looking at was a strand of DNA.

The strand grew till it was clearly the familiar twin helix shape. A portion of the strand was separated from the rest for analysis.

The computer began looking at the various sections of the strand. A portion would highlight and a coded label in tiny print would appear to the side of the image. After a few moments the entire segment had been scanned and the side of the screen was crammed with coded labels.

A larger tag came up. 'Human head hair; Lyubova Anastasia Chernov, Female, Age 14 years.'

Lyuba read the display quietly so her friend would know what the print said.

Madhura made a little clucking sound with her tongue on the inside of her mouth. *It's amazing.*

Lyuba grinned. *I know.*

Phil cleared the screen, pulled the sample out and placed the next sample inside. The process repeated and Lyuba's cheek cells were positively identified. He reset everything and then turned expectantly to face his two-person audience.

Daniela leaned over. "Lyuba. Do you think your friend would be willing to do the same thing?"

Lyuba shrugged and turned to Madhura. *Madhura. Would you like to see what your cells look like on the machine?*

Madhura looked doubtful. This was stranger than anything she'd imagined in her wildest dreams.

Lyuba had done it and it didn't hurt her. *I guess it would be all right. What do I do?*

Lyuba asked Phil. "May I have a couple of those sample cases?"

"Sure thing." He grinned as he produced them.

Lyuba took them and turned to Madhura. *OK. We need you to take a small bit of your pelt and put it in one of these containers.*

Madhura was hesitant. She looked about as if lost. Then she looked at Lyuba.

What's the matter? Lyuba's new friend ducked her head in a pose that looked too much like embarrassment. *Does this embarrass you?*

Madhura signed yes.

Lyuba looked around. "Dr. Jacob? Is there a smock or small sheet or blanket we can borrow?" Daniela looked at the girls, truly puzzled. Then she looked about. "Nancy."

A young team member approached. "Did we bring any sheets, blankets, anything like that?"

Nancy thought for a moment. Then she brightened. "Yes, we thought we might need to set up a tent."

"Very good. Please fetch a sheet for us?"

Nancy smiled. "Sure. I'll be right back" She hustled off.

Lyuba looked at Madhura. *Umm, how about the mouth thing? Is that OK?*

Madhura signed yes.

Good. Just do what I did. She handed over one of the little cases along with a couple of cotton swabs.

Madhura took a swab and, lifting her proboscis, awkwardly inserted it in her mouth. She swished it about and then dropped it into the case.

Lyuba snapped it shut and handed it to Phil.

Nancy came up and presented a sizable sheet. Lyuba took it with a big thank you.

Now. Madhura. How can I help you with this?

Madhura was a bit hesitant. She glanced about and pointed out by the surf.

Lyuba shrugged and motioned for her to lead the way. "We'll be right back," she said absently.

They stepped out and stood near the surf. *Lyuba. I'm sorry for making this difficult. We don't pick at our pelts in public. It's either a matter of personal cleansing, or for adults; it's part of the mating rituals.*

Lyuba blushed. *I'm sorry. I had no idea.*

Madhura did her little shrug with her arms. *How could you possibly know? Just hold the cloth up so no one will see.*

Lyuba carefully did as she was asked.

Uh...Lyuba. You too...don't look?

Lyuba blushed again and turned her head. *Sorry.*

After a moment, Lyuba heard the snap of the sample case being closed. *I'm done. Thank you.*

Lyuba quickly folded the sheet and they returned to the pavilion. She handed the case to Phil.

The look of curiosity on the doctor's face was impossible to miss. Lyuba smiled, "I'll explain later."

Daniela glanced at their guest and back. "OK."

Phil placed the sample of pelt in the machine, tapped in a few settings and swept the run icon.

After a few flickers, the screen focused on a short strand of hair. It was very fine, almost like the hair on a short-haired cat or dog.

The machine centered things and began zooming in. Soon they could see at the cellular level. The cells on this hair were somewhat different in shape from the one from Lyuba's head, but they were clearly basic cells.

The green lines moved around as if uncertain. Finally the computer determined the boundaries of one prominent cell. The green lines bracketed it and the cell zoomed up to dominate the screen. It was different, yet similar. There were two nuclei, one primary and one smaller secondary.

The dance of the green lines started to look a bit frantic. Finally, the larger nucleus was selected.

The zooming process continued until the nucleus was all they could see.

Lyuba remembered her biology from a few months back. The shapes inside the nucleus were similar. The computer zoomed out slightly so that the outer wall of the nucleus could be seen along with the inside of the cell. The green lines did a complicated dance. Finally they bracketed a promising strand.

Again, the computer zoomed in on the strand., drawing closer and closer until the unmistakable double helix shape came into view. Something looked different, but Lyuba couldn't figure out what.

The computer went quiet. About the time Lyuba thought it had decided to crash, the various segments along the ladder began to highlight. A tiny coded label appeared to the right. The computer was going very slowly. It seemed to take forever.

Lyuba noticed that some of the segments had been skipped and little question marks hung in place of the usual coded label.

Finally the 'run complete' signal sounded. She waited for the final description, her curiosity mounting.

The label finally began to fill in. It almost seemed like the computer wasn't sure what to call the sample.

Species: unknown, cell classification: hair, origin: unknown, gender: possibly Female, Age: unknown.

Special note: If sample is not contaminated, speculation suggests the sample is not of human origin. Sample does not match any known species of animal. Sample, a hair, appears to be structured for efficient existence in deep water. Sample has excellent thermal insulating properties.

Madhura pointed at all the text. *This is writing?*

Lyuba smiled. *Yes, Our machines communicate with us using writing, pictures, even voice.*

Madhura looked up at Lyuba. *We have writing; lots of very old writing too.*

Phil saved the information and then cleared it. He started on the cheek sample.

These results were similar. The computer was even more perplexed. The sample was strange enough that it couldn't even hazard a guess as to the classification of cell. It didn't know where the cell came from.

Phil mumbled something about informing the computer of the source of the sample. "...not that that would help."

He decided to try one more thing. He set up a comparison run between the two types of hair. The results were interesting. By correlating the differences and the similarities, the computer was able to fill in a few more of the blank labels.

Daniela grunted. "Well, this is all very interesting, but it doesn't help with the current problem."

She finally decided that a genetic testing of food samples would be quicker. She sent Lyuba to collect a few. Their hosts were going to get impatient.

This course of action was more informative. The samples, though unfamiliar to the computer, could be classified in broad terms as plant or animal life. Their composition seemed to be safe enough. Some of them would not be of much use nutritionally, but they wouldn't cause anything worse than minor gastrointestinal discomfort until acclimation had occurred.

Minor indigestion she could deal with easily enough. Daniela made her way across the pavilion to where Tolya and Tanya were conversing with the help of Felix and Sherry. She got Tolya's attention. "I believe, for the most part, the food will be safe enough. There may be some things that cause minor indigestion at first, but I have plenty of things to combat that."

She looked around at the group, then back at Tolya. "Just don't gorge yourselves too much. Even the meds can only do so much."

Tolya grinned. "Thanks Dannie. I think the natives are getting restless, wondering when to start the feast."

Daniela shook her head and grinned. "Then, 'let the revels begin'...or...'When in Rome...'"

In The Works!
From Starhome Books

Volume 2
Stars in the Deep
~Endeavor~

By David F. Snider

Our story continues as the colonists from *ECS Destiny* begin to build settlements along the islands among the Aambüka ... the 'Water People'.

Called 'Star People' by the Aambüka, the humans endeavor to create a new society able to function harmoniously with their unexpected neighbors.

Expect great adventure and discovery as obstacles and surprises develop to make life more interesting.

Visit Dave Snider at: DavidFSnider.com
          or: StarhomeBooks.com

E-mails accepted at: DaveSnider@DavidFSnider.com